Praise for *A Study in Silks*

"This book has just about everything: magic, machines, mystery, mayhem, and all the danger one expects when people's loves and fears collide. I can't wait to return to the world of Evelina Cooper!"
—KEVIN HEARNE, *New York Times* bestselling author of The Iron Druid Chronicles

"As Sherlock Holmes's niece, investigating murder while navigating the complicated shoals of Society—and romance—in an alternate Victorian England, Evelina Cooper is a charming addition to the canon."
—JACQUELINE CAREY, *New York Times* bestselling author of the Kushiel's Legacy series

"Holloway takes us for quite a ride, as her plot snakes through an alternate Victorian England full of intrigue, romance, murder, and tiny sandwiches. Full of both thrills and frills."
—NICOLE PEELER, author of the Jane True series

"*A Study in Silks* is a charming, adventurous ride with a heroine who is both clever and talented. The brushes with the Sherlock Holmes mythos only add to the fun of this tale, and readers are bound to fall in love with Evelina and the London she inhabits."
—PHILIPPA BALLANTINE, author of *Geist*

A Study in Silks

Emma Jane Holloway

DEL REY • NEW YORK

A Study in Silks is a work of fiction. Names, characters, places, and incidents either are the product of imagination or are used fictitiously. Any resemblance to actual persons, living or dead, events, or locales is entirely coincidental.

A Del Rey Mass Market Original

Copyright © 2013 by Naomi Lester
Excerpt from *A Study in Darkness* by Emma Jane Holloway copyright © 2013 by Naomi Lester

Published in the United States by Del Rey, an imprint of The Random House Publishing Group, a division of Random House, Inc., New York.

DEL REY and the HOUSE colophon are registered trademarks of Random House, Inc.

This book contains an excerpt from the forthcoming book *A Study in Darkness* by Emma Jane Holloway. This excerpt has been set for this edition only and may not reflect the final content of the forthcoming edition.

ISBN 978-0-345-53718-8
eBook ISBN 978-0-345-54564-0

Printed in the United States of America

www.delreybooks.com

9 8 7 6 5 4 3 2

Del Rey mass market edition: October 2013

For my good friends,
who know precisely when to administer tea,
common sense, or chocolate as required

A STUDY IN SILKS

CHAPTER ONE

EVELINA FROZE, A BREATH HALF TAKEN CATCHING IN HER throat, nerves tingling down every limb. She sat unmoving for a long moment, searching the shadows cast by her candle on the dusty attic floorboards.

Slowly, methodically, her gaze probed each corner of the space around her. Stacks of trunks and boxes made elephantine humps in the darkness. Furniture lurked phantomlike under dust covers. Attics were for storage of the useless and forgotten, for memories and the occasional secret. The only creatures that should be moving up here were ghosts and mice. Yet she'd heard something else. Or sensed it.

Still barely daring to breathe, Evelina carefully set the minuscule piece of machinery she held back into its box, resting her tiny long-nosed pliers next to it. Her fingers lingered on the casket for a moment, caressing her brass and steel creation almost tenderly. Most nights, she retreated to the attic to work in private after the rest of Hilliard House had retired. This was the one place, the one time, she enjoyed the absolute freedom to indulge her talents. No one else came up here, especially not this late.

And yet, she heard the creak of the door at the bottom of the attic stairs, then a footfall. Someone was coming. Odd, because the household had retired early—His Lordship had declared himself and his lady in need of a quiet night in.

Therefore, no one dared to so much as rustle a candy wrapper tonight.

So who was up and about? Apprehension prickled along her arms. In the privacy of her own mind, Evelina Cooper gave a very improper curse.

There were any number of reasons why a young lady, gently reared by a respectable grandmamma, did not want to be caught hiding in the attic in the dead of night. First would be the inevitable assumption that she was meeting a lover. Why was it that no one imagined a young lady might have more weighty interests?

Second, whatever trouble she got into would automatically rebound on her best friend, Imogen Roth. Hilliard House belonged to her schoolmate's high-and-mighty father, Lord Bancroft, and Evelina was a guest for the Season at Imogen's request. If she were caught doing anything even mildly scandalous, Lord B was more likely to mount both their heads on his study wall than to listen to excuses.

And an unladylike fascination with mechanics was enough to cause comment. It was time to vanish, thoroughly and quickly. She snuffed the candle with her bare fingers. Moonlight slanted through the window, painting the attic in a watery light. She gathered up the scatter of parts and tools she'd strewn about the floor and placed them into the box, careful not to make a clatter. After a last glance around, she closed the lid and silently hid the box and candle behind a rolled-up carpet leaning against the wall.

Evelina's stomach cramped with tension. There wasn't just one pair of heavy feet coming up the stairs. She definitely heard two. *Damnation!*

Her mind went blank for a split second, as devoid of ideas as a pristine sheet of paper. There was only the single exit. She had to hide, but where? The third reason she absolutely, categorically could not be caught was because her box didn't just hold tools; it held implements of magic. That fact would raise more questions than she was prepared to answer.

The footsteps were loud now, nearly to the top of the stairs. She could see the flash of a lantern swinging to and fro. Male voices filled the cavernous gloom. Servants, by their accents. The deep voices of big, strong brutes.

"Why the bloody hell is it always something in the attic they want moved?" one grumbled.

"'Cause if it were easy, they wouldn't be paying us to lug it down the stairs, would they?" said the other. "Now shut it and do your job."

With desperate haste, Evelina pulled off her shoes and stockings and stuffed them behind the carpet with her box. Then she bolted for the window and carefully pushed up the sash, hoping the noise the two men made was enough to hide the scrape of wood on wood.

A blast of night air ruffled her hair. Gathering her skirts tight, she crawled out the window, balancing on the narrow decorative ledge that ran along the outside of the house. It was lucky she was wearing a plain work dress, not much fancier than one of the maid's uniforms. If she'd been dressed in a dinner gown with a bustle and miles of petticoats, she would never have managed. Fortunately, she'd abandoned all that nonsense during her late-night sessions, letting herself bend and breathe free.

Her bare toes felt for the cool stone, sensitive to every dip and ridge. The ledge was just wider than her foot, easy enough to walk on if one had good balance. The voices were getting louder. Anxiety nipped at her heels. Her knees trembled with the effort to hold herself back, not to move too quickly. She had no trouble with heights, but haste could literally be her downfall.

Taking a breath, Evelina edged away from the window, not daring to take the time to close it behind her. One step, then two, and she was out of sight. Even if they guessed someone else had been there, no one would look for one of Lord Bancroft's houseguests clinging like a bug to the wall. Of course, how many graduates of the Wollaston Academy for Young Ladies numbered walking a tightrope among their accomplishments? Then again, how many were orphans with one grandmother in charge of a country estate and another who told fortunes with Ploughman's Paramount Circus? In some ways, Evelina had spent her whole life on a narrow ledge, balanced between two completely different worlds.

She gripped the wall behind her, inching farther still from the open window. With any luck, she would find another unlocked window and crawl back inside. While she was safe from the servants within the house, too many neighbors had a good view of her perch. The house had a large walled garden behind it, a legacy from a rural past, but now it faced onto busy Beaulieu Square. To either side of Hilliard House, arches of terraced homes flanked a circular garden.

Perhaps she would have been better off ducking under a dust cover? But then, she had always been more inclined to take risks than to hide. That was half her problem. She might have learned to act like a lady, but she still didn't think like one. Ladies didn't sneak about, and they certainly didn't attempt unheard-of experiments just to prove to themselves that they were every bit as smart as a man—and clever enough to attend a university college—but that was exactly what Evelina was doing in her attic retreat. She took risks, but not without a reason.

The wind snatched strands of her dark hair and whipped it around her face. She caught bits of sound: the clop-clop of horses, a distant pianoforte murdering a Chopin *ballade*, the muffled notes of a female voice coming from just around the corner of the house. Evelina caught a man's answering tones, harshly ordering the woman, half buried beneath the chime of church bells. *Eleven? How had it become so late?*

She edged along, curious to catch more of the conversation, but the voices had died away. Her path toward them was blocked anyway. An oak tree grew beside the house, one of its thick branches angling up to scrape against the gutters. Evelina could easily reach it with one hand. Then two. She pulled herself up, swinging one leg over the rough trunk. Her skirts hitched, bunched, and generally got in the way, but she got to her feet and was soon moving cautiously toward the heavy foliage nearer the trunk. It wasn't perfect cover, but a girl in a tree was a lot less visible than a girl silhouetted against a moonlit wall.

Evelina paused, crouching low and balancing with one

hand on a neighboring branch. Bits of bark scraped the tender soles of her feet, but she forgot the discomfort in a momentary rush of exhilaration. It was so rare that she got to really use her body since she had passed the divide between girl and woman. At Imogen's house, where she could roam almost at will, Evelina enjoyed the freedom to think and work. But even at Hilliard House, a lady did not clamber about in trees.

She let the April wind play with her hair and skirts. It was chill, the scent of rain reminding her spring was slow to give way to summer. From up here she could see a sliver of London, gaslights tracking in zigzags across the richer parts of the city. And, besides the lamps on the streets, individual homes sported their own displays beside their doors, on balconies, or wherever smaller globes could be mounted. The more prosperous a household was, the more of the fashionable—and expensive—lights it had, until the richest parts of the city sparkled like the jewels of a fairyland queen.

The lights nearby showed a faint gold tinge, while those farther away were blue or green or red. The color of the glass globes marked the district and the company that provided them—and, by extension, which of the so-called steam barons controlled the light and heat for the people who lived there. According to Lord Bancroft, the owners of the great coal and gas companies had divided London— divided all the Empire in fact—into uneven slices like a pie. Steam was their mainstay, but they had bought up other things, like coal mines, railways, and even some factories. She understood the colored lights were a symbol of their stranglehold, but it did make for a pretty sight when the lamps came on at night.

Of course, there were always exceptions—those houses that sat dark and cold. There were whole neighborhoods like that in the poor districts like Whitechapel, but the rich streets had them, too. They were called the Disconnected, these people who had either lost all their money or, even worse, lost the favor of the steam barons.

The thought went by in a moment, as fleeting as the

breeze, but it was enough to distract her. When she shifted her weight to move again, her foot slipped. For a wild, heart-stopping moment, she felt herself falling. Leaves and branches rushed toward her, clawing at her hair and face. Reflexively, she hooked a leg around the branch while her hands flailed for something to grip. Then, with a hoarse gasp, she caught herself.

Now Evelina hung upside down, a gentlewoman's version of a tree sloth. Waves of panic slid beneath the surface of her control, threatening to crack her to pieces. She squeezed her eyes closed, refusing to give in to the tears of fright and embarrassment prickling for release.

Hullo.

The voice came from inside her head, but she felt the light pressure of the greeting like a finger prodding her con-sciousness. She opened her eyes. A faint, slightly luminous green smudge hung inches from her face.

"Hello," she muttered.

The light bobbed, seeming to look her over. *What are you doing?*

Evelina bit back a scathing retort. The creature was a deva, a nature spirit. They seemed to bear the characteristics of different elements: wood or air, fire or water, or maybe a combination in between. Some were tiny and others huge and fierce. The countryside was thick with them, though city gardens sometimes had spirits, too. This one had probably claimed the tree as its home. Those of the Blood—like her fortune-telling grandmother's side of the family—could see them. Everyone else called them the stuff of fairy tales.

Just Evelina's luck if someone found her stuck in a tree talking to an invisible creature. Lord B would send her packing before she could say "Bedlam." Of course, it would be worse if anyone actually believed she could talk to na-ture spirits. That counted as magic, deemed by most as im-moral and by the courts as illegal. Just today, they'd arrested a witch who was also a renowned actress named Nellie Reynolds. If someone as popular as her wasn't safe, Evelina didn't stand a chance.

I asked, the deva repeated in a tart voice, *what you are doing in my tree?*

"I'm stuck. I was running away, and I fell." What had she been thinking? Evelina cursed her idiocy. She wasn't one of the Fabulous Flying Coopers anymore and hadn't been on a tightrope since she was a child.

You should leave climbing to cats.

She just growled by way of response. Using her legs for leverage, she started to squirm in an effort to haul herself upright. Unfortunately, there were no handholds to help her get to the top side of the branch. It was a matter of pure strength and balance, both of which seemed to be fading fast. Her arms were starting to shake. *I'm getting soft.*

The thought made her jaw clench. "Give me some help, deva!"

Of course, it didn't. They never did unless compelled, and her tools—the needle and grains of amber she used in the spell with which she bound a spirit—were in the wretched box, hidden where bothersome servants couldn't find it. Making a last effort, Evelina wriggled and twisted until she found new handholds. When she finally got her bearings, she was facing the other way, toward the house, but she was upright again.

The deva had vanished. "Thanks for nothing," she muttered. Now she had scrapes on her palms, and she was sure she'd heard her hem tear on the stump of a twig. Still, she had got herself back up on the branch. That counted for something.

She glanced toward the attic window, hoping against hope that the servants had left. No, she could still see their lamplight. What were they looking for?

More carefully this time, she moved along the upward-sloping branch just far enough to get a better view. Not too close, though. She didn't want them to see her looking in.

The men had hung their oil lantern from a hook in the ceiling. A pool of light spread over the scene, far brighter than that of Evelina's candle. Now that she saw the men's faces, she recognized them as Lord Bancroft's grooms.

From what she'd observed, he used them frequently for odd, hard-to-explain tasks.

Five huge brass-studded steamer trunks had been taken from a stack against the wall and moved onto the floor. Evelina remembered they bore a maker's mark from Austria, where Lord Bancroft had served as ambassador.

"What's in these?" asked one groom. She could just hear them through the open window.

"Don't know." The other stopped, wiping his forehead on his sleeve.

"Figure if we have to take them cross-country, we should know, eh?" The first one bent down, pulling out his pocket knife and worrying at the lock. She heard the click of the heavy mechanism. Heavy metal hasps sprang open, as if triggered by springs.

Evelina watched intently, fascination outweighing the cold and the discomfort of her seat. It took both men to lift the lid of the trunk. One of them stepped back, seeming to recoil with disgust.

"God in Heaven," the man cursed. "It smells like something died in there."

Evelina's eyes widened, and she gripped the branch even tighter. The scent didn't reach her, but her skin prickled as if doused with magnetic energy. Stale, bad energy that left her fearful of the dark.

The interior of the trunk was lined with blue satin and sculpted to hold the limbs, head, and torso of a dismembered body. Panic clenched her belly, and Evelina gasped loudly before she could stop herself. *Good God, what is this?*

Then she caught sight of the metal joints at the shoulders and hips. The body wasn't human. In fact, it was covered in coarse, dun-colored ticking, and the face and hands were painted porcelain, just like a child's doll. *An automaton.* But it looked just real enough to send another shiver down her spine. She must not have been the only one to feel that way. The man pulled the lid down with a bang, shutting the frightful thing from sight.

She felt an almost palpable relief. That had to be the ugliest automaton ever made, the face staring and slack-jawed. Was it one of Lord Bancroft's souvenirs from Austria? She'd never heard anyone mention such a thing. Did each of those trunks have a monstrosity like that inside?

Of course, the appearance of the clockwork girl wasn't the most interesting thing. Even from where Evelina sat in the tree, she could tell the automaton vibrated with magic. And not any magic, but sorcery of the wickedest kind.

A chill of relief, anxiety, and a peculiar kind of terror shivered through her. What she had just witnessed was both a shield and an Achilles' heel. Whatever secrets Evelina was hiding, she now knew the impeccable Lord Bancroft was concealing much, much worse.

CHAPTER TWO

SPECULATION FADED AS EVELINA, TRAPPED IN THE TREE, grew colder and increasingly disgruntled. It took another half hour before the grooms left, carting the trunks away to who knew where, then another thirty minutes to make sure all was quiet again. Finally, half frozen and aching, Evelina crawled back through the attic window.

Her first priority was safety. She willed her feet to make no noise as she crept down flight after flight of plain oak stairs to the soft carpeting of the second-floor corridor. Her box was nestled in a canvas bag slung crossways over her shoulder, and her breath was frozen in her throat. At every turn of the stairs, she paused to listen for the slightest movement, but so far her luck had held.

Her final task was to run the gauntlet of the family's bedchambers, where the row of doors stood like oak-paneled sentries. Behind each, a titled or at least honorable head lay on goose down pillows. Her bedroom lay at the other end of the long hallway.

Pausing to listen, she heard only the ghostly *tap-tap* of the oak outside the stairway window. At the end of the corridor, a longcase clock beat a rhythm half the pace of her racing heart.

She shielded the flame of her candle with one hand, the light etching her fingers in glowing red. The glimmer that escaped touched the pattern of the Oriental carpet, the dark paneling, the glint of brass on doorknobs and wall sconces. Evelina tiptoed forward, catching the scent of wood polish and lavender. Lord B's domestic staff ran his house with exacting efficiency.

She made it past Lady Bancroft's chamber, then the youngest daughter's bedroom. Poppy was in the country with her grandparents, so there was no need to worry about waking her. Then came Tobias, the handsome son of the family. Though he often sat up very late, there was no light under his door. There was under Imogen's, but then she always slept with a candle burning.

The clock made a chunking sound as something inside it shifted. As well as the time, it told the date, moon phase, barometric pressure, and occasionally spit out a card in a cipher only Lord Bancroft understood. Clockwork drove part of it, but tubes of bright chemicals were also nested inside, powering parts of the machine. Evelina had figured out some of the workings, but by no means all. Every dial and spring worked perfectly, except for the function that predicted the weather. For some reason, it was wrong as often as not.

At least the clock, unlike some of Lord B's other souvenirs, didn't give her the shudders. Her mind went back to the trunks in the attic, the thought of them raising a chill down her nape. Why did the ambassador have those automatons? And why was he moving them?

Then without warning, Imogen's bedroom door opened.

Evelina sprang into the air, barely stifling a squeak. The box rattled as if she had purloined all the silverware in the house.

Bollocks!

A figure stepped into the corridor, closing Imogen's door. Despite the hour, the young upstairs maid was crisply turned out in black and white, though dark circles sagged under her eyes.

"Miss Cooper! Have you come to check on Miss Roth?" Her gaze flicked over Evelina, but only for an instant.

Evelina felt herself coloring. She had the bag slung over her shoulder, her hem was ripped, and no doubt her hair looked like she'd been climbing a tree. Yet the well-trained servant pretended to see none of it.

"What's the matter, Dora?" Evelina asked. "Is it her old complaint?"

"I don't think so, miss."

"Is there a fever? Should Dr. Anderson be summoned?" The questions came out in a panicked rush.

Dora shook her head. "I don't know, miss. Miss Roth simply said she could not sleep. I was going to prepare the draft the doctor left for her, miss, just as she asked me to."

Evelina exhaled slowly. "Then you do that. I'll look in on her."

Dora nodded, visibly relieved to be able to share the responsibility. "Very good, miss. I'll come back in a tick with fresh candles."

Imogen couldn't abide the dark. Evelina pushed open her friend's door and stepped inside. The room was cool and spacious, a sitting room on one end and a large bed in an alcove at the other. Bed curtains of heavy sky-blue silk were looped back, framing Imogen where she sat propped against a mountain of snow-white pillows.

"Evelina!" she said. "What are you doing up and about at this hour? And why do you look like you rolled through a forest?"

Imogen's fair hair hung in long, thick braids against the pin tucks of her nightdress. Her face looked pale, but part of that was her porcelain complexion.

"Dora said you couldn't sleep." Evelina set down her bag and candle and crossed to the bed. "Are you unwell?"

Her friend's gray eyes searched the ceiling as if she expected to find poems scribed on the ornate plaster. "I had a nightmare," she said flatly.

Evelina was silent for a long moment. Night terrors were a symptom of the nervous ailment that had plagued Imogen since she was no more than five or six years old. The illness came and went, until finally her parents had sent her to the Wollaston Academy for Young Ladies, hoping the good Devonshire air could achieve what the doctors could not. That was where Evelina had met her.

More to the point, that was where Imogen had taken her under her wing and given her the social advantage of her companionship. Though Evelina's disgraced mother had tried to teach her how to act the lady, a lot of polishing had been required, and Imogen had taken it on with a will. Evelina owed her a great deal for that, as well as for being a steadfast friend.

"You haven't had one of your bad dreams for a long time."

"No." Imogen was still looking at the ceiling, seeming embarrassed. "It wasn't the usual one about being trapped. This time I was dreaming about the castle in Vienna, where Papa was ambassador. I was floating through the tower. Flying, you know, like a feather on the breeze. I was terrified because I couldn't find my way back to my bed."

Vienna. Mention of it reminded Evelina of the trunks in the attic. She thought of asking Imogen if she knew about them, then discarded the idea. Her friend was already having nightmares without bringing up ugly automatons. "My grandmother says that dreams of old houses mean you're trying to find a lost memory."

"Your circus grandmother?" Imogen finally looked at Evelina.

"Yes, Grandmother Cooper. She knows what dreams mean. I don't think Grandmamma Holmes would let such fancies through the door. She'd tell the footman to toss them out."

Imogen chuckled. "I can see her doing it, too. You're lucky, having two such different grandmothers. Mine are almost interchangeable."

Of all Evelina's acquaintance, Imogen was the only one who knew about Ploughman's. The circus was all very fine to watch, but the gentry would never embrace someone who grew up with knife throwers and clowns. The first thing Evelina had been forced to learn when she joined the gentry was to hide her past.

"Do you know you have leaves in your hair?" Imogen asked. "Are you coming as a dryad to Mama's garden party?"

Evelina felt through her tangled locks. "I had to climb a tree."

"Indeed?" Imogen hitched herself a little higher on the sheets, a smirk curving her lips. She reached over to her bedside table, picking up an ivory comb and handing it to Evelina. "I think you had better tell me all about it."

"I did something foolish, and I'm sorry for it." Evelina perched on the edge of the bed, pulling the pins out of her hair. "I was in the attic."

"Working on—whatever it is you're doing. I know you tried to explain it."

"My toys. I'm indulging my unladylike penchant for gears and springs."

"You wicked, wicked girl." Imogen settled back against her pillows, clearly ready to be entertained.

"Fit for nothing but Newgate Prison."

And she hadn't even mentioned the magic part of it. Imogen knew a tiny bit about Evelina's talent—it was impossible to hide such a gift from her very best friend, especially in the confines of the academy—but she had never told her everything. There were only so many secrets she could ask her friend to keep.

Evelina started to drag the comb through her locks, wincing as it snagged. "I was nearly caught by a couple of the servants. I crawled out the window to hide and ended up in the oak tree. I just about fell out."

Imogen laughed—a hearty chuckle that had nothing to do with her delicate looks. "I wish I'd been there to see that!"

"I beg your pardon? It was most distressing!"

That only made Imogen laugh the harder, a healthier pink rising to her cheeks.

"I'm being serious." Evelina frowned with mock severity.

Imogen gave her a scathing look. She looked brighter for the conversation, but shadows still smudged the skin under her eyes. She truly wasn't well.

"I'm sorry for being so thoughtless," Evelina said. "If I'd been caught, your father would have blamed you as much as me. I'm in this house at your invitation, and I have no right to risk its reputation, or yours."

Imogen shook her head. "Your escapades don't frighten me."

"They should. I'll land you in trouble yet."

"I can look after myself."

Evelina felt something tighten inside. At school, she'd been the one who'd nursed Imogen when she fell ill. She'd been the guard dog when schoolroom bullies loomed. She still felt fiercely protective. "I should know better."

"You can't be anything but what you are."

"And what is that?"

Her friend squinted in a considering way. "I'm not sure yet."

"But you're going to be brilliant, Imogen Roth. The belle of all London."

Now that they had completed their education—an event slightly delayed because of Imogen's illness and Evelina's late start—this would be their first Season. Evelina had promised to be her companion through the balls and routs and the inevitable string of suitors—or at least as much as her modest place in the world would allow. A champion until death, Imogen had called her, although Evelina suspected her role would be short lived. Despite her health, Imogen was too beautiful to remain unmarried long.

As for Evelina—she doubted she would marry. At least not now. Unlike Imogen, she would not be presented to the queen—the seal of approval that granted worthy young women access to Society. Just before Easter, the summons had been sent to those young ladies deemed suitable for the honor, and Evelina had not received one. That limited which parties she would be invited to, and which young men she would have the chance to meet, and how far she could accompany Imogen. Even though her heart yearned to dance at the Duchess of Westlake's ball, she would never set one slipper on that glorious polished oak floor. Grandmamma Holmes would give her a dowry, but nothing like what Lord Bancroft could bestow on his daughter. Barring a romance worthy of Sir Walter Scott, Evelina's future lay in something other than a brilliant match.

Perversely, that bothered her less than missing out on the fun of the Season. It was hard to miss a man she would never meet, but she itched to go dancing. As it was, she would have to content herself with family gatherings, like Lady Bancroft's birthday party, or improving occasions, like the opening of the Gold King's show of ancient Greek artifacts at the new Prometheus Gallery. All of the exclusive events, to which only the cream of Society was invited, she would have to experience from the sidelines.

The sense of passing time tugged at Evelina like a dull, persistent pain. She and Imogen had been inseparable for years. This would be the last few months before they went their separate ways into womanhood. No doubt Imogen would rise to a title. Evelina would . . . well, she had her plans.

Dora's light step sounded in the passage. Evelina squeezed her friend's hand. "Shall I stay with you tonight?"

"Stop playing the mother hen. It was just a dream. Nothing more."

Evelina rose, picking up her things. "Then I had better go to bed myself. Sleep well."

"Good night."

Dora entered with the sleeping medication just as Evelina left. The maid bobbed a curtsey as she passed, but gave Evelina another assessing look. No doubt looking for twigs in her hair.

Still, Evelina hovered outside Imogen's door, unease seeping through her flesh. For all her efforts to avoid getting caught in the attic, Dora had seen her wandering the house. Since Evelina had caught Dora kissing the second footman last Tuesday, the maid was unlikely to speak of her twiggy disgrace. Any good servant knew the value of a little quid pro quo. But what if she'd been found out by someone besides Dora? Someone with the authority to ask questions? Someone who knew what those little mechanical toys really represented?

Evelina stared into the candle flame, no longer bothering to hide its light. Naked, it flickered and dipped in the air currents, as exposed as she felt. She had to be more careful.

Imogen had opened the doors to her heart and her home, and offered it without reserve. But her friendship—the only one Evelina could truly claim—could not shield her if things went wrong. Lord Bancroft's pretty daughter was only a young woman, with no power or money of her own.

So much hung by a thread. Evelina listened to the rattle of

the oak branch on the window, the quick patter making a counter-rhythm to the longcase clock. The sense of passing time did nothing to soothe her anxiety.

She heaved a quick breath, her chest too tight for a proper sigh. How on edge was she that a small incident could over-set her?

Positive action was the only antidote to this mood. Her problems could wait. She would hide her box and then take her old place in the armchair by Imogen's bed—just in case the nightmares returned. No one, especially not Imogen, should wake up alone and afraid.

She'd no sooner finished the thought than a flicker of shadow caught the corner of her eye. With the candle held aloft, she scanned the corridor.

No one was there. The only movement was her own re-flection in a narrow mirror that hung outside Imogen's door. Maybe that was what she had seen: the swing of her skirts. Forcing herself to breathe, Evelina strode toward her bed-room door.

The candle blew out, leaving her in utter blackness. Evelina stopped midstride, nerves straining. Someone passed by to her left, leaving a scent of sweat and brandy. She didn't hear footsteps on the soft carpet, but felt the displacement of air—a light exhalation like the sound of a gloating smile.

Her skin shrank against her bones. Panic sent her skitter-ing a few steps. "Who's there?" she whispered.

But there was no reply, just the insistent *tap-tap* of the branches outside.

The silence shredded her nerves. She listened intently, straining every sense, but could detect no sound—no foot-fall, no whisper, no breath. Had the figure been going toward the stairs or away from them? She couldn't tell.

She retraced her steps, finding her way back to Imogen's door, but still she sensed nothing. At last, she decided it would be safe to leave for the time it would take to put her box away. The presence she had felt—if there had been one at all—was gone.

With one hand skimming the wall, she hurried to her door, groping to find the familiar shape of the handle. It rattled open and she plunged inside. Moonlight streamed in the windows, giving the impression of a photograph. For a long moment, Evelina stood with her back to the door, one hand grasping the key that she used to lock herself in.

Had she been imagining things? Should she wake the footmen and have them search the house?

No, that would be awkward. And she hadn't actually seen anyone. It was probably just Tobias, come home after a night of carousing. *Or a rampaging ghost. How mortifyingly Gothic.*

She allowed herself a wry smile. That had been no remnant of the dead. She knew spirits well enough—anyone with her gifts saw them once in a while. It had to be Tobias.

Her heart still pattered, but slowly the calm dignity of the guest room—the pale counterpane, the wardrobe painted in Italian scenes, and the heavy velvet curtains—had its effect. Finally relaxed enough to move, Evelina left her post by the door.

Still working by moonlight, she set the candlestick on the desk, then slid the box out of the bag and placed it carefully on the polished wood surface. The box was really a train case—one her Grandmamma Holmes had given her— covered in black leather and fitted with twin brass hasps.

The stern old lady would have an apoplexy if she knew what her gift concealed. Evelina studied the train case for a moment, her mind flicking from Imogen to her fright in the corridor. *Tobias. It must have been him.*

Sliding into her desk chair, she drew the candle closer, smelling the smoke from its extinguished wick. With gentle fingers, she touched the warm wax, noting the shape and texture of it, feeling the potential energy inside. She let her mind drift a moment, envisioning the bright veils of flame she desired. *Come.*

Light sprang back to the wick, flaring up a second before settling back to a normal flame. Evelina pushed the candle back, satisfied. Though the bloodlines that granted such magic were thin these days, she could call the essence of things: fire, water, perhaps the deva living in a stream or a tree.

And it was a power that could damn her. Science was the currency of the educated, monied, polite classes. With the rise of industry, magic—impossible to measure, regulate, or rule—was banned by Church and State, and especially by the steam barons who controlled so much with their vast wealth. Fortune-tellers and mediums were usually tolerated as amusing if immoral tricksters. Anyone claiming to use real power was subject to jail and probably execution or—if there was some suspicion they actually had the Blood—a trip to Her Majesty's laboratories for testing.

The specter of the latter terrified her into nightmares at least as bad as her friend's. When she'd read about the arrest of Nellie Reynolds, she had wept with fear. And yet, Reynolds was far from the first magic user put on trial even in the last twelve months. It was hard not to grow numb and, from there, resigned that someday it would be her standing in the dock.

Yet, dangerous or not, the power pushed at her as urgently as thirst or desire. It wasn't something a person could just shut down. Plus, it was the strongest link to her childhood. Denying it would be like denying half her flesh.

She put her fingers on the hasps of the box, breathing hard. There was too much going on. She needed to calm herself. *Everything's going to be fine.*

"Evelina." Breath stirred the fine hairs at the nape of her neck.

Shock vaulted her out of her chair. The candlestick wobbled as she braced herself to wheel around, sending shadows lurching over the walls and ceiling. Before she had fully focused on the intruder's face, Evelina was holding a paper knife inches from the speaker's eyes.

He held her gaze, as if daring her to look. Evelina obliged, cataloguing what she saw: straight dark hair falling to his collar, dark eyes fanned in lashes any woman would have envied, and skin the color of milky coffee. Candlelight sculpted a face like a young falcon, lean and hook-nosed. A faint bruise fanned his cheekbone, as if he had caught a fist there, and a thin white scar tracked like a tear under one eye. His clothes, a curious mix of homespun and silks, were threadbare and wet with rain. Wisely, he held his hands away from his sides, showing them open and empty of weapons.

The knife hadn't wavered from where she held it poised to strike. Evelina's hand was perfectly steady, but her pulse thundered like the sea in a typhoon. Her mouth drifted open in astonishment.

Doubting, hoping, she flicked her attention back to those liquid brown eyes. Yes, she knew the face, or a version of it. Same gold hoops in his ears. Same quirk at the corners of his mouth. But the strong, muscled body smelling of saddle leather and adult male was entirely new.

"Nick?" she said in a choked whisper. "What are you doing here?"

"Is that how your fine governess taught you to welcome guests?" He smiled, teeth showing white in his swarthy face.

She lowered the impromptu weapon, stepping back until the edge of the table pressed into her skirts. So it had been *Nick* in the corridor, frightening her half to death. He had the Blood, too, but a different bloodline than the Coopers. Somehow it had given him an annoying ability to sneak up on other people with the silence of a falling shadow. Gran had said she'd never seen anything like it—but then Nick was one of a kind.

But knowing who it had been scarcely improved matters. She kept her fingers curled around the wooden handle of the knife, if only for the feeling of something solid to cling to. Her breath was coming in short, sharp pants, but she forced her voice to be crisp. Five years. She hadn't seen him in five whole years. It felt like a lifetime.

The moment stretched uncomfortably until she saw the flicker of doubt in his eyes. In that instant, her heart cracked. She dropped the knife onto the table and stepped into him, flinging her arms around his neck as she had when she was no more than a child. He closed the embrace carefully, his touch far more cautious than his bold words. A hot ache filled her throat, yearning and sorrow mixed with dread.

And anger—because there was nothing safe or good in this reunion. All the anxiety she had felt during her earlier adventure flooded back. She would be disgraced if the household found a strange man in her bedchamber—and just as bad, her past with the circus would be revealed. There would be no chance to explain, not with her history, and Nick would be arrested whether or not he was actually committing a crime. She couldn't count on luck saving her this time. Surely she'd used up her store for the night.

Even more dangerous, she felt a familiar ripple of energy pass between them as Blood met Blood. A hot, heavy pressure stirred inside her, calling her own magic to the surface. As they had grown older, whatever it was that made Nick unique made her own talents almost impossible to hide when he was near. Now, after so many years, the pull was stronger than ever before. In the flickering candlelight, she could almost see a silvery glimmer where they touched. Power—raw and uncontrolled. Whenever they had called it, it had slipped its leash. That was the last thing they needed now.

Evelina shivered, and as Nick ran his hands down her arms in a time-honored gesture of comfort, magic tingled along her skin. Her throat constricted with unspoken pain. The very spark that made them who they were made it incredibly dangerous to be together.

Swallowing back a rush of sadness, she took a deep, steadying breath. It had taken so long to get over the loss of him that he couldn't—he just *couldn't* be there. The sight of him brought back too much pain. She pushed him away, wanting to stop the reunion before old wounds began to bleed. "You're damp with rain."

He pressed a hand over his heart. "That is enough to send me away? A little rain shouldn't frighten you. We've slept together under the open stars."

She crossed her arms, keeping her embraces to herself. "I was eleven, and it was disgustingly cold. And Old Ploughman was snoring a dozen feet away."

"Your memory lacks romance."

"I like accuracy." She shot the words back before the sheer physical presence of this new, fully adult Nick could cloud her mind. Her gaze roved over him, taking in the lean hips and strong shoulders, the long, lithe legs of the horse-man. There was nothing of the boy left in the hard muscles she'd felt under his shirt, or in the graceful power of his every gesture. Her skin felt hot and tight, as if she'd suddenly contracted a fever.

"You pierce my heart, fair lady."

"Rot. Don't waste your patter on me; you're impervious to a mere comment. I'm willing to wager you have more knives on your person than Lady Bancroft has place settings."

He shrugged—the gesture so familiar it brought a throb to her chest. Memories crashed in, stifling in their urgency. When they had parted, Nick had been seventeen years old; she had been not quite fourteen. If she had stayed with the travelers, they would eventually have wed as surely as summer followed spring.

But that hadn't happened. She looked at him now, wondering what he would have been like as a husband. Wondering what secrets this older Nick had hidden behind his cautious smile and those silken rags. The thought of it left her empty and aching.

"What are you doing in my bedchamber?" she demanded.

"Do you think I am here to ravish you, after all this time?"

She allowed herself a smile. His showman's persona never quite came off with the costume. "I doubt you've kept the image of my pigtails and pinafore etched on your soul."

"How little you understand me," he said with another flash of teeth. "I was not whisked away by a long-lost and eminently respectable grandmamma. Perhaps my memory can afford to be longer."

"Why are you here?"

"I asked for you at every stop the traveling show made, from Scotland to Dover."

"No." She had to deny it. She couldn't bear the idea of him suffering anything like what she had felt. But then Nick, for all his faults—including the foolhardy bravery that had brought him there tonight—had always been loyal.

"It's true." He reached across the distance between them, his fingertips barely brushing her cheek. They were rough, but she didn't flinch away. Instead, she felt turned to stone, mesmerized by his plain, almost coarse accent. No Mayfair polish here.

"Stop," she whispered.

"I knew you would grow into a beauty. Skin like the moon and hair like a starless night, as the old song goes." His voice was husky. "We were close once. Are you so far above me now? I suppose you are."

As long as no one burst in and found them together. At the very least, that would send her plunging back to the mud as fast as the laws of gravity allowed. She had to make him leave.

Still, Evelina wanted to know everything. Where he'd been. If he still devoured any and every book that fell into his hands. If he had found another girl to follow him around like a worshipful duckling. She had run away to find him once, when her courage failed at the beginning of their life apart. Her Grandmamma Holmes had locked her in the cellar.

The questions jammed up, tangling her tongue. "Are you still with the show?" she managed.

He dropped his hand, a mix of irony and pride flickering over his features. "Where else would I be? I'm the Indomitable Niccolo, supreme knife man and best trick rider in all Italia."

"You've never been farther south than Kent," she said in caustic tones. And she suspected his parents had been more Romany than Italian, but no one actually knew. He'd been a foundling who knew his first name and nothing else.

"Italia plays better with the crowd. Besides, it's no more a sham than you playing at gentlewoman. Your father was one of us."

There it was, the betrayal. She'd left Nick behind.

"But this," Evelina gestured at the elegant room, "was my mother's world." And she was caught between, half gentry and half vagabond, two halves that never knit properly together.

Nick's gaze roved over the bedchamber, lingering long on the silver candlesticks. Instinctively, she moved to screen his view of the box. "Why are you here?" she repeated.

"What are you doing in London? Ploughman's never wintered here." It wasn't one of the big, famous shows. She remembered when all the performers had taken a cut in wages so the show could afford to buy the lions.

"We've been here since November."

That meant they were moving up in the hierarchy of the circus world. That should have been good news, but Evelina's throat tightened at the thought of her Gran, of Nick, of all the circus folk she'd grown up with being in the same city and never knowing it.

"I've been watching the house, wondering what was the best time to come see you, if you might be happy to see me. But then I saw you climbing a tree tonight, and I knew that at least part of you was still the same girl I knew. What were you doing, little Evie?"

The old endearment stung, reducing her back to the barefoot girl picking up pennies the crowds threw for her elders. "It's none of your business anymore."

His face went solemn. "Perhaps. But I saw you two days ago. In the street. I had given up hope of ever finding you. But a little silver to your groom and a gardener let me know where you sleep."

The look Nick gave her was far too soft. She felt blood mount to her cheeks. How she had wished he would look at her like that, once upon a time. How it had finally started to happen when it was time for her to leave him. Now it was too late. "You know it's madness for us to be together."

"I do. I'm not stupid, Evie, but knowing you're safe is worth the risk."

She bit her lip. He didn't have the right to choose that risk for her. "Are you so certain about that?"

He blinked, his face falling back to his insouciant expression. "I don't expect you to come home with me. I just needed to know that you are happy. Is that so wrong?"

She took a breath, held it, and tried to find the right answer. "No. Are you? Happy, I mean."

He shrugged. "You know me. I am content as long as I am the best." He looked around the room again, as if trying to memorize it. "So what do you do with yourself now? Have tea parties? Look for a husband?"

It was a good question, and one Evelina asked herself daily. She was caught between her circus past, with its hidden magic and its poverty, and her present, with schooling and science and enough to eat. She'd thought long and hard about another option, a place where she might find a brand-new path. "I want to go to university. There are colleges for women."

His gaze came back to her, wide with surprise. "Why do you want that?" Probably no one in his acquaintance had set foot inside a proper schoolroom, much less a lecture hall.

"I'm good at learning. I want to see how far I can go. Maybe I'll figure out . . . things."

"What for?" Nick asked practically. "What don't you already know?"

How to be whole. In her daydreams, she had fabricated a place where she would finally fit in. There would be women like her who loved a book of chemistry more than a new ball gown, and who didn't care where she grew up. She could study with the finest scholars. Maybe, with their help, she could crack the code to why magic worked and how it meshed with science. She could finally solve the puzzle of her own nature.

At last, she would know where she belonged. And maybe that mattered more than anything else.

The look on Nick's face was hard to read, so she changed the subject. "I'm glad you came."

One corner of his mouth curled up. "Is that the truth?"

"It is." But she couldn't tell. She felt suffocated by an emotion that was not guilt or loneliness or irritation, but a painful mix of all three. *It's not my fault that I couldn't stay with you.*

Nick watched her with eyes that missed nothing. His mouth was a flat line, with the deliberate neutrality of someone hiding pain.

Please go. She wanted to say it, but that would sever everything between them. She didn't want that, either. Instead, she grasped his hand. It was warm and hard with calluses and the slow, languorous pulse of his power. It tingled up her arm, a sensual temptation to throw caution to the wind. It was hard to be the only one with Blood. Falling into Nick's arms would put an end to isolation—but also an end to both their lives. "We'll find a way to talk later, but now you should leave before you're caught. And don't go through the corridor this time. It's late, but there's a maid about."

Nick had been staring at her hand clasping his, but now he looked up in confusion. He jerked a thumb over his shoulder. "I climbed the wall and came in that window. I wasn't in the corridor."

Downstairs, a woman shrieked—a long, chilling wail of terror.

Evelina locked eyes with Nick. "Somebody was, and I think we know which way he went."

CHAPTER THREE

SHE GAVE NICK A SHOVE TOWARD THE WINDOW, BUT HE JUST leaned into the gesture, grabbing her wrist.

"Go!" she said, exasperation turning the word to a hiss.

"You think I'm leaving?" he growled. "What the blazes is going on out there?"

"Whatever it is won't improve if you're found." Her words came out short and tight, urgency vibrating in her veins. She planted her free hand on his chest and pushed again. "And I'll be sent packing right along with you."

He bared his teeth. "Would that be so terrible?"

"Do you wish me ruined?" Her chances for school turned to dust?

They held each other's glare. Evelina had to know what the scream was about, and there was no time for squabbling. Plus, she was terrified for him—far more than for herself. "It's the only way we'll both be safe. Nick, my conscience can't bear it if you're arrested when all you did was come to see me for old times' sake."

"Old times' sake." His lips curled at the last words, and he flicked a hand as if batting them away. "There's a woman screaming downstairs. You thought someone was creeping around the corridors. I would worry about more than your reputation."

Pounding shook Evelina's door, making her jump. Nick pulled a knife from his belt, the blade gleaming in the candlelight. She caught her breath and grabbed his forearm, feeling the play of lean muscle under layers of clothing. "Wait here, then. Get out of sight."

Nick didn't budge.

The pounding came again, making the door latch rattle. "Miss Cooper?"

It was Dora.

"Who is that?" Nick whispered.

"One of the upstairs maids. Hide! Quickly!" Evelina was already in motion toward the door. When she cast a glance over her shoulder, Nick had vanished. Only a flutter of bed curtains betrayed his hiding place. *Nick in my bed. Spectacular. I'll never explain that one away.* She turned the key in the lock and opened her door.

Dora stood with a candle in one hand. Her face was whey-pale, her lips bloodless. "Miss, you must come. I don't know what to do." The maid looked smaller than usual, as if her entire body had retracted in shock.

"What is it?" Evelina stepped into the corridor and pulled the door shut behind her. She wasn't surprised that she was the first port of call in an emergency. Although she had little authority in the household, she knew the servants relied on her for a cool head and practical advice. That was one advantage of growing up in Ploughman's Paramount Circus, where sword swallowing was a daily event. It tended to promote strong nerves.

Plus, the odd problem could be dealt with by one of Gran Cooper's spells. Not that the servants knew why Miss Imogen's friend seemed to be able to solve the unsolvable on so many occasions; they were just grateful that she cared about their lot. But, taking her cue from Dora's expression, Evelina was already having doubts that this situation could be rescued with a bit of herb magic.

"What is it, Dora?" she asked again.

The maid opened her mouth, inhaled, then closed it again. She gave a quick shake of her head, as if to say the words couldn't come out. Tears were leaking from her eyes, trailing beside her pink-tipped nose.

This wasn't getting them anywhere. "Show me," Evelina said, wanting to get away from her bedroom and the man hiding there.

Without another word, Dora led the way toward the stairs. Once on the main floor, instead of going left to the stately drawing rooms, she turned right toward the main entrance and the cloakroom used to hang the outerwear of the ambassador's many guests. Though now retired from foreign service, Emerson Roth, Lord Bancroft, still moved chess pieces around the board of the Empire's political scene, and that required lavish parties.

They were almost to the entrance hall with its gold sconces and coffered ceiling. Evelina walked two paces behind Dora, following the silent, hunched form. Shadows dragged at the hem of her skirts, reminding her that someone—not Nick—had passed her in the upstairs corridor. There had been those hideous, dismembered dolls in the attic. And then there had been screams.

Despite her vaunted nerves, a shudder slid down her backbone. *Why didn't I at least bring along some of Nick's knives?*

Evelina hurried to keep up with Dora, who was clearly on the verge of panic. She seemed to be heading directly to the cloakroom. The door stood open, light pooling on the marble floor beyond. Outside, one of the kitchen girls sat on a long upholstered bench, placed there so guests could change their footwear.

The girl, surely no more than fourteen or fifteen, was bowed nearly double, her face in her hands. The housekeeper sat next to her, wrapped in a quilted housecoat. She murmured softly, cradling the youngster in a motherly embrace. Evelina dragged her gaze away, giving them privacy. "What happened?"

"It was Maisie that cried out," Dora said, the statement jerking out in pieces. "When she saw what was in there." She pointed to the cloakroom.

It was no wonder that Evelina had heard the cry all the way upstairs. The sound, far from being lost in the high ceilings, would have carried right up the stairwell. But what had the young girl seen?

Evelina realized that her hands were icy and she badly wanted the water closet.

The door to the cloakroom stood open. The moment was so silent, she could hear the faint sibilance of the gaslights that had been laid in throughout the main floor. She took a step toward the doorway when Dora touched her arm. The maid's brow was knitted in concern. "It's a terrible sight in there, miss. It's . . . it's . . ."

Dora began to cry again, losing her power of speech.

Evelina squeezed her hand. "Sh. You stay here and help with Maisie. Has someone told Bigelow?" The butler—pillar of all things respectable—was just what the staff needed.

Dora nodded quickly. "He's gone to tell the master."

"Good." With that, Evelina went through the cloakroom doorway. The gas was turned up, as if someone had tried to banish what was in the middle of the floor.

That sight made her forget every other detail of her surroundings.

Evelina stared at the crumpled lump, gradually making out the still form of a woman in a plain jacket and skirt. Not the rags of the poor, but not much above that, either. Her face was turned away from Evelina, giving a view of the back of her head. Her pale brown hair had been torn from its pins, the long tresses trailing around her. A well-worn hat lay a little distance from the body. Someone had carelessly stepped on it, crushing the crown. From the looks of her wardrobe, it had probably been the only one she owned.

It was the last detail that struck home, clogging Evelina's throat with a trembling ache. As a child, she had never gone hungry, but there had been days when the proverbial wolf howled just outside the door. She knew what it was like to have few clothes, and how precious each item could be. It was something the Roths, for all their kindness, could never understand.

Slowly she came to terms with the fact that she was looking at a dead body. Not just dead, but violently dead. The straggling hair was matted with blood. A flutter of nausea worked its way up from Evelina's stomach. She'd seen plenty of funerals and even helped with the laying out, but this was different.

And Evelina was utterly alone in the room. The soul of the girl was gone. Sometimes the dead lingered, but this time Evelina's magic would be of no use. Death reigned over the tableau. Her nausea soured to a chill anger as questions began crowding in—a babble that threatened to turn into a roar. Foremost among them: Why was this dead woman here, at Hilliard House?

Anger thawed the first shock, and Evelina began a slow circuit, looking at the fallen figure from different angles. Suddenly the room itself came into focus, and what had been irrelevant noise turned to important details.

Clearly, the woman's life had been ended here, at this very spot. It was a good thing that the rows of hooks and hangers along the wall were empty of costly garments that night. The simple white paint in the room made the sprays of blood stand out in gaudy contrast.

Evelina's path took her past the victim's feet. A broken candle lay on the floor, as if it had dropped from her hand during the struggle. Wax stuck to the floor, still soft enough to feel greasy when Evelina poked it with her finger. *How long ago did this happen, then?*

When she finally caught a glimpse of the woman's front, Evelina gave a stifled gasp. The dead woman's face was obscured by the tumble of her hair, but Evelina could see the throat had been slashed from ear to ear. What was left of Evelina's dinner began rushing up her throat and she was suddenly aware of the sticky, meaty smell of flesh, thick with the coppery tang of blood.

She turned away, gulping. She had to skitter to avoid the slick of blood pooling under the body. Someone had already stepped in it—the partial arc of a shoeprint had been left just beside the dead girl. It was small—maybe it belonged to the girl herself.

Narrowing her eyes, she studied the skin of the victim. She knew blood pooled inside the body once someone died, leaving bruiselike marks. But there were other faint shadows— very slight abrasions, perhaps—around the neck and chin and along the jaw, as if the killer had grabbed her there. Perhaps in order to cut her throat? The fatal injury angled a tiny bit downward from left to right, seeming to trail away at the end. Did that mean the killer was right-handed? She was too inexperienced to be certain, but one thing was clear.

Whoever had done this had strength. The wound was so deep that it had cut clear through the trachea.

"Evelina? What the blazes is going on here?"

She whirled to face the door. Tobias Roth, Imogen's brother, leaned against the wall, his posture as bonelessly indolent as usual. He was handsome, golden-haired, and dissolutely rumpled, as if he'd redressed himself while leaping out a paramour's window. Even from where she stood, she could smell tobacco, brandy, and sweat. He'd been out at the clubs again and was probably half drunk. He'd also been in a fight, judging by one eye that was starting to purple and the tears in his waistcoat and trousers. His jacket was gone.

Nevertheless, Tobias still looked like the Archangel Gabriel. And even here, the sight of him made her breath hitch, betraying a weakness she refused to surrender to. Angels weren't always as advertised, and Tobias would definitely be of the fallen variety.

But now he stiffened, his face turning pale as he gazed at the corpse in naked horror. "Dear God, that's Grace Child."

"What?" Shocked, Evelina looked at the corpse again, this time seeing past the dreadful wounds. Gingerly, she pushed back the lock of hair that had fallen over the top part of the face. She hadn't recognized Grace out of her maid's uniform and away from the pots and pans. *No wonder Maisie and Dora were so upset.*

And death had made a strange mask of the features, robbing them of expression. The hazel eyes were mere slits, the mouth slack, the cheeks splattered with blood. *She was barely more than a girl.*

"You wouldn't know her to look at her, would you? She was so. . . ." Tobias trailed off.

Evelina said nothing, still astonished by how different the girl looked.

"Who would do something like this? And why?" His voice had gone quiet, a thread of anger giving it a darker edge.

"I don't know." Evelina shook her head. Despite the fact that she was suddenly cold enough to shiver, sweat trickled under her arms and between her breasts. She swallowed hard for the fortieth time, forcing her stomach back down her gullet. "But I think I know how they did it."

"What do you mean?"

"Someone seized her by the throat and choked her, most likely when her back was turned. That would have made sure she didn't cry out. Then he cut her open while she was down. You can see her hairpins have been pulled out. If I'm right, the murderer grabbed her jaw to hold her head steady."

Tobias went utterly still. "Bloody hell."

Evelina could see it in her mind's eye—but what about what came next? Or before? "Someone must have seen who came and went from the house tonight. There has to have been a witness."

Tobias was silent. Then he seemed to pull himself together. His silvery gray gaze lifted to search Evelina, taking in her unbound hair and torn hem. "Are you all right? How did you come to be part of this?" He stepped into the cloakroom, coming far too close.

"I'm fine," she said shortly, all too aware of his nearness. "I came to see if I could help." As if to prove it, she drew close enough to bend over the body, to touch it. She would never, ever play the vulnerable woman with Tobias. That was a trap she might never have the will to escape.

But, oh, it was hard. The top buttons of his shirt were undone, his collar gone. She could see the smooth pale arc of his throat. Beneath the scent of brandy, she could smell coal smoke, as if he'd been standing next to a steam engine. What had he been doing? The question dissolved—one detail too many to absorb.

He crouched next to her. He was so near, she could feel the heat of his body, and it was all she could do not to lean even closer. *And if Tobias is a fallen angel, what does that make Nick? A handsome creature of the shadow world, come to tempt me with visions of lost love?* Both men were desirable, and both were dangerous.

"What happened to you?" He frowned at the grimy stains on her clothes.

Evelina looked away. "What happened to *you*? You look a fright."

He made a noise that wasn't quite a laugh. "Touché. Nothing happened. The commotion woke me, so I came down to see what was the matter."

Evelina looked up. Tobias met her eyes, as if defying her to contradict him. And yet there he stood, with the black eye and rumpled clothes, the very picture of a rake fresh from his late-night carousing. The question crept into her mind like some hideous subterranean beetle: Did he have anything to do with Grace's death?

No, I don't believe it. I don't want to. She lowered her eyes, wondering if it would have been easier if he were guilty. Anything would be simpler than the hopeless longing she felt whenever he was close.

He must have read her expression. "I can promise you on everything I hold sacred that I had nothing to do with this. I might be a rascal, but I'm not evil." His tone was gentle, almost apologetic, but she saw a flash of anger flit under the surface of his gaze.

It took every ounce of strength to keep her own voice level. "I know."

"Thank you."

How many women, she wondered, had been tempted to reform Tobias Roth? "You startled me in the upstairs hall," she said.

"When?" His white, drawn face didn't change.

"Never mind."

If it hadn't been Nick, or Tobias, then whom? Her stomach lurched. *Dear Lord.*

"Do you know what to look for?" he asked, jerking his chin at the body.

"Are you asking me to name the murderer by looking at the body?"

"Why not?" His eyes were bright with emotion. "If anyone could do it, you could. You're smart enough."

There was his redeeming grace. He didn't treat her like a fool.

Evelina shook her head. "I'm not a consulting detective like my uncle. And be careful. You're nearly standing in the blood."

Tobias drew back with a sharp oath, then noticed the footprint. "Is that yours?"

"No. And I can't be certain it's Grace's. Maybe it belongs to the girl who found her. I need to look more closely."

"Well, I would suggest that you be quick about it. The police are on their way. They couldn't find their backsides with an ordinance survey, but you can be sure they'll toss everyone else out of the room."

"Someone called the constables already?"

Tobias spoke low, through gritted teeth. "Bigelow did, before my father could stop him."

"Stop him?"

"Someone crept into our house and committed murder. The scandal will be ferocious if it reaches the papers, so you can be sure the event will be buried faster than a plague victim."

His words stalled Evelina's brain. "How can you say that?" And then she realized that she was being naive.

Tobias made an impatient sound. "You know my father. Best to get on with your work."

What work? What am I looking for? And why?

There was no good answer, outside the fact that it was impossible *not* to look. Partially it was curiosity. Partially it was respect. This woman had died. She deserved attention.

Carefully, she ran a hand down Grace Child's arm, feeling for broken bones but not finding any. The limbs were still loose and slightly warm, the blood tacky enough to stick to Evelina's fingers. She shuddered, wondering if it would be bad form to wipe herself clean on the victim's skirts.

A small cross hung at Grace's neck, the gold paint chipped. A purse with tattered fringes still held a few pence. Not robbery then—though any thief in this house would be after a bigger prize. Mended stockings. A hem and boots with fresh mud.

Grace had been out before this had happened. Errand? Assignation? Just a night off work to visit with friends? Evelina sniffed near Grace's mouth. No telltale stench of gin. No scent of cheap perfume. Just a burned smell, as if clothing or hair had caught fire, but she saw no scorch marks on Grace's clothes.

She lifted the hem of the skirt slightly, trying to gauge the depth of mud the girl had tromped through. Not too bad. Probably paved streets, then. Moving the skirts revealed a long, careful mend in Grace's right stocking. And, oddly, a brand-new petticoat trimmed in Brussels lace. Where had she come by that?

Evelina had a sudden, sinking feeling. A girl clinging to the edge of society, one with no protection, one tempted to seek affection in the wrong places. But for the grace of God, it could have been Evelina.

She squeezed her eyes shut for a long moment, fighting back tears, imagining the terror Grace had felt and no doubt falling short of the real thing. Then she drew out her handkerchief and covered the girl's face, giving her some dignity. She tried to remember some detail about the girl, but knew woefully little about the servant who slept under the same roof.

She arranged Grace's skirts, smoothing them over the edge of her petticoats. *I'll do what I can for you.* It would be little enough. As she'd said to Tobias, she was no detective.

There was the stomp and shuffle of men's boots, and Tobias left Evelina to greet the newcomers at the door. A glimpse of tall, distinguished Lord Bancroft told her that time was running out. Even in a dressing gown, he had the look of a man ready to slap an unruly colony back into obedient servitude.

But he was a man with secrets. She knew that now. *Dark magic, Your Lordship? Now there's a tale you'll keep close at all costs.*

Evelina slipped her fingers under Grace's jacket, questing for anything the servant might have hidden. Too many assumed a woman always used her bodice as a hiding place, but there were other options. Sure enough, there was an envelope tucked in the waistband at the small of Grace's back, still moist with sweat. Evelina retrieved it and checked for the address. It was blank. Something hard was inside.

An unpleasant sensation swept up her arm. *Magic.* It had a strange, double-layered flavor, as if the envelope's contents had come into recent contact with not one, but two spells. Some substances, occasionally stone but more often metal, could absorb magical residue. *Where were you, Grace?* These were dark spells, unlike anything her Gran Cooper would have spun. Evelina squeezed the envelope, trying to guess what it held.

She was suddenly all too aware of the constables standing with Lord Bancroft. Her pulse began to speed. *There is evidence of murder and dark magic on your cloakroom floor, my lord.* With a little careful management, the death of a servant might not arouse undue interest, but a scandal involving magic would be ruinous. There would be jail, or worse, and the courts were swift to find a culprit whenever and wherever magic was found. Every year, the penalties grew harsher, and a lordship was no guarantee of safety.

And if Lord Bancroft were destroyed, his family would be, too.

The thought made Evelina stiffen. Faces flashed through her mind: Tobias, Poppy, gentle Lady Bancroft, and even Lord B himself. They had been good to her. And Imogen was her only real friend. She slipped the envelope into her pocket and out of sight. Guilt flushed her cheeks, but she wasn't handing it over until she understood what was going on—or, more precisely, until she was sure Imogen and her family would be proven innocent.

"What is Miss Cooper doing here? And not properly dressed?" Lord Bancroft asked in a brusque tone. A slight sibilance betrayed the fact he had been enjoying a late-night tête-à-tête with the whisky decanter. "Do I need to point out the obvious and say this is not a suitable scene for a young woman?"

"I invited her," Tobias lied coolly. "You know she has an excellent head for details."

"I fancied I heard something earlier," Evelina interjected, thinking about the voices she had heard while in the tree. The clock had struck eleven, drowning them out. And then there had been the figure in the hallway. "I thought I might prove helpful."

"Is that so, Miss Cooper?" Lord Bancroft lowered his

brow. "It has nothing to do with your taste for sensational novels? Perhaps you should return to your bedchamber."

She was about to protest, to say he had to listen, or at least the police did. But, with a lift of his chin, he effectively dismissed her.

Anger fired along her nerves, bright and sharp as lightning. She barely stopped herself from making a gesture unbecoming a lady—or shouting that he should be quiet and let her help him, because she might be the only one who saw the full danger his family was in. Instead, she turned back to the body, continuing with her inspection despite her seething.

Uncle Sherlock very rarely gave in to emotion. Now she saw why—she needed a clear head. It was impossible to concentrate when she wanted to snarl like a tinker's cur.

There wasn't a whiff of magic on the body itself, which meant some*one,* not some*thing* invoked by sorcery, had wielded the blade. That meant Grace Child had been killed by a purely human agency. Or did it? In Evelina's limited experience, it took time for magical residue to stick, especially to flesh, so was it safe to make an assumption?

That raised an interesting question. Was there a connection between this murder and those trunks in the attic? Two unusual events in one night could be coincidence, but it seemed unlikely.

Lord Bancroft gestured to the man on his left. "This is Inspector Lestrade." The former ambassador's voice was dry as he addressed his son.

Evelina started. *Lestrade.* She knew the name from her uncle's cases, but she'd never met him in person. She studied him carefully, thinking that Dr. Watson had described him well.

"I'm sure you and Miss Cooper will leave him and his men to do their work," Bancroft added.

All eyes were on Tobias, who had his mouth set in a defiant frown. Evelina was invisible, just a girl who had accidentally strayed into the affairs of men—even though she was the one getting her hands bloody. Piqued, Evelina rose to her feet.

The motion of her standing drew the eyes of the inspector. "Miss?"

He was a wiry man of middling height with dark hair, a sallow complexion, and the sharp, pointed features of a rat. He had dressed with the look of one eager to impress, but something in his air made Evelina uneasy. This was no fool. She wondered, with a sick feeling, if Nick had finally found the wits to leave the house.

She looked at him squarely. "This is Grace Child, one of the kitchen staff."

Lord Bancroft barely stirred at the news. There were doubtless more drudges where Grace had come from.

Lestrade narrowed his eyes—an expression that did not match his polite nod. "Thank you, miss, but I'd appreciate it if you stepped away. There's a chance you might disturb the evidence."

"Of course."

As she moved toward the door, the evidence in her pocket, she counted the uniforms Lestrade had brought with him. There were three, all crowding into the cloakroom with chests puffed out and brass buttons shining.

One had a chemical whistle strapped to his belt, set to give off a shrill alarm if its plunger was depressed. Her uncle, something of a chemist, had designed the prototype and given it to Scotland Yard. If only the coppers' brains were as sharp as their gear.

With a pang of frustration, she wondered if anyone had thought to search the grounds. Or was that too much a breach of His Lordship's privacy? Lucky for Nick, they weren't combing the upstairs rooms, but . . .

She thought again about that moment in the upstairs corridor. Had Grace surprised someone? The idea gnawed at her.

But Lestrade's eyes were on her. The only thing Evelina could do right then was retreat, so she returned to the hall where Dora sat. Maisie and the housekeeper were gone, but someone had brought tea, the universal restorative. A little steam-powered trolley sat huffing to one side, smelling of Assam and brandy.

Evelina sat next to Dora. "How are you?"

Dora sniffed wearily. "I'll be all right, miss." But she shook her head, as if nothing would ever be right again. "Poor Maisie'd done the last of the pots and was going to bed. Taking the short way rather than the servant's stairs like she was supposed to. Saw the light and went to shut it off and then there was Gracie."

Evelina thought a moment, trying to picture the scene in her head. "There was a woman's footprint by Grace, and I noticed she was wearing walking boots that would have left a much larger outline. It couldn't have been hers. Do you know if Maisie went right up to the body?"

"No, miss. She barely set foot in the room once she saw the blood. I didn't, either. I get all hot and shuddery at the sight of a scraped knee, to say nothing of . . . of this."

Then whose shoe made that mark? She would have to find out where all the servants were tonight. She moved on to the next question. "Do you have any idea why Grace was in the cloakroom?"

A flush crept from the neat white collar of Dora's uniform, turning her ears crimson. "I wouldn't know that, miss."

Obviously she did. Evelina softened her voice. "Was she going to meet someone there? After all, it is a quiet room, and no one was using it. A private place."

"I don't know, miss. She wasn't a careful girl."

"Careful how?"

"To hear her talk, you'd think her latest beau was the crown prince."

"What do you mean?" Evelina asked, more sharply this time.

Dora suddenly looked very frightened. "I don't mean anything by it, miss."

"Was she someone's . . ." Evelina trailed off, thinking about the fancy petticoat.

Dora tucked in her chin, resembling a turtle on the defensive. "If it were anything much, she wouldn't have been peeling spuds all day, if you know what I mean."

"But she was seeing someone who had money?"

A sidelong glance shot from under the maid's lashes. "That

would have been a bit of all right, but her bad stomach in the morning said there was trouble on the way."

Evelina caught her breath. Grace had been about to be ruined. She would have lost her place. There weren't many options open to an unwed mother, especially a poor one. Usually those stories ended with death or emigration. "Did she ever say who the father was?"

Dora shook her head. "She never said any names." There was clearly more she wanted to tell, but she pressed her fist against her lips, as if to hold back the words.

"What, Dora?"

The maid shook her head again, tears glistening in her eyes. "Oh, miss, I saw Grace barely a half hour before Maisie found her."

"Alive?"

Dora nodded in quick, jerky movements. "I saw her out the window. She was in the garden, as if catching a breath of air before coming in to bed."

Evelina automatically calculated the hours. That narrowed down the time of death considerably. "Right after you left Imogen's room?"

Dora nodded. "When I went to fetch the sleeping draft."

That would have put the time at around twelve thirty. Evelina again remembered the voices she'd heard when she'd been outside. That had been much earlier, almost an hour and a half before.

"Alone?"

"No, miss."

Evelina felt her scalp crawl. "Who was she with?"

The maid was silent, gaze falling to her hands, where they kneaded the fabric of her apron.

"Dora, I won't repeat what you say. You know me better than that."

That seemed to reassure her. Dora leaned forward, dropping her voice to a whisper. "Mr. Tobias."

Evelina felt her jaw fall open, but couldn't summon the presence of mind to close it.

What has the great ninny gone and done now?

Tobias chose that moment to walk out of the cloakroom,

pausing to look her way. Dora stiffened, obviously sharing Evelina's dangerous thoughts. His shirt and hands were pristine, free of blood, but the bruise on his face seemed darker in the shadows beyond the gaslight. Someone had fought him hard.

A paralysis came over Evelina, pinning her where she sat. Frustration bubbled up, a painful pressure in her chest. She wanted to jerk her chin away, to ignore the steady searching of his gray eyes.

They both had secrets. Even though he'd learned nothing about her girlhood in the circus, much less her magic, he knew other things about her—such as her unorthodox taste for science and mechanics, and that she understood far more of the world than any young lady ought to.

She knew more than was proper about his gambling and women. She didn't need to be a detective for that—just have the eyes of a girl half in love. Neither of them ever spoke a word about what they saw in the other, and yet they both knew that the mutual knowledge was there.

Any other day, Evelina treasured that shared complicity as something that bound them together. Tonight, with so much suspicion in the air, it felt unsafe.

Tobias's mouth twitched downward, as if he sensed her discomfort. He turned with a slight hitch in his shoulder— the merest suggestion of a shrug—and left the room. A moment later, Evelina heard his footstep on the stairs. Going to bed. Returning to bed, if one believed his tale, though how one got a black eye while snugly tucked beneath the covers beggared her imagination. *Of course he knew Grace. He saw her just before she died.*

Yes, keeping his secrets forged a link between them, but it wasn't at all the kind of intimacy she had dreamed of sharing with Tobias Roth. And for that merest sliver of time, she hated him for it.

CHAPTER FOUR

LET IT BE KNOWN that the Society for the Proliferation of Impertinent Events was formed this twenty-first day of September 1887, for the exploration of practical science. The charter members of this society are the Honorable Tobias Roth, Mister Buckingham Penner, Captain Diogenes Smythe, and Mister Michael Edgerton. Membership private and by recommendation only.

They have selected for their motto the phrase "Beware, Because We Can."

—Official Charter of SPIE,
filed in the archives of the Xanadu Gentlemen's Club

London, April 4, 1888
THE ROYAL CHARLOTTE THEATRE

8p.m. Wednesday

IN A JUST UNIVERSE, A SPECIAL CIRCLE OF HELL AWAITED bad opera singers. And lo, the self-appointed administrator of that justice was to be Tobias—but very few knew that just yet.

At four o'clock that afternoon, *The Flying Dutchman* dropped anchor in the Royal Charlotte Theatre with all the *gravitas* of Wagnerian excess: elaborate sets, a massive orchestra, and singers with the lung power of bull elephants. Following some logic that Tobias couldn't fathom, the performance had started at an uncivilized hour, too late for a matinee and too early for an evening performance—but all the better to bombard the poor audience with hours of Sturm und Drang. In short, the long-awaited London debut of the Prinkelbruch opera company was not so much entertainment as a juggernaut flattening the senses.

From his throne in the balcony, Tobias scanned the horse-shoe of gilt and velvet boxes. The Royal Harlot—er—Charlotte resembled a cross between a whore's boudoir and a stale wedding cake. There was not a single surface that was not swagged, tasseled, or crusted in flaking gold paint.

Anyone who mattered in fashionable London was there, and the scent of overwarm humanity mixed with competing perfumes like an expensive fog. The heat was making Tobias itch wherever the flannel of his perfectly creased trousers touched his bare skin.

His companion, Buckingham "Bucky" Penner, lolled in his seat as if fatally shot, fanning himself with the program. "I rather like opera, but would say this *Dutchman* is a *sinking* occasion. And I, for one, am ready to walk the gang-plank."

Tobias spared a glance for his friend. "We're not here for the music. We're here to win the bet."

"Ever the general, with your mind on the plan."

"It's certainly not on the opera. I'd run mad. That baritone oomphs his arias like a morose foghorn."

Penner snuffled a laugh. He reminded Tobias of a mischievous spaniel, always in search of food, soft pillows, and pretty young women to snuggle up to. About half the time, he was steady, sensible, and a good listener. However, behind those mild brown eyes lurked a talent for creative geometry. No one knew how to calculate the trajectory of projectiles quite like Bucky. Given a fulcrum and a sufficient amount of force, he made things go "splat" excellently well.

And splattage was key to their machinations. The preceding autumn, Tobias Roth had wagered that he could scandalize fashionable London, land on the front page of every important newspaper, and mobilize the armed forces of the Empire in a single night without being arrested or dropping his pants.

The reason he had done so had subsequently vanished in

an alcoholic haze. Nevertheless, a bet was a bet, duly recorded and witnessed at the Xanadu Gentlemen's Club. Thousands of pounds rested on Tobias's word, not to mention a stellar opportunity to annoy his father.

"You are mad," Bucky observed placidly. "But in a pleasant way."

Tobias lifted the chased silver handle of his opera glasses to once more peruse the audience. "A man needs an antidote to boredom. A man needs ambition."

"To do what?"

The question summed up Tobias in three words. At the advanced age of twenty-three, he was more familiar with all the things he *didn't* want to do with his life. The founding of the Society for the Proliferation of Impertinent Events was his one great accomplishment, and the most fun to be had since Diogenes Smythe tried to jump his father's prize stallion over a moving locomotive. *Sad. Really. Surely you're good for more than this?*

Or maybe not. That was the scary possibility, wasn't it?

"Abercrombie put you up to it," Bucky carried on. "I remember that much from the night in question."

"So?"

Bucky sighed with disgust. "Abercrombie is a jam tart and you were drunk. Note that jam tarts are sticky and prone to leaving stains."

Tobias hated the waiting phase of a plan. It always led to moments of doubt, and he was having a large one now. Not that he would admit that to Bucky. *Were eight tentacles enough? Did I bribe the stagehands sufficiently? What the blazes will I do if this goes all wrong? I can't put my hands on that much money. Dear old Dad will throw a wobbler. At least that has possibilities . . .*

He swung the glasses farther to the left. In the penumbra of the gas footlights, the diamonds worn by the ladies in the audience shimmered like the Flying Dutchman's faraway sea. At last, the girl who had caught his eye came into focus. A pretty thing, tall, slender, and crowned with a fall of walnut curls.

To his annoyance, he could sense Bucky leaning over,

trying to guess whom he was ogling. "I say, is that whatsit—I mean your sister's friend?" Bucky asked.

Tobias lowered the glasses, disappointed. "Miss Cooper? No. Just looks a bit like her."

"Ah." Bucky straightened, took a nip from an ornate silver flask, then passed it to Tobias.

"Ah?" Tobias feigned innocence, then started as he caught sight of his father in a center box. Now he knew how Macbeth felt during a Banquo moment. He pushed the image away before it spoiled his mood. Instead, he conjured Evelina's heart-shaped face.

"Ah." Bucky nodded sagely, giving him a sly wink.

Tobias took a drink, disgruntled.

Onstage, the bass-baritone imitated a dyspeptic tuba.

Tobias let the brandy linger on his tongue a moment before swallowing. Evelina Cooper would fit right in with Bucky and the rest of the society's charter members. That is, if one overlooked the girl part, which was plainly impossible. Evelina's girl parts were on his mind almost constantly of late. Imogen's school friend had suddenly come into focus after years of existing as blurry backdrop.

Given her scanty dowry, she wasn't the type of girl one married, not even with the Holmes name on her mother's side. They were just country gentry. All right for a barrister or a civil servant, but not quite the thing for the son of a lord. If it hadn't been for poor Imogen's obvious attachment, Evelina wouldn't travel in their set.

But she wasn't that other kind of woman, either, the kind one kept about just for larks. Things would have been a lot simpler if she were. The problem was, he wanted Evelina to *like* him. It was ridiculous. He never wanted that from a girl.

"Do you think Edgerton's in place?" he asked, mostly to distract himself.

Bucky pulled out his watch, flipped open the case, and peered myopically at the time. "Probably."

Excellent. As he folded away his opera glasses, Tobias looked down at the stage and made a quick calculation. In about fifteen minutes, the ghostly captain would be bemoaning his curse, which meant the heroine would be drowning herself shortly thereafter. After nearly four hours, it was about bloody time. "My friend, let us take up our stations."

Scandal, headlines, bring out the army. How hard could it be?

They exited from the back of the box to the gaslit corridor beyond. A few patrons stood chatting here and there, but none looked up at two impeccably gloved and top-hatted young gentlemen beating a path to the marble foyer. None saw them turn and go through a service door and out the back way.

Darkness had just fallen, the last traces of daylight just fading from the sky. The spring air was as crisp as an Italian wine, even if the alley itself was none too clean. Tobias could still hear the opera plodding along, muffled by brick and distance. They hurried down the muddy passage with one eye on the shadows. The Royal Charlotte, despite its wealthy patrons, was at the edge of a less savory part of London. Here, what few gaslights there were had pale indigo globes, showing that the Blue Boy gang of the steam baron they called King Coal ran these parts. Despite himself, Tobias looked over his shoulder. It wouldn't do for their plans to end with their heads broken and their pockets picked, although he always relished a good fight.

Bucky gave a low whistle that was answered in kind. A small crowd trundled an object toward them. Tobias made out the cheerful features of their friend Edgerton in the lead. Tall and athletic, he wore a shabby brown jacket and an odd round leather helmet. Over his shoulder, he carried a large bag.

Behind him were a half dozen hired men pushing and pulling a low-wheeled handcart. On it sat a metal contraption resembling a large and ugly brass lotus flower surmounted with a kind of seat. Four feet in diameter and as many tall, the lotus emitted a slight wheeze of steam every few seconds.

The lotus-thing had taken the four charter members of the society nearly three months to design. It had taken that long again—plus a good chunk of money—to oversee its construction in a town far north of London, where Edgerton's father had a foundry. It would have been impossible to build such an engine any other way, with the steam barons monopolizing anything that generated so much as a fart, and it had cost them yet more cash to smuggle it south. As Bucky said, Tobias was going a long way to win a wager, but if a bet was worth winning, he would do it right.

As Edgerton reached them, he grasped their hands, pumping them enthusiastically. "Well, here we are, gentlemen. Are you sure this thing is ready?"

"Utterly," Bucky replied. "We calibrated it to a fraction of a degree."

"You brought our gear?" Tobias asked.

"Here." Edgerton indicated his bag.

"Excellent." Fortunately, the alley was deserted except for the workmen who had come with the cart. Ignoring their curious stares, Tobias and Bucky stripped down to their shirts and trousers, then pulled on plain jackets, boots, and helmets much like Edgerton's. In a few moments, they were unrecognizable. Edgerton wore what looked like a quiver slung over his shoulders, the pole of a rolled-up banner sticking from the top.

Tobias felt his heart thud with anticipation, the wine-sharp night fizzing in his blood. Everything was going right. The wager was all but won. It had better be—the price of failure was enough to give the family's finances a serious jolt.

He suddenly thought of his sister's upcoming Season. All those gowns and entertainments cost money. Just how much was he gambling, really?

Too late to think about it.

"Let's do this," he said, sounding oddly hoarse.

Edgerton handed Tobias a pair of thick leather gloves. Slipping them on, Tobias clambered into the wagon, mounting the seat atop the brass machine. It wasn't very well cushioned, and he could feel the rolled edges of the metal beneath his rump, not to mention an uncomfortable warmth. He'd meant to fix that, but had run out of time. *And what else did you miss?*

Heat from the engine seeped through the soles of his boots. Tobias wiped his face with the back of his glove. Already he was starting to sweat, his lips salty as he chewed them in concentration. Some of the repetitive movements of the creature were punched into a rotating cylinder that programmed the gears. The rest were powered by pneumatic pressure, guided by the clump of levers that stuck out from the contraption like the quills of a porcupine. He knew each one perfectly well, but for a moment his mind blanked. *Slow down. Take your time.* He inhaled a long breath, then let it out slowly. *This is completely, boffing mad.*

Which was exactly why it was going to be so much fun. Suddenly, doubt was gone. He had this victory in his pocket, and it was going to taste as sweet as buttered cream.

A grin split his face as he pushed a button and the machine issued a gust of steam. Bucky fell back, putting some distance between himself and the scalding air.

"Anytime now," said Bucky, his voice subdued. "We're ten minutes from the final curtain."

Tobias thumbed the controls. With a smooth click and whirr, the petals of the lotus unfolded, slowly angling away from the core. *Click. Chirrrr.* The bottom ends of the petals detached and unfurled to reveal that the petals were actually eight multijointed limbs. Four slapped the sandy dirt with a scrunch, the other four reaching up with questing pincers.

Tobias paused long enough to wipe his face again. The grin, if possible, had only grown wider. He grabbed two of the levers, easing them back slowly. With a shudder, the bulbous body swung free of the cart, hoisting itself into the air as the legs drew themselves straight with a sigh of metal on metal. It had been designed to move quietly—or at least quietly enough to be drowned out by an opera. So far, they had attracted no unwanted attention to their secluded alley.

Thinking about too many things at once, Tobias pulled hard on one of the levers. One leg straightened faster than the rest, tilting the machine so Tobias listed in his seat. His rump sliding dangerously, he grabbed the edge of his perch with one hand and adjusted the levers with the other. With a

stomach-churning lurch, the mechanical beast righted itself.

Tobias took another deep breath, registering the fact that
everyone else seemed very far away. He had been lifted
seven feet into the air. The dim light of the gaslights slid
along the machine's riveted plates in an eerie glow. The
steam engine that powered the beast, hidden in the depths of
its belly, powered gears and pistons that ground and thumped
in a well-insulated murmur.

Tobias wallowed in dreadful glee. Or was that gleeful
dread? "Behold the great, riveted squid monster, bane of
ghost ships."

"It doesn't have enough tentacles to be a squid," protested
Edgerton. "And squids don't walk. It's a crab."

"It's a squid," Tobias insisted.

"Maybe it's a lobster."

Bucky consulted his pocket watch one more time. "Better
unleash the kraken, or we'll miss our cue."

Edgerton paid the workmen. They wheeled the cart, along
with the discarded evening clothes, back to the warehouse a
few streets away where the machine had been stored.

The leather helmets came equipped with masks and goggles that disguised the top half of the face. All three pulled
them down, adjusting the eyepieces. Tobias adjusted a lever,
and one leg gracefully lifted to take a step forward. As he
lowered it, the body of the beast swayed, sending Tobias
sliding in his seat again. He swore under his breath, giddy
with vertigo and pride in his own cleverness. He pulled the
next lever, moving another leg and lurching in that direction. The sliding around wasn't so bad once he learned to
compensate. Kind of like riding a camel, he supposed. Not
that he'd ever ridden a camel, but . . .

Leg one arced forward with a whoosh of metal joints.

Leg two.

Leg three. *Squeak!*

Leg four.

The tentacles waggled in the steamy air.

Beautiful! Tobias began guiding his nightmare down the
alley, as proud as a mother at her baby's first waddling steps.

Wagner oozed into the night air like heavy treacle. The wild energy surging through Tobias bubbled in his throat, urging him to bellow along. It was a night to imprint in his memory—the laughter of his friends; the stink of the alley; the cold damp on his cheeks; the power throbbing through the controls. Leg three of the beast needed more grease, but it was an imperfection that set off the magnificence of the whole.

Bucky ran ahead to the theater to prop open the high double doors used for delivery of lumber for sets and props. Beyond lay the warren of corridors and dressing rooms behind the stage. As they approached, Bucky and Edgerton stayed a few steps ahead to take care of any interference. The stagehands had been bribed to ignore the invading creature and its shabbily suited keepers, but Tobias wasn't taking any chances. He couldn't afford to lose.

Just as Bucky opened the door and Wagner's music boomed forth into the fetid alley air, a collective gasp came from the motley collection of dressers, understudies, carpenters, and stagehands crowding the backstage area. A huge towheaded brute, surely part of the Prinkelbruch entourage, swore in German. He bulled forward just as the machine made it over the threshold, blocking Tobias's path.

Bollocks!

Two equally beefy characters joined him, so similar in coloring and scowl that they must have been brothers. The other bystanders were clearing away, wanting no part of whatever was about to transpire. A gabble of conversation was rising, sure to disturb the performance onstage. Tobias was running out of time. The three ugly brothers would simply have to move.

With a flurry of levers, the machine swayed forward, one massive foot narrowly missing the biggest of the three. The wooden floor magnified the sound of the beast's movement with a thundering *clomp*.

The gabble of exclamations died at the sound. Tobias felt a surge of gratification. The three huge stagehands growled.

Tobias's friends surged forward, flexing their shoulders and undoing buttons for ease of movement.

Clomp. A papier-mâché breastplate died with a sickening *scrunch.*

One of the brutes lunged for Bucky, who promptly slammed his fist into the man's gut. "Get it on stage!" he roared. "Go!"

Edgerton dove for the other two, tackling them both at once.

Tobias frantically worked the gears, trying to squeeze speed out of the lumbering beast. The creature laboriously lurched forward, rudely blasting a puff of steam from its hindquarters.

It was time to change tactics. Tobias thumbed a control. Two panels in the top of the would-be sea monster whirred open, and twin cannons poked out like antennae. These were Bucky's contribution to the project. The ammunition was a reservoir of overripe oranges.

A few more thumping steps, and Tobias could see the stage. The backdrop was a painted ocean. Imitation boulders and cliffs flanked the set, discreetly hiding the thick mattress upon which the heroine was to leap to her death. The *Flying Dutchman* itself had been wheeled into the middle distance, where it supported a chorus of ghostly sailors.

The cursed captain was staring in horror at Tobias and gradually losing his pitch.

This was the moment they'd worked for. Tobias drove the machine from the wings and into the last act. *Thunk. Thunk. Thunk.*

A woman in the audience screamed—a wonderful, gurgling shriek. The cry was taken up by every female occupying the Royal Harlot's plushy seats. Tobias whooped in merriment.

As scandals went among the London ton, this beat yet another bedroom farce tentacles down. Tobias fired the cannons, sticky orange guts splatting the audience in a perfectly calculated parabola.

With a puff of steam and a flurry of levers, the tentacles of the monster grabbed the ghostly craft's rigging with a sickly sound of ripping canvas and splintering wood. The remain-

ing chorus jumped ship. Outraged, the baritone roared in
E flat major.

Tobias punched a button and the cannons fired more
oranges, one catching the conductor in the ear. The other
landed on the stage in a mighty squish, showering the principal singers in slimy fruit guts.

The next volley hit the brass section. Uproar coursed
through the audience like a wave. Half rose with a cheer.
The other half bolted for the exit before orange peel death
rained from the sky. Edgerton picked that moment to sprint
across the stage, a banner raised high on its pole.

It was emblazoned with the society's motto: *Beware, Because We Can.*

It was just enough of a distraction that Tobias didn't notice that the doomed captain had drawn his weapon, proving
that an operatic hero would indeed attack a seven-foot
steam-driven monster with a pretend sword from the cos-
tuming department.

At that moment, Edgerton collided with a fleeing sailor.
The rebound knocked the chorister into the captain, who
thumped into the ghost ship. The mast toppled and smashed.
Relentless, the squid stepped over the wreckage, but a jut-
ting spur of wood caught and jammed in a leg joint. The jolt
sent Tobias flying from his perch. He tried grabbing at the
levers for balance, but one came off in his hand as he grap-
pled for the steel frame of his seat.

It was the brake.

Damn it all to hell.

The leather gloves, so essential for handling the hot
metal, were hopelessly clumsy. His grip was slipping. Nevertheless, Tobias barely noticed his precarious position, the
conductor snapping his baton in two, even Bucky's wild
arm-waving. He'd caught sight of his father's enraged face.
Lord Bancroft looked in his son's direction, but as usual
didn't recognize who he was. Mocking anger twisted Tobias's
gut: that peculiar mix of love, shame, and disappointment
only a child can know.

Have I finally lived down to your expectations, Father?

At that moment, the only element of success thus far lack-

ing came pounding through the gilded doors at the back of
the auditorium. The fourth charter member of the society—
Captain Diogenes Smythe—had raised the alarm. Burly
men in tight uniforms were coursing down the aisle, faces
as grimly set as if they were storming enemy barricades.

Unfortunately, they were shooting. Apparently Smythe
hadn't bothered to mention specifics, like not killing anyone.

Death missed Tobias by an inch, smashing into the
machine's controls. Tobias dropped to the stage, his shins
stinging from the bad landing. Another bullet smashed
home, gears and bolts spraying in all directions. Tobias felt
the wound to his creation like a searing injury to his own
flesh. He hadn't expected it to survive the night, but still its
destruction was almost too much to bear.

However, the monster did not die easily. Something
jammed inside, causing it to fire volley after volley of rotten
oranges, drenching the ornate theater in a sweetish stink.
That should have been the most it could do, but some devil
had possessed the machine. There was no hand to steer it,
but pistons and gears kept churning in its brass gut. Sparks
flew as the creature blundered through the set, crushing the
ship with the nightmare force of a real kraken.

Tiny flames licked the cheap painted scenery. The *Flying
Dutchman* was about to become Siegfried's ring of fire.
Horror dragged at Tobias's limbs. With a vague notion of
steering the creature back into the street, Tobias ran beside
it, trying to grab a handhold and clamber back onto his
perch. Bullets whistled past his ear and smashed into the
brass panels of its sides.

He was ducking out of the way when a fist cracked into
his right eye. He staggered backward, crashing into the ply-
wood waves. He caught his balance in time to see the baritone charge, head down like a bull. Tobias raised his fists.

Hands grabbed the back of his coat, yanking him away.
"Don't be an idiot," Bucky hissed, dragging Tobias into the
wings.

"This is just getting good!" he said, as the baritone floun-
dered headlong in the scenery.

"They're going to drive a bullet into your idiot hide."

Bucky's words barely had time to sink in before the soldiers stormed toward them. Edgerton stood in the wings, waving frantically.

Tobias gave up and ran. The three friends pelted through the theater and into the alley, a flock of police and soldiers behind them. Muck and mud splattered under their pounding boots, smelling of offal and worse. A police whistle shrilled through the night. He had a horrible vision of one of his friends catching a bullet in the back. "Split up!" he cried.

It was risky, here in King Coal's alleyways, where the Blue Boys reigned over a patch of London little gaslight ever reached. Barely half a mile from the Royal Charlotte, the homes were a honeycomb of broken-down tenements and twisted alleys. Edgerton disappeared to the north. Bucky vanished into a tavern. They wouldn't pass for working-class Londoners, but in their dull brown jackets, they hoped no one would notice them right away.

Tobias kept running, leading the police away from his friends. He was young, fast, and a natural athlete. His pursuers fired but night and speed were on his side. He ducked and wove, making it impossible to aim. Curses filled the air.

A lunatic laugh escaped him.

The first few streets were empty, but the next was filled with traffic. Streetwalkers idled on the corners. Crates and barrels clogged the narrow throughway. Normally, no stranger could walk here in safety, but this time Tobias had a pass. The locals were all too happy to get in the way of pursuing coppers, resulting in a shoving match. A fist was thrown by a drayman, a copper's lip split, and chaos erupted. The chase was over.

Tobias plunged on with the instincts of a fleeing fox.

Eventually, he dodged through a gap-toothed fence, emerging into a cobbled alley scented with stewing lamb. With a jolt of surprise, he realized this place was behind a restaurant he knew well. Directly above him, a curtain fluttered from an open window, the source of the enticing smell.

Tobias stopped, trying to listen past the heaving of his breath. The globes on the gaslights here were Keating Utility gold, indicating a much better neighborhood. He could hear two men passing on the nearby street, amiably chatting about a whist party. A hackney went by in the other direction, drowning out their words. From above, a dull hum of conversation floated from the window, punctuated by the clatter of the kitchen.

No sound of pursuing feet. For the moment, he was safe. He wondered, with a wrench in his chest, if his friends were all right. There would be no way to know until morning.

Tobias shut his eyes, feeling the beat of his slowing heart. *We did it. I won the bet.*

Scandal. Soldiers. There was no way the event would fail to make the papers. Abercrombie had lost. *But was it worth it?*

The question hung in the chill air, draining the energy from his limbs. Suddenly, Tobias was bone-tired. The destruction in the theater had been pointless. The whole wager had been a mindless lark. So much of his life was.

But he'd planned and executed a mission fraught with both scientific and logistical complexity. He'd *done* something.

Satisfaction bloomed in his chest like a small, private sun. It was a new and wondrous sensation.

His pleasure deflated just as quickly. The four friends had forgotten one detail. With the exception of Smythe, they hadn't planned on splitting up. Now they couldn't vouch for each other's whereabouts. If they met someone they knew, their unfamiliar clothes would be hard to explain. In fact, the outfits would connect them with the invasion of the opera house. *Bad planning.*

It was clear that they weren't very experienced criminals. *I need an alibi.*

Tobias stopped in his tracks and then, after a long moment of contemplation, turned right up a long, winding lane that seemed to have been lost in an earlier century. The street was uneven, the houses tall and narrow with wrought-iron fences guarding them from passersby. His feet found their way to the top of the lane, automatically stopping at a door painted a deep purple—violet for the Violet Queen, who ruled the brothels with a fist of lace-clad steel. A brass lion's head gleamed against the dark paint.

Tobias lifted the knocker and rapped softly, knowing there would be a servant listening for callers. As expected, it swung open at once, revealing a Negro boy in a turban and spangled garb that spoke more of theater than of tribal origins. The boy bowed deeply, recognizing a good customer.

"I've come to see Margaretha," Tobias said.

The boy didn't blink, but opened the door wide so that he could enter. It was no less than Tobias had expected—the employees of any of the Violet Queen's houses could be counted on for silence, an alibi, or anything else that could be purchased for coin. So what if a gentleman at the door was wearing goggles and orange slime, not to mention what was starting to feel like a serious black eye? That would be the least shocking thing they were likely to see on any given night.

The boy closed the door and made another deep obeisance, causing the bright green feather in his turban to nod gracefully. He spoke in a soft, liquid accent. "Allow me to summon Madame Margaretha to attend you."

With a sweep of his arm, he invited Tobias to enter the sitting room through a set of etched-glass doors and then disappeared up the stairs. Tobias strolled through the doorway and helped himself to the selection of brandies on a heavily carved sideboard. The room was unoccupied but for a statue of Venus draped in a net of minuscule lights—an eerie feature of the place. Tobias sank into a thickly cushioned chair opposite the statue and swirled the liquor in his glass, letting the fumes soak through his growing fatigue. Venus stared back, a remote look on her perfect face that reminded him oddly of his mother.

That wasn't an encouraging thought. Nor was it helped by the realization that he didn't particularly want a woman right then. If he could have had the option, he would have chosen someone with a clever wit, someone who could understand what he had just accomplished, and maybe someone who could tell him why his achievement felt so hollow.

Margaretha was lush and beautiful, but she wasn't the woman he needed. The only one he knew with that quick mind and gentle heart—one who would listen without judgment—was Evelina Cooper. In some ways, Evelina was so much a part of the family that she had become like another sister—except that not all his thoughts about her had remained particularly brotherly. With every passing day, he was less certain how to approach her.

He swallowed the last of the brandy, feeling the heat of it flow into his veins. What was he to do about Evelina? Women usually made him lusty, bored, or annoyed—and in that order. The Cooper girl just confused him, but he enjoyed every moment of it—which was simply perverse and inconvenient and intriguing.

The door swung open, the Negro boy stepping forward with an obsequious bow. "Margaretha will join you momentarily."

To his surprise, Tobias found himself shaking his head. "I'm going to sit here awhile. Bring me a cold supper instead."

This time, there was the faintest trace of curiosity on the boy's face as he withdrew. Tobias was glad he didn't owe anyone under this roof an explanation, because there was no good way to explain himself. He was starting to want a girl he had no business even thinking about, and he wanted her badly enough that it was putting him off his game.

TOBIAS LEFT THE establishment with the violet door hours later. Margaretha and the boy received a generous sum to say that he had paid an unremarkable visit that had begun at seven o'clock that night. The next steps were up to him. Absolutely no one could see him sneaking into the house. He had to be careful—with the fashion for lights everywhere, it was extremely hard to find a shadow to skulk in.

Tobias rounded the corner, hurrying past a dark, shuttered house that stood a street away from Beaulieu Square. It had been Disconnected for a year and squatted like an inky blot beside its brightly lit neighbors. It was odd, but he couldn't actually remember the names of the family that had lived there. He was almost sure that he'd seen people coming and going until a few months ago. It was true—once the barons cut you off, you disappeared.

With relief, he saw the bright outline of Hilliard House come into view. He knew there would likely be a servant or two still up in the kitchen, cleaning up the last of the day's pots and pans, but the kitchens were at the back. His best bet was the side door. He had a key for that. It would be a quick trip up the stairs, into fresh clothes, and then out again to get rid of the brown coat he still wore.

Tobias began crossing the street at an angle, trying to aim for the house without looking as if that were his destination.

"Mr. Roth."

He wheeled, his stomach knotting. A young girl in shabby clothes was standing a few feet away, looking hesitant. One of the kitchen girls. *Damn it all to hell.*

"Gracie," he said, forcing his voice into pleasant tones. He knew the girl from the kitchen, where he'd sometimes roam in search of a bite to eat after everyone else had retired. She'd be there late, and up to her elbows in soap suds—something he'd found oddly fetching.

Surprise turned to simmering irritation. He didn't find her presence fetching now. It was damned inconvenient. The last thing he needed was a witness. Nevertheless, he'd have to make the best of it. There was nothing else he could do.

"Good evening, sir," she said, bobbing a curtsey. "Seems we're both out late tonight. Mr. Bigelow's gone and bolted the door. I meant to be here on time, sir, really I did, but the Chinaman was so slow and I had to run a long, long way."

He wondered vaguely who the Chinaman was, but then dismissed the thought. Excuses didn't matter. The butler locked up at midnight sharp. Any servant out past curfew was not only barred from the dubious comfort of their tiny bedrooms, but would be disciplined in the morning. Tobias felt sorry for the girl, and then relieved. It wouldn't be hard to convince her to keep quiet about his presence here since he was the one with a door key.

He gave her a smile. It made the flesh around his eye

throb, and he touched it gingerly. The hot ache told him he would have a black eye by morning. *Damn that baritone.*

"You've been in a scrap," she said, drawing a little closer.

"I'm afraid so."

"You need to put something cold on it." She reached up, barely touching his cheek with the fingertips of her shabby gloves. She had the most beautiful eyes, huge and long-lashed. The darkness muted the color and he couldn't tell if they were gray or blue, but their almond shape was exotic, tilted upward at the corners. "It won't swell up if you keep it cold."

"Then I'd better let you in so that you can find me some ice," he said.

"I'd be happy to, sir," she said with obvious relief. "Especially if it means dodging Mr. Bigelow's scolding in the morning when he finds me out here instead of peeling the potatoes."

She spoke carefully, as if trying to erase the accent that marked her as a girl from the East End. It fit with everything else about her—the carefully mended clothes, her tidy hair, the neat, dainty way she walked. She might only have been a scullery maid, but she was trying to move up in the world. The last thing she needed was to be dismissed from her post.

Tobias wasn't going to be the one to ruin her chances. "I won't tell Bigelow, but only if you promise never to say you saw me out here tonight."

She drew her hand away. "You sound deadly serious about that!"

"I am. So can we keep secrets?"

She looked up from under her lashes, a gesture that must have broken a good many hearts. "To be sure!" She had a triangular face with a tiny, bowed mouth and turned-up nose. With those eyes, she looked feline—and beautiful, even by the standards of the Mayfair courtesans. The figure under her shabby clothes was rounded and lush. Tobias felt his body stir. He never poached the servant girls, but that didn't mean he was blind to their charms. "I'll keep mum, Mr. Roth."

"Good girl." He began hunting in his pockets for his keys. "So what were you doing tonight? Making merry?"

She didn't answer at once, and he didn't push. It wasn't really any of his business. But just as the key turned in the lock, she caught his arm. "Mr. Roth?"

"What is it?"

Her voice came in a quaver. "You've always been a good sort. A kind man. That's what they say below stairs. Not too high and mighty to care what happens to the likes of us."

He felt a stirring of pride, but pushed it down at once. It was true that he did what he could for the people who worked at Hilliard House, but servants flattered when they wanted something. It was one of the few tools they had. "I'm glad you believe so, but why does that matter right now?"

Grace tightened her grip, as if he were a handhold against a raging wind. "I'm in terrible trouble, you see."

She's pregnant and needs money. Or at least, that was the most probable calamity to befall a young and pretty girl with no future. "A child?"

She gave a faint nod, as if that admission cost far more than he could guess.

"Oh, Grace," he said softly. There was no need to tell her she had been foolish. That painful awareness was written in every line of her body.

"That's not the half of it, Mr. Roth." Tears were starting to trickle down her face. Those beautiful eyes crumpled shut, as if holding her misery in. "I'm afraid."

Tobias caught her hand and squeezed it. "Of what?"

"Not just for me, but for my poor baby, too." She squeezed back so hard that his fingers ached. This was no dainty miss, but a hardworking girl.

Now he was alarmed, forgetting his own troubles as she started to weep in earnest. "Whatever for?"

She lifted her chin, forcing her eyes open. Tears shone on her cheeks, reflecting back the distant streetlights. It made her look as if her tiny, pointed features were washed in liquid silver. "Us girls got to takes their chances where they find them."

"What?" Tobias felt like an idiot, unable to put the pieces together.

Suddenly, she was sobbing. "I agreed to do something for some bad men. I didn't hurt anyone, I promise, but it was wrong. I didn't know it at first, I just went back and forth for them, but I saw what they were doing tonight! And now I know why he wanted me."

"What are you talking about?"

"I can't stop, or they'll hurt me. I can't keep on with it, because sooner or later, I'll be caught. And now there's a baby to think of!"

Tobias was losing the thread of the conversation. "Why did you do—whatever it was—at all?"

"I loved him, I did. What a foolish, foolish girl I am." She pressed her knuckles to her mouth, her shoulder shaking in silent grief.

He could feel it all the way to his guts. "You need to go far away from here."

She nodded, eyes wet. "But I've never been more than a few miles from home."

"Are you brave enough to try?" he asked. "For the baby?"

She nodded.

The Penners had an estate up in Yorkshire. If he asked, Bucky would find her a place up there—somewhere to be until the child was born, and then a position on their household staff. There were any number of young widows with babies in the world. Who was to say Grace wasn't one of them? "I'll get you away from here. Someplace good and safe."

"Do you really mean that?" She sounded like a small child herself. In truth, she was barely older than Poppy, who was still in the schoolroom. He tried to imagine his youngest sister with child, and his stomach turned.

He managed a smile. "I might be a rascal, but I'm not a liar. Now come inside and get to bed."

She grabbed his arm again. "Promise me you won't tell anyone about the baby!"

He stopped. "I'll have to tell something to the people in

Yorkshire. Not much, but enough to make them understand."

Tears filled her eyes. "But no more than that. I've my parents to think of. If I have to go, let them keep a clean memory of me. I never meant to bring them shame."

That was simple enough. "Of course."

He opened the side door and ushered Grace inside. The door was just down the hall from the cloakroom. The stairway to the servants' quarters was next to the kitchen, far to his left, the stairway that led to his own bed to his right.

They stopped in the hall, suddenly awkward. "Thank you so much, Mr. Roth," she said. "You've saved my life."

He felt suddenly confused, as if he'd glimpsed the edge of something far darker than he fully understood. Maybe she was taking advantage of him, playing on his sympathies, but every instinct said her distress was genuine. Suddenly, the entire escapade at the opera house seemed like a surreal nightmare, insubstantial and ludicrous. *This* was real—whatever it was.

He cleared his throat. "Good night, Grace. I'll find you tomorrow and we'll talk again."

"Good night." She gazed into his face a long moment. Now he could see her eyes were a luminous pale blue, the color of a hazy sky. Grace truly was a beautiful girl.

She turned and walked toward the servants' quarters, her hips swinging slightly under her skirts. *I saved her life.* Tobias felt oddly shaken, as if he had surprised himself. *But what have I saved her from?*

CHAPTER FIVE

FOR TWO WEEKS ONLY!
THE CELEBRATED PLOUGHMAN'S PARAMOUNT CIRCUS
MR. THADDEUS PLOUGHMAN, PROP. & MANAGER
LIONS! TIGERS! MAGIC! THE FABULOUS FLYING COOPERS!
AND THE INDOMITABLE NICCOLO, LATE OF ITALIA,
EQUINE MASTER EXTRAORDINAIRE!
THE HIBERNIA AMPHITHEATRE, LONDON,
EVERY EVENING AT EIGHT O'CLOCK,
MATINEES EVERY DAY AT TWO O'CLOCK.
CHILDREN UNDER 10 YEARS OF AGE HALF-PRICE
TO DRESS CIRCLE AND STALLS.
—Advertisement, *The London Prattler*

NICK TOLERATED THE CAGE OF FILMY BED CURTAINS FOR all of a minute. Those sixty seconds on Evelina's bed were enough to conjure a lifetime of fantasies—what with the fine, embroidered linen and distinctly feminine scents—but with no female to complete the picture, it was pure frustration.

Besides, there had been no more screams or pounding on doors. Either everyone was dead or the crisis was over, and he was doing no good hiding among the mountain of pillows that crowded Evelina's bed. How did anyone find room to sleep in all this fluff?

He slid out from the lacy bower, feeling his boot heels sink into the plush carpet. A Siberian tiger could not have felt more out of place. The dainty, fussy, and obviously expensive room was nothing like the caravans or railway cars he usually slept in. The silver hairbrush on the dressing table was worth more than Nick's entire stash of coin, and he was a good saver.

He ghosted about the room, careful not to make a noise. Evelina was right—he had taken a risk coming here. A stupid one. No one would believe he was there just to ensure his childhood sweetheart was safe and happy—or maybe, just maybe, hoping that she had missed him. Anyone sensible would take one look at his rough clothes and dark skin and assume the worst.

And maybe they wouldn't be entirely wrong. There was no mistaking the fact that little Evie was a woman now, and he wanted to feel her curves under his hands. He wanted to hear her murmur his name, to cry it out in the dark of the night.

He trailed a hand along the top of a chest of drawers. Everything in the room breathed her presence. Atop a lace-edged runner sat an array of tiny crystal bottles of scent with names like Guerlain and Houbigant on the labels. A bouquet of flowers sat on the dressing table: late tulips, tiny yellow roses that must have come from a hothouse, and other exotic things he couldn't name. The tulips were wilting, blood-red petals startling against the dark wood.

The bookshelf, however, was puzzling. Nick had learned to read from Evelina's mother, learning everything he could from the thin, sickly woman, but he had never seen books like these before. Here were texts on botany. Books on astronomy. Lots of books on chemistry and anatomy.

He ran his finger over the spines, wondering what kind of person Evelina had grown into. University? What sort of female did that? Weren't girls supposed to like horrid stories about highwaymen and ruined castles?

Ah. There they were, on the bottom shelf. A collection of cheap novels and penny-dreadful serial magazines, kept almost out of sight like guilty pleasures. So there was something left of the Evie he knew after all. It lived in her love of fabulous tales, in her quick wit and sharp tongue, in those blue eyes that told him far more than her words ever would. In the magic pulling them together.

But there was more—much more—about this new Evelina

that he didn't know. At their age, five years apart was an eternity. Nick gave himself a wry smile in the looking glass. He understood that his idealized Evie—the one who waved aside her life of privilege and joined him on the road—was just a fantasy. One that had little to do with the real girl, and much more to do with his own desires.

His chest felt suddenly hollow. Dreams, even foolish ones, didn't die painlessly. *What do you expect? You have no fortune, no name, no relations of importance. You may be the great Niccolo, but you are not a gentleman.*

That was bad enough. Worse, she had plainly wanted him to leave. Anger flashed through him, fueled by shame. He might have had no right to come here, but she had no right to shoo him away like a sparrow begging crumbs. He deserved more than that.

Nick's face heated. There was no point in waiting. No point in ever coming back.

The thought rammed into him, leaving a degree of shock, but no pain. Nick wiped a hand over his face. The hurt would come later, the way feeling returned to a finger just slammed in a door.

He'd stopped in front of the writing desk and was gazing at the train case she'd been about to open when he'd surprised her. It was the type women filled with toiletries, and he had no desire to investigate yet more feminine clutter. He was done with women for the night.

Instead, he picked up the paper knife she'd nearly stuck in his eye. It was slender, the handle made of ebony decorated with a silver crest. Probably the arms of the lord who owned the house. They liked to put their mark on things, like dogs claiming their territory.

The knife was too fancy for his taste, but Evie had used it like a fighter's weapon. He picked it up, flung it into the air, and caught it as it spun downward in a perfect arc. The blade was as balanced as one of his own. Whatever Evelina might say, her instincts hadn't changed. And that was how he preferred to remember her: canny as a street sparrow and ready for action. He thrust the knife into his belt. If the world thought him a thief, why not oblige? He deserved a souvenir of the one great love of his young life.

He would escape this cursed bedroom, make sure the house was safe for Evie, and then go on with his night. And every night thereafter.

Nick slipped out the window, easily climbing down the same stonework and ivy he had used to reach Evelina's bedroom. It was child's play for an acrobat like him.

Unfortunately, in his pique, he had left the safety of the house without checking the grounds. When his boots silently touched the grass, he recoiled. At the corner of the building stood the outline of a helmeted constable, dark against the patch of light seeping from one of the downstairs windows. He froze, gluing himself to the wall. His heart lurched into a gallop, forcing him to gulp in the cold air. *Damn, damn, and damn.* His fingers gripped the rough stone of the wall, clutching it as if that would flatten his telltale form just a little bit more. In Nick's experience, where there was one Peeler, there were always more.

It was then he realized the scream—whatever it had been about—had summoned half the world. Evelina's room looked out the back of the house, but he could still hear noise from the street. Carriages were pulling into the square, some driven by horses, more by steam, and bringing the loud, masculine voices of more police.

Good news for Evelina. Whatever else, she was protected from the threat that had disturbed the house. He released a breath of relief.

However, it was not good news for vagabonds hanging about in the garden. Nick made a quick assessment.

Hilliard House sat on a respectably sized swath of garden bordered by brick walls. Flanked on either side by arches of terraced homes, it made up one side of Beaulieu Square. He had to either climb the back wall of the garden, which would land him in Ketherow Lane; get over a wall to one of the neighboring properties; or make it to the front of the house and saunter out of the square like he belonged there. Given that lights were coming on in the windows next door, the lane was his most realistic option. At least it was dark enough to hide there. The gangs that ran through the London Streets—the Yellowbacks, Blue Boys, Scarlets, and the rest—could be trouble, but he'd take his chances with them before a magistrate.

There wasn't a moment to spare for dithering. Nick sprinted across the lawn and hurled himself at the brick wall. Just as he cleared the top, he heard a startled "Hoi!" from the vicinity of the constable. They'd be on him in no time.

He heard the piercing shrill of a chemical whistle. Nick swore at himself, at the gods, at Evelina. He landed on the cobbles of Ketherow Lane and straightened to find himself nose to nose with a tall gentleman in an opera cape. Nick fell back a step, ready to dodge around him. But the gentleman raised his walking stick, blocking Nick's escape. The light flashed on a heavy ring with a dark-colored stone, stark against the white of his glove. "Stay a moment. Please."

The last word made Nick hesitate. Those intent on making an arrest were rarely polite. On the other hand, who was polite to shabby young men obviously sneaking out the back way? Generally not men who wore top hats and carried silver-headed canes.

"What do you want?" Nick asked, his ears perked for the sound of running feet. "I'm in something of a rush."

"Is this the rear of Lord Bancroft's residence?"

"Yes."

"So I thought."

Nick tried to get a better look at the stranger, but the darkness shadowed the man's face. All he could make out was the curve of a high cheekbone. By the voice, he was not a young man, but not more than middle aged.

"And you were within the walls?" the stranger asked.

"Yes." Nick twitched in impatience. "And obliged to leave quickly."

The man laughed softly. Out of the darkness came a flash of teeth. Nick had worked with enough lions and tigers to sense the predator lurking beneath the fine clothes. As with the big cats, he knew better than to show his unease.

The stranger ceased blocking Nick with the cane. Instead,

he propped it over his shoulder as if it were a decapitated parasol. "Why, my good fellow, you've been walking with me this past hour."

"What's that?" Nick was incredulous and a bit alarmed.

"You need a character reference. One willing to say where you've been tonight. My word carries far more weight than that of a mere constable. Let me buy you a drink."

As good as that sounded—the drink almost as much as safety—Nick held up a hand. "What for?"

The stranger's voice turned sly. "As you say, if you had legitimate business inside, you would be leaving by the front door. You can't afford to quibble. You have the Blood—that fact alone would be of interest to a judge."

The threat caught Nick's attention—and the mere fact that the stranger understood Blood power. Once, that wouldn't have been remarkable. In the old days, every cave or river had its sacred spot, where the country folk left offerings to the devas—but all that was forbidden now. Few understood that despite what the mayors and the priests said, magic was just a different kind of energy. Like all power, it could be used for healing or harm if you knew how to harness it.

Of course, that wasn't as simple as it sounded. Nick's bloodline was different from anything Gran Cooper or the others had seen before, which meant their spells rarely worked for him. Of necessity, he'd gravitated to steel and horse leather, his magic as much an orphan as he was. But still, he'd been able to learn a few simple tricks—such as recognizing by the prickle along his skin that the stranger had power of his own. This was an unpredictable complication, to say the least. Nick's stomach formed a hard knot of tension.

He found the glitter of the man's eyes in the darkness and gave him stare for stare. The stranger didn't flinch.

Finally, Nick shrugged as if the law was a mere annoyance at best. "True enough, sir. I'm not a front door kind of man, and that has its price." One he was in danger of paying. Now he could hear the scuffle of running feet. He began walking backward, still not convinced he shouldn't be running at top speed—and yet too uneasy to leave the stranger with a clear shot at his back.

As Nick moved, the man took a step forward. "You mistake my intentions."

I'll bet, Nick thought silently, calculating the number of yards between them. It wasn't enough.

"I don't care what you were doing there," said the man, starting after him in earnest. "And I'm not particularly interested in your minuscule powers. I simply want some information."

"About what?" A stab of protective anger ran through him. *About Evelina?* He wasn't sure why, but every instinct he had said to shield her from this man.

He caught up to Nick and slapped him on the shoulder, a friendly gesture no doubt staged for the two policemen who rounded the corner at a run, puffing like overfed poodles. They'd gone around the wall instead of over it. How *did* they ever catch villains? Under ordinary circumstances, Nick would have been streets away by now.

Nick's retreat had taken them to a curve of the alley that was better lit, and he finally got a good look at the man. His strong features were aquiline, his hair dark and threaded with silver. His skin was nearly as brown as Nick's own. Definitely not of English ancestry.

The stranger lowered his voice, putting his face close to Nick's. "How well do you know the inmates of the house? Or were you merely there to burgle the place?" He said it so matter-of-factly that it took a beat for Nick to catch up to his meaning.

"I was there to talk to a girl." *And make a fool of myself.*

"Ah, good. I thought as much."

"Why?"

"You're young, handsome, and you aren't carrying a sack of valuables." The man twisted the ring around on his finger.

The constables thundered to a halt, wheezing. The one in the lead drew himself up, inflating a massive chest. " 'Scuse me, sir, did you see a thief hop the wall and scarper, like?"

Nick felt weirdly invisible. His clothes alone should have

given him away. He felt an irrational urge to dance a jig right under the policeman's nose.

"No, no," said Nick's new companion. "Though when I entered the lane, I thought I saw someone hurry that way." He pointed with the cane, indicating the opposite direction from where he and Nick were going. "A thief, you say? How very disturbing. I was just escorting a young lady to her rooms—imagine if I had not been there to take charge of her safety. What outrages might have occurred?"

Uncertainty crossed the big constable's face, as if he couldn't quite tell if he was being mocked. "Very good, sir. Much obliged." He signaled to his smaller partner, and the two jogged off after Nick's phantom doppelganger.

The man lowered his cane with a silent laugh.

"They didn't even see me," Nick said.

"I didn't want them to." Again, that matter-of-fact tone.

Nick's instincts itched, telling him to get away from this fellow as soon as he could. Curiosity, however, had a siren's pull. For starters, what sort of a young woman would this man be squiring about? Did she even exist, or had he invented her on the spot?

The man steered him toward the street, moving away from the pursuing police. "Where were we? Ah, yes. I am in need of an informant. Someone who can come and go less conspicuously than I can."

"Why me?"

"Because when I need something, it generally falls into my lap. You very nearly made that a literal event."

Nick mulled that over, finally placing the oily feel of the man's energy. He gave the heavy ring the man wore a suspicious glance, remembering that his savior had been fiddling with it the moment Nick became invisible to the coppers. Sorcery used objects to focus power—far more than the practitioners of folk magic ever did—and sorcerers were quick to use that power to control other people. Between the blind police constable and falling into Mr. Opera Cape's lap, Nick was getting a definite whiff of brimstone.

The man twirled his cane, the silver top making a lazy circle in the darkness. "An intriguing event occurred tonight. One even more fascinating than lovelorn swains dropping from the skies."

Lovelorn swains? Nick bristled, but held his tongue.

"I was at the Royal Charlotte attending a production of *The Flying Dutchman* when a large mechanical creature lumbered from the wings and launched upon an orgy of destruction. I'll grant you that Wagner engages in some fanciful devices—dwarves, bridges made of rainbows, and the like—but I don't recall a kraken in the libretto."

So it's not Evie he wants? "And how does that get us to your need for an informant?" They were reaching the mouth of the lane. The street ahead glowed with a soft golden light. Instinctively, their steps slowed, as if it was important to keep the conversation in the shadows.

"I want to locate the man who built the machine," announced the stranger. "Needless to say, executing such a feat requires an impressive level of expertise. Furthermore, the steam barons disapprove of private citizens building engines willy-nilly and have bought up most of the foundries. Materials are expensive and hard to get. So who can afford to waste so much money on an episode of mindless vandalism?"

"You already know who did it."

The man flashed another smile. "I suspect. I've seen Lord Bancroft's work, though it was years ago. He was a maker of rare distinction, and that creature would have been well within his capabilities."

Lord Bancroft? Nick couldn't imagine the stuffy ambassador getting his hands dirty. "But why would a lord do such a thing?"

"When I knew Bancroft as Her Majesty's ambassador to Austria, the heart of a rebel beat beneath his watch chain and waistcoat. However, you're right, there is no immediate logic that fits. I saw my old friend tonight, and though we did not speak, I could see that he was not pleased by the chaos."

"Then why assume he did this?"

The man gave Nick a look that said he asked too many questions. "Because what I saw was too like Bancroft's handiwork to ignore the possible connection. That is where my informant comes in. There is no workshop in Hilliard House, so does one exist elsewhere? If Bancroft is not personally flouting the will of the steam barons, then is it someone close to him? A hireling? A student? A peer, as I once was? Makers gossip together like fishwives in the market. If he is not the author of the creature, he may well know who was, even if he despises what he saw tonight."

"Is that all you want to know?"

"Is that all?" The man laughed. "It is the cornerstone to a vital foundation. Find out if Bancroft or one of his intimates has a workshop. If he does, tell me what he creates there. I will reward you well for that information."

Nick wavered for only a second. *What the hell.* He'd be in town for a little while longer. As the saying went, there was a sucker born every minute—and, truth be told, he knew accepting the task was far wiser than refusing a sorcerer. "Give me good silver, and I'll find out everything I can."

The stranger's words turned silky. "Excellent. You may call me Dr. Magnus."

CHAPTER SIX

EVELINA CLIMBED THE STAIRS BACK TO HER BEDROOM, HEAD spinning with fatigue and far too many unpleasant thoughts. If she closed her eyes, she listed as if slightly drunk. Not a good mix with long skirts, steep stairs, and the open flame of her candle.

The tall clock on the landing chimed the half hour. The hand that foretold the weather pointed to thunder and lightning. It was wrong as usual. Outside, the stars twinkled from a clear sky, with not a cloud in sight.

She stopped at Imogen's door, opening it just enough to see that her friend was sound asleep, her chest rising and falling in slow, steady breaths. She had slept through everything, thanks to the sedative that Dora had brought her. Relieved, Evelina turned her steps toward her own bedroom. The way her mind was scrabbling for logic, she wasn't going to sleep for some time.

Tonight her world had suddenly turned a corner. The question was—what had changed, and who had done the changing and why?

Her thoughts turned immediately to Tobias and his black eye. He was brilliant, handsome, and—for an idle rich boy—essentially kind. If he survived to maturity without drinking himself into the grave or contracting the French pox, he would probably become a better man than his father.

So why would he be involved in Grace's death? He had his pick of well-dowered debutantes, and kept mistresses one after the other like the links of a colorful paper chain. Many men took advantage of their servants, but she'd never suspected him.

She turned the door handle, still mired in speculation. *He seemed genuinely shocked to see that it was Grace who was dead.* And he'd promised that he had nothing to do with it, but—despite the fact she longed for and even *liked* Tobias— could she trust him? His room had been dark when she passed it on her way down from the attic. He hadn't been there. But why lie and say he was? If he was innocent, what did it matter what he was doing? Was he the man she'd heard talking outside? Or the figure who had passed her in the hall?

Closing the door behind her, Evelina stood in her own bedroom once more, heartsick and confused.

She knew instantly that Nick was gone. In the soft stillness, shadows settled in the corners like sleepy cats. The only motion was the wavering candlelight, the only scents cosmetics and old book leather. Nothing of Nick. The air was blander for his absence.

Evelina let out a disappointed cry, soft and private. Nick had always been a combination of older brother and dashing hero. He had taught her trick riding and knives and walking the high wire above a sawdust ring—not that she could do half those things any longer, not after so many years. Tonight's escapade in the tree had proven that.

Time changed everything, taking pieces of her life away, putting new ones in. When she had stood with Nick on the threshold of adulthood, Evelina had overheard the elders of the circus talking. Gran Cooper had been terrified that the strange energy that sparked between Nick and Evelina would become ever stronger. She had called it wild magic— by definition unpredictable because of the devas that flocked to it like butterflies to nectar. The effects could be benign or deadly, but so much power in one place was impossible to hide. Its inevitable discovery would be their downfall and, by extension, that of every member of the circus. The only answer was to send one of the two sweethearts away.

Nick—still an orphan and stranger, despite all the time he had spent with Ploughman's—would have been the one to leave. No one would ever have asked a Cooper to go. But then chance had intervened, and Evelina suddenly had another option. She could go to a new future, and Nick—who had already been cast adrift once in his short life—could stay. To save him, she'd had to leave him behind.

Not that she had ever told Nick—she had gone without a word. Although the circus was all he had, he would never have accepted her sacrifice. Even now, the knowledge would cut his fierce pride to the quick, and that was a bigger price than she was willing to pay.

And now she'd lost Nick once more. After finally seeing him again—and when she was at last of an age to look at him as a grown woman looks at a man—he had vanished like a flash of lightning, leaving barely an afterimage.

The older, wiser Evelina knew that was how it had to be, for his future and hers. Still, a mass of sadness pulled at her. *How could he be in London all this time and I never knew it?* She sank into the chair by her writing desk, suddenly exhausted, and picked idly at a spot of blood that had dried on her skirt before she realized what it was and snatched her hand away.

What a horrid tangle.

There was only one good thing to come out of the whole night. At least Nick had not run afoul of Tobias. Nick might be expert with a knife, but Tobias could shoot the pip from an ace half drunk and ragged from a night of whoring. The two of them bashing heads was the last thing she needed.

After so much exertion, Evelina was growing cold from sitting still. The candles had died down, letting the shadows creep from the corners.

A new thought cropped up unbidden. Had Nick really come in through her bedroom window? Like any showman, he could tell a good tale when it suited him. *No, it couldn't be him. Or Tobias. I know them both at least that well.*

But how objective was she? Wishful thinking, no doubt, was what got Grace Child with child, and then dead. Look at what had happened to her own mother, Marianne Holmes, eloping with a handsome captain only to end up disgraced and in an unmarked grave at five and twenty. No woman could afford willful blindness.

Evelina rubbed at the blood spot furiously. *No man is an angel, however handsome he looks.*

Her hands stilled. Evelina sat for a long moment, watching the candlelight flicker along the walls, licking along the metal tops of perfume bottles and glinting off their cut crystal sides. The silence quieted her nerves, letting her think.

Her first and most urgent fear was for Imogen and her family. The death of a servant was bad, but those automatons reeking of dark magic made things much worse. Magic and murder would bring any family down, but Lord Bancroft had political ambitions. That meant he had enemies, at least some of them rich and powerful. If suspicion of sorcery fell on any member of the household, Bancroft's ruin—and that of his wife and children—would be swift and complete.

The men would most likely be taken to prison, perhaps hanged, perhaps shut away forever. Imogen—beautiful and frail—would lose any chance of marriage. So would young Poppy. And Lady Bancroft—she was born and bred to be a woman of Society. What would someone like her do if she suddenly had no money and no friends?

I can't let that happen. Even if she wasn't a real detective, there had to be something she could do. But how would she stop Lestrade and his investigation? What if he dragged her Uncle Sherlock into it? Lord Bancroft was a highly placed man, and Lestrade would be under pressure to make an arrest. He'd want to get it right, because a mistake involving a peer could sink a policeman's career. Unless a solution came to hand right away, why wouldn't Lestrade employ his best resources?

Evelina had to find out the truth before anyone else did, and if she could solve the murder, then there would be far less reason for anyone—like her uncle—to uncover Lord B's secrets. That would give her a chance—somehow—to protect her friends. But common sense said that if she was ever going to find Grace Child's killer—and perhaps the father of her child—Evelina had to learn where Grace had been, and why.

The task would not be simple. There might be a connection between her murder and the magic Evelina had felt clinging to the envelope, or not. There might be a connection between the circumstances surrounding her death and the automatons in the attic, or not. Unfortunately, there was too little information to draw any satisfactory conclusions. As Evelina's science-minded uncle would say, she needed data.

And she had the means to get it. She could know everything the police knew.

She swiveled in the chair and unlocked the hasps of the train case. The cover swung up smoothly, showing a lining of watered pink silk. Nestled in the spaces made for glass jars and bottles were what looked like small brass toys: miniature birds, mice, and even a tiny dog. Under the lift-out tray containing these little marvels was a neatly organized supply of gears and springs, watchmakers' tools, and special magnifying eyeglasses to see their minuscule parts. They were expensive supplies, hard to come by and most of them salvaged wherever Evelina could find them.

There was also a collection of magical tools that Gran Cooper had given Evelina along with a promise to teach her their use once she grew into her power. One looked like a bracelet of twisted copper, another a wand no bigger than a pencil. There was a painted stone with a hole in it and a triangle of silver etched with tiny runes. Such objects were used only for the most powerful magic, and a student had to learn all the other spells first. Evelina had left Ploughman's before that had ever happened, so the mysterious objects sat against the pink silk, a mystery too precious to part with. Someday, somehow, she would learn how they worked.

But she didn't need them tonight. She dipped into the box, picking up the little bird. It nestled in the palm of her hand, barely four inches long. Her toys were all experimental designs, but this was the one she had labored over the longest. She'd given it eyes of paste emeralds and a beak that opened and closed to reveal a ruby-red tongue. A row of crystal chips tipped its wings. A useless bit of frippery, but the sparkle pleased her eye.

She had first learned her art from her father's father, who

built coin-operated wonders for Ploughman's Paramount Circus. Since then, she had devoured everything she could find on the subject and added her own twist. The same inherited powers that let her call flame from a cold candle could be used to animate the creatures.

Yes, magic was far from legal, but there were other, bigger implications.

These days, the steam companies had a stranglehold on almost every kind of machinery and the supply of parts, making it next to impossible for independent craftsmen to do their work. Only rich hobbyists, like Tobias, could afford their own workshops, and even he kept his out of sight. The less attention he attracted, the better.

The reason for the situation was simple: the steam barons didn't want even a suggestion of competition. Rivals had unsuccessfully tried other inventions to produce power, such as the combustion engine, only to see their companies crumble beneath the steam lobby's economic hammer. Others purported magic was the fuel of the future, but no one had yet successfully combined the supernatural with mechanics.

Except Evelina—which was why she worked in secret. When the time was right, her ideas might be the key to scholarly recognition and even financial independence, but she had to be careful not to move too soon. Nevertheless, this was the perfect opportunity to test her invention. She would never be allowed to join the official investigation of Grace Child's murder, but she needed to know what Inspector Lestrade found out. Ergo, her little gimcrack toys to the rescue.

She raised the hand holding the bird and studied it, visualizing a real bird and imagining the wind and sun in its feathers. Slowly, she fell into the image, losing herself in a fantasy of the bird's darting flight. Her vision broadened to take in a stream below, sparkling with white shards of light where the water tumbled over stones. Above, puffy white clouds seemed to snag in the leafy verdure of willow trees. She circled, sailing up into the green like another leaf caught in an upward draft.

With that strong, concrete image in her mind, she reached

out, seeking the half-conscious essence of a deva. It would have been easier in a garden. The only one nearby was slumbering beneath the flowers on her dressing table. It was small, even for a deva. When she reached out with her mind, she tasted the rich tang of earth and wood. Excellent. Earth devas were the easiest for her bloodline to work with. She hoped the little creature would be strong enough. With barely an effort, Evelina gently caught it in her Will.

She blew into the tiny beak, urging the deva into the tiny brass bird. The sleeping spirit drifted in, unawares. She sent her Vision of the flight along with it, giving it the dream of all a bird could do. A flare of light shone briefly in the emerald eyes, a spark of heat touched her palm. The metal began to warm as she held it.

The deva woke. Now she could feel it panic and struggle against her Will.

Help! The whisper came low and urgent, but the voice was in her head. Her heart tugged, a little sorry for the bewildered spirit. No one liked waking up in a strange place.

"Sh!" she whispered in return. "It's all right. You're safe."

What is this place? What is this prison? It's hard and cold!

"I gave you a body."

What for? The voice was indignant now. *I was asleep. Minding my own business. Then, bam, I'm stuck in a brass duck! What the blazes is this about?*

"Lark," Evelina said automatically. "I made you a lark."

There was a stony silence. *Not much of an artist, are you?*

Irritation reared in Evelina's heart, but she squashed it. The unfortunate thing about earth devas was their temper. They might be easy to catch and bend to one's purpose, but they were vocal about it. There was always a price in magic, and earth devas exacted it with sarcasm the way a hedgehog protected itself with prickles.

Taking a calming breath, she spoke the words of the old bargain as her father's mother, Gran Cooper, had taught her. "I summon you by Will and Vision to perform a task for me. If you do it well, deva, I shall set you free."

Sullen silence was the bird's only response. There was

just a shifting of the green eyes, which suddenly looked suspicious.

Evelina set the bird gently on the desk and retrieved a needle that had been poked into the lining of the train case. Catching her lip with her teeth, she pricked her finger deep enough that a bright ruby of blood welled up. She smeared it on the bird's back. "With Blood I give thee strength."

She lifted a glass vial from the case and shook some of the contents into her palm. It was tiny grains of aromatic balsam dried into a resin, perfect for a deva with an affinity for plants and green spaces. She sprinkled it over the bird. "With Tears of Trees I give thee wisdom."

The bird flicked its wings, shedding the amber crumbs over the desk.

"With Words I give thee direction. Go, and come back to me with what I need to know."

Picking up the bird again, she crossed to the window and opened it. "By Blood, Tears, and Words I direct thee. Go find Inspector Lestrade. Listen hard. Learn everything you can about the murder in the house tonight, then come back to tell me all. Do your best, and I shall reward you with wine and honey."

Blackberry wine with honey stirred into it?

"If that is what you want." Earth devas had a notorious sweet tooth. She wasn't sure how beings of energy consumed solid food, but every offering she'd ever made had been gone within the hour.

The brass bird stirred to life in her hand, suddenly far more flexible than any metal had a right to be. Gears inside began to churn like a tiny heartbeat, the wings a flittering blur more like a hummingbird than a lark.

All right, maybe ornithology *should* be her next area of study.

Evelina slipped her hand out the window, gently cupping the creature. "Ready?"

What about cats? The voice in her head was grumpy.

"You're too fast for them."

Are you sure? I've never had a body before. No one's ever tried to eat me.

"You'd break their teeth," Evelina said dryly.

What if there's a brass cat?

"You're stalling."

Am not.

Impatient, she threw the bird into the air. It arced up and, for a horrible moment, she was sure it would crash to the ground. After all, Gran Cooper said her generation of old wives and wizards was the last who could do the binding. The Blood was too thin to carry on the tradition. Gran had said Evelina was the exception—but maybe she wasn't. Maybe she didn't have the necessary magic. But then suddenly the air caught the bird, the wings blurring with effort. Evelina's lips parted, ready to shout with joy. It flew! All those hours pondering speed and weight and aerodynamics had paid off. Her design worked!

The flare of triumph heated her veins before fatigue rushed back to turn the emotion to ash. Too much had happened in one night to sustain even joy for long.

Evelina sank to her knees before the open window, leaning her elbows on the sill, her chin in her hands. The night air was cold and sweet, tasting of the uncomplicated freedom of childhood. She wondered if that would ever be hers again.

The bird streaked away, an errant scrap of gold, into the darkness.

CHAPTER SEVEN

**TERROR AT THE ROYAL CHARLOTTE!
STEAM SQUID SINKS WAGNER!**

A most insidious prank was visited on performers and patrons alike at the Royal Charlotte Theatre last evening. Just as Wagner's *Der Fliegende Holländer* was reaching its soaring climax, a hideous mechanical apparition invaded the theater and destroyed the sets. The crablike machine tore the rigging from the ship with giant pincers, all the while firing a barrage of oranges at the public. The masked culprits driving the monster fled the scene and remain at large. The Prinkelbruch Opera Company has suspended all further performances, denouncing English audiences as unready for Herr Wagner's greatness.

In this writer's opinion, musical criticism has finally gone too far. However, it is with some relief we see *The Barber of Seville* will occupy the stage of the Charlotte beginning tomorrow night.

—Front page of *The London Prattler*

THE NEXT DAY, TOBIAS APPEARED IN HIS FATHER'S STUDY, summoned as peremptorily as if he were nine years old. The room, like everything else connected with the pater—Tobias couldn't resist the disrespectful term, since it drove his father wild—was exactly what protocol demanded: dark, masculine, and slightly musty with the scent of leather and tobacco. A mantel clock kept up a steady, baritone *tock-tock*. Unlike many of the exuberantly ornate rooms in the house, this one had a plain coved ceiling with no mural or gold leaf. Books lined the walls, punctuated with the severed heads of big game. The snarling tiger over the desk summed up everything about his dear old dad.

His father stood looking out the window, velvet curtains framing his silhouette. Made the first Viscount Bancroft for his services to the Crown, Emerson Roth exuded respectability like musk. Though his father's hair had turned to an iron gray, his straight, lean form was that of a much younger man. Jove himself would have envied that commanding profile.

And his father was just as fond of throwing thunderbolts. He might have been Her Majesty's *former* ambassador to Austria, but the pater wasn't done mucking in politics. He was inching toward a seat in the government's inner circle. Worse, he knew every lawyer and banker of note in London. If Tobias embarrassed him, he could bid farewell to his allowance. He might be thirty before he could stand another round of drinks.

Bancroft turned, and the expression on his face tightened Tobias's stomach.

"What the hell happened to your face?" his father demanded.

Tobias touched his swollen eye. "Spot of bother last night."

His father grimaced in his my-son-the-idiot fashion. He stepped on the claw of a man-height, chased-silver Phoenix, and a tiny blue flame blossomed to life in its beak. He lit one of his pungent Turkish cigarettes. "Have you read this morning's *Bugle*?"

"About the murder?"

"No, thank God, not that."

Bloody hell, then he knows about the squid. Defiance and fear spiked through him. "I've just read the *Prattler*."

Bancroft harrumphed derisively. The *Prattler* was something of a renegade paper, printing the news as they saw it rather than as the Empire—or the steam barons—demanded. No one respectable subscribed. "Then you won't have seen this."

He shoved a folded newspaper, carefully ironed by the

staff to make sure the ink did not stain his lordship's fingers, across the desk. Tobias turned it around and noted the squid had made the front page of this newspaper, too, right next to an article about some actress taken into custody for use of magic. However, his father's finger was pointing at something else. Tobias read the headline and the first few paragraphs of an article detailing a purchase of shares.

Confused, he looked up at his father. "Keating Utility purchased majority stock in the Harter Engine Company. Why does that matter?"

His father sank into the chair behind his desk. The gesture spoke of a weariness Tobias was seeing in his father more and more often these days. It seemed to occur in lockstep with the steadily declining tideline of his whisky decanter. "How well do you understand the Steam Council?"

Tobias knew it was made up of the men and women they called the steam barons—those industrial magnates who owned the power companies. "I suppose as much as anyone else does."

"Coal. Steam. The railroads. The gas companies. Factories." His father put bite into every word. "Next they'll be controlling what bread we buy and what ale we drink."

Tobias had never seen his father drink anything as common as ale, but he took the point. The steam barons ran their companies and, by extension, certain towns and neighborhoods with a combination of bribes and threats. Each baron had one or more streetkeepers—bully boys who turned threats into broken bones. A shopkeeper sold what the local steam baron told him to, and painted his steps blue or green or gold to show which baron had his allegiance. If he broke the rules, his gas went out and his pipes ran cold—and there was no place to buy his own coal. If he continued in his disobedience, more than his lights would be snuffed out.

"What I don't understand," Tobias replied, "is why the law doesn't make a stand. Take away their fine clothes and fortunes, and the steam barons are little more than extortionists."

His father gave him a sharp look, as if they were finally getting somewhere. "Can you imagine what would happen if Parliament challenged them, and the Steam Council stopped supplying coal and gas?"

Tobias didn't have to think long. No industry. Dark streets. No railway. Cold houses. "There would be riots in the streets. If it went on long enough, the government would fall. The *Prattler* is always going on about how there's a rebellion just waiting to happen."

"Precisely." His father gave a fleeting smile. "And that is exactly why developing an alternative to their steam power is essential. Steam may be the engine that drives the Empire, but the steam barons are the knife at its throat."

Tobias was beginning to follow his father's logic. "And they bought Harter's, which was trying to develop an alternative type of engine."

"You can rest assured that now Harter's prototype of the combustion engine will never see the light of day. They will buy the patents and bury them. If Keating Utility and their like prevail, steam power will be our only future. Right now, Jasper Keating is determined to seize the defense contracts for a fleet of weapons-class airships. It will be worth millions."

Tobias frowned. "And?"

Here his father's chin dipped a degree. "I felt it was my moral obligation to invest in Harter's. It is in the best interest of England to break the stranglehold of the council. Unfortunately, I have just lost a great deal of money."

A cold chill ran over Tobias as he recalled the wager at the opera, and what might have happened had his plans gone awry. He took a seat in one of the studded leather chairs facing his father's desk. "How bad is it?"

"We should have been able to weather this better but, sadly, this is not the first such loss we've taken." His father fixed him with a steady look. "I need your help to ensure there are no further blows."

Tobias felt his whole body go still. Those were words he never thought he'd hear from his father. "What can I do?"

"We must remain respectable."

"The murder."

"Indeed."

"Shouldn't we concentrate on remaining alive? There was a killing under this roof."

"Don't be ridiculous. She was a servant."

"Are you saying only the servants are at risk?"

His father reddened with temper. "Absolutely. A disgusting affair. Use your head, Tobias. Why would anyone kill one of the family?"

"Why indeed?" Tobias asked, letting a smidgen of sarcasm into his tone. There were footmen on every door now. His father was nowhere near as confident as he was trying to appear. "I do notice you're not whisking your nearest and dearest to the safety of the country seat."

"And broadcast to all of Society that we have something to fear?" Lord Bancroft tapped the papers on his desk impatiently. "This unfortunate incident must never become common gossip. Keating will wield it like a sword."

Tobias unfolded the paper, checking the other pages. "He doesn't appear to have done so yet. There's no mention of it in the press."

"That is the one boon of that buffoonery at the opera. It has made an admirable distraction in everyone's minds. Utterly ridiculous."

It's not ridiculous. "Don't you find that it was an inventive sort of prank?"

His father's glare quelled his enthusiasm. "I find nothing admirable in that degree of pointless destruction. And there are more important considerations at hand."

Tobias lowered the paper. "Such as?"

His father narrowed his eyes. "Murder. Ruin."

"Oh, that."

"Do try to concentrate." His father leaned forward, his face intent. "If news of a murder under our roof gets abroad, the chances of Imogen making a good match this Season will wither on the vine. And that would just be the first of our troubles. Once Society scents blood, they turn like rabid dogs. If you love your mother and sisters, your life and this house—if you love *me,* my son—it is imperative that the death of that damned scullery girl never reaches the papers."

Tobias fell silent, thinking about Grace. Her beautiful

eyes, when she looked up at him last night, asking for help. Then her dead eyes, staring up from the floor as Evelina searched the corpse. The alteration had been horrific. It had happened in—what?—mere minutes? Less time than it took him to achieve a perfect knot in his tie.

As for loving his father . . . He'd always wanted to, more than anything, but his pater didn't make it easy. "What exactly do you want me to do?"

"There is a potential problem I have tried to anticipate. I want you to take care of it."

Tobias narrowed his eyes. As always, whenever he stopped resenting his father and began listening, he felt adrift between conflicting tides. Family loyalty. Justice. Honor. Pride. The desire for approval. They should all be pulling the same way, but they never were.

"What's the problem?" he asked.

Lord Bancroft rose and paced to the window. "That Cooper girl was examining the body last night. You know who her uncle is, don't you?"

"Of course I do." Then the breath stopped in Tobias's chest. "Oh."

"See to it that there is no investigation. I don't need to know how you accomplish it."

"She has no reason to interfere, much less invite her uncle to do so."

"She was curious." Lord Bancroft tapped his foot, a sign of nervousness that told more than anything else. "I would appreciate it if you distracted her. I assume you know how to hold the attention of a young woman?"

Tobias's gut began to knot. "What do you mean?" He rose from his chair, suddenly uneasy. He knew very well what his father wanted, and it made his stomach fold itself inside out. Evelina was innocent. Socially beneath him, certainly, but she was educated, pretty, and respectable—deserving of all the protection her status as guest commanded. And he wanted her in a way that kept him staring at the ceiling all night, which made this conversation all the more confusing.

Lord Bancroft said nothing, continuing to stare out the window.

"You want me to seduce her."

His father's tall, straight form didn't move. The clock ticked heavily, beating out the minutes of Tobias's life. Lord Bancroft reached for the decanter on his desk, poured himself a measure. He didn't offer any to his son.

I want to seduce her. You want me to seduce her. Do I give in and please us both, or do I refuse because you asked me to? Or am I really more honorable than you? That would be a lark, wouldn't it? His father made even basic rebellion a convoluted, steaming mess.

When it became apparent that Lord Bancroft wouldn't say anything more, Tobias left the room.

BANCROFT WATCHED HIS son exit, and then turned back to the window. The April wind tossed the branches of the old oak tree, plucking a few of the pale green leaves and scattering them to the lawn. *So what will happen if Tobias fails, and the girl or her uncle uncovers the wrong secret? Do I lose all this?*

Hilliard House had once been a large estate, but before Bancroft's time, it had been whittled down piece by piece over the years, one street or square at a time. Now only the core of the place remained, a green and gracious oasis in the middle of the West End where terraced homes, one cheek-by-jowl to the next, were the norm. Bancroft had bought the house and its extended garden on his return from Austria, a showplace to go with his new title and fresh ambitions. The previous owner had been a different viscount, one who had been ruined by the Gold King and forced to sell. Whenever Bancroft ran into the steam baron, the jumped-up mushroom always managed to remind him of that detail.

Bancroft began to pace slowly, moving from the window to the desk and back again. The tiger's head above his desk watched, unimpressed by the restless human.

The years as ambassador to Austria had ended gradually. Tobias had gone to England first to attend school, then, some-time later, Bancroft's wife and daughters. Just two years ago, Bancroft had come home to find the Empire he'd left a quarter century before had been taken over by the steam barons and their greed.

Right at that moment, his life had taken a sharp turn. No man of good conscience—and considerable political ambition—could stand by and watch upstarts take the reins of power, bit by bit, from the peers of the realm. And the Empire's leaders had all but lost the struggle for political supremacy. The steam barons might not sit in Parliament or the House of Lords, but they could buy almost everyone who did. In short, they were meaner, smarter, and richer than any duke in the land.

And, oh, how grateful those dukes would be if someone came along and put the barons in their place! So, with an eye on making an even greater fortune, Bancroft had put his talent for backroom deals to use. Harter's was only his most public scheme. There were others, buried deeper—the rebellion Tobias had alluded to was more than just talk—but the success of those depended on gold and secrecy. And both were difficult to get.

"And the very last thing I need is Sherlock Holmes or his niece investigating my affairs," he said to the tiger. The yellow eyes glared back.

He'd dismissed Evelina Cooper as his daughter's hanger-on. What he knew about her could be written on a calling card. The mother's elopement, of course. The harridan grandmother. The famous uncles. That was all. He didn't concern himself with schoolgirls. But it seemed that he was going to have to pay more attention—she'd been all over the corpse like a bitch on a scent. Cool as ice. Obviously, she had investigative ambitions of her own.

Bancroft's lip curled in distaste. Well, Tobias could keep the Cooper girl busy. She played coy, but anyone could see she fancied him. *As if such a mismatch would ever be acceptable.* The question was whether his son had the sense to understand that. It would be like him to get caught up in the game.

When he looked at Tobias, he saw far too much of himself. *Is it wrong to hate my son for being the same fool I used to be? Is it even worse to wish I had his soul, clean and un-*

blemished by all my sins? Well, perhaps the plan wasn't fair, but there was too much at stake to quibble over a maiden's virtue.

Bancroft had made exactly the same judgment when it came to Grace. *The corpse.*

His glass was empty, so he refilled it and drained it again, letting the harsh, sweet burn flame down his throat. *Think of her as the corpse, because that's all that's left.* But once his mind turned that way, there was no way to stem the tide.

It had seemed the easiest thing in the world, looking into her beautiful face, to convince himself that he *had* to seduce her. He had needed a messenger, someone anonymous. She had needed money. That was all very straightforward, but he had experience with spies and informants. She might sell his secrets for more money, but that kind of girl never betrayed the man she loved.

So he betrayed her instead, making her love him and then sending her into danger. That was what men like him—the deal-makers and throne-shakers—did.

Bancroft felt a harsh sting at the back of his eyes. He had felt oddly calm, looking at her body and hearing the news she was with child—possibly—probably—his. If he'd ever needed proof that his soul was dead after a career spent in intrigue, that was it.

The pity of it was, dead or alive, she would have been useless. Women with babies were too preoccupied for his kind of work—unless you took the child from them to focus their concentration. And, while by-blows were inconvenient for a man like him, servant girls with bastard babies were ruined for anything at all. At the very least, he would have had to pension her off, another millstone around his financial neck. He should be thankful to be spared that much.

But he didn't feel spared. Shadows were gathering around him, dank and dark sins rising up from their carefully concealed graves.

He poured himself another whisky. He would make this one last, because he must stay alert. Not like last night, after he had come home from the theater. He remembered breaking into a cold sweat when he saw Magnus there, sinister as a demon with one cloven foot outside the conjurer's circle. He remembered sending the grooms to move his trunks from the attic, praying that Magnus would have forgotten their existence. He remembered his first drink, and his third. But there was a blank period, before Bigelow woke him in the library. If he'd indulged less—well, Grace wouldn't have been waiting for him to come and get the envelope when someone had killed her for it. He couldn't even recall how he got to the library, or if he'd spoken to anyone along the way.

Could he have . . . no. *I've never killed an innocent.* He'd simply killed innocence along the way.

I'm sorry, Grace. Bancroft turned away from the window, unable to bear the sight of the fresh, green spring. *Somehow, I miscalculated.* That's how he would have to think of her death, to shrink it to something he could manage. A miscalculation.

He tossed the whisky down his throat.

Where had the sums and averages of risk and probability failed? Where had he gone wrong? He'd told Tobias there was no danger to the family. If he'd had to place a bet, he'd say that had been a lie. But he knew better than to run. Enemies hid everywhere, waiting for weaklings to lose their nerve. Then they pounced, their teeth in your neck.

Bancroft lifted his glass to the tiger's head, giving it a facetious salute. He kept the snarling thing as a reminder to show no fear.

When you ran, that's when the predators got you.

CHAPTER EIGHT

NELLIE REYNOLDS
ARRESTED FOR WITCHCRAFT

The celebrated actress Eleanor "Nellie" Reynolds, aged two and thirty, was taken into custody last night on charges of practicing magic. Scotland Yard arrested Mrs. Reynolds at her home in Hampstead, where detectives seized a wealth of magical implements. When questioned, the actress claimed they were props for the stage, but neighbors report unseemly "doings" under the light of the full moon. Formal charges are expected to be laid after a brief investigation. Reliable sources report that wagering on the outcome of the trial is split between a burning and remanding the prisoner for observation at Her Majesty's laboratories. Mrs. Reynolds was last seen on stage in *The Merchant of Venice,* playing the role of Portia.

—*The Bugle*

London, April 4, 1888
BAKER STREET

9 a.m. Wednesday
The day of the murder

JASPER KEATING, THE STEAM BARON KNOWN TO MANY AS the Gold King, snapped the newspaper shut. He was not a betting man, but long ago the Steam Council had agreed that given their considerable influence, it would be unseemly for them to wager on trials of magic users. That might be seen as a coercion of justice. Nevertheless, it was irritating, because whoever bet against the actress was on to a sure thing.

There wasn't a pulpit, a judge's bench, an editorial column, or a respectable dinner table where the voice of authority would not deplore the use of supernatural powers. Through careful cultivation and steady pressure, the industrial machine had seen to that. The only power in the land came from their fires. So why, when he was one of the handful of men who ruled the Empire, did he feel so uncertain?

Keating tossed the paper onto the seat beside him. He was not a man who suffered from nerves. Yet, rolling across Marylebone Road toward Baker Street in his very expensive carriage, he experienced a flutter in his stomach that had nothing to do with the breakfast he had just eaten. No, Keating was an abstemious man untroubled by such mundane foes as sausages. There were two things bothering him.

First was the prospect of having to ask assistance from that consulting detective, Sherlock Holmes—an individual well known for his independence. Being one's own man was a trait unwelcome in this day and age of allegiances and bargaining. But what could Keating do? Holmes was uniquely qualified to solve an urgent difficulty. And that was the second thing upsetting his stomach—the task itself. Just the fact that Keating was going to the Baker Street address rather than commanding Holmes to come to him said much about how profoundly Keating needed that brilliance at his beck and call. He hoped that a little condescension would be worth his while in the end.

The equipage slowed, the steady *clop-clop* of hooves breaking rhythm to shuffle to a halt. Bits jangled; horses blew. Keating could have had one of the new steam-powered vehicles for getting about, but he preferred flaunting the hallmarks of gentility his forefathers would have understood—and hopefully choked on, given that the sententious old bastards had expected him to come to nothing. Therefore, in Keating's eyes, anything less than his matched bays would be unforgivably short on elegance.

The carriage door opened and the footman folded down

the steps. Keating gathered his hat and walking stick and emerged into the slightly misty April day. He gave a nod to the servant, who stepped smartly forward to knock at the door. Keating's informants said Holmes lived in the first-floor rooms with the bay window overlooking the street. A landlady lived at street level. A fairly typical arrangement.

He took a moment to look around. A steam cycle whirred by, kicking up dust. A Disconnected house stood a few doors down, a sign on the gate advertising it for sale. Some rough boys had stopped to gawk at the carriage, but the groom was shooing them off. Uninterested, Keating kept a cool gaze moving over the street and its inhabitants.

Ah, this was more pleasing. Workmen from Keating Utilities were changing the globes of the streetlamps from red to gold. He'd just recently pushed the boundaries of his territory north, taking this street, among others, from the Scarlet King.

The mechanics of such a takeover were simple: central power plants had been adopted in London, and individual homes and businesses were now hooked up to their lines. Gaslight and steam heat were supplied by one or another of the utility companies, depending on which company served that street or square. Unhooking the pipes from one trunk line and reconnecting them to another was just a matter of valves and couplings and perhaps some excavation. And so, where Baker Street had once run off the Scarlet lines, now it ran off the Gold.

But the politics that made it happen were fierce—a matter of bribes, threats, and backroom deals. There would, no doubt, be repercussions for this maneuver, but that was a difficulty for another day. One didn't wrest possession of an empire from one's rivals with nothing but gentle persuasion.

The thought acted like a switch in his mind, and suddenly he was irked anew by his role of supplicant. What was he doing, standing in the street like a beggar? A wave of pique rushed through him, flushing his skin until the fine wool of his coat itched abominably. Keating wrestled with his top button, setting his jaw. The footman had sent his card up to the Great Detective, so what was Keating waiting for? Word that the man was receiving visitors? He was the Gold King. No one dared to turn him from the door.

But that unthinkable event might happen. A middle-aged woman—no doubt the landlady—was standing at the threshold talking to the footman and shaking her head regretfully. Bitter bile caught in the back of Keating's throat. This was insufferable.

With a barely polite nod, he marched up the walk and pushed past her into 221B Baker Street. Without pausing, he spotted the staircase and mounted the steps to the rooms above.

"Sir!" the woman bustled after him with a rustle of heavily starched petticoats. "Sir, Mr. Holmes is still at his breakfast!"

Keating was already at the top of the stairs, his impatience mounting with her every word. "I'm sure the man can eat his toast and listen at the same time."

"But Mr. Holmes . . ."

"Do you know who I am?" he thundered.

That took her aback, a glisten of fear filling her eyes. "But sir!"

Silly, twittering creature. He relented. "I'll be sure to tell Mr. Holmes you're not to blame for my intrusion." And Keating pushed open the door to Holmes's room.

His first impression was one of chaos. He looked from left to right, quickly cataloguing what he saw. In one corner stood a table littered with scientific equipment of some kind, racks of glass bottles hinting at research of a chemical nature. Next to that was a desk where no paper had ever been neatly squared. It looked more like a badger had been at the stack of papers, books, and empty plates piled there. Keating could not repress a shudder at the mess.

Straight ahead was a fireplace with a large bear skin before it. The skin was flanked by a settee and pipe rack on one side and a basket chair on the other. On the Baker Street side of the room was a table and chairs. The table was set with a breakfast redolent of kippers. One chair was occupied by a tall, angular man with an ascetic air and lean face.

"Holmes, I presume?" Keating said. "I am Jasper Keating."

"Indeed you are," said Holmes absently. "Might I offer you tea? Breakfast? Mrs. Hudson's scones are quite delightful." The man barely looked up from the copy of the newspaper he was perusing, instead awarding Keating an indifferent glance.

Stung, Keating narrowed his eyes. "I come in the character of a client, not a breakfast guest."

Holmes at last lifted his eyes from the very same article on Nellie Reynolds that Keating had been reading in the carriage. His brow furrowed. "I apologize for the informal reception, but I had no intention of seeing anyone for at least another hour."

"And I had no intention of waiting."

Holmes compressed his lips with displeasure, but a beat later a mask of politeness visibly slid over his features. It was somehow more demeaning than outright rudeness. "I take it you have a matter to discuss which you consider to be an emergency?"

"So it is."

"I should sincerely hope it is nothing less, since you have trampled my housekeeper and interrupted my meal." Holmes flipped his napkin from his lap and dropped it to the table. The gesture held all the irritation Keating felt.

Keating gripped his walking stick more tightly, banking his temper. *I must tread carefully if I want his help.*

"May I take your coat, sir?" The landlady was hovering uncertainly at the door, looking as if she preferred to bolt.

Annoyed at being caught wrong-footed, Keating shed his coat and hat and handed them to her, along with his walking stick, lest he be tempted to teach Holmes some manners. The woman gave a curtsey and left.

Holmes had risen from the table and crossed to the basket chair by the fireplace. With a sigh, he subsided into the chair with a graceful collapsing of his long limbs. With one hand, he indicated the settee with an airy wave. "Please be seated, Mr. Keating, and tell me how I may serve you."

Keating sat, suspicious of Holmes's heavy-lidded regard.

Annoyance prickled whenever the detective's gaze flicked to Keating's face, but in the end it didn't matter. Holmes was listening. The Gold King had power even with this contemptuous bounder, and that was all that mattered if he wanted this matter of Athena's Casket resolved.

But how did he explain the theft of the casket, which he had learned of only this morning, without actually explaining the item itself? It was a risk. Holmes was intelligent. He might find out more than Keating wanted him to know. *Don't be daft. Keep it to the facts he will understand. No one would believe the rest, anyway.*

"I have an interest in archaeology," Keating began.

"As did your father before you," Holmes countered.

Keating frowned. "I heard that you perform an amusing parlor trick, telling a man all about himself using seemingly insignificant details."

Holmes stretched out his legs, crossing his ankles, and made a steeple of his fingers. He looked utterly at home and relaxed. It was annoying.

"I can," he said with barely concealed smugness, "but it is your ring that gives you away. It is etched with a likeness of the Acropolis, and it is of an age that suggests you did not purchase it yourself, but rather someone from the previous generation. Your father, I understand, was a bishop in Yorkshire, and therefore well educated. It was not an enormous leap of logic that the ring would be his."

Pompous idiot. "You are quite right," Keating said, gathering up his train of thought once more. The interruption had distracted him and inserted unwelcome memories where his tidy narrative had been a moment before. Thinking about his father was never pleasant. "As I said, I have an interest in archaeology. I funded an excavation in Rhodes recently. You have heard of Heinrich Schliemann?"

"Of course. He claims to have rediscovered Troy."

"Among other sites. Like so many of his ilk, he is perpetually short of funds. I met the man some years ago. At the time, he had found another site, not so glorious as Troy, but of some interest. He petitioned me for financial assistance."

"Where was this site?"

"On the Greek island of Rhodes." Schliemann had found the site where Athena's Casket was believed to be buried. He had promised to fund Schliemann if the archaeologist would hand over the casket. Of course, Holmes would get a slightly different version of the truth. "I gave him the cash to do his digging on the condition that I be allowed to sponsor an exhibit of his findings here in London. It was my intention to open a gallery, and this seemed the perfect opportunity for an initial show."

Holmes smiled, looking too damned amused. "Ah, yes— the crowd of rich patrons, snowy-browed scholars, and all those reporters drinking far too much of the free wine. It would have been quite an evening."

"Indeed." That was, in fact, fairly close to how Keating had imagined it. There might have even been an accolade or two for his outstanding benevolence in the service of scholarship. Perhaps an honorary degree?

The abominable detective was chuckling. "How unfortunate it is that Dr. Watson is no longer resident here. I can almost see him coming down with writer's cramp in his haste to get every word of this committed to paper."

"This is entirely confidential!" Keating snapped.

Holmes sobered instantly. "As you wish. So tell me, Mr. Keating, what was to become of this treasure once the great reveal was accomplished?"

"My plan was to donate it to the British Museum."

Holmes raised an eyebrow. "You did not intend to keep and sell the items?"

Keating fidgeted with a throw cushion on the settee, settling it so the edge was level with the pattern on the seat cover. "May I be entirely frank, Mr. Holmes?"

"I count on it."

"I am first and foremost a businessman, but I have my ambitions. I also have a profound sense of what is the right and proper order of things. In this case, the two coincided perfectly. A generous donation to one of the Empire's greatest cultural institutions would do more for my reputation than mere cash."

Holmes nodded slowly. "I am inclined to agree with your assessment."

The knot of tension in Keating's gut eased a degree. Ridiculous that this man's approbation should matter. "So there you have it."

"Not quite. You have yet to tell me where this all went awry. Did Herr Schliemann cheat you?"

Keating plucked at a fleck of dust on his sleeve, feeling his anxiety rise once more as he contemplated the note he had received from Harriman this morning. "No. He packed up the treasure in Greece and shipped it in good order. I had trusted men present to ensure that all ran smoothly. They stayed with the crates all the way to London, but some of the articles never arrived."

"Where were the crates delivered?"

"To a warehouse behind Bond Street. The workers there are Chinese, incorruptible and utterly loyal to my cousin, who is in charge of that operation."

"And so?" For the first time, the detective looked truly interested.

"When the shipment arrived, several of the crates— including a large and valuable item—were missing. I only learned of it when my cousin sent word this morning." Keating pulled a piece of paper from the breast pocket of his jacket and handed it to Holmes. His hand shook slightly as he reached across the bear-skin rug. "This is the most valuable of the lost pieces."

The detective unfolded the paper, studying the sketch. It showed an ornate cube, flanked by sculptured owls and crusted with a fortune in precious stones. It appeared to have many gears and levers and dials on every surface. "I have seen this picture before. I believe it is a navigational instrument, though no one is certain how it worked."

Keating nodded. "Very good. It's a somewhat obscure piece."

Holmes gave a quick smile. "It has appeared in scholarly essays from time to time, often under the sobriquet of Athena's Casket—note the owls and the fact that she was the patron goddess of navigation—but it has not been seen since the first century."

"Until Schliemann dug it up."

Holmes actually looked impressed. "I had not heard that it had been found."

Keating had insisted on secrecy. In some shadowy, secret circles—it paid to have a good spy network—the casket was reputed to be the one perfect blending of magic and machine known to humankind. It had the power to command flight and the unerring navigational power of a migratory bird. Rumors like that were worth paying attention to, especially for a man with an interest in military contracts. Keating had grown up in the north, where the country folk still remembered the old ways, so he knew magic was potent—even if it was something he publicly denounced.

And if magic *could* work a machine? That meant mechanical power with no need for fuel—not coal, wood, gas, oil, or anything else that men could sell for money. It was exactly the sort of thing that would put the steam industry and all its investors into the garbage bin. The moment he had heard Schliemann had found the possible location of the casket, Keating's plan had been first to keep it from his rivals, and second to destroy it or harness its potential for himself. But now that the casket had vanished, it was an uncontrolled missile hurtling from the heavens straight toward his head.

And *uncontrolled* was not one of Keating's favorite words. He had to find the thing, and fast. Whoever figured out how to use it would make Nellie Reynolds look like a choir girl.

"What are the dimensions?" asked Holmes.

Keating held up his hands, measuring the air. "The case was solid gold."

Holmes frowned, letting the paper dangle from his fingers. "Are you telling me that a winged box the approximate size of a picnic basket, studded with gems and no doubt heavier than one man could carry, was stolen from the shipment and no one saw when or by whom?"

Keating sprang to his feet, the tension inside too fierce to sit still. He paced to the window, glowering outside. "Precisely."

Holmes huffed. "I suggest you question your employees."

"They are loyal. I've guaranteed it."

"No doubt you have, and no doubt that guarantee was arrived at in an unpleasant fashion." But the detective sounded bored.

Keating wheeled away from the window and glared at Holmes, who was already folding up the sketch. "You must find me this device."

"Who do you think took it?"

"If I knew, I wouldn't be here."

"Rebels, perhaps?"

Keating's stomach clenched. He didn't think much of the ragged bands of malcontents who broke into his factories and smashed the machines. "I doubt they concern themselves with archaeology. This is theft, and you must retrieve my goods. A great deal depends on it."

Holmes twisted in his chair to regard Keating carefully, obviously considering the words as if they were dangling bait. "You sound as if the fate of nations were at stake."

"Not nations, Mr. Holmes. Think larger. The pieces on the board are not just kings and queens, but industries and interests that cross conventional borders."

"And an antique artifact matters to these mighty powers? How intriguing."

Keating realized he'd said too much. "There is little more that I can tell you, Mr. Holmes, but let me say this. My opponents have little use for the social order you and I embrace. Others don't value the niceties of civilized life. They are not gentlemen."

"And you are."

"I am, and I will keep order, by force if I must."

"How very instructive." The detective's heavy-lidded eyes glinted with a speculative light. "I never took you for the defender of Sunday picnics and tea at five."

"Mock if you must, but I beg you to take the case. The opening of my gallery is within the month. The casket must be there." Actually, he had no intention of putting something so valuable on public display, but the detective didn't need to know that detail.

Holmes rose, tapping the folded paper against the side of his leg. His eager look faded, as if he were thinking twice. "Allow me to ponder this. I will send you a reply by tomorrow morning's post."

"I will make it worth your while."

The detective gave a thin smile. "I shall give that all due consideration, Mr. Keating."

Another very polite jab. He'd heard the man was a decent hand in the ring, but his verbal punches were lightning fast, too. Keating couldn't resist pushing back. "You are too smart to alienate someone with my reach."

"I said I will think about the case and write you in the morning. I wish to make some inquiries before I commit my energies to what might be a simple shipping error."

"No." Keating paced, stopping to straighten one of the candlesticks on the mantel so that it lined up evenly with its mate. "You are simply searching for an inoffensive way to refuse."

"You are not used to refusal." It was a flat statement. "Perhaps that is why I wish to do so."

The man's gall made Keating choke, as if a fistful of gritty mud were being jammed down his throat. His need to bring Holmes into line reached a screaming pitch. He changed tactics, going low to strike soft, vulnerable parts. "If you have no wish to gain my goodwill for yourself, think of those close to you. Yes, I like to know something about those with whom I do business. You have an elderly mother, I believe? A brother in the civil service? A niece barely out of school? I think she is the product of that sister of yours who left a stain on the family reputation."

A look of something akin to hatred rippled over Holmes's countenance. Perversely, it pleased Keating. That meant he finally had the man's attention. "Your niece has been dealt an unfortunate hand, always destined to struggle against her mother's legacy. It is the start of the Season, is it not? Think of what could happen if I spoke the right word in the right place. It is nothing to me—a favor owed, a debt paid—but to her? Well it could make all the difference, yes?"

Holmes was silent. Keating could see him considering the flip side of his statement: if the right word could help the girl, what damage could the wrong word do? *Everyone is vulnerable somehow. This one hides his affections, but they are there, exposed nerves that quiver at a touch.*

Keating allowed himself a smile. "I hear she is a fetching creature. Can you, or even your illustrious brother, offer her as much assistance?"

The man looked like he had just downed one of his own chemical experiments. "You know I cannot."

"Then help her by helping me find the casket."

"I shall consider it." The tone hadn't altered, but now Holmes did not meet his eyes.

I have you. It might take all night for the man to choke down his enormous pride, but surely the battle was won. Keating smirked inside, though he was careful to keep his face perfectly bland. "Then I shall expect results, Mr. Holmes. You have a reputation to uphold as well."

Holmes finally gave him the full effect of his icy gray eyes. "I do not guarantee that you will like everything I find. I go where the evidence leads."

A twist of anxiety spoiled Keating's mood. He was taking a huge gamble, and he could only pray finding the casket was worth the trouble of managing Sherlock Holmes. "Then I rely on your professional discretion."

"Truth has no discretion, but I shall keep what she says to myself."

It was as much of a surrender as the detective was likely to give. Jasper Keating left, descending the stairs with a brisk tread. He gave Mrs. Hudson the barest nod as he gathered his coat, hat, and walking stick on his way out the door, almost triumphant.

CHAPTER NINE

LATER THAT MORNING, KEATING WAS BACK IN THE CAR-
riage, his mind swinging from the aggravating topic of
Holmes, to his displeasure with one Lord Bancroft, and then
back again. His chest burned with the first fires of a dyspeptic attack, as if a miniature steam engine had lodged in his
esophagus.

If Holmes was annoying, the affair with the Harter Engine Company was infuriating. Oh, Keating Utility had
bought the firm and it would vanish without a trace; that
was not the issue. It was the fact that someone had dared to
oppose the steam barons so openly by attempting to build
one of those alternative combustion engines. It was next
door to treason.

Most of the investors had possessed the wits to use shell
companies or false names, but not that thrice-damned fool
Bancroft. Against all reason—as if anyone knew what the
ongoing wealth and order of the nation required more than
Keating himself—Bancroft had taken a public stand against
the steam monopoly.

A fool? Certainly. A martyr? Keating was too smart for
that. Bancroft was too important to beat to a pulp, but he
would have to endure a cleverly crafted public lesson. No
one thwarted the Steam Council. Harsh rules, but this harsh
world demanded a strong hand.

Keating was that fist. He regarded it as his duty.

And the whole sorry business reminded him how badly he
needed to get his hands on Athena's Casket, and that Holmes
was the best detective that money apparently couldn't buy.

"Sir?" a gentle voice asked.

He looked up, remembering that his daughter, Alice, sat across from him now. She had thick, curling hair, more copper than gold, and cornflower blue eyes, her face the heart shape of a porcelain doll's.

Alice was much like her mother, and not only in her looks. She was obedient and soft-spoken, attuned to Keating's every wish. The perfect daughter, just as her mother had been the ideal wife until the hour of her death. Keating was well aware how absolutely he had been blessed.

"A penny for your thoughts, sir?" Alice said in her quiet way.

Keating realized he was gripping his cane like a club. Self-conscious, he relaxed his hand, easing the strain on his finely stitched gloves of Spanish leather.

"I could use your advice, my chick," he said, his mind still on Holmes. "There is a man whose favor I would win, though he does not wish to give it to me."

"Why not?" she asked, as if that were the strangest notion in the world.

"He is like a growling dog. He will need a demonstration of power."

"You mean to ruin him, sir?" Her chin tilted down so that her gaze was bent on the ivory lace of her gloves. Demure, even as she cut to the quick of his thoughts.

"Tempting, but not yet. He has agreed to work for me, but grudgingly. It will take more than one show of force to keep him in line. As that is far from an economical use of resources, I would prefer to win him over with a show of generosity. He's not expecting that, and I won't get anywhere unless I surprise him."

Her bow mouth curved in a half smile. "What would a growling dog want, besides the opportunity to bite?"

Behind that pretty face and bright curls is a clever mind. There is no doubt she is my daughter. Even if that quick wit and frankness made Alice a bit too blunt sometimes, for all her feminine airs. "Something for himself would be too obvious. He has a niece about your age—from all reports an intelligent girl, but without your advantages."

"So you will do something for her?"

"And undo it, if he crosses me. The greater the pleasure, the more immediate the pain. My little gift will have to count."

"Poor girl."

"No girl matters but you. If you were this young creature, what would you wish for?"

"I do not know her, so that is an impossible question." Alice fiddled with the pale blue ribbons of her tiny and largely useless bonnet. "I, at the moment, hope my gown is ready for the presentation. The Season will get off to a bad start if it does not fit just right."

She had dodged the question, but then she had a soft heart. He'd indulged her and kept her close, perhaps too close. "The presentation is the thing for you young lasses, isn't it?"

Alice's eyes widened with exasperation. "Of course it is, Papa! Without that, what use is the rest of the Season? No one will look at a girl twice unless she's kissed the queen's hand."

The carriage came to a stop. Alice hitched forward on the seat. "This is the dressmaker's. I shall leave you here, sir, unless you have further need of my sage advice."

Keating gave her an indulgent smile. "No, my chick, you've quite inspired me."

The door opened, letting the sun stream into the carriage. The fog was gone now, and the April day was in full bloom. Alice's maid already stood outside, looking a little wind-blown from her ride up front with the coachman. Keating watched thoughtfully as the footman handed his daughter down to the street. The Season meant suitors, and Keating would have to watch his only child and heir with the vigilance of a raptor.

The thought filled his gut with ice. *I should not worry so much. She is no fool.* And yet all fathers worried, because that was the natural order of things.

The carriage took off again, the *clop-clop* of the horses gaining momentum, as did Keating's thoughts. Alice *had* given him a very good idea about what to do for the detective's niece. The Lord Chamberlain and Queen Victoria herself checked the list of eligible young ladies each Season, and only those who passed muster were presented at Court.

Daughters of scandal-ridden mothers were not received. Unless, of course, the Lord Chamberlain could be persuaded? It would take some finesse—the man was wound tighter than his hopelessly out-of-date cravat—but Keating had the means and a great deal of motivation.

I want Holmes very badly. No, he wanted Athena's Casket. Maybe to destroy it. Perhaps to keep it for himself.

If he were the only member of the Steam Council with access to the secret of combining magic and machines—even his mind boggled at the possibilities. What was a sop to the Chamberlain compared to that? He'd see every chit in London curtseying at Court if that's what it took.

The carriage stopped again, this time outside the Steam Makers' Guild Hall. Keating got out. No sooner had his foot touched the marble steps that swept up to the hall's monumental double doors than his aide, Mr. Aragon Jackson, exploded from the door in an officious fury. Jackson was tall and thin, with features as sharp as a weasel's. Although his talents as an inventor were beyond doubt, he thrived in the position of favored lackey.

A flock of other hangers-on trailed after Jackson in a frantic train, somber in their unofficial uniform of dark wool and sharply pressed linen. Keating liked his people tidy, and they knew it.

Jackson pulled out his watch midstride. The case flipped open at the touch of a button, releasing a puff of steam into the air. It was a most impractical trinket. Although it was something to possess the smallest steam engine on record, the heat from the case had entirely ruined the watch pocket of Jackson's waistcoat, discoloring the fabric and making it sag. It was only a matter of time before the silly thing melted its way clear through to Jackson's pink flesh.

Jackson snapped it shut again, drawing himself up to greet Keating. "Good afternoon, sir. It's a pleasure to see you, sir. The members of the Steam Council are gathering. I have your files in hand, if you'll follow me, sir."

The aide fell into step beside Keating, the skirts of his

coat swirling behind him as he moved to pull open the guild hall door. The entourage followed, a school of hopeful remoras following the shark. Jackson's steps were quick and eager, his gaze darting ahead to anticipate the steam baron's every need. Keating both loved and hated the subservience, but despised Jackson. Like a dog trained to do tricks, the man performed with one eye out for possible treats.

Not like my streetkeeper. Striker waited for them on a bench in the hallway, standing only as Keating drew near. He was ambitious, prepared to break bones if Keating asked it of him, but he wasn't interested in being liked.

"M'lord," Striker said, touching the brim of a disreputable brown hat that perched on top of his spiky brown hair.

Keating was not a lord, but he had the sense it was all the same to Striker, a matter of indifference more than respect. The stocky thug was a blunt instrument at best, a gutter rat trained to keep Keating's subjects in line. He wore a long overcoat, covered in bits of metal that resembled an improvised kind of armor. On the streets, where materials for fixing and building were scarce, the metal was a sign of wealth, and Striker was never seen without his portable hoard. The weight of it would have crushed a smaller man. He fell into step behind the others, the coat jangling slightly as he moved.

"What's the betting on the Reynolds woman, Striker?" Keating asked.

"Odds are in favor of cutting her open for a look inside, m'lord." It was long rumored that magic users had different organs than the rest of humanity. To be honest, Keating had wondered himself.

They moved as a unit down the broad corridors of the club, the soft carpet muting the sound of their feet. Once, the walls had hung with spears, scimitars, and other exotic weaponry from the Empire's far-flung holdings, but those had been removed as a precautionary measure. Sometimes these meetings became heated. Now, portraits of shaggy highland cattle glowered moodily from the walls.

When they neared the meeting room, Keating gave the order to Striker to deploy men around the perimeter of the building. No one would be allowed to make an unauthorized exit today. It was going to be an interesting meeting.

Keating checked his pace a degree, a sense of caution cooling his mood. King Coal and a half dozen of his Blue Boys were approaching from the other end of the hall. The enormously fat man reclined in a wheeled chair powered by an engine and steered by three strong retainers. As they drew near, Keating saw the contraption shed a cinder on the carpet, leaving a burned patch of wool like droppings in its wake. King Coal, too fat to look down or turn his head, didn't notice. A steady stream of sweat poured from the folds and mounds of the man's pallid flesh, as if the heat of the chair's engine were melting him like tallow.

If the Blue King was the picture of gluttony, the members of his entourage were the image of want. Striker was ragged, but nothing like the threadbare Blue Boys, their pinched faces and hollow eyes a mask of dull anger as they looked around at the club's opulence. Perversely, those starvelings not pushing the chair carried food and drink, since the Blue King lived in horror of starvation. He slept in the room next to his kitchens and had been known to fly into a panic at the notion of a missed meal. The man was a brilliant schemer, but in other ways quite mad.

And King Coal's boilers supplied the worst of London—the docksides and Whitechapel, the criminal dens, tenements, and stinking alleys where even the spiders starved—yet he ruled the area by choice. *What does he find there to eat?* Keating mused, eyeing the covered dishes the servants carried. *His tenants?*

They reached the conference room at the same moment. The two barons eyed each other, Keating wondering whether to assert precedence over the disgusting splot of lard or conspicuously flaunt good manners.

King Coal broke the impasse. "I think today would be the day to teach Green a lesson, don't you agree?" The man's voice wheezed like a punctured concertina—a high, thin death rattle incongruous with his massive size. "I want that bridge."

Keating gave a slow shake of his head. "She will not take it quietly. Besides, Green is ambitious. That can be turned to our advantage."

"You came with a plan for this meeting, something tasty and not on the agenda. I knew you would."

Keating was not sure if he was pleased because they were thinking along the same lines or annoyed for the exact same reason. "I have an idea. Perhaps we can strike a bargain and deliver justice at the same time."

His counterpart harrumphed, his gaze flicking greedily around them. "Do tell."

"Surely you know where they found the supplies for the Harter Engine Company?"

"Which you no doubt have under lock and key?"

"We don't want them falling into the hands of the rabble. We don't want them making their own engines, do we?"

King Coal made a wry face. "Definitely not, but I still want my cut of the proceeds."

"Of course," Keating said silkily.

A beat passed, in which the two men eyed each other like rival tomcats. The fat man rumbled with dark laughter, and Keating forced a smile to his lips. The tension broke with an almost audible pop.

"Then there will be tasty pickings before the day is out. I do love pickings." King Coal gave a ghastly, brown-toothed grin as he waved at his three cadaverous servants to roll him through the wide doors to the conference room.

And a merry old soul was he. Involuntarily, Keating shuddered, waiting until the last of the Blue Boys had passed before he led his own retinue into the room.

CHAPTER TEN

MEMBERSHIP OF THE STEAM COUNCIL, APRIL 1888

Mrs. Jane Spicer, Spicer Industries, Green District,
Madam Chairwoman

Mr. Jasper Keating, Keating Utilities, Gold District

Mr. Robert "King Coal" Blount,
Old Blue Gas and Rail, Blue District

Mrs. Valerie Cutter, Cutter and Lamb Company,
Violet District

Mr. William Reading, Reading and Bartelsman,
Scarlet District

Mr. Bartholomew Thane, Stamford Coke Company,
Gray District

Silence Gasworks, Black Kingdom,
represented by Mr. Fish

A vast mahogany table filled the room. Only the members of the Steam Council sat at the table, but their assistants crowded behind them, some sitting, some standing, adding their breath to the already stuffy air.

There were no windows, but gaslit sconces ringed the walls. The only decoration was an elaborate model of an airship suspended over the council table, one of the new transcontinental models, placed there as a reminder of what collaboration between the barons could achieve. A nice theory, but Keating thought it served as a goad to competition instead. The big passenger ships were the aeronautical equivalent of a barge. Every baron wanted to be the first to build a sleek and deadly warship to rule the skies. No doubt they all had plans for experimental ships hidden in their desk drawers, waiting for the right opportunity.

Keating had hoped he'd been the only one to pursue the legend of Athena's Casket—the Holy Grail of air flight. After all, even scholars thought it more myth than fact. Now he looked around the room, wondering if one of his rivals was the thief.

He took his seat. He was the last to arrive, but already he could feel the tension in the room, like some thick, sticky substance clinging to every surface. The Harter affair had put everyone on edge. There was little of the usual premeeting chitchat among the seven principals. The aides, flunkies, and hangers-on were restless, expending their energy in stormy glowers at their neighbors. Only the Violet Queen asked after Alice and the progress of his gallery. The woman never forgot her manners, despite the lines of tension bracketing her mouth.

The chair was a rotating position, and today Green had it. Jane Spicer was one of the two female members of the council, succeeding her late husband to the position. The softest thing about her was the bottle-green silk of her day dress. Otherwise, she ruled the commercial districts of the capital with a fearsome hand.

"Gentlemen. Ladies." She rapped on the table with her knuckles, reminding Keating of a stern governess. What little conversation there was dribbled to a halt, stemmed by the harsh grating of her voice. If that tone could have been distilled and used as a weapon, the Empire would have the entire globe shaking in its boots. "We have a long agenda, so I suggest we begin."

Keating listened with half an ear to what came next—an unnecessary roll call, the adoption of past minutes, and so on. He looked around the table. The Violet Queen, decked out in frilly violet ruffles, was as feminine as Green was not and was completely prepared to use that beauty when it suited her. Next to her sat Scarlet, an athletic, black-haired man with piercing blue eyes. Neither of these two worried Keating much—they were smaller players in the game, dangerous only if they forgot their self-interest long enough to work together, and that was unlikely. Keating and Blount were both too good at sowing dissent.

The next two did interest him, but for different reasons. Silence Gasworks was an enigma, operating in the underground. It was believed that a couple ruled the Black Kingdom, but no one was entirely sure. They typically sent a single representative—and not always the same one—who sat and listened, voted if required, and volunteered nothing. Today it was a gray-bearded man in a kind of cassock who had identified himself as Mr. Fish. Indeed, he contributed as much as if he had floated up on the Thames's polluted banks, belly to the air.

Keating would have been insulted by the apparition and thrown the lone man out, except he dared not. The underground was as large as the whole of London, and no one was sure how much power the Black Kingdom actually had. So Mr. Fish sat, silent, solitary, and unmolested.

The final member of the council was the Gray King, who occupied a smallish territory on Green's northern borders. His people were outdoor sporting types with red faces and bushy whiskers who no doubt kept hounds and drank vats of good amber ale for breakfast. Gray was a good businessman and a nice enough fellow, in the fine old tradition of English country squires. Unfortunately, he had made some serious mistakes for which he was about to atone. That included trusting his peers.

Green's shardlike voice fell silent, letting their ears rest a beat before launching into the new business of the agenda.

"Before we begin, I have something to add regarding the division of supply areas," Keating said, modulating his own tone between firm and utterly reasonable. "The junction of the Blue, Green, and Gold pipelines at Blackfriars Bridge is proving inconvenient."

"How so?" Green asked suspiciously.

"Simplification. Our gas and steam and rail holdings don't align. There are householders in the area who pay you for their heat, me for gas, and then board a Blue train to go to their workplace. That fails to promote loyalty with our client base, which is something we all aspire to." Sometimes that loyalty was inspired at the end of a streetkeeper's fist, but that was mere detail. "I propose Green retreat north of Fleet and leave the bridge as a clean divider between Blue and Gold territories."

The woman huffed. "I think not. That area of town provides good revenue, as you well know. And furthermore, there is a toll on that bridge that is currently split three ways. You mean to cut me out."

"Surely you are mistaken, madam." She wasn't, and they both knew it, but Keating plowed on. "The toll program has been purely experimental. We agreed not to institute charges that would impair healthy commerce in London. For a flat fee, anyone can buy a monthly pass and avoid individual tolls altogether. It only makes sense. Merchants have to move their wares. Farmers must get their goods to market. Fishermen . . ."

"Yes, yes, spare me the litany." She waved his words aside. "That all means nothing. The meaning is in the money."

She was right. Merchants paid not only for heat and light, but also to move their goods via railways, docks, and now bridges. The barons' stranglehold on the areas their companies served was all but complete. Keating's gaze flicked up to the sour-faced men standing behind Mrs. Spicer. They looked like clerks, doomed to a future of high desks and cold lunches. He knew for a fact she bled her businessmen of money before any of them got enough capital together to challenge her. Not a bad plan, but she didn't have the wits to be subtle about it. It would have worked better if she'd made them think handing over their fortunes was their own idea.

"Move your area of influence north," King Coal wheezed. "That will compensate you most handsomely."

She wasn't impressed. "I have a nonexpansion treaty with Gray."

"Perhaps a concession, then," Keating suggested smoothly. "You promised not to take him over if we left your southern borders alone. Give us your share of the bridge, and we'll let you expand north."

Gray jumped to his feet. "What is the meaning of this?"

"Indeed," said Green, sitting back in her chair. Yet she did not relax. Every angle of her body begged for an excuse to pounce on this opportunity.

Keating meant to give her that. He rose more slowly, letting his fingertips rest on the mahogany surface of the table. "It means that inquiries have revealed storehouses of machine parts within Gray's borders. Parts that any competent mechanic could use to construct his own boilers, gas burners, or batteries. Parts smuggled from unlicensed factories in the north and used in the workshops of the Harter Engine Company."

Green rose, a hungry look on her square face. "That contravenes the first article of the Steam Council's code of conduct. 'No one shall promote or enable the general populace to generate its own power or means of locomotion without the express approval of all.' "

Trust her to be able to quote chapter and verse. "We must protect our interests," said Keating.

"He's supporting the rebels!" Scarlet almost shouted in his fury. He was half out of his chair, but the Violet Queen pulled him back into his place by the sleeve.

"You're seeing rebels everywhere, my dear," she said calmly. "Calm yourself. They generally don't hide under the furniture, much less at our council meetings."

"You're wrong," Scarlet shot back, though with more self-control. "It's this damned Baskerville affair. It's not just the rabble anymore. The gentry are getting involved."

"That's nothing more than wishful thinking on the rabble's part." Violet pulled out her handkerchief, a delicate fluttering of lawn and lace, and dabbed at a faint gleam of perspiration on her cheeks. It was hot in the room, and tempers were making it worse. "All gentlemen of quality pass through my houses sooner or later, and if they have secrets my employees have a way of finding them out. I've heard nothing about the Quality taking up arms against us."

That seemed to reassure Scarlet, but Keating's interest was piqued. Whatever Violet thought, not every gentleman went whoring, and not every one who did struck up a conversation about politics with his doxy. More to the point, what was this Baskerville business? And why hadn't he heard about it? The gap in information irked him, especially so soon after his shipment went awry. He hated being caught by surprise.

But Gray saved him the trouble of asking questions. "What's Baskerville?"

"Don't pretend you don't know," snarled Scarlet.

"Baskerville is a phantom," wheezed King Coal, his chair letting off a gust of steam as he leaned forward. "A rumor. A vaguery. There are whispers of a shadow government that will sweep in and seize control when the time is right, and we shall all end up on the gallows."

A ripple of laughter went around the room, some voices less confident than others.

"It's all nonsense. The crown prince will never stand for it," the Blue King added. Victoria's pleasure-loving heir was deeply in debt to the Steam Council. "He will never make a move against us as long as we give him a golden teat."

"And yet they say Victoria is willing to oppose him in the name of duty. Turn him over to the rebels if need be," argued Scarlet. "They say those were the Prince Consort's final instructions to his wife."

That sounded like Albert, who had loved progress until he realized it rendered old institutions like the monarchy redundant. But even so, Keating doubted that the queen would do anything that risked her children or the throne. "The Prince Consort might have frustrated our fathers' version of the Steam Council, but he is dead."

Scarlet stared at Gray. "Let's not forget that he had faithful friends."

"Too true." Keating saw at once how he could use this Baskerville hysteria to his own advantage. Keating pointed a finger at Gray. "Mr. Thane, I believe your older brother was one of them. In fact, wasn't he one of the gentlemen who worked alongside the Prince Consort during the planning of the Great Exhibition?"

"That was more than thirty years ago!" Gray sputtered.

Green broke in, her harsh voice slicing the air. "But isn't your family motto something about remaining faithful after death? Your brother is a lord, and that makes you one of the aristocracy. You're one of them far more than you've ever been part of the business community, to be sure."

That was met with a rumbling of dissent, particularly from the Blue King's corner of the table. It was all Keating could do to keep from rubbing his hands with glee. This was too easy.

"Maybe if we dig deep enough into Harter Engine, we'll find a few more lords and ladies, and perhaps a duke or two." Keating gave a predatory smile as he piled assumption on wild assumption. Truth didn't matter once blood was in the air. "Old friends of the Thane family, every one of them. Imagine what they could do with those combustion engines. No doubt they'd be trying to light up their fancy houses without paying us our due."

"And that would just be the start of their treason," Scarlet muttered.

Gray flushed. "I have no idea what you're talking about. You have no proof of any of this."

"Of course we do, you little idiot," Keating scoffed.

"You don't!"

Which was true, up to a point. The Harter Engine Company had done its best to operate quietly, and Keating had next to no idea who was involved, outside of the public shareholders. Gray might be entirely unaware that the warehouse even existed. But none of that really mattered. Devious or stupid, Gray was weak and Keating's spies had done their work. The man had been caught with the one kind of contraband that mattered to the barons.

Contraband that Keating now had under lock and key.

"We have a treaty!" Gray looked wildly around the table. "You are supposed to protect me!" His retainers were already backing away, fear twisting their bluff, hearty features.

"Treaties matter," King Coal wheezed, "until they do not."

Green gave a smile as sharp and unpleasant as her voice. "Gentlemen, I think we have an agreement. My bridge in exchange for this traitor's lands."

Gray reached out a hand to Scarlet, who shrank back. "You're next." Flecks of spit flew from Gray's mouth, and he wiped his lips with his sleeve. "You or Violet. You know that."

"Not yet, little man," Scarlet said coldly. "I still have a pretty good hand of cards."

And the stakes are so irresistible. Fool. Keating turned and gave a nod to Striker, who gave a signal to the other streetkeepers in the room. At the same instant, the Gray party surged for the door, desperate for escape.

There was only one way treason against the council ended.

Keating's hand snaked across the table, catching Gray's wrist. A pitcher of water smashed to the floor, papers scattering into the wet. The man was strong, but Keating's fingers dug in as he tried to pull away, refusing to give even as Gray dragged him sprawling over the table. Tendons and bone slid under his grip as Gray cursed in pain.

The sound caused a twist of satisfaction in Keating's gut. *Got you.*

Then Striker was at Gray's side, wrenching the man's free arm behind his back. "Come on, guv'nor."

"No!" Gray squirmed, but it was pointless.

Reluctantly, Keating released his prey and let the street-keeper march him away. Seven steam barons walked into the guildhall that day. Six would leave. Harsh rules, but it was a harsh world out there, and it demanded a strong hand. *And someday there will be only two, and then one.*

There was another minute's commotion—a babble of voices, scraping chairs, the thump of a body hitting the door frame. Keating sat down again, gratefully accepting the glass of water Jackson set on the table, a doily underneath to protect the shining wood. Someone was already cleaning up the shattered pitcher.

Keating took a sip of the cool liquid, making a conscious effort to calm the pulse pounding in his ears. The crisis was over and the battle won, but he felt oddly sad that it was finished. Now it was just a workaday matter—Green taking over Gray's plants and gas lines, changing the streetlamps, hooking one pipe to another. The drama was over.

"Expertly done, sir," Jackson whispered in his ear.

Apparently King Coal thought so, too. He gave Keating an enormous wink. *A strong hand. That's what they respect. And it's better that I keep these dogs in check than let them run wild, however cruel it might seem.*

Mr. Fish leaned forward, speaking for the first time. "I'm curious," he said in a light, almost quavering voice and fixing Keating with damp, pale eyes. "What do you do with the corpses afterward?"

CHAPTER ELEVEN

MYSTERIOUS DEMISE OF BARON GRAY

The body of Mr. Bartholomew Thane, principal shareholder of the Stamford Coke Company and the *soi-disant* steam baron of the Gray District, was found floating near the Lambeth Pier in the early hours of the morning. It was estimated that he was in the Thames overnight and did not enter it of his own volition.

—Front page of *The London Prattler*

MELANCHOLY PASSING
OF A GREAT FRIEND

With great sadness we report the untimely passing of Mr. Bartholomew Thane, principal shareholder of the Stamford Coke Company. His noteworthy career was crowned in recent years by the seat he occupied on the Steam Council as representative of the Gray District. He was found this morning after having passed peacefully in the night. He is survived by his loving wife and two sons.

— Page five of *The Bugle*

London, April 5, 1888

HILLIARD HOUSE

11 a.m. Thursday

THE DAY AFTER GRACE'S MURDER, THE GARDEN OF HILLiard House glistened in shades of green and pink, which almost precisely matched Imogen's dress. She was perched next to Evelina on a stone bench at the corner of the garden wall. The sun warmed the masonry there, giving the illusion that summer had already arrived. The girls wore only the lightest of shawls over the flounced, bustled, and fluttery confections that passed for a plain day dress for a privileged young lady.

Imogen was looking far better today, almost back to herself. Evelina hoped the nightmare was an isolated incident. If she kept her health, Imogen would definitely be the belle to watch this Season, especially with that interesting air of fragility that made men melt and mothers cosset.

It was convenient camouflage. Evelina knew that beneath that languid demeanor, Imogen had the will and temper of a wolverine when roused. One didn't survive a dangerous illness without backbone.

Imogen reached over and clasped Evelina's hand. Little speckles of light fell through the holes of her straw hat, scattering like stars across her nose. "I can't believe you didn't wake me. You shouldn't have had to face the horrid incident alone."

Evelina laughed. "You're just sorry you missed out on the excitement."

"You can't blame me, can you?" Imogen caught her lip in her teeth. Her handwork sat idle in her lap, the needle poked carelessly into the cloth. "Mama sent Maisie home. She offered to let Dora have time off, but she wouldn't go. Not with Mama's birthday party the day after tomorrow."

A party seemed trivial, but Dora was right. The business of Hilliard House would go on. Guests would flood the lawns, play croquet, and eat too much. A herd of Imogen's hopeful suitors would no doubt descend in hopes of winning fair maid and fortune. Evelina looked forward to it. It was one event she could attend whether or not she'd been presented to the queen.

And yet, it would seem odd to sip tea and make small talk so soon after a tragic and violent death. "Do we know who Grace Child's people were?"

"Yes. They live over in Whitechapel."

"Has anyone told them?"

"Mama took care of that, too. Someone from here will go to the funeral, of course. Papa gave them a handsome sum to pay for the funeral and more besides. Or at least that's what Tobias said." Imogen turned to Evelina, the clean angle of her cheekbone catching the sunlight. Her gray eyes looked almost translucent, like the eyes of a wolf. Despite a discreet application of powder, Evelina could tell she'd been crying.

"I heard that Tobias was talking to Grace just before she was killed," Imogen added.

A bird warbled high in the branches, a throaty whoop of joy. Evelina squinted up, seeing only a black speck hopping through the elms that rimmed the lawn. Not her bird. It wouldn't be back yet—but she hoped when it was, it would have answers that cleared Nick and Tobias.

Evelina squeezed her friend's hand. "I know what Dora saw."

But Imogen went on anyway. "Maisie found Grace just after one o'clock. Dora saw him with Grace not long before."

Evelina frowned. She didn't like to see Imogen fretting. "Who told you all this?"

"No one. I heard Dora talking with Bigelow." Her friend swallowed hard. "I honestly don't think Tobias did it. He's my brother. But the timing looks very bad. The problem is, if it wasn't Tobias, who was it? No matter how you turn it around, there was a killer in our house."

"I know."

"Are you afraid?"

"Yes and no," Evelina replied.

"Yes I understand, but why no?"

Evelina hesitated. She didn't want to involve Imogen in any of this, but doubt was an insidious foe. That had to be worse than talking it through, and frankly Evelina welcomed the chance to go over what had happened. She wanted, even needed, Imogen's support.

Evelina's immediate problem was simple: she wanted answers, but she wasn't sure where to begin. She'd lain awake all night, trying to get the details straight in her own mind.

Uncle Sherlock would tell her to get her facts in order before making a single move. Anything less, and he'd give her that eyebrow-raise and accuse her of sloppy thinking. "There's more to Grace's death than meets the eye."

Imogen's brow puckered. "What makes you say that?"

Evelina reached into her work bag and withdrew the envelope she'd pocketed right under Lestrade's nose. In all the commotion last night, she'd all but forgotten it until she had undressed for bed. "I think there was a reason Grace died. She had this hidden in her clothes."

"And you took it?" Imogen's eyes widened.

"I had my reasons."

"But this is evidence!"

"The police aren't going to understand it."

At least, not until they started hiring experts who could detect the magical signatures—she was sure there were two—clinging to the envelope. The residue was so disturbing to be around, she'd packed the whole thing in salt to neutralize the bad energy. It was mostly gone now. Otherwise, she'd hesitate to let Imogen handle it.

She turned the envelope over in her hands, feeling her friend's curiosity like a flame. Despite the seriousness of the subject, Evelina had a showman's thrill anticipating the reveal. One could take a girl out of the circus . . .

"Look at what's inside." She tipped it and a bright silk bag fell into her hand with a clinking sound.

Imogen reached over and picked it up. "What is it?"

"Another layer of mystery. Keep looking."

Imogen pulled the drawstring open and peered down into the silk mouth. Evelina watched in amusement as her friend's eyes widened. "Oh! Oh, dear!" Imogen dipped her long fingers into the bag and pulled out a rectangle of bright gold. "This is . . ."

"Worth a fair bit of money, I'd guess. I weighed it. That's three ounces by the scale in the pantry. And there's more in the bag."

Imogen fished out a handful of tiny stones, looking at them curiously. Evelina could see the shock fading and curiosity taking over. Imogen had a mind every bit as good as her brother's, but was rarely pushed to use it.

"These are emeralds," she said, excitement thrumming in her words. "But roughly cut. Not like any I've seen. And the gold is so pure, but there are no markings on it. I've seen Papa with gold that has come from a bank. There's almost always a stamp to say where it was minted." Imogen's eyes were bright with interest. "It looks like someone melted this down."

Someone who uses magic, or else the gold and gems were close to magic long enough that it left a trace. Metal and gemstones would absorb the residue of power faster than almost any other substances. That was why there were so many magical swords and crowns and whatnot in folk tales. "Any of your family heirlooms have emeralds? Anything missing?"

"No. Nothing we have would boil down to this." Imogen slipped the items back into the bag. "The gold puts another light on the matter entirely. What was Grace doing with it? What had she got herself into?"

A bee zipped by, stirring the flower-scented air. In a moment, it was lost in the shivering shadows of the leaves.

"She was delivering it, probably."

"But why kill her and not rob her?"

"Maybe the killer was interrupted—or maybe she was killed for an entirely different reason." Evelina pulled a paper out of the envelope. It was plain, the cheap kind that could be purchased anywhere, and it bore a few lines of block letters. The words were printed by hand with ordinary ink. "Look at what was with the gold."

The paper was folded in half. Imogen flipped it open, the breeze fluttering its edges. Her chin tucked back as if the words had offended her. "This is pure nonsense."

"It's written in a cipher of some kind."

Imogen gave her a blank look. "One of your uncle's specialties, I suppose?"

"He's written what he describes as a trifling monograph on the subject in which he analyzes one hundred and sixty separate ciphers."

Imogen raised one fair brow. "He would have, wouldn't he?"

"He doesn't have many friends."

"Except that poor doctor he used to live with. He must be a very patient man."

Evelina gave a slight shrug. There was no point in trying to explain Uncle Sherlock. It just couldn't be done. "Anyhow, if I'm right about what this is, ciphers of this type are extremely hard to figure out."

A stubborn look came over Imogen's face. "But we have to, don't we? To clear Tobias?"

Evelina held up a hand, a wave of unease urging her to caution. "Nothing good can come out of poking around murders and thievery. You have your presentation and Season to worry about."

"So leave it to you?" Imogen shot back. "Not bloody likely, Evelina Cooper. You're not the only girl with wit and daring. By this time next year, I could be an old married lady. Give me an adventure to remember!"

Evelina's heart caught. After the Season, their paths were sure to part. They would still adore each other, they would write letters, but hours together would become a treat rather than the general rule. Their youth would end with all the predictability of a clock striking midnight.

Evelina swallowed an ache. "I don't want you to get hurt."

"Figuring out a code?"

"Cipher. There's a difference."

Imogen rolled her eyes skyward. "Deciphering a letter, then."

"It's not just that. There will be other things. There might be magic involved."

"Piffle. Don't try and keep me out of this. You need my expertise."

Evelina blinked.

"Don't look so shocked! I'm not useless." Imogen held up the bag. "I know my silks, and there is only one place this could possibly come from. A little shop in the West End. Whoever made this bag had to have purchased it there, and recently. It's this year's pattern. Check the fashion gazette if you doubt me."

A bolt of pleasure scattered her misgivings. Evelina threw her arms around her friend. "You are a genius! Only you would notice that."

"Probably, and only because I've looked at a thousand samples while picking out my wardrobe for the Season." Imogen murmured into her ear. "We can investigate and go shopping all at the same time. Isn't Papa always promoting efficiency?"

Evelina winced, wondering once more about Lord B's possible secrets. The magic on the bag was nothing like that on the automatons, but why was she encountering it at all? Where had the poor maid been, and on whose business?

They were interrupted by Dora, who came bustling across the lawn at a trot. "Miss Cooper, you must come at once!" The maid stopped a few feet away, puffing.

"What's happened now?" Alarmed, Evelina quickly put the silk bag, note, and envelope back with her needlework. *The last thing I need is yet one more ball in the air. Juggling was never my talent.*

The maid lowered her voice to a sepulchral whisper. "Your grandmother is here."

Imogen cast Evelina a sorrowful glance. "Oh, dear."

Bugger! I don't have time to appease her on top of everything else. Evelina rose, smoothing the skirt of her pale blue dress. She would have felt better if her embroidery bag contained a revolver. She was grateful to the woman who had taken her from poverty to a life of gentility. Nevertheless, Grandmamma was probably the reason her uncles had never married. She'd no doubt frightened the poor dears into permanent celibacy.

Evelina trailed Dora from the garden, feeling vaguely like a convict en route to execution. All the beauty of the morning, from the sunlit leaves to the bright spring flowers, faded to grays as her mind focused on the prospect of speaking with her grandmamma. *Where's a good tumbrel when you need it?*

Not surprisingly, Evelina's family difficulties were a legacy of her parents. Evelina's father had run away from Ploughman's circus as a child. He'd risen through the ranks by unequaled bravery and good luck, won an officer's title, convinced her mother to elope, and then got himself shot in Ethiopia less than a year later. He'd left Marianne Cooper, née Holmes, penniless and pregnant with their daughter.

Marianne's parents, with a sense of wounded privilege, cast her off without ever telling Sherlock and his elder brother, Mycroft, of her return. Thus Marianne was forced to find refuge with her husband's people, who proved much kinder than her own. But that had all happened long before Grandmamma Holmes had fetched Evelina and tried to turn her into a lady.

Not that the older woman was confident of success. The expectation that Evelina would also fall from grace—an event no doubt attended with all the aplomb and inevitability of cold gravy plopping from a spoon—was sufficiently acute that there were days when Evelina wanted to oblige and get it over with.

She took a deep breath on entering the house, reminding herself how grateful she was for everything her grandmamma had done for her. Really.

Evelina took an extra minute to go up to her room and make sure her hair and dress were beyond reproach. She paused in front of the mirror a moment, finding the proper expression for a meek and obedient granddaughter. Then she descended the stairs again, pausing to look at the long-case clock. The dial that showed the weather showed a smiling sun. It was more optimistic than she was.

As if aware it was being watched, the clock bonged and spit a card out of a slot. Evelina grabbed it before it fell to the floor. She turned it and tried to read the message embossed on the card. The letters were familiar, but the words they made were gibberish. It was a great pity—for all the clock's clever beauty, there was definitely something wrong with the workings. She set the card on the window ledge and continued down the stairs.

All the curtains of the morning room were drawn, casting the usually sunny space into an early twilight. Yes, Grandmother Holmes was a traveling storm cloud, plunging all into darkness and consternation. Light faded furniture, after all, so no one with any sense opened the curtains on a bright day. And, of course, poor Lady Bancroft had knuckled under.

Swathed in heavy black silk, Grandmamma sat in the largest and most comfortable chair. Though well into her seventies, her tall, spare frame was still ramrod straight. Her only ornaments were a mourning brooch woven of human hair pinned to the high collar of her bodice, and a jet comb skewering her smoke-colored coiffure.

Evelina stood in the bull's-eye of the patterned carpet, clasping her hands in front of her. With some anxiety, she noted that they were alone. Her grandmother wanted her all to herself.

A light fluttering occupied her stomach, as if she had swallowed a moth. "How pleasant to see you, madam. An unexpected pleasure, to be sure."

Mrs. Holmes set down her cup and saucer with a clatter. "Don't be pert. Lord Bancroft summoned me. I understand he found you prodding a dead body last night."

He must have telegraphed at once, to have summoned the old lady so quickly. "I was merely attempting to see who it was," Evelina protested, keeping her voice mild.

"Disgusting. Utterly unfeminine curiosity."

"My intent was to be helpful."

"I despair on a daily basis that you will end up like Marianne."

How anyone could equate eloping with examining the deceased escaped Evelina, but then again she'd never been married. "I'm sorry if I caused anyone concern. I assure you, it won't happen again."

"No. Fortunately, murdered servants are in short supply."

Her grandmother looked her up and down with eyes as dark and hard as the jet beads on her comb. Despite her ferocity, she looked tired from the journey. She was getting frail, Evelina realized with a pang.

The old lady plowed on. "But I do believe it is time to think of your future, as this visit is clearly *not* being spent with finding a husband in mind."

Evelina made a noise of protest. "There was only the one corpse."

Her grandmother slashed the air with one bony hand. "Tut."

"I shall work hard to please you better, Grandmamma. I always do."

"Pretty words are better with pretty deeds. I'd rather not think of my granddaughter putting herself in harm's way. You never know what might come of interfering with such vulgar affairs."

That sounded close enough to concern that Evelina experienced a moment of surprise. "Indeed, madam."

"But enough about the dead bodies. I have other things to speak of." Her grandmother pointed to a chair, as if accusing it of something. "Sit down and have tea."

Evelina poured from the Wedgewood pot, first remembering to refill her grandmother's cup and offer the plate of biscuits. If nothing else, no one could fault her manners.

Her grandmother pulled out her lorgnette, the eyepiece springing open so that she could examine the sweets through powerful lenses. She tutted at the macaroons, then pushed a tiny gold button to select a bird's nest cake with strawberry jam in the center. The automatic plate lifted it in silver tongs and deposited it neatly on Grandmamma's saucer.

Evelina lowered herself to the embroidered fauteuil, maneuvering her bustle with great care. A slice of light fell impudently across the carpet, as if thumbing its nose at the dictum against sun and air. Evelina thought quickly, wondering how to proceed. Perhaps it would be best to put the whole notion of marriage into the grave as soon as possible. She respected her grandmother enough to be honest.

She wet her lips, then finally gave voice to the idea she'd been formulating for months. "With reference to the future, madam, I would like to seek admittance to Ladies' College of London. I am, of course, desirous of your support."

Her grandmother jerked as if struck. "College? Whatever for?"

She'd braced for disappointment, but a sliver of panic slid under her guard. It was impossible to gain admittance without the support of her family. How hard was this going to be?

Evelina kept her face frozen in a polite mask. "To further my education."

"Utterly out of the question."

"Pray tell, what could be the harm in it?"

"Women in a college? A ridiculous modernity. Your grandfather would never have permitted it."

Evelina opened her mouth to speak, angry words aching to fly free. *Don't quote the old wretch at me, madam.*

If Grandfather Holmes had still held sway, she would be at Ploughman's giving three performances a day on the high wire. It was only after the unlamented bugger had died that Grandmamma had dared to rescue her—too late for Marianne, who by then was long dead of a putrid fever.

Evelina chewed a biscuit to keep herself from firing off a rude retort. "If I'm not to receive an education, then what sort of future do I have? Governess? Companion? Nurse?"

Her grandmother sniffed with disgust. "Nonsense! How can you think of such things when you have—against all my expectations, I might add—received an invitation to be presented to the queen? It seems the Duchess of Westlake herself has offered to sponsor you! No doubt she will invite you to her ball as well. That is quite a coup."

Silence resounded with all the majesty of an Oriental gong. Evelina felt her saucer slipping from her hand before she regained her wits enough to catch it. "Pardon me?"

"You heard me." Grandmamma raised her chin, clearly pleased to have asserted control over the conversation. "It is the next best thing to divine intervention. No one will dare to gainsay her choice of protégée."

Confusion clogged Evelina's thoughts. She had met the duchess, of course, during social calls, but there was no reason for the woman to single her out. *Why has she sponsored me?* Evelina should have been dancing around the room with glee, but instead felt . . . perplexed.

Her grandmamma, however, was gathering momentum like a chugging locomotive. She set her cup aside, rubbing her hands together with enthusiastic delight. It was an odd look on her. "I was certain that after your mother's fall there would be no presentation. It seems Sherlock finally did something useful and called in a favor from one of those steam men. Jasper Keating, he signed himself. He arranged the whole thing."

Evelina blinked. *Which means the Gold King convinced the Duchess of Westlake to sponsor me. Why? How?* What hold could Jasper Keating have over a duchess? Then again, from what Evelina had heard, he was a very powerful man. It could be anything.

A seasick sense of exposure swept her, as if she were suddenly a tiny bug on a very large display board. For all of her childhood spent in front of an audience, she didn't like being noticed by such important people. It felt dangerous.

"What did Uncle Sherlock do for Mr. Keating?"

Her grandmother gave a loud snort. "Such details are of no concern to me, but I brought your mother's presentation gown so it could be altered and brought up to date. May it bring you more presence of mind than it did her, my girl. Don't go wasting *your* chances on a circus performer."

An unwelcome thought of Nick popped into Evelina's mind. *He's not a waste. It's wrong to even think it.* She had loved Nick with all the fierceness of a girl's first passion and loved him still—but that way led to danger for them both. She couldn't risk him like that, and if she didn't move forward the temptation to run back to him would grow too strong. A presentation at Court would take her even further from the barefoot girl she used to be, further toward the side of the gentry—and further away from Nick's magic, and the risk of discovery.

And—though it sounded almost ridiculously commonplace, given everything else—where would college fit in? This piece of good luck—if that's what it was—added another layer of complexity to her future.

Her grandmother went on, oblivious to her inner turmoil. "This opens a lot of doors, you know. You could actually marry well. A younger son, perhaps. Or, with a bit of luck, I could find you an older gentleman, some minor title with a bit of money and in need of a nurse. That might suit."

Evelina gaped. *A life of bedpans and emetics? What larks!* But what if she could have someone like Tobias? *Or*

Tobias himself? Presentation meant that she was formally accepted into that small circle from which he would choose his wife. Imogen's clever, handsome brother wouldn't be so far out of her reach now. He would never be her first love—only Nick could have that place in her heart—but he held the promise of passion all the same.

A tiny rush of excitement stole through her, breathless and tender as a green shoot. *Could I? Would I dare?*

He's still a Roth. He'll still want a fortune, and Lord B will be looking for political connections. Don't overstep your good luck. Indeed, she stood on a cliff's edge, the ground crumbling under her feet, and for that moment she didn't care. Tobias was half a rake, but that was part of the thrill. Just once, she wanted to drop her guard with him, to see where that might take her.

"I don't know if I can," Evelina said quietly.

"Of course you can," Grandmamma snapped.

Evelina jumped in her chair, startled out of her daydream. "Pardon?"

Mrs. Holmes raised her eyebrows. "You don't look pleased. In fact, you look troubled. You should be happy."

"It's all rather sudden." Evelina swallowed the last of her third biscuit and washed it down with a swig of tea. *What an utter fool I am.*

"Didn't you eat breakfast? You'll lose your figure if you keep gobbling up sweets that way." Her grandmother pursed her lips, as if considering Evelina's prospects. "There is much to be done if you're to have a proper Season, and not a lot of time to do it. If you can refrain from encountering dead bodies, perhaps Lord Bancroft won't notice that you're still here. From the tone of his note, I'm afraid you quite offended his sensibilities."

"Odd. He doesn't strike me as the sensitive type."

Her grandmother gave a knowing snort. "He was alarmed enough to send for me to talk sense into you. I got his message at the same time as Mr. Keating's. Together, they made quite fascinating reading with my morning chocolate. You have a great many shortcomings, but dullness is not among them. It seems you've quite riveted these two fine gentlemen, if in different ways. I can't wait to see what sort of suitors you will attract."

Evelina bit her tongue, but her grandmother saw the look. Her eyes twinkled. "Finding a proper husband is rather like selecting a hound. They all have more bark than bite, my girl. One day you'll look across the breakfast table and realize the only option left is obedience training."

AN HOUR LATER, Evelina had a moment of peace in her bedroom. She sat on the edge of her bed and buried her face in her hands. Her skin was hot. Truth be told, she was verging on frantic. Her grandmother's visit had panicked her.

Presented? I am to be presented to the queen? It was beyond belief, even though it was something she had secretly hoped for. It granted her a mark of respectability. It meant she could fully participate in the Season with Imogen and— find a husband?

Most women assumed they would marry, but because of her uncertain social standing, she had deliberately formed other plans. College fit well with her curiosity about science and magic, and figuring out how she could bridge the two. But now, suddenly, she had another choice.

She had no idea what to wish for. She'd had no time to think.

Her mother would have been delighted. Evelina remembered sitting on her lap, listening to tale after tale of pretty dresses and assemblies. Marianne had done her best to raise her daughter well, tried to teach her how to use all the forks and spoons and "my lords" and how to address a duke's firstborn son. Evelina wished she could tell her that her lessons had not been in vain.

But one thing nagged at Evelina's mind. She had no illusions that a gentleman's son would want a magic user for a wife. She would have to keep her abilities secret forever.

She lifted her face from her hands, looking out her window over the back garden. She didn't see the pale green of springtime trees as much as she did a fondly desired future. One in which magic and science held equal sway, and no

one cared how many biscuits she ate or whether she preferred fixing a clock to embroidering handkerchiefs. Where
she could marry where she loved, or not at all. She allowed
herself a plaintive sigh. *That, Evelina Cooper, is what fantasy looks like. There's a murder to solve. Get to work.*

She immediately felt better. However morbid and terrifying, murder seemed easier to manage than suitors.

Where do I begin? She knew Uncle Sherlock sometimes
struggled to find clues. That wasn't her problem. There were
clues aplenty, but they all led to questions. What was Tobias
doing last night, and why wouldn't he talk about it? Was
there a connection with the automatons? Who was Grace's
lover? Why was a penniless scullion carrying a fortune hidden in her clothes? Why had Nick chosen that moment, after
five years, to visit? *And do I need to go to Ploughman's to
find out?*

The questions flickered, a luminous web in her mind's
eye. She could almost see the connection from one to the
next, but they eluded her vision if she looked at them too
hard—almost like the afterimage of a bright candle in a
dark room. The longer she stared, the blinder she became. It
would be delicate work to tease those will-o'-the-wisps into
concrete facts, and that meant a lot of investigation.

*But I have no authority to ask questions, because I am a
young woman barely out of the schoolroom. As it is, I'm
relying on a clockwork bird for help.*

And she wasn't one-quarter as brilliant as Sherlock
Holmes. One person had died already, and trying to solve
the case herself carried the risk that her inexperience might
put someone else at risk. She wanted to write to her uncle
for advice.

But that had its own challenges. Her uncle was never so
much invited into a case as unleashed on it. He would surely
uncover dangerous secrets—just as she feared in the event
Lestrade brought him in. Uncle Sherlock's involvement
could well negate any hopes Evelina had of protecting Imogen and her family. Even worse, he might decide a household visited by murder was unsafe, and insist she return

to the country to stay with Grandmamma Holmes. That
was . . . categorically unthinkable.

She had to find a way to ask advice in a very limited
fashion—only about the cipher. Puzzles and abstract problems were topics they corresponded about anyhow, and as
such it would not arouse his curiosity, especially since he
would make her figure it out herself. What she wanted was
a clue as to the type of cipher she was looking at. She sat
down at her desk, taking several pieces of writing paper
from the drawer. Then she copied out the cipher text, careful
to keep the nonsensical letters exact.

JEYRB AGZTL JLPWG WPPEF LEOZV ZI

Once that was done, she began a letter.

My dear uncle Sherlock,
*I hope this finds you well. I am enjoying good health
and a pleasant visit at Hilliard House.*
*To come directly to the point (as I know this is your
preference), I am writing to express my gratitude. I understand that through some act of yours, Mr. Jasper Keating has engineered my presentation. As you can imagine,
this has caused a great deal of happiness and excitement
for Grandmamma and me, your humble niece.*
*In addition, I have encountered the enclosed cipher,
which you might find of some slight interest. While I have
done my best to absorb such methods as you have cared
to share with me, I am afraid this is beyond my skill. As I
do not have the key, any advice you might offer toward its
solution would be much appreciated . . .*

CHAPTER TWELVE

London, April 6, 1888

HILLIARD HOUSE

11 a.m. Friday

My dear girl,

You are most welcome to your presentation. Quite simply, Mr. Keating has asked that I consult on a case for him. I agreed, and he made the arrangements. And that is all that there is to say on the matter.

As for your cipher, please consult my monograph. Everything I have to say on the matter of ciphers will be there, and it is best to make an attempt on your own at first. Write and let me know how you get on with it. The world would be a better place if more young ladies were so fond of exercising their minds instead of indulging in shoddy thinking.

I suppose it falls upon me, as your elder, to offer some gem of wisdom to guide you through your first London Season. What little I have, I am afraid, is based strictly on observation. First, no one looks intelligent dancing the polka. Second, fifty percent of masquerade balls are held in order to facilitate espionage. Third, and above all, do not attempt to engage dangerous men in flirtatious conversation. Whatever second-rate novelists might say, such individuals are called dangerous for a reason. There, that is the sum of my advice to young ladies.

I have been called away unexpectedly on a matter of some importance and shall be on the Continent for the

*next few days. Watson will be joining me in a day or two
and can bring any letters you send. I shall see you in person as soon as I can.*

HER UNCLE SIGNED THE LETTER WITH A SIMPLE *S.* EVELINA
refolded it, sliding it back into her pocket. A feeling of reassurance emanated from the heavy paper, easing the tension
that knotted the back of her neck. Her uncle was a complicated man—just witness the terse explanation about her
presentation—but he was as good an uncle as she could
wish for. Except that she wished he'd solved the cipher for
her instead of referring her to a book. She was no further
ahead.

Her fingers brushed the other piece of paper in her
pocket—a clipping from the *Prattler* that announced Ploughman's was performing at the Hibernia Amphitheatre. She
had told herself not to pay it any mind, but her fingers picked
up the scissors and cut it out anyhow. For some reason, the
prospect of being ushered into Society had made the urge to
revisit the past almost painfully acute—and, if possible,
even more unwise. If her past was found out, there would be
no presentation, no Season, no future. If her magic was
found out, that would be even worse. And yet . . . she couldn't
bring herself to throw the clipping away.

Light streamed into the morning room, bringing the soft
greens and yellows to shimmering life. The place smelled
of the freesias sitting in a blue and white jug Evelina had set
on the windowsill. Outside of her own room, this bright
haven was the place she spent the most time. As was often
the case, today she had the room to herself.

The table where she worked was littered with small pieces
of metal. Evelina had out her tiniest set of pliers and was
trying to shape a scrap of gold wire to match the loops in a
beaded necklace that had broken apart. It was an old piece
and not particularly valuable, but she needed every bit of
finery she had for the Season. Besides, working with her
hands helped her to think.

She picked up a coral bead no bigger than a lentil and slid
it over a piece of wire. With the pliers, she looped the wire

through the bottom chain of the necklace, leaving enough play so the bead could dangle freely. *We all love our pretty things, even poor Grace and her petticoat.*

An image of the girl's dead body floated through her mind—bloody, still, and pale. *It's been a whole day and I haven't figured anything out yet.* A sense of urgency gnawed at Evelina, but she pushed it down, concentrating on the mechanical movements of her fingers. Panic wasn't going to make her think any faster. *Think about the case. Blood. Corpses. Stolen treasure.* And she was going to have to figure it out on her own.

She tried to tell herself it was just as well she couldn't talk to her uncle about the case, because then she would be tempted to explain about the magic she'd sensed on Grace's package. She'd kept her abilities secret from the Holmes family, and not just because magic was banned. If Uncle Sherlock detested shoddy thinking, she cringed to imagine what he'd make of her fumbling descriptions of a nasty feeling in her tummy when she touched the envelope. No doubt that would end in a hysterical bout of opiates and bad violin.

"Hello." Tobias wandered into the room, managing to look impeccably turned out and rumpled at the same time. Evelina was not sure quite how he managed it.

"Good morning."

"You look like a goddess in that sunbeam, bent to your work." He sprawled into the chair on the other side of the table, blocking her view of the garden. He was dressed in a dark brown jacket and forest green waistcoat, a golden watch chain dangling against the silk. "Perhaps a goddess of industry, or the sylph of gears. If only I could sketch. The sight of you there, so feminine and yet so ready to ply your tools, is enough to give a man improper fantasies."

"Spare me." Evelina felt a rush of heat claw up her cheeks, and she forced her gaze to the necklace. If she looked at him, her wits would turn to oatmeal. "Young men are most imaginative creatures."

"You disapprove?"

She gave the wire a deft twist. "A pity so much good brainpower is squandered on idle yearnings."

"It is entirely up to you whether or not my yearnings are idle."

That made her look up, one eyebrow raised. Tobias flirted, but this was more obvious than usual. "I would never spoil your fun with disappointment."

"Disappointment?" He leaned forward, his elbows on the table. "I doubt that, Evelina. It is not in you to disappoint."

She froze, her pliers suspended in midair. It shocked her every time he used her name—and not just because first names were an intimacy between an unmarried man and woman, but because he made every syllable delicious, as if it were something made of cream. *Evelina.*

One corner of his mouth curled upward, giving a lopsided smile that was all charming self-mockery. He knew he was behaving like an ass and didn't give a fig.

Confusion deepened until it was next door to anger. "Don't waste my time."

He leaned an inch closer, so she could feel the warmth of his skin just a touch away. "No need to bring out your prickles. I hear you're going to the presentation. Congratulations."

She lowered the tools, giving up trying to work. "Thank you."

He pulled a box out of his pocket and slid it across the table. "I got you a present to celebrate. Anyone else I'd give flowers or a book of genteel poems, but you are a different kind of creature."

Evelina knew very well that a gift from her friend's handsome brother, no matter what, was in a very gray area of propriety. They shouldn't be alone, and should never spar the way they did. And yet, there had always been an alliance between them, slight but steadily growing. Confidences, secrets. Such things led to breaking rules. The notion enticed and terrified her.

The box was plain paper, dull and gray. Cautiously, Evelina flipped up the lid with one finger. What she saw made her give a tiny start, as if the contents had emitted a spark. Tobias chuckled.

She lifted the lid, and scooped the box toward her with an

eager hand. She couldn't help herself. Inside was a perfect, tiny piece of clockwork made of gleaming brass. "What is this?"

"German made. You said you wanted to try your hand at making moving toys."

"Ah," she said, happy and embarrassed. Tobias didn't know about the bird, or any of the others that were close to complete. The half-living creatures weren't something she could share.

"You've already mastered a lot, but I thought you might like another example to take apart anyhow."

His voice had lost its teasing tone. They were on different ground now, a place for plans and projects they both shared and that few understood. Ladies didn't work with mechanics, of course, but neither did a gentleman—at least not past the stage where it could be considered a passing whim. Blue bloods never dirtied their hands, lest they be considered vulgar.

Lord B's aversion to his son's tinkering was so severe that Tobias had hidden his workshop somewhere else in the city. And although the steam barons grew increasingly touchy about anyone but their own people making machines, Evelina still didn't understand Lord B's objections. Surely building engines was a better pastime than gambling and whoring, although Tobias did plenty of that, too. He was a versatile lad.

Well, clockwork was the one passion that they could safely share. Evelina dug into the box, closing her fingers around the cluster of cogs and springs. It was a generous gift. Even though the steam barons didn't directly interfere with the buying habits of the gentry, good mechanical parts were becoming expensive and hard to get.

In some ways Tobias knew her better than anyone else. "Thank you so much."

He fixed her with his gaze, disconcertingly direct. He was still leaning toward her, his head tilted at a considering angle. She could see the striations of his iris, the grays of ice and storm and mist. The huge purpling bruise around his eye was pretty spectacular, too. "I'm glad you're here this Season. Very glad."

And suddenly the uncomfortable tension between them was back, the scant few inches between them humming like an unresolved chord. *Very glad.* What did that mean? More flirtation? An honest desire for conversation? Or nothing at all?

Her discomfort must have shown, because he pulled away with a ghost of a laugh. She couldn't tell if it was aimed at him or her. "Oh, Evelina, you make this so hard."

Stung, she felt a moment of numbness before shame flared under her skin. She drew herself up, her hand instinctively closing around the handle of the pliers. Something to defend herself—not that anything could protect her from this kind of danger. "What do you want from me?"

His expression was unreadable. She searched his face, finding a jumble of emotions as confused as her own. "I don't want anything from you," he replied. "That would be too finite a request."

Tobias rose, a languid, lazy movement that didn't go with the troubled set of his mouth. He paused a moment, his hands braced on the table, and leaned over. The sun slanted across his face, gilding his hair and turning his features to a mask of highlights and shadow.

Then, suddenly, he moved. He did it so fast, she didn't have the wits to duck. Or maybe she guessed what was coming and didn't want to.

He kissed her at the corner of her mouth. Not full on the lips. Not hard, or long, but gently, almost chastely. But all at once, it was not quite chaste. His mouth was warm and softer than she had expected.

Shock gave way to desire. Evelina's breath caught almost painfully, her own lips parting in surprise. She looked up at him, feeling her eyes grow wide. Her body turned toward him, as if a magnet were pulling her into another kiss, but he was already out of reach.

Her reaction must have been what he wanted. He backed away from the table, a knowing look in his eye. "Have a pleasant afternoon."

With that, he spun, his jacket swinging with him, and sauntered out the door, the sound of his footfalls lazy against the carpet. They dared her to say something, to stop him from leaving the room.

Furious, confused, wanting, all Evelina could manage was a strangled noise deep in her throat. Part of her wanted to rage that she was not to be trifled with like some chit fresh from school. Except she was. She wasn't as ignorant as most of the Society misses, but she was hardly a sophisticate, either. Tobias, with his mistresses and his clubs, was far beyond her.

What did he want? If he was simply scratching an itch, he could do that anywhere and with a far more accomplished woman. There was at least one other layer to his game.

Evelina looked down at the mess of half-fixed jewelry on the table. The gleaming clockwork sat to one side, tucked neatly in its box, not quite belonging with the rest. Just like her, neither project was anywhere near complete.

She braced her elbows on the table and covered her face with her hands. *Above all, do not attempt to engage dangerous men in flirtatious conversation.*

Well, Uncle Sherlock hadn't said anything about kissing them.

BANCROFT SAT SLUMPED behind his desk. With the garden party looming, he was trying to write a birthday letter to his wife, something he'd done every year in the early decades of their marriage. It was the sort of thing women liked—soft protestations of devotion—and something he hadn't attended to in the last dozen years. He loved Adele, he supposed, as well as most men did their wives of nearly thirty years. Habit supplied what passion could not. Perhaps, with all the upset in the house, he missed that warmth a little.

Unfortunately, he hadn't made it past the opening lines and had more or less given up. His mind was scrambling. The trunks he had ordered removed from the attics had not been delivered to their destination. There was no sign of the footmen or their cart, either.

Who even knew about the automatons? Bancroft had been careful. He'd let all of the Austrian servants go when he returned to England, hiring new domestics with no knowledge of his past. That left the family. Poppy had been a babe in arms when he locked the hideous things away. The other two children would remember them, though Imogen had seen more of them than Tobias. The dolls had first been built to amuse Bancroft's sickly twin girls.

He shuddered, filtering the memories like a terrified child trying to look and cover its eyes at the same time. Imogen had lived. Anna had not. But his children would not know the full history of the automatons. Not even his wife knew their real secret—only Dr. Magnus. And he'd seen Magnus at the opera last night.

Bancroft had offered the police a reward if the trunks were returned unopened. That had been a mistake, sure to arouse curiosity, but he had been drinking when he made the offer. He knew alcohol made him take chances, but somehow that didn't make him stop craving the taste. And the specter of Dr. Magnus made him even thirstier.

Now it was a waiting game. Why was Magnus in town? Would he try to use the automatons against Bancroft? Would Magnus even come at all, or did he have schemes afoot that had nothing to do with the Roth family?

There was a knock at the study door. Bancroft started, the skim of liquid left in his glass sloshing up the side. Annoyance clenched his shoulders. "Enter."

Bigelow pushed open the door with an apologetic cough and extended a tray upon which rested a plain calling card of indifferent quality. "There is a Mr. Harriman to see you, sir."

Could this day grow worse? Bancroft snatched the card from the salver and read it, misgivings building like thunderclouds.

John Harriman, Esquire

*Warehouse and Shipping
Bond Street, London*

Damnation. The only thing he could do was see the man and get rid of him as unobtrusively as possible. "Show him in."

Bigelow vanished. Bancroft rose, put the whisky glass back on the tray and resumed his seat behind the desk. When the door opened a second time, the man who came in had much the same features as his older cousin, Jasper Keating, but in him they were expressed in a pale, watered-down way—his hair graying brown instead of white, his mouth a bit weaker, his nose a shade too long. Harriman had one redeeming feature. As Keating's cousin, he expected to share in the man's amazing wealth rather than to content himself with a modest position in the firm. Ergo, despite the family connection, he hated the Gold King and was quite prepared to rob him blind. That had made him easy clay for Bancroft to mold.

Without waiting for an invitation, Harriman dropped into the chair opposite Bancroft's desk. "I must speak with you."

"Apparently. Why do you need to do it here? You could have sent a note." They had a perfectly good cipher to use.

"Word travels fast among servants. I heard about what happened."

About Grace. Bancroft's stomach cramped with hatred, loathing this coward who barely had the nerve to deal with his own workers. Mind you, he had hired some terrifying characters. Could it have been Harriman's thug of a foreman who had followed Grace home and killed her for the gold? When Bancroft had approached Harriman at his club, he hadn't bothered to instruct the man whose services to engage—after all, it was Harriman who had worked around the docks for years, not Bancroft—but maybe he should have managed him a little more closely. "Go on, then. Say what you have to say."

Harriman shot a nervous glance at the door, as if he expected half of Scotland Yard to come crashing through the door. "I sent a note with—uh, her. Along with—what else she was carrying."

"The police searched her body and found nothing." One more time, he felt the sting of the loss like something physical. He'd been counting on the treasure Grace carried—not just to bolster the family fortunes, but because there were irons in the fire besides Harter Engines, and everything required cash.

"Then she was robbed." It was an obvious statement, but an almost crafty look crossed Harriman's features. It was gone too swiftly for Bancroft to give it much study, but something about it put him on alert.

"Was it the note that brought you here? A question you need answered?" Thank the gods they used an unbreakable cipher.

Harriman looked at the door again, clearly anxious. "The note hardly matters now. There are larger problems if proof of what we've done is in the hands of a killer."

"I hardly think a thief and murderer will turn *us* in to the police," Bancroft said dryly.

The man gave him an irritated look. Where Keating's eyes were almost amber, his were hazel and too small for his head. "The gallery is opening soon. We need to finish up our enterprise, and quickly."

Bancroft's fingers twitched, as if grasping for all the gold he'd hoped to extract from Keating's vaunted archaeological treasures. He'd needed to recruit four others besides himself and Harriman to put the plan in motion. Simple and elegant though the plan had been, when the wealth was split among so many, the proceeds hadn't gone nearly as far as he'd hoped. "Are we done so soon?"

"You always knew it was time-limited."

Heat flooded up Bancroft's neck. "Of course I did. I arranged everything." Each of the six partners had received four payments so far—each lot a bar of gold and some gemstones. Nothing so unusual that it couldn't be taken to a bank and used as collateral or sold as old family treasures. "How many artifacts are left to process?"

"The last few crates came in two days ago." They'd been expecting them, but hadn't known what they contained. "Two were just pottery, but one was jewelry and plate."

"Did you determine why they weren't shipped with the rest?" Bancroft asked.

Harriman gave a slight shrug. "I suppose the sender didn't have them packed up in time. They came by a different boat."

Bancroft supposed that could be true. Schliemann's treasures were shipped directly from Rhodes to Harriman's warehouse, where he was unpacking the crates and readying the contents for Keating's new gallery. The direct shipping route had been arranged to prevent loss, theft, or accident, and it did—right up until the priceless artifacts reached Harriman's hands.

"At any rate, I was the only one there when they arrived," Harriman added. "I never told Jasper that they came. In fact, I made a point of saying that they hadn't."

"Why the hell did you do that?" Bancroft frowned. "That's not how I planned this would work."

"I'd read Schliemann's letters about what was supposed to be coming." The crafty look was back. "It sounded like he might have saved the best for last."

Bancroft studied Harriman suspiciously. "What do you mean?"

"One or two really large pieces. The crates were so late, I wasn't sure we'd have time to make copies, so I thought if they were lost, who would be the wiser? If everyone thought the crates were lost, we could just keep the contents. So I hid them underneath the warehouse."

A sick feeling swamped Bancroft's entire body. He closed his eyes a moment, summoning patience. "If something valuable goes missing, people tend to look for it. That's a danger to us. If we supply copies, there is a reasonable chance they won't look, at least not right away. That means less danger."

"So what are you implying?" Harriman asked, a touch belligerent.

"I'm implying that you should get the workers to process these last crates immediately. If there is something that they cannot finish in time, we should simply leave it alone." Bancroft's tone was growing sharper. He sucked in a deep breath, forcing himself not to bang Harriman's head on the desk.

"Do you mean that I should tell Keating the last crates have arrived?"

"In a word, yes. We can't afford to have him looking high and low for his missing pots." Bancroft leaned back in his chair, doing his best to look relaxed and in control. "Will there be time to do your business before Keating wants these new arrivals for his gallery opening?"

Harriman shrugged, looking sulky. "For some of the items. I'll start the workers on them right away."

"Now is not the moment to get careless." The forgeries had to be meticulous, and for that Harriman had hired the finest company of Chinese metal workers. One or two were master goldsmiths who directed the others, but each one was highly skilled at some aspect of the work. They were excellent, obedient, and had been made available to work full-time on the project.

First, the craftsmen made casts of the solid gold and silver pieces Schliemann had unearthed from the dusty Greek soil and re-created them in copper. Then a thin layer of the original metal was applied over the copper using some sort of wizardry involving electricity and cyanide. Gems were replaced with glass. Bancroft didn't understand every last detail, but when the job was done, only an observant eye could tell the real object and its twin apart. Since Keating never saw the two together—and was not nearly the expert he thought he was—the deception was seamless. The Gold King became the Gold Plate King.

Then the originals were melted down and divided among Harriman, Bancroft, and four other investors who had bank-rolled the scheme. The return on investment was staggering. Unfortunately, this particular golden goose had a short life span.

Harriman folded his arms defensively. "But I didn't come here to speak of the schedule."

There was a surliness in his tone that made Bancroft clench his teeth. "Then why are you here?"

"To speak frankly."

"About what?"

Fear flickered behind Harriman's eyes. The man dropped

his voice so low he was barely audible. "To put it bluntly, your girl is gone. This isn't the time to break in a new courier. I need you to come and get the final payment yourself."

"You came today. Why not bring it to me?"

"No. I chanced it once. That might be interpreted as a social call by anyone watching. After what happened to the kitchen maid, I'll not risk it again."

"That's nonsense."

Harriman's gaze grew furtive. "You're in disfavor with my cousin. I can't afford to be seen seeking your company. This time, I need you to do what I say."

Bancroft bridled, but held his tongue. On some level he knew that Harriman, always the last and least of their pack of villains, was enjoying the moment. Finally, he had the power to give the orders. It was bitter, but it was medicine Bancroft knew how to swallow if it meant bringing the forgery scheme to a problem-free close. He would lie low and wait for his moment. "When do you want me to come?"

"I'll send word to come when the time is right."

Bancroft sucked in a breath. He could feel his gut roiling with anger, but his mind was utterly clear. *Let him have his moment.* "Very well."

Harriman's mouth tightened. "Bring a pistol."

The bugger has something in mind. "I shall do that, Mr. Harriman."

"Then I will bid you good day." The man rose.

Bancroft rose, reaching across the desk to shake the man's hand. It was clammy with perspiration. *Why do I bother with these cretins?* But he knew the answer already.

Gold and secrecy were both so damned hard to get. He wondered how much the bastard would make him pay.

CHAPTER THIRTEEN

London, April 6, 1888

WEST END

2 p.m. Friday

NICK STRETCHED HIS SPYGLASS TO ITS FULL LENGTH, BAL-
ancing its end on the window frame of his fourth-floor
perch. With a sense of satisfaction, he adjusted the brass
tube slowly, pulling and pushing the slide until the image
came into focus. There it was; the front of the tailoring shop
on Old Bond Street, the tidy facade washed in spring afternoon sunlight.

The street ambled through the West End—the section of
London that was home to the finest shops, gentlemen's
clubs, and fashionable residences. A steady stream of carriages and pedestrians passed up and down the avenues, but
it was a leisurely sort of bustle, and one with lots of coin at
its beck and call. Looking down on the scene, focusing in on
his quarry, Nick had a flash of kinship with a hawk spying a
flock of lazy, overfed pigeons. Lucky for them he was there
to watch, not to hunt.

His vantage point was perfect. He crouched in an empty
room in an empty building across the street and down from
the tailor's. It looked like it had been Disconnected. Dust
clung to the corners; the oak floors were gritty with sand.
By the few bits of furniture left, the place had once been a
counting house. From its empty shell, he could see without
being seen.

"Steam for a ha'penny," came the cry from the street. It

floated through the broken window like the fading memory of a dream. "Pennies for power."

Nick winced. That crier wouldn't last long if the street-keepers found him. Rogue makers sometimes cobbled together engines small enough to move around on a wheeled cart, selling the power for everything from illegal forges and machinery to powering back-alley surgeries. Some used the steam hawkers because they'd rather buy from a person than from a company. Some simply couldn't afford what the barons charged.

And there were always rebellious fools. From time to time, Nick got into trouble, but he was careful about whom he made his enemy. Speak courteously and finish every fight, that was his motto. Never leave an angry man behind you.

Two nights ago, Dr. Magnus had saved Nick from the police in return for information about Tobias Roth. Nick had spent the day paying that debt. He didn't fancy owing a man like Magnus.

However, in the first hours of his researches, Nick hadn't made a lot of progress. He'd followed Bancroft for a day and found nothing of interest, so today he'd decided to focus his attentions on the son and heir.

Nick knew next to nothing about the ponce, except that he occupied the same house as *her*. Breathed the same air. Ate the same food. Could see her every day, the way Nick had once done. Sudden bitterness flooded him, blotting out his senses. Nick ached to find some excuse to trip him up.

Unfortunately, today the rich boy had gone only as far as the tailor's shop. Roth was still inside, taking so long that Nick began to wonder if they were weaving the cloth for whatever His Nobship was buying.

Nick swung the spyglass a hair to the left. A pair of steam cycles whirred by, moving twice as fast as any horse. He followed the sight of a pretty girl until she was handed up into a freshly painted victoria drawn by a single gray mare. She was at least worth watching.

Although there was only one dark-haired beauty he truly wanted. Going to see Evelina had reopened wounds that were deeper than he remembered, and the fact that she'd grown to womanhood only made them throb the worse. All their history aside, the simple fact was that she had always been the only girl who'd ever made his whole being come alive just by walking into a room. He had recognized her scent like the return of spring. That alone should make her his woman. And now Evie was grown up, every curve and valley of her, and his body knew it. Even the thought of her made him ache in ways that could only lead to a hangman's noose. Evie was right. There would be no mercy if he were caught inside a rich man's house.

It had been a murder that had the place in an uproar the night he'd paid a visit. He'd found that out from one of the gardener's boys, and the news had left him worried for Evie's safety. Not that she'd appreciate his concern, he supposed, but that didn't matter. He couldn't just switch his heart off like an engine, all their history disappearing in a puff of leftover steam.

"Oy." The voice came from behind him.

Unconcerned, Nick turned his head just enough to see who had addressed him. The city crawled with street rats, both two- and four-legged. The rich districts were no exception. After all, they had the best pickings.

Nick had no fear of rats. This one was big, though, built in a thick, beefy way that had nothing to do with fat. Nick rose from his crouch, snapping the spyglass shut and sliding it into the leather pouch slung beneath his coat.

"What can I do for you?" Nick asked, polite with just a pinch of nonchalance. He was willing to bet this was one of the streetkeepers—bullies who were the lowest rank of authority in any steam baron's organization. Like all those who worked for Keating Utility, they called themselves Yellowbacks. Others called them Yellowbellies, but usually not to their face.

"The name's Striker," said the streetkeeper. "I don't know your vile mug, Gypsy. What are you doing here?"

"Mr. Striker." Was that a real name? Probably not. "As you so astutely observe, I'm a stranger to this neighborhood."

"Don't like strangers. What's your business?"

"My name is Nick, and my business isn't yours."

"Fair enough," said Striker.

"I'm pleased to hear it." Nick started to turn back to the window, already dismissing the man.

"Not so fast. You picked the lock to this here building."

With a sigh, he turned back. "So did you, if you're standing here."

"My territory, my lock."

No doubt the landlord of the old counting house would argue ownership, but Nick shrugged. "Just borrowing the window."

"No one breaks in nowhere without my say-so." Striker's voice dipped in a sneer. "The Gold King fines criminals who break the law."

Irritation prickled through Nick's limbs. "I owe you nothing."

Striker clapped his hands together, making the empty room ring with the smack of his fingerless leather gauntlets. "You do if I say you do. I'm the Gold King's law down here in the streets, and Yellow is the color a smart body fears most." He ducked a head, shoulders rising, clearly ready for a fight.

Sullen silence followed. Nick took the moment to examine Striker more seriously. Dark hair stuck up like a hedgehog's spines, framing a face that had been smashed in one too many times. His skin was the brown of so many of those born around the docks, making him perhaps the son of a lascar who had sailed to the western end of the Empire and took a local woman to his bed.

Nick's scrutiny went on. Striker wore the thick boots of a laborer. A tattered leather coat hung to his knees, covered in metal bits and pieces, as if he'd attached every bit of iron and brass ever lost in the city of London to improvise armor. It gave him status, when raw materials for building anything were in such short supply. Plus, the coat looked like it had already deflected a bullet or two.

Most telling were his big hands, held loosely at his sides,

ready to fight. Nick was about the same age and height, but Striker had at least twenty pounds more mass.

Nick cleared his face of all expression. If it was to be a contest of dominance, so be it. "There is no point to this conversation. We shall disagree, then fight, I shall probably win, and you'll go home with a broken head and tell everyone how there were five of me. I, on the other hand, will be annoyed because you interrupted my work."

Striker shifted from foot to foot. The chains hanging around his neck swayed and rattled, the flat surfaces of charms and keys catching the sunlight glancing through the window. One key was new, and flashed bright enough to attract Nick's eye. He wondered what a rat like this would lock up.

"I don't give a mouse's fart about your work," said Striker.

"You should. There is poetry in the satisfaction of a day well spent. I'm willing to include breaking your head among today's tasks."

Striker's thick brows drew together. "How about you shut your gob and hand over that pretty piece of brass you had in your hand a moment ago?"

Nick didn't bother to reply. He'd won the spyglass at cards, and it was one of the few things he had that was of any value. It would be a long, cold night in hell before he let it go—especially to this vermin.

He took a step to the right, just to see what Striker would do. The man took a diagonal step forward, closing the distance between them. The coat clattered as he moved, the chime of metal deadened by the heavy leather behind it. Nick's mind cleared, calling on the same sharp, calculating focus he used when he performed. He feinted back, then went left. As he suspected, Striker was nowhere near as light on his feet. There was no doubt he could beat him with speed.

"Stand still, Gypsy boy." Striker glared.

"Why should I? Are you too slow to dance?"

"I'm no wee street sparrow and this is no light dodge. If I say I want something of yours, you don't get to walk away."

Nick didn't doubt he meant it. The street rabble fought for

survival like starving dogs, and only the fiercest lived. If anyone challenged the streetkeepers and won, their master lost face. If Striker let his side down and word got out, he would be punished. He couldn't afford to let Nick go without taking something to prove he was stronger.

But Nick had no intention of letting Striker win. There was no way he could put his life on the line every time he performed without believing—without *being*—the best. Confidence was everything.

All this flashed through Nick's head in seconds. He had to fight and win, but there was a fierceness to this lout that made him uneasy. Tweaking his tail would be dangerous. And irresistible.

Nick's hand darted out, grabbing the shiny key and yanking it from Striker's neck. The man cried out as the chain broke, his fist hammering toward Nick's head. Nick ducked, his reflexes far faster. "A point to me!"

He stuffed the key into the pocket of his coat, curious to see what his adversary would do next. Slow and strong had few ways to beat light and quick.

The angle of Striker's body said he was going for a weapon almost before his hand was in motion. The coat swept back to reveal a studded leather harness. There were enough weapons strapped to Striker's chest to arm half the queen's dragoons. "A point to me."

Mother of hell! A jolt of alarm made Nick fall back. He only had a knife.

The weapon Striker pulled was nothing Nick had ever seen. He had an impression of a pistol mated with a bulbous brass gourd, horns of metal curling above the bulge of its barrel. Nick dove for the floor, using his momentum to somersault beneath Striker's aim. The bigger man whirled around, coat flying as Nick hurtled down the stairwell, half running, half sliding on the heavy oak banister. Striker flew after him, thundering down the stairs like a charging bull.

Nick's mind scrambled for sense. This was appalling. Since when did street rats carry bloody cannons? And since when did the Indomitable Niccolo run?

About three floors down, Nick realized the whine he

heard came from Striker's gun. It escalated to a tooth-rattling shriek. Nick grabbed the banister, vaulting over it to land on the dirty marble floor of the foyer. He landed in a roll, the breath leaving his body in a painful rush as pain shot up his shin. Cold, pale stone bruised his knees as he scrambled to his feet, looking for the door. A strange, scorched smell flooded the air as the hair on Nick's arms stood to attention.

Light flared, blasting through the dim building, scorching every last shadow to oblivion. Reflexively, he ducked. Somewhere above him, the banister exploded in a blast of toothpick-size splinters. Nick felt them scraping his cheek, raking through his hair. Hot blood trickled down his neck where one had flown by.

Dark Mother of Basilisks! The noise echoed long moments afterward. Nick glanced up, but the flare of light had blinded him. He blinked furiously, tears trying to wash away the afterimage of the explosion. A stink of chemicals clawed his throat. Before, he had felt healthy caution. Now, for the first time, real fear ran through his gut. No gun he knew could do that.

"Come 'ere, Gypsy boy." Striker's words were muffled. Nick's ears still rang from the blast. "Pay the piper, or I'll teach you to jig on a beam of light."

But Nick had no intention of surrendering. By this point, emptying out his pockets could hardly be enough to buy his safety. Striker was out for blood, and he was still coming down the stairs. Nick charged for the door, fumbling for the latch because he still couldn't see.

He breathed a prayer of thanks when the knob finally turned and the door cracked open to the world outside. Once he reached the street, he ran, aiming for the shortest way out of the Yellowbacks' territory. He'd turned his right ankle landing on the marble floor, but he was used to shutting off pain. For a moment, he actually thought he'd escaped.

Then he heard the high, shrill whistle common to every streetkeeper's gang. The universal signal for *Enemy Among Us*. He blinked hard, only able to see around the splotches in his vision, but it was enough to navigate the street. He pushed harder, aiming for the busiest streets, hoping the crowds could provide some basic protection. Nick's lungs burned with London's filthy air.

As he scrambled through the throngs of shoppers, his vision cleared. He almost wished it hadn't. The shadows between buildings suddenly teemed with ragged Yellowbacks. Nick dodged between carriages, behind barrows and signboards, doing his best to disappear from sight. It didn't work. A glance over his shoulder showed him a stampede of pursuers.

He turned down Piccadilly, then down Swallow, finally rounding onto Regent Street. He pounded past gentlemen's clubs and whorehouses—the best of everything could be bought and sold here—and slipped between two buildings just when his heart threatened to burst.

Nick leaned against the bricks, chest heaving. He was faster, but the pack of Yellowbacks wouldn't be far behind. Their blood was up and the chase begun. It would only end when they dragged him down like a wounded stag or he vanished into thin air.

Obviously, his choice was the latter. He glanced around and then up. The building was only two stories high, the mortar half gone from its sides. There was no time to hesitate; he jumped, grabbing at the worn grooves between the bricks, and started to climb, ignoring the protests from his ankle. His fingers dug into the gritty, cold crevices, his arms and chest bunching painfully as he dragged himself up. His toes scraped and pawed until the soft soles of his boots found purchase—and then he was away.

It was an easy ascent, and it gave him a moment to think. Striker had been spoiling for a fight and had been quick to give his name. And he'd been quick to show off his arsenal. All that told Nick he was ambitious. He wanted word to get out that the Gold King's streetkeeper was a man to be feared. The last thing he wanted was Nick noising it about that he had skipped away from Striker's net scot-free.

But where had a street thug got such weapons? The worst he'd ever encountered in London's back alleys was a crazy old soldier who had somehow stolen a howitzer left over from Waterloo. There were suddenly more important questions afoot than how Tobias Roth spent his idle afternoons—questions like how Nick would survive to taste his supper.

Nick grabbed the edge of the roof and pulled himself up. The pitch was mercifully slight, and he was able to crawl a few feet and collapse to catch his breath. All around him, roofs peaked and rippled like a slate ocean.

The key he had grabbed from Striker's neck poked him as he lay there. He fished in his pocket with stiff fingers and pulled out the bright key on its grubby chain of rusting gray metal. It had been foolish to grab it, a whim based on pride more than logic. Then again, pride was all he had. And curiosity. What was the key for?

That was a question for another day, when he wasn't scrambling to survive. Nick stuffed the thing back into his pocket, then prodded his sore ankle. It felt like it was swelling inside his boot. Bad news, when he had two performances on the morrow. He had to get back to the circus and take care of it.

Nick crawled cautiously up the roof, keeping low. Hot from exertion, he unbuttoned his coat, letting the spring breeze touch his skin. From a higher vantage point, he made out the route back to safe territory. Some of the buildings along the street hugged its curve, sporting flat-roofed porticos just made for Nick to run on. He could travel for some distance before he would be forced to drop back down to street level. He hoped by then Striker would have lost track of him. With luck, he had already.

He'd almost reached the peak of the roof when he heard a noise like a rifle shot. He thought he saw a plume of smoke, then a grappling hook shaped like a heavy, brass octopus snagged the gutter. Astonished, Nick stared as it clattered and scraped a moment before grabbing hold.

Nick drew the knife strapped to his hip, edging sideways down the roof toward the hook. A glance down showed the top of Striker's spiky head as the man swarmed up the rope dangling from the octopus. Other Yellowbacks were clustered on the street below, their faces turned up like pale blossoms. When they saw Nick, a derisive hoot rose up, making passing shoppers skitter nervously into the street.

Well, this was easily solved. Nick dropped to his knees and immediately hacked at the rope. But the thrust of his blade struck something solid, sending a shock up his arm. To his utter surprise, the knife glanced off it. The rope wasn't rope. It was made of dull metal fashioned in tiny flexible sections, jointed like a lobster's tail. If there was hemp involved, it was inside armor hard enough to turn a blade. Frustrated, he stabbed at the joints with the tip, trying to wedge the knife between them. The blade snapped in two.

With a spurt of alarm, Nick dropped his knife hilt and scrambled up the rooftop, building up speed for a leap to the next building. He made the jump easily, but when he hit the next roof, pain shot up his right foot as if he'd landed on a sword point. Nick rolled, a cry escaping him before he could stifle it. After a long moment of dizzying agony, he got to his feet, refusing to limp. If he lost command of his balance, he would never survive the next hour.

Pain turned him cold, then sweat began to trickle down his back. This roof was flat and easy to cross, but the seconds spent nursing his injury had cost him. Halfway to the next jump, he heard a thud that said Striker was just behind. His step faltered, agony slowing him down despite his refusal to accept that the chase was over.

"Stop, Gypsy boy."

Nick stopped. "Let me go." His hands slid over his jacket, looking for one last trick, one last weapon.

"Sorry, boyo. Too many eyes on you to give you a pass."

"How unfortunate." Nick's fingers closed on the long, thin shape of Evelina's silver paper knife. With a flutter of dark satisfaction, he pulled it out, wheeled, and threw it in the same smooth motion.

It was a trick he performed every night—sometimes blindfolded, sometimes standing on the back of a galloping mare. The knife sank deep into the soft meat of Striker's thigh, aimed right where the heavy leather skirt of the coat parted in front. The man yelped in pain, then fell to his knees, then collapsed on his side, moaning in agony. Another few inches, and he would have lost his equipment. A single inch, and the blade would have cut an artery. But Nick had put the knife exactly where he'd meant to.

Nick wasted no time. He staggered, hopped, and ran for the next rooftop, leaving Striker at the mercy of the other Yellowbacks. And he kept running, circling back almost to Old Bond Street, looking for a place where he could drop onto the roof of one of the steam-powered omnibuses, or maybe find his way down to an underground station where the trains ran beneath the streets. He had to get away—and soon—because the Yellowbacks would be out for his blood.

Unfortunately, he had let himself be led more by which rooftops were the easiest to cross than by which went in a direct path. He wasn't sure exactly where he was. He stopped, dropping to his stomach and crawling to the edge of the roofline. In a moment, he had found his bearings, but he had also found something else.

Tobias Roth, walking across a courtyard. They were several streets away from the tailor's shop, and whatever Roth was up to had nothing to do with fashion. He had shed his fine coat in exchange for a workmen's smock, his soft-soled shoes for a pair of shabby boots. What, by the Dark Mother, was Roth doing?

Nick inched forward, trying to get a better look. The courtyard was surrounded by high walls, making it invisible from the street. On one side was a warehouse. The large double doors stood open, showing the inside was full of mechanical detritus, a woodstove, and a few pieces of derelict furniture.

Nick sucked in a breath, half in wonder, half in bitterness. This was the workshop! Nick had thought Magnus half cracked, thinking His Lordship, his son, or both were playing with machinery. But the doctor was right. Nick had never heard of a toff playing with greasy springs and wheels—dirt might get lodged around his nails, after all—but there was Tobias Roth, dressed for honest work.

Roth stopped in the middle of the yard, falling deep into conversation with another man of his own age. They were discussing some sort of contraption that looked to Nick like a giant metal insect with most of its legs pulled off. It lay belly-up on the ground, a few limbs stuck straight into the air. That must have once been the opera-eating monster.

Look at all those parts, Nick thought. Where did Roth get them? Did he have the Gold King's permission, or did rich bastards get to build whatever they wanted? And all those resources were being squandered on a gigantic toy—not a generator for light, or a pump to move clean water uphill. He didn't understand the rich.

Nick pulled back, taking care not to be seen. *So, did the Golden Boy go in the front of the tailor's shop, then out the back door to come here?* Maybe Roth wasn't as stupid as Nick had assumed. But what was Tobias doing, and why was he trying to keep it a secret?

Nick pondered the broken machine, turning what he knew of the young man over and over in his mind, and then adding what he'd read in the papers over the last few days. A slow smile began tugging at the corners of his mouth, finally breaking into a grin. Perhaps the metal monstrosity wasn't an entire waste. He had to admit, Tobias Roth knew how to put on a show. Not at Nick's level, but not bad for an amateur. And as an inventor, the toff had a wealth of raw talent.

He knew instinctively that this was exactly what Dr. Magnus wanted to know.

CHAPTER FOURTEEN

Murder Most Foul! A local farmer made a gruesome discovery on a remote byway in Hampstead late this morning. Two hale young men were discovered dead on the roadside with their throats cut. When questioned, a local innkeeper claimed he had seen the men driving a wagon loaded with chests several hours before dawn. They had awakened the innkeeper looking for a smith, as one of their horses had thrown a shoe. No sign of the missing wagon, horses, or cargo has been found.

—*The London Prattler,* evening edition

EVELINA HAD JUST FINISHED REPAIRING HER NECKLACE WHEN the afternoon paper arrived. The two dead men were Lord Bancroft's grooms. Grace was no longer the only victim among the staff. The papers had made no mention of the men's names, or where they had worked, but the Peelers had come asking questions for the second time in less than a week. If Evelina wanted to keep Lestrade from finding anything that would hurt Imogen's family, she had to find answers, and fast.

Now Evelina stood in the dusty gloom of the attic, candle in hand, searching for a clue. The automatons hadn't reappeared with a sinister clap of thunder. The closest item was a headless dress form with a pincushion topping its neck. And an hour of searching had produced no more information than she already had.

It was time to go back downstairs. Evelina knelt, peering under a trunk. "Time to go."

A faint whirring was accompanied by the patter of tiny, tiny paws.

"Come on, stop mucking about," she said impatiently.

A minuscule nose popped out from under the trunk. Dust bunnies clung to its fine steel whiskers. *I discovered twelve misanthropic spiders and a nest of wary moths, but sadly there is a paucity of information on demon-possessed automatons. Mind you, this is an attic, and I am a mouse. You might have made me a researcher at the Bodleian, able to—let's be rash here—actually read and turn pages. But, no. You went for cute and amusing, ergo, I am a rodent. If you think I'm going to squeak adorably, you have lessons to learn.*

"Oh, do be quiet. And who said anything about demons?" The automatons had dark magic clinging to them, but thankfully they hadn't been demon-class evil.

I'm improvising.

"You're whining." That's what she got for using another earth deva.

But temperament aside, her latest creation worked beautifully. The mouse had been her idea for indoor spying. Its dark, etched coat looked almost real in the dim light. She picked it up gently, balancing it on her palm.

The lark she'd sent after Lestrade had not come back. She had forgotten to specify *when* it was to return with news. It might show up tomorrow, or sometime in the next century. A classic mistake when casting a spell. She didn't have time to wait, so she'd brought her second toy to life with the deva that had found her in the oak tree—a comeuppance for taunting her when she had slipped from the branch.

What did you expect to find here, besides old rags and broken armoires? The mouse sat up, cleaning the dust out of its whiskers. *Love letters? Or are you simply avoiding that fair-haired idiot? I've noticed your heart thunders every time that one prances by.*

"We're not talking about him."

Suit yourself.

"I shall." Evelina watched the creature groom, fascinated by the fact that it could move as if it were made of flesh and not metal. Something about the spirit overrode the reality of

their stiff bodies—maybe it was an affinity between the
deva's elemental nature and the metal that had been forged
from the earth. She wondered if an air deva would work
equally well. "Actually, I was hoping to find something that
would tell me about the automatons. Why did the family
keep them? Why would anyone kill for them?"

*You said they stank of undesirable magic. Maybe they as-
sembled themselves, killed their captors, and walked away
to wreak havoc on an unsuspecting metropolis.*

That mental image was going to haunt her dreams—if she
ever slept again. She glared at the tiny mouse. "Their magic
wasn't like yours. They weren't alive."

*Then perhaps you need to consult the family archives to
discover where they came from. They had to be purchased
somewhere.*

"Good idea." It gave her a place to start, anyway. "Though
I'm still not sure how Grace is connected."

The mouse ran up her arm and perched on her shoulder.
*My dear girl, I've been around since that tree outside was a
wee sapling and this house was a few blocks on a green
meadow. In the end, everything is connected. You must per-
severe. Dirty linens always show up in the wash.*

"Perhaps, but I don't want to drown in the laundry tubs
while looking." Evelina put the wriggling mouse into her
pocket.

The most curious part of the whole affair was Lord Bancroft. Not because he kept a placid mien worthy of a
cardsharp—that was to be expected of an aristocrat with an
eye on high office—nor even that he forbade the servants to
speak of the murders. No master wanted his staff so distracted they burned his toast and overstarched his shirts.

No, it was what the housekeeper had overheard and told
Dora, who had then told Evelina. Last night, Lord Bancroft—
more than a little tipsy—had promised Lestrade a reward if
the police would find his trunks. It was imperative that they
were returned unopened.

Why? No one knew. All of his servants had joined the
household after Lord Bancroft returned to England. No one
seemed to know anything about the trunks' contents, much

less why they mattered. Of course, the mention of a reward had made everyone twice as curious. If Bancroft's plan had been to keep the trunks and their magic-ridden contents quiet, that was the wrong way to do so. But whisky had never made men smart—and whisky was something she'd noticed on Lord B's breath more and more of late.

Evelina took one last look around the attic and descended the stairs, pondering her next move. Through the small windows of the stairway landing, she could see that an indigo dusk had just settled on the garden outside. When she got to the main floor, she blew out the candle, left it on a small table, and carried on toward Lord Bancroft's library.

The ambassador had a collection of volumes on mechanics— apparently a relic of his youth, since he reviled his son's interest in the topic. And displaying such books wasn't the done thing now that the steam barons held sway. Evelina had found them entirely by accident one day. There, behind the plays and poetry, high up on the library shelves, was a second row of books. Evelina had felt like she'd found Aladdin's treasure cave, and had read as many as she could sneak out unobserved. Maybe there was something in the collection—a pamphlet or a manual—that identified where the automatons had come from. Finding at least this answer might be simple.

She had learned about clockworks from her father's father, who made the mechanical wonders at Ploughman's circus. Through Lord Bancroft's library, she had studied every new innovation in automatons that had come along, including the elaborate punch-card probability sorters that were supposed to cause the machines to make simple decisions for themselves—a bit of a nonstarter, really. Even the most sophisticated engines seemed to produce machines only slightly brighter than a toasting fork.

From the glimpse she'd had, Bancroft's models were at least ten years out of date. Automatons came and went out of fashion, usually making a comeback when some manufacturer laid claim to a new innovation. *New! Improved! Same old bunkum as you've never seen it before! Guaranteed impractical and finicky to fix!*

Even a stupid servant was more versatile and cost a fraction of the price. Still, the idea of a wood and metal slave, willing to fulfill its owner's every whim—the more depraved the better—reliably parted the rich from their gold.

Which raised uncomfortable questions about anyone who had a whole collection.

The library was considerably warmer than the attic. A small fire was burning in the grate, more for cheer than for necessity. Gaslights filled the space with a gentle glow. Evelina walked into the room, her attention already on the tall shelves of books, before she noticed Lord Bancroft in one of the wing chairs. He was reading a newspaper, a glass of whisky on the tiny carved table at his elbow.

"Miss Cooper," he said without moving.

Most men stood when a lady entered the room, but he rarely observed that nicety with her. She occupied a gray zone halfway between servant and family member, which made his slight both an insult and a compliment.

"My lord," she replied, her nerves prickling with irritation. It was hard to snoop in someone's affairs when they were reading the paper only a few feet away. Nevertheless, she made a slight curtsey before she turned to focus on the books.

Lord B turned a page, happy to ignore her. She ignored him right back, finding the shelf she wanted, discreetly shifting the books so she could see the titles behind. She started reading the spines quickly, knowing she might be interrupted at any moment and directed toward Lady Bancroft's collection of insipid novels. Not that Evelina disliked fiction—far from it—but Lady B had a taste for do-good heroes and heroines with all the personality of a dust ruffle.

On the other hand, Lord Bancroft seemed to have a dozen good volumes on building automatons, though they were all in German. She pulled one off the shelf and opened it, struggling through the introduction. The book seemed to be a comprehensive study on creating walking machines. That made sense. The problem of balance and joint movement had plagued builders for years.

She lifted her gaze from the page and studied Lord Bancroft—or rather, the back of his newspaper. One hand reached out and picked up the glass. His ring gave a quick flash of gold in the gaslight before the hand and glass disappeared behind the wall of newsprint. For a man robbed of a prized possession, he looked utterly calm. Then again, knowing him, he might have a decent load of whisky on board by this hour.

She turned back to the shelf, pulling out another volume. This time it wasn't even German, but something she didn't recognize. With a huff of exasperation, she closed the book and slid it back on the shelf. There was no owner's manual for the automatons, so she drifted over to a collection of French plays. If she was going to pretend to be looking for a book to read, she couldn't leave empty-handed.

The newspaper rattled. "Finding what you want?" Lord Bancroft asked quietly.

There was a slight edge to his voice that made her think he knew exactly which books she'd been looking at and he wasn't happy about it. Her stomach clenched, and she quickly picked up a volume of Racine. "Yes, thank you."

She'd taken a hurried step toward the door when Bigelow, the butler, entered.

"A gentleman to see you, my lord." Bigelow intoned.

"Who is it?" Lord Bancroft let the paper droop so he could see his servant offering a silver salver with a calling card. He picked up the card without much interest, but as he read, his eyes widened with what looked like homicidal rage.

Evelina quickly made for the door, but someone was shouldering his way past Bigelow. She stopped, arrested by the sight of the figure. He was very tall, with a cape and silver-headed cane. Beneath the brim of his high-crowned hat, a dark, aquiline face made her think of exotic lands and fortunes in pirate gold. Not at all the type to play the lead in one of Lady Bancroft's novels.

Lord B's voice was hard as flint. "I heard you were in town, but prayed it was only vicious gossip. What are you doing here?"

Evelina jumped back, as if the angry words had been directed at her. The fine hairs on her arms rose. The man wasn't quite close enough to be sure, but she thought she detected a prickling of magic. *Who is this man?*

"Is that any way to greet an old friend?" said the stranger, sweeping off his hat and cape and thrusting them into Bigelow's arms. "I saw you at the opera, but you refused to acknowledge me. I had to come to you, since you would not speak to me in a public place."

Bancroft rose from his chair. "What are you doing in London? You swore to keep away."

The stranger laughed. "No, you swore at me until I left you alone. There is a difference. Tell me, how are the children? I haven't seen them in years."

There was a long pause. Bigelow cleared his throat. "My lord, shall I summon the footmen?"

Lord Bancroft's expression said he wanted exactly that. Instead, he waved Bigelow and Evelina away with a curt jerk of his hand. They went, Evelina pulling the door shut behind them as the butler's hands were full with the hat and cloak.

She could still hear Lord B's sharp tones. "Is it money you want, Magnus?"

"*Dr. Magnus.* I deserve at least that much respect. And what do you think the answer is?" The voice seemed far too intimate, as if he were whispering in Evelina's ear.

Bigelow and Evelina lingered outside the door, their eyes meeting in tacit agreement. So what if eavesdropping was a bad idea? Neither was prepared to move. But all that followed for a long moment was silence. Evelina's nerves began to twitch.

Finally, Dr. Magnus spoke. Evelina detected a slight accent she couldn't place. "I performed a service for you, and now I require connections in London. You must rectify that, with your influence. I am desirous of meeting your men of industry. What do you call them? Steam barons?"

"They would have no use for you."

"Nor I them, for the most part. But I require your influence on a small matter, and since I find you such a rising political star, that should be no great feat. Besides, you are very much in my debt. Refusing me would be unwise."

Bancroft swore viciously. "Is this blackmail?"

"Come, come. We go too far back—long before your censorious British morality pinioned your curiosity."

"Before you damned my soul, you mean," Bancroft snarled.

"I have nothing to do with your choices."

"How did you get into this house?"

Magnus laughed but it was filled with sly mockery. "Won't you offer me a whisky? You can exorcise me later."

Bancroft swore again, and then the conversation became muted, as if the men had moved to a different part of the room.

"Who is he?" Evelina whispered.

Bigelow's face was filled with concern. "I don't know, miss. I have been with the family since their return to England, and I have not seen that man before tonight."

"Perhaps they knew each other in Austria?"

The butler gave a slight shake of his head. "I do not know, miss, though when I think on it, I have heard Dr. Magnus's name. It was the night that poor young Grace died. When I went to wake His Lordship, he cried out that name, almost leaping from his chair when I touched his arm."

"His chair?"

"That night, he fell asleep over a book right there in the library. He does that sometimes."

After one too many drinks. "He saw Dr. Magnus at the opera, and then dreamed of it." *And nightmares at that—but at least Bigelow's story means Lord B did not slit Grace's throat. Not if he was asleep then.*

"That is not for me to say. I should return to my duties, miss."

Evelina glanced down at the book she had no intention of reading. "So should I."

She intentionally let the Racine fall, and stooped to pick it up. As she bent, she scooped the mouse out of her pocket, and it ran under the door to spy on the two men.

Bigelow disappeared down the corridor. Evelina watched him go, a knot of anxiety heavy in her stomach. The last few days had not been reassuring. Automatons coated in dark magic. Murder. Coded messages. Gems and gold. Mysterious strangers from the ambassador's past. *And the Season hasn't even properly started yet.*

Evelina began walking, barely paying attention to where her steps led. She turned and went back up the stairs to the second floor. The longcase clock struck eight as she reached the landing.

Tobias was there with his hands stuffed into his pockets, watching the mechanism with his habitual air of nonchalance. When he saw her, a half smile lazily curled his lips.

Her stomach flipped, but she took a deep breath, determined not to show her nerves. The mouse was right that she had been avoiding him since the kiss in the morning room. Did she want to see him or not? Common sense told her to run. Curiosity begged her to stay.

"The weather dial says there is a storm coming," said Tobias. "What a terrible blow. I shall be obliged to forego the pleasures of the racetrack."

"I hope there is no storm. It is your mother's garden party tomorrow."

"Blast, you're quite right." He laughed a little, making it hard to tell if he had really forgotten or was just putting on a show.

"The clock is always wrong, anyhow."

"So it is." He gave her a lazy smile.

"But there is a real storm brewing, I think," said Evelina. "Someone named Dr. Magnus arrived tonight to talk to your father. Lord Bancroft wasn't happy about it. They seemed to know each other."

The smile faded a little, a crease forming between his fair brows. "I remember the name from Vienna. He was a friend of my father's once—I believe he was a mesmerist. I vaguely recall that he gave me a wooden horse for my birthday when I was still in the nursery."

"What kind of a man is he?"

"I don't know. I was a child."

How old was Tobias? About twenty-three? Magnus barely looked old enough to be an adult mixing with ambassadors so many years ago. Then again, some men looked almost the same between thirty and fifty. Perhaps Magnus was one of the lucky ones.

Tobias looked down at her. "What are you thinking? You have the most puzzled expression on your face."

"There is a lot going on."

"Including the murder of Grace Child?" His smile was completely gone now. "And then the grooms?"

Evelina hesitated, then decided there was no point in avoiding what she most wanted to know. "Did you talk to Grace just before she died?"

For a moment, he looked almost as stern as his father. "Yes."

She studied him, thinking about their kiss and then about Grace and finally wondering what manner of man Tobias Roth really was. The only part of him she felt utterly sure of was his taste for pneumatics and magnetic currents. That seemed to be his one absolute truth.

Frustration itched along her nerves. She cursed inwardly, wishing she knew what hid behind those solemn gray eyes. He was so rarely still and never serious, always on his way out to a club or music hall or mistress. If they were alone, he seemed to smile from a point just out of her reach.

Her mouth had gone dry. "How did Grace seem?"

He shrugged, looking out the narrow window beside the clock. "What you'd expect. She had stayed out past curfew. She was afraid Bigelow would sack her. He locks all the doors at midnight. She wanted me to sneak her inside, so I did."

"That's all? She didn't say anything else?"

"She didn't name her murderer, if that's what you're asking. She muttered something about a Chinaman being idiotic or slow or something to that effect. I thought perhaps she'd been in the Limehouse area."

She tried to weigh his tone and expression, wondering if he lied. She couldn't tell. "Was Grace waiting outside or was she just arriving at the house when you met her?"

He ran a hand through his hair. "She was waiting. I think."

"For long?"

"I don't know. I don't think so."

"Did you say anything to Inspector Lestrade about your conversation with Grace?"

"No. Then he would ask me where I had been, why I was out, and I have no intention of answering that question until I absolutely have to."

"But—"

He put a finger over her lips, silencing her. "A man has to keep some secrets. And I swear to you it has nothing to do with Grace or the grooms."

Where had he been that late? With whom and on how many occasions? If it had no bearing on the problem at hand, her uncle would declare it immaterial to the investigation, so she had to as well, even if the questions burned like red-hot coals.

Still, Evelina gave a mutinous glare, pulling away from his touch. She could taste his skin on her lips, bitter with tobacco. He smelled of cigar smoke. "A girl died, Tobias."

"And I didn't kill her. We talked, we went inside."

"Did you lock the door again?"

"Yes."

"Then the killer was already inside." *Was that who passed me in the hall that night?*

He froze, as if the import of her words just sank in. Then he shook himself. "I can't believe that."

"Do you have another theory?" she asked, unable to stifle a shudder.

The killer could still be inside, right then. Hiding or, worse, wearing a familiar face. The clock ticked, loud and slow, as if prompting them to continue.

All of a sudden, he looked startled, then worried, his eyes widening. He'd thought of something. She would have traded her best bonnet to know what was passing through his mind.

Then his face changed again, becoming soft as he reached out a hand. "Evelina, this isn't something you should be getting involved in. Father assures me that there is no danger to the family, but I still think that it's not safe for you to be asking all these questions."

Not safe was balancing on a whisper of rope twenty feet from the ground. Not safe was being the maid carrying a fortune in gems at midnight through dark alleys infested with street rats. All Evelina had to worry about was dodging half-truths, and she was fairly sure Tobias was feeding her some now.

No, her biggest danger was desire, because she wanted to believe that look of concern on his face. She took a small step back, putting another inch or two between them. "You wanted me to examine the body. Why stop me now?"

His gaze lingered on her face, working lower and lower a degree at a time. "Honestly, I'm afraid for you. You're too important to me to take needless risks."

She raised her eyebrows, unable to keep the sarcastic edge from her voice. "I'm important to you?"

"Of course."

Long ago, lying in her narrow bed at the Wollaston Academy for Young Ladies, she'd daydreamed of Tobias Roth falling on his knees and declaring his love. Of course, her dream Tobias was an ideal—this man of flesh and blood was not. In her dreams he'd meant every word. Now she could not tell, and caution warred against her desire.

"Aren't I important to you?" he asked softly, angling his body closer. "Please say that I am."

"You are Imogen's brother." She had tried to make the words crisp, but they had come out far too breathy for comfort. He was standing too close again, the warmth of his breath brushing her cheek.

"No more than that?" His hand was on her waist. There were too many layers of clothes between them to feel the warmth, but she sensed the pressure of his caress. Was this how her mother had ended up eloping? A touch in a dark hallway?

The moment his arm was around her, Tobias lowered his lips to hers. Instinct urged her to run, but she ached to taste what he had to offer—and properly this time.

His mouth was soft, so soft and warm. Just like before, except now it was spiced with brandy. He smelled of wool and soap and smoke and just a faint undertone of machine oil. That made her smile against his mouth. Tobias was rich, spoiled, and willful, but there was more to him. He had an artist's urge to create that disarmed her.

Their noses bumped as they shifted, finding a better position. Her palms brushed the front of his jacket, feeling the soft, expensive fabric and the swell of firm, young muscle beneath. An ache throbbed deep in her body, blotting out common sense. A slow burn began low in her belly, tingling upward until she was sure she glowed with hot little sparkles of sinful sensation. Her stays suddenly felt too tight, too hot, too rough against her skin.

His mouth moved against hers, his tongue parting her lips. Evelina's knees were melting. In a moment, she'd sag against him, helpless and pliable as putty. She was losing. This was how reason drowned in the arms of a pretty young man. A moment's weakness, and she had forgotten everything: her caution, his half-truths, and—oh, yes—a killer in their midst.

Evelina backed away, nearly crashing into the clock. Her heart was pounding almost painfully hard. "You're Imogen's brother. You can't be more than that to me, and you know it."

His brows bunched with irritation. "Why not?"

She cleared her throat, forcing herself to feel the floor under her feet instead of billowing clouds of wishful thinking. "You're not a man I can marry, and I'm not a woman who can afford to take a lover."

Her frankness clearly startled him. "Why can't we marry? You're not a nobody, Evelina. You're being presented. You're getting a Season."

Her mouth twisted, hating that she had to explain. "Don't toy with me. Your father would never countenance it. He has ambitions for your family, and you're his heir. I'm neither rich nor titled."

Now he looked angry. "So?"

A flash of temper rescued her. "I'm not a tart, either. I can't afford you, Tobias."

The look he gave was filled with hurt confusion. Apparently the great oaf had never thought any of this through. And his eyes smoked with need. It was plain on his face:

Tobias Roth had just realized he wanted her, quite possibly because she'd just said no.

Oh, dear God. This was far too complicated. Evelina stepped around him cautiously, careful that not even her skirts brushed his leg.

"Evelina?" The one-word query held volumes of other questions.

"Good night, Tobias," she said quickly, and fled to her room. She'd completely forgotten to ask him about the automatons.

CHAPTER FIFTEEN

London, April 7, 1888

HILLIARD HOUSE

1:30p.m. Saturday

DESPITE THE CLOCK'S DIRE PREDICTIONS, THERE WASN'T A storm cloud in the sky. At least, not the literal kind. The walled garden behind Hilliard House sheltered the genteel gaiety of Lady Bancroft's birthday party. And although the April wind was still cool, bright sun and puffs of flowering cherry and plum trees made up for the sometimes brisk air.

Tobias looked wistfully at the table where the guests were served brandy and soda, and accepted a cup of tea instead. Spirituous liquors would help his mood but not his etiquette, and that sort of thing mattered to his mother.

The weather was perfection. Servants had moved the dining table and second-best Turkish carpets onto the lawn, so the ladies' kid slippers remained free of grass stains. An automatic samovar puffed dainty gusts of steam as it brewed individual cups of tea, dispensing razor-thin slices of lemon when one pushed the correct cloisonné knob. A small wind ensemble occupied one corner, spinning out Mozart divertimenti like so much musical frosting.

One would never have known a servant had been slaughtered just nights ago, and only a dozen yards away. Tobias couldn't drive the shadow of Grace Child from his soul. It seemed to cling to every bonnet, every macaroon, making the frothy cheer of the party feel obscene. The only thing worse was pretending that it had never happened—but his father had threatened to sack any of the help who breathed a word of it.

Grace's eyes had been lovely. They were the only part of her face Tobias really remembered. He hadn't even stopped to take a proper look at her. Not at first. He'd been thinking about the idiot prank he'd pulled at the Charlotte, and whether he'd be caught.

He took a swallow of the tea and nodded and smiled at the pretty copper-haired girl someone had introduced as the Gold King's daughter. He thought he might have met her before. What was her name? Alice? Did he care? Whatever the case, he gave her the full force of his insincere charm. She dimpled sweetly, reminding him of an insipid china doll.

She wasn't Evelina. *No, don't think about that.* Even the memory of the debacle by the clock made him cringe. Seduce her, said his father. Somehow, in the moment, she had seduced him instead—and then slapped him in the face.

But he had his pick of women, and he knew himself too well. He was fickle. He was over Evelina now.

Unfortunately, the idea of wooing her in earnest came and went like a fever. One of those nasty recurring ones. Ten minutes hence, he might be shaking with the dread sickness again. Only keeping his distance from her seemed to make things easier. He never stayed in lust long—at least that fact gave him something to hope for.

Unless he really meant to lay his heart at her feet? Tobias pondered for a moment. His father would hate it, which was a plus, but he actually cared about Evelina. He worried about her safety. He might be a bit of a rake, but he wasn't without some scruples. Still, what could a bit of dalliance hurt?

Maybe more than he had assumed. She was more than some demimondaine who knew the rules of the game better than he did. Those women never raised the question of marriage. She'd slapped it down before him like a gauntlet.

And what exactly had Evelina meant when she said she couldn't *afford* him? That made him sound like an overpriced pair of shoes. *Just admit it. She showed you how con-*

fused you are. You're a callous idiot and don't really know what you want.

He strolled through the crowd, nodding and smiling and utterly revolted with himself. The only thing he'd done right was keep Grace's secret. The word about the baby was out—there was nothing he could do about that—but not about her involvement in some sort of shady activity. It helped that his job was to keep Evelina from investigating, because he'd been able to keep his conversation with Grace private.

Nevertheless, if it hadn't been for the squid business— and he didn't want to trust his alibi at the brothel until he absolutely had to—he wasn't sure he'd have kept Grace's fears from the police. The longer he thought about his exchange with the maid, the more uneasy he became. The safety of the family was paramount, but he wasn't sure that silence was the best way to get it, whatever the pater said. Nevertheless, his father had a lot more experience of the world and had spent decades striking deals with emperors and kings. All Tobias knew was how to get a good table at a fashionable restaurant.

"A fine occasion," said Bucky, appearing at Tobias's elbow. He had a generous plate of food: lobster salad, foie gras, salmon in green sauce, and a little paper cup of ice cream that was quickly melting into a puddle. "Your sister looks radiant."

"Eh?" Tobias looked for Imogen, a little puzzled by the statement. Imogen looked like Imogen. She was fluttering around the row of chairs set in the shade, making a fuss over the dowagers no one else wanted to talk to.

"Your sister. London must agree with her."

Tobias gave a halfhearted shrug. "It's the prospect of buying nine and twenty dresses for her Season. That sort of thing puts a sparkle in a girl's eye."

Bucky speared an olive with his fork. "And no doubt this blazing insight arises from extensive discourse with the fair sex?"

"My observation, or shall we say interrogation, of any woman's wardrobe has little to do with shopping."

Bucky rolled his eyes heavenward. "So which was most informative, petticoats or knickers?"

"Both were most unreliable witnesses. They came undone beneath the slightest pressure."

Bucky dropped his voice. "One would have thought they'd keep their lips fastened. Or perhaps that's the girl I'm thinking of. Or perhaps I'm thinking of the wrong lips."

Tobias opened his mouth, closed it, and cast about for a change of subject before the conversation could get any more disgraceful. Most of the time, he found innuendo amusing, but not now. Today, he felt weirdly prim.

"Did you hear they're betting on the Reynolds trial?" Bucky asked, his merriment fading a degree.

"Who hasn't?"

They'd both known the woman from parties—not well, but enough to be shocked by the charges. Nellie Reynolds was a queen of the demimonde, a bastard daughter of some highborn lord. She was striking more than beautiful, but possessed of a resonant voice that captured one's heart and wrung it without mercy.

"I heard she's got a lawyer," Bucky said. "A good one. He's going to plead the evidence they found was all for the theater. Magic for entertainment purposes is allowed. Card readers and astrologers are exempt, so why not allow someone to own a crystal ball, if its only use is for playacting?"

"The whole thing is too macabre for me."

"An anonymous donor is paying for a defense." Bucky shifted uneasily. "Someone is brave, to go against opinion like that."

They both stood silent a moment, sharing uneasy thoughts. The wish to rebel was easy. Facing the reality of it was something else. Eventually, Bucky saw someone he knew and hurried away.

Abandoning his teacup on the table, Tobias worked his way through the crowd to where his mother was accepting birthday wishes. Her pale gray and pink gown was accompanied by a tiny hat crowned in curling feathers. Lady Bancroft was tall and slender, but her fair hair and pale skin seemed faded, like a painting left too long in the full glare of the sun—or perhaps in the glare of her husband.

"Dear Mama, happy birthday." He bent and kissed her cheek.

"Tobias." Her hand automatically touched his face—a maternal gesture she'd never quite surrendered.

"My congratulations on the party. You always put these affairs together with such exquisite taste."

She waved a dismissive hand. "After so long in the service of your father, it becomes second nature."

Tobias met her pale blue gaze, experiencing a slight twinge of apprehension. "I have a birthday gift for you."

When finding a present for his mother, Tobias faced an age-old problem. She never complained about what he gave her, and never seemed to favor one year's offering more than any other. It made it hard to tell which ones had truly hit the mark.

He pulled a small parcel from his jacket pocket and placed it in his mother's lace-gloved hands. Then he watched for her reaction as she unwrapped the blue tissue paper with agonizing care. Inside was a delicate silver brooch shaped like a butterfly.

"How lovely!" she said, tilting to examine the garnets and pearls set into the wings.

Tobias reached down, pressing a tiny button on the butterfly's body. The wings began to slowly fan. He pressed it again, and a soft, silvery chime rang as the creature moved. His mother's lips parted in wonder, and she smiled. It was a wonderful smile—a real one that warmed him from the heart outward.

"You made this, didn't you? It's so delicate," she murmured. "And so clever."

"I had a jeweler set the stones," he said, struggling to sound nonchalant.

"You're as brilliant as your father was when he was your age."

The words seemed to catch in her throat, and the smile stopped. Tobias scanned her face, wanting to bring back that instant of rare, genuine pleasure. Somehow, in his infinite genius, he had managed to please her and stir an unpleasant thought at the same time. There were days when he marveled at his own ineptitude.

"Thank you so much, darling." She put her hand to his face again, the pleasant, impersonal mask of Ambassador's Wife firmly back in place. "Help me put it on. I want to wear it right away."

Obediently, he pinned the brooch to her shawl and accepted a kiss to his cheek. He wondered how many hours he had to remain sober.

Too many. His father was advancing, shirt so crisp beneath his cutaway coat it made one's eyes water. A violent urge to flee seized Tobias, but with the eerie telepathy of mothers, Lady Bancroft took his hand. Lord Bancroft gave him a cool look and turned to his wife.

"My dear, you look lovely as always." He lifted her free hand, kissing the air just above it. "Felicitations of the day."

"Thank you, Lord Bancroft. I hope the arrangements meet your expectations."

His father gave a perfunctory smile. "It's a shame the prime minister couldn't attend, but I had a very satisfactory discussion with the ministerial liaison to the Steam Council."

"I'm pleased to hear it, my lord."

Tobias clenched his teeth. Of course his mother's birthday party would be used to further his father's social connections. That was the way the world worked. But it still bothered him.

"What's this?" Lord Bancroft indicated the fanning butterfly.

Her hand cupped it protectively. "A gift from Tobias."

He shot his son a contemptuous look. "I would have thought you had outgrown your artisan phase."

Tobias heard his mother's indrawn breath, but knew she would not contradict her husband. She was too proper to even address him by his first name in public. Instead, she gently squeezed Tobias's hand, offering covert sympathy. He returned the pressure and then took a step away. Otherwise, it felt too much like he was a child again, hiding behind his mother's skirts.

"I'm still fascinated by the possibilities of the imagination," he said to his father, keeping his tone reasonable. "Not just the possibilities, but how many of them I can manifest."

His father's tone was low, but held the sting of acid. "Better if you manifested a career."

"Perhaps I shall invent something that will make me a wealthy man."

"Then you would do well to raise your sights above butterflies."

"But it is merely a gift!" his mother interjected.

Both Tobias and his father stared at her. She had never, as long as Tobias could recall, intervened in one of these debates.

"What did you say?" Lord Bancroft demanded.

The moment hung in the sunny garden. At the other end of the lawn, someone smacked a croquet ball. Lady Bancroft looked away, hiding her face. Casually, as if merely moving to keep the sun out of his eyes, Tobias put himself bodily between his parents.

His father's displeasure radiated like the blast from a furnace. "I've given you my opinion of your tinkering. It's not an acceptable pastime any longer. Not with men like Jasper Keating, and their opinions count. You attract the wrong kind of attention to this house."

"I have talent. How can that bring anything negative?"

"Unless you intend to mend pots for a living, you had best find other pursuits."

"You were good with your hands once, too." Tobias turned his head to look his father full in the face.

But Bancroft looked more drawn than angry. "This is no time to mock me."

Tobias frowned. "I don't understand."

With a derisive huff of breath, his father stalked away. By the time he reached the drinks table, he appeared to be his smooth, urbane self once more. From what Tobias could see, whisky always improved Lord Bancroft's mood. But once he had refreshment, he wasted no time in moving to the far end of the property, away from his son.

Tobias stuffed his hands into his pockets, and then turned to his mother. "At risk of repeating myself, I don't understand."

Lady Bancroft gave him a searching look. "Perhaps that is for the best."

"He did wonderful work. He made that machine that cut out those pastries you like. And do you remember those odd dolls he made for Imogen and Anna?" As a child, he'd thought them hideous and frightening, but now he could appreciate the skill it had taken to make them.

His mother shuddered. "Ugh. Don't mention those automatons. Those were what made him give it all up."

Tobias just had time to wonder about that before they were interrupted by a tall man wearing an elegantly cut dark suit.

"Forgive my intrusion," the man said, sweeping off his top hat to make an extravagant bow to Lady Bancroft. "Madam, I come to pay my respects."

Everything about the man was foreign, from his looks to his accent to his presumption that he could address a respectable woman without proper introduction.

"Who are you, sir?" Tobias demanded.

His mother answered with a laugh. "Why, this is Dr. Symeon Magnus. It has been far too long. You have not aged a day. You must tell me your secret."

Tobias looked on in astonishment. Now that they'd been introduced, he recognized him, but only vaguely. His childhood memories were jumbled at best.

When Magnus bowed a second time, Lady Bancroft offered her hand. He lifted it to his lips in such a way that it brought color to her pale cheeks. Whoever he was, the man was smooth.

"This is such a pleasant surprise. Have you been in England long?" she asked.

"Not so long," he replied easily. "Rest assured that I would not delay the pleasure of renewing our acquaintance, my lady."

"Do you remember my son, Tobias?"

"Indeed, but he is now grown, I see."

As they exchanged a nod, Tobias catalogued the man's features. His dark, saturnine face was set off by a neatly trimmed goatee and mustache. His hair was too long for English fashion, but was thick and dark. From the quality of his dress and the fine silver carving on his walking stick, he was very well off.

"What an exquisite ornament." Lord Magus indicated the butterfly brooch. "It operates on a spring, I assume?"

"Yes, it does." He'd had enough of the man smiling at his mother. "What brings you to our fair country?"

"There is something here that I seek." Dr. Magnus leaned both hands on the head of his cane, studying Tobias like a piece of prized horseflesh. "And if what I hear is true, I have come to see you."

A jolt of surprise raised his hackles. "What business have you with me?"

The man grinned, teeth white in his dark face. "Allow me to render you pleasantly astonished."

"How can I refuse such an offer?"

A flock of his mother's friends were descending, so Tobias led the man out of earshot. They came to a halt underneath the oak tree.

Magnus leaned idly on his walking stick. "I have reliable information that you were the creator of the machine that destroyed *The Flying Dutchman*. An associate of mine observed you in possession of the remains."

Tobias tensed, folding his arms. "You are drawing a great many conclusions."

"Perhaps, but that pin your mother wears confirms all."

"What associate?"

Magnus gave an enigmatic smile. "You have an almost magical facility for creation in your blood. I was there at the Royal Charlotte. It was a juvenile act, but such imagination promises enormous potential. Even more, I think, than your father, and I knew him at the height of his powers as a maker."

Instinctively, Tobias reached out for the tree trunk, needing support. He'd never had more of *anything* than the illustrious Lord Bancroft, much less a quality he valued. But who knew about the workshop? Had one of his friends spilled the tale?

He finally pushed past the surprise enough to speak. "Your praise is very generous, given that it was, as you say, a juvenile prank."

"You are defensive." Dr. Magnus tilted his head, studying Tobias with dark, fathomless eyes. "I suppose I cannot blame you. Few understand real talent."

The man's undiluted attention made him want to squirm, as if he were no more than a boy in knee pants. "Let me be blunt. What might I do for you?"

"What do I want?" Dr. Magnus flicked at the grass with the tip of his cane. "Always a dangerous question, fraught with unexpected perils."

"And yet you clearly want something from me." Hadn't he had this conversation with Evelina just yesterday? He'd given her an answer that seemed clever at the time, but surely gave her no more satisfaction than Magnus was giving him now.

The man studied the ground, his voice slow and measured. "I have a great deal of money, and a great deal of knowledge. What I require is your artistic and mechanical talent. I'm wondering, if we pool our resources, just how far we might go."

"Go?" The word promised everything, but specified nothing. Tobias was afraid to let himself become too interested.

"I have a number of projects in mind. When I first came to England, I meant to approach your father, but he seems, um, preoccupied."

"My father?" Tobias asked in surprise. "He's no maker. Not anymore."

"So I've heard, sadly. He used to be, but I'm sure you know that."

"I do."

"Of course, we all used to be young. What I have in mind are young men's projects, full of ambition and adventure.

They are somewhat esoteric." Magnus smiled, and the smile was filled with mischief and a little wistful sadness.

Tobias was intrigued. People had wanted him for his name, or his looks, or what he might do for them, but never for what he loved about himself. "And in return for all this money and knowledge, all you want is my talent? And I assume that of my associates? I cannot claim to have built the squid on my own."

He couldn't leave his friends out of this stroke of good fortune.

Magnus raised a brow. "Yes, if they are willing, they are included. I want all your skill and imagination. I want your very best efforts."

Suddenly, Tobias felt drunk, the ground seeming to shift under his feet. He clutched at the tree again, then tried to turn the move into a casual lean. *Someone wants me. For me. This is what a proposal must feel like to a young girl. Maybe one from a prince.*

Tobias laughed, and he could hear the note of giddiness in it. "Our best efforts? That's all?"

"And absolute secrecy, of course. Some of my ideas are quite revolutionary. Nevertheless, I'll be pleased to share them with bright young minds." Magnus smiled warmly. "As I have been a friend of your family for so long a time, I hope you will agree to look on me as an honorary uncle."

"I shall." And he would do more than that, because he felt like the prodigal son finding a home where he least expected it. A home, and—Tobias tried to stifle the thought because it seemed so young and weak—just maybe the father he'd always yearned for.

CHAPTER SIXTEEN

THE PITCH OF GENERAL CONVERSATION WOUND HIGHER, LIKE an orchestra changing keys. Evelina turned to see what was the matter.

An impeccably dressed man breezed directly onto the back lawn, not even waiting for acknowledgment before he made himself at home in Lord Bancroft's garden. She recognized Jasper Keating, the Gold King. From his white hair to his almost military bearing, he fit the aristocratic idea of a powerful man—no doubt one reason he was able to do business in the wealthier quarters of London.

The fact that he had been the author of her invitation to be presented at the Court Drawing Room only increased her suspicions about the man. She had written her thank-yous to express her gratitude, but it had felt as if she were a pawn thanking the king during a game of chess.

"Every time that one shows up someplace, he reminds me of Death coming to visit," Imogen observed under her breath. "A scythe in one hand, and in the other one of those awful tuppeny books of jokes. His audience wants to groan as he reads them, but they're too terrified not to laugh."

Evelina eyeballed the newcomer. "Death at least has a sense of irony. This bloke looks like he believes his balance sheet."

However, what set Keating apart the most was the crowd of dark-suited men that trailed after him. Although it was none of her affair, the sight of all those servile hangers-on irritated her.

The best antidote was tea. Evelina placed an empty cup under the automatic samovar. It spit out orange pekoe in a gurgling whoosh, then hurled in a lemon slice after. Hot liquid slopped into the saucer. "I didn't ask for lemon."

"Those things never do what you actually want, but they do what you *don't* want with amazing efficiency. That's called progress." Imogen popped a tiny square of cake into her mouth, then sucked frosting from her finger with a guilty glance to see if anyone watched.

"This reminds me," Evelina said with all the casualness she could muster. "You recall what we were discussing earlier?"

"Yes." Imogen filled her own teacup. "I'm not likely to forget."

They'd been poring over the latest reports in the newspaper about the death of the grooms. Somehow, the papers had found out about Grace, too, and that had kept the story alive for another day, although it was still buried in the back pages. Nevertheless, she had seen Lord B's face at the breakfast table when he found the column. He was not a happy man.

Evelina leaned close. "Why do you think your father still had those automatons?" Though she'd told her friend what she'd seen inside the trunks, she hadn't mentioned the magic. The fewer people who knew about it, the easier it would be to keep that aspect of the affair quiet.

Imogen shrugged, unperturbed by the question. "Until this horrid affair with the grooms, I had no idea they were still around. I would have thought they'd have been left behind in Vienna along with the majority of my father's other old projects."

"Your father made them?" Evelina asked in astonishment. It was a big leap from tinkering with machines to making a working device like that.

"Certainly. He made them to amuse my sister and me when we were tiny girls. He was very accomplished, but he gave up tinkering around the time Anna died and I fell ill. I think that's why he hates such things now. It reminds him of a time he'd rather forget. I don't think my parents ever got over her death, and the dolls bring it all back."

It made sense of a sort. Anna had been Imogen's twin.

From the ornately framed daguerreotype Evelina had seen in Lady Bancroft's sitting room, the two had been identical.

Evelina fished the lemon out of her cup with a spoon. "Maybe that's what Lord Bancroft means when he complains that the Steam Council lacks finesse. He knows as much about machines as the barons do."

"But there's more to it than finesse. It's one thing to be able to build a beautiful butterfly brooch like Tobias, but quite another to put up a power plant that gives you the means to light up half of London—or plunge it into darkness if the mood takes you. Everyone wants power. The barons have it. Therefore, they win." Imogen leaned close as one of the guests paused to pick up a watercress sandwich. "All the political hacks follow them around like sad little spaniels waiting for a crumb to drop. The *Prattler* said so."

"For shame. You've been reading the newspaper again."

"Don't tell my father. He thinks absorbing too much information will ruin my marriage prospects."

But she was right about the spaniels. Evelina looked over at Keating again. "What's His Steamship doing here? I thought he and your father were at odds."

"My father has taken a sudden interest in making new friends. He's up to something, as usual." Imogen shrugged. "As for why Keating came, I suppose even if you own half of London, a free meal still tastes best."

"So cynical."

"Pessimism is the basis of all sound expectations. If you foresee nothing good, no outrage can shock you."

Evelina choked back a laugh. "I pity your future husband."

"Only if he can't keep up—which is a depressing likelihood. I suspect there's a factory in Yorkshire turning out insipid young men by the box load, and they're all clamoring to be on my dance card."

"Poor Imogen."

"Bah." She ate another piece of cake. "Oh, look. Here comes Alice Keating in yet another Paris frock."

Evelina turned to see the copper-haired girl was indeed drifting their way, chatting airily with a brace of young bucks. She wondered what it would be like to have the Gold King for a father.

"What is this vision I see before me?" cried the buck to Alice's left when he caught sight of Imogen. He raised one hand to shade his eyes and extended the other with the air of a sailor spotting a tropical paradise. To Alice's credit—or the young man's demerit—she didn't seem to mind the competition.

Imogen blushed and Evelina sipped tea to keep from giggling. The tall, gangly young man's name was Percy Hamilton. As the younger son of Lord Bushwell, he'd been destined for the navy, but never quite made it there. He'd taken a wrong turn somewhere near a gaming hell and lost his commission before he'd even reported for duty.

The other was Stanford Whitlock—tall, dark, muscular, and a renowned pugilist. A good one, if one judged by the pristine condition of his handsome face. His father was a well-to-do banker, so the Whitlocks were on everyone's guest list. He remained by Alice's side, but stared at Imogen like a starving man suddenly spotting a perfectly cooked roast.

If one was nonverbal, the other would not stop talking. "Oh, Disconnect me, you are so lovely, Miss Roth!"

Evelina turned to Alice Keating and searched for something to say. "How pleasant to see you here."

Alice released Whitlock's arm and opened her parasol. It had a fringe of tiny yellow pompoms that matched her dress. The breeze caught them and they bobbled merrily. "Indeed, I am delighted to attend. Shall we take a turn about the garden, Miss Cooper, and leave these swains to worship at the feet of their goddess?"

Evelina shot a look to Imogen, who widened her eyes in feigned panic. Imogen claimed to hate her gaggle of suitors, but Evelina thought she secretly enjoyed the attention.

Evelina set down her cup. "Certainly." She didn't know Alice well, but the invitation seemed innocent enough.

Abandoning Whitlock with the sandwiches, Alice began skirting the lawn. "I see Lord Bancroft has begun adding more lights to the house and garden. It will be quite lovely at night."

That was true. Some of the new additions were tall lamp standards, others just tiny globes that hung over windows and doorways. At the prices the barons charged for gas, the fad for outdoor lighting displays was also a symbol of how much money one had to waste.

"It's the fashion," Evelina replied noncommittally and then gestured at a turning in the path. "If we go this way, you will see the tulip beds. They are quite lovely this time of year."

Alice complied, her eyes as much on her feet as on the world around her. Evelina got the impression that she hadn't mixed much in company until the last year, and was a little shy.

Evelina changed the subject. "I owe your father a debt of gratitude."

"What for?"

"He arranged for my presentation."

"Oh, that. It's his pleasure, I'm sure." Alice gave her a sidelong glance. "You're quite right, the tulips are spectacular."

Evelina agreed, gazing at the riot of pinks, reds, and yellows, and wondered why Alice had singled her out. Now that they were in private—too far away from the food to attract many partygoers—she didn't have to wait long to find out.

"We do not know each other well," Alice began, the sun seeping through the fine silk of her parasol and turning her hair to a red flame. "But I met some of your schoolmates from Wollaston's at a musicale the other night."

"That can't be good," Evelina replied lightly, trying to sound less alarmed than she felt.

Alice chuckled. It wasn't the silvery laugh Evelina had heard the few times they had been at the same dinner tables and drawing rooms, but an earthy chuckle that sounded much more real. "On the contrary. They all said you were smart and very much your own person. Also, honest to a fault."

"I wonder whom I offended by that."

The girl's tone was droll. "Well, I understand the school closed the year you left."

Evelina cringed at the memory. "The headmistress retired after an unfortunate incident with the walking dead, but that's a tiresome story."

Alice looked up from the flowers, her eyes alight. "How very intriguing. My informant left out that detail."

Evelina was growing uncomfortable. "Why is the Wollaston Academy of interest to you?"

"Not the academy, but you. You interest me."

"Why?"

Alice gave a little huff of breath—less a sigh than someone working up to a confession. She twirled the parasol, making the yellow bobbles fly. "When I heard you were the niece of Sherlock Holmes, I grew curious. I'm my father's daughter. When I wish to resolve a problem, I research it thoroughly."

"Do I disappoint?"

"On the contrary." Alice's face changed, a small pucker appearing between her brows. "I wish I had the opportunity to know you better."

"I'm flattered."

"No, you're not, and I say that utterly without rancor. You're wondering why we are having this conversation." Alice finally met her eyes. Unlike her father's golden gaze, Alice's were a startling blue. "I'm concerned about my father. I want to know why he is using your uncle's services. And I want to know if you're likely to tell me the truth about it."

Evelina's breath hitched. She'd heard Alice Keating was sometimes blunt, but she hadn't expected this. "My uncle does not discuss his cases with me. He holds his clients' confidentiality in high regard. In any event, I don't know what they spoke about."

Alice frowned. "Would you tell me if you knew?"

"They aren't my secrets to share."

For a long moment, Alice glared at the flower bed as if it had offended her. "And my father tells me nothing of substance. My welfare depends on his. I should know."

"He has not taken you into the business?" Some of the steam barons were female.

"No." The single word spoke volumes.

"Ah." Evelina swallowed hard. It wasn't her affair, but she suddenly understood far too much. Like so many women, Alice was smart, but her capabilities were undervalued by her family. "I wish I could help."

"Thank you." Alice lifted her head. The elaborate coils of her copper hair resembled some mysterious invention. The sun sparkled on the diamonds in her combs. "You are frank, Evelina Cooper. I like that. Perhaps someday we shall be friends."

Evelina smiled, suddenly deciding she could like the Gold King's daughter. "I would be honored."

"Good." They started back toward the main party. Alice made a long-suffering face. "I suppose I should get on with the business of finding a husband my father will like."

"Find one *you* will like," said Evelina firmly. "You're the one who has to live with him, after all."

Alice gave another laugh, but this time it was high and nervous. "Very true, but he will have to live with my father. He will have to be a very strong man to dare that."

Evelina could well believe that. "Then when he comes along, you will have to snap him up."

"That sounds very carnivorous."

It was Evelina's turn to laugh. "My grandmamma told me the marriage mart is not for the fainthearted."

"Well, then," said Alice, "let us break out the cutlery and have at it."

IMOGEN EYED STANFORD Whitlock uneasily. He was nice to look at, but had the unhappy habit of licking his lips. The sight of that large pink tongue reminded her of a mastiff they'd once owned. She was tempted to toss him a hunk of beef just to see if he would catch it in his teeth.

"But you see," piped Percy Hamilton, who kept moving forward an inch with every breath. He was very close to crowding her against the tea table. "Buttercup was the favorite in the fourth race. She had a beautiful gait, she did. I was sure she could take Rake's Flagon by at least a head."

"And did she?" Imogen asked politely. "How fared the gallant Buttercup?"

"Disconnect me if she didn't throw a shoe on the curve, and I lost my last shilling that day," Percy said cheerfully. "But I got it all back at the next meet. It's all a matter of trusting the numbers will come your way again."

Imogen didn't entirely disagree. Unlike Evelina, who planned for every last contingency, she was more patient with the universe. However, Imogen had also learned that life could be fleeting, and ought not to be wasted on irritating young men.

If he said "Disconnect me" one more time, she was going to shriek.

Percy inched forward again, and her bustle connected with the table. There was a faint rattling of teacups. "Mr. Hamilton, would you please be so kind as to withdraw a few steps?"

Before he could reply, Whitlock grabbed him by the scruff and dragged him backward. Percy made a faint gargling sound as his feet bobbed above the ground.

"Better?" Whitlock asked.

"Yes, thank you," Imogen returned brightly, scanning the horizon for Evelina to come to her rescue. She was beginning to feel fatigued. She'd never been unduly strong, and the stress of the last few days was wearing on her. "You may set him down now."

Whitlock released his grasp and returned to his former stance. Stolid. Wordless. Imogen felt herself growing tense even as Percy launched into a new tale of equine glory. She was beginning to think of Whitlock as The Stare. She wondered if this was what rabbits felt right before a fox bagged them.

"Miss Roth." A third voice made her start. She turned to her left. Bucky Penner was grinning down at her. He always had the look of a man planning an outrage, and right now it was directed at her.

"What may I do for you, Mr. Penner?" she asked a bit

tartly. He was Tobias's longtime friend, and familiarity—
not to mention his ceaseless pranks on his best friend's sisters, like the time he had glued the edges of Poppy's shoes
together when she had fallen asleep under the pear tree—
had rubbed away the top layer of good manners between
them.

"Your furbelows are blocking access to the tea." He stared
pointedly at her bustle.

"Indeed, sir." Only he could make a factual statement
sound so improper. "Are you even certain of the definition
of a furbelow?"

"I know they are an ornament prized by ladies in all
conditions of life, and that they have come between me,
a humble supplicant of the teapot, and the object of my
desire."

The only thing to do with Bucky was to hand his impu-
dence right back. "Like a goddess of old, perhaps I demand
obeisance before letting supplicants pass."

"Is this man being a bother?" The Stare demanded, proving he could actually speak.

Ignoring him, Bucky raised an eyebrow. "Are you truly
going to deprive me of my refreshment, Miss Roth?"

"You cast yourself in the role of supplicant, Mr. Penner. I
would like to witness some groveling, if you please."

"You are a cruel deity, madam, to sport the fair and innocent visage of Venus and yet possess the unforgiving temper of a Juno."

Imogen folded her arms, starting to enjoy herself at long
last. "How badly do you want your tea, Mr. Penner? Hom-
age must be rendered when and where it is due." And she
prepared to stare him down.

Which was a mistake. He shamelessly stared right back.

Imogen's stomach fluttered and heat rose up her neck and
cheeks. How mortifying. She knew her pale skin showed
every blush like a bright red flag. Still, she refused to budge.

"I say," began Percy uncertainly, but no one paid him the
least attention. As far as Imogen was concerned, Percy and
Whitlock might as well have been struck by a thunderbolt
and dissolved to dust.

Imogen had never noticed how delicious a shade of brown Bucky's eyes were, like the very best dark Belgian chocolate. Or how his hair curled at the tips, begging her fingers to smooth it down. Or how the corners of his mouth quirked with ready laughter. Bucky Penner had always struck her as Tobias's foil—not as handsome, not as adventurous, but the one with his feet planted firmly on the ground. Now she saw that was only half the truth. Everything about him was full of life.

She was elated by the discovery, as if one part of her soul had figured out what the other half already knew. And she was dismayed, because she wasn't quite prepared for this. The Season hadn't even begun. Her heart was supposed to remain in its white tissue wrapping a little longer.

Don't be a goose. This is Bucky. Even his name is ridiculous. Imogen wanted to withdraw from their contest of wills very badly, but wasn't sure how to do it without making a cake of herself. *Ugh!* If this kept up, she might finish by actually *liking* Tobias's best friend. Now that would be embarrassing.

Almost as bad as the moment when Bucky swept off his hat and fell to one knee, for all the world like a suitor begging for her hand. "My glorious goddess, you have carried the field. I declare myself undone by your majesty. Is there something you would like me to kiss as part of my supplication? Your hand, or perhaps your feet? I believe I saw that once in a badly rhymed poem—though perhaps we could manage something more befitting your furbelowed glory. An offering of lemon ices and love letters to be spread upon your altar?"

"Mr. Penner! Get up at once!" Imogen gasped, looking about in abject mortification. Bad enough that a young man was pretending to propose, but it was *Bucky*. Everyone would know he was mocking her. "Stop this foolery and get your wretched tea!"

He was up in an instant, diving for the cups so fast their bodies collided. She felt the solidity of his like a warm, hard wall as she let out a faint "oof!" He caught her arm, steadying her before she fell into the cream.

"Are you all right?" he said, laughing.

"I'll survive." Her skin tingled as if he'd doused her in a magnetic field. The heat of her embarrassment gathered in her belly and grew . . . well, as odd as it sounded, the feeling was rather nice. *Lemon ices and love letters.* Yes, she had to admit, it sounded rather pleasant.

She gathered as much dignity as she could muster and looked around. Percy and The Stare were gone. She tried to regret the fact, but couldn't quite manage it.

When Bucky looked down at her this time, the grin had turned to something far more speculative and intriguing. "Be sure when you begin a conquest, Miss Roth, that you actually mean to win."

Imogen swallowed. Her mouth had gone dry and it felt like she had a croquet ball stuck halfway down her throat. "It's a question of standards, Mr. Penner. I may not be a real goddess, but even so I expect flowers before a kiss, even if it is only my feet involved."

He narrowed his eyes, one corner of his mouth curling up. "I'll remember that, Miss Roth."

"MR. KEATING BROUGHT toys," Imogen said to Evelina a few minutes later.

Evelina noticed she was flushed, but in a way that spoke of excitement rather than fever. She somehow didn't think it had anything to do with the Gold King, and she wondered what had gone on while she was talking to Alice.

One of Keating's spaniels was setting up some sort of sci-entific equipment. "Let's go over there to get a better view," Evelina suggested.

Imogen made a face. "I'm sure it's going to be dull. No one ever brings anything fun if Papa is around. It's probably something to do with that new gallery of Keating's. A lot of Greek pots, from what I hear."

"Let's go anyway."

They wandered across the lawn, Evelina a pace or two behind her friend. Imogen stopped next to Tobias.

The sight of him made Evelina's stomach twist with an

unpleasant mix of regret and anger. She instinctively veered to the left, keeping Imogen between them. After their scene by the clock, she had no desire to be anywhere in his vicinity.

He stiffened as she approached, his shoulders as rigid as the knot in her gut. That just annoyed her more. She wished she could take back that kiss. No, that wasn't right. She wished she could make it mean something to Tobias beyond a bump to his pride.

She'd been watching him all afternoon. She'd seen him arguing with Lord B earlier, then talking earnestly with Dr. Magnus. Whatever Magnus had said had acted like a tonic. Tobias stood with his shoulders squared, an air of barely contained energy wrapping him like a cloak. Something was afoot.

But now the doctor was nowhere to be seen. In fact, Lord B and Magnus hadn't come within a dozen yards of each other, but that was no surprise.

The mouse had come to her room a good half hour after she'd left Tobias last night and reported that Magnus wanted leverage with Jasper Keating. There was something he thought Keating possessed, or was about to possess, and Magnus wanted Bancroft's help in getting it. Bancroft had refused, but Magnus had been insistent. According to the mouse, the doctor had eventually backed down with the air of someone playing the opening hand in a long game. The mouse had heard no open references to the automatons.

Her thoughts were broken by the fact that the man setting up the curious contraption appeared to be finished. He dusted off his hands and trotted back to Keating's side with an eager expression.

"What's going on?" Imogen asked her brother.

"The Gold King's man, Jackson, is about to give a demonstration of some kind. They have an enormous dry cell battery."

Evelina's gaze traveled from Jasper Keating to Lord and Lady Bancroft. They all stood only a few sociable feet apart from each other, and yet the air between them seemed to crackle with enough tension to combust. Although it was politically expedient to invite the Gold King, the pall it cast on the company hardly seemed worthwhile.

"Ladies, gentlemen." Jackson opened his arms in a gesture reminiscent of Old Ploughman about to announce the high-wire act. "Gracious hostess." He turned and made a bow to Lady Bancroft, who gave a graceful nod.

Evelina quickly catalogued the items on display. Battery. Wires. A pair of glass globes flickering with crazy arcs of electricity.

"Some fool is going to get a nasty shock," Tobias muttered under his breath.

Evelina glanced up, realizing the buffer between them was gone. Imogen had sidled to a different position and was frowning at Bucky Penner, who was chatting with two other young bucks. Evelina wondered what nonsense Bucky had got up to now, and returned her attention to the unfolding drama.

"For those who do not know me, my name is Mr. Aragon Jackson, and I am fortunate enough to be in the employ of Mr. Keating. My purpose at Keating Utility is to come up with new ways to make gas, steam, and other types of power a useful part of your households. Today, ladies and gentlemen, I have something entirely new!"

Evelina half expected Jackson to whip out a bottle of cure-all tonic.

He pointed to the crowd, making a slow arc to capture them all in his gesture. "I ask you, who here has rung and rung the bell for lazy servants who never came?"

With an inward groan, she wondered if they were about to endure another new model of automaton.

"Who here has waited for refreshments, or the newspaper, or for the lights to be adjusted? Who can bear to bother with dull and inattentive servants one more day?"

A murmur rippled through the party. Evelina cast a nervous glance at the staff standing still as wax figures around the periphery of the crowd. Three of their number had just been murdered. This was not the time to persecute them.

"This invention is the answer!" Jackson swept an arm toward his creation. "I require a volunteer."

Two of Keating's men dragged forward a maid in black and white. Evelina's stomach clenched. It was Dora. Jackson strapped something to her arm, then placed an odd-looking circlet on her head. It had a pair of antennae sticking up that reminded her of a bug. A wire ran from the headgear to the armband, another from her wrist to the enormous battery sitting on the lawn.

"What is this?" Tobias growled under his breath.

"Using the very latest in wireless radio transmission, your summons can be communicated directly to staff on duty." He pointed to what looked like a telegraph key sitting on a table beside the battery. "No more pulling on a bell rope only to have your desires lost in an empty servant's hall. Now they have no excuse to ignore your wishes."

Jackson leaned over and tapped the key. Dora cried out, fingers flying to the wristband.

Evelina started, looking around for an explanation. "What's happening?"

Then she realized she was the only one who spoke.

"Yes," Jackson announced to the suddenly silent audience. "This new invention wirelessly delivers a soundless summons anywhere within your house. No more shirking, no more hiding. All that is required is the equipment you see here, with the addition of one of our new patented portable energy cells, small enough for an active servant to strap onto her waistband. Obviously, the staff can't be tethered to a large battery such as the one you see here."

He paused, waiting for a polite chuckle to ripple through the crowd. Then he tapped the key again. Dora yelped a second time.

This time Evelina saw sparks. Smoke. *There's something wrong. Surely he can't mean to hurt her!* But maybe he did. There was something in the way Keating was glaring at Lord Bancroft that held a warning.

The crowd had fallen raptly silent again, except for someone who tittered. Evelina scanned the gathering. Imogen had turned pale. Bucky was gone. Lord Bancroft looked outraged, Lady B horrified. Yet no one made a move as Jackson bent to adjust some dials. The crowd all looked at Jasper

Keating, as if they understood a subtext Evelina could only guess at.

Then she heard an older woman behind her murmuring to her friend. "I would be careful if I were Bancroft. He's been on thin ice this past week, ever since they caught him putting his money in the Harter Engine Company. Betting on the competition is hardly wise, especially with all the chit-chat about the Quality throwing in with the rebels. I'd say that shock was meant for him, not his parlor maid. Keating's just sending a warning through her."

No one moved, no one objected. It was as if they had all silently agreed that the public torture of servants was entirely normal. *They're all too afraid of the Gold King to tell him to stop.*

So was she. She was there at the invitation of Lord and Lady Bancroft. It would be the height of ingratitude to embarrass them in front of London's elite. Crossing the steam barons would mean not just embarrassment, but punishment. And, unlike most of the richly clad guests, Evelina actually knew what being cast down to the gutter would mean.

But she also knew what it meant to have no power. No one had stood up for Grace Child. What would happen if no one spoke up for Dora now? Evelina's heart pounded in her throat, afraid to move, too horrified to keep silent.

Her foot, as if with a mind of its own, was already poised to take a step off the social precipice when Tobias grabbed her wrist, pinning her to his side. He shot her a glance, shaking his head slightly. His eyes were wide with exasperation, but maybe with a touch of admiration, too.

"Mr. Jackson," he said, raising his voice. "Surely you mean to summon the staff, not cook them."

Nervous laughter went around the garden. Tobias slowly released Evelina's wrist, as if he was unsure if she would bolt forward anyway to cause a scene.

"Thank you," she whispered.

A fleeting smile touched his lips, but he turned and strode toward the machine before she could say any more. On the way past Dora, he unfastened the device from her wrist, plucked the odd-looking tiara from her head, and gave her a gentle push toward the house. She didn't need to be told twice.

Tobias turned to face his father's guests. "This demonstration is done. The unit is clearly defective."

"Tobias!" his father barked.

But the spell was already broken. A general hubbub broke out as the guests scrabbled for a sense of normality. A great many of them nearly ran for the table with the brandy. Evelina used the milling bodies as cover to get a closer look at the machine and, even more, to see what Tobias would do next. *He always surprises me.*

"Does the young gentleman care to demonstrate his superior skill?" Jackson said with a hint of insolence. He might not have Tobias's blue blood, but he had Jasper Keating as a protector, and that counted for much these days. "Does he have some acquaintance with machinery?"

By way of reply, Tobias shouldered him out of the way and crouched down to examine the machine. He turned a dial to his left and glared at Jackson. "You idiot, you had this set high enough to give the young woman a fatal shock. Wireless technology is far from perfected yet."

"Obviously that is not the case," Keating said. He stood closest to Jackson and near enough to overhear Tobias's muttered remark. "As you can see, she did not die."

"Tobias," Lord Bancroft said again in a low, strained voice. The single word held a world of warning.

Be careful, Evelina thought. If Lord B was worried, so was she. Keating was in motion now, closing the brief distance to the Bancrofts.

The younger man ignored them both, intent on checking the wires connecting to the battery. Evelina knew that when Tobias was working on something mechanical, he was lost to the mortal world. "I could make this work, though," he said.

"Perhaps," said Keating. "Although you assume the device wasn't set exactly the way we wished it to be."

The furious expression on Lord Bancroft's face sent a chill down Evelina's spine. "Tobias is merely young, Mr.

Keating. Hot blood will sometimes outweigh good sense at that age."

There would be words between father and son before the day was over.

"Such an independent temperament can also bring unpleasantness." Keating laid two fingers on Lady Bancroft's butterfly brooch, stopping its wings. The brooch's gentle chime stuttered to a sickly chatter. She stepped back, and Keating let her. He had crossed a thousand social lines by touching her at all, but once again no one dared to utter a word.

Grace Child's still form hovered in Evelina's mind. Not that she believed Keating had played a role in her death or that of the grooms—why would he? Still, he and the other industrialists, with their streetkeepers and their hunger for power, had encouraged a world where that kind of brutality could happen. A maid could be slaughtered. A maid could be repeatedly shocked in front of her employers and they would make no move to protect her. A lady could be insulted at her own birthday party with her husband standing mere feet away.

Her thoughts were mirrored in the disgust stamped on Tobias's face. He rose, his glare moving from Keating to his father and back again before he pressed the wristband against Jackson's chest and tapped the key. The man started, but it was nothing like Dora's violent jerk.

He cast a final icy glance at the Gold King. "I think you'll agree that's a little safer."

He turned away, letting the wristband fall. Jackson reflexively caught it, giving himself another shock. Tobias let him fumble, then stalked back toward the house in the same direction Dora had gone.

Evelina wanted to cheer.

CHAPTER SEVENTEEN

Sequence of events:

April 4	10:45 p.m.	Grooms enter attic to fetch five trunks containing automatons.
	11 p.m.	Male and female voices heard from ledge.
	11:30 p.m.	Grooms leave attic.
	Midnight	Climbed back through window and went downstairs. Spoke to Dora and Imogen.
	Midnight	Outside door locked by Bigelow at curfew.
	Past midnight	Grace returns home, then Tobias (where from?).
April 5	12:30 a.m.	Dora sees Tobias talking to Grace in the garden. Nick arrives?
	12:45 a.m.	About this time, encounter someone in hallway.
	1 a.m.	Maisie discovers Grace's body. Nick leaves.
	1:10 a.m.	Bigelow wakes Lord Bancroft in the library.
	1:15 a.m.	Tobias arrives on scene, claiming to have been in bed.
	Before dawn	Grooms wake up innkeeper, looking for smith.
	Late morning	Bodies of grooms discovered in Hampstead, robbed.

Survey of household indicate all were accounted for on that night except Tobias.

—From Evelina's private notebook

THEY'D BEEN DISCONNECTED.

Evelina's stomach was in knots. The heat had gone off five minutes after Jasper Keating departed, leaving the kitchens and baths cold. The cooks had been forced to wash up in frigid water. Then the gas had gone out the moment dusk fell. Fortunately, candles were one staple that was still easy to get, and there were plenty on hand. Lord B had never run gas to the upper floors, only lighting the rooms that guests were likely to see.

Apparently, Tobias's outrage had warranted retaliation. There was no need for raised voices or displays of temper. All Keating had to do was send workmen out to turn off the lines running to Hilliard House, and his point was made for all to see. It was hard to miss a pitch-black house among all the brilliantly lit yards.

Of course, no one had said *Disconnected* out loud—the Gold King was too crafty for that. So just as Dora had been the screen for Keating's first retaliation against Lord Bancroft, a mysterious—and simultaneous—failure in the gas and steam lines disguised his second. "Just one of those things," said the mystified leader of the repair crew from Keating Utility, loudly enough for all to hear. "It'll be fixed just as soon as the right part arrives." Which meant five minutes hence or never, depending on the Gold King's pleasure.

The less suspicious guests who overheard the crewman accepted that the failure was a malfunction. The cynical looked askance and said nothing. The only question in Evelina's mind was how long a house could be "out of order" before it became officially "Disconnected." Not long, she guessed. As warnings went, the situation was abundantly clear. Bancroft had better watch his step.

To top everything else, Inspector Lestrade and his men arrived just as the bulk of the guests were leaving. Evelina was fairly sure the Gold King had arranged that, too, because Lestrade seemed unconcerned about either the party or the Gold King's move to cut the power. Normally, the police trod more carefully around the gentry than this.

"It's just routine, you understand," he promised.

Lestrade sat on the chair opposite Evelina's place on the sofa, not mentioning the Disconnection by word or deed. She couldn't guess whether that was strategy or sensitivity. They were in the same drawing room where she had met her grandmamma, but there was no tea and biscuits this time. Just some candles, the rat-faced inspector, and her. Normally, a young lady would have a chaperone, but everyone else was dealing with the utility crisis.

The inspector had out his notebook and pencil. "Tell me again exactly how you came to be with the deceased."

If he was speaking to her, that meant he hadn't found more promising leads. Evelina wondered about her bird. It had been gone three days. It was supposed to have spied on Lestrade, but it hadn't come back. Worry made her stomach knot.

"What were you doing when you heard there was trouble in the house?" he asked.

She'd been with Nick in her bedroom, wanting him to stay and wishing he would go. Her mind cast about for a different answer. Anything to deflect the question. "You don't have a recording cylinder?"

"I don't need one, miss," he replied a little testily.

"But you can get verbatim statements from the punch rolls."

"Sometimes it's not the words that matter, miss. It's what lies between 'em."

The look he gave her chilled her to the bone. Uncle Sherlock might cow Inspector Lestrade, but Evelina related the events of the night—the ones she saw fit to tell him, anyhow—without further ado. It would be little more than he already knew.

"If you don't mind my saying miss, you don't seem terribly upset by all this."

Evelina stared at the candle on the side table beside her. "Swooning won't help you or Grace."

"No, miss."

"You think me unladylike."

"I find you an unusually calm young lady."

Whatever his opinion, Lestrade was a good listener, taking copious notes. When she was done talking, he reread them silently, tracking his progress down the page with the tip of his pencil.

"You say you heard voices outside earlier that night. When was that?"

"I heard the church clock strike eleven."

"You're very precise, miss. I appreciate it."

She gave a small smile. "I have it on good authority that cases can be solved by the observance of trifles."

He gave her a sour look. "You sound like Sherlock Holmes."

"He is my uncle."

"I know." He lifted a brow. "He told me to pay special attention to what you might say, and promised to be my undoing if you came to harm before this case was done."

"Really? He knows about this case?" Chill dread rose.

"Oh, aye. He had to go haring off to the Continent, or he'd be here, I'm sure."

Panic engulfed her, making her shift restlessly in her chair. She'd meant to get ahead of Lestrade, solve Grace's murder, and steer the police away from Lord B and his automatons, but every tick of the clock seemed to make matters worse. At this rate, there would be nothing left of the family before she had her first real break in the case.

Suddenly the shadows in the candlelit room oppressed her.

"By the by," Lestrade said casually, "do you happen to know when young Mr. Roth came home that night?"

He nearly caught her off guard. "I didn't see Tobias come home."

"Did he tell you when he came home?"

The scene by the clock came back to her. The kiss. His nonconfession about coming back from somewhere that night. Somewhere he wasn't going to speak of. And the kiss. If she was smart, she'd give him up. Tell Lestrade everything, and show Tobias she wasn't a stupid girl who could be silenced with a few soft words and a grapple in the shadows.

But then, he'd stood up to Jasper Keating to protect Dora. Tobias wasn't perfect, but he didn't deserve to be tossed under the charging locomotive of Lestrade's investigation. *No matter what the inspector finds out, it will be wrong because I know about the gold and the magic, and he does not.*

"Tobias didn't tell me anything. Young men don't confide in their little sisters' houseguests."

His lips twitched, or maybe that was just the shadows of the candle flame shifting over his features. "I take your point, miss. In that case, I think I have everything I need from you."

He flipped the notebook closed, but reached into the pocket of his overcoat. "I just remembered—I spoke with Dr. Magnus on my way in tonight. He asked that I give this to you."

It was a plain paper box from a bakery, complete with grease stains and string. "What is this?" she asked.

"I have no idea, miss. I suggested that he give it to Lady Bancroft, as that would be more proper when a young lady was involved, but he said that the contents were yours and that he's merely returning something you lost."

Evelina took the box and slipped off the string. When she flipped open the lid, there was her bird, laying stiff and flat.

She couldn't stifle a gasp of surprise. Her hands felt suddenly clumsy, her arms numb and heavy. Instinctively, she closed the lid, hiding the contents.

"You weren't expecting this, were you, miss?" Lestrade said with a searching look.

"No. I wasn't sure where this had got to. How clever of him to find it." Her voice sounded flat in her own ears, but beneath her control was a deal of panic. There was something terrifying about Dr. Magnus, and he had handled her invention. Had he killed it? *How did he know it was mine? No one has even introduced us.*

Her stomach turned to stone, remembering her first meeting with Magnus in the library. She'd felt magic on him, just like she'd felt it on Grace's envelope. Had he done the same with her? Was her signature on her creations? She'd never really thought about that particular danger.

She longed to pick up the bird and examine it minutely, but dared not arouse the inspector's interest. Instead, she forced herself to set the box aside, as if it didn't matter, but her hand lingered near the table. She couldn't quite bear to have it outside her reach.

Lestrade rose, and she followed suit, clasping her hands so he would not see her fingers tremble.

"Shall I ring for the footman to see you out, Inspector?" she asked. "Or is there someone else you would like to interview?"

"I can see myself out. I think I'm done for today." A grim smile played across his lips. "You've given me the most complete account so far, miss. Not too many people seem to notice what goes on with the staff, even when they're dying."

"Have you found anything out about those poor grooms?" She knew it was unlikely he'd answer a question from a witness, but hoped her uncle's reputation would loosen his tongue.

It seemed to work. "We've recovered the horses and the wagon. They turned up for sale at a fair. We're questioning the bloke who's selling them. He claims to have found them abandoned in his farmyard."

"How odd! Was there any sign of the cargo?"

"Not a jot." Lestrade's face darkened. "His Lordship says the trunks are packed with souvenirs of his time in Austria. Seems to want them back most urgently. Do you know anything about what's inside?"

"No." She didn't, really. Not in any way that would help Lestrade.

He met her eyes, and must have been satisfied with what he saw there. "Do you know if those grooms had dealings with the dead girl?"

"Again, I don't know."

He was still holding her gaze. "They were killed the same way, throats cut."

Evelina went ice-cold.

"I'm sorry if that shocked you." He actually looked contrite. "You seemed to be taking so much of this in stride."

It wasn't the manner of death that bothered her, though. It was the connection. "Are you saying the murderer was the same? That he killed Grace—maybe because she surprised him—and then followed the grooms and stole the chests?" Which would explain why the gold had never been taken. That wasn't what the killer was after. He wanted the automatons Lord Bancroft had made years ago. But why were they significant?

Lestrade blinked. "It's a possibility. I'm not ruling anything out."

"No doubt, Inspector. That is of course the correct way to proceed." She sat down, too overwhelmed to remain standing a moment more.

"Very good then, miss." Lestrade bowed slightly, and left.

Evelina sat still a moment, her thoughts spinning too fast to pin down a single one. Then she heard a familiar scrabbling. She glanced down to see the mouse poking out from between the sofa cushions. Its fine wire whiskers quivered inquisitively.

Bird has been returned to you?

She swallowed down an aching lump. "I think he's broken."

Let me see.

She scooped up the mouse and placed it on the edge of the table, then lifted the lid of the bakery box again. The mouse placed its front paws on the side of the box, levering itself up to peer over the rim. *Oh, my! Look at those wings. You gave him gemstones. Why Bird and not me?*

"You're an indoor spy. I needed you to be stealthy."

The mouse snorted—a strange mechanical exhalation. *Such is my lot, that I am forced to spend my servitude grubbing under furniture while this one floats around the air like a bloody Fabergé confection. Well, fat lot of good it did you, Bird.*

Evelina reached over to pick up the inert device. The bird lay with its wings outspread and toes in the air, belly exposed. It looked pathetic. "Do you know what I mean by bedside manner?"

Do you know what I mean by malingering?

Bird suddenly righted itself and surged out of the box, darting through the air in half a tick of the mantel clock. *At last! I never thought I'd get away from that sorcerer.*

"You're alive?"

Always good to state the obvious. Bird fluttered into her hand.

Pride and excitement exploded inside her as she felt its delicate claws curl around her fingers. "Are you all right?" she murmured, examining the bird all over. There was a slight scratch along one wing, but otherwise it looked unscathed.

Of course. I'm fast.

"No brass cats?"

It opened its beak and gave a disgusted chirp. That was interesting. She hadn't built in a voice box; that must have been something the deva figured out for itself. *Just the sorcerer. He nicked me out of the air right as I landed in the garden this afternoon.*

Evelina cursed under her breath. "The sorcerer? Do you mean Dr. Magnus?"

Bird spread its wings in a gesture that looked like unease. *He should never have been allowed in this house. The moment he had me I pretended to be dead. I told him nothing.*

"And yet he knew you were mine."

He caught the scent of your power. The metal I'm made of absorbed your magic. Any wood-witch worth their salt knows that much.

Evelina had been right. He'd felt her just as she'd felt him.

Bird chirped again. *He'd never learn it from me, anyway. I'm a professional. What's that mouse doing there?*

"Reinforcements."

The bird and the mouse stared at each other. Perhaps they were silently communicating, perhaps it was just a contest of wills. Evelina couldn't tell, but she suddenly wished Gran Cooper could see what she'd made with her magic.

Well, Ploughman's was in town. Involuntarily, her hand slipped into her pocket to feel the newspaper advertisement for the show. If she could sneak away, she could go see them all. But after she'd tried so hard to forge a new life, to give both her and Nick a chance at a fresh start, it would be the height of folly to return, even to visit. She'd made her choice, and circus girls were not presented to the queen . . . and yet it was a chapter she felt she had to reread before she could close the book on that part of her existence.

Bird broke into her thoughts. *You're going to have to watch yourself. Sorcerers are a bad lot. Their magic doesn't work with life. They work with death.*

Evelina sank back in the chair. "Is Dr. Magnus the murderer?"

Bird flew to the top of the box and poked its shining beak at a feather. *How should I know? You're the amateur detective.*

Mouse lashed its skinny tail. *You might have the gemstones, brother, but you lack manners.*

It's been a hard and dirty few days on the streets. Only the surly survive.

Mouse's whiskers bristled. Evelina intervened. "What did you find out?"

I followed your policeman. He spent a lot of time talking to the staff who work in the houses around here. They only had the usual things to say about the dead girl.

"Like what?"

Worked hard. Liked her bit of fun. There were a few men she walked out with, but lately seemed to favor a particular sweetheart.

The one who got her pregnant, no doubt. "Is that it?"

Your man went to see a lout he called the streetkeeper of the Yellowbacks, but he was in bed with a knife wound to the leg. He wasn't much good for talking.

"Why did Lestrade question him?"

It was to do with something else, but the girl's name came up. The Yellowbacks had been watching her come and go across their turf. It sounds like this sweetheart of hers convinced her to deal with some unpleasant people, but she would never reveal the man's name.

Was it love that had Grace running gold and jewels across London? Risking her freedom, if not her life, for a few kisses? Evelina was disappointed, and on many levels. "I'd hoped for more specifics."

So did Inspector Lestrade. You're lucky that you have me. I made one more stop. By then I was starting to get curious.

"Really?" Anticipation twinged in her chest.

Your policeman made much of the fact that she had just returned home from a journey the night she died.

Yes?

So I talked to the deva who lives in the hedge by the gate. He says he saw her with a man.

"Tobias."

That's right, but then the hedge deva said something else. They weren't the first couple outside the side door that night.

"I heard a man and a woman talking there earlier."

The hedge deva said the man and his shadow came here more than once.

"His shadow?" Evelina asked.

One doesn't get the best quality information from a shrub.

Just then Imogen put her head through the door, scattering Evelina's thoughts. "There you are. I thought I saw the inspector leave." She slid inside the room and closed the door behind her. She was still in the pale pink and green gown she'd worn in the garden. "All those questions! What a dreadful way to finish off a horrible day. Why couldn't that all have waited? Poor Mama! I had to put her to bed. This was all too much for her. A utilities failure? Anyone with an ounce of sense knows we've been Disconnected!"

Imogen's mouth quivered, but she swallowed hard and bit her lips together, refusing to cry. Evelina rose and took her friend in her arms. "Imogen, I'm so sorry this happened."

Imogen took in a long, shuddering breath. "It's not your fault. I don't know what we're going to do."

Evelina released her and made her sit down in the chair where Lestrade had been. "Your father is a clever man. He'll think of something." *And so will I.*

"It's one thing to have offended Mr. Keating, but with the detectives arriving on top of all that . . . What do you think it means, Lestrade arriving tonight of all nights?"

It meant nothing good, but she wasn't going to add to Imogen's woes. Evelina glanced at Mouse as she resumed her own seat. Mouse had jumped inside of the box and was sitting as still and stiff as Bird. "I think the police delayed questioning the family as long as they could. They started with the servants, but I don't believe they learned anything of value. Otherwise they would have arrested someone and spared us the ordeal."

As if conscious of being watched, Mouse twitched the end of its long, steel tail. It made a scraping sound against the bottom of the box.

Imogen leaned forward, peering at the side table where the box sat. "What have you got there? Oh, what clever, darling little devices! I need to see something wonderful right now."

Device? Bird grouched. *I'm more than just a lump of brass!*

"Do you like them?" Evelina replied airily. *Be quiet! She's not supposed to know you're alive!*

She did say darling and clever. I can forgive a lot for that.

"Of course I adore it." Imogen scooped the bird out of the box, then nearly dropped it as it fluttered its wings, trying to balance. "Good gracious, it moves! Did Tobias make it?"

The bird squawked derisively. Evelina did not reply, wondering why the devil the bird wasn't playing dead. Of course, it was a deva. Or perhaps diva. Neither were predictable.

"You made it, didn't you?" Imogen gave her a sly look and stroked the bird's shining head. It bobbed with pleasure, gems flashing in the candlelight. Then it gave a coo of adoration. Evelina watched as realization dawned on Imogen's beautiful face, freezing her expression. "This creature is full of magic."

Evelina's breath caught, her whole body suddenly a block of ice. She leaned forward so quickly she nearly launched from the chair. "Hush!"

Imogen stared at her. She dropped her voice to a murmur. "Mechanics and magic. Living machine! Do you realize what you've done? This is genius!"

Evelina looked away, only slowly finding the courage to meet her friend's gaze. She couldn't help thinking of Nellie Reynolds dragged into court for witchcraft. "You can't tell anyone. Promise me!"

Imogen was too excited to be serious. "Is this something your father's people know how to do?"

Evelina waved her hands in a negating motion. "Only some of it. Promise not to tell."

"Evelina—"

"Promise me!" Evelina gave in to her panic, grasping Imogen's wrist.

Imogen yelped at the force of her grip. "Yes, I promise. Of course I promise!"

Evelina leaned closer. "You saw what the Gold King did to Dora. What do you think he would do if he discovered I have a whole new means of making machines work? Have you heard about the actress they arrested?"

Imogen closed her eyes a moment, turning pale. "I promise. I've heard about Nellie Reynolds's trial."

I knew she would promise. This one is good. Bird bumped its head against Imogen's hand, like a cat begging to have its ears scratched. She stroked it, then squealed as Mouse ran up her leg so it, too, could beg for attention.

Imogen looked at Mouse with wide eyes. "This is your secret."

Evelina released her breath. "It is."

"I wouldn't ever share it, if I were you." Imogen's tone was serious as she touched Mouse's nose with her fingertip. "Some things are too wonderful to be safe in this world."

"You know me. I'm careful." Only once, faced with life and death, had Evelina given away her secret. During the worst of Imogen's illness at school, Evelina had felt her slipping away, and she'd spent hours coaxing Imogen's essence to stay with her body. She had won that battle, but even the memory of that horrible night made her hands tremble. That was how Imogen had a hint of what she could do, though they rarely spoke of it—at least until the dark of night, when Imogen had nightmares about her soul wandering away from her pale, cold body, or of being trapped in some dark, smothering place. Then all pretenses stopped.

Her friend's fingers stilled. "I knew you could do magic, but nothing like this."

"You were keeping too many of my secrets already. It didn't seem fair to burden you with another."

Imogen made a rude noise so loudly that the bird hopped to Evelina's hand. "I don't accept that. You'll have to make it up to me."

"Of course." Evelina hadn't felt guilty before, but now she did. "What can I do?"

Imogen closed her eyes, her soft fingers still cradling the sleek form of Mouse. "Someday I'm going to ask you for an enormous favor, and you'll have to say yes."

"Of course. But what sort of favor are you thinking of?"

Imogen gave a crooked smile. "Just as he was leaving tonight, Stanford Whitlock proposed. When Papa learns that I turned down an eligible young man, I shall have to pay the piper. I'll need a clever friend on my side."

"But it's Stanford Whitlock," Evelina said derisively. "Surely Lord Bancroft can't want him for a son-in-law."

"His father is in banking and has an indecent amount of money. Any father would drool like a starving dog at the prospect of that amount of wealth in the family."

"But you could hope for money and a functional intelligence in the same man. Surely your father is not driven onto the ropes that badly."

Imogen buried her face in her hands, letting Mouse run down into the silky nest of her skirts. "I don't know, Evelina. With Papa, I never know how much is threat or truth or simply his ambition at work. The only certainty is that if this whole business of being Disconnected goes on, I'll be lucky to marry the butcher's boy."

"Well, then you can rely on a steady supply of bacon." Outrage prickled under Evelina's skin. She had been hoping to spare Imogen distress, and so far her investigations had only revealed more questions.

Imogen looked up, her brow puckered. "Bacon?" Then she started to both laugh and cry, all the tension of the last dozen hours bubbling up at once.

Evelina folded her in her arms, biting her lip to keep from sobbing herself. With so much at stake, she couldn't let herself falter. Not for an instant.

CHAPTER EIGHTEEN

London, April 7, 1888

WEST END

11 p.m. Saturday

THE NEXT NIGHT AFTER HIS FIGHT WITH STRIKER, NICK scanned the throng near the Savoy Theatre, finding his mark. The playbill on the door proclaimed Gilbert and Sullivan's *Ruddigore,* and from the mood of the crowd swarming into the Strand, it had been a successful performance. The crush made it necessary to thread between other pedestrians coming and going from the restaurants and playhouses. Carriages clogged the road, the brass and gold of harness and crest glinting in the uncertain light. Fine evening clothes, so bright inside the opulent buildings of the district, were muted to shades of indigo and wine.

Ah, there he was. Nick had been following him for hours, having picked up his trail quite by accident on Oxford Street in the late afternoon. Dr. Magnus, of course, wore nothing but black from top hat to the shining toes of his dress shoes, a raven among the peacocks. He blended with the shadows, at times visible only because of the glint of his silver-headed cane. Unlike most of the evening revelers, he walked alone, his stride quick and purposeful where the others ambled and chatted.

Another look around, this time for Yellowbacks. There were plenty of street rats lurking about, but none that Nick recognized from his rooftop chase. Best of all, there was no sign of Striker—Nick's ankle was still sore and swollen and nowhere ready for a rematch. Of course, it could be the streetkeepers kept away from this no-man's-land southeast of the Strand. The area represented an uneasy truce between the Yellowbacks and the Blue Boys.

Nick detached himself from where he leaned against the brick wall and sauntered after Magnus, careful to keep at least two clumps of people between himself and his quarry. And careful not to limp. Showing weakness was the surest way to make himself a target.

Nick watched the tall man as he strode from gaslight to gaslight, swinging his cane in rhythm with his steps. There was something jaunty in his movements, as if he were reliving the closing song of a comedy—and yet Nick could never imagine Dr. Magnus enjoying such simple pleasures. Coupling the man with any innocent impulse was simply impossible.

Nick had met with Magnus the night after the incident with Striker, or rather Magnus had found him at the place where Ploughman's was performing. The doctor had been very interested to hear about Tobias Roth's workshop, and even more that the young man was going there in secret. Obviously, the information played nicely into whatever plan Magnus was brewing.

With his report delivered, Nick considered his obligation paid. He had agreed to provide information on Tobias Roth in return for Magnus's protection from the police, and that was done. Now he could satisfy his own curiosity. Who was Dr. Magnus and what was he up to? *Whatever it is isn't jolly clowns and toffee. There's something grim going on.*

As Magnus's long strides took him from one pool of gaslight to the next, the capes of his coat merged with the shadows as if he walked in his own aura of darkness. It was a trick of the eye, but there was something unnerving in the sight, as if any moment he might dissolve into a cloud of fluttering bats.

Magnus turned left down a street that was far less crowded. Nick started to trot to catch up, and then thought better of it when pain lanced up his injured leg. He caught his breath, hopping on one foot to catch his balance. To his surprise, Magnus stopped and turned.

"Are you coming, Mr. Niccolo?" the doctor said, making himself heard without seeming to raise his voice.

Heat surged to Nick's face. He was an expert sneak. How had the man known he was there? From a distance, he couldn't feel Magnus's aura of magic, but perhaps the doctor's senses were sharper? Nevertheless, he swaggered forward—not quite hiding a wince as he stepped on his throbbing ankle— as if this was exactly what he'd meant to happen.

"Good evening, sir." He swept an extravagant bow.

"I take it you wish to make another report?"

Nick cocked a smile to cover the panicked scramble in his mind. How could he explain himself? "I was wondering if you had any further need of me."

Of course, that was the opposite of the truth. He wanted to pin the man to a card and study him like a bug. He couldn't exactly say it, though.

"I'm sure you were." With a sardonic look, Magnus beckoned. "Then come. My lodgings are this way."

Nick hesitated, momentarily startled. He was going to get a look inside the doctor's home? If he wanted to know who the man was, this was an excellent beginning. But if he crossed that threshold, would he ever leave?

The question skittered down his spine, leaving his stomach cold. Did he dare to match wits with Magnus? Who knew what strengths the foreigner possessed, besides a lick of dark magic? *And a curiosity about the people Evie is with.*

That was no good.

A distant clock bonged the hour, and Magnus shifted impatiently.

Fortune, be my whore. Nick fell in beside him, wondering what steps there would be to this dance. Magnus said nothing, and Nick said less.

They went for some blocks, finally stopping in a small, elegant street of tall Georgian homes with wrought-iron fences and tiny front gardens. The redbrick facades were broken by narrow windows framed in white. The effect was at once understated and in impeccable taste. There was no sign to give the street name, but Magnus approached the town house marked 113.

"We'll keep this brief," Magnus said, unlocking the door. "I have had a long and complicated day."

"I am devastated to hear that, sir." Nick stepped into the house behind him. The place was silent, no manservant rushing to take his master's coat.

Magnus tossed his hat and cloak onto a velvet-covered bench by the door and placed his cane in a large china urn patterned with blue chrysanthemums. "Your cheek is uncalled for. Why were you really following me?"

Nick didn't answer right away. The foyer was not large, but it had a marble floor and gold-leaf scrollwork framing the door. He hadn't been inside a rich man's house before—not through the front door, anyhow—and the sight of so much wealth threw him back on his heels. It was one thing to know he was poor, quite another to feel the full force of everything he could never have. A bitter taste invaded his mouth, as if he had been chewing the ashes of his own dreams.

Anger robbed him of caution. "I'm curious to know what you want with Tobias Roth, sir. He may be clever, but he is little more than a pretty boy."

"And you are, no doubt, infinitely more clever and capable." Dr. Magnus turned a mocking sneer his way as he opened the door to the rest of the house. "Nick with no name and less education."

The barb stung, but Nick responded by strolling into the doctor's rooms as if he already owned something much finer. The trick wasn't to swagger, but simply to fill the space with his presence. No great feat for a showman.

He schooled his face as he looked around, observing the tooled green leather on the walls, the carpet so thick the toes of his boots disappeared as he walked. The center of the room was filled with a huge table, bow-legged and carved with zephyrs at every corner. It was piled high with books and contraptions Nick guessed were scientific in purpose.

His stomach roiled with an emotion he couldn't name.

Envy was part of it, but there was more. At least one other ingredient was rage so acute that bile burned in his throat. *What did he do to deserve this? How can one man ever hope to enjoy so many things?*

Magnus turned a device mounted on the wall, and a gigantic chandelier came to life overhead. Glass baubles rattled in the drafts of the high, high ceiling, but the light remained bright and steady. Now Nick could make out a balcony of sorts all the way around the room, where tall bookcases lined every inch of wall space.

Nick swallowed down his emotions for the sake of curiosity. "That doesn't look like gaslight."

"It's not. It is electrical incandescent light operated from a generator. Nothing here is gas or coal. I refuse to do business with the so-called steam barons."

"Were you Disconnected?"

"No. I never bothered to have the place hooked up to their utilities."

"For what reason?" Nick looked around uneasily, noticing the dusty odor in the place, the cobwebs clinging in the shadowed corners. Perhaps the man really did have no servants. But if he had only been in England a short time, where had this library come from?

"Let me answer that in a roundabout way. The Savoy is an interesting playhouse," Magnus said. "Apparently the original plan was to light it entirely with electricity. They'd got as far as hiring someone to build a generator."

"And?" Nick couldn't care less, but danger lurked at the edges of Magnus's words. No doubt he would care in a moment or two.

"D'Oyly Carte, the proprietor, is still using the Gold King's gas. Evidently there was a sudden change of direction after his electrical man was found dead. Bled to death after swallowing a dozen broken lightbulbs. The chap who designed the bulbs, some fellow named Swan, suffered a similar fate. There were a great many jokes about the Savoy being his swan song."

Nick swore under his breath. "Why does one playhouse matter so much to the steam barons?"

"The steam barons? No one accused them of a thing."

"Who else would do it?"

"Precisely. And if they let one establishment do what it liked, anyone who could get away would wriggle out from under their collective thumb. They are greedy masters, after all. One pays once for light and again for heat and thrice if you are so lucky as to receive electricity for your business— but woe betide the customer who tries to cut costs by converting the steam to electricity or the gas to a boiler without the express permission of the utility. They might miss an opportunity to collect their fee."

"What's your involvement, sir?" He asked the question boldly, not like a servant to his master but man to man. As usual, the only tool he had was his pride.

Magnus studied him, obviously weighing what he saw. "Me? I am but a humble doctor who practices the art of mesmerism. My involvement counts for nothing—and yet like every man, woman, and child of the world, my involvement is everything. There are plenty of theaters in Paris, New York, Florence, Vienna, and Saint Petersburg. There are also hospitals, universities, and racetracks. The entire world is watching what happens in the Empire with avid interest. Should Europe simply sit back and watch a mighty power bleed to death? Should they go to war? The question of when to intervene on Queen Victoria's behalf, and how much, is greatly debated."

"And if they don't step in?" Now Nick was actually curious. He rarely had occasion to think much beyond his own horizon, but this intrigued him.

"Someone will, eventually. I might say inevitably. But will it be too late? Your steam magnates already have tentacles in the German states. I would rather like to lop those tentacles off, and I might even be able to do it if I play my cards cleverly enough."

Since when did a mere mesmerist interfere in international affairs? Dr. Magnus was clearly more than he admitted to. "You care about what happens in Germany?"

The man laughed, showing white teeth. "Before you accuse

me of philanthropical leanings, let me say first the barons have something I want."

"What is that?"

"My own affair."

Magnus fell into a red velvet wing chair that framed his head like a peacock's fan. He waved Nick to a footstool. Instead, Nick leaned against the table and folded his arms. He wanted to stay light on his feet.

"So you will fight them?" he asked, watching Magnus's dark face. What would the steam barons have that this creature would want?

"I'm not a rebel in the accepted sense. I work alone. But I do plan to poke a stick in their wheels. You might say that right now I am looking for the best possible stick for the job."

Nick looked down at the stacks of books on the table. Most looked very old, the leather corners worn away to expose fraying cloth. The titles contained words he didn't know, or maybe they weren't even in English. "So, Dr. Magnus, do these ancient books say that Tobias Roth is a good stick?"

"He has an exceptional talent for mechanics, as well as the ideal family connections. His father, in particular, has access to Society. That is part of what I need. But I am also curious about Miss Cooper. I saw something of hers, an invention that quite took my breath away."

Nick froze inside, but he refused to let the least twitch cross his face. "She's barely out of school." Relieved, he heard his voice was even, not showing the alarm he felt at the thought of Evie in this dark stranger's crosshairs.

"She is the girl you climbed the wall of Hilliard House to see, is she not? Old enough for stolen kisses?"

Nick turned away from Magnus, pretending to examine one of the contraptions perched on the stacks of moldering tomes. This one looked suspiciously like a miniature still, but there was no way he would ever drink the greenish liquid in the tiny flask beneath the mile of tubing.

By the time he turned back, Nick had prepared his lie. "No, sir, I'm rather more interested in Tobias Roth's sister. The fair-haired girl."

Dr. Magnus gave a sly smile, as if he were playing along with the lie. "Ah, so the golden-haired beauty likes a bit of rough, does she?"

Nick shrugged. "She is pretty and has money."

"And who can fail to appreciate such straightforward charms?"

Nick wandered idly down the length of the table. He wanted to put distance between himself and Magnus before his worry for Evelina showed on his face.

Halfway down, a set of plans was unfurled from a clock-work scroll. He'd seen such scroll devices before. Lengths of specially prepared silk were used like paper and could be wound down to cases no larger than a pocketbook. He leaned closer to see what the plans were for.

He caught his breath. The design was a cutaway drawing of an airship so graceful Nick thought it might float off the page. The detail was so fine, he could almost imagine walking the deck. Looking away was almost physically painful.

Magnus kept talking, his chin resting in his hand. "I would like very much to know everything about Evelina Cooper. I want to know what she's capable of."

"In what way?" Nick struggled to keep his voice casual.

"Every way possible. I want to know every detail about the girl, no matter how trivial." The words came out not as a statement, but as a command.

Nick looked up sharply. "Why would I?"

The doctor's voice grew sly. "Shall I tell the fair-haired girl that you are secretly in love with Miss Cooper? It was Miss Cooper's window you climbed from that night, was it not?"

Nick didn't answer. He didn't know how Magnus knew that, or what invention of Evie's he had seen, or what he in-tended to do with the information he wanted Nick to find. All he knew was that the man was a threat.

Magnus lifted one brow. "Or perhaps I should simply tell the world that Miss Cooper entertains Gypsy showmen in her bedchamber."

Shame burned so hot that Nick flinched. His desire to see

Evie had trapped them both. "How would ruining her serve your purpose?"

"And how would it serve yours, I wonder? Would it bring her within your reach?" Magnus rose, tossing a handful of silver onto the table. "There is an advance on your wages, Nicholas No-Name. Are you going to play the cad or the truehearted knight?"

Nick stared at the silver as if it would burn him with its touch. His fingers curled, aching to grab one of those huge books and smash the doctor's sneering face. There was no choice here. He could spy on Evie and betray her to Magnus, or refuse his silver and ruin her future. *I could refuse. I could have her then.* But that was a lie. She would never thank him for sending her back to Ploughman's, and there was no hope of keeping it a secret. Sooner or later she would find out what Nick had done. They had never been able to hide the truth from one another.

He forced his hands to relax, joint by joint. There had to be a way to outwit Magnus. He couldn't afford pride. Not right then. He would plan, first. He was a hawk, and would carefully select his moment to strike. *You owe me one, Evie.* He scooped up the silver and made a show of counting it.

Magnus's lip curled in disdain as Nick fondled the coin. "There will be more if you bring me something I can use."

"For what?"

"That is not your concern. You wouldn't understand even if I took the time to explain."

It was one insult too much. For a second, Nick's vision went white with fury, and his fingers clenched around the coins, trembling with the urge to throw them in Magnus's face. Evelina might not want him in the way that he had hoped, but she was his—friend, sweetheart, the closest thing he had to a sister. And no refusal of hers could stop him loving her in every way a man might love a woman. Nick might have had little more than the clothes he stood in, but he had loyalty.

If Nick had entertained any ideas about walking away from Evie, they were gone. She still needed him. He forced his face into a nonchalant mask. "Whatever you say, sir."

"See what you can have to me in the next few days. There is a dinner party at Lord Bancroft's that I shall be attending. I would like to go equipped with as much information as possible."

Nick gave a mocking little bow. "Very good, sir."

"Now get out of my house."

Nick glanced around, memorizing everything he could, before sauntering for the door. Magnus did not realize it, but he had just declared war.

CHAPTER NINETEEN

London, April 8, 1888
WEST END

10 p.m. Sunday

BANCROFT LEFT HIS USUAL CLUB—THE APOLLONIUS NEAR Grosvenor—at his usual time and strolled into the clammy spring night. As always, the warmth and comfort of the smoking room clung for half a block, dissipating slowly under the plucking fingers of the breeze. The only difference between this night and any other was that instead of turning left to go to the theater—the excuse Bancroft gave for dismissing his carriage—he turned right and went to find out what Harriman wanted.

For once, he had waved away the offer of liquid refreshment. He wanted a clear head to aim the Enfield revolver that sat comfortably beneath his coat. Tension sparked in his blood, both exhilarating and frightening. There was something about the prospect of danger that took a decade off a man's age.

Bancroft's thoughts paused as a scatter of raindrops drummed on his hat. He opened his umbrella, angling it against the breeze. Showers had come and gone all day, the pavement barely drying before the sky grew dark again. Now the rain flashed across the golden globes of the Keating Utilities gaslights—bright needles that disappeared into the dark. The air had that heavy feel that promised fog before the night grew much older. Bancroft quickened his step.

If tonight's trip was to retrieve his last share of the gold, this was likely to be his only visit to Harriman's lair. That meant he had to absorb every detail, catalogue every nuance of the operation he saw. Harriman, despite the boldness he showed by participating in this scheme, lacked experience. And Bancroft knew from his own past mistakes one didn't end an enterprise like this with a toast and a fare-thee-well. There were always an astonishing number of details to tidy up, beginning with the servants who knew—literally or figuratively—where the bodies were buried.

Grace would have been just such a loose end. He tried to imagine her face, but all he could remember was her body when he'd taken her in his private dressing room, her white limbs draped languidly across the red velvet of the chair. Her hair had smelled of Cook's baking bread, and for a week afterward his dinner rolls had carried an erotic thrill.

Bancroft turned a corner, hiding his face with his umbrella as he passed a crowd of young officers. Here and there dark shapes lurked in doorways and voices called softly from upstairs windows, enticing him to linger awhile. Bancroft walked on, doing his best to appear a busy man with things to do when he really wanted to stop and forget the cold and rain and memories. There was no room for weakness now.

Does my situation make me so vulnerable that I must do what Harriman says? Before he even finished the thought, he knew he wouldn't like the answer. *Yes.* The twin devils of Need and Greed made him hungry enough to risk all for success. His family, his career, and his private plans demanded it. Without those, there was no Bancroft—and he wanted that name to mean something. Talk was flying about a coup against the steam barons, a plot that went all the way to the throne and that was organized under the code name of Baskerville. A shadow government was being hand selected, and a place at that table was everything that he had been scheming for. He wanted in, and that would never happen if he were perceived as vulnerable.

And God knew, he needed to make a move if he was going to survive Keating's wrath. The steam baron had hit him hard by cutting him off from the network of pipes and valves that ran like life-giving veins beneath the London streets. No steam or gas meant cold and darkness—and, more important, invisibility.

So far Keating's official fiction about a faulty gas line had held, half disguising the truth like a sheet covering a corpse. Everyone knew Bancroft was on notice, but so far the clubs were still open to him, and the merchants who sold meat and vegetables still delivered to his kitchen on time. At a word from Keating, though, the period of grace would end, and he would be finished. Without the ubiquitous blaze of light around Hilliard House, he was marked as beyond the pale, no better than the beggars hiding in the alleys—and his dreams of a political career would be utterly obliterated.

He had to fight back—against Keating, against the barons, against everything that stood between him and his future—and if that meant playing Harriman's games tonight, so be it. And there wasn't much he wouldn't do to achieve his ends. As an ambassador, Bancroft had sat down to dinner with men who had slaughtered villages for sport and bartered their virgin daughters for a strip of barren land. He had always been willing to face the unthinkable if that meant getting the right result.

Bancroft stopped, having reached the end of the civilized portion of his journey. *And I am about to enter the underworld.* The mouth of the alley was a narrow crevasse between two buildings off Bond Street—one the first in a row of shops, the other the offices of an insurance broker. Behind the respectable facades was a seemingly uneventful string of small warehouses and other utilitarian structures. Those needing access could enter by a large gate kept locked at night by a watchman, or this small gap between the buildings.

Bancroft folded his umbrella, which was too wide to fit through the entrance. Then he felt for the hilt of his gun, listening to the street noise and trying to pick out stealthy footfalls or the whisper of drawn blades. After another heartbeat of procrastination, he angled sideways and slid between the buildings, careful not to brush against the sooty bricks.

After a dozen steps, the alley widened until it was almost a small street on its own. Unlike most of London, it was eerily empty. And it was very dark. Confident that he was out of sight of the main road now, he pulled a brass tube from his coat pocket and twisted it, then waited as chemicals mixed and a faint green glow began to radiate from the glass window in the side of the tube. When it was bright enough to see, he began walking again, scanning every shadow and niche. He could hear distant hammering, a man and a woman hurling heated words, and far away, someone squeezing out a sad tune on a concertina. But those noises were distant. In the alley itself, his only company was the sound of his own feet. *Grace walked here, along these very same cobbles.* The thought unnerved him more than he cared to admit. *Was she frightened?*

The warehouse he wanted was on the right. The front was guarded by a large automaton—he could just make out the hulking shadow—so his instructions were to circle the warehouse and knock on the rear window. He rounded the corner, picking his way carefully through weeds and refuse, and then rapped on the dirty glass with the ebony handle of his umbrella.

A smear of light flared, as if someone had moved a light closer to the glass. For a brief instant, he saw the pale outline of a face, and then it disappeared again. In another moment, a lock rattled and a narrow door opened a few feet away.

"You're punctual," said Harriman as Bancroft entered. The man had stripped off his jacket and rolled up the fine white sleeves of his shirt. The silver buttons of his waistcoat glinted in the wavering light of the old oil lamp he held.

"I see no point in delay." Bancroft looked around. A mop and bucket leaned against the wall close to where they stood. The rest of the warehouse was a cavernous jumble of packing crates, a few workbenches, and inky shadows. His gaze traveled back to the bucket. "I smell blood."

"I was just cleaning it up," Harriman said with a shrug, hooking the lamp over a nail in the raw planks of the wall. "Unfortunately, the wood is old and thirsty and the stain is impossible to get out of the grain. I'll scatter some sawdust from the crates to hide it."

An uneasy tingle crept up Bancroft's spine, making him scan the warehouse a second time. Suddenly, everything looked a good deal more sinister, especially Harriman. "Whose blood is that?"

"Big Han was taking care of some details. I told him to keep it in the underground, but he let things get messy." Harriman picked up a rag and wiped his hands. "Then I was left with the unfortunate task of mopping up."

Big Han was the mountainous foreman Harriman had hired to look after the craftsmen who did the actual work. Bancroft had met him but once, and that was enough to last a lifetime.

"Is *details* your word for loose ends?" Bancroft asked. Perhaps he had underestimated Keating's weakling cousin.

"Loose ends," Harriman laughed uneasily. "If you like. We couldn't risk them talking. I debated, you know, wondering how far I really had to go. There aren't that many Chinamen in London to speak up if one of their own went missing. Still fewer officials who would care if they did. That's why we used them."

Used. Not *are using.* Bancroft didn't need a slide rule to figure out which way Harriman's decision had gone. The twelve workers had died. It wasn't just Grace anymore, but thirteen souls who had perished to buy his gold. A wash of dizzy nausea swamped Bancroft, but he let it pass through him. He'd had years of practice at this sort of thing. "All the workers were unknowns? There won't be family pounding on the door?"

"No. The Chinese here are a transient group. Sailors— here one day and gone the next. Many of these were fresh off the boat. No one to recognize their handiwork, even if there was something in the replica pieces to recognize."

"But surely master goldsmiths cannot be that common amid a population of sailors?"

"I'm not sure how Big Han found them. He has contacts that stretch back to Canton. But in any event, we only had two masters. The rest were 'prentices and laborers plucked off the ships."

Bancroft's mind raced, looking for weaknesses in the plan. "All the workers are gone? All twelve?"

"As Han put it, he fed them to Mother Tyburn tonight. In pieces." Harriman threw the rag onto a pile of debris stacked against the wall. "Come. I will show you."

"Is this something I really need to see?" Bancroft asked warily.

"If you want your gold," Harriman answered. "If I had to mop up blood all night, the least you can do is take a look at the pit I've been suffering with for all these months."

Bancroft bristled. Harriman had been the workhorse while he had been the instigator of the plan. That had been the deal, and the man had no grounds for resentment. But all too often, that wasn't how things worked—especially now that Bancroft was having difficulties with Harriman's powerful cousin. It was far more expedient to appease Harriman than to try to put him in his place, so Bancroft made himself nod. "If you wish."

Harriman gave a derisive laugh. "Good of you, Your Lordship."

He kicked aside a pile of sawdust, exposing an iron ring in the floor at least three hand spans across. It clattered as he gripped it and then, with a grunt, he heaved a trapdoor open. There was a light on below, because a faint yellow wash illuminated a crude flight of wooden steps. Bancroft caught a dank waft of sewer stench. *It stinks as badly as the rest of this.*

Harriman watched him closely. "You have no taste for what lies below the surface?"

"Are you trying to be metaphorical, Harriman?" Bancroft growled. "Leave it to poets."

The man had the gall to smirk. "I'll go first."

Harriman's footsteps echoed on the stairs. Bancroft followed, one hand on his pistol, the other holding a handkerchief to his nose against the acrid smell. "Does this lead right to the banks of an underground sewer?"

"Not quite. That's some ways off."

"I hear water."

Harriman reached the bottom and turned. "We're near the Tyburn down here, or that's what the locals say."

Now Bancroft could see the basement clearly. It seemed to wander far beyond the confines of the warehouse—less part of the warehouse than a cavern under the street. There were proper walls on two sides of the space, but ahead of the stairs and to the right, the space seemed to wander on forever. It looked as if the street might have been raised at some point, covering over older levels, or perhaps man had simply added to nature's plan for underground caves. The ceiling was rough stone, higher in some places than others. "I had no idea this was down here."

"London is full of surprises."

And some of them are nasty. Bancroft reached the bottom of the stairs and froze. Now he could see what Harriman had referred to as the pit. It occupied the space directly under the warehouse. Here the ceiling was high, showing the wooden supports of the building above, and lighting was in place. Gas lines ran along the wall and supplied a small generator. A series of workbenches made a loose square. A forge, equipment for electroplating, a kiln, and a plethora of other tools neatly lined the work area and hung from the rafters above. Had it been upstairs in bright sunlight, it was the sort of workshop Bancroft might have used himself in long-ago days. But that was not what caught his attention. It was the row of cages that ran along two sides of the room. They were the source of the stink—the combined odors of unwashed humanity, airless quarters, night soil, and despair.

Wordlessly, Bancroft walked toward them. On some level, he knew Harriman—or rather, Han Zuiweng—had kept the workers secure lest they run away or tell someone they had been forced into an outrageous forgery scheme. He just hadn't let his imagination conjure what keeping them secure might mean. *Caged. Forced to slavery. Killed. Welcome to the Empire.*

A coldness took root in Bancroft's belly, spreading like frost through every vein. Despite his years of supping with villains, he shuddered. Then he hated himself for the weakness. "Is this what you wanted me to see?"

"There is one final detail." Harriman crossed the floor to stand beside him. "We have taken care of the workers, but there is still Han."

Bancroft remembered the conversation they'd had at Hilliard House. *I wondered why you insisted that I come in person, and now I'm about to find out.* "What do you want me to do?"

"Han is more dangerous than the rest put together."

"So kill him." But Bancroft knew that was more easily said than done. Big Han, Han Zuiweng, Drunken Han, Han the Devil—whatever one called him—was a huge creature who stood a head taller than Bancroft and was at least twice his weight in solid muscle.

Harriman paled. "If you help me, I'll make good what was stolen from your girl. I'll share my cut of the gold."

Despite himself, Bancroft's pulse skipped. He stood a bit straighter, but was careful to keep any emotion out of his voice. Harriman was the underling, the one who should be taking orders instead of giving them—but this was clearly the kind of detail he couldn't manage. If Bancroft wanted Han silenced, he would have to get his hands dirty. "Do you have a plan?"

Harriman gave a reptilian smile, but it faded quickly. Sweat dewed his temples. "Yes. I drugged his wine. It made him compliant enough that I could lead him into a cage before he passed out. But he's been sleeping for hours, and I don't think the drug will last much longer."

He waved a hand toward the last cage in the row. It was deep in shadow, but when Bancroft squinted he could just make out a shape slumped against the rough stone wall. "What do you want me to do? Shoot him?"

Harriman made a helpless gesture. "Someone has to. Hiring another killer to take care of it would merely complicate matters."

"Why not you? You could have done it the moment he fell asleep."

Harriman's helplessness turned to steel. "I've done enough."

"And if I do the shooting, then I'm implicated further. Another reason my silence is guaranteed and you are protected." Bancroft nearly laughed. "Oh, don't look so abashed. These moves are as predictable as a cotillion. I've been at this far longer than you. And none of this is more than my word against yours if you don't have witnesses."

Harriman's eyes flickered. "Well, I wonder if you *predicted* that I put your share of the final payment of gold in the cell with Han. If you want it, you need to deal with him. I told you to bring a pistol tonight. I hope you did."

A spike of fury blanked Bancroft's vision for an instant— an anger so acute that he sucked in a hiss of breath. Bancroft considered shooting Harriman instead, and gold be damned. Unfortunately, he didn't want Keating to get curious when his cousin turned up missing. "You have no idea who you're playing with."

"Oh, I do. And I'm taking no chances, milord." Harriman's voice was icy. "And you're quite correct. I shall make sure that you keep your part of our bargain."

Bancroft stopped before the cage. The bars were old, rusted iron woven in an ornate pattern that made him think of an antique menagerie. But what he'd thought was a sleeping man was just a pile of old clothes. "Harriman, what is this?"

The man had gone pale as a mushroom. "Dear God, he's loose." He grabbed the cage door and swung it open. "He broke the lock clean off."

Bancroft swore under his breath. "Suggestions?"

The shadows seemed suddenly thicker, as if they were congealing into smoke. Harriman wheeled around, as if trying to look in every direction at once. "Bancroft, listen to me. Han has a pet."

"A pet?"

"A creature to call. It guards this place, but somehow he controls it."

Bancroft was growing irritated. The cavern seemed to be growing darker. "A dog?"

"No, it's a thing. A foreign thing. He spelled it into the warehouse to keep out thieves."

"You're making no sense," Bancroft snapped.

"Harriman," a voice growled behind them. "You broke honor."

They spun, and there was Big Han. He had moved as silently as the shadows that wreathed him. His only garment was loose-fitting trousers, leaving his massive chest bare. Heavy leather bracelets studded with brass clasped his wrists. He was bald as a rock, but thick black mustaches drooped past his chin. His eyes were dark and cold as a December night. Bancroft had no trouble believing Han had torn a dozen men to pieces and tossed them into the Stygian waters of the hidden river. *I should never have let Harriman handle the hiring.*

Everyone froze, as if unwilling to see what would happen the moment after the tableau dissolved. Tension screamed up Bancroft's neck. He longed to reach for the Enfield, but he forced himself to wait. Timing was all.

The darkness began to crackle, as if something burned. All around them, the smoke roiled, starting to solidify, and it became clear what Harriman had meant about Han's pet—it was some sort of conjured beast. A clawed foot raked the air, a hairbreadth from Bancroft's head. Bancroft swore, barely getting out a single pungent syllable before terror clogged his throat. Violence and blood he could bear, but not sorcery. Every man had a private fear, and magic was his. He felt himself begin to shake.

Without warning, Harriman shoved Bancroft toward Han and bolted for the stairs. Bancroft stumbled, losing his hat and falling to one knee with a painful crack against the stone. Han lunged for Harriman, catching the man's shoulder in one huge hand. Harriman spun, limbs flailing like a doll tossed by a child.

Harriman dangled in the air as Han stomped a foot into Bancroft's face. Bancroft toppled backward, trying to draw the pistol but flopping helplessly from another brutal kick before he could reach it. Harriman landed in a heap beside him, his lungs emptying in a wheeze.

Han made a growl like a Rottweiler. The congealing smoke twined up his legs, a slow, sensual caress. The huge man stepped forward, as graceful as he was massive, and reached for Bancroft. An image of the bloodstained floor upstairs flashed through Bancroft's brain.

Bancroft groped for the Enfield, slapped and fumbled for the butt beneath his coat, got tangled in his watch chain, and finally discovered it under his hip. He rolled as Han's paw clutched the back of his coat, pinning him for a second, but Bancroft kicked out, twisting hard enough to rip the seams that held the fabric together. The motion brought him directly under the man's ugly face. Bancroft drew the Enfield, cocked it, and fired. The sound blared against the stone walls, echoing as if a dozen charges fired. A small, round hole appeared on Han's forehead. Brains and skull spewed into the air behind him. Bancroft squirmed out of the way just in time to avoid the crushing fall of Han's body.

Something screamed, long and fierce. Bancroft staggered to his feet with a grunt, feeling every bone and muscle in searing detail. He clutched his weapon and swept the muzzle in an arc, aiming toward one corner, then another, but the shadows were fading, seeping back into the stone and fetid air. He realized he was breathing too fast, and forced himself to slow. He was shivering, his gut cramping with fear, but the crisis was past. *I lived.*

A quick look down told him Han wouldn't be getting up again—not without the back of his head. For good or ill, Harriman would fight another day. After pawing the ground a moment, the man hauled himself to his knees with a moan. "Is it over?"

"Yes."

"That was fast."

Bancroft grimaced as he felt his shoulder protest. He picked up his hat, which had rolled into a puddle of shadow. "It doesn't take long to die from a bullet to the face. Your detail is taken care of, it seems."

Harriman didn't answer at once, but licked his lips. "The shadow beast will be back. Han set it to guard the warehouse."

"Han is dead."

"But it is not. It will still guard what it believes belonged to its master."

Bancroft's skin crawled and he took an involuntary step back from Harriman. "You're a fool to dabble in magic. Sooner or later, it turns on you."

Harriman let his head drop forward. "How is that different from the rest of our existence?"

Bancroft snorted. "Courage, man. So far you have made everyone else do your murdering for you. That's a sign of talent even your cousin could be proud of."

Harriman straightened, annoyance on his face. Then he took one look at the ruin of Han Zuiweng and heaved out his guts. Determined not to leave without the gold, Bancroft left him to it and set about searching the broken cell. He turned everything over, using his boot to topple the heap of stinking rags and cursing as fleas jumped in every direction. By the time he emerged empty-handed, Harriman was upright and bracing himself against the wall.

"Where is my gold?" he demanded.

"If it's not there, Han took it. If he took it, he put it with the rest of his things." Harriman's voice was weary.

"And where are they?"

The man turned to look at the endless shadows that stretched under the streets. "He was a secretive bastard. He kept his lair somewhere out there, which means it's as good as lost. There are miles of tunnels, and very few of them are empty, if you take my meaning."

Fury burned like acid. Bancroft launched himself at Harriman, smashing his fist into the man's jaw. Harriman reeled, the back of his head smacking the wall. He slid down until he sat on the floor, knees crooked awkwardly before him.

Pain shot up Bancroft's arm, sharp as a sword, but it cleared his head. He pulled the Enfield, pressing it to Harriman's forehead. "Tell me why I shouldn't kill you."

The man shook. "I'll pay you everything. I swear."

"How? You've killed all your workmen."

Tears flooded Harriman's eyes, snot glistening on his

upper lip. "But Jasper doesn't know. I've fooled him once. I can do it again."

"You've seen what I can do if you fail me. I need money. I need it fast."

Harriman nodded frantically.

Bancroft weighed his decision. He'd killed one man already tonight, and he had no taste for killing another—but that was the least of his considerations. Letting Harriman go was a risk. The man was weak and treacherous. But if he killed him now, there would be no chance of recouping one shilling of his loss. And there was some appeal to having a pet viper so close to the Gold King. *I'm so far on the edge now, what is one more throw of the dice?*

Bancroft put the gun away. "I'm leaving."

Perhaps it was the look on his face, but this time Harriman didn't argue.

BANCROFT LEFT THE way he had come, turning back onto Bond Street and toward home. The rain had stopped, but mist was creeping between the buildings, reminding him uncomfortably of the shadow beast. As he had left, Harriman had been weeping at the prospect of cutting up the body and dragging it to the underground river, but Bancroft had been unmoved. If Harriman was going to cheat his cousin, he was going to have to develop a backbone. That was the way of secret wars. Every player had to learn the lesson of consequences, and tonight was Harriman's turn.

As Bancroft walked, he fingered the empty space in his pocket. There should have been gold there. Some would have gone to repairing his personal fortunes, but most had been earmarked for his private projects—the many irons in the fire he had organized and funded in hopes of crushing Jasper Keating and the other steam barons. The schemes that would buy him a place in the shadow government. Someday Lord Bancroft would rise, stepping on the rubble of their industrial juggernauts to accept the wealth and titles due to a savior of the Empire. Counselor to the queen, perhaps. Prime minister?

Bancroft allowed himself a dry smile, amused by his own fantasies—but no one ever made great strides by dreaming modestly. He had been born a second son—heir to nothing—and had dreamed his way into a title and lands. He had married the daughter of an earl. Was there a reason he shouldn't be victor in the struggle against a handful of shopkeepers-turned-thugs?

The only constraint was that his fight had to be invisible—and there was his own lesson in consequences. He had been too public with the Harter's affair, and now his whole family was paying the price, with the lights off and their future hanging by a thread. Adele and the children were right at the core of his tangled motivations, and he knew with bitter certainty that he had let them down with that mistake. Bancroft had to fix matters and see that they stayed fixed—and, among other considerations, that meant ensuring that Evelina Cooper and her detective uncle kept out of his affairs.

Bancroft's path took him south. Ahead, he saw a crush of carriages that meant someone—Lord Hansby, by the address—was having a party. Bancroft crossed the street to avoid meeting the throng crowding the sidewalk, and took a quick glance over his person to check for unwanted pieces of Big Han. He was rumpled, but relatively clean. There was nothing he could do about the rip in his shoulder seam, though, or the fact that every joint throbbed from the struggle.

His attention was caught by a figure waiting in the golden glow of a light standard just ahead. *Keating. Speak of the devil and he shall come.* Keating's head turned and he straightened. It was clear the man had seen him, so Bancroft approached. There was no point in hiding.

Keating was wrapped in a cape of soft black wool. His eyes, always a peculiar shade of amber, looked yellow in the gaslight. They slid over him in a quick, dismissive glance, as if he was hardly worth looking at. "Enjoying the night air, Bancroft?"

Bancroft forced a smile to his lips, thinking again about

his empty pocket. "Just out for a stroll after a quiet evening at the club."

"Too dark and cold at home, eh?" Keating tilted his head, his expression saying that he only half listened to Bancroft's words. "I trust I've made my point. I don't like seeing you out in the cold, but it had to be done. There's only one way the wind blows anymore, and that's where I send it."

Bancroft swallowed down a quip about poor digestion. Instead, he regarded Keating with studied calm, even though his heart was pounding with nervous excitement. Apparently the moment for polite fiction had ended, and Keating was prepared to speak openly about what he'd done. That was a bit nerve-racking, but if the Gold King was utterly done with him, he wouldn't be starting up a conversation. Bancroft hated himself for feeling a twinge of hope, but he had to survive.

He forced his voice to be bland and pleasant. "Are you looking for a show of defiance or submission, sir?"

"That's your choice. I'll give you a second chance, but never a third."

The gall of it was breathtaking, and Bancroft found himself momentarily robbed of words. The noise of a passing steam tram covered his lapse long enough to recover. "What does a second chance entail, Mr. Keating?"

Keating made an expansive gesture, clearly enjoying the moment. "I'll forgive your boy his outrage over the affair at your garden party, but bring him in line, Bancroft. He does you no credit."

Bancroft bristled. It was one thing to wish he could still smack his son's backside at times, but no one else had that privilege. Still, he felt Keating's eyes on him and held his peace.

The Gold King flicked a speck from his cape. "And I'll overlook your bad judgment with Harter's Engines. The lights at Hilliard House go back on this one time, but it stops there. We're friends, or you're finished. Am I clear?"

"As crystal." *He's right. As long as I have no money, he has power over me.*

Bancroft had hoped to leave Harriman's workshop with

more gold tonight, but his luck had run out. Big Han had stowed it somewhere in the maze of underground tunnels that made up the territory of the Black Kingdom. Bancroft could search for it, but it was a poor gamble that he would come out alive.

That left Keating in control. Anything more Bancroft could do—at least until he had a new fortune to pour into his plans and projects—would be no better than a suicide. And Keating was no fool. He would watch Bancroft like the proverbial hawk and ensure he never got his hands on fresh resources.

The realization crept through his veins like venom, the agony of it so acute that his breath hissed through his teeth. He was trapped as surely as if he were locked in Harriman's underground cages. He had fought so hard and so long for his career, and this money-grubbing boilermaker had taken everything. *It's not possible. Surely I have cards left to play.*

But he didn't. Not right now, at any rate.

Keating smiled affably, but it didn't reach his eyes. "I think we understand each other perfectly, Lord Bancroft. Ah, here comes my carriage at last."

Bancroft watched the steam baron climb into the vehicle, noting the arrogant set of Keating's shoulders. Clearly, the man thought he owned the Empire. If he could get rid of the other barons, he would be right. The driver snapped his whip and the carriage drove away.

Bancroft watched it go, waves of fury pounding through his body until he went numb. Sickness welled up, driven by pure hate. He turned and heaved his guts into the gutter.

Gods above, thought Bancroft, saliva dangling from his lips. *I need a drink.*

CHAPTER TWENTY

London, April 9, 1888
WEST END

1 p.m. Monday

IMOGEN AND EVELINA LEANED BACK IN THE VICTORIA, THE picture of idle elegance in perfectly turned-out day dresses and brand-new hats. It was a time to be admired. The low vehicle was just large enough for the two young women to sit side-by-side, with the driver perched on his raised box in front and managing a pair of grays.

The calash top was down. They might as well enjoy the fine weather; the fashionable West End streets were jammed with shoppers. The driver had been forced to slow their vehicle to a crawl.

"How long do you think it will be before someone invents an inflatable bustle?" Imogen asked, her tone filled with ennui.

"Excuse me?" Evelina replied, her mind snapping to the here and now with an almost audible twang. She'd been inwardly cursing the fact that a young lady's life, with dress fittings, at-homes, the garden party, and then church yesterday—not to mention the time lost to dealing with the blackout at Hilliard House—left little room for discreetly hunting down leads. It had taken the most determined effort to wrestle free an afternoon to follow up the clue of Grace's silk bag. *Never mind the automatons and Dr. Magnus and all the rest of it. Thank Heaven Lord B hasn't learned about The Stare's proposal to Imogen.* At least they hadn't had to deal with that crisis.

It was becoming rapidly clear that proper detective work meant organizing one's schedule. Uncle Sherlock hardly slept or ate while working a case, and now she knew why. Daily life took up too much time. If she was going to be an effective investigator, she was going to have to do a much better job of managing her routine—though she doubted she could give up meals.

At least Lord Bancroft—who looked and moved like he'd fallen down the stairs this morning—had made his peace with the Gold King and the utilities had been reconnected overnight, which meant the glorious luxury of a truly hot bath. Although she had lived for years without such indulgences, Evelina had to admit she had grown very fond of them.

"I was just thinking how convenient dirigible underthings would be. One could self-inflate with hydrogen and sail over this bothersome traffic." Imogen winked. "I can think of a hundred uses for your scientific skills, you know."

Evelina imagined flocks of well-dressed women dangling from their posteriors, then wished she hadn't. "Steering could be a problem."

"Propellers?"

"Wouldn't they make one look fat?"

"You have a point there." Imogen leaned forward, peering out at the street. "I believe the shop we want is over here on the right. Applegate, you may let us out anywhere along here."

The driver, an older man with a comfortable girth, brought the pair of grays to a stop and then handed the ladies out of the victoria.

"Wait for us here," said Imogen. "We shan't be long."

"Certainly, miss. Take your time." He smiled fondly. Imogen had all the manservants wrapped around her little finger.

"It's not always easy to choose just one pair of gloves," she replied. "Or hat. Or parasol."

"Never mind me, I've brought my pipe. I can wait as long as you need."

Imogen gave Applegate her sweetest smile, then led

Evelina toward a little shop with steps painted in the Gold King's bright yellow. Almost every shop along the street had yellow somewhere on its front, showing its allegiance to the steam baron. Of course, that also meant that a percentage of every sale went into Jasper Keating's pocket, and in the wealthy West End, that meant thousands or maybe millions of pounds a year. Evelina couldn't begin to guess.

She took in every detail. The district fascinated her, from the theater to the gentlemen's clubs to the so-called universal providers—one could buy everything from boots to biscuits there—to what were supposedly the most fashionable whorehouses in London. Not that she was supposed to notice those.

The streets were crammed with women from respectable and wealthy classes, including many that looked like they'd escaped the protected suburban family enclave and taken the train into London for a day of shopping. Wide-eyed and open-mouthed, they ran from merchant to merchant in a positive orgy of acquisition.

That only put Evelina's senses on alert. With so many easy targets on the loose, there were undoubtedly expert pickpockets in the crowd. She glanced warily at the shadows between buildings and in the corners behind waiting cabs and a pie-man's stall. There were urchins aplenty, and there were older toughs. One boldly caught her eye and winked, as if he knew exactly what she was thinking.

Evelina stuck close to Imogen's side. Her friend, of course, hadn't noticed the street life. The rich never did.

A bell chimed as they entered Markham's Drapery. Behind the polished oak counter, cubbyholes were stuffed with bolts of every imaginable fabric and spools of trim. Cheval glasses stood to the right and left of the desk, allowing the customers to hold up the silks and calicos and imagine them made into a dress.

Imogen began working her magic the moment she parted her lips. "Mr. Markham, I know you have the most complete selection of fine Eastern silks. I've known that ever since my mama brought me here when we first returned to London."

She gave him the full benefit of her charming smile. The

stout shopkeeper flushed with pleasure right to the crown of his balding head.

"Well of course, Miss Roth, and it is a pleasure as always to serve your family. And you, too, Miss Cooper. It has always been an honor to have the Quality as my customers. In this day and age when people travel willy-nilly on the railways, it's not a given anymore that a merchant will know his clients and his clients will know him."

"Indeed not, sir," Imogen replied with a slight widening of her eyes. "I've never seen such a crush on the street as there is this afternoon."

"It's sheer mayhem," Evelina put in, playing the role of chorus. "I imagine it's been ever so much busier since Keating Rail has put half-price fares on for special shopping days."

He puffed out his cheeks. "That it has, with special trips straight from the countryside to the local station twice a week. Mr. Keating promised to increase local trade if we agreed to show his colors hereabouts, and he's kept his word. Can't say that he hasn't."

Which meant that the Gold King not only solidified his hold on the wealthiest shopping district in London, but also tithed the merchants on the increased sales and collected the extra rail fares. Evelina remembered Old Ploughman's maxim never to do a piece of business unless it earned money three ways. Jasper Keating could have a future in circus management if his plans for dominating the Empire's economy fell through.

"These new days are busier to be sure, although there are times I miss the old, slow way of doing business with families I know," Markham admitted. "What with these special trains and the department stores drawing in all manner of people with their advertising and their cut-rate prices, there's no telling who might wander through my door."

Or which ladies have husbands with good credit, Evelina thought dryly. Some stores only accepted cash these days, a departure from the times when it was normal to run an account and settle up only a few times a year.

"Nothing's the same as it once was," he said. "Except our

fine merchandise, of course. Markham's has never compromised on excellence."

"Or selection, I'm sure," Imogen replied, sounding a little relieved to be returning to familiar ground. "I'm looking for a very particular pattern, and I'm sure you will have it."

She began to describe the fabric from the bag of treasure Grace Child had been carrying. They had agreed not to show it to Markham, just in case. It was one thing to turn up asking for a particular fabric, another to wave evidence of crime under his nose. They had no idea how deeply the shopkeeper might be involved.

While Imogen rattled on, Evelina examined the draper's shop in more detail. She wished she'd been able to bring Mouse and Bird to help her look, but she'd rewarded them both with the promised wine and honey. On slurping down the sticky mixture—which seemed to disappear without actually reappearing inside their clockwork stomachs—the devas had fallen into a contented sleep so deep that Evelina had no idea when they'd rouse themselves. She'd had to pack them away in the bottom of her drawer beneath a pile of underthings, because it turned out the idiot creatures snored.

So Evelina had to do her own investigating. She let Imogen carry on her conversation and began a slow circuit around the room, affecting the air of a bored young lady too polite to tell her friend to hurry up. The public area was tiny, every inch of wall covered with shelves, and every shelf filled with bolts and boxes. In one dark corner, there was a clockwork machine for sale for tightening the laces of one's stays—the very idea made Evelina cringe—and a space of wall covered with the yellowing cards of various dressmakers. Beside that was a dusty velvet curtain that separated the front of the store from the back. She pushed it aside a few inches.

She caught a glimpse of more shelving with more merchandise as well as a steam-driven sewing machine and ironing press. She also heard voices, low and hurried. At first she couldn't make out what they were saying, but then she understood why. She recognized the language, or something like it, from a team of acrobats she had met years and years ago. Markham didn't just sell Chinese silks; he had Chinese tailors.

She wouldn't have thought anything of it—there were plenty of foreigners of all kinds living in London, especially near the docks—except that she caught a whiff of powerful magic. It wasn't at all like what she'd sensed on the automatons. That was dark, somehow slippery and oily, and if she had to describe it, she would say that it was made up, like a recipe. This was more like her devas, a living entity pressed into service. Actually, when she thought about it, there might be elements of two different magical beings.

And that combination—as unique as a vintage of wine—was exactly the same as what she'd sensed on Grace Child's stolen treasure. Excitement bubbled through her. This was a clue. A real, tangible link with the dead girl and whatever she'd got herself into. Evelina clenched her hands into fists and nearly bounced on her toes with excitement. Suddenly a lot of things didn't matter—circus girl or lady, debutante or bluestocking—she was in her element, doing what she was made for.

But Grace was dead, and that meant danger lurked nearby. Evelina swallowed hard, bottling up her glee, and turned back to see how Imogen was doing. Her friend gave her a significant look. A bolt of green silk was spread out on the counter with exactly the same pattern as the bag.

The door chimed as two more ladies came into the shop. Markham greeted them obsequiously.

"This fabric is exactly the thing, Mr. Markham," Imogen said brightly. "I'm just not sure there's enough here for my needs. Do you have more in stock?"

"Well, miss, this is the last bolt of it, I'm afraid."

"No remnants?"

"Not of this, or of any of the finer silks. My tailors make any remnants into bags for shoes and jewelry and the like and sell them to the other merchants for their stock. I'm afraid what you see here is all I have left of this fabric."

Imogen furrowed her brow. "I'm not sure it's enough. Allow me to consult with my friend."

"Of course, Miss Roth," he replied with a bow, and turned his attention to his new clients.

Evelina beckoned urgently, and Imogen strolled over, fingering a length of trim as she passed by.

"That's it," Imogen said casually, as if she were talking about no more than the material for her next dressing gown. "That is exactly the bolt of cloth we were looking for."

"There's more." Evelina kept her voice low, glancing at the shopkeeper, who was completely absorbed in making his next sale. "Are you up for some mild exploration?"

Imogen lifted a brow. "Always."

Evelina grabbed her sleeve and pulled her to the other side of the curtain. The back of the shop was larger than the front, with wide double doors open to the sunlit alleyway. Evelina barely caught more than a fleeting impression of worktables and machinery before two pigtailed men in Chinese garb jumped to their feet, exclaiming loudly. One held an enormous pair of shears. She heard Imogen's quick intake of breath and felt an answering flutter in her own stomach.

Evelina grabbed Imogen's hand and lunged for the open door. "'Scuse us. Just passing through."

The men looked confused, as if caught between ordering them out and bowing graciously because they were clearly patrons of their employer. Evelina wasted no time hurrying past.

"Where are we going?" Imogen demanded, nearly bumping into Evelina when she stopped running. "What are we looking for?"

Evelina wished she knew. Her immediate goal was to find the source of the magic, but what that would be was a mystery. She spun on her heel, looking around.

"What?" Imogen demanded.

"Hm." Evelina adjusted a hat pin, making sure the jaunty angle of her *chapeau* hadn't budged. She didn't actually care about the hat, but wanted an excuse to stall and think for a beat.

The alley was fairly typical—smelly and dirty, brick walls black with soot and age. Some of the bricks and cobbles looked scorched, like there had been a fire. Wider than some, it got enough sunlight that a few weeds grew beside the trough of filthy water trickling down the middle of the path. What was less typical was that no one was in sight. There should at least have been stray dogs and grubby children. Not a good sign. With a cold shudder, she suddenly wished she were alone and Imogen safe at home. Imogen wanted adventure, but didn't truly understand what that meant.

"Come on." She took Imogen's hand and started walking. A few doors down squatted a barnlike building she guessed was a warehouse. As they drew closer, she got a better view of the strange pile of metal outside the warehouse door. She'd assumed it was a pile of scrap.

Unfortunately, it was a nine-foot automaton. It had no head per se, and had clearly been built for brawn, not philosophical rumination. *A guard dog.*

The nervous fluttering in her stomach stilled into a deep apprehension. She was close enough to sense the warehouse was the source of the magic. *Why can't it be a nice tearoom? Why always the nasty, grotty places?*

Evelina cleared her throat. "That's where I'm going."

"Um—why?" Imogen looked dubiously at the metal figure.

Evelina wet her lips, suddenly feeling like her stays were far too tight. "Because the residue of magic that was on the gold came from there."

"Skipping past the fact that I was handling something with magic on it, and you knew and didn't tell me, how can you tell it's the same?"

"It feels prickly."

"Prickly?"

"Like a mustard plaster. Hot and irritating."

"Are you sure that's not my irritation you're feeling? You should warn people—"

Evelina twitched with impatience. "Imogen! Worry about that later. I cleaned the magic off the bag before you ever touched it."

Her friend pulled a face. "Oh, very well. And this sensation is coming from over there?"

"Right."

Imogen sighed, toying with the handle of her reticule. "I think I'll just have to take your word for it. To me, the place feels wrong, but that's not really proof of anything."

"But it is. It explains why there's no one in this alley. Everyone can feel magic, even if they don't realize it. And if it's a charm to keep people away, that's exactly what it's going to do." Evelina looked at her friend, trying to weigh the slight mockery in her voice. "You're taking this very much in stride."

Imogen gave a low laugh. "There's something about nearly dying a few times when I was little that makes everything else look very manageable. Although that ugly automaton is giving me pause."

"Most storerooms or warehouses have them. Go down near the docks and they're all over the place."

Imogen, who had never been anywhere so exciting, gave her a look brimming with curiosity. "Are thieves that much of a problem?"

Evelina nodded. "The bigger the machine, the more important the merchant." She couldn't help thinking of Lord Bancroft's stolen automatons, and wondering one more time what was so important about them.

Imogen looked impressed. "This one is plenty big. I wonder who owns it?"

"Someone who's putting it there simply for show. It's rusty."

"Does that mean it will leave stains on my skirts while it mashes me into the dust?"

"Only if it catches you."

"How sporting."

"You stay here."

Evelina marched toward the huge metal figure, stopping a few feet away. With a great groaning of metal, it shifted one leg so that it could face her—rather pointless, since it didn't have eyes to see or a head to put them in if it did. As a result,

Evelina wasn't sure where to look, and had a disconcerting sense that she was somehow being rude.

A good five seconds and a lot of noise later, it completed its change of direction. The huge, dull gray foot made an enormous *clump* and sent up a puff of dust. Things clunked inside as the internal logic engine churned away, cycling through a complex wheel of punch cards for an emergency marked "impertinent young women."

Then it gave a puff of steam—a signal that the boiler was ramping up for action, and also that the unit was in need of repair. The coal-fired boilers inside these units were small but highly efficient as long as the housing was tight. If the system was losing pressure, it was no wonder the unit was slow.

Evelina tapped one foot. The thing was obviously just a warning. The real guardian was whatever magic she sensed inside the warehouse. "Pardon me? Mr. Automaton?"

It ignored her salutation and ponderously lifted one fist high above its head. Metal creaked, flakes of rust raining down as it strained to move. She supposed if she stood very still and didn't bob about, it might have been able to deliver a mighty blow.

Meanwhile, the automaton had become stuck. The arm had reached its highest point and couldn't seem to reverse course, the joint sticking at the zenith. The thing shuddered with the robotic equivalent of dry heaves. Calmly, she reached up to examine its chest. There was the usual plate that could be removed to expose the workings inside. She touched the metal skin and found it hot and slippery from the escaping steam. The fingers of her gloves came away soaked.

"Evelina!" Imogen cried.

She darted aside as the automaton finally unstuck and thumped its fist into the ground where she had been standing a moment before. Then she waited patiently as it creaked to an upright position again.

"I'll be done in just a tick," Evelina replied.

As it raised its arm for another attack, she unlatched the chest panel—standing on her toes and cursing as she burned her thumb—and disconnected the main pneumatic line. The automaton froze, arm raised. She squinted up to read the date of manufacture on the back of the panel: 1856. No wonder the thing was so slow. It was ancient. The maintenance label read *Fitzgerald's Gravel Works*.

"I think this fellow was designed for breaking up rocks," Evelina announced when Imogen reached her side.

"It's not much of a guard."

"It looks impressive. That's probably good enough for casual passersby. One look at this and your common bully-boy would stay away—at least until he figured out he could run circles around this thing." *That means the real antitheft protection is inside with the magic.*

Evelina's palms were sweating.

"Well," Imogen said brightly. "That wasn't so hard. Now what?"

"Now I have a look around."

"I'm coming with you."

Evelina stepped away from the machine, dread crawling up her scalp. The sunshine seemed suddenly thin as watered soup. "No, there's no telling what's in there."

"I'm not going back to the carriage to sit there like an obedient spaniel."

Evelina gave her a baleful look, but Imogen didn't budge. Evelina relented, imploring the gods that she wasn't putting her friend in danger. "Then stay close."

The warehouse door wasn't locked, but came open with a creak of hinges. Sunlight fell in filmy banners from windows set high in the unfinished walls. Evelina felt a prickling against her face, as if she'd walked into a swarm of biting insects. Whatever caused that was the real guardian. She swallowed, but there was nothing to ease her dry throat.

She held up a warning hand, listening for movement, hearing nothing.

"Go slowly," she spoke in a whisper. "There's definitely magic in here."

Imogen stopped. "What kind did you say it was?"

"I don't know yet." Evelina tugged her close. "Just stay with me. We might have to leave in a hurry."

Crates were stacked at one end of the space, some with the lids pried off to reveal tufts of packing straw and sawdust. A crowbar leaned against the wall.

"This doesn't look like the draper's stock," Imogen said. "I don't see any cloth. I actually don't see anything that looks like merchandise for a store. What is this?"

"An importer's wares, perhaps? There are all kinds of languages on the labels of these crates. I think that one is Greek."

They stuck close together as they moved quietly between the rows of wooden boxes. The loudest sound was the hem of their skirts dragging through the old sawdust that littered the floor. As Imogen said, there were no stacks of dishes or furniture or other household goods. It was as if whatever had been unpacked had already been removed.

"What's all that?" Imogen asked, indicating a workbench and racks of carpentry tools at the other end of the building.

"It looks like a workshop, maybe? Perhaps some items are sent in parts, and they assemble them here?" There was a fascinating pile of old gears and wheels, as if someone had disemboweled an entire showroom of clocks. "I wonder if the Gold King knows about all this machinery. You could build half a factory from these scraps."

"He knows about everything, doesn't he?" Imogen said dryly. "I checked the list, you know. He was never invited to Mama's party."

Evelina drew closer, wanting a better look. Some of the parts were shiny and new, others old and misshapen with time. Corrosion reduced what might have been gears to jagged skeletons. Images of shipwrecks and treasure hunters played in her imagination.

"There are bloodstains underneath the sawdust," Imogen said with disgust, scraping at the floor with her boot.

"One of the workers must have been hurt."

Evelina barely gave the blood a glance. She'd seen plenty of mishaps at the circus, and even had a few of her own—like the time she'd tried one of Nick's knife tricks without supervision. She still had a faint scar across the palm of her hand. *I want to see Ploughman's again.* The truth was, she wanted to see Nick again. The need burned inside like a fever—consuming everything, leaving nothing but pain and weakness behind.

It was folly. Wanting Nick was selfish, hurtful to her and worse for him. She had gone over it in her mind a thousand times, and she'd decided to take the hard road for both their sakes. She had a future, better than what she'd left, and she should be grateful. Still, sadness lanced through her like a knife.

She bowed her head, slowly forcing away the idea by concentrating on the jumble on the shelf in front of her. And something reached out to her mind. She recoiled as if she'd been shocked with Aragon Jackson's evil machine.

"What's wrong?" Imogen demanded.

"There's something here."

"Your magic mustard plaster?"

No, it wasn't the biting, swarming sensation. It was something more. Something very, very old. She drew near once more to the shelf with the clock parts, summoning the courage to tentatively open her awareness a bit further.

There it was again, reaching up like a baby wanting to be held, but oh so ancient. So lonely. It wanted her to find it, amid the wreckage and dross of forgotten machines. It was one of them, but much, much more. It told her all that, not with words, but with an ache in her heart so sharp her eyes stung with sorrow.

She inched nearer still, reaching out her hand.

"Evelina?"

She brushed aside a litter of screws and wheels, sending them bouncing to the floor with a clatter and ping. Her fingertips sought the source of the thoughts, blindly groping to quiet its plea. She felt her hand connect with it. The sensation was odd—a duality of cool metal and warm energy, not unlike the combination of the mechanical bird and its deva. Curiosity vibrated through her as she realized that this was another combination of magic and machine. Someone else had done what she had done, and put a spirit into a mechanical body—but long, long ago.

She brushed away the surrounding bits and gears and

lifted the chunk of metal in both hands. It didn't look like much, just a brass and iron cube about eight inches across. The surface was lumpy and irregular, as if molten metal had been dripped over a piece of crude clockwork, or else the surface of the cube had corroded away to expose what lay beneath.

Whatever was in the cube reached up to her with a profound and archaic intelligence. Now that she'd found it, was holding it, she could sense more than just its loneliness. There was a feeling of depth, or maybe just vastness. It was like reading an entire library at once. It was like falling into a sky of stars.

"Evelina!"

She started, looking up at Imogen. "Pardon?"

"What is that thing?"

"I'm not sure, but it wants to come with us."

Imogen looked dubious. "It does?"

"I think someone was about to put it in the scrap bin."

"Really?" Her friend's face said that was a reasonable plan.

"But it's alive," Evelina explained. "Like my bird, only much more sophisticated than that."

Imogen blinked. "Sophistication which sadly didn't extend to wings or wheels. Or much else, for that matter." She pulled off her shawl. "Knot this around it and it will make a reasonable carrier."

Evelina took the shawl almost hesitantly. "Thank you. I'm afraid your shawl might be soiled, though."

Imogen shrugged. "Just hurry. This place is starting to give me the shivers."

She was right. The warehouse seemed to be growing darker, the shadows creeping in from the corners. It was also growing warmer, as if a boiler had been switched on beneath the floor. Evelina felt a sense of alarm from the cube, and shared it. The stinging, biting presence that must have belonged to the guardian of the place was no longer merely annoying. It had increased from the scrape and poke of crawling ants' feet to something sharper, like a thousand tiny blades glancing along her skin.

"I think we had better leave," Evelina said quietly, folding the cube in the shawl and knotting the ends of the soft fabric into a handle. Once again, she was sorry she'd brought her friend.

Imogen opened her mouth to answer, but no sound came out. Evelina spun to see what her friend saw, and froze. Straight ahead, their path had vanished in a haze, as if night had fallen on the far end of the warehouse. It took a moment to figure out why, but when Evelina did, her gut turned icy with alarm. The shadows were moving, rolling end over end to form a long tube of smoky darkness.

CHAPTER TWENTY-ONE

"WHAT IS THAT?" IMOGEN ASKED HOARSELY.

"Remember I told you about the devas?"

"Yes."

"This is the biggest damned deva I've ever seen."

Imogen didn't even blink at the curse. There were far greater things to worry about. The rolling shadows were arching up from the floor with serpentine grace, seeming to grow thicker and more solid every moment. The front end wavered in the air like a questing worm. The back end grew a long, snapping tail as she watched. *A fire drake.*

This was no countryside deva of tree or spring, small and formless and more or less harmless, but something ancient. The ability to assume physical form took enormous power, and such creatures were rare. She'd only met an eyewitness once before—an old man who told of the great bear spirit who roamed the north. The rest were just legends—until now. This creature had powers straight out of Gran's fairy tales.

The touch of its magic grew sharper, scraping along her flesh. Evelina glanced down at her arms, half expecting to see a tracery of blood seeping through the fine sleeves of her gown.

"Back the way we came," she gasped.

"Sounds good."

They turned tail and scampered for the door, the rustle of their petticoats loud in the cavernous space. They had gone a half dozen yards when Evelina caught darting movement from the corner of her eye. The roll of shadow slid, gliding along the floor with an undulating slither. Evelina caught her friend's arm, stopping her just as the thing reared up, blocking their escape.

She had the impression of vast, whiskered jaws and eyes the color of peridots. Red scales glittered from the darkness like flakes of burning coal, as if the thing were made of a living hide of banked fire.

Imogen shrieked, jumping backward in terror. Evelina pushed her to the side, stepping in front, ready to defend her just as she had in the school yard. Evelina weighed the cube in its sling of fine cashmere. She wondered how the entity inside that would feel about doubling as a weapon.

"We can't go back," Imogen said, her voice quaking. "It will just outrun us that way, too."

The thing lunged, snapping fangs that curled up and outside its mouth like tusks. Short, muscular legs churned the air as it reared and lunged again. Evelina ducked, pulling Imogen down with her into the safe space between two piles of crates. The beast lashed its tail, leaving a trail of heat behind it. Evelina could smell sawdust burning. All it would take was the right spark, and the creature would set the whole warehouse on fire.

The tail lashed again, and a small crate crashed to the floor. A clay jar broke open, spraying tiny glass beads everywhere. Evelina ducked, wincing as one stung her cheek. What looked like a giant paw smashed down on the rolling spheres, curved talons emerging from the dark, glittering form. She heard the glass crunch as it was ground to powder.

The urge to flee wafted up from the cube. Run fast, run desperately, run into the jaws of the beast, but definitely *run*. She wasn't about to argue.

Evelina began to inch backward, thinking they could sneak out the other side of the crates. Suddenly, hot breath blasted her back. She whipped her head around to find herself staring into the creature's glowing green eyes. They were slitted like a cat's. The long, sinewy body was wound over the pile of crates, feet on one side, head peering in the other side.

Evelina's pulse thundered in her mouth, coppery fear fouling her tongue.

"What do we do?" Imogen was panting, her fingers digging painfully into Evelina's arm. "What can it do to us?"

Frozen with fear, Evelina could barely move her lips. "The only reason it would be here is because someone bespelled it into serving as a guardian. If we want to leave, we have to make sacrifice."

"Such as?"

"I need something sharp. Something metal."

"I have a hat pin."

"Something more like a blade."

"That's more in your line."

The next words came out in a croak. "Anything that will slice. I need blood and lots of it, so it has to be more than a poke or a scratch."

She heard the rustle of Imogen searching. It was ironic, given the amount of gears and wheels and metal debris in the warehouse, that they would be stuck in the one spot without a scrap of anything useful. "I just have my card case."

"Give it to me."

Imogen did as she was told. The case was a pretty thing of gold and blue enamel forget-me-nots. Evelina peeled off her gloves, flipped it open, and emptied out the calling cards into Imogen's hands, spilling them so Imogen had to scrabble to pick them up. Then she snapped off the lid. It was a thin sliver of metal, and the broken hinge was sharp. In one quick swipe, she dragged it deep across the meat of her palm, using all the strength she could muster. Blood welled up in a red gush, and she let it drip onto the floor.

The beast began lapping it up like a cat, the thick black tongue darting.

"Run," Evelina said in a tight voice, her throat aching with tension.

Imogen ran. Evelina wormed her way from between the crates and followed, the cube swinging in the shawl and banging against her leg. The beast bounded after with a hungry mewl, its back humping as it half ran, half slithered on its stumpy legs.

It was fast. Evelina barely made it across the threshold

before the blare of sunlight stopped it in its tracks. They kept going, putting the length of the alley between them and the warehouse before Imogen had to stop. She was wheezing, the exertion too much for her.

"That. Thing. Was a deva. Like your bird?" she gasped.

"No. It was far more powerful." Evelina cradled her hand, feeling her heartbeat pulse in the wound. She realized her teeth were chattering, fear finally catching up to her body. "I remember Gran Cooper talking about creatures like that. Some call them demons. Some dragons. I don't know if either is the right name, but they can be summoned and controlled if you're strong enough and know the right spells."

"And they can't go into sunlight?"

"That's not it exactly. They're set to guard something. As long as you're off their territory, they don't care, unless . . ." Evelina looked down at the cube-shaped lump in the shawl.

"You took something."

Evelina swore, feeling hot, wet tears trickle down her cheeks. "Oh, no."

The strange, mewling cry echoed through the alley. The dragon was considering its options. What little noise there was in the alley went dead, as if all of London was holding its breath. There was no one and nothing in sight but the singed brick buildings.

She looked around, realizing they had run farther than she'd thought. The smell of baking perfumed the air. It seemed surreal, a homey touch that clashed with the grim, sooty space. Then, as suddenly as it had disappeared, the chatter of excited voices started up from the open door ahead. She cudgeled her brain for an idea. "Isn't that the back of the tea shop?"

"I think so."

Evelina grabbed Imogen and pushed her through the open door. "Go straight through the shop to the street, find the carriage, and wait for me there. Don't argue."

Imogen gave her a startled look. "What are you going to do?"

"I'll be fine, and I'll tell you all about it later."

"Why don't you just run?"

Evelina swore under her breath. "That thing's not going to stop coming for me, no matter where I go. I can't leave here without putting other people in danger."

Evelina gave Imogen another shove, bodily moving her along as she marched through the door after her. Her hand was bleeding again, no doubt drawing the beast with the smell of her blood.

A blast of heat smacked her skin when she pushed through the door, floating tendrils of hair back from her face. Two burly bakers gawped, eyes wide, at the sight of the disheveled Society ladies. Evelina gave Imogen a last shove, sending her trotting through the curtain to the front of the shop.

Evelina stayed behind, glancing frantically around the worktables. In moments, she saw what she wanted—a bag of salt, still half full. She snatched it up. One of the bakers shouted a protest, but she was already in motion, diving back into the alley. The contents poured over the lip of the bag into her cut, stinging hard enough to make her eyes water.

It was an odd weapon, but the only one she could think of to confront the dragon. Evelina wasn't sure how the salt worked—chemistry or magic or rules of engagement—but it seemed to nullify the energy that kept creatures like the garden devas alive. One sure way to kill earth or fire spirits was to drown them in the sea. An ocean sprite, of course, was a different problem.

She made it back to the alley in time to see the dragon's approach. In the sunlight, it looked less distinct, like a cloud of thick smoke, but its magic was no less powerful. *This is insane.* For a moment, she considered simply tossing the cube its way and running.

The moment she formed the thought, a wave of panic roiled up from the bundle dangling from her shoulder. It wasn't her emotion, but Evelina's knees quivered as the terror struck through to her heart, sharp and deep.

It's all right. I won't leave you. She clutched the shawl, barely resisting the urge to cradle it in her arms to comfort it. She could no sooner abandon it than drown a sack of kittens.

A wave of gratitude rose up, sweet as incense. Tears stung her eyes.

And then the beast was there, rising high on its hindquarters and opening its great, black maw. Energy pounded out from it with excoriating force, as if the magic were a thousand flexible blades designed to flay the skin from her body. Evelina couldn't breathe as its teeth—now suddenly, horribly solid—gleamed in the sunlight.

The thing's size made her look up and up and up. She had been afraid, but had forced herself through the fear because she had a job to do. Now all that went out the window. Her legs shook like the bones were dissolving. The fingers holding the bag of salt were losing their power, the coarse cloth sliding away.

But heat from the monster's breath lashed her face, snapping her back to herself. She had to act, and now, before it destroyed her and then anyone else it deemed guilty for violating its hoard. Evelina stuck her hand into the bag of salt, pulling out a fistful and scattering it in a line between them.

"With salt I bind you."

Her voice shook, the words seeming to fall to the ground under the weight of her panic. Nevertheless, the dragon drew back with a snarl sharp as ripping silk. Evelina drew in a shuddering breath, backing away just in case the binding hadn't worked.

It had stopped its advance, but not the attack. Sudden flame erupted from the creature's throat, blackening the cobbles. Evelina hurled herself to the left, diving into a roll that sent her crashing into one of the sooty walls. She came up on her feet, tripping over the hem of her dress so she staggered into the edge of a stairway.

She'd lost a lot of the salt, and the cube had dropped to the ground. Imogen's shawl was a lace of smoldering cinders. With jerky, desperate motions, Evelina dug into the bag and hurled another handful of salt.

"With salt I banish you!"

She fell to her knees, screaming the words. Their effect was instant. The giant of smoke and scales and teeth furled inward, contracting more and more, like an ink blot sucked back into the nib of a pen. Ears and claws and lashing tail were the last to disappear with a feathering of shadow, and then all that was left was a spinning ball of fire hovering six feet from the ground. Evelina blinked, her eyes not quite taking in the sight. The ball throbbed and crackled, making a noise like bacon frying in the pan.

She got to her feet, sweat running from her temples. Warily, she approached the ball. It wasn't a solid red; there were lights of yellow and orange in it, too. The surface was veined with black, like bits of ash clung to it.

"I'm sorry," she said softly, "but you can't run around London scaring people. But if I guess right, you had no choice about coming here."

Like the cube, the guardian didn't have speech that she could understand, but anger burned there, as red-hot as the thing looked. Who knew how ancient it was or where it had come from? Somewhere along the way, it had been captured and bound by magic to serve the owners of the warehouse.

She emptied the last of the salt into her palm, and sprinkled it over the ball.

"With salt I send you to your home. Be well."

It vanished with a sound like a popping cork. Then Evelina was standing in the empty alley, dirty and exhausted, her hand shedding blood down the front of her ripped and filthy dress. She turned to look at the back of the tea shop, realizing with horror that the bakers were standing there staring. *Now I've done it.*

One shook his head with wonder. "Thank you, miss. We've been plagued by that thing for months. All that smoke got into the bread and made it taste burned—but neither the watch nor the vicar would do aught. Told me I was imagining things. As if I couldn't tell a great fiery lizard right in front of my nose."

None of that surprised her. The common folk knew magic when they saw it, even if they'd forgotten how to protect themselves. What did interest her was the timing of it: not years or days, but months. What had happened months ago that brought the dragon to this alley?

Far down the alley, she saw the Chinese tailors running

out of the back of Markham's shop. They were lifting their hands to the sky. She couldn't tell if they were rejoicing or cursing.

Evelina turned back to the bakers. "I'm sorry, but I used all your salt."

"A small price to pay for a good service."

Evelina walked stiffly toward the shop door, pausing to pick up the cube. It was still warm to the touch, but it didn't burn her hands. "Please don't say anything about this."

The baker touched the side of his nose. "Of course we'll keep mum. We've heard about the actress. That won't happen to you—not on our account."

The bakers stood aside to let her into the back of the kitchen. She dropped the empty salt bag on the table, nearly mute with fatigue.

The more talkative of the two bakers wasn't done. "Of course, this is what you get when folks from strange parts move into the neighborhood. All sorts of nasty goings-on. People wandering in and out of that warehouse at the strangest times. Banging like a thousand elves are at work. The tales I've heard."

"Just remember to take them with a grain of salt." Evelina pushed the hair back from her forehead, then wiped her face with the back of her wrist. Tears. Maybe it had just been the smoke.

The baker made a face. "Salt. Right you are, miss."

Evelina went through the tea shop and out the front door without looking at the other patrons. She could only imagine them staring at her soiled dress. She knew she'd wither with shame in about an hour, but at the moment she was too tired to care.

WITH HER STOMACH in a hard ball of anxiety, Imogen watched the front of the tea shop. Her hands were shaking as she clutched the edge of the carriage seat, a thousand awful scenes running through her mind. Evelina dragged out by police constables. Evelina carried out on a litter. Imogen knew her friend had a knack for finding the oddest kind of trouble, but she had never dreamed of dragons.

I saw a dragon! She wanted to run and tell anyone who would listen, but knew better. For everyone's safety, it would have to be a marvelous secret she would carry to her grave. *What an interesting gift she's given me. Who else would show me something like that?*

No one Imogen was likely to meet. Half the time Evelina seemed to hang back, as if unsure of her welcome in the world. It seemed odd in someone who was so capable and so protective of other people. In Imogen's opinion, the world was a far better place for having her friend in it—with the possible exception of the amount of fretting Evelina caused at moments like this.

"Oh, come on, Cooper!" she muttered under her breath, frustration sharpening her tone.

There was nothing Imogen wanted more than to fight at her friend's side, sword in hand, a battle cry on her lips. But while she might be a good pawn in her father's empire-building schemes, she was really still a sickly girl whose only real talent to date lay in picking out dresses and avoiding her math lessons. Perhaps she could chat up a shopkeeper, but her chest hurt even from the slight bit of running she'd done that day. In a real battle, she would only be in the way, a danger to Evelina and herself.

Disgusted, she flung herself back in the seat, nearly squashing the paper sack of buns she had bought inside the shop. It was the only action she could think of to quiet the flustered proprietor when Evelina shoved Imogen out of the kitchen. Imogen had stumbled into a table displaying a dozen different types of tea, knocking half the packets to the floor—but shopkeepers rarely minded one's behavior as long as money changed hands. At least the buns smelled good.

Imogen scanned the street to either side of the door, alert in case Evelina emerged from a different building. Applegate walked around the carriage, fussing with the harness and keeping a watchful eye on his charge.

"Shall I go and see if Miss Cooper requires assistance?" he asked for the second time.

"Oh, no," Imogen replied airily. "She cannot seem to choose fabric for her gown, so I went for tea."

He gave Imogen a suspicious look, perhaps because she was watching the door of the tea shop and not Mr. Markham's store. She shifted her gaze accordingly. "Unless, of course, you enjoy looking at trims and laces."

That made him pale and return to his perch up front. Imogen chewed her lip, nearly twitching with nerves. *Come on, Cooper, slay your dragon and get back here!*

Then she saw Bucky Penner strolling down the street, a faint smile on his lips as if he had just heard a cheeky story. Of course, he always looked like that. It was one of the many things that charmed and irritated her about the man.

Imogen's icy stomach eased a notch. Nuisance though he was, the sight of Bucky made her feel better. He spotted Imogen and that smile widened to a grin, but then he turned aside to look at the blooms in a flower stall.

So I do not even merit a proper greeting. Imogen shoved the paper sack aside and sank into the seat cushions, her irritation with Bucky swirling into her anxiety over Evelina in a sickening stew. She wanted to scream, rage, do anything but sit like a good girl in the carriage. But then Bucky left the stall, a small bouquet in one hand. With a lift of his hat, he crossed over to the victoria.

"Good day, Miss Roth," he said pleasantly, his eyes darting to Applegate for just a moment. There was no doubt that anything he said would make it back to Lord Bancroft. There would be no discussion of goddesses today.

"Good day, Mr. Penner," she answered very properly. "I trust you are well."

"Indeed I am," he gave her a sly look. "I see you are once again guarding the supply of tea, this time with an entire equipage."

Imogen's eyes narrowed. "Indeed, I am not. Let there be tea for all. Here, have a bun." She unrolled the top of the paper sack and held it out defiantly.

The corners of his mouth twitched, but then a furrow of

concern appeared between his eyebrows. Imogen looked down to see what he was looking at and saw with horror that her lace cuff was torn. Dirty streaks covered her pale gloves where she had scrabbled to safety in the warehouse. She felt the color mount to her cheeks as Bucky's brown gaze lifted to meet hers, a question clear in his eyes.

"You've had an eventful morning?" he asked blandly and with another quick glance at Applegate.

"Nothing untoward," she said, widening her eyes in warning. "Just a bit of shopping."

He fished a bun out of the bag, his look turning conspiratorial. "Far be it from me to question the mercantile conquests of the fairer sex. But do keep in mind that I am always available to carry parcels if the occasion requires. I hope it is not too forward a sentiment, but I've been a friend of your brother's far too long not to consider myself your friend as well."

Imogen swallowed, her mouth suddenly dry as the sawdust on the warehouse floor. She rolled up the paper sack briskly, refusing to show that she was flustered even if her face was hot clear up to her eyebrows. *Ugh. How sophisticated.*

But after a brief struggle, she found her tongue. "That is most gentlemanly of you, Mr. Penner." And there was something about his manner that said she *could* trust him if she needed to. Intense gratitude unlaced the tight feeling that had left an ache in her stomach and she took the first proper breath she'd had in what felt like hours.

And then Bucky held up the bouquet. It was a small, round confection of primroses framed in a paper lace doily. Reflexively, she accepted it, even though there were a thousand warnings about accepting flowers from young men. It was a signal that he was courting her, and that simply wasn't possible. Not Bucky. At least, not in any world she was familiar with.

"What is this?" she asked, thinking the question stupid even as she said it.

"Flowers," he replied dryly. "Or, if you prefer, an earnest

against future events." His mouth curled wickedly as he bit into the bun with strong, white teeth.

Imogen gulped. She'd demanded flowers before he kissed her, she recalled now. The realization made her fingers clumsy, and she nearly dropped the bouquet into her lap. "Primroses. How lovely."

"My sisters claim flowers have a meaning. I do hope I made an appropriate choice."

Primroses were the flower of the silent but enduring admirer. Did that mean Bucky had been nursing feelings for her? With a sudden flood of panic, Imogen raised her eyes, but Bucky was looking away.

"Here comes Miss Cooper out of the tea shop," he said jovially, and raised his hat as the dark-haired girl approached.

Evelina! And Evelina was alone—not in leg irons or on a stretcher—looking a little disheveled but otherwise unhurt. Relief crashed into Imogen, but somehow got tangled in this new worry over Bucky. She parted her lips to speak, but no sound came out. *Am I making too much out of a simple bouquet?*

Bucky still had his face turned away. "Miss Cooper looks a trifle harassed. What is it about refreshments that obtaining them seems to be fraught with complications?"

Imogen's mind flashed back to the garden party and her encounter with Bucky beside the tea urn. She'd felt something stir inside her, a recognition of attraction for this man who had been no more than her big brother's teasing friend. She looked at him seriously now, realizing that what she felt for him promised hours of interesting contemplation.

"Tea is never as simple as it appears, Mr. Penner."

He finally turned to face her, that smile of his a bit less certain now. This was the moment she could end this flirtation before it began. *And this is Bucky Penner, the one who rigged my pianoforte so that it set off a miniature explosion every time I hit the D below middle C.* Her heart had nearly stopped the first time he'd done that. She still flinched every time she played that particular piece by Czerny.

"Then perhaps I should take my leave," he said with an edge of disappointment.

"As Miss Cooper has returned, I must be on my way," Imogen agreed.

"You do not wish me to stay and assist in any way?"

"Thank you, but no." His face contracted a minute degree, but she held out her hand, torn cuff and all. "Until another day, then."

That was clearly the message he wanted to hear. With a spark in his brown eyes, he took her dirty glove in his, kissing her fingers lightly. "Until another day, Miss Roth. And thank you ever so much for the bun."

He straightened, bowed to Evelina, and set off down the street, eating the sweet with obvious enjoyment. Imogen watched him go, unexpected butterflies in her chest, wondering if she had wakened a second and even more unpredictable dragon.

WHEN EVELINA REACHED the street, the victoria was in front and waiting. With—of all people—Bucky Penner looking like a canary-eating cat. He departed quickly enough that she got the impression he was doing his best to appear a chance passerby. But despite everything, she couldn't help a prickle of curiosity. Was she missing something? It was hard to tell. She had the feeling that like so many who appeared easygoing, Bucky was expert at hiding what he was really thinking.

When she reached the safety of the carriage, Evelina's strength ebbed. She grabbed the edge of the victoria, refusing to let her knees buckle. Suitably dismayed, Imogen and Applegate bundled her into the vehicle.

"Good gracious, what happened?" Imogen scolded, looking pale as paper. "You were gone so long, I was about to summon the cavalry!"

Since Captain Diogenes Smythe was one of Imogen's admirers, that wasn't an entirely empty threat. "I took care of our smoky friend."

"Pardon me, Miss Cooper," the old driver broke in, "but may I ask what happened?"

It was a polite way of warning her that Lord Bancroft

would get a full report on the day's events. He clicked to the horses and eased them into the busy traffic.

"There were ruffians." That sounded lame, but it was the best Evelina could think of on short notice.

"They were bothering me," Imogen put in. "Extremely rude."

"Ruffians with a giant, um, dog," Evelina elaborated. "I stayed behind to point out the villains to some baker's boys who took care of the matter. It got a little rough."

"You always were adventurous for a young lady," the driver replied easily. "It would have been better if you had come and fetched me to sort them out. But as long as you're not hurt, there's no harm done I suppose. Though I can't imagine what ruffians with a giant dog were doing in a draper's shop that caters to fine ladies like yourselves."

There was no good answer. The two young women exchanged a conspiratorial look. Evelina smothered a nervous laugh. "They weren't in the draper's. They were behind the tea shop."

Imogen held up a paper bag. "Tea bun?"

"You bought buns? I was fighting for my life and you bought buns?"

Imogen shrugged. "I thought I might as well, since I was in the shop anyway. The currant and lemon ones are excellent."

Evelina pulled one out and bit into the soft, sweet bread. Ladies didn't eat in the street, but Imogen grabbed one, too, dropping sugary crumbs all over her dress. Something about danger and derring-do negated even the best table manners.

"So what did we learn?" Imogen asked.

Evelina glanced toward the driver. "That's where the, um, cloth sample came from. It must have something to do with the warehouse out back."

Imogen leaned close, lowering her voice to the point where Evelina was mostly reading her lips. "Do you mean the foreign connection? Are they importing something they shouldn't? I thought opium and the slavers and all that was down in the East End."

"So did I." Not that crime stopped at even the steam barons' borders. If a crook could make a shilling, he'd do it anywhere he could get away with it. Evelina put her lips to Imogen's ear. "But I don't think we'd be out of line to speculate that whatever they're importing has a connection to the contents of Grace's bag."

"But we don't know that for sure, do we?" Imogen replied.

"You sound like my uncle." She could almost hear Uncle Sherlock intoning, "Speculation is not fact."

Imogen cast a nervous glance at Applegate, but he was shouting at a clutch of street urchins to get out of the way of the carriage. "So what can we be certain is true?" she whispered to Evelina.

"Whatever was in that warehouse was well-guarded. There was no chance the locals were going to bother it, and even if a determined thief figured out the automaton was no better than scrap metal, there was a guardian inside. The merchandise has to be valuable, or why go to all that trouble?"

But what did any of it have to do with Grace Child, the Roths, or anything else? She felt the hard surface of the cube against her foot, where she'd set it on the floorboards of the victoria for safekeeping. Tobias had said that Grace mentioned something about a Chinaman. Was it significant that there were Chinese workers near the warehouse? Probably, since her bag had come from the area—no doubt one of the ones made up from Mr. Markham's scraps. And Evelina had figured out what she'd sensed on Grace's gold was a combination of two magics, and found them both: the dragon and the cube. She'd conquered one and absconded with the other. Evelina had learned a lot in one visit to the shops.

But now that the rush of triumph was fading, the implications of what she'd done slithered over and under her courage like cold, slimy eels. How vulnerable was she?

The people using the warehouse knew enough magic to control the guardian, yet they had buried the cube in a pile of scrap. What did that say about them? Didn't they know it also had magic? If only the deva in the cube could talk! But as much as she could feel its presence, it knew no words that she could understand. It couldn't tell her who had put it on that shelf, only that it had to get away.

By all rights, Evelina should have been able to count the adventure a success, but she'd raised too many new questions and might well have poked the wrong hornet's nest. *Who would know how to trap a fire drake? Magnus, perhaps?* He was a sorcerer, but something told her he wouldn't have left the cube in a scrap heap. He would have felt its magic.

"What next?" Imogen asked.

Evelina didn't hesitate. At least now she had an idea where to start looking. Applegate had stopped shouting, so she leaned over to whisper in Imogen's ear. "We need to discover who owns the warehouse and what on earth was in those crates. I'll bet you your lace mantelet that Grace's gold was in those shipments. I want to know who sent them and where they were going."

CHAPTER TWENTY-TWO

London, April 9, 1888

HQ, SOCIETY FOR THE PROLIFERATION
OF IMPERTINENT EVENTS

4 p.m. Monday

"A MAN HAS NEEDS BEYOND A STUFFED SHEEP," TOBIAS SAID with the certainty of the extremely drunk.

"I'm relieved to hear it," Bucky replied, refilling his glass and proffering the bottle. He'd been in a fine mood since he'd arrived at the clubhouse an hour ago, rather like someone who'd won large at the gaming table. Tobias wasn't sure what sort of a state he was in—except drunk.

Tobias waved the bottle away. The clubhouse—with its ratty furniture, litter of tools, and half-finished machines— was already rotating in that irritating way things had when one was snockered. The condition had crept up on him. He'd thought he was safe, since they weren't actually drinking anything that had come from the in-house Steam-Accelerated Special Compression Distillery. That had exploded with spectacular gusto last week.

The accident had produced tragic results. The sheep, never of reputable appearance, was now minus one ear and several handfuls of fleece. Hence, Bucky had raided his father's cellar for a supply of Bordeaux.

"What I'm saying is . . ." Tobias trailed off, forgetting what he had in fact been saying.

Bucky resumed his habitual sprawl. "The squid adventure is done, and now you're bored."

"That's it," Tobias pointed his wineglass more or less in Bucky's (or one of the Bucky's) direction(s). "That's it exactly. We did the *Dutchman*. We need another sip to shink."

Tobias looked proudly around the clubhouse. The Society for the Proliferation of Impertinent Events met in a converted outbuilding that looked over a walled patch of scrub a block and a half behind his tailor's. It was everything his home was not. Except for the tools, there was nothing they had not built or scavenged. It was a house of imagination, not money. It was freedom from their birth and an opportunity to discover their merit.

Which, of course, was not the way most would view their pursuits. It was one thing to dabble with engines when one was a schoolboy, but real gentlemen didn't actually get their hands dirty. Not with grease and rust and the guts and bones of machines. That went beyond even the politely eccentric.

Never mind that Tobias was happiest when he was deep in the bowels of a machine, the sharp smell of steel and oil grating on his lungs. He was actually affecting something, not talking or planning or critiquing, but actually *doing*.

It seemed a rare state of bliss. Not even the poor people got to do much tinkering anymore, since they weren't able to buy parts to fix anything, thanks to the steam barons and the sneaky way supplies seemed to disappear on their way to store shelves. Even the fact that SPIE could get its hands on whatever parts it liked was proof they were a bunch of lunatic toffs and not real makers at all. Which made no sense, but then nothing did anymore. When did it all get so complicated?

"We need a new project," he said. "We did the squid. We did the still—sort of, until it blew up."

"Nearly did us in, that one did."

"There was the special vegetable launcher."

"The horse trapeze."

"The autocravat self-garroting device." That one had been meant to produce perfectly formed bow ties. Tobias snorted, then coughed when wine went up his nose.

"I make my toys."

"Yes." Bucky had three sisters, and Tobias envied his friend's small army of nieces and nephews. They appreciated all the mechanical marvels SPIE could invent. Making a child laugh wasn't the worst way to spend an afternoon. "I need to build something."

He wished that Magnus would surface—wished it with an almost childish ache. The foreigner had promised to give them all something exciting to do, but the man had vanished partway through the garden party and hadn't been seen since. It had been like getting a bite of a divine iced dessert, and then having the bowl snatched away.

"An idea will come up," Bucky said contentedly. "It always does."

"I'm bored."

"For the love of Babbage, don't make a complicated bet like the last one! Do something easy. Get a new mistress."

"Spare me. My father wants me to seduce Miss Cooper."

The words were out before Tobias knew he was going to say them. Damn. He grabbed the bottle and filled his glass, knowing he should be more sober, not less—but if he got drunk enough, then he wouldn't remember his transgression.

Bucky set down his drink. The afternoon light fell across his face, giving him the look of one of Rembrandt's younger cavaliers. "I thought the pater wasn't in favor of the girl."

"Forget I said it." Tobias rubbed his eyes with the hand not clutching his wineglass.

Bucky looked suddenly sober. "No, I won't. What's going on?"

Now that his mouth was engaged, it wouldn't stop. "It's this bloody affair with the maid. The Cooper girl's uncle is that detective, Holmes. My father's afraid she'll somehow dig up something embarrassing. You know how he is about his political career."

"So he wants you to keep her busy? Maybe on her back?" Bucky sputtered.

"Don't be vulgar. She's not like that."

"So you'll just make her think she has a chance of landing Lord Bancroft's heir? That's a bit low, isn't it?"

"Drawing-room intrigues happen all the time."

"Which makes it all perfectly fine."

Tobias's temper prickled. "Since when are you a moralist?"

"Someone has to put in a word for common decency." Bucky gave a mirthless laugh. "What if I did that to your sister?"

"Imogen?" Tobias was horrified. "Why? She doesn't have an uncle."

Bucky rubbed his face with one hand. "Good God, there are days I'm glad to be an upstart merchant's son. You aristos are utterly crazy."

Tobias checked the bottle, only to find it empty. "My father just got his title a few years ago."

Bucky uncorked another bottle. "They say there's nothing worse than a convert. Do you even like Miss Cooper?"

"Of course I do. She's a perfectly decent sort." And pretty. She reminded him of a roadside briar, all the more lovely for a little wildness. *Bloody hell, I'm drunk.*

"Do you like her enough to do your father's bidding, or too much?"

"I tried, you know. It didn't work. All that detecting or what have you. She knew not to trust me. My heart wasn't in it."

"Oh." A frown puckered Bucky's face. "Where does that leave things?"

Tobias laughed bitterly. "The minute she walked away I wanted her."

There was a long silence. Worry radiated from Bucky like waves of heat. "This doesn't sound like you. Have you been getting enough sleep?"

"I know how this sounds." Tobias set down his glass. "Don't make too much of it. She's just a girl." The lie coated his tongue like something rancid.

Bucky shook his head. "Forget your father."

"Do I have a choice? She doesn't want me near her."

"I doubt it's as bad as all that. But if you keep pushing, and she keeps pushing back, you're just going to become more invested in the game."

"So? I need a project."

"Before you know it, you'll propose."

Tobias actually thought he felt his heart stop. He buried his face in his hands, feeling the world tilt through his alcoholic haze. He imagined Evelina's soft skin beneath his fingertips, her breath on his lips. If he proposed, would she refuse him?

The question mushroomed until it was the only thing that filled his brain.

EVELINA SAT IN her bedroom just after dinner, hunched over the tiny writing desk. She'd received a short note from Dr. Watson that her uncle was back on the Continent after stopping in Baker Street for barely a day. The only thing he'd let slip was that her uncle was headed for Bohemia, tying up the aftermath of who-knew-what debacle. Intriguing, to be sure, but what it really meant was that she had a bit more time to find answers.

Not that she relished the thought of working alone, given her adventure in the warehouse. She still wondered what would happen when the owners noticed their dragon was missing. She might have enough magic to send it packing, but what kind of power did its masters have? What on earth had it been set to guard? How much danger had she and Imogen actually been in? *Too much.* She would have to go carefully as she followed up her questions about the warehouse.

The fact that there were other magic users in the mix worried her more than she cared to admit. She was used to having that as her secret advantage, but now she couldn't rely on being the only one with tricks up her sleeve. Once again, she thought of the mysterious Dr. Magnus. She remained convinced that he wasn't directly involved with the warehouse, but his fingers were in this pie somewhere. *What should I do about him?* What *could* she do about him? She had so much to sort out already, he was going to have to stand in line.

Evelina rubbed her aching eyes and tried to focus on the

papers in front of her. The window was open a crack, and Bird—wide awake now—hopped along the sill. Mouse was curled into a ball next to her inkwell, its jet nose tucked beneath its etched steel paws. The cube sat on her dresser, shrouded in the remains of Imogen's shawl. Evelina had hidden it, along with her train case of clockworks and magical implements, at the very back of her wardrobe. But tonight she had it out, thinking it might like the fresh air and company. Beyond that, she had no idea what to do with it or what it wanted.

In the meantime, she was trying to work on the letter Grace had carried in the silk bag. She had her uncle's pamphlet open on the desk, the letter, and a piece of notepaper in front of her. By everything she could determine, the document was written in a Vigenère cipher.

According to the pamphlet, a tabula recta was a series of alphabets staggered by one letter. There were variations, but she'd drawn the basic one.

A	B	C	D	E	F	G	H	I	J	K	L	M	N	O	P	Q	R	S	T	U	V	W	X	Y	Z
B	C	D	E	F	G	H	I	J	K	L	M	N	O	P	Q	R	S	T	U	V	W	X	Y	Z	A
C	D	E	F	G	H	I	J	K	L	M	N	O	P	Q	R	S	T	U	V	W	X	Y	Z	A	B
D	E	F	G	H	I	J	K	L	M	N	O	P	Q	R	S	T	U	V	W	X	Y	Z	A	B	C
E	F	G	H	I	J	K	L	M	N	O	P	Q	R	S	T	U	V	W	X	Y	Z	A	B	C	D
F	G	H	I	J	K	L	M	N	O	P	Q	R	S	T	U	V	W	X	Y	Z	A	B	C	D	E
G	H	I	J	K	L	M	N	O	P	Q	R	S	T	U	V	W	X	Y	Z	A	B	C	D	E	F
H	I	J	K	L	M	N	O	P	Q	R	S	T	U	V	W	X	Y	Z	A	B	C	D	E	F	G
I	J	K	L	M	N	O	P	Q	R	S	T	U	V	W	X	Y	Z	A	B	C	D	E	F	G	H
J	K	L	M	N	O	P	Q	R	S	T	U	V	W	X	Y	Z	A	B	C	D	E	F	G	H	I
K	L	M	N	O	P	Q	R	S	T	U	V	W	X	Y	Z	A	B	C	D	E	F	G	H	I	J
L	M	N	O	P	Q	R	S	T	U	V	W	X	Y	Z	A	B	C	D	E	F	G	H	I	J	K
M	N	O	P	Q	R	S	T	U	V	W	X	Y	Z	A	B	C	D	E	F	G	H	I	J	K	L
N	O	P	Q	R	S	T	U	V	W	X	Y	Z	A	B	C	D	E	F	G	H	I	J	K	L	M
O	P	Q	R	S	T	U	V	W	X	Y	Z	A	B	C	D	E	F	G	H	I	J	K	L	M	N
P	Q	R	S	T	U	V	W	X	Y	Z	A	B	C	D	E	F	G	H	I	J	K	L	M	N	O
Q	R	S	T	U	V	W	X	Y	Z	A	B	C	D	E	F	G	H	I	J	K	L	M	N	O	P
R	S	T	U	V	W	X	Y	Z	A	B	C	D	E	F	G	H	I	J	K	L	M	N	O	P	Q
S	T	U	V	W	X	Y	Z	A	B	C	D	E	F	G	H	I	J	K	L	M	N	O	P	Q	R
T	U	V	W	X	Y	Z	A	B	C	D	E	F	G	H	I	J	K	L	M	N	O	P	Q	R	S
U	V	W	X	Y	Z	A	B	C	D	E	F	G	H	I	J	K	L	M	N	O	P	Q	R	S	T
V	W	X	Y	Z	A	B	C	D	E	F	G	H	I	J	K	L	M	N	O	P	Q	R	S	T	U
W	X	Y	Z	A	B	C	D	E	F	G	H	I	J	K	L	M	N	O	P	Q	R	S	T	U	V
X	Y	Z	A	B	C	D	E	F	G	H	I	J	K	L	M	N	O	P	Q	R	S	T	U	V	W
Y	Z	A	B	C	D	E	F	G	H	I	J	K	L	M	N	O	P	Q	R	S	T	U	V	W	X
Z	A	B	C	D	E	F	G	H	I	J	K	L	M	N	O	P	Q	R	S	T	U	V	W	X	Y

Then she'd copied out the message letter by letter, leaving a space below each letter for the key.

J	E	Y	R	B	A	G	Z	T	L	J	L	P	W	G	W	P	P	E	F	L	E	O	Z	V	Z	I

Decoding was simple if one had the key, which would be a word or phrase of some kind. All she had to do was find the first letter of the key along the top of the tabula recta. Then she followed the column down until she found the first letter of the coded message, and then follow that row to the left-hand margin. Whatever letter was on that row along the left-hand margin was then the first letter of the decoded message. Then repeat with the second letter of the key to find the second letter of the message, and so on. The key would keep repeating until all the letters of the message were decoded. Dead simple, if one had the key. Which she didn't, and it could be absolutely anything.

Bugger. A sense of helplessness crept through her as she stared at the letters. There was no magic spell, or foul word, or temper tantrum that would make the nonsense phrase suddenly resolve into sense. *Bugger. Bugger. Bugger.* Frustration was fast eroding her boarding-school gentrification, at least inside her own head.

Evelina felt the cube reach out, touching her mind gently. The emotion in the wordless contact was as soothing as someone stroking her hair. It reminded her of Gran Cooper.

Long ago, Evelina had sat beside her fortune-telling grandmother while the old woman turned over card after card for the patrons who came to her tent wanting to know the future. The air would grow still and strangely hushed, the candlelight softer, as if the magic of the reading pulled the noise and brightness from the air. That was when little Evie would cuddle closer to her grandmother's side, glad of the warmth of the woman's rough woolen shawl against her cheek. The worn cards would turn, *snick, snick, snick*, and the fortune-teller's soft voice would spin stories about what was to come.

Evelina could still remember the smell of the tent: damp earth and animals, incense and the perfume of herbs from the old woman's medicine chest. An extra sixpence could buy the customers a love potion or a lucky charm. When Gran sold one of those, their supper might be just a little bit bigger.

At the time, the cards had been just as mysterious as the cipher, but she'd eventually learned their language: love, deceit, success, defeat. Nothing, however, could untangle the web that bound her to that tent. The threads might stretch, but nothing could cut them. She would always be Gran Cooper's baby girl, no matter how hard Wollaston Academy tried to scrub that from her soul. *And yet I am not the same girl anymore. She is part of me, but there is more to me than her. You can't put a plant back into its seed.*

Evelina blinked the cipher back into focus again, realizing her mind had wandered. *This is hopeless.*

Bird gave one of its odd mechanical chirps. *Someone is coming.*

Evelina shuffled her papers into the desk drawer and slammed it shut. Bird flew out the window and perched in a nearby tree. Mouse stayed where it was, looking much like a paperweight.

A soft knock sounded at the door. "It's Tobias. May I come in?"

"All right."

He entered, closing the door behind him. Evelina rose uneasily. Propriety demanded an open door.

"I must speak with you," he said quietly. "Forgive me, but I must do it privately."

He didn't look particularly sober, which didn't reassure her at all.

"What about?" she asked.

He paused, giving her a distracted smile. "So serious. Do you know I almost never see you laugh?"

She raised her eyebrows. "Is that what you came here to say?"

"No, although it's definitely worth saying."

He pulled the stool from her dressing table and sat down on it, resting his elbows on his knees. He looked suddenly exhausted. "I . . ." he trailed off.

Evelina waited, her apprehension turning to worry for Tobias. "What is it?"

"I don't know where to start."

She turned her desk chair to face him and sat down, clasping her hands in her lap. She wanted to reach out to touch him, to offer comfort, but that would have led down a dangerous road.

"Are you still angry with me?" he asked, looking up under his brows.

The question caught her off guard. She felt her cheeks heat. "Does it matter?"

"To me. I'm sorry. There are things you don't know."

She was tired of his secrets. "Then you can't blame me for making what judgments I can."

He winced. "Fair enough. I'm asking you to believe I'm being honest when I . . . well, it's trust for trust, isn't it? I need to trust you if you're going to trust me. But I need you to keep what I say to yourself."

Evelina heard the scrabble of Bird's claws on the ledge outside. Panic tingled through her, and she shifted to block as much of the window as she could. *Secrets. There are just too many secrets.* "I can keep a confidence, but don't tell me if you will regret it later."

To be honest, she didn't want to know about his mistresses, or the gambling hells, or any of the other depravities that went on in his clubs. Her imagination could supply all that well enough without his assistance.

Tobias hunched his shoulders, his hands braced on his knees. "That night—the night Grace died—I built a giant squid and tore down the opera." The words came out in a muffled mutter.

For a moment there was nothing but stunned surprise.

Bloody hell. Evelina clapped her hand over her mouth. "Oh, dear Lord, that was you?" she mumbled from behind her hand. "I should have known!"

"You can't tell anyone or we'll all be arrested!" he hissed.

She clamped her other hand over her mouth, forcing herself to stay silent. Her shoulders were starting to shake. She'd read about it all in the papers. Tears of laughter started to leak from her eyes.

He was turning red. "It's not that funny!"

"Yes, it is." She hiccuped. "Was your father there?"

He nodded, starting to grin himself. "Like Jove remembering he left his thunderbolts back in the chariot."

Then they both started to giggle, the cramped, hushed noise of two conspirators afraid of discovery. Evelina couldn't stand it, and got up to look out of the window. She needed to laugh out loud, but they might be overheard. And there was no way to settle down as long as Tobias was right in front of her, looking as guilty as the boy who'd stolen the pie.

Of course that was him. Who else would ever do such a thing? She shook with an aftershock of mirth, wiping tears from her eyes.

"Is that why you had bruises on your face that night?" she asked.

"There was quite a fight," he nodded, looking sheepish.

A huge knot of worry came loose from under her heart. If he was wreaking havoc at the opera, full of high spirits and mischief—well, it just didn't fit with a cold-blooded, gruesome murder. *Tobias has to be innocent.*

How could the man who had defended Dora before the Gold King be anything less? Tobias Roth was handsome, clever, and original. There was no room in her universe for him to be anything but good and kind.

Bird had flown off and was flashing through the branches of the trees, bouyant as her spirits. Behind her, she heard Tobias moving and was about to turn around when she felt his hands come to rest lightly on her shoulders. She tensed, afraid to move, afraid that he would move, afraid that he would leave. As if he sensed her uncertainty, he stood perfectly still.

"At least now I've seen you laugh." His voice, deep and soft, came from right behind her. His breath tickled her ear, tart with the scent of wine. His fingers were warm, gentle—though there was strength just beneath that softness.

"You are a wonderful idiot," she whispered, wanting him to touch her even if it made every instinct alert and wary.

He chuckled. "You're probably the only woman in the Empire who knows who I am and still thinks so. The wonderful part at least. The idiot part is a generally accepted truth."

Evelina bit her lip, afraid to disturb the moment. *Would you think I'm wonderful if you knew everything about me?*

Tobias went on, his voice low and urgent. "I want you to know I'm dealing honestly with you."

Instantly, caution assailed her. "Your father—"

"Never mind him." Tobias squeezed her shoulders lightly.

"He is your father. Don't hurt yourself for my sake."

"He is important to me, but I have my own heart to follow. I know who I am now."

She thought of her own situation, of the roads she had traveled and how many she had yet to go down. Her chest ached for Tobias. "That's not always as simple as it sounds. There are a lot of false paths."

"Yes, I know. I've been on quite a few of them."

Evelina swallowed, wondering what any of this meant. *Don't read more into it than is there. He just came to tell you about the opera house. The rest is as reliable as quicksand.* "Right now everything is more confusing than ever."

He made a wry noise. "I have a feeling a lot is going to happen before the Season is over, and I don't mean just a lot of balls and tea parties."

Champagne, proposals, and—oh yes, a triple homicide with a garnish of sorcery. What larks. "I think you're right."

"You'll keep me honest." He pressed his lips to the tip of her ear, then backed away.

She turned to face him, catching her breath at the soft look in his clear gray eyes. "I can't be your conscience."

He gave a lopsided smile, his face pale as if the drink were finally catching up to him. "Some of us are better if we're held accountable."

She smiled, shaking her head. "You have to do that for yourself."

That's the thing with real professionals. They can work without a net. But he had trusted her enough to tell her his secret. Never mind he was quite clearly drunk, it was still something. Perhaps it made her trust him a little. "Good night, Tobias."

The lopsided grin widened with a version of his habitual mischief. "Good night, fair Evelina. Talking with you always makes me a better man."

"It doesn't take much," she muttered, pushing him away.

He barked a laugh as he disappeared out the door.

CHAPTER TWENTY-THREE

London, April 10, 1888
KEATING RESIDENCE

9 a.m. Tuesday

THE GOLD KING WAVED AWAY ALICE'S OFFER OF ANOTHER cup of tea. She set the Wedgewood pot back on its trivet and subsided into the chair opposite him at the tiny breakfast table.

She had eaten earlier and returned, it seemed, for the sole purpose of cosseting him. A lovely gesture, but he was enough of a businessman to know it didn't come free. If she had nothing to ask, she would have left him to his morning papers.

The sunlight made her hair burn like copper fire. She was dressed to go out, neat and tidy in a fawn walking ensemble Keating had ordered from Worth in Paris. Alice wore his money well.

"A busy day ahead, Papa?" she asked sweetly.

"Exceedingly. And you?"

She folded her napkin with an air of delicate ennui that made him tense. His darling daughter used that languid air the way a leopard used its spots—camouflage to hide her stealth. All right, then. She wanted something she knew he would not easily surrender.

"My day consists of a dress fitting, a musicale, perhaps a ride in Rotten Row, and if I feel energetic enough, the heir to the Westlake fortune has encouraged his mama to invite me to the theater tonight. Some Italian opera at the Royal Charlotte."

"I thought they were doing Wagner. Someone was talking it up to me the other day."

"The production was eaten by a giant squid."

Keating paused, his egg spoon poised in midair. *Only in London.* "Italian it is, then. Have a lovely time."

"I would rather be with you." She gave him a coy glance.

He raised an eyebrow. She was definitely angling for a favor. "Not where I am going today."

"Another brutal, bloody battle in the name of commerce?"

Sometimes he wondered if she knew how literal that was. "Several, in fact."

"How thrilling. Then I shall leave you to muster your troops." She bent, kissed his cheek, and made for the door.

Too easy. He looked up at her slim, stylish figure outlined against the heavy wine damask of the wallpaper. "Are you fond of the Duke of Westlake's boy?"

She paused, turning slowly. Her skirts followed with a silky swish. "Not particularly. He has a title, though. And his mother's annual ball is one of the choice events of the Season."

Her chin tilted at a dismissive angle, and he understood the game, at least in part. She had set her sights on someone and wanted him to approve—but his Alice was too subtle to blurt out her heart's desire. Not, at least, during a negotiation. He'd taught her to be a better businesswoman than that. *Maybe I should let her take a modest role in the firm.*

A glow of pride—and a bit of fatherly worry—warmed his chest. "Would you rather marry money or breeding?"

A ghost of a smile played across her bowed lips. They understood each other. "Both are pleasant attributes, but I'd rather have a man with a mind of his own."

He experienced a pang just under his watch chain, as if a knife had slid neatly into his gut. Was it the sudden sense that she was looking toward a future that didn't always include him? He slammed the feeling down, but could not help thinking she might be a bit too much like him, and too little like her poor obedient, dead mother.

Keating snorted, turning back to his egg. "Best of luck finding such a man at your musicales."

Her blue eyes held just a spark of triumph. "Exactly so."

He set down the spoon, growing irritated. "And pray tell, miss, what does that mean?"

"I would want someone with wits enough to help you. Someone who won't merely lick your shoes."

She was right, of course, but the statement shocked him. "Since when do I need help?"

A lift of her delicate chin signaled defiance. "You are a great enough man to build a legacy. I refuse to take a husband who will simply squander it."

Keating felt the net of her logic closing in. He could tell her straight off that she would marry where he told her to, since that was the way of things, but he let her keep her pride. "Of course."

She ducked her head, a little shyly. She thought she had won and was trying to hide her pleasure. "That's why I have you to look out for my interests, Papa. You are a most admirable guard dog."

"You flatter me." He watched his daughter go, already hating the man who would take her away.

And then, eyes suddenly vulnerable, she said the last thing in the world he expected.

"I fancy Tobias Roth."

And Alice all but ran from the room.

Pure dismay curdled Keating's breakfast to a hard, greasy lump. He sat motionless, his mouth slowly drifting open.

Roth! That was the fair-haired idiot who'd made a fool of Aragon Jackson. *Of me.*

Surely she jests. And yet, he understood the attraction. The boy had all the usual qualifications: education, looks, good pedigree, the trappings of a successful family. Plus, he was just enough of a rebel to catch the female eye.

And he clearly understood machines.

But Keating planned to eventually ruin the father for that Harter's debacle. Bancroft was obedient now, but that was only because he knew he was under scrutiny. He'd try something the moment Keating's attention wandered.

And yet—ruin wasn't the only means of revenge. Perhaps he could be inventive and steal the heir to Bancroft's imagined legacy right out from under his aristocratic nose. He savored the idea, cataloguing the nuances of its flavor as if it were a fine wine.

He did so like to please his daughter.

KEATING WAS STILL mulling over the idea as he settled into his study on the main floor of his Mayfair address. The London house was not as large as his town house in Bath or even the estate he had purchased near Truro, but it had the smell of old aristocracy about it. It was the perfume of age and money, as if the pedigree of its former owners had seeped into the brick and timbers.

The rooms had high ceilings and gilt, with delicately painted panels in the bedchambers and marquetry on the floors. The fireplaces were framed in porphyry and the enormous paned windows were draped with velvet so heavy that it took two strong men to remove each panel for spring cleaning. The house had once belonged to a duke's mistress, but she'd been old and ill and Keating had seen his opportunity to drive a hard bargain.

He'd added modern conveniences, of course—like the pneumatic tracks that ran like a narrow shelf all along the wainscoting. Tiny silver cars ran along it, much like a toy railway. They allowed food, drink, or any small item to be delivered at the touch of a button without the annoyance of intruding servants. If one really wished privacy, one had merely to place one's order to the butler's pantry through a speaking tube, then wait for the requested item to appear via the Lilliputian railway. It was the finishing touch on a house that was no more than the founder of Keating Utility deserved, and one that he would be proud to settle on Alice someday.

But how did he feel about the Roth boy putting his feet up on the fender? Keating expected his daughter to marry high up the social ladder, and it was worth noting that Tobias would inherit his father's title. *Alice could be the next Lady Bancroft.* Not bad, though the next Duchess of Westlake sounded even better.

And Keating wasn't sure that he approved of her ideas about marrying a man with brains. *Too much intellect could be problematic in a son-in-law.*

He'd barely finished the thought when the dark paneled door swung open, and his first appointment strolled in with the air of a man on a scenic tour. Keating studied his visitor. Tall, wearing a black suit tailored with a Continental flair. Goatee. An emerald the size of Keating's fingernail flashing in his stickpin. *Flashy, verging on tasteless.*

"Dr. Magnus, I presume," Keating said. "I saw your name in my appointment book, but I do not recall setting this meeting."

"Your secretary did so at my request," his visitor replied, sinking into one of the oxblood leather chairs without invitation.

"I recall that Lord Bancroft introduced us at his wife's birthday party."

"Indeed he did. And as I do not flatter myself that you recall every detail of the conversation, let me say again that I am a man of science recently arrived in London."

Bully for you. "What can I do for you?" Keating took the other chair, doing his best to make the seating arrangements look like his idea.

"Seeing as we are both busy men, I thought perhaps a polite conversation could save us both a great deal of skulking and snarling, however recreational that prospect might seem."

"Snarling about what?" Keating felt a moment of confusion. It usually took a few minutes to arrive at hostility, but this man seemed to have gone on without him.

Magnus waved an airy hand. "You had Herr Schliemann dig up Athena's Casket and ship it to London. As soon as I had word that it had been located, I was on its trail."

"How did you know that?" A wary feeling formed in the pit of the Gold King's stomach. He had done everything possible to keep the discovery of the item a secret.

A hollow, almost ravenous look came over the man's dark face. "I have my methods and my watchers within the archaeological community. I've been searching for the casket for a great many years."

Wariness grew to worry. Keating shifted uncomfortably on the horsehair padding of the seat. "Indeed? Your interest must be great, if you traveled from—wherever you came from—to follow up on what must be a slender lead."

The foreigner's brows contracted. "Please, do not play me for a fool."

Affronted, Keating pulled himself up in his seat. "I beg your pardon?"

"I know Schliemann found the casket and had it shipped to London, right to your warehouse. The archaeologist's work has long been of interest to me. He has investigated many sites I thought long lost to memory. I have kept a member of Schliemann's crew in my pay, well rewarded to notify me if anything of interest comes to light. He gave me every detail of the treasure found in Rhodes, down to the name of the ship it traveled on."

Damn him. Keating would be having words with Schliemann via the next post. "Very well. What is your interest in the casket?"

"It is unique."

"I would say it was large and gaudy." *Just like your tiepin.* "That hardly makes it worth crossing oceans."

"Again, you are needlessly coy." The man gave a white and somehow carnivorous smile. "So let me say why it is of such interest, to spare us the dance. Only a handful of ancients knew how to harness an ambient spirit within a mechanical device. Athena's Casket is the only surviving example of a lost art."

It was all Keating could do not to flinch at the words. "I am well aware of the legends around the item." *And how it could destroy my fortune or make me master of the Empire.* "That does not answer why you are sitting in my study."

"For the obvious reason. I want the box."

That surprised a laugh out of the Gold King. "Do you, now?"

The foreigner leaned forward, his expression slightly mocking. "I do, if only to study its workings."

Keating crossed his legs and bent a sliver of truth to fit the situation. "I do not have the casket here. The shipment was delayed."

Keating had, of course, contacted Holmes as soon as a problem reared its head, but that hadn't been the end of the story. A handful of the boxes had been separated from the rest, arriving late. The shipping manifest claimed those last few crates had been delivered days before Harriman was able to confirm their arrival. Keating had visited the owner of the shipping line with a most urgent request that his goods be found—but to no avail.

Keating's frustration must have shown on his face. Magnus's eyes narrowed. "Surely you did not let such a valuable object slip through your fingers?"

"That is not the case. There was merely a logistical difficulty."

Harriman had looked into the matter, and eventually found the crates had gone to a different establishment down the street. Everything had been in order—except the casket. It was still missing. Keating's men were quietly taking aside the owners of the other local warehouses for some very pointed questioning.

He'd sent an update to Holmes, but the detective wasn't at Baker Street. No sooner had he accepted the case than the pompous idiot had rushed off to Bohemia on some other errand. He didn't seem to understand that Keating needed him in London, now, finding out what happened to Schliemann's shipment. If Keating did not see results soon, he would be obliged to yank Holmes's leash.

"So you are admitting that it was lost," Magnus said again in a soft voice.

Shame and anger crept up the sides of Keating's neck. His fingers dug at the brass studs in the arm of the chair, as if to rip them out with his nails. *Lost* was further than Keating was willing to go. Surely Holmes would solve the case, when he troubled himself to get on with it. "No. I simply do not have the casket here."

"Then send for it. Allow me to examine it."

"I think not."

Magnus steepled his fingers, his brows furrowing with annoyance. "I can tell that you are hiding the truth from me. Either you are lying and you have lost it, or you are lying and you have it squirreled away for your own purposes. You prevaricate well enough that it is hard to tell which is reality."

"Believe what you like. The casket is not here."

"Then for today we are at an impasse."

"As you wish."

Magnus gave a small, dry smile. "I think you have it, sir. I shall make it my business to make you surrender it to me."

Keating had put up with enough. He turned his words to ice. "I will not attempt to dissuade you. I can only warn you that I am a dangerous man to annoy."

A moment of silence followed. Warm sunlight filtered between the heavy green drapes, gleaming on the brass fire screen. Keating saw their reflections ripple in the polished metal surface, one silver-haired and elegant, one dark and strange. Outside, a carriage clopped by.

Keating's thoughts tangled: Alice, the Roth boy, Holmes, the casket. He was trying to weave a future with threads that kept breaking. Now there was this Magnus fellow, knotting everything still further. The doctor had to go, with as little fuss and bother as possible. *One can only be at an impasse with equals. This posturing crow is beneath me.*

Fury clutched at Keating. "I think it is time you left, sir."

"Not yet. Two days ago, I visited the place where you house your treasure. Chinese workers, closely guarded, and your own cousin in charge of operations. There is no opportunity for a thief to worm through your security measures. They are, shall we say, extreme."

How closely has he been studying me? And what does he mean by extreme? He left the operation of the warehouse to Harriman, who seemed competent enough at his job— until now. They weren't expecting any further shipments, so Harriman had let the Chinese go back to their families for a week or so. But then yesterday someone had got into the warehouse after disabling the automaton at the door. The only blessing was that the pieces for the exhibit sat packed in crates in the gallery, so nothing more had been taken. Did Magnus have something to do with the break-in? If he had, would he be here? Keating just couldn't tell.

His mouth twitched with ire. "What can I do to make you leave?"

Magnus gave an unpleasant chuckle. "Give me the box. Sooner or later, you will accept my viewpoint on the matter."

The Gold King's mouth twisted into a snarl. "And why should I do that?"

Magnus rose in a single graceful movement. "Because of who and what I am."

Bancroft stood, not liking the sensation of Magnus looming over him. Unfortunately, the doctor was taller by inches, and leaned down into his face.

Magnus grinned, and it wasn't pleasant. "Eventually, it shall be a relief to place the casket in my hands, because that is the price—the only means—of obtaining peace."

He touched the green gem that pinned his necktie. The sun leached out of the room, leaving it cold and dank and dark. Shadows crept from the corners, leaving all in shades of mildewed gray. Keating felt a chill move up his legs, as if cold hands were reaching up from graves hidden beneath the carpet. Keating felt a sudden, craven urge to beg the doctor to let the light back in. He bit the inside of his cheek, refusing to let his teeth chatter. "This is magic. The use of magic is illegal in the Empire. Punishable by death."

The doctor waved a finger. "Oh, tut. You are credulous, for a man of business. I am merely a mesmerist."

"Mesmerist?" Keating's voice sounded shrill. "This is more than tricks of the mind, sir."

"Are you so certain of that?" Magnus laughed softly.

Fear lanced through Keating at the sound. He jerked back, as if Magnus were poisonous to the touch. "You will regret this."

Magnus turned his eyes to the ceiling in a gesture of exaggerated patience. "Please, threatening me is unwise in the extreme. Don't force me to fall back on the obvious blustering tropes of penny-dreadful adventures."

Keating was a brave man, but there was something in the darkness that recalled every boyhood terror. "All men bleed. Is that a trope?"

Magnus pulled a face. "But not all men have daughters, Mr. Keating. And yours is so lovely. Think on her while you ponder my request."

There was a moment of stunned silence while Keating's breath choked in his throat.

"Good day, Mr. Keating. I shall be seeing you about town. Often." Magnus gracefully bowed from the room.

Keating fell backward into his chair, glad of the light that came rushing back through the window glass, but not feeling one bit warmer.

Until his rage breached like a furious kraken.

CHAPTER TWENTY-FOUR

THE ONLY ANTIDOTE TO DR. MAGNUS WAS ACTION. AND THE Gold King had resources for this kind of thing. He had Striker.

South of Marlborough and East of Regent Street lay one of the poorest parts of the Gold district. St. James Workhouse formed one corner of a neighborhood made up of people surviving on a few shillings a week. For a few shillings more, Keating had bought himself an army of Yellowbacks.

Striker, as their leader, had been an even greater find. He was strong and hard and ambitious, but he also had a talent for firearms. Not just to use them, but to make them from bits and scraps. Illiterate, barely articulate, Striker was a natural savant, a primitive Mozart of weaponry.

Keating had snatched him up, a rare and useful specimen to keep close by—but not too close. A streetkeeper had privileges—a place of his own and enough money for regular food, liquor, and the occasional whore—but Striker could still see the workhouse from his rooms. A useful reminder.

Striker's home was not the kind of place Keating preferred to go, but some orders were better delivered in person. Still, he took extra grooms to watch the carriage, and another pair to follow him into the rooming house where Striker lived, just in case.

It was daytime, so the place felt oddly subdued, as if the very bricks of the ramshackle building were sleeping off last night's gin. The main floor had a communal parlor to the left of the front door, probably where whores entertained their customers. Above that were three floors of supposedly private quarters. Striker was up a long, steep flight of the narrow, filthy stairs in one of the corner rooms.

Keating followed behind one of his men, another bringing up the rear. The middle of the steps sagged and creaked, so he found himself walking close to the wall for safety, and then leaning away so his sleeve wouldn't brush against the grimy paint.

The first man, who had moved up the steps more quickly, pounded on Striker's door.

"Go away," came the streetkeeper's growl, muffled by the wood.

The man pounded again.

"What the bleeding hell do you want?"

By that time Keating had caught up, puffing a little from the climb. "It's Keating."

"Then do come in, sir." More polite, but not exactly welcoming.

Keating turned the rattling knob and pushed open the door. The sight reminded him of an illustration to a cautionary tale, something to do with the wages of sin. The stench was worse—cheap gin cycled through the human body and sweated out again.

Striker sat at a wood table littered with odds and ends, his ragged shirt half buttoned and his bandaged leg stretched out in front of him. His dark complexion had a gray cast, his eyes pink with lack of sleep. Perhaps pain was keeping him up nights.

If so, the man had found his solace. An open bottle hung loosely from his hand. Striker shoved the other through his spiky hair, as if dimly aware of his disheveled state.

It was the first time Keating had ever seen him without the metal-encrusted coat. Now he could see the outline of heavily muscled arms beneath his filthy shirt.

Striker began to struggle out of the chair, but Keating waved him back. "Don't try to stand." If he didn't fall from his injury, the drink might do the job.

Striker subsided. "Thank you, sir. Right kind of you."

Keating looked around, the floor crunching as he shifted his feet. There was almost no furniture. There was an unmade bed in the corner and a fireplace with a cook pot, but little else. Something had crusted inside the pot that added to the malodorous fug hanging in the room.

Keating felt his gorge rise. "How's the leg?"

Striker's face darkened, but he shrugged his bulky shoulders. "It'll heal. The wound's clean enough."

"Glad to hear it." *Probably the cleanest thing in the room.*

Keating looked down at the table. Among the plates and string and garbage were several of Striker's weapons, the housing cracked open and the guts spilling out like cornucopias of gears and wires. Fixing, inventing, improving—he was never done with his creations. They were always works in progress. Always better than anything Keating could buy for his street rats, no matter the price. *He's an asset, if an ill-mannered, grubby piece of work.*

He flicked through the mess with one gloved finger, until he uncovered the handle of a silver paper knife. Not something a streetkeeper would own. "Is this the weapon that hurt you?"

Striker grunted and took a pull at the bottle, wiping his mouth on his sleeve.

Keating saw the crest on the handle of the knife and frowned, first shock, and then a worm of anger, sliding through his guts. He picked it up, making a fist around the elegant coat of arms. *Bancroft.* What was his knife doing in Striker's leg? The Roth family kept turning up these days like an invasive weed.

"May I keep this?" he said, already sliding the knife into his pocket.

Striker's lip curled. "Why not? I've got others. A knife's a knife, and that's not the sharpest. Did for me well enough, though. Gypsy bastard who had it was a professional."

Interesting. What was Bancroft doing with a professional knife man? Or was this the work of bizarre coincidence? It was one more thing to follow up on. He watched Striker take another swig and decided to get down to business. "I have a job for you. There's a man who needs killing."

The streetkeeper glanced at his bandaged thigh. "How soon?"

"Now. The man's name is Dr. Magnus. I expect he'll be staying somewhere close at hand. He means to annoy me, and I won't have it."

"Give me another day or two and I'll be back on my feet."

"Get others and do it now. Use some of those interesting guns you've made. I know you have plenty stored at the dockyard."

He'd only just arranged for Striker's excess arsenal to be moved to a locked and guarded shed at a yard owned by Keating Utility. The streetkeeper had been stockpiling his lethal inventions in a seaman's chest at the foot of his bed. Given the neighborhood's reputation as a den of thieves and cutthroats, it was only a matter of time before the guns found their way into the worst possible hands. Peace of mind was worth the price of cutting a new key.

But at the mention of the dockyard, Striker flinched. He covered it quickly, but Keating caught it all the same. "What is it?"

"The Gypsy bastard took my key."

Keating's vision went white, the room disappearing for a beat. Then it was back, red-tinged with rage. *"What?"* He spat the word with such fury, the two grooms who had come with him backed away. They knew his temper.

Keating could barely breathe. The Harter Engine supplies were also in that locker, and much more. But that wasn't the point. It was the disappointment. "That was careless, Striker." This time it was a whisper. "I trusted you to guard my back. Do you understand me? I *trusted* you, and you let me down."

Striker's mouth pressed into a hard line. "I'll get it back. I've got a thirst for payback. A terrible thirst, sir."

Keating leaned in closer, smelling the stink of the man, but he didn't recoil even when his lips nearly touched Striker's ear. "Why am I just hearing about this now? Why didn't you come and tell me right away?"

Striker's gaze flicked his way, but didn't hold his regard. "I couldn't walk, sir."

Keating swore softly. The street value of the supplies from Harter's was incalculable. If the thief knew what he was about, the locker was already empty. Rogue power vendors sought to rob the steam barons at every turn—and every barber, baker, and candlestick maker wanted to pay the filth to do it. The only way to exert control was to ensure that nothing—no machine, no generator, no wind-driven device—would ever be built in the sheds and alleys of the city's underbelly.

"That's a poor showing for a man who is supposed to run my streets. You could have sent a note."

"I never learned my letters. And I couldn't send a runner, 'cause then they'd know my business."

"Excuses." And the delay meant that changing the padlock would be an afterthought at best. Still, he turned to one of his men. "Grimsby, get someone down there to check the shed. Get a new lock on it."

With an air that verged on insolence, Striker pushed the bottle onto the table. It was empty. "My apologies, again, sir."

The statement was as sincere as he was likely to get, but Keating felt as chill as January ditch water. Apologies meant nothing. They were an epilogue to carelessness.

"You're lucky I let you live to say you're sorry. Do you know what my father did to me when I failed as a boy?"

"No, sir."

Keating ground his teeth a moment before he replied. "He would not permit me to eat until the fault was corrected. Oh, I was allowed at the table, and the food was set before me, but I was not to touch it. If I did, I would be beaten until my back was raw. So I learned to sit and smell my supper, and my mouth would water and my belly would cramp, but there would be no eating. Not until whatever sin I had committed was sponged away. And just to be sure I felt the full force of my shortcomings, my mother would not be allowed to eat, nor my brothers or sisters. We would endure together, if any one of us erred. Father was evenhanded that way."

Keating looked into Striker's eyes and saw nothing but a kind of dull curiosity. Whatever Keating's lot had been, it was fair to say a brown-skinned bastard from the dockside had seen worse. That just made Keating angrier, his resentment gnawing from his groin to his throat.

"My father was a holy man," he spat. "He dressed up his punishments in scripture. It was hard for a child to argue with chapter and verse."

As he was speaking, Keating took a step away from his streetkeeper. It gave him the chance to find firm footing. When he struck, he put his weight behind a perfect left hook. Keating's knuckles cracked against the side of Striker's head with a meaty thud. And he was fast; too fast for the man to block the unexpected blow.

Striker sailed from the chair, sprawling facedown on the floor, sliding like a sack of meal through the grit.

Didn't expect that from me, did you? Keating's blood fizzed, the violence of the moment like a tonic. He flexed his throbbing hand, grimacing with pain and the beginnings of a smile. *Sometimes blood is a better release than a whore.* "You'll get no sermons from me. I prefer to keep things simple."

Striker rolled to his side, cradling his face in one hand. Keating's groom moved forward, just in case he planned to fight back. Striker's eyes had gone dark with murderous anger, but he stayed down.

Keating moved closer so that he stood with the man at his feet. He nudged him with a toe. "Sometimes dogs need a good beating. Now get up and start hunting."

CHAPTER TWENTY-FIVE

"HOW DO I LOOK?" IMOGEN ASKED, EXECUTING A SHARP turn so her train curled around her feet like an affectionate kitten.

"Lovely as always," Evelina replied. "Every man in the place will faint dead away, overwhelmed by your astonishing beauty."

Imogen made a face. "I'm not too pale for this color?"

"No. It suits you."

Imogen wore a shell pink, a shade just off cream, the bodice embroidered with pale green and pink roses twining around a shimmering latticework of tiny brass gears. The style was called *à l'automate,* the latest mode since *à la girafe* and *à l'égyptienne.* There was no possibility anyone would mistake Imogen for an automaton, but the glittering effect was lovely.

"And why are you so particular about your toilette?" Evelina asked airily. "Have you set your cap at some fine young peer of the realm?"

Evelina had chosen a simpler dress in a shade of rose that set off her darker coloring. Imogen's face flushed until she almost matched it. "No special reason."

They linked arms, starting down the stairs. "Is Mr. Penner going to be in attendance?" Evelina asked, thinking of what she had seen as she had come out of the tea shop. Bucky had been kissing Imogen's hand, and the look on her friend's face had been anything but displeased.

But now Imogen was the picture of innocence. "I assure you I have no idea."

Evelina let the matter drop, making up her mind to keep an eye on matters that evening.

The two girls had spent the afternoon getting ready for the Season; the presentation was only days away. Evelina had collected three new dresses she had ordered when she first got to London and, at her grandmamma's insistence, ordered three more. The seamstress had also finished altering her mother's presentation gown, and now that was spread out on the bed—too pretty to put away quite yet.

To be sure, there were many, many more important things to do than buy new clothes—such as find out who owned the warehouse where she had found the cube. There seemed to be no way of finding out without drawing attention to herself, which was the very last thing she wanted. In addition, a copy of *Barrett's Guide to the Mechanics of Ancient Europe* sat on the desk, waiting for her to do some research on the mysterious cube—but she was only human. No young, bright woman on the threshold of life was immune to the fascination of a months-long orgy of parties, and there was something wonderful about seeing her name inscribed on so many invitations. She'd had to order more calling cards.

And, to be honest, the encounter in the warehouse had made her cautious. She had lost none of her determination to protect Imogen and her family, but whoever had kept the dragon would be scouring London for news of other adepts. And by returning Bird to her, Magnus had shown that he knew more about Evelina than she liked. She was no coward, but she had an increasingly sharp urge to dissolve into the crowd of innocent young debutantes and concern herself with nothing more than waltzes and bonnet ribbons and blessed security.

They arrived at the parlor door, where many guests were already milling about. Now that the lights were back on and the Gold King was smiling on Hilliard House, it looked like the cream of London had come out for Lord Bancroft's dinner party. At a quick calculation, Evelina counted a dozen men who were a baronet or better. She spotted Lord B, surrounded by monocled men in dark suits and gray whiskers. Seated here and there at the periphery of the room, their wives bloomed in hothouse colors. After a shared glance, Evelina and Imogen sought out the younger crowd, who were clustered in the smaller room next door.

Evelina caught sight of Tobias and Bucky, along with a handful of the other young men in that set. Tobias was grinning his familiar fallen-angel smile, laughing at a jest. Evelina's chest tightened with a painful burn of wanting. When he turned her way, his eyes went dark with interest as he appraised her. Evelina's cheeks heated at the thought that Tobias Roth found her beautiful. She looked away, her heart too full to hold his gaze, and let herself drift on a complicated surge of hopes.

Imogen gave an exclamation of pleasure at the sight of her friends, and dove into the group with a broad smile. "Gentlemen, we have arrived, and you may prostrate yourselves."

"Beautiful ladies!" Bucky cried, making a sweeping bow, while Percy Hamilton fell to one knee, clutching his hands to his chest in exaggerated adoration.

Imogen said something in reply, but the words were lost on Evelina. She was too busy watching Imogen's carefully schooled expression, and how her gray eyes brightened whenever they turned Bucky's way. No wonder Imogen always lost at whist. She could never hide her feelings—not when they mattered. Bucky, in his turn, was easing his way through the throng of young men, shouldering his rivals aside without their fully realizing what was happening. Evelina smiled to herself as a rosy pink spread over Imogen's cheeks.

The next moment, Tobias was at her elbow. "My compliments to your dressmaker. She almost does you justice."

Evelina raised her chin, feigning a confidence she didn't quite feel. "Do I require justice? Perhaps I need a defender, if I am to mix in such witty company tonight." She said it with a touch of dryness.

"Undoubtedly. I understand good *couture* is a woman's armor." Tobias gave a sly smile. He looked every inch the diplomat's son, dressed in a formal black coat and snowy dress shirt mounted with pearl studs.

She tried to reconcile this man with the creator of the mechanical squid, and felt a pain behind one eye, as if her head were about to explode. "I thought a woman's armor was her virtue."

"That is a fallacy perpetuated by the underdressed. The only time virtue prevails is in light opera." He leaned closer, lowering his voice and drawing her into the embrasure of the bay window. His hand on her arm sent a pleasant shiver down the back of her legs. "And I'm sure there will be a touch of melodrama tonight. Father has proclaimed the Gold King the guest of honor."

"What?" Evelina whispered, turning so her back was to the room. She had always wondered how many Society gossips were effective lip-readers. "I know your father has to be civil—the man turned off his lights, for pity's sake—but what about that horrible scene with Dora in the garden?"

"It's all politics. At least he didn't bring that fool Jackson." Tobias made a sour face and tugged at one of his perfectly starched cuffs. "Keating's suddenly very interested in Father's doings. It brings to mind that old saw about keeping friends close and enemies closer."

Her throat tightened. "What does Lord Bancroft say?"

"What choice does he have but to smile and bring out the best wine?" A worried crease formed between his brows. "It's complicated—all markets and investments and patents. The barons are catching us, one by one, by holding our pocketbooks hostage."

She blew out a frustrated breath and glanced out the window, longing for the freedom of the high wire, where she could dance above all the complexities. It was a fine springtime evening, the sun just dipping below the London rooftops. The small patch of sky she could see was scattered with clouds, their bottoms burnished gold by the light. Tobias's tone made it sound like the sun might never come up again.

"Hello," he said suddenly. "Who's that coming up the walk?"

Evelina leaned an inch to see around the fold of the heavy velvet drape. Panic stopped her breath. "That's Dr. Magnus!" she hissed.

She got a sudden flash of the bakery box with her bird. Gooseflesh ran up her arms and she jerked away from the window, nearly bumping into Tobias. "Why is he here?"

But Tobias gave her a chuckle, his mood visibly lifting. "With luck, Dr. Magnus is here to see me."

"Why?" Evelina nearly gasped the word, making a few heads turn.

"He looks a bit exotic, I'll give you that, but you don't need to be skittish. He has some old feud with Father, but he's all right, you know." Tobias gave a boyish grin. "He wants me to help him build something."

She remembered the garden party, and how happy Tobias had been after talking to Magnus. "Be careful!"

"Of what?" He gave her a puzzled smile, then squeezed her arm and left her standing at the window, an anxious lump just under her heart.

NICK HAD A plan. He was, after all, the Indomitable Niccolo.

A handful of silver—or even a fistful of rubies—would never buy Magnus the kind of information he wanted about Evelina. Not from Nick. He wasn't a hero by anyone's definition—he'd done his share of surviving and had even killed a man who'd shown up at Ploughman's with evil on his mind—but Nick had his lines in the sand and Evie was one of them. Money was useful, but he was used to the lack of it, and it couldn't buy what he most wanted.

He hadn't recovered from seeing Evie in that soft and lacy bedroom, her dark hair tumbling down her back and her skin as fair as lillies. He would give his soul to touch her again, and have her touch him back the way he wanted—the way he knew in his bones was the way they were supposed to be—and he would never get that with betrayal.

It had been four days since he'd followed the doctor home from the theater, and he'd got away with making only one innocuous report. He still didn't know exactly what Magnus wanted with her, any more than he understood the man's interest in Tobias Roth. However, when it came to shady foreigners using death magic, it couldn't be good.

Withholding real information was easy enough. Warning Evelina was another matter. After the murders, the grounds of Hilliard House were now discreetly guarded by men with firearms. No nipping into her bedroom now—even if his ankle was mostly healed—unless he was going to parachute from a dirigible onto the roof.

Or, not until tonight. With guests arriving and the staff all busy with the carriages and endless deliveries to the kitchen, he'd been able to sneak across the garden and through an open window—not an easy task with the fashion for so many lights everywhere. He had to get into the house, because that's where Magnus was going, far too close to Evie for Nick's comfort. She had to be warned. He wanted to let her know he was there in case she needed help. If the doctor went too far, the Indomitable Niccolo was expert at discouraging ruffians with a knife.

Nick was crouched in a room that he guessed was used to store cleaning supplies. He'd picked this window because he could get to it, but also because no one had passed by for some time. There were pails and brooms in one corner, and shelves with sacks of borax and washing soda and jars of polish against the other. Some kind of mechanical device on wheels sat mutely across from him—perhaps one of those steam-powered things that sucked dust from the floor. The rich were strange. After all, wasn't the ground where dirt was supposed to be? Nick gave a mental shrug. Whatever the case, no one was wanting to suck dirt now, with company in the house, and that made the room a good hiding place.

He shuffled to the door, reaching up to turn the knob and opening it a crack. He peered out, barely daring to breathe.

Two men were walking away from his position, speaking in low voices. Nick went completely still, recognizing Dr. Magnus's familiar form. Magnus, who seemed to have eyes in the back of his head. He'd caught Nick following him once. Something told Nick it would be a bad idea to let that happen again and he shrank back another degree, his eye pressed right to the crack of the door.

Then the two figures stopped, facing each other. Nick

froze, recognizing the other man as Lord Bancroft. He'd been watching Evie's comings and goings long enough that he knew almost everyone at Hilliard House.

This is interesting. What were they doing in the downstairs part of the house? The toffs weren't supposed to hang about here. Not even the servants were in these quarters, with the dinner party in progress—they were with the food and drink and horses. Nick had made sure of that before he'd slipped inside—at least as much as he could tell from a lot of listening and creeping about.

But of course that was the answer, wasn't it? No one was supposed to know the men were here. Nick realized he'd been holding his breath for too long and wanted to cough. He sucked in air as quietly as he could.

"I understand you are the Gold King's latest acquisition," said Magnus, his voice carrying a snide edge. "His new friend, or at least his newest lackey destined to help him with his political connections. How odd, because the gossip I heard just days ago said that you were bent on challenging the man. Some ill-advised dabbling with a new kind of engine."

"He has chosen to invite me to work with him rather than against." Bancroft's tone was impatient, hot to the other man's cold.

"In other words, he's put you under his thumb. How merciful, but a lord does qualify as big game, even for a steam baron. Crushing one altogether might cause him to break a sweat."

Bancroft snorted. "Good to hear."

What's this about? Nick could almost taste the tension between the men, the roots of it clearly deeper than this single conversation. *And what does the Gold King have to do with all this?*

"Keating's prudent. You could be useful. Plus, he wants a title for himself, after all, and that will be hard to weasel out of Victoria if he's mounted the head of a viscount on his study wall. In broad terms, aristocrats find the public ruin of their peers off-putting." Magnus smoothed his goatee, looking thoughtful. "Count your blessings this happened now. In a few years, Keating might have enough power that he won't need to show restraint."

"Thank you for pointing out my precarious position." Bancroft folded his arms, leaning back an inch to look into the taller man's face. "But I assure you, I was entirely aware of the abyss yawning at my feet."

The ambassador was a tired man, Nick thought, adjusting his position to see the man's face better. For all the crisp quality of Lord Bancroft's garments, his skin looked as rumpled as clothes that had been slept in for a week. He also looked like he'd been in a fight. There was a bruise on the side of his face and he was moving like a man who ached.

Bancroft curled his lip. "But something tells me you aren't here to offer me advice."

Magnus nodded. "True. I require your assistance with Keating."

"Are you mad? I have no influence with the man!"

"You always find a way, Ambassador. You are not a diplomat for nothing." Magnus made a gesture that whisked away all objections. "Keating has something I want. You must convince him to relinquish it to me."

"I will not!"

"No?" The doctor's voice was suddenly low and dangerous, like velvet soaked in contact poison. "I knew you would say this, and I am far, far ahead of you. I have something you want back. Not just for your sake, but the sake of your family."

"You!" Bancroft's exclamation was a snarl. "You murdered my men."

Nick started. *Murder?*

"I did not." Magnus shrugged. "Not that you are required to believe me, but I swear to you it was not my hand that held the blade. But I do have your trunks and their cargo."

What the bloody hell are they talking about? Nick's legs were starting to cramp, but he didn't dare move.

Bancroft lunged at Magnus, as if he were going to strangle him where he stood. Magnus sidestepped the attack, grabbing the ambassador's lapel and using it to push him against the plain white paint of the servants' corridor. "Get a grip on yourself, man!"

Nick could hear Bancroft's breathing, the heavy, gasping whistle of someone whose strength is all but spent. Nevertheless, Magnus held Bancroft pinned until the older man went limp with submission.

The doctor spoke between clenched teeth. "Keating has Athena's Casket. I need it."

Bancroft's face twisted. "What are you talking about?"

"Keating is building a gallery. He intends to put the casket in his show of archaeological treasures, but I want it for my research. It is too important a piece to waste on him."

"Why don't you simply ask him for it?"

"I did. He prevaricated, spinning some nonsense about how the shipment was delayed. It's clear that he wants to keep it for himself."

Nick was growing boggled. Too much information was flying too fast, and he wanted to—had to—straighten up. The urge to flee was growing by the second. Getting caught spying was bad enough, but there was no question he'd heard something of value, even if he didn't grasp it all now. He started to stand, moving inch by inch, praying his knees didn't crack.

"It was from Greece?" Bancroft asked, a cautious note in his voice.

"From Rhodes."

Bancroft said nothing, his breath hissing in his throat. Nick wondered what that silence meant.

"Come now," said Dr. Magnus, releasing Bancroft and smoothing out the lapel, "you'll get it for me, won't you? All I want is the casket. I'm not an unreasonable man."

Bancroft made a panicked noise, as if that was not his experience of Magnus.

The sorcerer chuckled.

A flicker of defiance crossed Bancroft's face. "What do you want it for?"

"My work. Benevolence. Order."

"Benevolence?" Bancroft spat. "Call it tyranny. No, vanity. You and Keating want the same thing. You both want to see your reflection everywhere you look. Maybe if the world is remade in your image, you'll believe you exist."

Magnus muttered something that sounded like a curse. "And you are disintegrating into a shadow of the man you were. Get the casket for me, and I'm gone. Beyond that, I don't care what games you and Keating play."

"And if I can't?" Something new resonated in Bancroft's voice. To Nick, it sounded like a mix of anger and dawning realization. He would have laid good coin that a penny had dropped for the man, though he couldn't say what had prompted it.

"I have your trunks. Jasper Keating is not the only man who can hurt you. I trust that you do not need a demonstration."

"I remember what you did in Austria."

Nick's muscles screamed with tension, frozen with fascinated horror. It was like watching a terrible accident, where one could not stand to bear witness, and yet could not turn aside.

Suddenly, Bancroft pushed away from the wall, making Magnus fall back. The ambassador spun on the heel of his glossy shoe, striding stiffly away. Not another word. Not a single nod of acknowledgment. Just his back, straight and square and impeccably garbed in black.

It didn't matter. Even Nick could tell that he had lost. Magnus laughed, low and long. After a minute or two, he followed at a slow saunter.

Nick gripped the wall, finally rising to his full height. He was sweating, a sick, greasy sensation in the pit of his stomach. Part of it was the aftermath of tension. That had been a close call. By the Dark Furies, in what sort of a place was Evelina living?

IMOGEN NOTICED THE way her brother looked at Evelina, and a tiny thread of worry disturbed her contentment. The evening was perfect in so many ways—she and Evelina were safe from dragons, the power was back on, her dress was perfect, and the company couldn't have been more congenial. And she was watching Bucky Penner with intense interest, because he never seemed to be more than a few steps away. However—the very same thing appeared to be happening between Evelina and Tobias, and that concerned her.

There was no doubt that Imogen loved her dashing brother, but she had no illusions about what he got up to at his clubs. Bucky did the same things, true, but some young men seemed to treat such shenanigans as a rite of passage—a moment in time that was folded away and revisited years hence for nostalgia's sake. She could hardly blame someone for that. But Tobias never seemed to have that sense of a future, and that frightened her both for him and for Evelina. She drifted in their direction, knowing what they discussed was none of her business, but somehow unable to stop herself.

She never got far enough to overhear their conversation. Instead, her father's low tones came from somewhere behind her.

"What do you think you're playing at?" he growled.

Imogen froze, her hand poised over the tray of sherry glasses one of the footmen offered. Then, she realized it wasn't her to whom Lord Bancroft spoke. She took a glass and angled her body as she sipped, realizing that she was standing with her back to him and that he was addressing a man she recognized as Jasper Keating's cousin. What was his name again? Harrison? Hartman?

Whoever he was answered in a strained voice. "I did exactly as you instructed, no more and no less. I returned the crates to my warehouse and informed my cousin of their arrival."

She felt, rather than saw, her father's flinch. His next words came out as a furious rasp. "We'll talk about this later."

"You must believe me. Whoever intimated that there is a missing article is quite mistaken."

"Mad, perhaps," her father conceded. "But he has never been careless about his facts. In any event, this is not a conversation for tonight."

And her father walked away, leaving Imogen with an

intriguing—and disturbing—scrap of information. She casually glanced in the direction of the other speaker, appearing to look for someone else. Harriman! That was his name. Despite his connection to the Gold King, he was a nobody. What would Father be doing with a man like that?

Whatever it was had to do with a warehouse and crates—Harriman's warehouse, apparently—and one of her father's schemes. Cold terror prickled up her arms. She had long been aware—probably far more than Tobias—that Lord Bancroft always had his fingers in a dozen problematic pies. That was the fate of a girl with some intelligence who was forced to be quiet and polite and part of the furniture. One learned far more than was appetizing.

Now a thousand details came flooding back. Harriman had come to the house about four days ago, slipping in to see her father and slipping out again without the usual stay-for-tea sociability a home visit implied. Were Harriman and her father involved with the boxes she'd seen in the warehouse? The blood on the floor? Grace Child's death? Imogen suddenly felt weak, the taste of the sherry sickly and cloying on her tongue. *Dear God, what if he's guilty of something?*

Evelina had said the next step in the investigation was to find out who the warehouse and those crates belonged to. *Those crates were for Harriman's cousin, the Gold King.* And her father seemed to think Harriman was responsible for an object going missing. Lord Bancroft had instructed Harriman to return some crates. Return them from where? And why? *And do I tell Evelina?*

The question hit her like a physical pain. Her first instinct was to share everything she had just heard, but caution brought her up short. It was one thing to hunt down a killer, believing it would clear Tobias from suspicion. It was another when the murderer might be your father.

Ridiculous! She pushed the idea away vehemently. *That can't be true. I won't have it.* Her father was a schemer, but that was all. The best thing she could do was forget she ever overheard him talking. That was the problem with eavesdropping—it was too easy to get the wrong end of the stick. Imogen trembled, caught between what her mind knew and what her heart was willing to accept.

"Miss Roth?"

She jumped so violently that her sherry nearly spilled down the front of her dress. "Mr. Penner!"

"I interrupted your thoughts." He regarded her with steady brown eyes.

"They weren't very good ones." She guessed that he'd watched her all evening, weighing every nuance in her attitude toward him. It had made her jumpy until now—but after the incident with her father, she didn't have the energy to edit every twitch of her eyelash. "I would welcome some distraction."

His mouth quirked. "I'm pleased to have some useful function."

"I seem to have lost mine." She cleared her throat. "There is no teapot nearby for me to guard."

They stared at one another for a moment. Imogen grew increasingly uncomfortable, unsure what to say. Her mind groped for subject matter—the weather, the liveliness of the guests, the handsome brocade of his waistcoat. It all seemed boring enough to make anyone scream and run away, and she wanted him close right then.

"How fare your sisters?" He had three—one older, two younger. She'd visited with them last summer.

"They flourish," he said with a polite nod. "Noisily and with gusto. How is Poppy?"

"She is well and remains with her grandparents at Horne Hill."

"In Devonshire?"

"Yes." Miraculously, Imogen's shoulders were starting to unknot, although part of her mind was still occupied with her father's discussion with Harriman. "I trust in another year or two Poppy will recover from the catapult trauma."

"Ah," Bucky looked away. "Well, it *was* the season for plums, and my father had just given me a book of da Vinci's designs."

"A parent should know better," Imogen said with mock

severity. The Plum Affair was the outrage of several harvests ago, but she never tired of teasing him about it.

He smiled at the memory, his eyes crinkling at the corners. "On the contrary, Miss Roth. My father makes guns for a living. The idea of his son and heir shooting at things is hardly a source of parental concern."

The Penners might have been—as her father put it—common as turnips, but their large weapons manufactories in Yorkshire had turned a tidy profit for the last three generations. "I suppose the future magnate has to learn his marksmanship somewhere, although Poppy is still a trifle disturbed by your efforts. She regards fresh fruit with the utmost suspicion."

He made a dismissive sound. "I was determined to hit every pane of glass in her bedroom window. There were fourteen, as I recall. Excellent target practice, but it was only for one afternoon. She will recover."

"Are you as rotten to your own sisters?"

"Rotten?" he grinned. "Such attentions are the highest mark of my regard."

Imogen cocked an eyebrow. "It must be extremely sincere regard, to sacrifice so many wormy plums."

Then he bowed, all courtly courtesy. "Where it concerns ladies I regard as diamonds of the highest water, I would far rather shower them with more appealing attentions."

Imogen felt herself flushing and turned away to set her sherry glass on the tray of a passing servant. "Ah, of course. Your father also has some breweries, I think?"

He laughed at that, a hearty sound that made her grin in response. She simply couldn't help it. "That is very true, Miss Roth, and I do prefer my father's beer to my father's weapons. But before that statement causes you concern, I promise to spare you a bath of good Yorkshire ale."

"That is a relief."

He then gave her a look that still held mischief, but of a much more adult kind. "I trust that you will not object to attentions of a dryer nature."

"They may be dry," she returned, "but is that the extent of their wholesome qualities? A lady in this day and age must be careful that there is no rotten fruit involved." *In other words, Bucky Penner, what are you up to?*

Bucky took her hand, bowing over it with all the grace of Sir Walter Raleigh making obeisance to the queen. "My lady, you may rely that my every intention is earnest and honorable, and entirely fruit-free."

Imogen sucked in a breath as his lips touched her gloved fingers. This was as serious as she'd ever seen him, and his manner said far more than his words. *So he does want to court me!*

Something in her chest gave a tiny pang, and she realized what made Bucky different from the other young men who begged for a dance or a chance to turn pages while she played the piano. Like Evelina, Bucky had spent a good deal of time at their house for years. They had jokes that spanned years. She was the girl who always had to have her toast slightly burned. He was the boy always up to messy mischief. Who they were formed part of the equation between them, not just how much of a fortune she had to offer.

Bucky straightened, his eyes meeting hers with unusual seriousness. With the lightness of a swift's shadow, an understanding passed between them that something had turned a corner. They agreed to share more than banter now.

And then Percy Hamilton's voice cut through the air, shattering the moment. "Disconnect me! There you are, Miss Roth!"

Blast. And in that moment, her other anxieties came tumbling back down on her soul—her father, the murder, the steam barons—all summoned by Percy's shrill voice. Beneath that discomfort was the fearful certainty that she would be sold to whoever could do the most for her father's career.

As if reading her need for reassurance, Bucky gave her hand a squeeze.

CHAPTER TWENTY-SIX

EVELINA HAD SPENT THE LAST HALF HOUR PRETENDING everything was normal. Guests had come and gone from the room, each arrival making her start, afraid it would be Magnus. Her first instinct was to plead a headache and slip from the gathering, but the crowd made her feel safer. Besides, giving in to abject cowardice was a bad way to begin the Season.

Courage was sometimes the only meaningful weapon. Back at the Wollaston Academy, on that first day of school, the headmistress had made her stand on a stool at the front of the class while she was introduced, stiff and awkward in ringlets and petticoats. One look at the sea of spiteful faces, and she knew she would never fit in. They'd take her down like a doe among wolves at the first sign of weakness. Only Imogen had shown the least curiosity about who Evelina was. School did prepare a young person for life, but never in the ways parents expected.

So Evelina smiled and made light conversation, determined to look bright and happy. A champagne fountain appeared, wheeled in by two of the footmen. Evelina wasn't sure it was quite a success. The pump was steam operated, the heat melted the ice too quickly, and a few of the guests complained behind their hands that the wine was a shade too warm.

"I just don't think these new inventions are the thing. I mean, certainly the trains are efficient and industry finds them useful, but steam has no part in a gentleman's home," said a whiskered man named Sir Darius Thorne.

"I rather like the novelty," protested another. "Something

new. Tradition can stand to be shaken up a bit from time to time."

"Tradition might be dull, but it is seldom smelly, noisy, and greasy, not to mention vulgar."

"You should come 'round to my in-laws at Christmas dinner. They might prove you wrong about that. Nevertheless, I'd watch what you say. With talk of the gentry joining the rebels, it's best to love steam and all its workings, at least in public."

She edged around the room, looking for someone she wanted to talk to. She thought she'd seen Alice Keating's red head go by. Unfortunately, she got stuck in a crush near the doorway before she could find the Gold King's daughter.

There was a conversation going on behind her. "Did you hear the Reynolds trial is set for next week?" asked a basso voice that sounded like a human tuba.

"That was fast," someone responded in a light tenor.

"They don't expect it to last more than a day or two. They're already clearing the prison courtyard for the pyre."

"I hope it lights faster than the last one."

"You mean the sorcerer from the boys' school?"

"I paid good money to get in to see that, and the man died of smoke before we got to see him burn."

Agitated, Evelina inched back the way she had come, nearly locking bustles with Lady Liverton. When the clockwork trolley bearing drinks rattled by, she took a glass of sherry to fortify herself. There were just too many people in the room.

She'd just sipped the sweet liquid when a fat, jolly laugh sounded behind her. She turned to see the commissioner of the Metropolitan Police chatting amiably with Jasper Keating. *No wonder Uncle Sherlock is sometimes wary of the police force. They're cozy with the steam barons.*

"It was the damnedest thing," the commissioner was saying. "At least half a dozen bodies found in pieces yesterday, washed up by the tides. So sorry they turned out to be your cousin's Chinamen. Damned inconvenient to lose a whole set. Some sort of tribal war, I suppose. Can't get anything out of that bunch. Can't understand a word they say. Some babble about a dragon. Their kingpin, perhaps?"

"They've been smoking their own opium." Keating sounded put upon. "Harriman will have to hire a fresh crew. I'll tell him to make them local boys this time."

Chill horror drove the warmth of the sherry from her stomach. Evelina bit her lip, recalling the blood Imogen had seen on the floor of the warehouse and the Chinese tailors who worked in the area. *Dragon? Bodies?* There hadn't been anything in the papers, but then the death of foreigners, however gruesome, never seemed to count as much as someone like the Gray King.

She didn't have time to think further. With a sudden start, she saw Dr. Magnus bowing over Alice Keating's hand, giving the red-haired girl a lingering look that seemed more scientific curiosity than male appreciation.

Evelina calculated the distance to the door, but before she could react, he had seen her. His tall, dark form was coming her way, the force of his personality preceeding him like a wave. Evelina braced herself.

"My dear Miss Cooper, well met." He bowed low, his dark eyes crinkling pleasantly. "I was hoping we would meet again. Our acquaintance has so far been limited to passing in doorways."

"No, we've not been properly introduced."

"I know such things are properly done by a mutual acquaintance, but they all appear to be having a splendid time elsewhere. I am Dr. Magnus, an old friend of the Roth family."

He stood so close that she could feel power radiating from him. Evelina looked him in the eye, doing her best to hide the fact that she felt the prickle of his magic against her skin. It wasn't a clean, bright power, but dark and somehow oily.

She was tongue-tied for a long moment, and then gave in to her impulse to come to the point. If he was as dangerous as she surmised, games were useless. "I understand you are the one who found my toy bird. I'm extremely grateful for its return."

He gave a long, slow smile. "It was my pleasure to be of service."

"How did you know it was mine?" She supposed that it was the feel of her magic that had given her away, but she was interested in his answer.

He flashed white teeth. "I have my means, which shall hopefully be made plain as the evening progresses. I do believe we are being called to dinner. Shall we?" He offered Evelina his arm.

She didn't want to be near him a moment longer, but it would have been the height of rudeness to refuse. Gingerly, she slipped her gloved hand over his sleeve and let herself be led into the dining room. She heard Imogen's laugh somewhere ahead, and wished she had stayed close to her friend, even if Imogen had been dogged by Stanford Whitlock and Captain Smythe all evening. The captain had nearly poured champagne down his front when Imogen had smiled in his direction—although that smile might have been meant for Bucky, who was standing directly behind him at the time. It seemed Imogen and Bucky hadn't been more than a dozen feet apart all night. If there had been any doubt that something was going on between the two, it had been dispelled in Evelina's mind.

And she felt just as overset as Smythe, but for quite different reasons. Dr. Magnus had a hungry look that reminded her of one of Ploughman's tigers.

The room was large and elegant, the gaslights softened to cast a gentle glow on the glittering company. The table decorations were tastefully simple arrangements of spring blossoms set into chalices of silver. Footmen glided to and fro, all efficiency in their white gloves and stony faces. Evelina found her place card, done in Lady Bancroft's elegant hand.

With a twist of anxiety, she discovered it was next to her escort's. She swallowed hard, barely resisting the urge to tear up the offending scrap of paper. Dr. Magnus wanted a conversation with her, and she guessed he left nothing to chance. In some men it would be endearing, but after the bird in the bakery box, it was creepy.

"Are you going to sit, Miss Cooper?" he asked in a faintly mocking tone.

She didn't like to be toyed with. Evelina's vision blackened around the edges, anger and the tight lacing of her stays strangling her. She took a step back from the table.

Magnus raised an eyebrow. The room was filling with guests, the light shimmering on jewels and silks. A babble filled Evelina's ears like a spring stream, making it hard to think. If she caused a scene, she would never find the nerve to return. *Courage. He's just another bully to be faced down.* Evelina swallowed down her discomfort and settled into her chair.

The evening did not immediately improve. The first course was a chilled green soup the color of pond scum. There was no way it would pass her lips, so she had to look busy or get dragged into a chat with the doctor. She tried talking to the man on her left, but he was a banker who had no idea what to say to young ladies.

Bored, she looked around the table. Lord Bancroft had the flush of a man who had been drinking steadily. To his right was the Gold King. Despite their smiles, the air between them sparked with tension. If there had been any other option, Bancroft would clearly have tossed his guest into the street.

Both men were older, proud, and perfectly dressed, but there the resemblance ended. Where Keating was hard and clean-edged as steel, Bancroft was old stone, porous, and crumbling, his features blurring as time and drink had their way. Mind you, there was nothing indistinct about his bad temper that night. Lord B was watching Magnus with a look akin to hatred.

Keating's perusal of Tobias reminded her of a scientist scrutinizing a new form of algae. Tobias appeared to be doing his best to entertain Keating's red-haired daughter, but she could tell it was just good manners. He was restless and trying to hide it, while poor Alice was making every effort to charm him. Evelina felt a pang of dislike that had nothing to do with Alice herself and everything to do with her proximity to Tobias.

Seeing Evelina unoccupied, Magnus moved in like a polite shark. "To answer your earlier question," he said in a quiet voice, clearly meant for her ears only, "my first clue about your bird was easily obtained from the vibrations left on the metal it was made of. I think you and I recognize each other for what we are."

She remembered Bird saying that Magnus had caught her scent. *So it's true. Magic users can tell each other's traces apart.* She'd been able to track the magic from Grace's gold to the warehouse, but she'd never known enough practitioners to test the theory to any greater degree.

He smiled gently. "I am a mesmerist by profession, but we share an interest in imaginative mechanics."

She wondered just how imaginative he meant. Up to and including bringing them to life? She struggled to find polite words. "Is that so?"

"How were you introduced to the subject?"

"Here and there. Machines are like puzzles to solve." She gave what she hoped was a convincing smile. "And I do like a good puzzle."

He met her smirk for smirk.

"Perhaps you will find this of interest." He reached into his pocket and withdrew something. He kept it hidden in his palm as the soup plates were whisked away and turbot drizzled with lemon sauce was served. This dish smelled of cracked pepper and parsley, and Evelina's stomach perked up.

When the footmen had retreated, Magnus set the device down on the white damask linen of the tablecloth. It was a tiny beetle, made of a black, shiny metal. He made a gesture with his fingers, uttering a single word under his breath. With a faint clicking sound, the beetle scuttled across the snowy table, hiding under the gold-edged lips of the plates. Evelina tensed, certain one of the ladies was going to scream and faint dead away.

"Put that away!" she hissed. "Lady Bancroft doesn't deserve to have her dinner ruined!"

And that was the least of it. He was using magic. In public. Hadn't he heard about Nellie Reynolds? Evelina started to breathe hard and fast, her fingers digging into the edge of the table.

"I am a mesmerist of great renown, Miss Cooper," the doctor all but purred. "People expect to have their perception dazzled when I am in the room."

"You're taking too great a risk."

Magnus ignored her. The beetle burrowed unobserved through the wilderness of centrepieces and butter knives. It actually ran over Mrs. Fairchild's wrist, climbing up and around her emerald bracelet, but she was too fascinated by her conversation with the younger Mr. Bellamy to do more than absently rub her skin after the beetle had been and gone. It puddled through some dropped sauce, tracking tiny dots of green behind it, before it finished its grand loop around their end of the table and returned to Magnus's hand. He made another word and gesture and set it ceremoniously before Evelina.

"What do you make of that?" he asked.

Panic-stricken, she picked it up quickly, hiding it in her lap. It buzzed with the same slippery energy as she sensed from Magnus, and that made her want to wipe her hands on her napkin. She turned the creature over, half hiding it beneath the edge of the tablecloth and wishing the lights were brighter. A careful examination, however, revealed no way to wind the thing up. "How does it run?"

He bent close, so that his lips were close to her ear. He smelled of an exotic cologne. "A relatively simple spell."

There is no deva!

"It's a mere charlatan's trick. The thing has no mind of its own, no independent intelligence. It burns with no more meaning than a match."

Sorcery. When she turned to stare, his face was far too close to hers. She could tell from his expression that he saw the mix of curiosity and alarm on her face.

Magic was life. If it didn't come from a trapped deva, there were only two other sources of power. One was the magic user's own energy—dangerous, but still ethical. The other was life stolen from another. The blackest spells came from murder.

Folk practitioners like Gran Cooper used devas. The rest was the shadowy domain of sorcerers. Evelina set the beetle down on the table as fast as if it were a live scorpion. "A dangerous toy, my lord, if the wrong person saw you at play." *You could get us both imprisoned or killed!*

To her vast relief, he scooped it up and put it back into his pocket. "Perhaps I am rash, but this demonstration saves a very long-winded explanation of what I am, and the fact that you comprehend the discussion tells me a great deal about you, Miss Cooper."

His words jolted her like a hot needle.

"What do you want from me?" she demanded under her breath. If he found her understanding informative, she was learning a great deal by the fact that almost every word they'd exchanged had been in a whisper. Dr. Magnus wasn't suitable for public conversations.

He waved his hand in the air. "My interest is in the search for truth. I have long believed that perfect truth will be found not as an abstract concept, but in living consciousness. Incarnate, so to speak."

Magnus paused, surveying the next course. "Beef. How very English."

Evelina tasted her food, but was too nervous to register the flavors. "And?"

"Mm. The rosemary is a nice touch. Where was I? Oh, yes. Truth is as old as creation. If you adopt the notion that man strives to reach perfection, to return to that perfect state of truth that existed at the moment of creation when spirit and flesh became manifest, you will have to concede that the rational mind, as demonstrated by our burgeoning level of technology, is an expression of our desire for truth and the blissful repose of perfect wisdom."

"Excuse me?"

A flicker of impatience crossed his features. "Our inventions equal our desire to realize divine truth."

"Because they're rational and capable of perfection." Despite her caution, Evelina was interested.

"Exactly." He raised a finger in the air. "Machinery is rationalism meeting creativity. What's missing from that equation is spirit. If we could infuse spirit into a machine, we would have achieved the perfect balance of truth. Not like my toy bug, but true union of mind and machine. A completely rational flesh with all the godlike intelligence of spirit."

Evelina tried to envision Bird as the expression of divine truth and failed. Still, Magnus was as equally curious as she was about blending magic and machine. The apprehension in her chest was joined by a fugitive flutter of excitement. Even better, he was willing to discuss it. "What would the combination of machine and spirit accomplish?"

Magnus put down his fork, his expression deadly serious. "Freedom from pain, for those who suffer it. Unlimited mechanical power, for those who need it. Genius, for those who know how to find it."

"Genius?"

"Imagine the swiftness of human thought combined with the tireless strength of brass and steel. What brilliant computations could not be achieved then? And that would just be the beginning. Imagine the wisdom to be gained by true immortality."

Evelina stabbed a bit of potato with her fork. She couldn't decide if Dr. Magnus was insane or a revolutionary genius. "Is this philosophy of your own making?"

"Not solely. I seek to further my work by studying ancient writings, and by creating my own examples. Old devices and new freaks of nature, you might say."

Something in his expression said that was a private joke. Irritation pricked her, but she moved on. "Have you applied these theories?"

"I have. My greatest limitations have always been my mechanical abilities. I have as much talent as the most accomplished of the makers, but tire of tedium of practiced application. My greatest achievements have always occurred when I work with another who takes up that share of the burden."

Does this explain his interest in Tobias? "And then?"

"Oh, there have been a few solid victories. I made some automata, truly fine ones in their day. And there was a longcase clock that had some of my best work. I wonder if Bancroft still has it."

"He certainly does." Evelina put down her fork, suddenly glued to Magnus's words. "I have always been fascinated by that piece. Would you please explain it to me?"

"THERE IT IS," said Magnus, once they had escaped the dessert course. "It's been many a year since I saw this beauty."

The clock on the second-floor landing was a familiar part of the house. It was a large, walnut affair with an arched top framed by carved finials. It was the most complex clock that Evelina had ever seen, with seven moving dials besides the regular face and chimes. The top part of the arch showed the zodiac. The lower part showed the phases of the moon, each with a delicately painted face.

Below was a slot where punch cards emerged at random intervals, usually fluttering to the floor to the annoyance of the maids. Only Lord Bancroft seemed to understand the cards' meaning. Evelina detested the fact that she could never figure them, or the rest of the clock, out. And so her curiosity pushed aside all caution about Dr. Magnus. This man had *built* the machine and that frustrating gulf of ignorance could be bridged within minutes.

She turned to him, forced to look up to meet his dark eyes. "The face shows everything. Time. Date. Barometric pressure. Every second of every minute. And it's accurate. Lord Bancroft said that he has to adjust the workings only once every year, and that by only a matter of seconds, and then only due to the slope of the floorboards affecting the balance of the pendulum."

Dr. Magnus bowed slightly, accepting the acknowledgment of his superior creation.

"But," Evelina said, tapping the side of the glossy case, "the dial that shows the weather has never worked. In most clocks, the weather reading follows the barometric pressure, fair if it is high and foul if it is low. But here it seems to operate independently—and it's wrong. Tonight, the sky is perfectly clear and yet the clock's hand is pointing to storm clouds."

"Indeed?" Magnus smiled.

Evelina frowned at his amusement. "It is a critical flaw in the design. Perhaps the technology is lacking. I've opened up the case to see that part of the mechanism is connected to vials of fluid rather than to a recognizable barometer."

Magnus stroked the side of the clock as fondly as if it were a favorite cat. "Who is to say that the reading refers to literal weather?"

"What other kind of weather is there?"

"The predictive value of this feature is metaphorical."

"Metaphorical?" Evelina parroted in disbelief.

"Have you not seen the cards it emits?"

"Of course I have. They've been coming fast and furious of late. They're gibberish."

"Not gibberish, a cipher Bancroft and I wrote together. The cards are prognostications and warnings. This clock is of my own design and is attuned to currents in the aether. Whenever there is a disturbance, the clock reports it."

Evelina put a hand to her forehead, as if trying to ease her pounding thoughts. "Let me understand this. Those vials of colored fluid inside the clock somehow detect fluctuations in the aether?"

"Simplistically, yes. They are chemical compounds of my own devising with varied levels of viscosity. They are tuned to detect the slightest energetic vibrations. If someone ill-wishes you in Turkestan, this device will know of it. And it will tell you, if you understand the cipher."

Twenty more questions crammed into Evelina's skull, including why Lord Bancroft was so anxious to know what was coming his way. Of course anyone wanted to know about bad luck, but was he expecting particular trouble? *Three murders. Enemies all around his table. Of course he is.*

"Why did you make this clock?"

"Because I could. And, at the time, Lord Bancroft was a friend. I was happy to give him a tool designed to aid in his political ambitions. Unfortunately, he now professes to revile the magical arts."

"Magic is forbidden in the Empire."

"That is like saying the air is forbidden. It will be there whether you approve of it or not. I can tell you possess a talent, Miss Cooper, the same way you can sense mine. The question is whether or not you have the courage to learn how to use it to its fullest advantage."

She thought of the implements in her train case—all the magical tools Gran Cooper had never explained. Someone like Magnus could teach her much about her birthright.

"Perhaps it is you who will find perfect wisdom." The look he gave her devoured her face. He lowered his chin a degree, giving her the full force of his eyes. "Perhaps it is you that I have sought for so many years."

"Um." Evelina had been doing fine until he returned to the topic of perfect wisdom. That struck the same sour note as a huckster selling a bottle of cure-all, promising too much. "If I had the potential for such impeccable wisdom, I would not be standing on a dark staircase with a stranger, unchaperoned."

She turned to leave, but he caught her arm in a bruising grip. Fear lanced through her. She gasped, jerking herself free.

He surged toward her, eyes flashing. "Don't be a fool. I can open doors of impossible wonder. I can answer your every question. I can make your life remarkable."

Evelina skittered away, cursing the encumbrance of her heavy dress. "If I live a remarkable life, it will not be at your whim, my lord!"

Magnus's lips thinned. "Is that so?" And his hand snaked out to grasp her wrist so hard she thought the bones would break.

Chapter Twenty-seven

NICK GHOSTED PAST THE PARLOR WINDOWS, KEEPING TO what shadows he could find, his feet silent in the soft flower beds. He raised up just enough to peer inside. A lone maid mopped up a spill from the carpet. He ducked out of sight before she noticed him, feeling like the thief from a comic farce.

Where had Evelina gone? He'd caught a glimpse of her leaving the dining room with Dr. Magnus, but it hadn't been possible to see where they went. And his near-encounter with Magnus and Bancroft had proved that creeping into the ground-floor rooms wasn't practical. Looking in windows wasn't getting him very far, either.

Bloody woman. What was she thinking, going off alone with Magnus? *You should have warned her about him. You should have found a way.*

Should have, would have. The story of Nick's life. Well, now he was going to act, even if that meant embarrassing himself or tackling Magnus to the ground. Every instinct said the man was trouble on a demonic scale, and Nick's self-appointed task was to keep Evie safe. It had been since the first day he'd seen her, a cherubic imp with long, dark ringlets and mud on her skirts. He wasn't about to abandon her now.

He heard the maid leaving the parlor, her mop, bucket, and broom rattling as she shuffled away with her burden. Nick squirmed through the flower beds and around the corner, heading for deeper shadow.

This was the same side of the house as Evelina's bedroom; he knew this wall well. There were a great many casement windows, all easily opened with a knife just like the one he carried. And, it was nighttime now, with this side of the house relatively free of ornamental lights, which meant he could climb without being seen.

Most of the upper windows were dark, but those on the first two floors were lit, stained glass panels floating like jewels in the darkness. Nick pulled himself up, using a drainpipe and the frames of the windows as handholds. After all that crouching and lurking, he appreciated the flow and stretch of muscle, even if his ankle was starting to complain again.

His line of ascent was between the stairway windows and the bedrooms. At the first bedroom, he saw one of the ladies' maids repairing the hem of a gown for her visibly impatient mistress. He ducked out of sight, then clambered across, hand-over-hand, to peer in the stairwell window.

Shock speared him, making his hand slip an inch. *By all the dark gods!*

Dr. Magnus was dragging Evelina toward him by the wrist, making her stumble as she tried to twist away. In a flash, Nick had his knife out, working at the latch of the casement. With a hiss of pain and disgust, Evelina raised her free hand and slapped the doctor hard across the face. As the man's face clouded with rage, the latch gave way and Nick pulled the window open, sliding through to the stairway and landing feet-first. It was farther to the floor than he'd bargained for, and he landed with a loud thud.

"Nick!" Evelina's startled squeak echoed in the high vault of the ceiling.

Magnus wheeled around, a scowl of rage on his face. "What the devil are you doing here?"

He had a sudden instant of clarity. Magnus: powerful, wealthy, dangerous. Nick: half in rags, entirely out of place. Words deserted him. He raised the knife, figuring that would have to suffice.

"And you are her Galahad?" Magnus asked incredulously.

"Nick, be careful," Evelina said in a low voice.

He could only spare a glance at Evelina, but he saw her look of gratitude. He was there, defending her, fighting by her side as he was supposed to be. The knowledge gave him courage as he crouched, knowing by sheer instinct that Magnus was waiting for an opening to strike—but how he would fight was anyone's guess. Nick was no practitioner, but he had enough of the Blood to feel the prickle of magic in the air.

"Dr. Magnus, I would very much appreciate it if you left this house," Evelina said in a tight voice.

Magnus's expression grew even more dangerous. "You are not the owner of this place, nor are you one of his children. You have no power over the threshold here."

Nick's heart jerked in his chest, but a flood of white-hot anger surged through his blood, half of it at himself. He should have found a way to stop Magnus the moment he had misgivings about the man—which was mere seconds after meeting him.

Could have, should have. He was done with all that. "You heard the lady. It's time to go," Nick said.

"I think not," Magnus replied coolly.

Nick lunged forward, one hand extended to push the man back, knife in the other as backup. An altercation would attract unwelcome attention, but under the circumstances what did it matter? Getting thrown out on his arse was the least of their problems.

But suddenly Magnus wasn't there. Nick wheeled to look for him, and was gripped in wild, white-hot agony. The pain was so great, he felt suspended in the air, left arm extended, right fingers curled around the knife, knees bent, weight balanced on his toes. Every fiber of his body seemed to curl inward, retracting as the pain crawled up every nerve, biting, clawing, flaying him one shred at a time. Nick was aware of the knife falling from his fingers, the searing flash of light on the blade, the distant thump as it hit the carpet. Somewhere to his left, there was a rose-colored swirl as Evelina turned to grab for him, but he could not move his head—not even to spare his life. The roots of his eyelashes hurt too much to glance to the side.

A crawling sense of evil poured over him, questing fingers tickling his skin, looking for openings into his core.

Frozen, unable to move, he cringed with horror at the feel of it clawing at his ears and eyes, wriggling up his nose and between his teeth, hunting for a way into his soul.

And then, something gave way inside and he crumpled. It didn't happen quickly, but one muscle at a time lost its resilience, letting bone and tendon fail. His right knee hit the ground first, jolting his teeth and making him bite his tongue. Then his hip hit the carpet, and finally the rest of him. When his head smashed to the ground, the world had already gone black.

He had a distant, puzzled thought that he'd expected to die in a performance or maybe of old age and drink, not breathing his last on a rich man's carpet.

"YOU BASTARD!" EVELINA hissed, lunging for the knife.

Magnus grabbed her arm, bruising the flesh above her elbow. They were both crouched on the landing, almost knee to knee. Nick lay in a heap to her right, his chest barely moving.

Fury flamed through her blood, leaving her light-headed, delirious with the need to strike back. She snarled into Magnus's face, baring her teeth.

His smile was nearly as savage. "So there is a tiger inside that soft white skin. Good for you."

"What did you do to him?" She had the blade, the curve of it familiar in her palm. It was an old one, the ivory handle just as she remembered it from long ago, warm and smooth against her skin. Like Nick, it was part of a past that made her strong now.

Magnus answered by digging his fingers between her tendons, making it impossible to keep hold of the weapon. "Give it up, Evelina. You can't fight me."

"Watch," she spat, but her grip released, dropping the knife to the carpet. She couldn't help it. So she swung with the other fist.

He caught that hand, too, and shoved her backward with as much ceremony as if she were a bale of straw. She fell with a soft cry, too hampered by stays and skirts to resist.

Magnus rose, his tall form looming over her, the knife in his hand now.

"You're mine," he said quietly, "as surely as if I bound you in chains and carried you away. I've been looking for a great many years. You hold the secrets I want. Give them to me, and I will teach you in return."

Too angry to speak, Evelina glared.

"You want what I know. That simple fact will be magic enough to lure you."

"You don't know me at all."

He gave a sepulchral smile. "If that thought comforts you, keep it."

The need to deny his words swamped all common sense. She spat, the fat glob clinging to his elegant pant leg and sliding down like a glistening slug.

The look he gave her turned her bones to putty. "I can see I shall accomplish nothing more tonight. I'll be visiting with you soon, Miss Cooper."

He drove the point of the knife into the banister. It quivered and stuck, poised like an unexpected bird.

Then Dr. Magnus turned and descended the stairs. In a flurry of skirts, Evelina scrambled to her feet, pulling the knife from the wood with a grunt.

He must have heard her, but didn't turn. Magnus was clearly confident that she wouldn't throw it, even though his back was right there, just a few yards below.

Evelina rubbed the knife handle with her thumb, watching his form disappear step by step.

"NICK!" SHE HISSED.

His eyelids flickered, the only response a weak, "Huh?"

Fear cramped her stomach. She looked up the stairs and then down, terrified they would be caught. After three murders the police couldn't solve, she didn't fancy Nick's chances with a judge. She had to wake him up.

For a long moment, she stared at his handsome face, the hawklike bones and smooth, olive skin. The gaslight glinted on the gold of his earring. An ache filled her—a mix of longing and remembrance, of sadness for things that would never be. *He risked everything to save me.*

Now she had to save him, and there wasn't time to play the soft and innocent girl. She wanted to touch his face, to run her fingers over the graceful angles, to press her lips to his. He was asleep and would never know. She would never have to admit to her weakness.

But giving in to her feelings would never save him. Instead, it would most likely condemn them both. Ignoring the prickle of tears, Evelina smacked his face with a stinging slap. The noise alone made her wince.

His eyes snapped open.

"Wake up, damn you!" she muttered.

He slowly put a hand to his head, eyes crinkling as if it hurt to move. He worked his mouth a moment, as if he'd forgotten how to talk. "Where is he?"

"Gone." Vanished with an evil look and fierce silence. She shuddered at the memory of the doctor's face, grimacing down on her with a scowl that froze her to the bones. It was over that fast—one last glare and then down the stairs—but it had seemed to go on forever. Long enough that she'd died a tiny bit. Long enough that she'd nearly prostrated herself, burying her face against Nick's fallen form, like a child clinging to her parent and begging not to be left alone.

She tried to keep all of that off her face. She had to be stronger than that. "He left."

"Huh."

Evelina got to her feet and grabbed Nick's arm, trying to pull him with her. He was too big, and she might have been a girl of six again. "Get up. You're not safe here."

He staggered upright, weaving slightly and then nearly falling when his ankle gave way. He grabbed the wall to steady himself. "You know, a kiss would have worked as well as a blow to the face." His voice was hoarse, but a spark of himself was coming back into his dark eyes.

She wanted to cry with relief. "Then you would have sprawled there till next Sunday, hoping for another."

His mouth curled into a lopsided grin. "I made the villain go away. Surely that's worth something."

Tears stung her eyes. *Damned idiot*. "That was a close-run thing. Can you walk?"

"Almost."

She grabbed him, one arm around his waist, and steadied him. He smelled of horses and the cold, clean wind of the spring night. She closed her eyes and swallowed hard, trying her best not to notice how warm he was and how his lean form moved against her. Sooner or later, a servant would come by. They had to get out of sight.

"My knife," he said.

"I've got it." Her voice was tight.

The clock made a sepulchral bong, followed by a long grinding noise. A card spit out of the slot. Out of long habit, Evelina grabbed it before it hit the floor.

"What in damnation?" Nick squinted at the clock.

"Never mind."

She stuffed the card into her pocket and moved away, helping Nick hobble to a small sitting room at the end of the corridor. The fire was out and the room was chill, but at least there they'd be undisturbed for a little while. The tiny room wasn't used much, having no view, little furniture, and only a few bookshelves of almanacs from years long past. When she got Nick inside, she locked the door. He sank gratefully onto a settee.

The only illumination was the glow from the blazing display of lights outside the window, proving that Lord Bancroft was far from Disconnected. Evelina lit one of the oil lamps, turning the flame down low. As the light spilled over her hands, she used the ritual of match and flame to steady herself.

Her fingers felt thick and clumsy as she worked, each breath coming a little too quick. Panic was just around the corner, but as long as she kept moving, she didn't have to dwell on the fact that Nick was right there, just a few steps away, hurt and vulnerable—and he'd put himself on the line for her sake. It was her responsibility to get him out of there in a fit state to dodge the police or Magnus or Lord Bancroft's footmen. It wasn't going to be simple. No matter what she did next, there would be risk.

She stood before him a moment, her hands on her hips, running her gaze over his long, lean legs and sweep of black hair. Looking after him came naturally. She'd always relied on Nick, but she'd also been the one who mended his shirts and made sure he came in to dinner. It was how she'd earned her bread and milk as a girl, but those were also the things she'd done for love. She felt an echo of those days now, the bond between them as strong as ever.

She cleared her throat. "How are you feeling?"

"It's stopped hurting." A gray pallor clung to his skin, but he shrugged and leaned forward, bracing his elbows on his knees and propping his head in his hands. "Mostly."

She stood uncertainly, fidgeting with the trim on her gown. "I'm not certain you can shake this off with a moment's rest. It's not that kind of an injury."

"What else is there to do?" He looked up, a fine sheen of sweat clinging to his cheekbones. "Are you going to call a doctor and ruin everything for yourself?"

"I would if I thought it would help." He made a noise that said he didn't believe her. A spike of anger made her flush. "Don't be daft. None of this is worth spit if you're dead."

With a jolt, she realized it was true. Nick was terminally loyal, but in her own way, she was, too—and there lay the danger. *I still love him. I won't ever stop.* But none of that mattered when there was no future for them.

"At any rate, you're limping. You can't do the show like that." She knelt before him, running her hands over his ankle.

He gave her a sharp look, half astonished, half suspicious. "What are you doing?"

Wordlessly, she pulled off his boot, ignoring the sand and mud clinging to the worn, supple leather. Then she placed her hands on the rough wool of his stocking, trying not to think about the fact that it looked like Gran Cooper's work. If she started missing her old home too much, there would be no hope of concentration.

As she expected, the moment she pulled down the sock, putting her hands on his skin, power flooded under her fingers as if she had suddenly summoned a hot, prickling river of silver fire. It didn't happen with a casual brush of the hand, but now—when she touched him with intent, when she *meant* to call his soul to hers—the energy opened like a floodgate. This was the combination of their powers, the thing no one could explain when their two bloodlines met. And it was no more possible to be together and keep from calling it than it was to stop breathing.

The flow was impossible to describe—it was almost like cinnamon was to the tongue, or a distant birdsong to the ear, bright and sweet and filled with urgent longing—but there was no language that could quite wrap around the sensation. It felt like heaven and yet still brought tears to her eyes. It was everything she and Nick were when they were together. Everything she had given up to keep them both safe.

She heard the hiss of Nick's indrawn breath. It was a sound of anticipation mixed with reluctance. He knew what might happen, too.

"You need healing," she said, trying to sound brusque. "You can't climb out a window like this. You'll fall and break your neck."

"Evelina," he said, pulling his foot from her hands, "just let me leave. You know better than this."

Nick was right, but if he slipped and broke a bone crawling out the window, there was every chance he'd never ride again. He'd starve to death on the streets. If she could bring steel and gears to life, surely she could heal a simple injury. "I'm stronger than I was. I can control it."

Doubt filled his eyes. "But I don't know how to help. No more than I ever did."

"Trust me," she said softly, hoping she wasn't promising too much.

Even in the few seconds since Evelina had summoned their energy, she could feel how much stronger the power was than the last time they'd called it. They were adults now, not children, with all the intensity that implied. She took his foot and put it back in her lap. "You have to get out of here in one piece. This is the only thing I can think of."

Her words were matter of fact, but her stomach was in

flutters. It wasn't just fear of discovery, but also the thrill of feeling this addictive power again. And she had the best excuse—Nick's ankle was swollen and hot. She pushed the energy into it, envisioning the intricacy of bone and muscle, joint and blood and tendon, and directing it to heal.

The silver fire began to glow brighter, the look of it growing solid as she worked. That was part of the danger—when their two bloodlines operated together, it didn't act like normal magic. It should have been invisible, but anyone, whether or not they had the Blood, could see this power at work. She had locked the door, but a niggle of worry still wound around her heart. *Please, let no one come into the room.*

Evelina glanced up to see Nick's eyes drifting closed. Her own head was spinning, the electric sensation acting like strong wine. Sensations were far more acute—the crush of carpet under her knees, the rasp of clothing on her flesh, the scent of dinner seeping up the stairs. Every breath intensified the feeling, eroding caution in the pure delight of her senses. *No, no, no—keep your mind on the task at hand.*

Of course, Nick himself didn't help. It was improper for a young lady to touch a man like this, and the strong, supple muscles of his leg prompted all sorts of impure speculation. She found her hand drifting up to his knee, almost of its own accord. And then he was bending down, his hand on her cheek. The silver fire spread, engulfing them in its light.

She let go of his ankle and was suddenly leaning upward, reaching toward him as he reached down, winding her arms about his neck. The splash of power as they touched made her gasp. With each beat of her heart, the silver fire expanded into a nimbus, the edges thinning to a mist that filled every corner of the room, engulfing it in the electricity of their shared emotions. It felt like the most natural and the most wondrous thing in the world, to be moving in for an embrace, to share their powers fully and with no inhibitions.

Evelina felt control—both of herself and of her magic—slide through her grip like satin ribbons torn away by a sudden breeze. Suddenly, she was back at the circus in the simple, constant springtime of girlhood, and Nick was her whole world. She leaned forward, aching to touch her lips to his as if that would seal the past into the present and make her whole.

Then, a handful of the old almanacs shot across the room, pages tearing with the fury of the motion. The volumes hit the wall with a resounding thump, then fell to the floor like birds shot from the air. Nick pulled back with an oath, leaving her bereft. Like Evelina, he was breathless, sweat beading on his olive skin.

A fire burst to life in the grate, rushing up the chimney in a gust of flame—and then a sudden wind snaked around the room, fluttering curtains and tearing at her hair.

Now that a fire lit the room brightly, she could see the emotion in his dark eyes—desire, fear, and wonder. "We've called devas," he whispered. "Dozens of them."

Slowly, reluctantly, Evelina sank back to her heels and turned to look around the room. Tiny balls of light whisked through the air like sparkling dust motes, intoxicated by the sudden surge of energy in the room. They were beautiful, fuzzy balls of gold and blue and green no bigger than her hand—and yet filled with destructive potential. Normally, devas were too small to throw a book or light a flame by themselves, but the silver fire changed everything. *We called devas. Drunk, delirious devas.*

A clump of tiny blue lights pushed a candlestick off a tabletop. It fell with a heavy clunk to the carpet, the mercifully unlit candle falling out and rolling away.

Apprehension turned Evelina cold. She wondered how far away the devas had felt the surge of power. Mouse and Bird were locked safely in her bedroom. Had they felt it? Or had the scent of energy reached the nearby parklands? How many might yet come? This was exactly the kind of thing her Gran had feared would give them away—and why she would have turned Nick out into the cold before the authorities arrested the entire circus for harboring demons in their midst.

Evelina pulled away from Nick entirely, struggling with her skirts as she got to her feet. "No, no, stop that!" She batted at the devas frantically, as if they were troublesome flies. "Stop it at once!"

Or what, little witch? One of them buzzed around her head, tugging at a hairpin.

She clamped down on her power, willing it back inside her until she thought she might choke. The silver fire shrank inward, dragging the devas with it. That only concentrated the problem. The tiny spirits buzzed around them like gnats, sucking the last of the energy like sots crowding around the bar at last call. One dove through Nick's ankle, riding the strongest current of power and making him curse at the sensation as it popped out the other side.

Evelina backed away, putting even more distance between her and Nick, breaking their connection altogether. As the last silver light disappeared, the sudden wind died. As she moved away, the fire in the grate sank back to a dull glow of coals. *And that happened only from a touch. What if we had kissed? What if we had lain together, as man and wife?* They might start another Great Fire of London.

Nick massaged his ankle. "This feels better."

But Evelina held up her hand, silencing him. Then she heard it more clearly—the rattle of the door handle. Her mind flew from detail to detail. They'd been speaking in quiet voices. The fire was low now, so little light would escape under the door. But there had been a great many thumps—all the noise must have attracted attention. Both of them remained frozen, playing statues.

But the devas were pushing another candlestick to the floor. Nick looked her way to see the horrified expression on her face. Wordlessly, Evelina pointed. Just in time, he dove to catch the falling object, his feet silent on the carpet.

Evelina's gut twisted into a cold knot. She fell back another step, as if her body were seeking a place to hide even if her mind had frozen, unable to form a complete thought. The ornate brass door knob turned again as someone pushed against it on the other side. She bit her lip and watched the devas, deprived of their feast of silver energy, drift aimlessly about the room. Nick, still holding the candlestick, looked from the door to the window and back. His only escape was the window, but if he raised it, whoever was outside the door would hear it for sure.

The door handle stopped moving. "Locked," someone whispered. "Let's try somewhere else." The words were followed by a barely heard giggle.

Evelina released her breath. It had just been two guests— or maybe servants—taking advantage of the after-dinner confusion to slip away for a moment or two. As she heard footfalls moving away from the door, her heart gradually slowed. They were safe—for now.

A few of the devas slipped beneath the sash of the window. Another glowing ball turned to a needle of light, sliding between the floorboards at the edge of the room. The rest were fading away like snowflakes, disappearing into thin air.

The crisis was past.

Sharing power had felt so good, but now Evelina's body ached with the release of tension. She hastily picked up the volumes, shoving them back onto the shelf. Her hands trembled, aching to drop the books and return to Nick, starting the folly all over again. It wasn't just the power. All of her old feelings had reawakened. She wanted to touch *him*.

"You should go," she said softly. *Before I give way and fall into your arms and destroy us both.* "You see what happens when we're together."

"I know," he said.

She turned to him. His features were perfectly calm. To him, one more peril was just business as usual for a showman, another chance to pit his wits against fate.

She didn't walk the high wire anymore. "I wish I had your nerve."

He shrugged. "What did you expect would happen? We've never learned to control the power."

"Exactly."

He took a step forward, lifting a hand to reach out, and then letting it fall. Gran had said control wasn't possible, not with Nick's strange bloodline. And if anyone knew about magic, it was Gran Cooper. Evelina said nothing, her chest too tight to speak.

Even without the wild magic, she wasn't sure they could stay together. She didn't belong in his world anymore, and he'd never belong in Mayfair, and love wasn't everything. Her parents had been a similar mismatch, and she'd watched her mother fade like a flower cut off from its sustaining vine, shriveling until she died. That had left a shadow on Evelina's soul that was impossible to dispell. *I wish I knew what was the right thing to do.* But there were no guarantees, and with the magic in the mix, it didn't matter. They had to stay apart.

He must have seen her thoughts on her face. "Very well. I'll go."

"I'm sorry." It was all she could think of to say.

His features were a neutral mask, giving away nothing. "One thing before I leave. I overheard Bancroft talking with Magnus."

"When?"

He sank back onto the sofa. Perhaps he was healed, but he was clearly still exhausted. "Earlier tonight. I've been trying to find a way to speak to you. I wanted to warn you about Magnus, but this place is guarded like Buckingham Palace."

She hugged herself, afraid to come any closer to him. "I'm glad you stayed away. It's too dangerous for you to be here."

He leaned forward and peered up under his brows. She knew the look—it was the one he used when he spoke from his gut. "Evie, we go too far back for me to stand by and watch you sail into a storm."

There was no answer to that. Her throat ached too much anyway, filled with unshed tears—of gratitude, of regret, and mostly of confusion.

"Magnus wants something," Nick said. "I don't understand what it is, but he thinks he can make Lord Bancroft help him get it from the Gold King. And he's stolen something from Bancroft, and he's holding it over his head. Something—he said trunks and cargo—that sounds like it would ruin him."

The automatons! Evelina tingled with excitement. "That fits. Bancroft and Magnus were friends once, but now they hate each other."

"Why?"

She shook her head. "I don't know how it started. Whatever it is, Lady B and Tobias don't seem to mind him. It's between the two men." She thought of the conversation she'd overheard in the library. Lord Bancroft had looked like a haunted soul from that night on. *That was why. He knew Magnus had his dolls.*

"Evelina." Nick's face was pale and serious. "Wherever you think your life is going, what we did tonight is who you really are. Magic is in you, and it's something your new people can't help you with, even the few who wouldn't hang you just for having it. And as much as I want to be by your side—and I would cut the heart out of my chest if I thought it would buy me the privilege—I can't protect you. Not where you're bound. You'll be walking alone. That frightens me."

Her breath caught in her chest, too painful to move. She knew all this, but she didn't want to hear it in words, least of all from Nick. It was hard enough without adding the memory of his pain-wracked face. Tears blurred the sight of him.

He reached out, taking her hand, the faintest silver light gloving their fingers. His palm was rough and hot, the hands of a man used to work. "Magnus wants you—or what you can do. I'm not sure what he's planning, but it sounds like a play for power dressed up in big words and mumbo jumbo. He'd dead set on a spat with the steam barons, so you can bet there's bad news coming."

His voice was gentle, low and rough and familiar as the smell of horse and the earth under her bare feet. "I know you want to be careful and keep this new life of yours clean, but you're going to have to be ready for a fight. And tonight was just the start. This isn't over."

She barely understood her magic, much less how to fight with it, but that probably didn't matter. "What's this all about, anyhow?"

"Power and money." It was more or less the same thing Tobias had said. "Magic is just a way to get it."

"I'm in the middle, aren't I? I'm caught between your world and theirs. Gran Cooper and Grandmamma Holmes."

That might have been too frank. Nick pulled his hand away, looking down at the floor. She flexed her fingers, already feeling his absence.

"I won't tell you what to do. I love you too much to keep you in a box, however much I long to keep you safe. But I beg you to be careful."

The words shook her to the bone, bringing a sting to her eyes. "I will."

"If you ever want to come home to Ploughman's, I'll defend you to my death. But if you stay here, Magnus will know where you are, Evelina."

Her heart pounded beneath her stays. "I can't run forever."

A long pause followed. It was plain to both of them that she wasn't going back to the circus, though Nick would never know the whole reason. All those years ago, she wouldn't let him give up the one home he knew for her sake. Magnus or no Magnus, she wasn't about to do that now.

Nick rose from the chair stiffly. "I have to go."

She took a step forward, longing to hold him but knowing that meant never letting him go. "What do I do?"

Nick shook his head. "I can't answer that for you."

He touched the side of her face lightly, just dusting her skin with magic. She wanted to lean in to the touch, to feel the comfort of his familiar warmth. The earthy salt of his skin called to memories deep in her bones. *I can't let him go. He's part of me.* And yet that was the one thing she absolutely had to do.

Tears stung her eyes. "I don't want to run or hide or be used by someone else. I just want to be who I am."

He stepped back, letting go of a sigh. "Then be prepared to fight for it, because only the strongest get to stand on their own."

Chapter Twenty-eight

"THERE MUST BE A WAY TO MAKE THIS WORK."

Tobias stood back from the stuffed sheep and switched on the device. He was in a mood and more than a little drunk. The late afternoon had been spent at the clubhouse behind the tailor's shop, trying to make sense out of, well, pretty much everything.

His hoped-for reunion with Dr. Magnus had not occurred beyond a polite greeting at dinner. Magnus had been put at the other end of the table and had disappeared just after the meal. Evelina had apparently taken to her bed with a headache. The two had clearly spoiled each other's digestion and had left Tobias stranded with Alice Keating. Alice was nice enough—well, actually quite pretty and a definite wit—but she wasn't Evelina.

Altogether it had been a miserable meal. The tension among his father—who for some reason looked like he'd been in a fight—Jasper Keating, and Dr. Magnus had worn away at his nerves. He had been counting down the minutes until Keating had whipped out some new invention to torture the guests. Perhaps steam-powered thumbscrews, or a spring-loaded guillotine designed for a faster slice.

He hadn't seen Evelina or Magnus since. He fervently hoped this afternoon would be less of a waste. He was testing his version of Aragon Jackson's contraption, last seen electrocuting the upstairs maid. It was his firm opinion that whatever the Gold King wrought, the Society for the Proliferation of Impertinent Events could do it better.

The mission might have been more personal to him than to the rest of SPIE. Smythe had his regiment, and Bucky and Edgerton were destined to take their place in their fathers' manufactories. Tobias alone had no plans and, just speaking statistically, he couldn't be a blot on the universe every hour of every day. There had to be something constructive he could do.

He stopped to take a swig out of his hip flask and then considered the sheep in its technological finery. Tobias remembered some Serb had recently published a paper on wireless transmission, and Jackson had put the cutting-edge theories to bad use. The device consisted of a wristband strapped to the forearm—in this case foreleg—and a receiver that circled the head, a little like a tiara with an antenna on top. Tobias had stitched it awkwardly onto one of the frilly white caps the maids wore. On the sheep, it looked slightly rakish.

A small voice at the back of his mind reminded him about grounding wires, but the alcohol garbled the message. Bucky was standing nearby, and he thought vaguely of mentioning it to him, but decided against it. Forming a complete sentence would cost more effort than he wanted to exert right then. And, well, the stuffed sheep couldn't actually feel pain, after all.

Tobias bent over the main control unit, set a dozen steps' distance from the sheep. He flipped the transmission switch. There was a crackling noise, sparks flew, and Fleecy's head burst into flame.

"Bugger," grumbled Tobias as he emptied a bucket of water over the experiment, which resulted in further pops and sputters.

Bucky folded his arms, tapping one forefinger to his chin. "Unfortunately, SPIE will have to amend the name to include *incendiary* as well as impertinent events."

Tobias made a rude noise.

A tall figure emerged from the clubhouse behind them.

"Can't see the maids going for that one," observed Michael Edgerton, pushing his dark hair out of his eyes. He still had one arm in a sling from the squid incident. He'd fallen into the trombones. "Gar, that stinks."

Tobias stomped on a stray scrap of smoking wool. "Smell of progress, Edgerton."

"There's a gentleman here who says he knows you, Roth."

Tobias shared a look of confusion with Bucky, and then strode across the yard. Surprise morphed into annoyance. Hardly anyone knew of the existence of their private workshop. He guessed the only reason the Gold King tolerated their operation was because they were rich and kept the operation very, very quiet.

Tobias shouldered his way through the door, ready to snarl. Then he stopped in surprise. Magnus sat inside, looking as comfortable in one of their ratty, discarded chairs as he had prowling through the dinner crowd at Hilliard House. His cane leaned against the arm of the chair, holding his high-crowned hat.

"Dr. Magnus!"

He rose when he saw Tobias. "There you are. And I've met Mr. Edgerton. But I do not know you, sir."

"Penner." Bucky shook his hand.

"I am delighted to meet you all." Magnus smiled warmly. "I admired your work at the Royal Charlotte. Such spirit is not to be underrated."

Tobias's mood lifted with the praise. Bucky and Edgerton looked equally flattered.

Magnus gestured around the room. "And now that we have been introduced, perhaps I should explain why I am here."

They sat, Edgerton turning over a crate to use since Magnus was in one of the few actual chairs.

Magnus began in a confidential tone, as if he were picking up a conversation with old friends. "I am currently in pursuit of a—how should I put it?—a *part* for the main project for which I will need your collective talents. And trust me, this is a large and marvelous thing for which I require a crack team of makers. But it is taking some time for me to acquire this part, and in the meantime I am eager to see what you gentlemen can do."

"You want a demonstration?" Bucky sounded amused. "The squid was not enough?"

The doctor gave a gracious smile. "It showed competence and power of invention. I also require delicacy of execution. Consider this first commission as a type of audition for what comes next."

Edgerton, who liked nothing better than a challenge, shifted impatiently on his crate.

Magnus nodded toward a trunk sitting against the wall. It was plain black, neither old nor new, the brass bindings dull with use. There were a thousand just like it on any train in the Empire. "The contents are your assignment. They require repair and assembly. With your extraordinary talents, I believe this test is well within your reach."

The members of the society exchanged "after you" gestures. Growing impatient, Tobias crossed the room and released the clasps of the trunk, wondering vaguely how Magnus had got it there without a servant anywhere in evidence. The thought dissolved into unimportance the moment he lifted the lid. "What in blazes?"

"What indeed, Mr. Roth." The words rolled out like a dare.

Inside lay the disassembled parts of a perfect woman. Tobias caught his breath, his brandy-hazed brain barely making sense of what he saw. It was clearly an automaton, but not one like he had ever seen. It was nothing like his father's grotesques, nor at all like the steel monstrosities used in factories.

The hair, a long, lustrous auburn, had to be real. He reached in, fingertips brushing the soft, ruddy waves, discovering a tiny part that seemed shorn away. The slightest flaw, but it somehow gave the breathtaking features individuality. The face was porcelain and painted with such subtlety it was hard to believe that it was not hot blood that pinked her cheeks. The limbs were smooth and white, the hands perfectly molded and tipped with dainty nails. What jarred Tobias was that all those exquisite parts were jumbled into the trunk's interior. He picked up a foot, the shining joint poking out where the shin should have begun—but the naked toes were exquisitely detailed.

A shudder took him. This wasn't a machine. It was a dismembered corpse made of ceramic and steel. His stomach suddenly disapproved of the brandy.

"I need you to put her together," said Magnus. "I need you to make her live again."

Edgerton had come to stand behind Tobias, the technical challenge clearly drawing him like catnip. "Is she clockwork?"

"Yes, that is the basis of her workings. And yet the design of my angel is imperfect."

Imperfect? That word didn't fit the creature he saw, despite her disassembled condition. Yet Tobias wasn't sure if he felt excitement or revulsion. The others had gathered around, crowding him where he knelt by the trunk. The clubhouse suddenly felt stifling. Sweat soaked his shirt, making it cling to his back.

He picked up the head. The eyelids had soft lashes glued on in tiny tufts. They flicked open with a click, leaving him staring into glass eyes of an impossible blue. Goose pimples rose along his neck. The creature looked vaguely like Alice Keating.

"What's her name?" Bucky asked.

"Serafina. She is meant to be the first of a troupe of life-sized puppets, if I can master the logistics of her workings. That is where you young gentlemen can assist me."

Edgerton picked up an arm and was examining the tiny cables that worked the joints. "We may need some additional parts."

"Buy what you need, and please factor in a cost in consideration for your time."

The young men shifted self-consciously. There wasn't one among them who didn't have debts. Though gentlemen technically didn't work for pay, the offer of money caught their attention.

They cleared the worktable that sat at one end of the clubhouse and began ferrying parts from the trunk one by one, laying out the body in proper anatomical position. Some of the limbs were scratched or mended, as if the doll had met with violence. There were many tiny bits left in the bottom of the trunk, not all of which made sense to Tobias. He would need to spend a good deal of time studying the design before he knew where everything went.

He looked down at the automaton, trying to ignore the gaps where she should have been whole. The torso had a layer of sawdust stuffing beneath taut, flesh-colored silk that felt unnervingly like female skin. Whoever had made her had left no detail of female anatomy to the imagination, right down to details of the cleft between her legs. He had an irrational urge to cover her up to preserve her modesty. "Who built her?"

Magnus waved a dismissive hand. "A young Italian made it to an existing plan. Alas, consumption took him before he perfected her. The first trials showed flaws in the design, and I was obliged to make repairs. She walked and talked to perfection, but her ability to reason occasionally proved primitive, even aberrant—a common difficulty with automatons, as I'm sure you've heard. I have just now recalibrated that portion of her workings and would like to embark on a new trial at once."

"So she outlived her first maker." Tobias laid the final hand at her side. The fingers slipped coolly over his, as pliable as if she merely slept.

"She is an orphan and an only child. How long she stays thus is up to you."

"If you took her apart, can you not reassemble the pieces?" Edgerton asked.

Magnus smiled. "Of course. But I believe that an essential bond is formed between the maker and the made. You will nourish her in the act of bringing her to life and be, if you will, her bridegrooms in her passage back to the world. Or, you will not and she remains but a puppet."

"Bridegrooms?" Tobias asked, his thoughts straying to Serafina's detailed anatomy. He yanked them back, somewhere between disgusted and amused.

"I am being metaphorical, of course." Magnus lifted the

head and admired the painted face. "Do not mistinterpret my meaning as some piece of low comedy. Serafina represents a test, as I said. The questions she poses are not a matter of springs and gears, much less of the flesh."

Bucky lifted his eyebrows, but said nothing more. Of all of them, he seemed the least interested in the doll.

The exchange was entirely lost on Edgerton, who was all about the mechanics. He squinted at the steel socket of her left hip, his concentration absolute. "The wear here is bad. She's going to be arthritic before her time if we don't replace these. The curve is wrong for the shape of the joint."

"How hard will that be to fix?" Tobias asked.

He shrugged, taking measurements with a protractor square. "It's finer work than we can do here. My father's man is in town today. I'm going to talk to him before he catches the evening train for Sheffield. Either he'll have something we can use, or I can get him to order some custom work."

He cast a glance at Magnus. "If I have to bring something in from Sheffield, it might mean a bribe to the Gold King's officers. You know how the barons are about machinery."

Magnus simply nodded and flicked his fingers, as if the cost was nothing. Edgerton left.

Tobias and Bucky remained at the table, one on either side. Bucky cast a look at Magnus, his face doubtful. "What are you going to do with her once she's operational? You say you want a troupe of these puppets?"

"There are specialized kinds of theater that require a durable cast." Magnus rose and began pacing the floor. He wore no cape, but one seemed to swirl about him anyway as he stopped, reaching into the trunk. "These are the designs."

He drew out a dull brown portfolio and unwound the string that secured the cover. He withdrew a handful of sketches, laying them out on the edge of the worktable. With a start, Tobias recognized his father's handwriting.

"Yes," said Magnus. "She is of the latest technology, but the original concepts were your father's work. You come by your talent honestly. My hope is that, unlike him, you do not become entangled in mundane considerations. A gift like yours demands freedom to fly." Magnus met his gaze and held it, as if to make sure Tobias grasped the full import of his words.

"I'm just a dilettante."

Magnus's mouth curved in an expression that said humility was sweet, but utterly unnecessary. It made Tobias taste the lie on his tongue.

He didn't want to be a mere dabbler. Tobias felt his skin heat with a sudden desire to live up to the task Dr. Magnus had set. It felt like a hunger, or the thirst after an entire night of drink. He was a rich man's son. His life might not depend on proving himself, but something else, something important inside him, did.

Magnus replied without taking his eyes from Tobias. "My goal has always been to unite artifice and animus."

"What does that mean?" Bucky asked with a nervous laugh.

"There are a thousand ways to construe the concept. I like to think that we always put a little bit of our souls into what we create. In turn, creations feed their creator by seducing the public with their beauty."

"You make your puppet sound like the bride of a vampire," said Bucky.

Magnus laughed, but it wasn't a reassuring sound. "An apt comparison, in a way, though I would not put it in such graphic terms. Creators need the awe and wonder of their audiences the way a revenant needs blood."

Bucky's face twitched, as if he were trying very hard not to laugh. "I hope you don't expect children to play with your dolls."

Dr. Magnus narrowed his eyes. "I don't let just anyone play with my toys." Then he chuckled. "Serafina is dear to me. I owe her much. Creating a thing of beauty purifies the soul, don't you think?"

Tobias winced. "I wonder what a flaming sheep says about my chances for salvation."

Bucky scratched his chin. "Perhaps slightly more than the exploding still. But not much."

CHAPTER TWENTY-NINE

I SHOULDN'T BE HERE. THIS IS UTTER AND COMPLETE FOLLY.
Evelina stood across the street from the Hibernia Amphitheatre, looking up at the marquis—THE INDOMITABLE NICCOLO! THE FABULOUS FLYING COOPERS!—and tried to identify the burning in her chest. Regret? Jealousy? Relief that she had escaped that life?

Much of it was loss. She was going to be presented the next day. After that, there was the Season and perhaps college, if she could manage it. Evelina carried magic within her, but her path was clearly pointed toward a life within the gentry. She'd made that choice long ago.

Yet seeing Nick again last night had left her hollow and uncertain. He still watched over her. In the complicated world she lived in now, she was terrified of never finding that kind of unconditional affection again. Of never deserving it. Of never loving any man, not even Tobias, as much.

It wasn't only Nick that she missed. She desperately wanted to see Gran Cooper, but would Gran want to see her? In Evelina's dreams, sometimes the old woman turned a look of reproach her way that made her start awake in tears. Evelina felt like two people—one scrambling away from Ploughman's toward the safety of Society, the other screaming in her face that lopping off that part of herself would never be possible.

Evelina took a shaking breath, gripping her beaded reticule until it crushed against the dark navy stripes of her skirt. *Damn you, Nick.* She knew she couldn't go back, but he had still managed to shake her. She *would* be presented and she *would* take her place in Society, but she had to go back to Ploughman's and take one last look before she could go forward to the queen. It was a rite, a ritual, and perhaps a final good-bye.

Evelina had meant to come alone to make her farewells, but had invited Imogen at the last minute. Her friend had seemed too quiet, almost haunted, since last night. Evelina put it down to the stress of the presentation, or perhaps that she had endured another nightmare, perhaps the one about being trapped inside a box. Those were the most frequent and the ones Imogen hated the most. At any rate, she needed a distraction, and Ploughman's was excellent for that. It seemed to work.

"What are you waiting for?" Imogen tugged excitedly at her elbow. "Let's buy our tickets! Where do we get them? Oh, there's a little booth by the door over there."

Evelina looked to where Imogen pointed and, sure enough, there was a tiny automated ticket office. The Hibernia was an up-to-the-minute venue, painted in brilliant vermillion and gold. A large clock soared from the roof, brass gears flashing as they whirred inside the enormous glass case. The entire place looked like a child's toy.

"You'd think I would feel like I am returning in triumph," Evelina said quietly. Her voice was barely audible above the sound of steam cycles purring past and a boy selling hot pies.

Imogen visibly reined in her excitement, putting on a dutifully sympathetic expression. "But you don't."

"I feel a bit ashamed. It's like by leaving I said they weren't good enough for me, and that is so far from the truth . . ."

"But you had no choice. Your Grandmamma Holmes took you away."

Evelina didn't reply, but studied the sun slanting across the front of the theater.

"In any event, you did what made sense to you at the time. How could it not?"

Evelina laced her arm through her friend's. "There were things I lost. I didn't see it at the time."

One of the steam cycles streaked through a puddle, sending up a cloud of pigeons.

"Your friends and family? They're not lost. They're right here."

She thought of Gran again. Maybe it would be all right, if she could just see her. Just hug her again and chat over a cup of that strong, strong tea. "It's not just the people. It's such a different life, Imogen. I was one of the Flying Coopers. I miss the circus itself. There's a moment in the routine when you're holding nothing but air. The crowd may roar, but all you hear is an absolute quiet. All you can count on is your own equilibrium and that silence to carry you to the bar of the trapeze. It's life or death."

Imogen gave her a sharp look. "I've never heard you say that."

Possibly because she had been too young to be a performer when she'd first been part of the show. Not legally, anyhow, and she'd always been careful of saying too much. Evelina's gaze slid back to the marquis. "I don't think I wanted to admit that I missed it. Leaving was like taking a knife to a limb."

She started toward the ticket booth, Imogen matching her step. The carriage had dropped them off at the shops a few streets away and was scheduled to pick them up in two hours. With luck, no one at Hilliard House would be the wiser about where they'd spent the afternoon. Imogen broke into her thoughts. "What will you do if you meet Magnus on the street?"

Evelina had told her about last night, though nothing about the magic she shared with Nick. That wasn't entirely her secret to tell.

The thought of Magnus blackened everything, like a cloud coasting in front of the sun. "For now, I'm not going anywhere alone."

"And for the long term?"

A young man turned to look at Imogen and walked into a lamppost. She seemed entirely unaware of it.

"He's got something to do with the murders. I'm sure of it." She wasn't about to say that Lord Bancroft was tangled up in everything as well, not until she absolutely had to. Imogen was his daughter, after all.

"So Magnus is part of the investigation." Though she kept her words soft, Imogen's voice was filled with excitement. "It might take some doing, but we'll get him."

As far as Evelina could tell, they weren't getting anyone or anywhere, just coming up with more questions. "If my Uncle Sherlock were doing this . . ."

Imogen poked her in the arm. "He'd be coming at the problem in his own way. You have resources he can't touch. He might have even been eaten by that wretched dragon, although he undoubtedly would have deduced who it had for breakfast three weeks ago by the residue stuck in its fangs. Never mind your uncle. Look at everything we've learned so far."

"Which at the moment is a lot of unrelated facts." They hurried to avoid a steam dray moving too fast for the crowded street.

Imogen waved a hand. "That's the trouble with gathering truth. It's never neat and tidy, whatever that nice Dr. Watson writes. I still want to know what kind of goods that importer was receiving. There was nothing there but empty crates and mechanical jumble." The strained look was back on Imogen's features.

Evelina frowned. "Are you sure you want to be involved with my investigation?"

"Of course I do!"

Imogen sounded almost testy, which wasn't like her at all. Evelina would have said more, but they'd stopped at the ticket booth. It was coin operated, the clockwork ticket seller inside made to look like a tabby cat wearing a green bow tie and bowler. Imogen fed her shillings into the slot and pulled the lever. The cat's tail waved frantically, a paw lifted the bowler, and a ticket shot out of a slot in the front of the booth surrounded by embossed gold scrollwork. Imogen took her ticket, and Evelina repeated the procedure.

The ticket read: EQUESTRIAN DRAMA: THE KNIGHTS OF TATIANA VICTORIOUS OVER THE FORCES OF KING OBERON. Evelina felt a twinge of relief. At least they weren't still doing Waterloo. There were only so many times one could watch Wellington defeat Old Boney, especially decades after the fact.

"I think we're too late to see the battle," Evelina said. "That's all right, though. I prefer the second half."

The afternoon performance was well attended, but the theater was large and there were plenty of places to sit. Imogen insisted on finding seats in the lowest tier of boxes hanging right next to the sawdust ring. Evelina angled her chair, using the curtains on the box to shadow her face. She wondered how many of the troupe would recognize her, or her them, and wasn't sure she was ready for that moment.

Imogen gave her a sly smile. "I'm looking forward to seeing this Nick of yours. Is he really so very indomitable?"

"He'd love to think so."

The next act was setting up. A young girl was walking along the seats selling ices. Evelina wasn't hungry, but she could taste the cold sweetness in her memory. The circus smelled the same—churned dust, animals, the lingering sharpness of sweat. A sense of displacement swamped her, skewing her perception of time and place and leaving her lonely as a ghost that has outlived its century.

Imogen pulled out a dainty white leather case that unclasped on one side and popped up to reveal collapsible opera glasses. She studied the faces in the other boxes. "I see the Whitneys, but no one else we know. Oh, wait. They're leaving."

That was a relief, but Evelina had barely unclenched her shoulders when, moments later, the show began. Old Ploughman strode forth, arms raised as if to conjure. He stopped in the middle of the ring, bowing to one side of the auditorium, then the other. The knees and elbows of his suit were a little shinier with wear than Evelina remembered, the fit a little tighter in the waist, but his grandiloquence still rolled like thunder. "Gentlemen! Beautiful ladies!" his introduction began.

The sound of his voice straightened Evelina's spine, as if she were still bound to his orders.

Just as Ploughman finished his prologue, Maximilian the

Fierce paraded his lions and tigers through the ring, the cats fluid as tawny liquid as he jumped them over his stick. Evelina recognized the old, scarred lion and shivered a little in her seat. Xerxes was many things, but the padding giant could never be called completely tamed.

No sooner had the tip of the last feline tail disappeared then the Maharaja appeared and made Bessie the elephant stand on her hind legs and balance a ball on her trunk. That was the odd thing with elephants—why would a creature that big ever do anything for a mere human? And yet they did, so they must have their reasons. They were complex beasts.

When Evelina had been no more than eight or nine, she had hidden one night in the soft warmth of the elephant's pen. It had been after a bad day—she'd done something wrong and Gran had scolded, and she'd leaned up against Bessie and cried and cried. The elephant had wound its trunk around her, as gentle with little Evie as if she had been Bessie's own calf, rocking her gently from side to side until she was all but asleep. The memory pierced her, fixing her to the past with links of unbreakable sweetness.

By the time the elephant left the ring, the Maharaja and his monkey swaying on her back, Evelina was clutching her handkerchief in a tight, moist ball. Imogen gripped her other hand.

The riders came next, two bay horses side by side. Young men stood in the saddles, and atop their shoulders stood Nick. His dark hair streamed behind him, showing the clean lines of his face. He raised his hands triumphantly in the air, the brilliant silks of his costume rippling in the breeze created by the horses' steady canter. The crowd cheered, the sheer bravado of the cavaliers a joy to behold.

Once they made a circuit of the ring, another horse pranced into the arena. This mare was slightly smaller, gray with a flowing mane and tail bound in colorful ribbons. Nick called something from his perch, and the horse reared, dancing for a moment with her front hooves churning the air. In one glance, Evelina knew this would be Nick's special horse. He had always trained his mounts to do that trick—sometimes it was almost as if he had the ability to talk to his horses, the way he could understand almost any deva. That affinity with animals was part of what made Nick who he was.

As the other two horses galloped once more around the ring, he caught one of the trapeze bars hanging from the ceiling. In one smooth move, he lifted off the shoulders of the other two riders, then swung around the trapeze to balance above the crowd, his hands stretched out to show only his hips touched the bar. Evelina looked up, knowing how skilled he was but nervous all the same. There was no net, and he had been badly hurt the night before.

He whistled, and his mare trotted over with a toss of her head. Like something more liquid than human, he whirled around the bar, somersaulted in midair, landed in a crouch on the sawdust floor, and, with no pause, vaulted into the saddle. The horse took off, moving around and around the ring at a clip faster than the other riders.

Then Evelina realized the others had vanished, and she hadn't even noticed. The walls of the auditorium could have fallen away unheeded. The Indomitable Niccolo, his face taut with concentration, completely commanded the stage.

Evelina had seen plenty of trick riders, but Nick's style was his own. He rode standing, then using a handstand to rotate so he faced backward, then hung from the saddle to trail his fingers through the sawdust. The audience applauded and Imogen clutched her hand so tightly that Evelina had all but lost circulation, but he was just dispensing with the preliminaries.

A young juggler in motley came out tossing a cascade of four balls while two clowns carried out a brightly striped pole on a stand. As the clowns left, the juggler took his position before the pole. While the horse cantered around the circle, Nick brought out a fistful of knives and threw them between the balls. Each blade hit the red stripe of the pole, never once grazing a ball—or the juggler.

The audience was silent, not even the sound of a single breath escaping from the hundreds of gaping mouths. And then the sequence of the balls changed, one bouncing from the ground and fountaining into the air like a grouse flushed from cover.

Thwack! A knife skewered it to the pole.

A second ball made a bid to escape. *Thwack!*

Thwack! Thwack!

The juggler raised his empty hands, the balls pinioned in a neat vertical line above his head. Nick jumped to stand in the saddle, accepting the sudden roar of applause. Evelina and Imogen clapped as enthusiastically as the rest, Imogen giving a very unladylike whoop. One of the female members of the troupe ran out with an armful of roses, and the juggler immediately began to toss them into the air. The flowers weren't particularly good candidates for the job, but they worked well enough for Nick to snatch one from the air as he rode by.

He finally slowed the horse to a halt beneath Evelina's box. All eyes were on the lithe, hawk-faced young showman as he raised the rose in salute.

And then all those eyes were on her, the object of his tribute. For a moment, she quailed. Still, he was impossible to refuse. She rose, leaning over the edge of the box to accept the flower. He was breathing hard, the throat of his damp shirt open, the dark skin glistening beneath. His eyes held her, electric with the triumph of the performance.

Evelina was mesmerized. Her fingers closed over the rose petals—soft, sensual velvet. Nick said no words, his fingers grazing hers as she took the flower, and she felt the prickle of shared magic. Even if she could have heard him speak over the wild audience, nothing was necessary. Everything was clear.

She'd been blinded by memory, not seeing the present. In their years apart, he'd transformed into a magician of air and steel. She had risen to new heights, but now she understood that he had, too. This was his kingdom, and he ruled it.

I see you now. A tremor passed through her, followed by a flood of unwelcome heat. His sheer physical prowess made her mouth go dry.

She raised the rose to her face, breathing in its scent. Nick made a graceful bow of his head, finally breaking that dangerous gaze. He spun the gray mare, giving a final wave to the roaring beast of the crowd as the horse reared and snorted. And then he was gone.

Evelina fell as much as sat down. Her heart thudded as fast as the mare's hooves.

"Good gracious!" Imogen exclaimed, fanning herself with her handkerchief. "So that is your Niccolo. My, my, my."

Evelina gave a weak nod, and then touched Imogen's arm. "Please wait for me here. There's something I need to do."

What she had just seen had broken her heart a little, or maybe it had just broken the fear around it. Now the past gripped her like a riptide. She had to see Gran.

CHAPTER THIRTY

London, April 11, 1888

HILLIARD HOUSE

6 p.m. Wednesay

LORD BANCROFT LOOKED ACROSS HIS DESK AT HIS SON. THE tiger's head mounted on the wall above somehow managed to mimic his expression, perhaps because it was frozen in its usual snarl.

"I received a note from Markham's drapery this afternoon wanting to know whether or not Imogen wished to purchase a certain length of silk brocade, as there was another customer interested in the same bolt of cloth. I thought nothing of it at the time." Bancroft's fingers twitched.

"Imagine my consternation when, not a half hour later, Jasper Keating arrived in person and brought two items to my attention." His father opened a drawer, pulling out the offending objects and setting them on the desk. One was a silver paper knife. The other was a calling card with Imogen's name embossed on it.

"This," his father pointed to the knife, "was pulled from the leg of the Gold King's streetkeeper—some creature named Striker—just days ago. It came within an inch of severing the artery in his leg."

"Unfortunate, but what is the significance?"

"Look, you dolt." His father held it up so that Tobias could see the handle. "It bears the Bancroft coat of arms. According to the staff, it belongs in the guest room Miss Cooper is currently using. I would like to know what it was doing embedded in the flesh of a back-alley thug."

"Oh." Tobias shifted in his chair, deciding he had best pay attention.

"This," Bancroft poked the calling card, "was found in a warehouse belonging to Keating. One of his cousins, Mr. Harriman, runs it for him—and Mr. Harriman brought it forward to the Gold King's attention."

Bancroft's mouth worked as if he wanted to spit. "Harriman was considerably upset by the fact that there was clear evidence of intruders in the place. He has, consequently, hired toughs to guard his person."

Tobias doubted his sister could inspire that kind of response. There had to be more to this Harriman's paranoia than finding a young girl's calling card on his warehouse floor. However, he knew better than to interrupt the pater when he was on a tear.

Bancroft slammed his palm on the desk. "What, I wonder, was my daughter doing there? The only clue I have is that Markham's Drapery is nearby, where Imogen was shopping *in the company of Miss Cooper.*"

His father put heavy emphasis on the last phrase. "Your function was to keep the girl distracted and out of our affairs, not to allow her to roam free and drag my daughter into God only knows what difficulties."

Tobias opened his mouth to protest, but then closed it. He usually felt guilty about something—and probably was—but he couldn't quite work up a feeling of responsibility for Imogen's escapades. She was responsible for her own damned guilt, with or without Evelina helping her along.

His father gave him his special glare. "So? What are you going to do?"

Tobias wished he'd leave off about Evelina. He wanted her right enough, but not on his father's terms. He took a painful swallow. "She's an innocent girl, and our guest. Don't expect me to dishonor her. I'm better than that."

There, he'd said it. He'd stood up to his father.

"Don't be an idiot," Bancroft snapped. "Innocent girls don't stab street thugs and go traipsing through back alleys.

I want to know what she thinks she knows about the murder of that wretched serving girl."

The change of subject startled Tobias. "What does that have to do with Imogen?"

"I'm thinking it is time that Imogen learns to do without her. I want Miss Cooper gone by week's end."

Tobias frowned, not liking this turn in the conversation at all. "What makes you think she knows anything?"

His father glared.

What are you afraid she will find out? Tobias wanted to ask, but wasn't sure he wanted the answer. Instead, he took his turn changing the subject.

"What is it between you and Dr. Magnus? Why do you dislike the man so much?"

His father's face turned to the color of ash. "Don't ever speak to me about him. Ever."

It was Tobias's turn to narrow his eyes. A strange feeling was coming over him, almost a dislocation. He was used to being the one in the wrong. The one whose affairs were in disorder. Now everything was suddenly different, as if he were standing on solid ground and watching his father flounder for a change.

"Keep your mind on what's important," his father snapped. "Such as this attack on the streetkeeper with our knife. I can't apologize to Jasper Keating for one more thing. Not if I intend to keep this family afloat."

"Which is another way of telling me, sir, to behave like a cad," Tobias said dryly.

"Why not? You're good at such things, from what I hear." His father swept the knife and card back into the drawer. "How hard can it be to distract one young woman?"

Tobias sat in stunned silence. He wanted to rage and bluster, but a horrible embarrassment stilled his tongue. *He's guilty!*

The only question was how deeply Lord Bancroft was involved in Grace Child's murder. Tobias had a sudden urge to retch or get very, very drunk. Maybe both. His father had always been terrifying, oppressive, but he had been a standard, the thing Tobias could never live up to. His father wasn't supposed to be beneath contempt.

Lord Bancroft broke the silence. "Now get out of my study and do your duty to this family."

And what is that? Evelina was right when she said it would be hard to find his true path. After a life doing little beyond drinking, whoring, or building a giant squid, he wasn't sure what to do next. He'd never been taught how to be useful. Quietly, Tobias got up and left the room, wishing he would never have occasion to return.

BANCROFT SCOWLED AT the door as it closed behind Tobias. The last thing he needed was to give Keating another weapon to use against him, and there seemed to be no way to impress the importance of the situation upon his son. Why hadn't he simply caught the girl in a secluded corridor and shown her what a strong, healthy young man was good for? Now even that expedient was too late.

The fact that the Cooper girl had been at the warehouse—no doubt dragging Imogen into the matter—was intolerable. The fact that Keating had arranged for her presentation was a complication, but surely she could be moved on after that. There had to be a polite way of showing a single nosy girl the door. And once she was out of the house, anything could happen to her. Something would, if Bancroft had his way.

He couldn't take a chance that she would learn what had gone on at the warehouse. He wasn't even sure he was content to let Harriman live. Unfortunately, it seemed that Keating's cousin had second-guessed him there.

He'd told Tobias the truth about Harriman's bodyguards. They were all over the weasel's house now, and Bancroft thought he knew why. According to Harriman himself, the last crates had arrived in the early morning around the fourth of the month. Thinking they contained something especially valuable, the idiot had kept them underneath the warehouse and had not told Keating that the final pieces of the shipment had arrived.

That night Harriman had sent a coded message with

Grace. The message had disappeared along with the package of gold she was carrying, but two days later—and here things got interesting—Harriman had said the note didn't matter. Bancroft remembered his words: *I'd read Schliemann's letters about what was supposed to be coming. One or two really large pieces. The crates were so late, I wasn't sure we'd have time to make copies. If everyone thought the crates were lost, we could just keep the contents.* But then he'd described the crates as nothing but pottery, jewelry, and plate.

A crafty look had crossed Harriman's face right then. It had come and gone too quickly for Bancroft to be sure he'd seen it, but he'd been on the alert ever since. As it turned out, caution was justified. He'd produced the crates when Bancroft had ordered him to, but now something was missing—this thing Magnus had called Athena's Casket.

Bancroft rose from his desk, staring out the window at the circular garden that graced the middle of Beaulieu Square. The garden was ordered, trimmed, the paint on the iron railings immaculate. He was filled with a sudden urge to run outside and dig his hands into the cold spring mud and tear that perfection to ruins. On some primal level, he wanted the outside world to match the chaos inside his mind.

What was this blasted casket? Magnus wanted it, and had approached Keating to get it. It had to be valuable. That meant both Magnus and Keating would be on the hunt—and the gods only knew what they would turn up in the process. But it was obvious that Harriman had melted it down and kept the gold entirely for himself.

So Bancroft had gone around to Harriman's house, which was when he'd discovered that the little cretin had hired a pair of very dangerous-looking men to guard his modest town house. Only a trained eye would spot them, one smoking under the streetlamp, another drinking a glass of wine outside the shop across the way—but both had gone on the alert when Bancroft had approached. Evidently, Harriman was afraid he would figure things out and make a move.

Fury rushed through Bancroft at the memory, making him wheel away from the window. He didn't want to look outside, but inward, where he could nurse his rage. Anger was better than fear.

Magnus has the automatons. There was no better bargaining chip to be sure Bancroft helped him get the casket from Keating. *But Keating doesn't have it. There is no casket to get anymore.* How would Magnus react to that news? Would he give them back? Destroy them out of spite? Would he even believe the truth? With a shuddering breath, Bancroft buried his face in his hands, wishing he could scream in frustration without attracting a dozen servants.

Bancroft picked up his decanter and glass, setting them before him on the desk, but pausing there, his fingers tracing the elaborate geography of the cut crystal.

He was tempted simply to tell Magnus to go get his magical toy from Harriman and be done with it. Unfortunately, then he would have to explain more than he wanted Magnus to know, and Harriman was sure to squawk to Keating with some lie about being bullied into going along with Bancroft's plans. There was no way to emerge the winner from that scenario.

What had started as an elegant plan to grab money and insert himself into the inner circle of aristocratic rebels had devolved into a house of cards that threatened to topple with the slightest gust of ill wind. Unfortunately, he had blowhards on every side. Bancroft, as the brains of the plot, had to stay the course until the forgery scheme was complete. There was one more piece, one more phase that he had to see through. One that, thankfully, Harriman knew nothing about. That was the way to do things—always have a trick up the sleeve that only you knew about.

Bancroft had started out as the fox stealing from the henhouse, and ended up as Reynard on the run. The only way he could survive was to duck between Keating and Magnus and let the two of them beat each other's brains out over this mysterious casket.

Well, he was clever and lucky. It just might work. He wanted his share of that gold, and he absolutely had to retrieve the automatons from Magnus's clutches. He could only pray that his luck held.

I'll drink to that. He lifted the stopper from the decanter and poured a measure into his glass. It tasted like victory, but unfortunately didn't give rise to any brilliant ideas.

That thought drove him to another, and he picked up a letter that had been sent half in jest from an acquaintance at the club who knew Bancroft liked a bet. *Here you are,* the note had said, *the long shot of your dreams. A few of us contrarians are getting in the action. The odds don't get any longer than an aging actress with no paint, nor lines, nor boards to tread. If La Reynolds comes out of this alive, the heavens will have set on the Empire as we know it.*

Bancroft picked up his pen and applied it to a clean sheet of paper. *Put me down for ten pounds.*

Given the precarious state of the Roth purse, it was a lot of money for a losing bet, but if anyone prayed to the goddess of lost causes, it was Bancroft.

WHEN TOBIAS REACHED the hallway outside his father's study door, he wasn't sure where to go. There were times when he confided in Imogen, but she was out with Evelina. He would have to figure this out on his own.

Or perhaps not quite.

He turned his steps toward his mother's sitting room. Once, she had ruled over the house every minute of every day. She still oversaw all the entertaining, but more and more she came to this small, quiet room with only her thoughts for company.

When he opened the door and peered inside, he nearly overlooked her. The soft gray of her dress blended into the muted tones of the walls and drapes. She was sitting on the sofa, holding a book, but staring out at the garden.

"Mother?" he said softly.

She turned, the sunlight silvering her wealth of golden hair. With the light behind her, she looked so much like Imogen it made him blink. "Yes?"

"May I sit with you a little?"

She motioned him to the other end of the sofa. "Problems with your father?"

Was that the only time he came to talk to her? The thought made him wince. "Yes, but I wanted to talk to you about something that's been on my conscience."

She furrowed her brow. "What's that, Tobias?"

"The servant girl who died. Grace Child."

"What about her?" Her eyes took on that perceptive sharpness he remembered from being a small and naughty boy. Back then, she had never assumed his guilt, but never ruled it out, either.

"I saw her just before she died. I've never spoken of it to the police."

"Why not?"

"I had nothing to do with her death, I promise, but I was out doing something, well, a bit unwise."

Her smile was wistful. "And if I can't keep my son's confidences, what kind of a mother am I?"

Tobias closed his eyes for a moment, realizing how badly he needed to hear those words. "Maybe you can help me understand what Grace said."

Lady Bancroft set down her book, then reached over and grasped both his hands. The spring light fell around her gently, glinting off the stones in her wedding ring. "Tell me."

Tobias thought carefully, his gaze on the ring. He hadn't told Evelina everything. He hadn't told anyone this part of her story. "I was coming home late and went to the side door. She was outside."

His mother waited patiently while he sorted his thoughts for a moment more. "They'd locked the doors and she couldn't get in. At first it seemed all she wanted was to get to her bed without Bigelow finding out she'd missed curfew. I didn't mind. What was it to me if one of the maids was making merry? I liked the idea of doing her a good turn. But then, just before we went inside, she held me back, asking for a word."

"What did she want?"

"She said she was in terrible trouble." Tobias wet his lips. "At first I thought she meant she was, um, in a family way and needed money."

His mother drew her brows together. "The talk below stairs says that was the case."

A surge of nausea left him hot and prickling. Grace had been so afraid, and not just for herself, but for that unborn child. "Maybe. But that was not all that troubled her. She said—"

He stopped, distracted by his memory of her piquant features, bold and fragile at once. *Us girls got to takes their chances where they find them,* she'd said in her common accent, raising her chin. And then she had started to sob.

He cleared his throat. "The long and the short of it was that she'd become mixed up in some sort of illegal business and wanted to get free of it. She thought it was only a matter of time before she was caught."

His mother was starting to look alarmed. "What did you say to her?"

"I asked her what she wanted me to do. She seemed to think that I could find her a position someplace far away. I said I'd try. The Penners have a house in Yorkshire. Maybe she could have gone there. But by the next day, she was dead."

His mother squeezed his hands and let them go. "Poor girl. That was very generous of you, but would never have worked out. We could never have recommended a servant who had obviously involved herself in something disreputable. But I see why you couldn't tell any of that to Inspector Lestrade. It wouldn't do to have it rumored that we had a criminal element in the house."

Uncertainty crept over Tobias. His mother was clearly missing the point. "Grace was afraid that if I said anything, she would be dead for certain. I think she was afraid of someone in this house."

He watched his mother's face carefully. Bewilderment faded to consternation, and she shook her head. "Impossible."

"I'm not so sure."

"How can you say that?" she exclaimed.

"Who are we, Mother?" he snapped, hating the sharpness of his voice. "Do you recall the housemaid being electrocuted at our garden party? How many steps is it from torture to murder?"

"Tobias!" His mother's eyes were wide and a little afraid. "Whatever put that thought in your mind?"

He had felt the fissures in his world widening under his feet even then. Perhaps Grace had seen them even before he did. "Father is guilty of something."

"How can you say that?"

"I don't know," Tobias said dryly, wondering how the conversation had turned to his father. Then again, everything in their lives revolved around the man.

His mother's face had gone white. He decided to let the subject of Grace drop and try a different tack. "What is the connection between Father and Dr. Magnus and automatons? They both seem obsessed with them."

"Automatons? What do you mean?"

"The ones we had in Vienna. The ones that were stolen."

She sat back slowly, every movement carefully controlled. "Oh. Those."

"What is so valuable about them?"

"Dr. Magnus helped him build them, long ago," his mother said dully, avoiding the question. "It's a part of your father's life that he will never willingly revisit."

"Why not?" Tobias gave a harsh laugh. "Science is the one thing we have in common, and he won't even talk about it." Anger jammed in his throat, too thick to let out. He fell silent.

His mother looked stricken. "Some things should never be disturbed," she whispered. "Whatever it was that happened came at that terrible time when your sisters were so ill."

"A girl is dead. Two of our grooms are dead. A little discomfort is a small price to pay."

His mother blinked rapidly, refusing to meet his eyes. "Tobias, stop this. For my sake, if not for your own."

"Did he kill Grace Child?"

His mother looked up, her lips parted in shock. Guilt seared through him. He hadn't meant to go this far. His mother was the last person he wanted to hurt. She bore too much of his father's burden already. And yet he held his breath, waiting for the answer.

"I don't know," she said. The words held so little force, he could barely hear her.

"I'm sorry." He wasn't sure what for. Maybe everything, like the sacrificial scapegoat.

She drew herself up, folding her hands in her lap. She refused to look at him, but sat with the light gilding her hair and casting her features into sharply limned shadows. "What are you going to do?"

Tobias didn't know. What would the future hold if Lord Bancroft were hauled off for murder? Or even if his career collapsed? Imogen would never make her brilliant match. His youngest sister—scholarly, awkward Poppy, happier in the country than enduring the London social whirl—would suffer, too.

If his father fell from grace, so would his mother. How long would she last in genteel poverty, forced to manage her husband's thwarted ambitions, before the shadows finally blotted her out altogether?

How much depended on Tobias keeping his suspicions to himself? Bile burned in his gut. He didn't want this much responsibility. "I have to find out what happened to Grace," he said quietly. "Until I do, I can't know where my duty lies."

"Duty?" his mother asked in a stiff voice, finally turning to look at him. "To whom? To what?"

"Honor, then."

"There is no such thing," she said hoarsely. "It's time you grew up and learned at least that much."

"Mother?"

Her face twisted. "Honor is what people use when they can't bring themselves to face their own weakness. Then they grasp their honor like Michael picking up his holy sword and cut their loved ones off at the knees in the name of the greater good."

Tobias sat, numb and silent. His mother worked her tiny handkerchief, kneading it into a tight ball. "I'm sorry," she said. "I can't bear this conversation a moment longer."

She stood up, waving him down when he scrambled to his feet. "Sit."

"Mother—"

"Sit and think about the calamity you're going to cause before you do a single thing."

"But what if he is guilty? What am I supposed to do then?"

She turned to look down on him, her face taut with misery. "Guilty he may be, but am I? Are your sisters? If you punish him, you punish us. That's the way of the world. Does his guilt matter that much?"

The worst part was she thought her husband capable of murder. He could see it in her eyes. He could hold his tongue, but he couldn't protect her from her own suspicions. "It matters to you," he said.

"Only so far." She held up her finger and thumb, a scant inch apart. "I have children. That makes me blind to everything else."

Tobias could find no words to say. His mother left the room.

He stared at his hands, lying idle in his lap. All he wanted in his life was to build interesting machines. Instead . . .

Outrage crept over him. He wished he wasn't part of his family anymore, but there was nothing he could do to change his blood.

CHAPTER THIRTY-ONE

THE CLUBHOUSE WAS SILENT AS THE PROVERBIAL . . . WELL, Tobias was depressed enough without the comparison. The conversations with his mother and father had left him raw.

The bottle of brandy he had taken from his father's private reserve at first tasted like hot, smooth ambrosia. Then rank as poison, as he drank past the point of pleasure. Finally, he tasted nothing at all.

The remains of the iron squid looked lonely in the yard. He and Edgerton had quietly retrieved them from the scrap heap behind the Royal Charlotte, where old sets went to die. The scavengers had been at it, picking the metal like a carrion bird cleaned a corpse. He had mourned the thing with all the intensity of a bereaved parent. It had been his one real triumph.

Now it lay on its back, the remaining three legs stuck in the air, a fly carcass from a giant's windowsill. Tobias sat on its steel belly, bottle in hand, and fondly patted one of its knees. "That was some night."

He had barely escaped. And then that wretched girl had died. Tobias raised the bottle to his lips again, accidentally banging it against his teeth.

He squinted up at the sky. Coal smoke dimmed the stars, but he had the impression of a vast, awe-inspiring heaven. It seemed like a good moment to wax philosophical, but tilting his head back reminded him how much brandy he'd consumed.

What options did he have now? He could fall into line with his parents. Take up a profession his father approved of. Abandon his talents. Protect his family. Use Evelina's affection to trick her. Most important, bury any uncomfortable truths she and her uncle might uncover. As options went, they all sounded disgusting.

In truth, he thought he might love Evelina. It wasn't because she was pretty or clever, though that didn't hurt, but because she actually cared who he was. That was worth fighting for, taking risks for. He hadn't lied when he'd said she made him a better man. He needed her if he meant to keep his soul. No, there would be no betraying the woman he loved.

He could help Evelina find Grace Child's murderer and whatever other horrors might be hiding in the Roth family closets. But that way led to ruin not only for his father, but also for the innocent women of the family.

The first alternative—dishonor—was unthinkable and the second—utter ruin—unbearable.

He rose, desperation giving him a second wind. The dark swirled around him, the shadows unpleasantly intimate. With a final affectionate caress to the squid, he walked with careful steps toward the clubhouse, where a gentle pool of light spilled through the door.

He had left a candle burning in the lantern that hung from an overhead beam. Tobias half sat, half fell into the ragged chair. There was an inch of brandy left in the bottle, but he set it aside. He was at that state where the world tilted if he closed his eyes. Instead, he stared at the floor, focusing very hard on the cracks between the boards to keep the room from spinning.

Tobias needed a mentor. Someone who knew who he was and could help him turn that to practical ends. To be perfectly honest, Magnus's intensity was daunting. But, with knowledge, money, and ideas, he was a lifeline. Tobias's best option was to surpass the foreigner's expectations at every turn and hope somehow to make a name for himself with his talent. That might lead to an independent income, which meant the freedom to make his own choices.

Feeling slightly steadier, he rose and crossed to the work-table. Serafina still lay there, naked. Edgerton must have come by, because her legs were properly attached, the issue with the hip joints solved in record time. Again, Tobias had the irrational urge to cover her. *It's cold in here. Magnus should have brought her some clothes. Surely she must have some?*

Tobias picked up the drawings, shuffling through them. There must have been more reasons why the doll had been disassembled. Oh, yes, something with the logic system. Magnus had said he'd fixed that, hadn't he? She was ready for a new trial.

If he had doubts about his inebriation, those moments quashed them. He could feel Serafina's eyes watching his every move. It had to be his imagination, because in his own mind those eyes belonged to one of his many mistresses, and then another, and then Evelina.

When he looked up, the doll's eyes were peacefully closed. He made a disgusted noise, fed up with his own weakness. He needed to work. If he could turn his hands and mind to a practical problem, everything wrong with the world would fade away. It was the only time he was truly at peace.

He peeled off his coat and settled to work on Magnus's doll. At first his fingers were clumsy, drink-addled, but concentration pushed past the fog, sending him into a state that was almost hyperalert. The arms attached easily, only needing an hour's effort. The head was another matter. It was missing a pin that slid from ear to ear, unlocking the spring-driven programming mechanism that served as Serafina's brain. That had to be one of the bits and pieces at the bottom of the trunk.

It was too dark to see inside the box, so he knelt and searched the bottom by touch. He didn't find the pin right away, but instead found the trunk was lined with thick black card. Wedged halfway beneath the card were papers that looked like they'd escaped the portfolio of sketches.

Tobias pulled them out, finding the pin stuck between two sheets of paper. He carried the lot back to the lamplight and then began sorting the pages into order, looking for any further instructions on how to activate the automaton. He couldn't see a proper power source, and that made him curious. In terms of appearance, she was a superior product, but the real test of manufacture came when the gears were in motion.

Tobias leaned with his back to the worktable, his legs crossed at the ankles. The spidery writing on the pages was in Italian. Not his best language. Still, it didn't take him long to realize it was the notebook of Serafina's original maker.

"I am dying," he read. Lovely. He was distinctly not in the mood for someone else's brooding. "I stole the pin and threw it in the holy well before the cathedral. God willing, this theft will save my life."

Holy well? What was he afraid of? Tobias flipped over the page, frowning. The man was a complete lunatic. Moreover, his plan had been a failure because the pin—or its replacement—had been in the trunk, along with the notebook pages.

Tobias dropped the pages back into the trunk and picked up the brandy bottle, returning to the table to stand looking down at Serafina. *Well, let's see what this lady can do.* Lifting the soft, waving locks of red hair, he slid the pin into place. Nothing happened. He was oddly relieved.

It was hard not to be rattled by something that looked so alive, but wasn't. In the flickering light of the candle lantern, the porcelain features seemed soft as flesh, the intersections of jaw and joint nearly invisible. Whoever had sculpted her had loved the female form, down to the details of her perfect, pink-tipped breasts, and the swell and dip of belly and thigh. Shadows seemed to press in around them, the silence in the room profound. He could hear the pulse of his own blood.

Tobias blinked, his fingers tightening on the bottle. He could swear the shadows were actually seeping into the doll, like a thick, dark smoke. Weird, roiling darkness was rising from the floor, creeping up the legs of the table and worming under the inanimate form like something insectile. The doll was absorbing it into her sawdust flesh.

And Tobias felt himself growing weaker, as if he were losing blood. *This can't be happening.* He set the bottle down, pushing it away. He was drunk. He was just feeling that sudden fatigue that comes a few hours after a hard drinking session. That point where a nap sounds like the best thing in the world.

He unhooked the lamp from the hook on the ceiling, bringing it closer to the worktable. Details jumped into focus. The patch of Serafina's hair that was uneven had not been cut, but burned away, as if she had leaned too close to a candle.

He leaned close. The hair smelled of smoke, but there was a fresh scent, too, as if she had been out of doors not long ago. He would have expected staleness, but she could not have been locked in the trunk long. Magnus must have taken her apart for repairs very recently.

And brought her to SPIE to be put back together. The task the doctor had set wasn't to challenge their skill—that was certain. It had taken a delicacy of touch to hook the doll's fine workings back together, but Tobias could have done the whole job himself in an afternoon. So what had the doctor said? *Serafina represents a test. The questions she poses are not a matter of springs and gears.* What did that mean?

He didn't have long to wait for an answer. The sawdust chest rose in a breath.

Terror bolted up his spine. Tobias skittered back from the table, his disbelieving cry bouncing off the lowering shadows. *Magic!*

The following silence was suffocating. Suddenly, there seemed to be no air in the place, despite the doorway open to the night. He rubbed his eyes, sure his imagination had run riot. But his mind raced anyway, trying to straighten out what he'd seen the way a maid tidied an unmade bed. No rumples. No wrinkles. Just rational, tidy corners.

I'm not in a nursery tale. This was London, a real London

full of real monsters like his father and Jasper Keating. With them around, dark magic was superfluous.

No, but the last man who worked on Serafina took out the pin and sunk it in holy water. That can't be good.

Nausea robbed the strength from his legs. He sat down hard in the chair. *If this was a nursery tale, the power source she doesn't have would be magic and Dr. Magnus would be a sorcerer. After all, didn't he say artists put a bit of their soul into their creations? Isn't that theft of life how sorcery works?*

"Sorcerers don't trick men into assembling evil dolls." He said it out loud, trying to forget all Magnus's prattle about bridegrooms and nourishment, and all Bucky's talk about vampire brides.

He needed to reject these thoughts out loud, because he was quite clearly drunk and nearly swallowing the nonsense whole. But he might have also said that strangers didn't unexpectedly mentor talent that rested on the fame of a single prank at the opera. Good Samaritans didn't lure talented young men by appealing to that hurt in their soul left by a bitter father.

If Tobias wanted a fairy tale, he had to look no further than his own wishful thinking. Magnus had taken an interest because he wanted Tobias for his mysterious other project. *And he only wants me if I pass the test that is Serafina.*

He rose, approached the worktable, and put his hand on the doll's chest, ready to convince himself that it wasn't actually moving—but he felt it lift. Tobias started to tremble, tears filling his eyes. *The breathing must be part of the mechanism.* He hadn't really had a good look inside the torso.

"I am dying," the Italian had written. Death magic worked by stealing life. Did Serafina survive by draining her makers? *Don't be ridiculous!*

So . . . what was he looking at? A mechanism? A miracle? The stirrings of a creature set to devour him? In the nursery tales, there was always a test of faith. Was he supposed to trust Dr. Magnus, no matter what? To keep courage and accept whatever dark, shadowy horror the doctor threw at him, because that was the only way to move onward to the bigger project, to the next level, and to get the support he needed to be his own man?

Serafina's eyes snapped open, the relentless china blue fixed on his face. Then one hand lifted, the delicate, porcelain fingers reaching out and grazing his cheek in a slick, chill caress. Then her jaw opened with a slight click, showing the white tips of tiny, perfect teeth in an eerily charming smile.

Tobias made a sound between a groan and a cry of terror. Before he could stop to think, he pulled out the pin. He stood with it in his hand, tears hot on his cheeks. *The questions she poses are not a matter of springs and gears.*

He'd wondered who he was. Now he knew.

Tobias Roth was a desperate coward.

CHAPTER THIRTY-TWO

London, April 12, 1888
HILLIARD HOUSE

8 a.m. Thursday

EVELINA SAT BEFORE HER DRESSING TABLE MIRROR, NOT seeing the image before her. She was aware that it was a sunny morning, sparkling as champagne on ice. She could hear Imogen's excited voice down the corridor, exclaiming about a button or a feather or some crisis of absolutely national import. She could feel the heavy richness of her presentation gown, the white folds like a blanket of snow around her.

But none of it could quite penetrate the haze in her mind. She was adrift, spiraling like a twig down a stream, powerless against the rushing force. Evelina had known even as a child that leaving the circus would take her away from all she knew, but now she understood how irrevocable that act had been. There would be no return. Even if she could go back to Ploughman's, it would never again be the place she knew.

Gran Cooper was dead. Nick hadn't told her. She had learned it from Old Ploughman himself, his manner kind and delighted to see her again, but unsure what to say. The winter had taken the old woman barely two years after Evelina had left. All her other kin was gone, too, taking up regular occupations or moving on in search of richer shows, though Ploughman had kept the Fabulous Flying name of the Coopers' old act.

She hadn't asked for any more details. Too shocked to prolong the visit, too afraid of whom else she might have lost, she'd left at once, collecting Imogen on the way. Without Gran, nothing would seem right anyway.

Evelina still hadn't cried. She would, eventually, but the pain had gone too deep, like a splinter the flesh couldn't eject until it had festered. All she could do was go forward, a twig in the stream, anchored to nothing.

Behind her, Lady Bancroft's maid pushed another pin into Evelina's dark hair, fastening in the headdress of feathers required by the Lord Chamberlain's precise dress code. Usually Dora dressed her hair, but for the presentation Lady B was taking no chances.

"How does that look, miss?" she asked.

It would look fine, Evelina knew, because the girl was excellent at her work. Nevertheless, she forced herself to focus on her image in the mirror. A stranger looked back, the formal hairstyle and her mood conspiring to disorient her. "Lovely, Jeanette. Thank you."

The maid left. Evelina stayed seated at her dressing table, feeling the morning flowing downstream. She was grief stricken, but nothing had changed. Not really. She would go to the presentation, make her bows, and go on. Marriage or college.

Why didn't Nick tell me Gran had passed?

His omission hurt. But then it was old news to him, wasn't it? Who was she to think that everything had remained the same just because she had left? And she hadn't exactly taken the time to sit down with him and chat. *No, I can't blame Nick.*

The rose was pressed between the pages of *Barrett's Guide to the Mechanics of Ancient Europe,* the cover safely closed over the scarlet softness. A keepsake, and a token of what might have been. Nick was the king of his own world now, and she had no right to drag him into danger. His weakness was his constancy, and she had to be wary of that for both their sakes. If she could wish for anything on this presentation morning—supposedly the *open, O sesame* to a young girl's future—it would be a secure future for them both. Sadly, that meant leaving him be.

The clock—Magnus's clock—chimed the quarter hour. Numbly, she rose, picking up her long white gloves and her fan.

Her mother had talked about Court. It had been Evelina's bedtime story—the pretty dresses and nice manners, the gentry and glittering palaces, the assurance of heat and light and enough to eat. Being presented was the culmination of her father's dreams when he ran away and took the queen's shilling, signing up for a life of war just so he could better himself.

Evelina was completing the family mythology. She had won the brass ring.

She wished she could have been happy. To top off her gloom, there had been word that morning from Dr. Watson. Uncle Sherlock was back in England, but had stopped overnight to see Grandmamma Holmes. The old lady wasn't well, and it was more than her usual complaints.

Despite their sometimes stormy relationship, the news had worried Evelina, but the last thing her grandmamma would thank her for was to forget Court and rush to her bedside in an excess of sentimentality. Grandmamma was expecting Evelina to eclipse her mother's transgressions. Still, the timing couldn't be worse, after hearing about Gran. *Don't make me lose them both. Not now.*

A profound sense of loneliness engulfed her. There would be no one from either side of Evelina's family to see her triumph.

Imogen and her mother had already departed in their carriage. Evelina would ride with the Duchess of Westlake—her sponsor and a woman she barely knew.

The duchess arrived on time, gathered Evelina into her grand equipage, and drove at a brisk pace to Buckingham Palace, where the Court Drawing Room was to be held.

The duchess was a large woman, gray-haired and without an ounce of nonsense about her. She looked Evelina up and down as if she were the latest addition to her stables. Whatever the woman's willingness to be her sponsor, there was no doubting her preparation. She had brought a maid and two large bags filled with brushes, powders, ribbons, sewing equipment, spare gloves, and stockings. She was apparently an old hand at the debutante business and approached the affair with the vigor of a general contemplating the battlefield.

"Did you refrain from drinking tea with your breakfast?" the duchess asked sharply.

"Yes, Your Grace," Evelina answered meekly.

"Good."

Evelina had guessed why, and it turned out she was correct. The crush of carriages outside the palace was unimaginable. They ended up waiting for hours before they could alight and enter the stuffy antechambers, only to wait some more. The place was jammed to the rafters with women growing hungry and restless. There were no facilities of any kind for the comfort of the debutantes and their sponsors.

Evelina looked around for Imogen and Lady Bancroft, who was her daughter's sponsor. The duchess spotted them first.

Despite the splendor of the occasion, Imogen was herself. "I can't believe we're doing this! And you're doing it with me! I'd embrace you but we'd both wrinkle our gowns!"

Evelina laughed. The sheer bizarreness of the situation was lifting her mood a little, and the happy excitement of all the girls around her was contagious. Still, she wasn't going to believe this was happening until she'd actually kissed the queen's hand. "I'll celebrate after, if I have any strength left. Apparently they mean this to be a test of endurance."

"I went through this with my own daughters," the duchess said with a sigh. "Each time I wonder how an empire that rules the world can manage to make a fifteen-minute job last all day."

"I'm famished," Imogen grumbled. It was nearing the three o'clock start time. They had left the house before nine that morning.

"The Lord Chamberlain is evil," Evelina returned darkly. The Lord Chamberlain ruled the presentations, and he did so with an iron sense of tradition. No newfangled inventions were found at these events, for all Queen Victoria's fascination with clever devices and clockwork toys. The Lord Chamberpot—not everyone was equally in awe of the man—dictated who was acceptable to put before the queen, and what they should be wearing when it happened. To Evelina, it seemed like he had confused the whole thing with a wedding.

All the debutantes wore white dresses and long, gauzy veils. All the gowns had short sleeves and low necks. No wraps, shawls, or scarves were permitted without a doctor's certificate. Apparently the Royal Court liked to see a bit of young female skin.

The regulation headdresses featured white ostrich plumes—three for the married ladies, two for the unwed—worn slightly to the left and curling grandly in the air. From the amount of fidgeting going on, it seemed most had trouble keeping them in place. The pins pulled at Evelina's hair, dragging because of the weight of the ridiculous veil and feathers.

The girls were presented in order of rank. Evelina—daughter of an army captain—was near the end. Finally, it was time, and a sense of occasion infused her. Now was the moment she truly crossed into the world of the Quality. This was the mark of acceptance they recognized and her admission into Society. *Thank you, Uncle Sherlock.*

Evelina stepped into the drawing room and handed her card to the Lord Chamberlain with her left hand and clutched her bouquet with the right. The gentlemen-in-waiting rushed forward to spread out the wealth of her long train—regulation three yards long, fifty-four inches wide—behind her.

"Miss Evelina Cooper," announced the Lord Chamberlain.

Evelina was suddenly faced with a large room filled with the pale butterfly forms of the court ladies and debutantes. Men in dark suits and uniforms punctuated the scene like exclamation points. But what fixed her attention was the group of figures at the opposite end of the room. Queen Victoria and two of the princesses were there, flanked by their attendants.

Small, plump, and gray-haired, the queen had celebrated her Golden Jubilee the summer before. Now, in her dark dress, she reminded Evelina just a little of Gran Cooper, a thought that brought a fresh wave of sadness.

As she drew closer, Evelina could see the old woman's face. Shrewd eyes held a glint of humor. There was something in the endless parade of girls bravely struggling with their feathers and trains that amused the queen. *She's just like Gran. Stern, but there's kindness there, too.*

Evelina came to a stop before Queen Victoria, and nearly forgot what to do next. Her hesitation only lasted an eye blink, but it was enough to jolt her back to the task at hand. Now came the curtsy. It had to be low, almost until her knee touched the ground, but only almost. She bowed, and the queen presented her hand to be kissed. Daughters of aristocrats received a kiss on the brow. Those who came from common stock did the kissing.

Evelina bent her head over the plump hand with its glittering rings, feeling the drift of her veil as she moved. The queen smelled of rosewater.

"The Duchess of Westlake is your sponsor," Victoria said. "Where is your mother? I do not remember her."

That, she supposed, should be a relief. Evelina had heard the queen reviewed the list of girls before each ceremony. She must have grown curious when she came across an unknown as the protégée of a duchess.

Evelina bowed her head, tears suddenly springing to her eyes. She hadn't cried yet, so why, oh why was it happening in front of the queen?

She blinked hard, sternly banishing the wetness before it could fall. "I'm afraid my mother died of a fever long ago, Your Majesty."

Victoria raised Evelina's chin with the hand just kissed. "Poor chick. You've a pretty face. A difficult thing to have when there is no mother."

"I do my best to keep my wits about me, Your Majesty."

"We are pleased to hear it, Miss Cooper." That thread of

sharp—but not unkind—wit was in the queen's voice now, as well as her bright eyes.

Evelina rose again, careful not to lose her balance or trip on her gown and its huge train. Then she curtsied again to the other royals. They looked slightly bemused. Her Majesty rarely spoke to the girls. Evelina finished with another, brief curtsy to the queen.

One of the gentlemen-in-waiting hurried forward to retrieve Evelina's train and drape it over her arm. From there, with a bouquet and feathers and a deal more bowing and scraping, she had to walk backward away from the throne and successfully exit the door without turning. One did not turn one's back on royalty.

Evelina counted her blessings that she had spent her early years studying acrobatics. She needed that good sense of balance. By the time she had left, the next debutante was already making her way forward. Evelina finally turned, to find the duchess already at her side.

"So, young lady, do you feel any different?"

No. She had expected more, and was vaguely disappointed. And yet she did feel a change, as if the twig she'd been thinking about that morning had gone over a waterfall, never to find its way back upstream, for good or ill.

But that was too complicated an answer to give, so Evelina reconsidered. "I feel that I have been granted an extraordinary privilege."

"You have." The duchess looked down her impressive nose at Evelina, sizing her up anew. "I will be pleased to see a bright thing like you in my drawing room."

They were leaving the palace, moving outside so their carriage could be brought. Food, drink, and—best of all— a water closet were in their future. The breeze caught Evelina's veil, and for a moment it blinded her.

Evelina dragged it out of the way. "Thank you. You're very kind."

"I knew your mother, you know."

That startled her. "You did?"

Some distance off, a steam tram huffed by on the public

roadway. The passengers hooted and waved at all the feathered girls standing about waiting for their rides.

"I'm sure the queen does as well, whatever she says. She's giving you a chance." The duchess's iron-gray eyebrows drew together. "You look just like Marianne. Mind that you don't make the same mistakes."

Evelina's lips parted, an angry retort coming from deep in her belly. All her grief about Gran came back, darkened by anger and too raw for politeness.

The duchess must have seen it on her face. She put a gloved hand on Evelina's arm, quelling whatever disastrous thing she was about to say. "Don't mistake me. I understand wanting love and happiness, believe me I do, but Society is a treacherous sea. I say the same thing to my own daughters. A young woman must find a ship that can weather the storms. Choose your husband as much for durability as for fine rigging."

Evelina lowered her eyes. "I understand."

The duchess smiled almost fondly, tapping her fan in an admonishing gesture. "I want you to be thinking about that at my ball tonight, because I think Society will take to you, Evelina Cooper. There will be no shortage of young men wanting to dance. Look, here is our carriage."

And a surprise to finish off the afternoon. They got in, but there was something on the seat. The duchess picked it up, after almost sitting on it.

It was a single flower tied with a white bow. "How did this get here? There is a tag on it for you, Miss Cooper."

Evelina raised a hand to take it, but the duchess chose to read the message first. She held it at arm's length to focus on the writing. "To congratulate you on this auspicious day. How proud you must be to have achieved so much."

The duchess flipped the tag over with a sniff. "Rather pompous, whoever it is. Aha, it is addressed from Dr. Magnus. Can't say I like the fellow."

Evelina accepted the flower as gingerly as if it had been a viper. The words were all civility, but the rose was identical to the one she had received from Nick. Somehow Magnus knew where she'd been and what she'd done yesterday. And he was here now, somewhere close, showing her what he could do.

Tension prickled across her shoulders, knotting the muscles in the back of her neck. She felt exposed in the low-cut dress, as if her magic and her past at Ploughman's were tattooed on her skin. "I don't like him, either."

"That shows you've got some wits," the Duchess of Westlake said crisply. "For all his fine airs, there's something dodgy about the man. To go back to our discussion of men and ships, that one reminds me of a doomed vessel, like the *Flying Dutchman*. All very fascinating until you find yourself keelhauled straight to hell."

Despite the tension cramping her stomach, Evelina had a sudden impulse to laugh. *Well, then, Tobias had better start building another squid!*

Chapter Thirty-three

THE DUKE AND DUCHESS OF WESTLAKE'S BALL, HELD AT their grand address in Mayfair, was the first big event for the debutantes of the Season. Although most of the girls, including Imogen, would also have a debut ball hosted by their families, this first whirl on the dance floor was as eagerly anticipated as their visit to the palace earlier that day. The duchess made full use of her guest list, and her power as a hostess was formidable—few dared to refuse her summons. The cream of Society would all be there to welcome the newcomers fresh from Queen Victoria's Court Drawing Room. And with this event, the hunt for husbands was officially on. Evelina had ached to go to the Duchess of Westlake's ball—yearned for it with her whole heart ever since she knew it existed. But now she understood how fillies felt, carefully brushed and with ribbons braided in their manes, before being led to the auction block.

Nervous, she was waiting outside for the carriage, catching a breath of air before they were due to depart. Maybe it was a risk, but she still felt asphyxiated after the long hours at the palace. She wanted to climb something, to feel the wind from twenty feet above the ground.

Clouds deepened the dark of the sky, promising rain to come, but thankfully it had not yet arrived. Custom required debutantes to wear white for the Westlakes' event, so Evelina stood almost immobile, her dancing shoes in a dainty sequined bag, her cloak covering every inch of the pristine white ruffles of her skirt. Somewhere in the elaborate mass of her coiffure, a hairpin was digging painfully into Evelina's scalp.

It was her first real ball, and she was so apprehensive, her stomach hurt. She wouldn't mind if a few spaces on her dance card went empty, but what if no one asked her at all? She wasn't a great beauty or a great heiress. What if all the men walked right past her? What if she was left standing alone all night? The thought of it made a corkscrew of her insides. She'd already fought off one attack of the hiccups. Give her a tightrope to walk, or a dragon to vanquish. This was agony.

A low whistle sounded from beyond the gate—a long note, then three short ones. *Nick!*

Or not. With Magnus lurking about, she wasn't taking anything for granted. Cautiously, she crept a few steps down the walkway to the metal gate that opened onto the street—or would have opened, had it been daytime. Since the murder, Bigelow had taken to locking it at sundown. She didn't cover more distance than she could make in a quick dash back to the door.

"Nick?" she said in a low whisper.

He suddenly appeared on the other side of the iron bars. "Evie."

The rough sound of his voice was like a familiar touch. With a stifled cry, she ran the rest of the way to the gate, but she didn't have the key to open it. She studied Nick's face, the oblique glow of the yellow gaslights limning the clean lines of his face.

"Why are you here?" she asked.

A frown put a vertical crease between his brows. "Watching for Magnus. What are you doing standing on your own outside?"

"I'm waiting for a carriage."

His hands waved in exasperated arcs. "You might as well have a sign over your head saying: *Damsel in distress, get 'em while they're hot.* You should get yourself back inside."

Nick had suffered the last time he'd met Magnus. The memory of it raised the hair on her nape and sharpened her tongue. "Oh, fine, and what are you going to do if he shows up?"

"I'll think of something."

She made an impatient noise in her throat. Tears started to her eyes, and she was grateful the darkness covered them. "Nick, be careful. Use your head. He left a rose in my carriage this afternoon. One just like yours."

The conversation froze in place, not only from the implication of the doctor's gesture, but also because of the memory of that moment in the ring: Nick the triumphant knight, Evelina the queen of love and beauty. He reached through the bars of the gate to catch her hand.

His grasp was hot enough to feel through the silk of her glove, and he pulled her forward a step. Her cloak fell open, revealing the form-fitting shape of her low-cut ball gown. His gaze ran down to her toes and back up again, lingering appreciatively.

Heat seared her cheeks. She wondered if he was there for Magnus at all.

"Aren't you a picture?" he said, his voice dipping to a deeper timbre.

Her mouth went dry. "You have your costumes, I have mine."

He stepped closer to the bars, leaning into them like a prisoner trying to see out of his cell. He lifted her fingers to his lips, brushing them lightly.

"Nick, stop," she breathed.

His gaze kept devouring her, but now it mocked as well, reminding her of that other, powerful Nick she'd seen in the ring. The one that made her insides melt.

He didn't let go of her hand. "Is there something wrong with worshipping a fine lady?"

"Don't tease me." She wanted to be angry, but it came out more as a plea.

Nick's eyes narrowed, the corners of his mouth twitching downward. "Where are you going tonight?"

"The Westlake ball." She could hear voices, and glanced over her shoulder. If they weren't careful, they'd be caught carrying on a conversation through a locked gate like lovers from some witless romance.

The pressure of Nick's hand brought her attention back to him. "Going dancing, are we?"

There was a tone in his voice she didn't like. Jealousy? "What else does one do at a ball?"

He shook his head, something akin to pain in his eyes. "Look at you, little Evie Cooper."

"Nick! Let me go," she begged. She could hear the carriage coming. She pulled her hand away.

And then he was gone, quick as one of his own flashing blades. She turned and ran back to the house, cursing him.

CONFUSED AND FEELING somehow guilty, she was nearly silent all the way to the Duke of Westlake's elegant mansion. When Applegate handed her out of the carriage, she was confronted with the sheer scale of the event. Vehicles of all kinds—steam and horse-drawn—jammed the street for half a mile either way. Every titled head in London was crowding into the pool of golden gaslight flooding from the mansion's front door. Evelina barely resisted the urge to cling to Lady Bancroft's elaborately ruffled bustle like a toddler afraid to lose her mother. The crush lasted until they were safely inside.

"There are twenty-four dances," Imogen said brightly, examining the dance card once they shed their wraps and put on their dancing slippers. "Twenty-four chances to sort the toads from the automatons."

About four inches tall, the tiny booklet had a richly colored cover ornamented with gold leaf, as well as a miniature pencil dangling from a cord. The whole works hung from a ribbon loop. What made this Season's cards unique was the novel way they opened. If one pushed the button to the left, only pages with unclaimed dances fanned out for viewing. The right-hand button showed them all.

Evelina slipped the loop of her card over her wrist. "Do you have a preference for dance partners?"

"I'm partial to the toads. At least they have personality."

"And prince potential?"

"Unlikely." Imogen made a philosophical moue, despite the flush in her cheeks. "Sometimes a toad is just a toad, but he might be a very nice toad. I think we'd get farther if we just accepted that and got on with things."

Evelina wondered if that particular amphibian was heir to the Penner factory fortune, but diplomatically held her tongue.

Their party gathered at the top of the grand staircase that swept down to the brilliantly lit ballroom. Evelina felt the heat shimmering up from the dance floor below like a palpable cloud. A footman took their invitations.

"Lord and Lady Bancroft," he announced in a stentorian voice. "The Honorable Imogen Roth and Miss Cooper."

Tobias, of course, would arrive with his friends, hopefully before everyone else went home. The interesting young men always arrived late.

The Bancrofts started down the stairs at a sedate pace, Lady Bancroft's gloved hand resting on the ambassador's arm like a hovering bird. Imogen descended next, all gold beauty, then Evelina. The coolness of the marble stairs seeped through the soft soles of her dancing shoes. Faces turned up to look at them, at her floating down the staircase in her fine dress of whipping-cream white. She lifted her head a fraction higher.

The descent gave her a good view of the company. Many of the same men who had been at Lord Bancroft's table were there, including Jasper Keating. In the opposite corner of the room, almost hidden by the crowd, was an attentive Dr. Magnus. It struck her as odd, because she doubted the duchess would have invited him—but then, it seemed, he had a way of going where he pleased. Despite the heat in the room, she shivered, remembering the bruising crush of his hand on her arm. It took everything she had to keep the fear from her face, but she would be damned if she'd let him see her panic.

When they reached the ballroom, Evelina reached into her reticule, feeling the cool steel fur of the mechanical mouse. *Watch Dr. Magnus. Find out who he is talking to and everything he does, but be sure to come back to me well before the dancing is over.*

She bent as if to adjust the lace of her dancing slipper, and quickly released Mouse next to the heavily carved base-boards of the wall. It disappeared in a streak of gray, a dozen times as fast as any regular rodent. She straightened to an-swer a question of Lady Bancroft's, careful to preserve a neutral expression.

At least I'm in a crowd, and Magnus would not dare to threaten me here. And with luck, she might learn something useful.

She needn't have worried about her dance card. The dip-lomatic service could have taken notes from Lady Bancroft and her cronies. They knew how to steer likely young men toward the young ladies without seeming to do so, winnow-ing away the chaff with a precisely placed word or tap of the fan. Within minutes, Imogen was the most sought-after belle of the ball, and Evelina not far behind.

As Imogen had predicted, there were some interesting toads and quite a few automatons. The first name on her card that she actually knew was one of Tobias's friends, Michael Edgerton, who asked her to partner him in the quadrille. It was one of the dances where conversation was practical and expected.

"You dance so gracefully, Miss Cooper," he said. He must have known how banal it sounded, because he looked faintly embarrassed.

On her side, Evelina fumbled for a response, because re-turning the compliment was out of the question. The tall, lanky Edgerton moved like a giraffe on ice skates. She tried to think of something she knew about him. Men were sup-posed to like talking about themselves, after all. "Are you still interested in the domestic application of an alternating current power supply?"

Edgerton fumbled his step, narrowly avoiding a collision. "In theory," he said shortly. "It hasn't been licensed for use."

Which in translation meant that the steam barons hadn't figured out how to monopolize it yet. She remembered some fellow named Ferranti had tried and been run out of Lon-don. Evelina executed a turn as she searched for an innocu-ous reply.

Edgerton broke in instead. "How on earth did you even remember my interest in that?"

"Because it interests me."

He gave an awkward smile. "How unusual, Miss Cooper. A fellow doesn't think to meet with that sort of thing on a dance floor. It's typically all posies and ribbons."

The way he said it left her unsure of his opinion. Was he pro- or antiposy? The dance ended and Evelina curtsied, then accepted his escort from the floor.

She decided to hazard a bit of honesty. "Do you truly find my question so off-putting Mr. Edgerton?"

"Heavens, no, Miss Cooper." He paused, leaning closer to lower his voice. "I'm just careful, you know, about my interest in new technologies. You should be, too. Someone might mistake curiosity for something else. You know what they say—if you really want to try new science, it's best to go to the Americas."

It was an oblique reference to the steam barons. She bit her lip, cursing her thoughtlessness. "My apologies."

Edgerton gave a surprisingly dimpled smile. "Don't apologize for being interesting, Miss Cooper. It only increases your allure."

ELSEWHERE IN THE room, Imogen had been cornered by The Stare. Despite the fact that she had turned down his proposal—and most young men would know enough to withdraw their suit—Stanford Whitlock had taken it as a challenge. Sadly, unless she wanted to alert her parents to her refusal, she was forced to endure his attentions. Such was the price of liberty.

Always handsome, The Stare was even more impressive in evening clothes. Unfortunately, he had consumed enough liquid courage to loosen his tongue. Still worse, some well-meaning Cyrano must have written his lines for him.

"My dear Miss Roth, how is it possible that you are so radiant?" he asked in his curiously monotone voice. The question concluded with a smile that might have been the effects of a mild stomach cramp.

"I only used the very purest of soaps," she replied helpfully, accepting the glass of lemonade he offered. "It is quite impressive what the cosmeticians can do with oil of almonds."

"Indeed?"

"Yes, indeed." Imogen felt sorry for the man, who had been born without the least talent for conversation. Or dancing. They had made it around the room once before she complained that she was too exhausted to continue the polka. In truth, she had feared too much for her personal safety—and that of any breakable object within a square mile. "Although I have read in a ladies' manual that steel wool brings an attractive pinkness to the cheeks."

His eyes widened. "Would that not be painful?"

"But a good girl will do anything to make herself attractive. That is our first duty to Society, Mr. Whitlock."

He appeared to search his memory for a moment. "You are certainly an ornament to our company tonight, Miss Roth. Would you like some lemonade?"

"Thank you, Mister Whitlock, but you just brought me some."

"Of course." He got that searching look again, as if mentally flipping through a notebook.

She looked frantically about the room for rescue. "And you, Mr. Whitlock, do you still engage in pugilistic pursuits?"

"Yes, Miss Roth, I do." There was a flicker of life in his voice, but it died quickly. "Of course, a fine young lady like yourself would not be interested in such a brutish sport."

"No?" Imogen bridled. "I'm not afraid of a little blood."

"Heavens, Miss Roth," he laughed—a strangely wooden sound that went with the rest of his manner. "The fights are too coarse. There are men who place bets there, you know."

"How savage. You must be very brave to attend. Oh, look, there's Captain Smythe. We were going to have the next waltz. Hellooo!" she trilled, waving her lace-gloved fingers.

Diogenes Smythe was dashing in his blue Hussar's uniform, with silver and gold braid glittering in the gaslight. He was slighter than Whitlock, but just as tall and darkly good-looking. Most important, he had all the verve that Whitlock lacked. He answered her summons in a trice.

"My snow queen," he purred, bending over her hand. "White becomes you like a poem. I am positively ravished that you are released from the schoolroom and into our midst."

He straightened, one hand at his waist, the other resting at his side where his saber usually hung. All that was lacking was a photographer, ready to capture his image. He smiled, teeth white and strong beneath his closely trimmed mustache. *From the automaton to the peacock,* Imogen thought. *There are precious few princes in this bunch.*

But he was at least a good dancer. After bidding farewell to The Stare, they set off around the floor in a seductive whirl. The captain made sure to execute a turn every time they passed a mirror, as if to check his profile from every possible angle. Imogen didn't mind. He was amusing, though all his stories were about himself and his swashbuckling military adventures. As Smythe was clever and daring and a friend to Tobias, she was predisposed to like him, but not enough to give him a second thought once he very properly walked her back to Lady Bancroft's side.

Imogen hummed a little as he strutted away. The exertion had left her feeling a little unwell—she would never have Evelina's stamina, and would have to pace herself carefully through the Season. Nevertheless, she was having a lovely time, with all the bright lights and pretty music.

It was a relief from worrying about her father and what he might be up to. She'd been on edge ever since she'd overheard his conversation with Mr. Harriman—afraid to speak of it to Evelina, and afraid of what trouble she might cause by holding back the information. There didn't seem to be a good answer.

And with so much going on—murder, the Disconnection, the affair at the warehouse—a night of entertainment was a blessing. There were a lot of people she was worried about—all of her family, for starters, and Evelina, who was more or less family anyway—but those worries would still be there on the morrow. All the villains and dragons could cool their heels tonight. She would experience her first ball only once in this life, and she meant to savor every moment—silly young men and all.

She popped open her dance card, so fascinated by the smooth snap of the fan that she closed it so she could do it all again. When she finally settled down to reading the name of her next partner, she saw the next space was for a *schottische*—and she loved those—but no one had put his name down. Her heart drooped.

"May I have this dance?" a voice asked softly.

She looked up, her stomach doing a pleasant little flip. "Mr. Penner. I'm sorry, I didn't see you there."

He gave a self-deprecating nod. He was tall and well made, but didn't loom like Whitlock or strut like Captain Smythe. Instead, he had the air of someone biding his time—a little amused, and a lot forgiving. And he did look very nice in his best clothes. "Now that you've cast your lambent gaze upon me, will you deign to take my hand?"

She gave her first real smile of the evening. "Are you going to be horribly annoying and tease me mercilessly? Or step on my toes? Or talk about nothing but the weather?"

He returned her smile with a warm grin of his own. "Are you going to be an imperious brat?"

"Shall we simply dance instead?"

"Excellent."

He led her out onto the floor, his brown eyes full of mischief. She let her hand rest lightly on his arm as they took their places, making sure her every move was exactly correct. Shoulders back, neck long and swanlike, arms graceful—just like the dancing master at Wollaston had decreed.

Then the moment came when she was supposed to say something infinitely clever. But this was Bucky, and she'd known him forever. Words should have come naturally, but unexpectedly, every brilliant quip she knew dribbled out her ears. *He's making me nervous? Impossible!*

So she said the first thing she could think of. "I heard that the duke and duchess put up over three thousand of those tiny gaslights for the night."

"No wonder it is so very warm in here." He raised an eyebrow. "But I suppose I shouldn't have seen you nearly so well with a mere fifteen hundred."

"Dazzling lights are the fashion."

"It's still silly."

She felt a tiny stab of annoyance. It was an extravagant, expensive fashion, but she rather liked it. "Bow ties are silly, and yet you're wearing one."

"Most of my existence is unforgivably comical. That is the lot of a young man of purposeless wealth." With an easy grace, he turned her about the floor. He was more muscular than her brother, almost as strongly built as The Stare. He made her feel slight enough to snap in the wind, and yet incredibly safe.

That feeling of security was most welcome after the last few trying days. It made her bold. "Are you one of those who mock everything and yet do nothing to improve it?"

"Heavens, no. I'm sure there must be something I have not yet mocked. I am strongly in favor of sausages. And buttered toast. And Mrs. Braithwaite has a highly appealing Yorkshire terrier."

Imogen bit back a laugh, struggling to remain poised. "I appreciate a man with standards."

She was a little short of breath, but it seemed to have more to do with Bucky than with any exertion on her part. Everywhere he touched her felt extraordinarily sensitive, as if her skin had been magnetized. It made her shiver with the sensation, a delicious flutter that made her warm and cold at once.

He smiled in a way that made his eyes crinkle nicely. "And where do you stand on sausages, Miss Roth?"

But by then the ladies had to make a star in the center of their quartet, circling around with a swirl of skirts. It gave her just enough time to find her sense of equilibrium, and when the figure deposited her back in Bucky's arms, she was decidedly glad to feel his touch again. He was relaxed and confident, which was the essence of a good dancer. They moved forward, changing partners, then changing back, her feet barely touching the gleaming marquetry of the floor. His gaze never left her for a moment, watching her with that special intensity that made it nearly impossible not to preen. No one, not even The Stare, had watched her quite that way. It made her feel like Venus swanning about on her sea-foam cushion.

When the last bars ended and she gave a final curtsy, they were near the doorway to the refreshment area. Imogen realized that she had abandoned her lemonade several partners ago, and she was parched. "I would very much like something to drink," she said plaintively. "But it looks like half the world has had the same idea."

"Fear not, fair lady. The first duty of a resourceful knight is to find alternate routes to the punch bowl." He tucked her arm through his, his gloved fingers warm and strong, and led her away from the throng. "I've been here many a time, and know a back way."

"You're removing me from the ballroom? Is this an evil scheme to lead me astray?" she asked suspiciously—but at the same time couldn't deny the prospect had appeal.

"To claim that I scheme would be to give me too much credit. The best I can manage is a desultory plot from time to time."

"How sad."

"I shall have to try harder. Never let it be said that I lacked ambition, even if it is intriguingly misguided from time to time."

His grin stayed a whisker away from impropriety. Imogen answered it with one of her own, feeling impossibly daring.

He led her into another hallway. There were fewer people, and suddenly walking was much easier. A servant hurried toward them, guiding a steam trolley with a tray of something that smelled delicious. Since the passage was narrow, Bucky pulled her into another doorway to let the man pass. Imogen noticed the considerate gesture—many wouldn't yield to a servant, no matter how impractical it would have been to force the trolley out of the way.

As Bucky had made way, he'd pushed the door open so they had more room to stand. The room where they'd taken refuge was one of those catch-all spaces necessary for large gatherings—this one was filled with stacks of extra linens,

instrument cases that no doubt belonged to the small orchestra, and a rolled-up carpet. There was another door on
the far wall that must have opened into yet another room,
because Imogen was suddenly aware of voices on the other
side.

"No, no, and no!" It was a woman's voice, and tinged with
panic.

Bucky and Imogen exchanged a glance. He pulled her
all the way into the room and shut the door to the hallway
quietly, leaving it open just enough to admit a sliver of light.
Then he raised a gloved finger to his lips. "I think someone
is in trouble," he said in low tones. "I'm not sure, but I may
need to interfere."

Whatever could be going on? Imogen wondered, her
heart pattering with alarm.

JASPER KEATING SAT in the small, fussy sitting room where
the Duchess of Westlake had bid him go. He was to wait
there until she could slip away from the ball unnoticed. The
separate-exit-and-rendezvous maneuver was standard protocol for romantic intrigue—as ridiculous as it seemed, the
old harridan was still too careful of her reputation to be seen
entering a private chamber with a man who was not her husband.

That was not—*not in a million years*—why Keating was
meeting her, but he still had to cool his heels in the fussy
pink-striped room that reminded him of something built out
of marzipan for a little girl's birthday cake.

It was an odd contrast to what he had been doing at this
time yesterday—marching through the dockyards to check
the locker where Striker had stored his weapons. His man
had inspected it already, but Keating wouldn't rest until he'd
looked himself. The lost key still felt like a betrayal, a spurn-
ing of the favor he'd showed the piece of street trash. If
Striker hadn't been so good at his job he would have been
today's refuse, left in the gutter for the rats and dogs.

Keating clenched his fist, watching the seams of his
gloves strain with the fierceness of his grip. *A careless, un-*

grateful fool. He got up to pace the room, a panther trapped in a nightmare of pink and cupids.

The sky above the dockyard had been pale gray blotched with inky clouds, the sun dying behind the rows of warehouses. Keating and his men had moved quickly between the brick and wood buildings. Many of the docks were under the control of Keating Utility, but not all—and every edifice was carefully guarded. Automatons loomed outside each doorway, a reddish light smoldering in the pits of their eyes and the slash of their mouths. Some rolled on tracks, others lumbered on two or four feet. No one in Keating's party was foolish enough to set foot beyond a competitor's property line. Men died for less.

By the time they'd stopped at the building in question, the sun had fully set and the lamps around Keating's structures were lit. The yellow glow washed the cobbles and brickwork in a sepia haze—a color that matched the river's cold and choking stink. Keating still felt the raw wind from the Thames on his face, a bite that seemed to go clear to the bone. He had cursed Striker all over again for making the trip a necessity.

And he'd cursed again when it turned out to be a fool's errand. The warehouse lock had been undisturbed, just as his man had said. They had opened it, pulling the heavy oak doors wide and lighting up the vast space within. The enormous building was a maker's daydream—a whale's maw crisscrossed with twelve-foot shelves heaped with machinery parts, engines, gauges, equipment, and all the materials seized from the Harter Engine Company, including the working models of their combustion engines. Deep in the whale's belly, filling three shelves end to end, was Striker's armory of fantastical weapons—enough firepower to set London alight. The warehouse as a whole could have supplied a revolution.

But every nut, bolt, and cog was untouched. Keating—not one for tears—had nearly wept with relief. Not that he let his men see the slightest hint of his distress. He'd simply ordered the locks changed and marched out again. Striker would be getting no more keys.

Keating continued his circuit of the Duchess of Westlake's room, vaguely conscious of the distant orchestra and the murmur of conversation. It was hot and stuffy, made hotter by his recollection of the cold dockyard wind. And yet, as unpleasant as the warehouse task had been, he'd enjoyed the action more than this elaborate minuet of secret meetings and whispered plans. Out on the docks, things were simple, clear, and brutally quick.

He paused in front of a painting—some pastoral scene involving sheep and a pair of lovers. The sheep looked bored. He looked up almost hopefully when the sitting room door swept open.

The Duchess of Westlake sailed in, closing the door behind her. "Mr. Keating, thank you for meeting me on such short notice, but as you know my needs are most urgent."

Keating bowed, waiting until she took a seat before settling himself back in his chair. Not for the first time, he wondered why the rest of the Steam Council was so worried about the so-called Baskerville conspiracy. They should take note of the way he handled the duchess, if they were worried about the aristocrats. People with titles were just as vulnerable to bribery and threats as everyone else. And once they were caught, flies—no matter how many fancy titles they had—couldn't rebel against the spider. "It is my pleasure as always to serve you as best as I am able. However, I'm not sure how much more I can do."

She lifted her head, the gesture more imperious than pleading. "No, no, and no! You must help me. Surely there is some arrangement we can make."

"That will be difficult."

"You are a man of business, are you not? Isn't making deals what you do?"

"Your Grace," said Jasper Keating, utterly irritated. "You are in no position to bargain."

The Duchess of Westlake glared back at him, her square form reminding him of a crudely carved figurehead that had somehow escaped its ship. "I've paid everything I can." Her voice was harsh. "My personal fortune is not limitless."

Keating didn't care, but tried to keep the annoyance from his manner. The woman was bent on saving her cousin's life, but it was a lost cause. Nellie Reynolds was an actress, of value only when she was the apple of the public's eye. Once that adoration was finished, she was little better than a drab walking the lowest streets of London. Keating had no use for trash, and wasn't sure why the duchess bothered.

But he put a look of concern on his face, and carried on. "Barristers are expensive, and Sir Philip Amory is the top man in London. I engaged him as you asked, but I don't think more money is the answer even if you had it to give. The public has turned against her."

"Nellie is my cousin. I can't give up." The duchess rose, sweeping around the private drawing room in agitation. The fine white-and-red shot silk of her ball gown glimmered as she moved, the fabric rustling like the surf on a beach. "She might not be my uncle's legitimate child, but we grew up in the same nursery. I taught her to read and write her name on the same slate I used. She was the prettiest child you could imagine."

Keating hated sentimentality only one degree less than tales of childhood bliss. Such things were too far removed from his own experience to sound credible. He sat back against the stiff upholstery of the armchair and wished etiquette permitted him to light a cigar.

"Why has the world gone mad?" the woman complained. "Anyone with sense can see Nellie is as unmagical as a lamppost. She wouldn't even let me drag her to a Gypsy at the fair to have her fortune read. She is as pragmatic as mud."

And common as mud, too. Keating said nothing. The duchess was probably right about her bastard cousin's lack of magic, but that was far from the point. Actors, poets, and the like were far too prone to making mock of the steam barons. One of their number had to pay the price for that mockery, and Nellie Reynolds was the easiest target. Even better, he owed Amory a favor, and handing him a client like the actress, with the duchess so ready to pay the barrister's egregious fees, evened that score nicely.

And the benefits of the entire business kept on multiplying. Securing Amory put the duchess in his debt, which had come in handy when it came to presenting the detective's niece—although that piece of business had yet to bear fruit. He would have to follow up on that first thing tomorrow.

The woman was still talking. "Besides, we grew up together. We've never lived more than a few miles apart. If she were a witch, I would know of it!"

It was time she heard the truth. It was a kindness, really. "My lady, forgive me for speaking my mind, but the Reynolds woman is an illegitimate relation, an actress, and a magic user. You need to let her go."

Outrage widened the duchess's eyes. "She is innocent, sir! Where is the evidence of this magic? A few props from her acting trunk? It's all poppycock. They say she has a crystal ball for summoning demons. It's a garden ornament I gave her out of my own yard last March. I know these accusations are baseless."

Even Keating had to wince at that.

"I can't just let her burn." The woman's voice hitched. She fell back onto the divan, which creaked alarmingly. The duchess was well beyond the day when swooning was a delicate business.

Keating steepled his fingers. "Madam, she is all but convicted. The association will taint this house. You will end up as one of the Disconnected."

"I am the Duchess of Westlake," proclaimed the woman. "You cannot turn off my steam."

This was the moment he had been waiting for. Keating moved in for the kill without emotion. "Your Grace, I make the steam. I have helped you as a friend and a gentleman. I have kept your confidences, and acted as intermediary on your behalf. I completely understand that some things you could not do yourself as a titled woman. It was not fitting that you personally meet with jailors and police."

So he had taken on all those distasteful tasks, winning her trust one bit at a time. Waiting with the patience of a cat at the fishbowl and scooping up pieces of business whenever they came his way. Now the Westlakes' affairs were firmly anchored with Keating Utility—all because the duchess loved her cousin. He supposed he owed Nellie Reynolds something after all. Pity he had no intention of paying that debt.

The duchess pursed her lips, looking a bit like that proverbial fish. "And I appreciate your efforts, Mr. Keating. You have been a friend."

Keating's reply was cool. "But first I am a man of business. I will not hesitate to do what is necessary to maintain harmony among my clients. I won't have the whole upset by the actions of one, however illustrious that one might be."

Disbelief filled her eyes, then pain, then a resignation thickly veined with hate. Keating felt a pang almost like regret. *This is the moment when she realizes her cousin is lost. When she realizes that I hold all the cards.*

Her voice rose in pitch, growing almost shrill. "Are you saying that if Society cuts me for trying to save my cousin from the stake, you will turn off my heat and light?"

"You come quickly to the point, my lady. But rest assured that I would only do so as a last resort. I know your son has a *tendre* for my daughter, Alice. She is a good girl, and will wed where I ask." She might fancy the Roth boy now, but that could change—with the right encouragement.

And there was the foundation of his scheming. The duchess would be pliable where her son's hand was concerned, if the entire Westlake fortune was in peril—and he would see to that. For Alice, the match would be brilliant, linking fortune to title.

"How comforting." The duchess's tone was dry. "No doubt you have brought your daughter up with the expectation of marrying well."

The comment nettled him. "Alice has nothing to be humble about."

The woman sniffed with all the hauteur of her title and pedigree. "Indeed, Mr. Keating. I understand she wears Paris fashions with great aplomb."

Keating narrowed his eyes. It was amazing how an aristocrat could insult without actually saying anything one could point at. Well, he was the one with his hand on the switch. "As you say, Your Grace."

Her face turned to stone. "I would appreciate it if you left me now, Mr. Keating."

Keating looked down to hide his smile. He had won. "Very well, Your Grace."

"YOUR GRACE," SAID a male voice. Whoever it was sounded utterly irritated. "You are in no position to bargain."

Eavesdropping from the room next door, Imogen touched Bucky's arm, feeling the fine cloth of his sleeve through her lace gloves. "Your Grace?" she whispered.

He put a hand over hers, and leaned close to her ear. His breath was warm. "Be careful they don't hear us before they need to."

Worry clutched at Imogen's chest, and she hugged her arms across her middle. They were in the awkward position of overhearing something they shouldn't, but Bucky was right. There was trouble. They couldn't walk away, in case there was real danger—but no one wanted to raise the alarm until it was absolutely necessary. A mistake could be mortifying for everyone involved.

Bucky began prowling the room, picking up a broom, and then setting it down in favor of a sturdier carpet beater. He weighed it in one hand, clearly testing its weapons potential. Bucky might not have had Captain Smythe's uniform, but he was a practical thinker who wasn't wasting any time. *But what if there is a gun?*

"I've paid everything I can," the woman said, her voice harsh.

"Barristers are expensive, and Sir Philip Amory is the top man in London. I engaged him as you asked, but I don't think more money is the answer even if you had it to give. The public has turned against her."

"Nellie is my cousin. I can't give up."

Bucky turned to look at Imogen, astonishment plain on his face. He mouthed the words, "Nellie Reynolds?"

Imogen felt her own eyes widen as the conversation came to a tense silence. She barely dared to breathe. Bucky made a questioning gesture. Imogen shrugged in reply.

"And I appreciate your efforts, Mr. Keating. You have been a friend."

Keating! Imogen's breath hitched—but she suddenly understood why the duchess had sponsored Evelina. If Keating was helping the duchess save her cousin, she would do anything he asked.

The duchess's voice rose in pitch. "Are you saying that if Society cuts me for trying to save my cousin from the stake, you will turn off my heat and light?"

"You come quickly to the point, Your Grace. But rest assured that I would only do so as a last resort. I know your son has a *tendre* for my daughter, Alice. She is a good girl, and will wed where I ask."

The threat was so bold, Imogen's jaw grew slack.

"How comforting," the duchess's tone was dry. "I would appreciate it if you left me now, Mr. Keating."

"Very well, Your Grace."

Imogen's throat closed with panic. What if he left through the back way and found her and Bucky within earshot?

Bucky silently set down the carpet beater and was at Imogen's side in a heartbeat. "Come on!" he whispered, and took her hand. He pulled open the door to the corridor and dragged her into the passage, barely closing it again before Imogen heard the interior door open.

It was just a piece of luck that the corridor was empty at that exact moment. No one saw Imogen emerge from a darkened room, towed by a young man who ran with a fast set. It would have been enough to destroy her reputation before the Season even began.

But their good fortune ran out before they made it more than a few more steps. Jasper Keating swept out of the room, as casual as if the house were his. *Maybe that's what he has in mind.* Imogen had already seen the duchess's son dancing with the Gold King's daughter, Alice.

But she barely had time for that thought to form before Bucky roughly backed her into the wall, shielding her from view with his body as if he were moving in for a kiss. Imogen's breath left her in a whoosh, and when she dragged it back in, all she could smell was him. It was a male smell—

tobacco and whisky, soap and wool. Intoxicated, Imogen allowed desire to overcome her fright for just that moment. Keating moved by, paying no attention to them.

But even as the Gold King disappeared down the corridor, Bucky didn't move away. Instead, he leaned forward, his deep brown eyes searching her features as if she were a precious artwork. She could feel his breath on her face, hot and quick, and felt her own grow shallow with excitement. Slowly, he raised one gloved hand and touched her cheek with his fingertips, the gesture almost reverent. Imogen was mesmerized, her entire soul lost somewhere in the tiny space of air between them.

When he spoke, the words were rough and low. "Whatever you do, don't say a word about this. Pretend you never heard it at all."

The statement brought her back to herself, breaking the spell of his touch. "But . . . shouldn't we do something?" She wasn't sure what, but the Duchess of Westlake was trying to help her cousin, and at considerable risk to herself. That won her points in Imogen's book.

Bucky shook his head, his brow furrowing with concern. "Not here and now. As you just saw, there is nowhere truly private at these events. You and I will talk about this some other time. Maybe many times—but I don't want you taking any risks before we've thought this through. There are some things that are too dangerous to know."

He looked into her eyes then, and she could see the urgency in their warm, brown depths. "Promise me," he said. "And we'll figure this out together. Don't run any risks alone."

"I promise," she said, but at least part of her mind was entirely on the fact that his face was so close to hers, their breath mingled at every word. *Is he going to kiss me?* She wasn't sure she wanted it now, when everything was so grim, but she was growing tired of waiting for him to make a move.

Something in the set of his mouth made her wonder if he was thinking the same thing—whether this was the right moment. She shifted just a little, putting herself just a smidgen closer, stretching her neck just a touch longer.

Then his eyes widened a shade, and the decision was made. He pressed his mouth to hers, hot and hungry. As much as Imogen had anticipated the moment, she gave a tiny start, and then leaned into it, tasting him as he tasted her. A fire began low in her belly, rushing to her head with a sudden, heady blaze. She rose up on her toes, not letting anything stop her from the full enjoyment of the moment.

And Bucky was an enthusiastic kisser. In that moment he proved that just like her, he could set aside the darkness in the world to enjoy life. When they finally broke apart, she nearly had to gasp for air. *So this is what they mean by kissing a girl senseless!*

"There is one thing I regret," she murmured. "I would have liked to have seen you challenge the most powerful man in the Empire with no more than a carpet beater in your hand. It would have made an enormously heroic picture."

Bucky chuckled, his eyes alight with pleasure. There was a touch of possessiveness in the look that nettled her and delighted her at the same time. "My dear Miss Roth, if that impresses you, I will be sure to demonstrate what I can do with oranges."

And then he gave her a smile that made her go wobbly in the knees. The world might be threatening to crumble about her ears, but Imogen felt something more powerful than the gathering storm.

JASPER KEATING STOPPED by to exchange guarded pleasantries with Lady Bancroft. Evelina thanked him again for his support for her presentation. At first, with a distracted air, he looked at her as if he couldn't quite recall who she was. Then, as he wished them a pleasant evening, he asked after her uncle, seeming to want to know the detective's whereabouts. Once again, she itched to know what on earth had gone on between the two men.

A few minutes later, Tobias arrived, as late as was permissible without actually being rude to the hostess. He was freshly shaved, his hair still damp from the bath, and impeccably dressed in formal black. He came bearing Evelina a glass of lemonade. Nevertheless, when he smiled it was not his usual wicked expression. He looked troubled.

"What's wrong?" Evelina asked.

"I've been distracted."

She wondered how much she should say, and then decided to speak her mind. "You didn't sleep at home last night."

"I was—disassembling a project."

She smiled. "You lost track of time."

"No—it wasn't that." He rubbed his eyes with his free hand. "It went all wrong. I took it apart. Chopped it. I tried to burn it but the wretched thing wouldn't light. I went back today to try to finish the job."

He actually looked shaken. She put her hand on his wrist. "Tobias?"

His mouth formed a hard line, and he looked down at his hands. "It's all right. I simply had a look down a path I can't follow. There was a price there I wouldn't pay."

A small, selfish part of her wanted to say this wasn't the right conversation for her first ball. She wanted romance, flowers, and celebration. She swallowed back the feeling, counting it as selfish. "I don't understand."

He gave a quick smile. "I'm glad to be here, with you, in the bright lights. In the end, that's all there is to it. Really."

Evelina squeezed his wrist and let her hand fall away. Any other comfort was hard to give when she didn't comprehend the problem. "Tonight is for music and dance."

Tobias recovered himself, affecting a semblance of his usual manner. "Have you any openings left on your card? If there are, I will have them all. And I *will* have the waltz."

Her heart skittered beneath the lace-covered sheath of her bodice, stopped midbeat by the seriousness in his gray eyes. The effect was more striking than mere mischief. In an eye blink, Tobias had introduced a new element: what was between them hadn't been a game for a while, but the stakes had somehow been raised.

Evelina stood pinned by his gaze, unsure of herself and

yet desperately certain she wanted him. She wanted to believe that desire so plain on his face. *He promised that he was being honest.*

She cleared her throat, reaching for the lemonade. "I'm afraid Captain Smythe has already claimed the waltz," she said.

His finely sculpted mouth turned down. "I shall have to call him out for pistols at dawn. I am a crack shot, you know."

"Is that a wise plan, Mr. Roth? Crack shot or no, I should remind you that he is a military man."

"Mr. Roth? So formal? You cut me to the quick."

"I think an element of formality is called for when a man proposes to get himself killed in such a harebrained fashion."

He lifted a brow. "You call the field of honor harebrained?"

"Yes, I do when the cause of the fight is three minutes of Johann Strauss at his most relentlessly cheerful."

He plucked the dance card from her wrist. "Then what time do you have left for me, Evelina?"

For a moment, a flutter in her stomach interfered with her wits. Then she snapped herself back to reality. There were dark circles under his eyes, strain around his mouth. Tobias sometimes looked ragged from carousing all night, but this went much, much deeper. The events of the last week were telling on him, too. He needed a night of light and laughter as much as she did. The least she could do was be entertaining.

She tilted her head. "What time do I have? I think it is received wisdom not to use words like *anytime* and *always* with young men. Absolutes terrify them."

His mouth quirked. "Speaking as a young man, allow me to correct you. Absolutes have a dread fascination. The question of how much dread and how much fascination depends entirely on the speaker."

He carefully penciled his name against the remaining dances and ceremoniously slipped the ribbon loop over her glove. Her heart began to speed. It was not the Done Thing for a young man to ask for so many dances in a night, much less write his name over another's. It was rude, unheard of, and coming from Tobias, the next best thing to a proposal.

Through the soft fabric, she could feel the strength in his long, clever fingers as he replaced the card. Then he raised her hand to his lips, his gaze never leaving hers. "Let's test the absolutes of anytime and always."

Her pulse raced like an overwound clock. She touched the icy glass of lemonade to her cheek to cool her flaming skin. "You are being selfish, Mr. Roth. I see Alice Keating, for one, casting a longing look your way."

"I don't want anyone but you. You are light and life, and I have been in a very dark place." He took the glass from her hand and set it on the side table as the orchestra began a medley of Chopin's waltzes. "Shall we?"

Evelina floated to the dance floor beside him, conscious that she was fulfilling all those fantasies she had nursed since first meeting Imogen's handsome brother years ago. Back then, Tobias had seemed more an untouchable godling than a real young man. All that awe came flooding back to her, giving the moment a solemnity that far outweighed the reality of a simple dance. She let him take her in his arms, and gave herself over to the sensual pull of the music. When his body commanded hers to lean into the first turn, for the first time in her life she was tempted to swoon. It was quite delightful. Evelina Cooper never had the luxury of being giddy, and she rode the feeling for all it was worth.

But of course, she didn't faint dead away in his arms. Nor did she curse when the last cadence rose like mist into the torrid ballroom air, though she was sorely tempted. It was intermission, and Tobias went in search of something cold for them to drink. A mechanical orchestra started up, filling the place of the live musicians with a pitch-perfect but utterly lifeless Gilbert and Sullivan pastiche. No one even tried to dance to it.

The dreadful music brought her back to reality, and her extravagant happiness abated a little. She wasn't sure what had got into Tobias, but she was going to have to restore her dance card to good order. The Duchess of Westlake wouldn't thank her for precipitating a scandal at her ball. *I owe it to Tobias to behave properly. I owe it to myself.*

She then realized Mouse hadn't reappeared since her arrival. She looked around anxiously, searching the floor for the familiar gray shape.

"Is something the matter, Miss Cooper?" asked Michael Edgerton, who was passing by.

Evelina started. "I, er, believe I dropped a button."

"What color is it?" he asked helpfully, staring at the floor intently.

Bother. She couldn't blame the lanky young man for helping, but she wished him speedily away. "Oh, I think I must be mistaken. Look, my glove has all its buttons after all." She held up her arm, proving her point.

"All right then," he said dubiously. "As long as you're sure."

"Absolutely," she said brightly. "Thanks so much."

Edgerton took his leave with a slight shake of his head. She'd handled that badly, and heaven knew what he was thinking, but Evelina was too uneasy about Mouse to care. A twinge in her stomach said something was amiss.

She looked around for Tobias, who was still in search of refreshments. The room where they were set out would be mobbed—he wouldn't be back soon. That gave her time to hunt for Mouse. With a last glance at the floor, she slipped through the door that led away from the dancing and toward the games room, where fortunes were lost and regained in an evening by the turn of a card or a toss of the dice. She could just see the doorway to that chamber, and the corner of a table with three or four young men clustered around. Halfway down the passage, she passed a room where men lounged around a low table, drinking and laughing. Some had cigars, and tiny clockwork hummingbirds whirred around the room, driving the smoke toward an automatic ventilation unit. Then came a room where two young girls, giggling and groaning in equal parts because they had danced so much that night, had taken off their shoes to wiggle their toes. They were so much like Evelina and Imogen, she stared for a bit, jealously wondering why they weren't sharing a similar moment. Life had become too serious all of a sudden.

She shook off the thought and kept moving. Other doorways, most standing open, led to rooms with less defined uses. Evelina began to walk past the doorways, searching for Mouse with her senses as well as her eyes. She was sure the little creature was somewhere nearby, and the feeling grew stronger as she moved farther from the dancing. It was there, a bright spark ahead and to her left, but there was something in the way, like a line along the floor that Mouse could not cross to get to her.

Then she knew what room she wanted—the room set aside for ladies to rest and refresh themselves in private. It was empty, the force that was keeping Mouse inside no doubt keeping everyone else out. Evelina swallowed hard and peered through the doorway.

The room was lit by a pair of branching gas sconces reflected by gold-framed mirrors hung on the opposite wall so the light bounced back and magnified the brightness. There was a painted Japanese screen, a few low couches, and a steam trolley piled with cakes and lemonade for the ladies' refreshment. Evelina stepped inside, feeling Mouse's presence like a piece of herself that had wandered astray.

The moment she did, the barrier she had sensed disappeared, and she felt a light tugging on her hem. She looked down to see Mouse pulling at her dress with its tiny forepaws. On the pretext of adjusting her slipper, she bent and scooped it into her reticule. *Dr. Magnus is right behind you,* said the little creature.

She whirled around, feeling Mouse squirm as the reticule swung with her movement. Mouse was right. Dr. Magnus gave a small bow, resplendent in his black and white formal attire.

"You are a vision, Miss Cooper."

And he was an apparition. An emerald stickpin skewered his lapel like a glittering eye. "Dr. Magnus," she replied with a stiff curtsey, uncomfortably aware that they were in the room alone.

"Pardon my methods of getting your attention. I would

speak with you, but we meet in an inauspicious location for any conversation of substance."

Evelina bristled. "I have no wish to speak with you."

"But I have much to impart." He gave her a significant look. "As I said before, you possess a talent that interests me greatly. I have been studying the infusion of spirit into machine for a great many years, struggling to accomplish the task at even a primitive level. Yet you, as in the case of your bird and of the little mouse you even now carry in your bag, are able to achieve this effortlessly. I would teach you all I know if you would return the favor."

Evelina started as if shocked by Jasper Keating's machine. The last thing she needed was someone to overhear them. "Dr. Magnus! Have a care what you say. We might be alone, but there is every chance someone might chance by."

He gave a meaningful nod. "As I said, this is an inauspicious location. It would be far better if we met in private. Perhaps at my rooms on Pemberton Row?"

"I'm not a fool!" she whispered. She always ended up whispering to the man. "Why should I trust you, here or anywhere else?"

"Shall I give you an earnest of my intentions?"

"What do you mean?"

"It is obvious to me that you pursue an answer to what has swept your corner of creation into such sad disarray. I will put you a step closer to your goal."

Evelina frowned, wary of anything the man might say. "My lord, your meaning is far from clear."

"That tends to be the case with random puzzle pieces." He waved an airy hand, all grace and elegance. "Attend. You are not the only avenue to learning, and I am not a man to neglect an opportunity. In addition to you, my living example of a rare talent, there is also an ancient artifact called Athena's Casket that forms part of the archaeological exhibit Jasper Keating has acquired from Greece. I would very much like to study the casket, but Keating claims that he does not have it."

Evelina narrowed her eyes. Nick had said Magnus was after an object of power, and he was trying to force Lord

Bancroft to help him get it from the Gold King. That object had to be the casket—and if it was from Greece, what about the crates she had seen with strange writing on them? She took a wild gamble.

"And he stored that exhibit in a warehouse?" Evelina's neck ached from the tension in her body. She kept her face utterly blank, hoping he would give up and leave her alone. Instead, he assumed his most charming smile. If she didn't know better, she would have found it devastating.

"Yes, the warehouse you so neatly exorcised. Well done, Evelina."

"How do you know that?"

"I visited the place after you. With all the metal in the vicinity, it stank of your battle with the guardian. You need to have a care, throwing your magic about like that. You leave a wide trail for those who can read it."

Evelina flushed, but refused to be baited. This was the man who had done his best to lure her to become his student in the dark arts. He had hurt Nick, and he was the one who had tricked her into this room tonight. She should have been fighting her way from the room.

Instead, she seized the opportunity to ask questions. That was the problem with Dr. Magnus—as much as she loathed him, he was the only person she knew who understood magic better than she did. It was an insidious attraction. "What went on in that warehouse? I heard something about Chinese workers connected to the place." Their deaths had finally made it into the papers. "And Mr. Markham, the shopkeeper, uses Chinese tailors."

Dr. Magnus shrugged. "Markham's men may well be honest tailors, merely plying their trade, or they might be lookouts. I don't know. The only concrete fact I have is that I discovered living quarters beneath the floor of the warehouse."

Evelina's eyes widened. She'd missed that—but then again, she'd been running from the guardian. "There was blood on the floor," she added. "Bodies were found in the Thames."

"Then the Chinese who worked for Harriman were killed."

The scraps and bits of information she had gathered were suddenly forming a pattern. "How unbelievably horrific."

"I agree." Magnus frowned. "But I think you have your answer. The warehouse is empty. No traces have been left of what went on there." He folded his arms, his face dark with displeasure. "There were workbenches beneath the warehouse, and signs that equipment had been in place, but what they were actually doing there remains a blank to me. I do not like that."

That at least was something Evelina could agree with him about.

His mouth twitched irritably. "I am not convinced the casket is missing."

That logic puzzled her. "Why don't you know?" He seemed to know everything about everything. The fact that he was unclear about this point was odd.

He gave her a disgusted look. "I have tendrils everywhere, but I am not *quite* omniscient."

"I still don't understand why Keating would say he doesn't have it if he does. Won't it form part of his exhibition anyhow?"

"Perhaps he means merely to keep it from seekers such as I am. Perhaps, like so many collectors, he cannot bear to share that which he has made part of his private hoard. The potential reasons are many. I simply know the man is lying to me, and must draw my conclusions from that."

"Of course," she said slowly, fascinated but horrified. So much was sliding together—Nick's half-understood account of Magnus's conversation with Bancroft, what she had seen in the warehouse, Magnus's interest in her bird. More questions exploded in her mind like a flock of startled pigeons, but the doctor spoke again before she could grab even one.

His face softened, his expression almost amused. "And now I've given you what information I have to solve this mystery. Will that buy me some trust, my Helen?"

"Helen?"

"A figure of speech. Helen is the wise woman, the divine

truth made flesh. Read the histories of the Magus, and you will understand. Helen was the key to universal love."

"You have an odd notion of flattery."

"I merely seek to win you over to my cause. Your knowledge and mine added together would be a powerful force."

"Not in this century or the next," Evelina shot back.

"Never?"

"Never."

"You sound like the heroine of a bad novel. *Never* is a long time to shy away from something you do not even understand." He swayed closer, shrinking the distance between them.

Evelina braced herself, refusing to give ground. "You deal in death magic. That's what sorcerers do."

"So I'm a sorcerer. What does that mean to you?"

"That you deal in darkness."

"You are so very fond of your light, aren't you?" Magnus replied, touching the green stone of his pin. "But you have no notion how to preserve it. Perhaps you don't understand how badly you need me as a teacher."

The air seemed to congeal around Evelina, raising the gooseflesh on her arms. Her heart began to patter with fear. *Dr. Magnus is calling his magic.*

But then all logical thought stopped.

The lights in the chamber began to dim. Even though the flames in the gas brackets and the chandeliers burned just as tall, they lost their luster, leaving the atmosphere a dirty and forbidding gray. The sound of the mechanical orchestra in the ballroom seemed to fade, but whether that was perception or reality, she couldn't tell.

Evelina could feel the rising tide of panic. Her stays felt suddenly tight, her hands clammy and cold. She clutched her arms, hugging herself as the atmosphere whispered of fear. "Dr. Magnus, please!"

His head turned slowly to regard her with the measured pace of a coiled snake. "You need to recognize my strength. You need to understand that you cannot stand against my will." Then he reached out and grabbed her forearm—the same crushing grip that had forced her to drop the knife.

If the fear floating through the room was soft and insidious, creeping like mist, this was a waterfall. It shot up her arm as if injected, coursing straight to her core. This was death. This was the terror, the moment when the dying knew their fate was sealed—the final breath caught halfway down their throat, the last thrashing thought as darkness closed in.

Evelina gasped, her pulse racing so hard it hurt. Instinct screamed to pull away, to run, but her numb limbs could barely support her, much less move. Like a cornered animal, she bit with the only weapon she had.

Her magic reared up, slamming into the invading horror like a sudden wall. It wasn't much—there was no flaming sword or blast of lightning, just refusal. "Get out!"

Magnus gave his soft laugh. "No."

Her barrier wasn't enough, and she had no training beyond what Gran Cooper had told her as a child. Magnus was right that she needed lessons. The room was growing darker still, dim and murky. Terror pervaded the space, as if it had turned breathable.

Her stomach lurched, panic skittering like bugs past the barricade she had built. Evelina shut her eyes, blocking out as much as she could. Inside was blackness itself, but this was her personal night, solid as mud. She thrust her energy into it, making it thicker still. Magnus pulled back, only the merest fraction, but it gave her hope.

In her mind's eye, she filled the mud with life— earthworms and burrowing things, roots and rivulets of water. It smelled rich, full of the sharpness of loam and the goodness of bursting seeds. The seeds burst, stretching up and out, driving out of the soil and exploding into leaves.

Magnus pulled back, yanking his hand from Evelina's arm as if it scalded him. She stumbled, bumping against the wall. Exhaustion flooded her, her lungs barely finding strength to suck in air. She still felt afraid, but this time it was her own emotion. She could live with that.

Surprise lurked in the doctor's eyes. "An interesting demonstration, Miss Cooper. You would be such an apt pupil, if you would only release your grip on accepted wisdom. Death always trumps life in the end."

"Life eats death," she retorted, her voice weak. "Neither way is final."

His shock turned to condescension. "How little you know of the cosmos."

The lights came up again. The mechanical tea trolley wheezed to life and began to trundle around the chamber. Evelina shuddered and looked around, reassuring herself the room was still intact. No one was screaming or stampeding through the building. That had to be a good sign.

She had no idea how much time had passed. Probably only seconds, but it felt like weeks. Suddenly she saw Keating and two of the Westlake footmen standing just inside the threshold of the room, staring at the lights in consternation.

Evelina turned, falling back a step at their unexpected arrival. The motion made her bump into Magnus and he steadied her with a gentle touch to her shoulders. That made her skitter to the side.

The look on Keating's face was one of unholy rage. Evelina might as well have been invisible. Keating looked right past her, his attention fixed wholly on Magnus.

The doctor sighed. "Alas, the prospect of a public unpleasantness erupts. Here comes the villain of the piece."

A quip about pots and kettles sprang to mind, but the idea died before it was fully born.

Keating spoke. "Get out, Magnus. No one invited you."

"And on what authority do you order my removal?"

"The duchess is my friend."

"Come, Keating. Men like you don't make friends."

Keating's face twitched. "Leave. You weren't invited."

"And yet here I am, finding exactly what I need." He gave a sidelong glance to Evelina.

She stepped back, even more uncomfortable than she had been moments before.

Keating filled the room with his anger. "Get out, before I remove you by force."

"Is this a threat? I think we had a chat about that, did we not, Mr. Keating?"

"I'm calling your bluff. You don't get to slither through my streets. Not anywhere you see my lights." Keating's voice was hard and steady. He stopped a few feet away, his henchmen a step behind. "To find you accosting a young lady of good reputation doubles your offense."

There was a pause, then Magnus made a languorous bow to Evelina. "Good night, Miss Cooper, we shall speak again. No doubt your dance partner awaits."

Tobias! She cast an anxious glance at the door. He had to be waiting for her. As she looked away, Magnus grabbed her elbow and pulled her close one last time, putting his lips to her ear. "Until next time."

He spun away, shouldering past Keating and striding through the door. The moment he was gone, Evelina heard the first strains of a lively tune. The regular orchestra was back, like birds bursting into song the moment the storm had passed.

Evelina sagged against the wall, sweat dampening the small of her back beneath the countless layers of muslin and whalebone. Fatigue blanked her mind, except for one tiny idea, small and green as one of the sprouts in her wall. *I beat him. Maybe just for this time, but he's not invincible.*

The Gold King gave a nod to the two footmen. They followed after Magnus, no doubt making sure that he actually left.

"Who is Dr. Magnus to you, Miss Cooper?" Keating demanded.

Evelina shuddered again, looking around for Tobias. He was still a dozen strides away. "Dr. Magnus is the Flying Dutchman."

The Gold King gave her a narrow look. "You know what happened to the girl in that story, don't you? She finished by throwing herself into the sea."

She gave a laugh that sounded slightly lunatic. "I like the version where she ran away with the kraken."

Then some subconscious instinct made her reach for her reticule. Her fingers closed on the soft beaded sack, crumpling the cloth into an empty ball. It was covered with a film of Magnus's oily magic, and Mouse was gone.

CHAPTER THIRTY-FOUR

NICK CURSED. EVIE WOULD BE SAFE AT A BALL. IT WAS PUB-
lic, and the Golden Boy was sure to be there, anxiously hovering at her elbow the minute someone stepped on her toe.

After leaving her at the gate of Hilliard House, Nick had
gone back to Ploughman's. Immediately, he went to the stables, picked up a brush, and began grooming his mare. The
light seeping into the stall was dim, the air warm with the
horse's heat. When she whickered, he felt the wash of her
sympathy. Anyone who said animals couldn't talk weren't
listening.

There was no performance that night, and he had time to
himself. He had no appetite for carousing, and for once, the
routine and the earthy smell of horse failed to soothe him.
His jaw clenched as he struggled with resentment. *Tobias.*
Nick knew the type. Pretty boys who came to the theater
one night with their sweetheart, the next night with their
whore. She deserved better than that.

His hand slowed, breaking the rhythm of the brush. The
mare turned her head in inquiry.

"That damned white dress," he grumbled. "She looked
like the virgin from a bloody melodrama."

The gentle swell of her breasts above the low-cut neck of
her gown—it crushed reason beneath the heel of masculine
possessiveness. He should let her go. He should move on.
But he bloody well couldn't make himself do it.

The mare flicked her tail.

"It's not safe. Not with Dr. Bleeding Magnus around."
And not with Tobias Roth looking at her as if she were a
pastry in a shop window.

The weary look the mare gave him was every bit as pointed as one of Gran Cooper's lectures.

THE OPULENT WESTLAKE home was a long way from the Hibernia Amphitheatre, but Nick was on the street outside in under an hour, dodging the crush of carriages. He could hear the faint gabble of merriment from inside the house, and the occasional scrap of music. It should have been reassuring, but his skin itched with apprehension. Or maybe it was just unquenched desire.

Or maybe it was the odd sense of being followed. He had first felt it around Portman Square, and it hadn't left him since. It left him fingering the knives he had strapped under his jacket.

The Duke of Westlake's mansion was a fortress, and his place was outside with the errand boys and street sweepers. There was no chance of getting close, so he hung back, keeping away from the pack of footmen sharing an illicit cache of their masters' brandy. He had no appetite for a fight.

And the distance from the front door didn't matter. If he did find Evelina, was he going to bundle her back to Ploughman's like a runaway? She wouldn't stand for it, and he wouldn't expect her to.

So what the bloody hell was he doing loitering outside the ball? Irritably, he slouched against a brougham that had been temporarily abandoned by its crew. He wasn't used to being still, and his fingers itched for something to throw, or fix, or juggle.

Nick was about to give in to reason and go back to the Hibernia when Dr. Magnus hurried down the front steps, still adjusting his tall hat as if he had left in a rush. Nick straightened out of his despondent slouch, suddenly alert. As if on cue, a pair of footmen stormed out of the Westlake's grand entrance and stood there like Rottweilers deprived of their prey. Given Magnus's penchant for stirring up trouble, it didn't take much to link the two exits together.

A blur of gold swooped out of the darkness, landing on

the wheel of the brougham. Startled, Nick nearly swatted it away.

Hey! The voice shrilled in his head.

Nick blinked, trying to absorb the fact the gold object was actually a brass bird that appeared to be alive. It hopped from side to side, peering up at him with one sparkling eye, and then the other.

"Hello?" he asked tentatively.

The bird fluttered its wings in annoyance. *Oh, good, it talks. You're the only one out here with a drop of the Blood. You must be the one she wanted.*

Squinting at the thing, he tried to reconcile what he was seeing with the voice in his mind. "You're a deva."

He could communicate with most devas, although he had no talent for calling them—unless it was when he touched Evelina.

And you smell like a horse. She told me to get help if I needed it. Since you seem to have nothing to do, maybe you could pitch in.

"She?"

The one who made me, horse boy. You know, the dark-haired chippy who makes you climb through windows.

"Evelina made you?"

Who else?

It was a valid question. Nick folded his arms, staring down at the bird. He'd seen the brilliance of Grandfather Cooper's coin-operated wonders. Gran Cooper had been one of the Blood. If Evelina had inherited both talents, why not create a fusion of the two?

That would explain Magnus's interest in Evelina. *Dark hells, what could a sorcerer do with that kind of knowledge?*

The thought expanded like a malevolent bloom in his gut. Nick's skin went cold. He scooped up the bird, stuffing it inside his jacket. He received a peck to his thumb that made him wince.

"Stop it!" he growled. "You have to stay hidden."

Bag that and smoke it, Gypsy boy. Sorry I bothered you. I just thought since you had enough of the Blood to hear me, you might be useful.

Nick gave up trying to hold the squirming creature still as it crawled out of his pocket and up the front of his jacket. It finished by digging painfully into his shoulder, the tiny talons like needles.

Nick winced. "What do you want me to do?"

The sorcerer.

"Magnus?"

He took Mouse. Neat as a pickpocket.

"Mouse?" Nick was beginning to feel like an echo.

The creature flicked its brass wings, the sound ringing like a tiny chime. *Mouse does the indoor work. I'm the outside spy. I can't exactly fly around a ballroom, so your girl kept me in her shoe bag as backup. Good thing or he'd have both of us.*

Nick's skull clogged with questions they had no time for. He settled for the basics: Mouse. Gone. Bad. "All right. I'll follow Magnus on foot, you take the air. I know where he lives."

Got it. The bird was off with a musical whirr.

Nick pictured a map of the streets in his head. He was about two miles from Magnus's home. It stood to reason the doctor would go there with his prize.

With new purpose, Nick slipped through the streets, ears attuned to every footfall. When he got to the steps of Magnus's town house, he slowed. Nick had no intention of blundering into a trap; nor did he relish the thought of cornering a sorcerer without some kind of plan. He knew what Magnus could do.

The home of Dr. Magnus was still and dark. He crept up the stairs on silent feet, scanning the shadows. Either Magnus hadn't returned home, or he was sitting inside, waiting.

A memory of pain drained his strength, leaving him panting. Forcing his feet up, step by step, Nick slid a knife into his sweat-slicked palm.

When he reached the top, he paused, listening. Nothing. His senses weren't as keen as Evelina's, but he probed inside as best he could and found nothing living. He'd just about convinced himself the place was empty when he heard metal scrape on metal. He glanced up, expecting to see the bird. Instead, he felt the kiss of a gun barrel beneath his ear.

"You took my key, thief."

Frustration blanked his mind as he recognized the voice. Striker. *Bloody black hells!*

"Didn't I kill you already?" Nick snapped. Now he knew who had been following him.

"Just left me gammy as an old cart horse, but what's one more score to settle?" The metal ground against his jaw. "Now where is it?"

Nick pushed away a skitter of fear. "My inside jacket pocket."

The pressure of the gun went away and a strong hand spun Nick around. *Perfect.* He pushed away, using the momentum to slam his foot into the wound right where he'd previously thrown Evelina's paper knife. Once Striker was off balance, Nick moved in and struck again. Striker didn't scream, but made a choking gurgle as he doubled over in agony.

Nick grabbed the gun. It was a blessedly ordinary revolver, not the bulbous monstrosity Striker had the last time they'd met. He checked it. Fully loaded. "How the blazes do you sneak up on anybody in that metal coat?"

"Give me my key," Striker wheezed.

The last thing Nick wanted was a prisoner, and the key was no use to him. Exasperated, he fished in his pocket and found the chain he had ripped from the man's neck. He tossed it to him. Striker caught it midair, his face brightening a moment before resuming his usual scowl.

Nick raised the revolver in two hands, wanting to be rid of the fool now. "I'm here to stop a man before he hurts someone I love. Be useful or be gone."

"And I've been hunting the doctor for two solid days but found you. Seems my time hasn't been a waste after all." With a swift movement, Striker pulled a second gun from beneath his coat and hit a switch on its side. It came to life with a whirr. It was sleeker than the one he'd had before, and to Nick's eyes, seemed even more deadly. Blue lightning arced in a glass dome at the top, giving off a faint crackle.

"You ever killed a man before?" the streetkeeper asked.

"Once," Nick said through clenched teeth, refusing to show fear.

Striker smiled, and in that blue-white light from the gun, it was a ghastly leer. The nose of the hellish weapon didn't waver. "You get better at it with practice. I would know."

A sinking feeling took Nick, that same sensation as when a trick went wrong and he knew that a fall was coming. Twenty feet of air and fragile human bones, his stomach somewhere up around his ears. *Oh, bugger, this is it. I'm done.*

There was a moment of regret. So much he'd never done in his short life.

He'd barely finished the thought when his eye caught a gleam from the street. He flicked his gaze up and saw Dr. Magnus there, the streetlight glancing off the silver head of his walking stick.

Nick's eyes met Striker's, and he saw his own doubt. Maybe they wouldn't be killing each other after all.

"I see you two have met," Magnus said with an amused air. "You've been dogging my steps, Mr. Striker. I take it that the Gold King is displeased with me."

Striker's face hardened. "I'm not the one he sends if he's asking you to tea." He raised the strange weapon, but before he could fire, the doctor raised his stick.

Reflex made Nick duck. He grabbed Striker's arm, pulling him to the ground at the same moment. Then the front of the house exploded. Shards of wood and brick sprayed into the air. Glass crashed and frame splintered. Pale fire licked down the door, pouring over the steps like something liquid before it was slurped back into the darkness and extinguished.

The flame missed Nick's boot by inches. His ankle smarted from the heat.

"Holy fardlin' hell," Striker cursed, rolling into a crouch and pointing toward the street. "What was that?"

"I think he plans to defend himself," Nick muttered, scrabbling to take cover behind the porch pillar. Magnus's shot had badly damaged the front of his house, but hadn't breached the door. Nick had the sinking feeling that Magnus had been holding back in hopes of saving his property.

And the doctor was walking toward them now, a thick, dark cloud gathering around him. No light glanced off the buttons of his coat or the silver of his walking stick. Everything around him was stark blackness.

Striker snorted. "Any ideas?"

Nick's mind scrabbled for something he could use. "He's smart. He knew he was going to be followed. He waited until we showed ourselves. He's probably dealt with people trying to kill him before."

"Like that matters now," Striker said with contempt. "Any *useful* ideas?"

Nick was dimly aware of noise and lights up and down the street. Neighbors. They didn't have time to get fancy. "Blow his head off."

"Heh." Striker discharged the weapon in Magnus's direction. It made a kind of *zzooop* noise followed by an iridescent flash. Across the street, a cherry tree blew to smithereens. Striker gave the gun a dirty look. "Range ain't right yet."

"What in all the dark hells is that thing?" Nick asked.

Striker gave an evil smile. "Aether disruptor."

"What is—" He didn't have time to finish the question. "Watch out!"

While Striker's shot had smashed the tree, the force of the explosion bounced the energy back on itself. When the rebound careened into Magnus's black nimbus, the sound was like the rip of a tearing bed sheet. Nick saw the doctor stumble forward, obviously taken unawares. The next instant, the dark cloud around Magnus sparked pale blue, washing him in a ghastly light as he staggered forward.

Nick was hard-pressed to understand what happened next. Magnus thrust out his hands, as if warding off a blow. Squiggling snakes of energy crawled over the nimbus around him, seeming to suck up the shadows Magnus had gathered. The arcing energy wadded into a bright knot of lightning, shooting arrows of electricity into the night sky.

"Bugger," Striker muttered under his breath. "Bet I've made him mad now."

Magnus wheeled, the pale blue light making a terrible mask of his face. Nick's stomach turned to ice as the doctor clutched at the swirling, crackling energy Striker's gun had set loose, and seemed to thrust the sparks into the air.

The door behind Nick flew to pieces with a resounding crack. A foot lower, and it would have been Striker spraying into the air.

"Get off the porch!" Nick cried, dodging out from behind the pillar with the sole intention of leaping out of the way.

Another blast came their way, landing in front of them this time. The force threw Nick backward into the house, mud hitting his face and blinding him. He was dimly aware of sailing clear through the doors into the big room with the worktable and all the books. He landed hard, facedown and skidding across the carpet, coming to rest just in front of Magnus's peacock chair.

Everything hurt. Deaf, dizzy, he made a vague swimming motion, figuring out where the floor was. The gun was still in a death-grip in his right hand. He supposed that was good. Somehow, he pushed himself up and got his knees under him. His back hurt horribly. When he tried to straighten, he found the left side of his jacket was soaked in warm, sticky blood.

Nick searched for an emotion, but didn't find any. Raising his left arm was hard, but he managed to peel back his jacket. A huge gash had opened up from his armpit diagonally to his hip. If he had to guess, he'd say that something sharp had caught him in the blast, slicing him cleanly as a kitchen knife. The wound was seeping rivulets of blood. *Will you look at that?*

Then he started to feel hot and sick and a surge of terror kicked his heart into high gear. He stumbled to his feet, weaving slightly and grabbing a cloth from one of the side tables and pressing it against the wound. Then he grabbed another cloth, then papers, stuffing whatever he could under his jacket and buttoning it closed. Hurt or not, he still had to rid the world of Dr. Magnus.

He had no idea what was going on in the street. He staggered forward, alternating between an urge to hide and the need to storm out the ruined doorway and back into the street, revolver blazing. He compromised by listing against what was left of the front doorway and peering into the darkness. The street was all but invisible, drowning in a fog of darkness. Somehow, the doctor's influence was keeping people away, blocking what was happening from sight. Good. He didn't want to shoot someone by accident.

And then suddenly Magnus stood right there, halfway down the front walk.

"You've become something of a nuisance, Nick with no name," he said.

Hey! Nick heard the panic in the bird's voice. It was near enough to touch his mind. Nick pulled the trigger, but Magnus had vanished. He thought he heard the bullet hit, but he couldn't be sure. In the next second, he heard the peculiar sound of Striker's gun. *Zoop! Zoop! Zoop!*

Nick ducked, covering his eyes from the flashes, his breath hissing in because it hurt to move. But even through his hands he could see the the air around Magnus catch fire, the bright illumination showing blood-red between his fingers. Whatever Striker's gun did, it reacted to magic like a spark to gunpowder.

The doctor's roar of pain escalated into a scream. Nick dropped to one knee, blinking white blotches from his vision. The scream faded to a whimper, and then to silence.

Nick's skin crawled, the hair on his arms standing straight up. He'd only ever heard that kind of cry once, when a tiger tore open the underbelly of one of the horses. *Gods forgive us.*

A dark shape lay on the ground where Magnus had been. It stank of cooking flesh, a shade too similar to what Nick had eaten for supper. Bile rose in his throat, but he stubbornly swallowed it down. He couldn't stand the thought of heaving with his side bloody and raw.

Striker stood to the left of Magnus, the gun casting a pool of oscilating blue light around him. With an almost mechanical motion, he reached over and hit a switch. The gun powered down with a whirr.

Nick found his feet and jumped to the soft grass below

with a grunt. There were no stairs anymore. "You got the range sorted."

Striker rubbed his forehead. "That I did."

Neither man sounded triumphant, because they weren't. There was nothing there to celebrate. Magnus was lying on the ground, his chest a burned mass of bone and blood. He'd fallen on one side, his tall hat adrift on the paving stones, his fingers helplessly trailing in the dirt. From his staring eyes, there was no question he was dead. Striker had shot him in the back, blowing his heart through his breastbone.

Well, he wouldn't be bothering Evelina anymore. Nick bent with a shuddering intake of breath, and searched Magnus's pockets.

"You robbing the bloke?" Striker sounded more curious than judgmental.

Nick found what he was looking for. A tiny steel mouse. He could just sense a consciousness inside, shivering in terror. He slipped it into his own pocket. "I've got what I want."

Striker hesitated an instant, and then made his own search, letting out a gratified grunt when he found the doctor's purse.

Nick looked away from the puddle of blood darkening the ground, a sudden foreboding taking him. A few yards away, brass gleamed dully in the uncertain light. The bird lay in pieces, shattered by the force of the blasts. He had no idea if destroying the mechanism freed the deva, or if it was trapped inside a broken shell.

The street was in chaos now that Magnus's magic was gone. The black fog was lifting and people were streaming out of their houses and coming their way. They would be on them in seconds.

"Come on," said Striker. "Time to run."

Forgetting his wound, Nick dropped to his knees, sweeping up the shards of Evelina's creation. He pulled the kerchief from around his neck, using it to gather the pieces.

"Come on!" Striker repeated, his voice rising.

Nick tucked the kerchief inside his shirt, feeling the bundle of cool brass against the heat of his body.

"Bloody hell, mate." Striker hauled Nick up by his collar,

then his eyes widened as he saw the blood-soaked side of Nick's clothes.

A police whistle shrilled.

The streetkeeper swore viciously. "You just keep making my life interesting, don't you?"

Chapter Thirty-five

VIOLENT EXPLOSION DESTROYS HOUSE

A respectable neighborhood in the Yellow District was shattered last night as a detonation of unknown origin destroyed 113 Pemberton Row. The owner, Dr. Symeon Magnus, was found dead in his front yard, clearly the victim of a vicious attack. Police are investigating the matter, but will give no further comment at this time.

—*The Bugle*

London, April 13, 1888

HILLIARD HOUSE

3 p.m. Friday

EVELINA WAS ATTEMPTING TO READ *BARRETT'S GUIDE TO the Mechanics of Ancient Europe*. However, the events of the day before had taken their toll, and she was exhausted, anxious, and unable to concentrate for more than three words at a stretch.

And the problems just kept mounting. A whole week had passed, and she still hadn't found out who had killed Grace Child and the grooms, or why the automatons were so valuable. And she had a hundred questions about the ancient Greek object they called Athena's Casket. She'd looked it up in what books she could find, but they all said it was an instrument used for navigation. Magnus had suggested it had magical properties—infusing spirit into mechanics and all that—but none of the volumes in Lord Bancroft's library mentioned any such thing.

And what had been going on at the warehouse? A lot of people were dead, including the Chinese workers, but what exactly had they been doing there? Whatever it was, somehow Grace Child and her silk bag of gold was the link between the warehouse and Hilliard House.

Evelina had started to investigate in order to protect Imogen and her family from scandal. Unfortunately, all she'd managed to do was piece together a reason someone in the house was guilty. It was simple math. Gold artifacts arrived at the warehouse in crates, and melted gold and unset stones were carried away by a servant who worked at Hilliard House. It didn't take a huge intellect to make a connection. Clearly, someone with no respect for archaeology was melting down the treasures. And since Keating was mad for all things Greek and Roman, it would be out of character for him to allow the destruction of historical treasures. And besides, the wealth was showing up in Lord B's cloakroom, not Jasper Keating's bank. Everything pointed to the fact that he was being robbed.

So who was doing it and how? Was that where the Chinese came in? So why had they been murdered? If she had to guess, they were the worker bees and their usefulness had expired—and that meant the villain was beating a retreat. If she meant to find out who that was, she had better do it now.

For more reasons than one. Her Uncle Sherlock was back in London and had written to say that he had begun work on Jasper Keating's case. He planned to stop by that afternoon to see her. At any other time, she would have been delighted by a visit. Now, with so much at stake, it was a glaring reminder of her failure to preemptively solve Grace's murder.

And Lestrade would be sure to contact him, because Scotland Yard was having no better luck than Evelina. There had been no progress in solving the murders of any of Lord Bancroft's servants, the dozen Chinese, and now Dr. Magnus. Public opinion was growing foul.

If Uncle Sherlock got involved, the question of the magic-infested automatons would be sure to come to light. The only thing Evelina could do was try to deflect her uncle from that part of the puzzle. It wouldn't be easy, because Sherlock Holmes was not a man easily fooled.

Evelina buried her face in her hands, summoning her strength. It was hard to believe, but her uncle was only one problem. There were others.

She'd sent Bird for help, hoping the creature would find Nick, but it hadn't returned. She'd seen—with the sense of an answered prayer—the article on Magnus's death, but there had been no sign of Mouse scampering back home. A frantic need to find the two creatures gnawed at her, but London was a vast city. She'd search the sorcerer's house, or his personal effects at the morgue, but she'd need her uncle's help to gain access. Explaining her need to search a corpse was going to take some doing.

Then again, it was Uncle Sherlock.

"Evelina?"

Tobias came through the door of the sitting room. She greeted the interruption with relief, and set the book aside. "Yes?"

"There is, um, a person who wishes to see you."

"Uncle Sherlock?"

"No. Mr. Keating's streetkeeper, I understand." Tobias frowned. "Highly irregular, so I told Bigelow I'd see to this personally. I don't like the looks of him. Says his name is Striker."

"What does he want from me?"

"He won't say." Tobias was clearly irritated. "Since he's Keating's man, it's harder to simply toss him down the steps."

She was intrigued. "Then I suppose I must see what he wants."

A minute later, the man called Striker was standing in the middle of the sunny green and yellow room, with its flowers in the pretty china jug. At first glance, he resembled a cross between a pugilist and an armadillo masquerading as a rusted-out boiler. He smelled of grease, gunpowder, and gin with an underlying tang of dried blood. A man who lived hard.

If one looked closer, however, there was a quick and wary

intelligence in the man's brown eyes. He held his hat in his hands and studied Evelina with some curiosity.

"Miss," he said. "Pardon the intrusion."

He was clearly minding his manners to the utmost of his ability. Tobias was watching from a few feet away, arms crossed and a disapproving scowl on his face that made him look alarmingly like his father.

"Consider it pardoned," said Evelina, wanting to ease Striker's discomfort. "What brings you here?"

"I came to give you these." He held out a cloth bundle in one grease-stained paw.

She recognized Nick's neckcloth immediately. It was the one he had been wearing last night. Alarm ran chilly fingers over her body. *Why does a streetkeeper have it?*

A coppery taste of fear flooded her mouth. She darted forward, reaching for the bundle, but Tobias got there first. "Tobias!"

"Let me see," he said, setting the package on the table and working at the knots. "Before you go touching whatever is inside." The contents gave an interesting metallic sound.

Evelina looked from Tobias to Striker, who looked unimpressed.

"It's quite safe, sir," the streetkeeper said.

The corners of the neckcloth parted. Mouse and Bird sprawled on the table, frozen as wind-up toys that had lost their keys. Both looked the worse for wear, Bird in particular sporting unfamiliar patches of metal that looked like they might have come from Striker's coat. She reached out with her mind. They were still and silent, but they were both alive.

Evelina whirled to Striker. "Thank you! Thank you so much!"

Flushing slightly, the young man shifted, the coat giving a faint rattle. "The bird was in bad shape. I tried a bit o' repair, miss, but I don't have the tools for work that fine. Nick said you could take it from here."

Tobias was intrigued, picking up Mouse and turning it over in his hand. "Did you make these, Evelina?"

She suddenly realized her secret was slipping out of the

bag. She shot Striker a look, but his face was completely neutral. A man used to keeping his mouth shut.

"Yes," she forced her voice to be calm. "As you know, I have an interest in clockwork toys."

Tobias picked up the bird, peering at its repaired wing. "Was there anything else you wished to say, Striker?"

"No, sir."

"You may go."

"As you wish, sir." The streetkeeper clapped his hat back on his head and started for the door, moving with a visible limp.

"Wait!" Evelina cried. *Why didn't Nick come?*

Striker stopped, one brow lifting, a bit of a tease lurking somewhere behind his eyes.

Questions formed and dissolved in her mind. She didn't know Striker, and wasn't sure what was safe to ask. "I appreciate that you came. And tell Nick thank you from the bottom of my heart. I hope everything is all right with him."

Striker's mouth twitched, as if understanding far more than she would have liked. "I'll do that, miss. And don't you worry about him none."

Evelina watched him go, then closed the sitting room door. It wasn't proper to be alone with Tobias in a closed room, but nothing about this situation was normal.

He was still examining the creatures. "How did a streetkeeper come to have anything of yours?"

"I lost them. A friend found them."

"This Nick person?" Tobias asked, a protective edge in his voice. Obviously, he'd missed nothing.

"Yes, Nick." And where was the Indomitable Niccolo? Being told not to worry was the fast road to indigestion.

Tobias set the bird down with a guarded expression, but he had questions. They were almost visibly swarming around him. "You're entitled to your secrets."

He told me his, after all. Evelina drew a ragged breath, explanations and excuses crowding up in a rush, but she didn't answer right away.

My secrets are even more dangerous to share. Striker's connection to Nick meant that Evelina's two worlds had unexpectedly intersected. Worse, her old love for Nick—hopeless, but reawakened—had collided with her fascination for Tobias. There was no good way to explore that mess with either one of her would-be suitors.

But the need to confess was almost a physical pain—to explain about her magic, about her fears, about what Magnus had wanted from her. If they were to succeed at all, there should be nothing between her and Tobias, nothing to hinder what was blooming into real affection. Magnus was gone. Surely, enough danger had passed to make confidences possible?

No. Caution held her back, at least from letting him all the way in. Still, she felt safe enough to give him something. "Nick is a childhood friend. He travels with Ploughman's Circus."

She felt sick the moment she said it, but there was no taking it back. Tobias's gaze traveled the length of her, to her toes and back up again. She fought the urge to squirm in an agony of disappointment and defiance. Her knees trembled as the blood mounted to her face.

"And you?" he asked.

Her fingers twitched, wanting to make fists. "I spent time there as a girl. Imogen knows all about it, but you can understand why I never talk about it."

"You think it appears too common."

"I'm sure your father would say so. It's enough that everyone knows my mother covered herself in scandal by eloping with a base-born soldier, even if he was made an officer in the field for bravery."

"My father is sometimes an idiot." He stepped closer, putting his hands on her shoulders. "You're unconventional, Evelina. I've always known you came from someplace different, and it doesn't surprise me that it was a circus. You're lighter than air when you move."

She swallowed hard, unable to answer.

He bent his head so his face was close to hers. "Remember, I saw you when you first arrived at Imogen's school. You were out of your element then, but you aren't now. My parents already know your mother had an uneven history—this won't matter to them as much as you think."

He was wrong. She had to say it plainly, though she could not help ducking to hide her eyes. "Your father will never let you court me."

He lifted her chin with his finger. "I can wave my father's title out the window and a dozen perfect girls will come running. You, by contrast, always have me asking whom I'm trying to fool. I'm smart enough to know to whom I should pay attention."

The shock of confession was receding, to be replaced by surprise that he was accepting it. Then she realized that they were standing very close, mere inches apart. Scandalously close. Her pulse quickened.

"Whom are you trying to fool, Tobias?" she asked gently. "I grew up at the circus. I learned to dance on a rope and fly on the trapeze. You're going to be Bancroft one day and sit in the House of Lords."

His eyebrow lifted. "A trapeze? That does conjure some fascinating imagery."

"Think, Tobias!" She took a step back, needing the space.

"I have." He sobered, looking weary, and closed the distance she'd just made. "I don't want to follow in my father's footsteps, however comfortable that might be. I don't want to be a steam baron's pet. I want to be my own man. And I don't say that casually. There will be difficulties. I had hoped Magnus would support me while I struck out on my own. Sadly, I was wrong—more wrong than I care to say."

She thought about his mood at the dance, and wondered if Magnus was the cause. "I'm sorry."

He shook his head. "Perhaps it is a lesson. Independence doesn't come easily, not when one has enjoyed the privileges of rank. It would be simpler if I were a plain tradesman, or a lawyer, or a doctor, but I'm not."

"And your plan?"

He sighed. "I shall manufacture an immense amount of character in record time?"

"And what if your father's plan is to marry you to an heiress?"

"I knew I could count on you for the practical question."

"I'm a bore that way." Still, she waited for the answer. The sun was streaming in, painting the room with a wash of honeyed gold.

He smiled wanly. "There is only one thing I can do: build. Surely that is of value to someone."

"I could applaud a man who builds."

Tobias's smile vanished. "Could you love him?"

It was a cautious question, a foot set gingerly on a newly frozen pond. The power of it weighed on her; he had laid himself bare. Her mouth went dry as she searched his face. Her emotions were a bonfire, but her mind was alert, weighing everything. *I could love him. In time, I think I could build a future with him.*

He was handsome, as he had always been, but she saw the harder lines beneath the prettiness now. There were the beginnings of maturity in his expression, and she liked what she was hearing. He wanted something different. She was different. If she could let go of the past, it might, just might, work.

"I could," she answered, barely above a whisper. "Building means something."

She had come so far, making it into her first Season. She had done the presentation and her first ball. But this was the first moment that felt like it belonged to the real Evelina, not just Evelina the debutante, the woman her Grandmamma Holmes had done her best to invent. Tobias wanted her, not just the ideal of a well-trained Society girl.

"I'm glad," he said, taking her hands. "Making is good. Making a life with you will be even better."

With that, Tobias leaned down that last inch, pressing his warm mouth over hers. Evelina's mind went hazy, all her critical faculties melting like snow on a hot stove. He smelled of soap and the linen of his shirt. Her fingers instinctively sought out his face, tracing the clean line of his jaw and lean, freshly shaved cheeks.

And then he deepened the kiss, and a shiver ran through her, sending an electric pulse that melted her core. She arched into it, letting him run his hand over the side of her ribs, down the curve of her waist. Her breasts crushed against him, deliciously sensitive. It was as if her whole body were suddenly awake.

When they broke the kiss, she was panting like she'd run a mile. There were no devas or silver lights, but his kiss was definitely magic.

His grin was pure wickedness, as if the shadow on his spirits had been lifted. "Testing out your investigative skills?"

For a moment, she couldn't form words. She thought she might need to lie down. "Are you a mystery that needs solving?"

"Perhaps I'm simply a crime about to be perpetrated."

That seemed all too likely. He'd scrambled her wits to custard. "Then perhaps I shall call Inspector Lestrade for an arrest."

Tobias squeezed her hands, his grin turning a little rueful. "A spell in the lockup might do me good. I have some plans to make."

CHAPTER THIRTY-SIX

Detection is, or ought to be, an exact science, and should be treated in the same cold and unemotional manner.

—Sherlock Holmes, as recorded by
John H. Watson, M.D., *The Sign of the Four*

EVELINA HAD LOCKED HERSELF IN HER ROOM, DISGUSTED with herself. She had spent the last hour elated, and then agonizing over what seemed to be the next best thing to a formal proposal. And then elated again. How she managed to be shocked and riven and desperately buoyant all at once was boggling. No wonder so much paper was covered with love poetry. People were just trying to make sense of the turmoil of emotion.

Young men were extremely complicated creatures. The Duchess of Westlake had compared them to ships. She didn't know much about the sea, but Tobias would have been something beautifully crafted and elegant with lots of white sails—the meeting place of tradition and innovation. Evelina turned the image around in her head, wondering where she fit into that metaphor without it sounding rude.

Nick, on the other hand, would have been a sleek pirate ship. He already had the gold rings in his ears.

Speaking of unfathomable young men, now there was this Striker, who—according to Mouse and Bird—began as Nick's foe and ended up his comrade in arms.

Nick and Striker had killed Magnus together—one saving the other's life and then vice versa—drunk an enormous amount of Blue Ruin, ogled over some airship plans Nick had accidentally stolen from Magnus in an attempt to pack his bleeding wounds, and then ended up visiting a surgeon when it became absolutely clear Nick required proper medical attention, which the Gold King's streetkeeper could command for his Yellowbacks at will. Keating at least did something for his people.

In the end, everyone was fine—except Magnus.

And how do I feel about any of that? Happy that Mouse and Bird were back. Ecstatic that Nick would be all right. Relieved that Magnus was gone. Gratitude— enormous gratitude—to Nick for seeing it done.

And yet? Loss yawned inside her and unexpected tears dimmed her sight. Magnus had known what she was. He could have told her much, although probably for a price she would never willingly pay. He had threatened her, stolen from her, and tried to seduce her. Still, knowledge and life were never lightly lost.

She gave a shuddering sigh. In contrast, the logic of gear and spring was soothing.

The gimcrack bird stood on the edge of her train case, pecking at the screws and wheels as if they were seeds.

She'd had to rework some of Striker's repairs, but most were as good as she could have managed without a complete recasting of the brass. The patches gave Bird a rakish air a bit like Striker himself. Mouse had been nowhere as badly damaged, but had experienced a rough ride during Dr. Magnus's last stand.

Evelina polished a scratch out of Mouse's belly.

I don't know why you're bothering with that—thing, Bird complained.

"Don't you want a friend?" she asked.

What do I have in common with a rodent?

As part of the repair, she'd tipped the little paws in velvet so that its scampering would be utterly silent. Now they waggled in the air as she rubbed.

"You can complain about brass cats."

Mouse piped up. *And after that extensive conversation, perhaps we can move on to the cricket scores? How am I supposed to work with something that but for the grace of the gods might have been an omelet?*

"You're both just jealous. You want to be the only living mechanical device."

Nonsense, Bird replied stiffly.

I am unique, huffed Mouse.

"That you are," she replied dryly, still rubbing at the scratch.

I protest this illogical servitude, Mouse complained.

"Yet you do seem to like sneaking about." She set down the cloth. "I might go so far as to say you relish it."

It has a certain sensationalist interest.

Evelina pulled off her magnifying lenses. "If you really want to go, I won't make you stay, but then you won't get to find out how the case ends."

They were both silent.

"I'm serious. In his own way, Magnus tried to catch me like I caught you, and I didn't like it. I don't want to do that to anyone else."

Bird hopped from the train case to the desk, feet skidding on the smooth surface. *We'll let you know.* Which seemed to say complaining was more fun than actually getting their way.

Evelina could feel another presence prodding her consciousness. The cube reminded her of a cat wanting to be stroked, the gentle tap-tapping of a paw to get her attention.

She'd hidden the cube at the back of her wardrobe, but brought it out when she was sitting in her room. It seemed to like the company, even though the other devas couldn't understand it any better than she could. No amount of scrubbing had made the thing attractive. It was still a rusty mass of partially melted gears and wheels, but the intelligence inside it was so much more.

It perched on the corner of the desk. Mouse had climbed it, and was cleaning its whiskers of metal polish. She touched the cube's surface with her fingertips, feeling the pitted roughness of the cool metal. In return, it reached out to her mind, gentle and almost adoring. There was something feminine about it, almost maternal.

"What are you?" Evelina whispered. "What do you need?"

An answer came, the voice clear and firm in her head, but it was in no language she knew. She'd never thought about the fact that nature spirits spoke different tongues—or perhaps there was another reason they couldn't understand one another. Devas spoke to those of the Blood, but Gran Cooper said that in the old days there were many different tribes, and each had different talents and an affinity for different types of devas. That seemed to make sense. Over the years, Evelina had talked to one or two air spirits, but hundreds of devas of earth and plant and tree.

Of course, none of that helped her now. "I don't understand."

The voice came again, husky and sweet but vibrant with urgency. It pulled at her heartstrings. It wanted her to understand—something. Tired as she was, tears of frustration pricked Evelina's eyes.

"I wish I could help."

Helen.

Evelina started. "What did you call me?"

Helen? The second time sounded hopeful. It wasn't much, but it was a speck of real communication. It was also the same name that Dr. Magnus had used at the ball.

And he had told her about Athena's Casket at the ball, and hinted that it combined magic and machine. She stared at the cube, wondering who had tossed it among the junk in the warehouse. Someone with no ability to hear devas talk. A careless worker? Definitely someone who was blind to anything that did not glitter. *If the cube were shiny and gold, I would wonder if this was the object everyone was hunting for. But if I'm right, and some of Keating's treasures were stolen and melted down, the story might be quite different. Is this all that remains of the casket?*

The idea was staggering. She grabbed the edge of her desk, as if contact with the hard edges would keep her from floating off into wild speculation. *I must go slowly here, and not jump to conclusions!*

A knock on her bedroom door shattered her thoughts.

Evelina grabbed Bird and stuffed it into the pocket of her skirt, stifling its indignant peeps. She dropped Mouse into the train case, slammed the lid, and picked up the watch she was pretending to repair. As an afterthought, she tossed a doily onto the cube. The effect was odd, but the best she could do at a moment's notice.

"Come in!" she called out, turning around so that her back was to her desk.

Imogen put her head around the corner of the door. "Your uncle has arrived."

"It's about time." Evelina shook out her skirts and hurried after her friend.

SHERLOCK HOLMES, CONSULTING detective, stood in the front hall of Hilliard House, somehow occupying every square inch of the space without moving a muscle. Tall and wiry, he looked enviably at ease in a light summer coat, as if he had just happened by after a stroll.

Evelina's step hitched. Though he was impeccably turned out, dark circles bagged under his eyes, as if he'd been up for the past three weeks. What had he been working on? Something to do with Bohemia?

"Lord Bancroft is not at home, sir," Bigelow intoned.

"I did not ask to see Lord Bancroft," Holmes said evenly. "I came to inquire after my niece."

"Here I am, Uncle." Evelina stopped and dropped a slight curtsy. If it had been Dr. Watson, there would have been hugs and smiles, but Sherlock Holmes wasn't the type of man one automatically embraced.

"I stopped to see your grandmother on the way back from the Continent." Holmes doffed his tall hat. "She is much better. I believe news of your success at the palace was the best tonic available." He said it dryly, but not unkindly. "During the course of the conversation, I established that she knows every dress regulation and step of the procedure by rote."

They exchanged a wry smile, sharing volumes of commiseration without speaking a word. "It's a fine day. Shall we take a stroll?" he asked. "I believe there is much of interest to review."

Five minutes later, Evelina walked down the street, hurrying to match Holmes's long stride. They were making a circuit of the round garden that graced the middle of Beaulieu Square. "I stopped by here specifically because Lestrade wrote me a letter," he said. "I understand three of Lord Bancroft's servants have been murdered. I vacillated between utter confidence that you could manage anything and anxiety that a knife-wielding maniac was stalking the halls. Then I wondered why no one else had bothered to inform me." He awarded her a sour look.

Evelina swallowed. It had taken him under a minute to begin the conversation she least wanted to have. "What would you have done had you known? You were out of the country."

"A necessity. My case proved to have unexpected dimensions."

"No doubt you found that of interest."

He flushed slightly, as if those dimensions might have been personal. *A woman? No, not possible.* "Not a pleasant sort of interest, I'm afraid. I cannot go into a great amount of detail, so let us just say that a few months ago, there was a scandal of sorts involving an adventuress and a member of the Bohemian aristocracy. It was averted and, as far as anyone could foresee, the matter was put to rest."

"And?"

"The steam barons have interests in several countries abroad, Bohemia among them. They found this woman, Irene Adler, and attempted to coerce her into advancing the barons' interests with Bohemia by every means at her disposal. She knew that if she agreed, none of the parties involved would come out of it unscathed."

Evelina was intrigued. She'd heard oblique mentions of Irene Adler before, and her uncle fell silent every time Dr. Watson mentioned the name. "What happened?"

"She requested my help. I gave it."

"And the steam barons?"

Holmes swung his walking stick almost jauntily. "I had

best stay well away from the Scarlet King for some time to come. He accused me of belonging to something called the Baskerville conspiracy. Imagine that."

It wasn't easy, because Holmes rarely worked well with others—which was usually what a conspiracy required. Nevertheless, Evelina filed the name in her mind. Knowing her uncle, he might have let the name slip for a reason. One never knew, but it would be useless to pepper him with questions until he was ready to talk.

They walked a moment in silence, letting a few chugging steam cycles pass. On the skyline, hydrogen balloons bobbed like colorful birds in the late-afternoon light. Keating Industries was experimenting with aboveground telegraph, stringing wires through the sky in anticipation of skyborne dirigible communication stations. But so far, birds and weather were proving a nuisance.

She cast a quick glance at her uncle. He sometimes stirred up chaos in his wake the way a maid stirred dust kittens with her broom, but people turned to him to bring order, to restore society to its norm. For once, she wondered at what cost that order came. As she'd notice before, he looked wrung out, the bones of his face stark beneath pale skin. "You've been working too hard."

"I'm sure Watson will write all about it," he said derisively.

She let it go. If he didn't choose to elaborate, pushing was a waste of energy. There was no point in arguing with a man who considered food and sleep an impediment to intellectual exercise. "I'm glad you came."

He gave a quick smile that was almost a grimace. "Then let us get down to business. In the matter of this murdered serving girl, tell me again everything you remember, skipping nothing."

Evelina flinched. "I thought you were working a case for the Gold King."

He looked surprised—something she didn't see often. "You are living in a house filled with danger. Do you honestly think I would ignore that, now that Lestrade has seen fit to enlighten me?"

"Keating is not a man who likes to be put off."

"So evidenced by the many unhappy letters he has written this past week. Never mind, I will deal with Jasper Keating in due course. His mystery is nothing more than a matter of lost and found. Now, tell me what you know."

She did, every tiny detail she could remember. The recital was almost therapeutic. Here was no complicated morass of emotion, no wrestling with decisions or choices. Everything was just cold, hard fact. Her job was to be a conduit, not an interpreter.

He absorbed her monologue with half-closed lids: Grace's death, the gold and emeralds, the automatons, the grooms, the clue that had led her to the warehouse, Lord Bancroft's conversation with Dr. Magnus, and Magnus's description of the underground living quarters, and finally, his death. She mentioned nothing of her own use of magic or the true nature of the automatons.

"Fascinating," he said after she had finished. "Athena's Casket seems quite the desired object. Keating came to see me about recovering it. It appears my case and yours overlap."

My case. Evelina felt almost breathless. It was silly and juvenile, but the fact he had not scoffed at her fumbling investigation thrilled her. "That seems to argue the casket is not in his possession."

"Magnus thought Keating had it, Keating believed it stolen, and Bancroft was caught in the middle. All the aspects of a *commedia dell'arte* farce, which tells me we are missing a player."

She looked at him in fascination. This was why he was the great detective. "We are? How do you know?"

"Find the holes in our story, and you will see the passage of our mystery player."

"How?" She squinted up at the sun, guessing the time. She wished he'd come earlier, because this conversation could take hours. She would scream if this chance to work through the clues was cut short.

"What don't we know?" He clasped his hands behind his back, assuming a professorial air.

"Who killed the Chinese?"

"And?"

"Where the casket is." *Unless I have it?* But she couldn't explain that the reason she suspected it was because the cube talked to her.

He nodded. "Good. And?"

"Why Grace was carrying gold, or who her killer was, if we believe Magnus was not the killer himself. He admitted to stealing the automatons as a threat to Bancroft."

"Did you ever see him carry a knife?"

Ah, good point, pardon the pun. "No. I don't know what kind of guns or knives Magnus favored." He was a sorcerer, but that was a piece of information her uncle would most likely question—and that was a road she wasn't ready to take. Not yet, at least. "We don't know most things, in fact."

Holmes shook his head, seeming almost irritated. "Not true. But you are missing several points: the voices you heard, or who was in the hallway, or who was the father of the poor girl's child."

Evelina laughed unhappily. "Just a few details."

"Any luck with the cipher?"

"Sadly, no." She felt utterly defeated.

"No matter. Believe it or not, you've done a passable job of assembling information. All that remains is to arrange it properly. I see the passage of not one, but two unknown parties."

They had circumnavigated Beaulieu Square and were back in the gardens of Hilliard House. They stopped outside the door where Tobias had met Grace Child the night she died. Holmes crouched to search the grass, pulling out a magnifying lens to check every blade. Evelina stared down at him, a little incredulous.

"What are you looking for?"

"There is some interesting cigarette ash."

Now there was an oxymoron. "There must have been fifty people at the garden party. At least half were men, and half of those smoked. There is no shortage of ash, interesting or otherwise. And it has been a week since the murder."

Holmes rose, dusting his knees. "You are correct, sometimes ash is simply ash. I never know until I look. And I'll have you know, most find that performance impressive."

Evelina raised an eyebrow.

"However," he said, putting away his glass, "let us return to the sequence of events for the moment. Grace Child was waiting outside until the young Mr. Roth let her inside shortly after half past twelve. Then she is discovered dead at approximately one o'clock."

"Yes."

"She had a candle, you say, that had dripped a quantity of wax on the floor?"

"Yes, where she dropped it."

He raised a finger. "Why was she standing with a candle in the cloakroom? She wouldn't have had one unless she went and got it once she was inside. Why didn't she simply go to bed?"

Understanding dawned. "She was waiting for someone. A few minutes, in fact, if that much wax melted."

Sherlock nodded. "Who was she waiting for? There are three possible candidates: an inmate of the house, the unknown who passed you in the hallway at twelve forty-five, or whoever was talking outside at eleven o'clock. The first is the most likely to have met with the girl. There is a good chance the second was her killer."

"They aren't the same person?"

"There is the fact that she still had the gold. I believe the person she meant to meet failed to show. Perhaps, while waiting, she surprised someone else."

Evelina's blood flared with excitement. "Of course! Magnus meant to steal the automatons! Could that have been him prowling the halls that night?"

Holmes shrugged. "Perhaps, and maybe more than perhaps. It will be easy enough to reconstruct events."

"Then where do we start?"

He looked up at Hilliard House. "With dinner. I believe I smell an excellent leg of lamb, and perhaps it is high time I exchanged pleasantries with the other players in our little game."

CHAPTER THIRTY-SEVEN

HIS FATHER STARED AT HIM IN OPEN-MOUTHED SHOCK, A look Tobias hadn't seen on the pater before. It made him yearn to back out the study door, the way one would retreat from a savage dog.

"What's this I hear about Holmes?" Bancroft rose from behind his desk, his snarl matching the stuffed tiger head on the wall above. "Here? Under my roof?"

The sun slanted low through the study window, glinting off the brass adornments on the desk. It gave the setting an extra dramatic flare, as if the place was about to catch fire. Maybe it was. "Mother just invited him to dinner."

Bancroft sat back down abruptly, as if he had suddenly run out of steam. "All I asked of you was to distract the Cooper girl."

"I apologize for not proving the cad you wish me to be."

His father gave him a withering look.

Tobias found his apprehension warping into annoyance. "What do you think Holmes is going to find?"

"None of your affair."

Something inside Tobias broke, letting loose a flood of anger. There was only so much contempt he could swallow. "None of my affair, and yet you feel compelled to lob one dark hint after another in my direction, somehow insinuating that it's my duty to help you cover it up."

His father sat straight, eyes flaring with anger. "What did you say?"

"What is this dark secret? I bloody well know it's all to do with the automatons." Tobias leaned across the desk, drunk on the sensation of finally speaking his mind. "I know, because Magnus had a puppet, a vile creation. Yours are nowhere near as pretty as his toy, but they shared a stink of evil. Even I can tell that much, and I know nothing of magic."

He fell back into his seat. The talk of automatons sickened him. His inner sight was veiled by the image of Serafina's breast rising and falling in a mockery of human sleep. It had imprinted itself like a stain, a blot that he had to look through to perceive the world. The only time it faded was when he was with Evelina.

Stiffly, his face a hard mask, Bancroft opened a box sitting on his desk. It was about the size of a loaf of bread, a fragrant wood covered in a latticework of silver. The lid folded away, revealing a double row of scalpel-sharp steel knives attached to a frame. He pulled a lever and the entire box telescoped up so that the blades sat on top of a box about two feet tall. "Be very careful what you say next. There are some parts of our family history that are best not probed."

Tobias swallowed hard as his father picked up a piece of correspondence from a stack at his elbow. Lord Bancroft held the letter above the knives and pushed a button on the contraption. The knives began a slashing frenzy, sucking the paper into their elegant, glinting maw and cutting it to bits.

Chopitty-choppity-choppity. And the letter was in scraps no larger than the nail of Tobias's smallest finger. Someone's secrets gone forever. Or maybe there was a not-so-subtle message there, in those shiny bright knives.

His father's head was darkly silhouetted by the sunset beyond. He could believe his father capable of cutting off his allowance, but he had never considered that the man might feed his heir to the MacDonald's Patented Correspondence Destruction Unit.

Chopitty-choppity-choppity went a second page.

Tobias was tired of this game. "Bugger that."

His father looked shocked, but then vaguely approving. "I'll tell you this much. Those automatons represent the worst passage of my life."

It was as personal a statement as his father had ever made.

Tobias hoped it wasn't the prelude to feeding him to the office equipment. "Why? And what do they have to do with Dr. Magnus?"

He didn't expect an answer, but the question deserved to be asked. Bancroft's hand trembled, and he sacrificed another piece of crested bond, letting his fingers come dangerously close to the blades. Tobias's stomach swirled.

"They are the means by which Magnus secured his hooks into the fabric of this family." The intensity in his father's voice shook him almost more than the flashing knives.

"He's dead now," Tobias said gently. He suddenly wondered if his father had orchestrated the murder.

"I won't believe that until I see his heart stop beating."

"What did Magnus do to you?"

"He dabbled in the darkest of magics."

"I know." Folk tales said magic was risky. The law called it treason. Tobias called it evil, plain and simple. He'd seen it looking back at him out of that demon's blue glass eyes.

Sometime in the night—obviously before he was blasted to smithereens—Magnus must have retrieved her. When Tobias went back to the workshop this morning, with oil and a match to try burning her one more time, Serafina and her trunk were gone. She was still out there, somewhere, disassembled and waiting to feed on her next caretaker.

"Tell me about the dolls that Magnus stole from you."

Surprisingly, his father answered. "I built them. At first they were nothing more than mechanical servants."

"I remember that." Not fondly. The clanking, blank-eyed things had spooked him as a boy. "I remember them being in the house."

Chopitty-choppity-choppity.

Tobias wet his lips. Perhaps a seaside holiday was in order for the parents. Somewhere restful. Somewhere far, far away where all the sharp objects were locked up.

"Magnus had ideas about infusing them with his magic. They became tainted, so I was forced to take them out of service." Bancroft switched off the machine, the last letter reduced to confetti.

As the blades slowed to a stop, Tobias sat back in his

chair, weak with relief. "That was around the time Imogen and Anna were ill."

His father looked up, eyes guarded. "Yes."

"Why not simply destroy the automatons? Why bring them back here?"

For a moment, his father looked wistful. "Magnus's experiments were at first amusing, amazing even. He could make the dolls walk, or dance, or perform household tasks."

He shook himself, his tone growing harder. "But when they became too independent, I began to fear for the safety of my family. I told him to stop. He claimed that I had asked him to enhance my creations, and he had done it all at my request."

"And?" Tobias prompted.

"He demanded payment. Exorbitant payment. I didn't have that kind of money. I threatened to chop them to bits. He claimed the magic he had infused them with would rebound on the family if I so much as chipped the paint. I was forced to drag them from one end of Europe to the other like millstones around my neck. Still, I thought if I could keep them a secret, we would all be safe."

"And then Magnus turned up here."

His father slumped in his chair. "When I heard he was in London, I tried to move the trunks from this house to a tiny property I purchased under a false name. And yet, he still managed to steal them from me. Magnus knew what his silence was worth. I didn't dare anger him, and he used that advantage to the fullest."

So that was why he showed up at the garden party and as a dinner guest. Magnus had kept his father at a metaphorical gunpoint. *And I trusted him. What a fool. I should be put away in a straight waistcoat to keep me from making a mess of anything else.*

His father got up, walked to the window. "Now he is dead, and I have no idea where they are hidden."

"He can't expose you now."

"Magic is forbidden in the Empire. One word of their existence, and I shall be ruined. The family will be finished."

"Then we have to find them."

"Of course." His father didn't sound hopeful. Instead, he found two glasses and poured whisky into both. He passed one to his son.

The story of the dolls made sense, and matched what little Tobias remembered from so long ago. Yet for someone trying to keep the automatons a secret, Lord Bancroft had offered a generous reward for their return. This was their tale all right, but not all of it. His father was still holding something back.

Anger singed what was left of his mood. He left the whisky on the desk, sickened by the smell of it.

"There are other things to talk about," Bancroft said, returning to his chair. "The Gold King was impressed by the brooch you made for your mother."

Tobias blinked. "When did he tell you that?"

"When he came to complain about finding our knife stuck in his streetkeeper's leg."

"Ah."

"He's taken an interest in you and mentioned that he may have an opening on his staff. I told him you would think about it. It seems your tinkering might have a use after all."

"You found me a job?" Tobias asked incredulously. "With a steam baron?"

The pater's eyes narrowed with the full force of Jovian thunder. "The family needs Keating's favor. The fact that his daughter has taken a shine to you doesn't go amiss, either."

"Ugh."

"She's a pretty girl. You just need to be civil."

It was never that simple, but Tobias was tired of arguing right then. *It seems my value as a pawn is not yet over.* Magnus. Keating. His father. There was not much to choose among them. He had come to hate them all because, despite what he said to Evelina, he could see no realistic way to escape them. Not without throwing his mother and sisters to the wolves.

He'd been surprised to find he possessed a sense of duty. And rather less pride than he expected, too. He had the makings of a good man, but not a great one. Not the rebel with the burning torch of truth.

In his mind's eye, Serafina's chest rose, and it fell. Was that a smirk on those red, red lips?

"In the meantime," Lord Bancroft said, topping up his glass, "there is Holmes to consider."

Tobias had nearly forgotten the detective. "Feed him dinner and send him on his way. There's nothing here to find. Magnus is gone. Let our bad luck die with him."

Bancroft's face set. "If only it were that simple."

The words were an eerie echo of his thoughts.

Tobias left his father's office a few minutes later, his head pounding and his stomach queasy. Nothing for Holmes to find? Of course there was. Only the great Lord Bancroft wasn't telling his son what that was, so how the blazes was he going to forestall disaster?

Tobias stopped outside the parlor, listening to the murmur of voices. The last of the daylight was fading, painting the corridor in washes of gray. Inside the room, drinks were being poured, relaxing the guests the way the color was relaxing out of the sky, leaving behind a blurred, twilight mood.

Evelina had said it was someone in the house who had killed Grace Child. It had been a violent, frantic act. Wasn't that usually done by someone driven to the brink, lashing out like a drowning swimmer? Someone with secrets? Someone under the thumb of powerful enemies and in danger of ruin?

Tobias turned and looked at the study door, wondering.

CHAPTER THIRTY-EIGHT

You know my method. It is founded upon the observance of trifles.
—Sherlock Holmes, as recorded by John H. Watson, M.D., "The Boscombe Valley Mystery"

"QUITE SIMPLY, MR. ROTH, I CAN SEE AT A GLANCE THAT YOU are an aficionado of things mechanical by the condition of your fingernails." Holmes set down his soup spoon, enjoying his display far too much to bother with mere consommé. "And your last mistress was an Italian opera singer. I can tell that by your shirtmaker, who uses a distinctive pattern of buttonhole on your front placket. The only seamstresses who know that trick come from warmer climes and generally work where their skills are most appreciated, which would be near the costume shops of the Italian opera. No doubt you purchased that garment on your way home some morning when your own was the worse for wear. However, you had a falling-out with the lady, and then a contretemps with your valet."

Holmes was just warming up, but Tobias was nearly at the boil. "How do you know that?"

"Your shoes."

"My shoes."

"Indubitably." Holmes folded his hands over his waistcoat, not even bothering to hide his gloat.

"Is he always like this?" Imogen whispered under her breath.

"Wait for it," Evelina muttered. "I feel a coup de grâce coming on."

"Let's have it." Tobias waggled his fingers with a come-hither gesture, turning a furious red about the ears. "How do my shoes betray my amorous missteps?"

"There is a scrape of gold paint along one heel. Your valet would have caught it if he paid closer attention to his duties. The mark is a particular gaudy shade used only in one establishment in town that has been—until recent events—devoted to German opera. I would think only a young man banished from the exquisite delights of *bel canto* would resort to the Royal Charlotte."

Tobias cringed at the name, which meant Holmes had scored.

"Isn't that the one attacked by a giant crab?" Holmes put in, mischief at the corners of his mouth.

"Squid," Tobias said.

Everyone looked at him. His gaze darted around the table. "Or so I read."

Holmes raised an eyebrow in the curious silence.

"What a delightful roast of lamb, Mother," Imogen said brightly to Lady Bancroft, who fielded the comment with the expertise of a world-class cricketer.

While his wife prattled about mint sauce at the other end of the table, Evelina noticed Lord Bancroft staring moodily at his plate. Flushed with too much wine, he had the air of someone looking for a fight. She picked at her food nervously, never entirely letting her attention wander from him.

However, he opened with an innocuous gambit. "I had no idea a consulting detective would also be acquainted with the musical arts."

She relaxed a degree. Her uncle liked musical discussions.

"I have my favorites," he said. "I am particularly fond of Tartini."

"Violin?"

Holmes took a sip of wine. "*The Devil's Trill* is a quite magnificent piece."

"A rather sensationalist title."

"That does not lessen its beauty."

"I understand that someone in Copenhagen has invented

a type of closet that will play *Don Giovanni* on a mechanical mandolin while it rotates," said Lady Bancroft enthusiastically. "One can be serenaded while selecting the day's wardrobe."

Holmes looked like he'd accidentally bitten into a lemon.

Bancroft's silverware clattered on the china plate as he attacked the lamb. "I am not a devotee of the Italian aesthetic."

The detective forked up a bite of potato. "That's right. You were ambassador to Austria. Mozart and marzipan."

"The Viennese tradition has much to recommend it."

Holmes smiled, but it was disarming. "I'll grant you Beethoven, but you must keep Strauss out of my path."

Bancroft grumbled something, but it was muffled by his wineglass. He was drinking a great deal, but had obviously had practice. His speech was barely slurred. Evelina bent her head over her plate, paying careful attention to her peas. Her uncle was a little too fond of his own opinions to make a comfortable dinner guest—at least not when there were other equally dominant men in the room.

She carefully picked up the silver container of mint sauce, aimed it at her plate, and pushed the button on the nozzle. A puff of steam gently curled from the lid, and a dollop of sauce plopped onto her lamb, warmed to exactly the correct temperature. A chased-silver boiler sat in the center of the table, connecting a half dozen such condiment dispensers, including butter, gravy, and red currant sauce. As a consequence of this latest invention for dining *en famille,* there were no servants hovering in the room. A little steam whistle sat atop the boiler, with a dainty pull-chain one could use to summon the next course.

"What did you think of your dance with Captain Smythe last night?" Imogen murmured.

"He's used to cavalry charges."

"You didn't dance after the intermission. You sat with Tobias instead. Mother noticed." Imogen poked her under the table. "I noticed. Is there something I should know?"

"I wasn't feeling quite the thing. That was after Dr. Magnus made a nuisance of himself. Tobias was being kind."

Imogen sobered for a moment, but it didn't last. "Is that all? Nothing more than that? Did you waltz with him?"

Evelina blinked, feeling her ears going hot as Tobias's had a moment ago. "Once. Your brother is an adequate dancer."

"Evelina Cooper, you have no romance in you!"

She looked across at Tobias, feeling her chest tighten. He was so handsome it was hard to keep her girlish thoughts from dribbling into the rest of her brain like runaway treacle. "I beg to differ."

Imogen rolled her eyes toward her father. Evelina returned her attention that way. The conversation had turned to more serious matters, and the ambassador was pontificating.

"How can you question the prime minister's decision? You are one of the new men, Holmes. Science all the way. No room for sentiment."

Her uncle could—and would—argue with anything if it satisfied a point of logic, but Evelina held her tongue. What were they talking about?

Holmes shook his head. "I do not argue with science. I might quibble with its misuse by demagogues."

Bancroft reacted like a bull spotting a red flag, nostrils flaring. "One of the gentlemen rebels we hear so much about lately?"

Holmes's eyes went wide for a split second. Bancroft had surprised him. "I beg your pardon?"

"Are you one of those who would see the steam barons blasted from their own engines?"

"As diverting a sight as that might prove, why should I wish that? What would it gain?"

Tobias hitched forward on his chair, visibly inserting himself into the debate. "Do you find it logical that one group of manufacturers has been allowed to acquire so much power?"

Holmes gave a dry laugh. "To play the devil's advocate, there is precedent. England has seen the great lords of the middle ages and the ascendancy of the Church. The public has simply consented to a different type of feudalism. Regardless of where my own sentiments might lie, who am I to question the public will?"

"I've heard that theory." Tobias looked grave. "Some believe the nation will go so far as to crumble into petty kingdoms, each with its own baron. Such will be the demise of the Empire."

Bancroft was turning pale. From what little Evelina knew of his politics, not long ago he would have agreed with his son. However, Jasper Keating had been his guest not many nights ago. If he'd switched sides to further his career, it wouldn't sit well to have his son arguing against the Gold King in front of strangers.

Unfortunately, Uncle Sherlock had a mischievous look in his eye. "If the nation is in danger of breaking into factions, it is best that we preserve what unifying ideals we can."

"Such as?" asked Lord Bancroft.

Holmes looked around the table. "I play my small role in the upkeep of justice, and can speak first hand of the deficiencies of the system. If we as a community cannot give the people justice and the rule of law, can we blame them for looking to men like Jasper Keating for protection?"

Lord Bancroft narrowed his eyes. "Is that how you see your role? Supreme upholder of justice?"

Holmes lost his air of mockery. "I do not flatter myself so much. However, I have become increasingly conscious of the precarious balance of the nation. Power breeds resentment, and there is plenty of both in the air."

"I ask again, are you advocating revolution, Mr. Holmes?"

The word made Evelina shiver. She wanted to think it was just the cool air from the window behind her, but she dreaded the idea of riot in the streets. Too much would be destroyed—businesses, homes, schools, hospitals. She remembered what it was to be only a step ahead of hunger.

Her uncle inclined his head, considering. "I am merely sounding a note of caution."

"To whom?"

"To the guilty. To those who will not pursue the solution of a crime, especially when the poor and helpless have been victims."

Evelina tensed, catching the allusion to Grace Child. So did everyone else. The room became deathly still, only the distant bustle of the rest of the house audible.

Her uncle turned so that he faced Bancroft. "Don't you agree, Lord Bancroft?"

Lord Bancroft frowned. "You overreach yourself. No man can be judge and jury."

Holmes gave a dry smile. "I am a consulting detective. I detect."

"And in doing so, you restore the natural order of things?"

Sherlock's eyebrows drew together. "So I would hope."

"Then I would ask you to restore order to my household and remove your niece."

Shocked, Evelina's fork slipped from her fingers. "My lord?"

"She has been throwing herself at my son."

"Father!" Tobias exclaimed.

Evelina's heart froze. She was half out of her chair before she realized she was standing. A protest formed on her lips, but she realized with horror that she had no grounds to defend herself. She hadn't thrown herself at Tobias, but she'd not discouraged him, either. Not really.

Tobias was on his feet, too, features rigid and angry. "How dare you! Evelina is innocent."

Bancroft drained his glass, pointedly ignoring his son. "Forgive my boy, Mr. Holmes. He enjoys his dramatics. Should have been on the stage, like all his whores."

His statement was so stunningly clumsy that no one spoke. A heavy silence followed, broken only by the sound of Bancroft's glass hitting the table. *He's drunk.*

Imogen grabbed her arm and pulled her back to her seat. Evelina felt her friend trembling, but her own hand was oddly steady. Maybe she'd been expecting this moment all along.

Her uncle remained seated and silent, watching everything like a cat about to pounce. "I understand the maid who was murdered was with child."

Bancroft snorted loudly. "No doubt it would have been a waste of air, like all my children."

Tobias turned to his father, his face white. "A waste of air, *like all your children*?"

Bancroft's face slackened. Evelina couldn't believe what she had just heard. *Lord Bancroft was Grace's lover?* Lady Bancroft sat frozen, like a woman turned to marble.

Tobias looked around the table, his gaze quickly touching on each person there, and then landing again on his father with a look of horror. Then he stormed from the room.

Bancroft lurched to his feet, his napkin slithering to the floor. He swayed a moment, as if letting the wine fumes settle. He turned to Holmes. "You're nothing but a busybody with a chemistry set."

Holmes gave a slow blink. "Indeed. And I know how to make an admirable stink."

Wordlessly, Lord Bancroft marched for the door, staggering just a little to navigate through the opening. Silence fell, breathless and seemingly endless.

Evelina caught sight of Lady Bancroft's pale face. The woman was distraught. "I'm so incredibly sorry. I have never . . . he's never . . ." Words failed her as her chin began to tremble. "I've not seen him like this since . . ."

She seemed incapable of finishing a sentence. Evelina exchanged a quick glance with Imogen, who rose to comfort her mother. Uncle Sherlock was staring after Bancroft. Evelina fingered her water glass, half temped to throw it, if she were only certain whom to blame.

"Very instructive," Sherlock said almost to himself.

"How?" Evelina demanded.

"Judging by the evening as a whole, Bancroft would be a formidable opponent when sober. But of course, that is just the start of it."

Imogen was helping Lady Bancroft from the chair, no doubt to assist to her bed. Evelina rose to help. She had barely taken one step to the side when she felt a rush of air skim her cheek. At the same moment, glass shattered behind her. Instinct made her drop to the ground, letting the soft carpet cushion her fall. A chair crashed, and Lady Bancroft screamed, high and shrill. A cascade of smashing china cut her cry short.

Sour fear filled Evelina's mouth. She blinked, trying to look around without moving her head. Was it safe?

The pool of light cast by the gas chandelier spilled over the edge of the table. Evelina was curled on her side, knees tucked to her chest. She had dived for the dark space beneath the dining table, and the forest of chair and table legs made a comforting barricade.

Glass littered the carpet like misplaced chips of ice. Carefully, she rolled to her hands and knees, bumping her head on the table as she went. The cloth had been pulled halfway off the far side of the table, making a tent. It blocked her vision, but she could hear everything. Running feet. Servants' voices. Lady Bancroft crying. She crawled for the edge of the table, but pierced her hand on a shard of glass. Cursing, she eased out from the lip of the table, rising cautiously.

It was chaos. Lady Bancroft was swooning in a chair, Dora cradling her head while two footmen braced to lift her limp form. Imogen was down on the floor, bending over the dark shape of Sherlock Holmes.

"What happened?" Evelina demanded.

"He's shot!"

Evelina was around the table in a moment. Imogen looked up, her eyes huge. She was pressing a napkin against his shoulder, staunching the blood. Her hands were slick and red, the skirts of her dinner gown splattered beyond repair. "What do I do?"

Heart hammering, Evelina knelt for a better look. Her hands shook, and not just from the shock of the attack. For all her uncle's frustrating habits, she genuinely loved him, and not just because he was a genius. He understood her. They never tried to fix each other. They never played games. She couldn't afford to lose him.

His face was in shadow, but she could see his teeth were clenched against the pain of his wound. No spurting blood, no shards of bone glistening in the lamplight, but it was still serious. She found his good hand and squeezed it. To her surprise, he returned the pressure.

"I'll send for Dr. Watson," she said, forcing her voice to sound level.

He gave a barely perceptible sigh of relief. "Preserve the scene. Do it. I'll survive."

Exasperated, Evelina swore under her breath. "I don't want to leave you."

"Miss Roth can hold my hand, but she cannot investigate. She doesn't know my methods. You do."

Evelina wanted to protest, but instead, she nodded. Evidence didn't seem to matter now, but it would later.

His mouth twitched. "Good." It was so faint she might have missed it.

A dozen thoughts jammed as the last moments replayed themselves. The bullet had nearly hit her. If she hadn't stood, would she be dead? Or had the shooter been waiting for her to move? Evelina rose just as Bigelow hurried into the room.

"What is happening, please?" he demanded in the voice of a man whose universe was imploding.

"Send for Dr. Watson," she said, struggling to recall where the doctor lived now that he was married. The mental exertion helped. She was calmer by the time she remembered the address and wrote it down. "And help Miss Roth to make my uncle comfortable."

She slipped out the side door of the house, moving as silently as she could. Some of the servants had run into the garden, but none had gone far. There was someone out there shooting people. Without one of the men of the house leading the charge, who would put themselves in harm's way? *Me, apparently. No one else is looking for clues.*

The garden was bathed in the eerie glow of a full moon. The gold-tinged gaslights that lined the street didn't cast their beams that far. Evelina shivered in the cool night. She didn't see anyone moving in the yard. Were they already gone?

Memories stole over her—of the garden party, of sitting with Imogen looking at the gold and gems in the tiny silk bag. Too much had happened in the last handful of days. People were dead. She prayed her uncle wouldn't be next, the victim of a fevered wound.

She struggled not to let her thoughts go further than that,

but they did. If the father of Grace Child's baby was Lord Bancroft, that gave him a very close link to the victim. But that wasn't what bothered her, because plenty of men slept with their maids and then tossed them into the street when they grew round with child. It would play badly during a political campaign, but it was a scandal most men could survive, though it might cause a few cold silences at the dinner table. And no doubt Lord B had appetites like any man.

What bothered her was that Lord Bancroft, as far as she knew, would have been more likely to seek out a sophisticated woman for his pleasures. What would a serving girl, however pretty, have to offer? It was the gold that complicated things. As her uncle had pointed out, Grace had probably been waiting for someone when she had been killed. *And Lord Bancroft had fallen asleep in the study.* If she was right, he was the one who was to receive the gold.

She had desperately wanted to protect the Roth family. She still did. But what if Lord Bancroft was guilty—maybe not of murder, but of some other crime? Her uncle's unerring instincts had already ripped the matter open like a surgeon exposing an infected wound. He could be brutal, but he was very rarely wrong. And so someone had shot him.

A shaking deep in her gut found its way to her limbs in a long, horrified shudder. She had been strong inside the dining room, wishing herself to be as steady as Imogen, as cool as her uncle. Now it would be too easy to sit down and wail like a scalded cat.

Which accomplished exactly nothing. She clenched her jaw and forced herself to think rationally, one step at a time. There was a sundial surrounded by a clump of low bushes that sat a stone's throw from the side of the house. It was the only possible cover. From there, the shooter could have seen straight into the dining room window.

"Evelina."

She turned to see Tobias coming from the front of the house. "What are you doing out here?"

The moonlight silvered his hair. He'd taken off his tie, so the open collar of his shirt showed the strong muscles of his throat. She felt his heat as he drew closer, tantalizing in the cold air.

He put his hand on her arm. There was no mistaking the affection in his touch. "You're cold."

"I came to look for evidence," she said.

"Oh." He looked around, as if expecting to see a smoking gun on the grass. He smelled like whisky. "I'm sorry about what Father said. I went to try to talk to him. He's passed out in his study. There's no point tonight." His voice was so tight it sounded painful. "But I will. I promise you that."

"My uncle . . ."

He leaned close. "I know. Terrible."

"The police . . ."

Tobias made a resigned motion, but he sounded strained. "I'll send word to Inspector Lestrade. I just wish that they didn't need to see Father this way. It will do his career no good."

There was a bit of irony, given how Bancroft had tried to conceal Grace's death. She bit her lip, holding the words back. "I've sent for my uncle's friend Dr. Watson."

"That makes sense." Tobias's tone eased. "But Evelina, forget what Father said about Grace's baby. Don't tell anyone, for Mother's sake. It's just too hard for her. And don't tell Lestrade. That would just make things look bad, and it doesn't prove anything."

His fingers brushed her cheek, coaxing. She looked away, too confused to answer.

"Please." Gently, he turned her face back so that she looked into his eyes. "Do this for me. For Imogen."

"All right," she said, her heart winning over reason. He brushed his lips to her forehead gently, but she still felt miserable.

The ground had shifted between them. The dizzying happiness had been sullied. She wanted to argue, to rage, to plead the last hours away until they were back to that brief second where everything looked possible. But not even magic could do that.

She tried to gather her wits. "We should check the grounds for clues so I can get back to Uncle Sherlock." Though she wondered, if she did find traces of the shooter, whether it would be anything she could take to Lestrade.

Tobias studied her for a moment, but then his face relaxed. "Lead the way, my pretty detective."

Evelina nodded, desperate to trust the affection in his eyes.

Chapter Thirty-nine

WITCH TRIAL ENDS IN GUILTY VERDICT

Actress Eleanor Reynolds was found guilty of use of magic and, with unexpected lenience, sentenced to an indefinite term as a guest of Her Majesty's Scientific Laboratories. Sir Philip Amory, who represented Mrs. Reynolds, had no comment. Illegal betting on the outcome of the trial was reported to be fierce.

—*The Bugle*

QUALITY OF MERCY STRAINED, SAYS FOREIGN CRITIC

The opinions of our peers from other nations are always instructive. Pietro Costanzo, Conte del'Arco and learned commentator on the Continental judiciary, has been in London during the arrest and trial of the celebrated dramatic actress Mrs. Eleanor Reynolds. His official observations of the one-day trial are as yet unwritten, but in conversation his opinion is nothing short of scathing. "The charges are based solely on a trunk of props left in her house after her company's last production of *Macbeth*. That, and witness testimony from a hostile neighbor. Where are the fruits of her crimes? Where are her accomplices? Where are her motives? And how can citizens of any other nation confidently do business with an empire that disregards the basic rule of law?" In this writer's opinion, it is unfortunate that the spirit of the trial did not heed the actress's last play, *The Merchant of Venice*, which contains the Bard's famous lines on mercy and justice. Sentencing was carried out immediately, and in a surprise move that smacks more of medical curiosity than mercy, Mrs. Reynolds has been sent to Her Majesty's Scientific Laboratories. Farewell, dear Nellie, we do not expect to see you again.

—*The London Prattler*

London, April 14, 1888
HILLIARD HOUSE

2p.m. Saturday

EVELINA WAS SLUMPED OVER HER DESK, HER HEAD IN HER hand. Her stomach felt queasy, as if she had eaten a bucket of grease, but it was actually a constant, barely manageable case of nerves. She needed sleep. She needed to not be worrying about Uncle Sherlock, who was lying in a bedroom down the hall. She needed to lose herself in a problem so she would stop thinking about the fact that one or both of them had narrowly escaped death.

Helen. The cube repeated it, interrupting Evelina's thoughts yet again. *Helenhelenhelen.*

She was cradling the cube in her lap like a cat. It seemed happy there, as if physical contact was necessary to the metal thing. Mouse and Bird were playing tag on the bed, getting tangled in the pillows and coverlets. The window was open to the garden, the cool morning fresh and sunny. It would have been idyllic except for the constables roaming through the garden, trampling any available clues.

With an effort, she dragged her attention back to the coded letter. Every time she had attempted a solution, she'd given up in despair. This time looked to be no more successful. She had her uncle's pamphlet open on the desk, the letter, and a piece of notepaper in front of her. In the middle of the desk, she'd pulled out her copy of the coded message with spaces below it for the key.

J	E	Y	R	B	A	G	Z	T	L	J	L	P	W	G	W	P	P	E	F	L	E	O	Z	V	Z	I

Helenhelenhelen.

She patted the cube absently.

HELEN.

She paused, thoughts bumping together to make a new combination. She got up, setting the cube on her dresser, and opened her wardrobe. With one thing and another, she hadn't yet sent the silk dress she'd worn at the dinner party to be cleaned. She rifled through the clothes until she saw the familiar rose-colored fabric. A search of its pockets produced what she wanted. She returned to the desk with the card that had spit out of the longcase clock. She had put it into her pocket when she'd been helping Nick back to her room after Dr. Magnus had left.

It was the one other cipher that she'd seen recently. She studied the card and compared it to the note from the gold, but that was a pointless exercise. Perhaps her uncle might have seen similarities and differences, but they both looked like a jumble of letters to her. But what had Magnus said? The cipher from the clock was one that both he and Bancroft knew.

So she could point to two people who knew a cipher. A twinge of satisfaction brought a half smile to her lips.

Helen, the cube repeated.

Evelina furrowed her brow, inching the problem forward a degree. She didn't know what the deva in the cube could perceive, or whether it was more or less than Mouse and Bird because they could understand the cube no better than she could. But for the moment, she would assume it had a similar range of perceptions. Therefore, if the people writing the ciphered message had been in the warehouse, and the cube was in the warehouse, it could easily have seen or heard them use the key. That opened up possibilities.

"Helen," she murmured.

The whole idea of Helen as divine truth was something of a hobbyhorse of Magnus's. In addition, the cube kept calling her by that name. It might have been the cube's way of trying to help.

While it was unlikely that a mysterious metal box possessed by an ancient spirit would give her the key to a coded message, not much that had happened in the past week could be construed as terribly logical. There was nothing to lose by trying, so she wrote in "Helen" as the key.

J	E	Y	R	B	A	G	Z	T	L	J	L	P	W	G	W	P	P	E	F	L	E	O	Z	V	Z	I
H	E	L	E	N	H	E	L	E	N	H	E	L	E	N	H	E	L	E	N	H	E	L	E	N	H	E

The typical way of decoding these ciphers was to find the letters of the cipher text at the top of the table and the letters of the key along the left-hand side. Where that row and column met in the table would spell out the solution. Evelina followed this method for a while and simply got more nonsense. She was ready to give up in disgust, but there was one last trick to try. Uncle Sherlock's book pointed out that sometimes those positions were rearranged various ways, and the key to the code could be found in the columns, and the letters of the message itself along the rows, so she tried that.

She found *H* at the top of the table, ran her finger down to *J* and left to *C*. She wrote *C* in the first block of the solution. Then she dithered a bit around the fact that *E* led to another *E*, but finally settled on the fact the solution letter was *A*. Then it was *L* to *Y* to *N*. She started to get excited by five letters in, tingly by the time she was halfway through, and almost dizzy when she got to the end.

J	E	Y	R	B	A	G	Z	T	L	J	L	P	W	G	W	P	P	E	F	L	E	O	Z	V	Z	I
H	E	L	E	N	H	E	L	E	N	H	E	L	E	N	H	E	L	E	N	H	E	L	E	N	H	E
C	A	N	N	O	T	C	O	P	Y	C	H	E	S	T	P	L	E	A	S	E	A	D	V	I	S	E

"Cannot copy chest please advise," she said aloud, and then said it again. "Cannot copy chest. Please advise." Copy? That opened up more questions—many, many more.

She picked up the cube, staring at it. "Are you Athena's Casket?" she asked.

She felt it pondering the statement, struggling with how to make itself understood. Inspired now, she set down the cube and returned to her desk and quickly decoded the message on the clock's card. It read, "Beware the untruth." She made an impatient noise. That was about as specific as a fairground fortune-teller. One couldn't throw a dinner bun in London without hitting a liar.

There was a frantic knocking on the bedroom door. Mouse and Bird dove into the bed cushions. Alarmed, Evelina shuffled away her papers and all but tossed the cube into her wardrobe before she unlocked the bedroom door.

Imogen rushed in, her face streaked with tears. "Evelina, have you read the newspapers?"

A rush of fear made Evelina clutch at her friend's arms, pulling her close. "No, what's happened?"

Imogen thrust a copy of the *Prattler* at her. "Read this."

Before she did anything else, she drew Imogen inside and made her sit on the bed. The girl was shaking. Mouse and Bird emerged from the cushions, curious to see what was going on. Evelina turned her desk chair around and sat, reading the article about Mrs. Reynolds's trial and conviction. "Somehow I knew this was how it would go. Hardly anyone accused of magic is ever acquitted."

"But she's innocent!" Imogen cried. "I overheard. At the Westlakes' ball. Mrs. Reynolds is an illegitimate cousin to the duchess!"

"Hush!" Evelina waved urgently. "Keep your voice down!"

Imogen put a hand over her mouth, realizing what she had done. When she spoke again, it was more quietly. "I was with Bucky when I overheard. The Gold King had been trying to help her, but he was warning her to stop. He said nothing was going to save Nellie Reynolds and it would just drag the duchess down if anyone found out she was helping."

"He was probably right." A cynical part of Evelina thought Jasper Keating could save or condemn anyone he pleased and was just pulling the duchess's strings, but dwelling on that would only upset Imogen more.

Her friend was crying in earnest now, her slender shoulders shaking with distress. "We knew she was innocent and we didn't say anything! Surely we could have done something. Why didn't we?"

Evelina closed her eyes for a moment, feeling a pang of regret. She moved onto the bed, sliding her arm around Imogen's shoulders. She didn't speak. There wasn't a lot she could say.

"Why?" Imogen whispered harshly. "Why is it so hard to object if something is unjust? Why isn't the duchess allowed to support her cousin? She's a *duchess,* for pity's sake. People should listen to her."

But the old aristocracy's sun was setting, and a ducal coronet didn't mean as much as it had in their grandparents' day. The steam barons dominated the Empire now. It wasn't as if Imogen didn't know the facts, but these last few days would have been the first time she'd felt the full measure of her helplessness. "I'm sorry," Evelina whispered. "How did you and Bucky hear this?"

Imogen bit her lip. "It was an accident. He said not to do anything, and to keep it all a secret because we should never have overheard. He promised to talk to me about it later."

"He gave you good advice."

"I thought somehow we'd find a way to prove her innocent—figure it out the way your uncle does. If Nellie Reynolds did nothing wrong, we should have been able to show that to a judge."

"It's very hard to prove a negative."

"I know," Imogen said bitterly. "In the moment it seemed a heroic idea. When I think about it now, it sounds incredibly naive."

Evelina winced, thinking Imogen sounded very much like she had at the start of her so-called investigation of Grace Child's murder. "Bucky is no fool and you read the papers, Imogen. Barely a month goes by without the trial of some magic user. If the steam barons keep everyone afraid of magic, no one will try to use it against them. And the betting just keeps the public appetite sharp."

"I know," Imogen said miserably. "I overheard Father tell Mother that he unexpectedly won a great deal of money on Nellie Reynolds's trial. Enough to pay for my Season. He laughed."

Evelina felt sick as Imogen turned even paler. How was

any girl supposed to feel about her parties and dresses, knowing they were paid for like that?

"Worst of all, I haven't been able to talk to Bucky." Imogen turned her silvery eyes on Evelina. They were bright with tears. "There was no opportunity to decide what we could or couldn't do, so our chance slipped away."

Evelina pondered that, trying to catch up to the fact that Imogen's heart was readying itself for more than a battle of wits with her brother's best friend. "Where is Bucky?"

Imogen pulled out a dainty kerchief and mopped her nose. "Papa heard that I turned down Stanford Whitlock. He's furious. Now, if I want to go anywhere without him or Mama on my heels, I'm going to have to climb out a window."

That made no sense. "But the Penners have plenty of money, and Bucky is a hundred times more capable than Whitlock. Surely they can see that."

"Whatever the Penners have, the Whitlocks have more. His father owns a bank. And Stanford isn't the only prospect on Father's list. The Westlakes' son has a title. Buckingham Penner is very much a second choice by those standards."

Evelina cursed under her breath. "This isn't fair."

Imogen's eyes filled with tears. "I won't marry someone I don't like, much less love. I won't." Lord B probably had no idea how stubborn his daughter really was. They were in for a storm. "This is all my fault! I knew something was wrong, but I didn't want to believe it!"

Evelina was bewildered. "What do you mean?"

"There is something going on between my father and Keating's cousin, Harriman. I overheard them at the dinner party." Imogen closed her eyes, as if recalling the scene. "Harriman said he'd done exactly as Papa instructed, no more and no less. That he had returned the crates to the warehouse and informed Mr. Keating of their arrival. And then he went on to say that whoever said there was a missing article was quite mistaken. Does that make any sense at all?"

Evelina had gone numb. "A bit."

Imogen had known this for days. A feeling of betrayal

swamped Evelina for a moment, but it didn't stay. What daughter would want to believe her father was at the core of a crime? She couldn't blame her friend.

But Imogen looked hollow with grief. "If I'd said something, maybe this would all be over by now. Maybe your uncle wouldn't have been shot."

Evelina's chest ached with a brew of anger and sadness. "We can't know that."

Imogen took another shuddering breath. "This week has been so horrible! First Grace and then . . . everything. Then what Papa said about Grace. After last night, Mother won't get out of bed."

It was true. Lady Bancroft had retreated altogether. The revelation of her husband's infidelity had been bad enough. That it happened at the dinner table, follow by a shooting, was intolerable. After the murders and the Disconnection, it had been the last straw.

"It all reminds me of my nightmares," Imogen said, taking quick gulps of air in an effort to keep control of her words. "I'm trapped in the dark, and I can't get away from whatever is coming."

Then the dam broke. Imogen wept and wept, her heart breaking. Evelina held her, feeling unutterably sad, but she had nothing to offer. As long as she had known Imogen, she'd been able to protect her, but over the last week, she'd lost that ability. It felt strangely like exile.

"Oh, Evelina," Imogen sobbed. "The worst of it is how little courage I seem to have. I thought I was braver. What if they had you on trial, instead of Nellie Reynolds? Would I still be too much of a coward to speak out?"

Evelina shivered and squeezed her tight. "Promise me that you'll be that coward."

LATER, EVELINA HOVERED at the door of the guest room. Wounded as he was, Holmes had been cared for overnight at Hilliard House. Evidently, one didn't evict even the most provoking dinner guest after he was shot at the dinner table.

"Dr. Watson?" she called softly.

She slipped inside. The second-floor quarters were divided into a bedchamber and sitting room overlooking the back garden. They were meant for a male guest, with green walls and substantial leather furniture. A tiger skin rug sprawled in front of the fireplace.

Holmes was propped in a leather chair, an ottoman supporting his slippered feet. She looked around for Watson. He had collapsed in another chair, a frown darkening his deceptively benign face. Not that Dr. Watson wasn't benign—he was one of the best souls in the Empire—but a man didn't get to be her uncle's right-hand man without a good uppercut and the stamina of a draft horse.

Just not enough to outlast her uncle. Watson had the look of a man at the end of his rope. "Stop talking nonsense, Holmes. You've been shot."

Uncle Sherlock glanced down at the sling meant to hold his right arm still. "So I have. It's a tremendously motivating factor."

"For what?" Watson snapped. "Bleeding to death? The only motivation you should have is a desire to sleep."

Her uncle subsided a little. "I want a report, niece of mine. What have you found out about last night?" After casting a guilty glance at Watson, he fixed her with the look of a schoolmaster asking his student to recite lines, then his face softened. "What is the matter?"

"Imogen and Lady Bancroft are in a sorry state this morning. I'm worried for them." She could have added Holmes to that list, but he wouldn't have appreciated being included with two frail women.

"I have looked in on Lady Bancroft," Watson said. "I prescribed a dose of laudanum. The sleep will do her good. I offered the same to Miss Roth earlier this morning, but she declined."

Evelina nodded. "Thank you."

"I would think," said Holmes, "that a speedy resolution to this affair would be the best medicine. The longer it drags on, the more of a toll it takes upon a delicate constitution."

He was right. Worry alone helped nothing. She cleared her throat, picking a place to start her report. "I had a thorough look at the grounds before the police arrived this morning. There was a single set of footprints leading to and from the sundial in the garden to the back wall. The shooter approached by the back alley and used the sundial to hide while he took his shot."

"Anything else?"

"There was no litter or debris left behind. The prints looked to be from a fit adult male."

"The weapon was most likely a handgun," Watson offered, "judging from the size and velocity of the bullet." The doctor looked up at Evelina, his expression somewhere between fondness and exasperation. "You are looking lovely, my dear, although it pains me to find you mixed up in this gruesome affair. Really, you're too pretty a young lady to concern yourself with violence."

Evelina remembered a girlhood crush she had nurtured for the doctor and consoled herself with the knowledge that had the romance flourished, she would have eventually been obliged to smack him over the head. She sat down, smoothing her skirts. "This matter may be unpleasant, but the sooner it is solved, the sooner we can put it behind us."

Sherlock gave a razor-thin smile. "Just don't develop a taste for murder."

"Solving murders, you mean."

Watson heaved a tired sigh. "There are days I begin to think they are one and the same thing."

"There is one other piece of new information," she offered. "I have solved the cipher."

Her uncle's eyes lit up. "Indeed?"

Evelina pulled a folded scrap of paper from her pocket and reread it. "Cannot copy chest. Please advise," she said aloud to Sherlock and Watson. "I'm not sure what it means by copying."

"Ah," Holmes replied with a feline smile. "This grows interesting."

"I would have thought we were talking about someone melting down valuables for gold," said Evelina cautiously.

Holmes gave her a sharp look. "Perhaps theft is but half of it."

The doctor took the paper from her uncle and read it over. "How did you determine the key?"

"The clock on the landing uses one, and I knew both Magnus and Lord Bancroft knew it. The key is the name Helen. Dr. Magnus is obsessed with Helen as the personification of divine truth."

Watson handed the paper back to Holmes and gave her an avuncular smile. "Very observant."

"Excellent." Holmes tapped the fingers of his good hand on the chair.

"A lucky guess," she countered.

Her uncle gave a brief shake of his head. "Luck is percentages. Good percentages are aided by good deduction. The value in this is not the message but the key. I entertained the notion that Keating might have been at the heart of this matter after all, but it appears that is not the case. And again, the cipher could have been added to this stew of intrigue by Magnus, but my guess would be our host."

Oh. Evelina closed her eyes a moment, dreading the consequences for Tobias and Imogen and even young Poppy. She recalled the conversation with Tobias in the garden and his desire to shield his father's liaison with the murdered maid. "Are you sure? I know that Lord Bancroft was involved with Grace Child, but still . . ."

"Let us go over the facts again." Holmes said, a touch irritably. "Then we can decide what Lestrade does and does not need to know."

Her heart lifted a little at that, though it was hardly a guarantee. "The fact that he slept with Grace doesn't prove anything." But it implied a lot, and she could see from her uncle's face that he had already considered that.

And then that sense of hope crashed when she thought about the cipher. "Nonetheless, Imogen came to me with information this morning that I'm afraid does her father no good."

"Do tell."

So she did. Holmes listened carefully. "What an unfortunate burden for so lovely a young lady. But how do you think it fits with what else we have learned?"

She knew very well that he had already made his conclusions, but spoke anyway. "If Bancroft was giving the owner of the warehouse instructions, there is little doubt that he is involved. To me it sounds as if whoever sent Grace with the gold was seeking instruction from His Lordship, since the note came in the same package."

"Quite. And I would suspect that receiving no answer, the author—most likely this Harriman—acted on his own and so set the cat among the pigeons."

"But what exactly was going on in the warehouse?" Not even Magnus had been sure. "Was it more than just melting down Keating's gold as shipments arrived?"

"Indeed it was more. First and foremost, this was a very elaborately staged theft. There are a half dozen criminal masterminds in London who will be jealous of our host's acumen once they read it in the papers."

Panic surging, Evelina shot to her feet. This was exactly why she hadn't wanted her uncle involved. "That can't be done. Exposure would ruin his family, and they are my friends. There has to be another way!"

"I have been shot," her uncle said sharply. "I am not in the mood for you to make excuses on behalf of a man who just last night was doing his best to cast aspersions on your character."

Evelina bit her lip, searching for a way to distract him. "I have a theory about why they haven't found the casket."

"Later. I will listen to it all when I am ready to do so. Right now I want to hear everything from the top," Holmes snapped.

Evelina bridled at his tone, but held her tongue in a mutinous silence.

"My pipe, Watson." Her uncle held out his hand irritably. "You brought it, I hope."

"Of course, Holmes."

There was no way to pack and light a pipe one-handed, so the dutiful doctor searched the mantel and picked up a briar pipe. The ritual of preparing it took a moment, so Evelina closed her eyes, searched her memory, and began once again with the night she was surprised by the grooms in the attic.

Watson paused at the fireplace, lighting the pipe from the perpetual flame that burned in the mouth of a carved stone dragon. The feature had been installed just days ago, a gift from the Gold King. Holmes accepted the pipe from Watson and nodded to Evelina to continue.

She went through the investigation, step by step. Apart from smoking, Holmes appeared asleep. Watson, however, listened carefully, and she realized this was the first time he had heard it—which was no doubt why her uncle was having her recount it all again. He would have remembered every scrap.

She had just reached the part about Magnus's death, when Sherlock raised a hand to halt the flow of words. "I want to talk to Lestrade, and I want to see your friend Nick. They will have the last pieces of this puzzle."

"NICK!" EVIE'S HUG damn near killed him, but he forced himself not to whimper like a beaten puppy. The embrace was worth the pain. She was soft in all the right places, the brush of her sweet-smelling hair reminding his body he'd slept alone too long. But she backed away before they sparked magic from each other.

He took off his hat, his hand over the cracked spot on the brim. His wardrobe and daylight weren't good friends. "Your bird found me. I came. It said someone here wanted a word."

She looked up at him with wide eyes. He looked a sight, he knew, with black eyes and bandages and more bruises than skin. He wasn't going to be performing for a few days, that was for sure—and that would be hard on his purse.

"Thank you for what you did," she said simply. "That was a terrible risk you took."

It had been, but he shrugged. The one good thing was that the Gold King had wanted the sorcerer dead. There was a chance he'd step in if they were caught, though Striker had his doubts about anything Jasper Keating promised. There was no love lost between master and man.

Evie took his arm, guiding him through the big house.

He'd been inside a few times now, but never with permission. With no active threat to counter, it was all he could do not to stare around him like a farmboy on his first trip to market.

"My uncle wants to talk to you."

"Sherlock Holmes?" He stopped in his tracks, bringing her up short. Her skirts swung like a bell.

"Who else? Uncle Mycroft never goes anywhere, much less to visit me."

Let himself be grilled by Evelina's genius uncle? Not bloody likely. But then he'd always had a curiosity to meet the man.

"Please, Nick." Her eyebrows puckered the same way they had when she was two feet tall. "He's trying to solve this once and for all."

Nick's side hurt enough that he was sure it was making him stupid. "All right."

He'd walked into Dr. Magnus's lair. He could do this. But pain and fatigue had robbed a lot of the swagger that had seen Nick through that encounter.

Still, Sherlock Holmes was alone, and he was not the imposing figure Nick had expected. The Great Detective was swathed in a silk brocade smoking gown, looking bloodless and weak, but his eyes glittered with the kind of focus Nick had seen in birds of prey. Evie said Holmes had been shot, and he believed it. Every so often, the fine skin around her uncle's eyes contracted as if he managed a wave of pain.

She marched Nick forward, a bit like a mother presenting her child. "This is my friend Nick."

Friend. He had been more than that, it seemed, the night they'd called the devas. Was there ever going be a chance for truth between them?

The man's uninjured fingers drummed briefly on the arm of the chair. "The Indomitable Niccolo."

"The world's greatest consulting detective, I presume." Nick's side throbbed. He had been stitched and bandaged, but he was running a fever and the colors in the room were a little too bright.

Holmes studied him, and Nick looked back. There was a family resemblance between Holmes and Evelina, something in the shape of the eyes, but he had to look for it. The bigger resemblance was in their circumstances. They were gentry. He was not. His envy tasted bitter on his tongue.

Holmes flicked his fingers, as if dismissing preliminaries. "I asked you here because you knew the man they called Magnus better than the rest of us."

Evie released him, stepping back until she found a chair to sit on. Keeping a safe distance between them.

That left Nick standing like a prisoner in the dock. "I did a bit of work for him, that's all."

Holmes lifted a brow. "My niece is very discreet, and avoids telling me a great many things I already surmise. Magnus threatened her, so I will agree for now that you worked for him, and had nothing to do with his death."

Nick kept his face utterly still. Evie remained immobile as the potted fern in the corner, her expression worried.

Holmes nodded, as if this was no more than he expected. "Magnus was, for want of a better term, an inventor. What was he working on? I understand he has made clocks and automatons, but what else?"

Nick brought the town house with its massive library into his mind's eye. "A lot of things. He had electric light. Chemical experiments. He had plans for an airship."

"The police found no such plans in Dr. Magnus's possessions. It was the one thing I had expected them to find."

Once more, Nick kept his face perfectly still.

"May I see them?" Holmes asked. He beckoned impatiently. "Come, come."

The plans were incriminating, stained with his blood and fresh from the house of a dead man. Nick had been afraid to leave them with his gear at the circus, just in case anyone went through his things, so he'd kept the plans inside his coat. He should have thrown them in the fire, and would have to eventually, but they were too beautiful to destroy. Slowly, he drew out the mechanical scroll and unlocked the mechanism.

"Please unfold them," Holmes asked, nodding ruefully at his injured arm.

Nick did as he was asked. The brass arm unrolled in sections and unfurled the silk drawings from what seemed an impossibly small space. "This seems a long way from a dead kitchen maid."

"But it is all of one piece, and this is perhaps a closer link than most."

Evie rose, moving to the other side of her uncle's chair. The three of them studied the plans.

"There has been much talk about Athena's Casket and its special powers," Holmes said. "Mycroft first brought the rumors to my attention when word got about that Schliemann had discovered where it had been buried. The casket seems to be a mythical beast-machine that holds the secret of limitless power by uniting magic with gears and pistons. But the one fact that keeps getting ignored is what Athena's Casket was actually used for."

"What do you mean?" Nick asked, forgetting about whom he was talking to and falling into the beauty of the neatly drawn airship plans.

Evelina tucked a strand of dark brown hair behind her ear. "Wasn't it for navigation?"

"If you believe the approved texts. Possibly more, if one accepts sketchier accounts." Holmes scowled at the plans. "And here we are. This ship has no power source."

"But that's the boiler there." Nick pointed. He could read and Striker understood mechanics. Together they had figured out most of what was on the scroll.

"The boiler is not big enough for significant propulsion. Furthermore, this has a large balloon, but it's not enough to lift a gondola this size. It would need an alternate source of lift." Holmes indicated a spot at the very front of the ship. "Here. All the power, lift, and navigation needed. An air deva."

Nick and Evelina both looked at him, startled. Nick found his voice first. "Pardon me, sir, but what would the likes of you know about that?"

Holmes's voice was sharp. "I have no affinity or understanding of the magical sciences. That does not mean I do not know of their existence, or of the theories surrounding certain inherited abilities." He gave them a significant look.

Evie opened her mouth, then closed it again when Holmes lifted a quelling finger.

"For now," he said, "all I need to know is that Magnus and others gave credit to old legends. So did Archimedes of Syracuse, who wrote the first accounts of flying ships and devices with the speech of men."

Nick's pulse quickened, which set his wound throbbing even harder. "But other men—here and now—want the casket, don't they?"

"An airborne war machine that requires next to no fuel? One with native intelligence?" The detective barked a laugh. "I can safely say that talk of it extends clear to Bohemia. Armed airfleets exist, but nothing with this potential. The steam baron who acquires the knowledge to create such ships will possess the nucleus of an unstoppable invasion force."

"Magnus said he wanted to put a spoke in their wheels."

"Dr. Magnus was a madman who would have used our outrage at the barons to open the doors to his own invasion." Holmes gave the plans back to Nick. "You had best keep these safe from official eyes. There is no telling who might wish to make use of them."

"Where is the casket?" Nick asked. "Do we have any idea?"

"You tell me." Holmes indicated a table with a lazy wave of his good hand. A book lay upon it, open to an engraving of a small chest richly decorated with gems and carved owls.

Nick shook his head. "I don't remember seeing anything like this in Dr. Magnus's things."

Holmes leaned back, clearly tired. "He never found it. An archaeologist named Heinrich Schliemann excavated it in Greece and shipped it to London. It was closely guarded, but supposedly never arrived. What do you think happened?"

Nick couldn't see why his opinion mattered, but he gave it anyway. "Who is to say that is true?"

"Precisely," Holmes replied. "I am beginning to suspect

that the entire operation was an elaborate scheme to harvest the gold from the artifacts. No one took the casket from the warehouse, because someone on the inside—someone with no idea what the casket could do—melted it down to nothing."

"Not quite," said Evelina.

Both men turned to look at her.

"The gold was just for show." She gave a sly smile. "They threw the insides out as scrap."

CHAPTER FORTY

8 p.m. Saturday

EVEN JASPER KEATING MUST HAVE KNOWN THE OLD AXIOM that the show must go on. With or without Athena's Casket, the gallery with his show of Greek treasures was due to open that night. Fashionable London was invited to experience the glory of the Gold King's archaeological bounty. Or, as Imogen quipped, booty.

The Roths—minus Lady Bancroft—went on ahead while Evelina got into a hansom with her uncle and Dr. Watson. No one except Sherlock Holmes thought he should be going anywhere, least of all his long-suffering doctor, but the game was afoot.

"I arranged for a wheeled chair to meet us there," the doctor said in a grumpy tone. "Lest the game no longer be afoot but prostrate."

"Did you bring it?" Uncle Sherlock asked Evelina, ignoring his friend.

"I did," she said, patting the basket in her lap. "Gold, gems, device, and decoded letter."

"Excellent," he said. "This should be most entertaining."

Evelina wasn't so sure. "What will happen to the casket?"

Holmes closed his eyes, leaning his head back against the cushions of the cab. "I imagine it will find its way into a ship. That is why it was originally created, after all."

"But do we really want to give such a marvelous thing to someone like Jasper Keating? What about armies of invading airships?"

"Holmes?" Dr. Watson piped up.

Her uncle didn't reply, but put on his inscrutable face and opened one eye.

"I would think that if the casket were designed to fly," said Watson, in his kindest voice, "it would yearn for the skies. It would be unkind to keep it locked in a museum."

Evelina gave him a grateful smile. The doctor had known almost nothing of devas until that afternoon, but was keeping up with the conversation like a trooper. "What about the gold and the letter?"

"I mean to expose a theft. You are holding the evidence. Athena's Casket is only one of many missing items."

"I follow the part about melting down the ancient objects for the gold," Watson said. "That explains why the maid had raw gold and jewels on her person. But wouldn't the melted objects be missed?"

"No," said Uncle Sherlock. "I surmise that Keating will see every item in his collection except the casket. That was too unusual a piece, with all its working parts, to replicate, but of all the pieces, it was the largest and most valuable. That made it far too tempting a prize for our thief to ignore, and so it was pronounced lost."

"Are you saying Harriman took it for himself?" Evelina asked.

"Assuredly."

"You say the other pieces were replicated. Replicated how?" asked Watson.

"I have my theories. I have but to test them."

"You're being cryptic again, and it's tiresome."

Sherlock closed his eye again. "I can promise you a good show, Watson. Mr. Keating will be one very angry man."

"But won't innocent people be hurt by that anger?" she asked, thinking again of Imogen and Tobias.

"Truth is impartial," her uncle replied evenly. "Even so, I will do my best to keep as many of your friends as I can from harm's way. I am not without my methods. You have my word on that."

That was somewhat reassuring, although she had no idea how her uncle would manage the Gold King. Evelina was starting to form an idea of what might happen, but it was like squinting through mist. There were outlines, but no details.

Lestrade had come by after Nick had left and reported that he had followed up on the matter of the Chinese workers. It turned out that Mr. Markham's observant tailors were a wealth of information. One had chanced to speak with a worker who had been allowed outside the warehouse to repair a window. He had said that the workers had been hired by Harriman. Their foreman—one of their own countrymen—kept them in virtual slavery. The most interesting fact was that some of them were goldsmiths.

The cab arrived at the gallery just as the sky was turning to indigo dusk. Evelina alighted, the basket over one arm. Keating's gallery wasn't in a large building on its own, just one door along a curving row of Georgian storefronts. The facade was pale stone, flanked by Corinthian pilasters. Through the door she could see a large open space, dotted with marble plinths holding statues and other objets d'art.

The streetlights were on, washing the front of the building in the gold light of Jasper Keating's empire. Her uncle waved away the wheeled chair and walked her toward the door. He moved slowly, but steadily.

Lestrade waited inside, his sharp face full of anticipation. "You're just in time," said the inspector. "The gang's all here."

"I'll be with you in a moment," her uncle said. "I have one small detail to attend to."

"Right you are."

Sherlock led her down a side corridor that opened onto a row of offices. One door was marked Curator. The room was empty, although the desk looked like someone had been there recently. Letters and invoices littered the surface.

"Wait here," he said, and left.

Evelina set her basket on the desk and looked around. The

cube had been curiously silent since the code had been solved, as if its work was done. Now she pulled aside the cloth she had wrapped it in, and slid her hand onto the cold metal surface.

"Do you want me to leave you here?" she asked it.

At first, she felt nothing. Then there was a faint stirring of consciousness, like a breeze rippling across a pond.

Then suddenly Evelina was in the clouds, mist and free air all around her. It was the first time she'd truly connected with its essence. *It is an air deva, all right!* Weightless, she soared, land and water an insignificance below. Wind tickled her feet, bouncing her gently as she surfed along its waves. All she had to do was wish herself higher and she could climb the brilliant beams of sunlight . . .

"Evie?"

The spell broke, and she was suddenly grounded and heavy, glued to the earth. For a split second, she had truly merged with the air deva. The loss of that connection, the loss of that freedom, left her bruised and leaning on the desk for support.

"Nick," she said breathlessly. "Why are you here?"

"Your uncle told me to come. He said I should be here for the finish, since I was involved. That was decent of him." Nick looked at his feet, a frown pulling at the corners of his mouth.

"What's wrong?"

"It's near the middle of April, and that means tenting season. Ploughman's is moving on. That means it's time for me to leave London."

Loss wrenched a cry from her lips. The hollowness that followed seemed achingly final. She closed her eyes, willing back a sudden rush of tears. "I'll miss you. More than you know."

He gave her a hard look. "Are you sure about that?"

There it was: he was jealous. It was in every line of his body, every angle of his face. He was moving on with the season, the way the circus always did. For Nick, lush spring would fade to a sweltering, dusty summer traveling to every market square and mining town, while Evelina would have her Season of balls and parties and then retire to a country manor for the hottest months. No two lives could be more different.

She had once looked up to Nick. He had wanted her to ask him to stay, but she hadn't. Now he thought he was beneath her notice.

But it wasn't like that. He was her Nick, and always would be. "I will miss you. I am sure about that."

"What about Roth?"

She knew what he meant, but she pretended not to. "What about him?"

"I've seen you with him." He looked away, as if the corner of the desk was intensely interesting. "Do you love him?"

"Nick." Sadness congealed in her throat.

"I would never expect you to come back. But if you did, if you wanted to, I would do everything . . ." He trailed off, hope dying, or already dead.

"Oh, Nick." She couldn't say any more.

Rousing himself, he took one step, closing the distance between them. He grabbed her shoulders, forcing her roughly against the desk. The edge of it pressed into her hip with bruising force. She started to protest, but suddenly his mouth was on hers, crushing her lips against her teeth. He tasted more of anger than affection. There was no magic this time—it had never come for them when they were angry with each other, as if that drained the life out of everything.

Evelina strained to push away, not wanting him like this. Not wanting the memories of him tainted by rage.

"Stop!" She managed to get the word out. "Stop, please."

"I'm not good enough for you?" His lip curled away from his teeth in a sneer, but he took a step back. "I saved you from Magnus. I *killed* for you."

"You've been good to me."

"The whole time you were a girl I never touched you. Anyone who tried would have had me to deal with. Doesn't that count?"

"Of course!"

"Your Golden Boy is rich. That's it, isn't it? He's rich and educated and smells better than a man who has to get dirty before he can eat. Nothing but the best whores for him."

Evelina slapped his face. The crack of it was loud in the little office. Nick's hand went to his cheek, hurt and mockery warring in his eyes. "Are you saying you don't love me, Evie girl?"

She swore under her breath. "Not like this."

She couldn't go backward. She wasn't the same girl who had clung to his hand in the dirt yards where they trained the horses.

"How then?" He leaned in. "Is there any way I could ever measure up?"

Was there? Their shared magic would condemn them, but that wasn't the only stumbling block. She'd gone to school. Her clothes were new, not bought from a barrow at the back of the market and crawling with lice. He was the king of Ploughman's, but she had a future. "The day Grandmamma Holmes came for me," she began in a dull voice.

Nick reached up, grazing her cheek with his rough fingers. "They took you away."

She shook her head. "I always told myself that, too."

Maybe it was time for the truth, or at least part of it. This would be the death of his fairy tale, the one where his lost princess was reclaimed. She could see him starting to understand, the hurt encroaching on his dark, liquid eyes. "No."

"I begged Gran Cooper to let me go, Nick." She put her hand over his, wishing she could soften it for him. Even now, after all these years, she was still torn between what she had and what she'd lost. "And Gran agreed. Oh, I ran away a time or two and tried to find my way back to Ploughman's. I cried myself to sleep for months. I didn't know what leaving would mean, and how many losses I'd suffer, but I knew I wanted more than Ploughman's. I still do."

Nick stared at her. "You wanted to go."

"Just like my father did, when he was a boy." Evelina looked away, unable to meet his eyes anymore. She felt a sob tremble in her throat, but swallowed it down. "That's the truth."

"Evelina, no." He grabbed her wrist, as if that would keep her. "No. It was the magic. That was why we couldn't be together. We had to be older and learn how to hide it."

But they couldn't. There was no turning back their power any more than they could command the sea.

"I'll find a way, Evie," he whispered. "I'll figure out how to make it work."

"Gran said that wasn't possible."

"I'll prove her wrong."

There was so much loneliness in the words, the tears that had threatened began to slide down her cheeks. She couldn't cry. She'd lose whatever ground she'd gained.

And she couldn't tell him any more than she had. He was the king of Ploughman's, the Indomitable Niccolo. The circus was the only place he could call his own—but those people he loved had been willing to cast him out in order to stay safe from wild magic. She couldn't tell him that was why she had chosen to go. What good could come of tainting his memories of the only home he knew? It would only make what had to be worse.

And that meant telling him only part of the truth. "I would die for you, Nick. You're my oldest friend. But I want a different life."

He didn't answer. His breath was coming hard, like he had run miles, and his hand crushed the bones of her wrist.

"You're hurting me," she protested.

He let go of her with a curse. She look a long, shaking breath, her thoughts sputtering under an onslaught of grief. The anger in his eyes sliced through her like a knife. He'd killed for her. He would do it again, if she asked, and maybe that loyalty was one of the reasons she couldn't stay. Deep down—maybe not so deep—she was afraid of him. Or herself.

She had left Ploughman's once to save his life. She would do it again to save them both.

"I can't continue this conversation." She pushed past him out the door, shrugging off his hand when he tried to stop her.

When she reached the corridor, she started to run toward the sound of her uncle's voice.

And away from Nick calling her name.

TOBIAS CONSIDERED A pot sitting on a plinth. Much of the exhibit was gaudy, covered in gold and jewels—the sort of things people had at coronations or funerals or trotted out to impress the neighbor barbarians during the sacrifice. This was just a pot, brown with some zigzags of white and red paint, but it was beautiful in its proportions. The name of the maker was lost in time, but his soul knew that potter's soul and sent its thanks.

Something simple and lovely was exactly what he needed after listening to his father crow about winning a tidy sum on Nellie Reynolds's trial. The money made up for what had been lost with Harter's Engines. Like any inveterate gambler, Lord Bancroft was expansive in the afterglow of victory. There would be dinners and gowns and nights at the club, thanks to the unfortunate actress. The good times were back.

In contrast, Tobias wished he could find the peace to create something as baldly perfect as the pot on the plinth. He was willing to bet—to continue the gambling theme—that the potter had been an orphan.

His communion with beauty lasted less than a minute. Then the crowd closed in.

Oddly, it was the Gold King who broke his reverie. Keating spoke in a confidential tone, putting a fatherly hand on his shoulder. "I'm sure you've heard that the Magnus question is resolved. I recall you expressed concern about the man the night of the Westlakes' ball."

"I did, yes."

Keating had given Tobias a law-and-order speech that would have done the prime minister proud. Having grown up around diplomats, Tobias was something of a connoisseur of such things.

"It wasn't the conclusion I had anticipated," Tobias added, "but I can't say that I'm sorry. The man was a menace."

"Some people invite fate to deal with them irrevocably." Keating inclined his head, a little sorrowful, a little cocky.

Oh, he is good, thought Tobias. *Chilling, but he has the amused statesman nod down perfectly.* The only flaw was that Keating watched his audience's reaction a little too closely. He was still testing out his mask. *Is he going to make a play for a seat in Parliament? A ministerial role? Maybe more?*

"I don't waste time, Mr. Roth. And I admire your willingness to speak out and identify a problem. In fact . . ." he fished in his pocket and drew out a watch.

To Tobias's surprise, he handed it to him. "What's this?"

"The world's smallest steam engine. What do you think of it?"

He struggled to collect his thoughts, which were still parsing through newspaper accounts of Magnus's demise. There hadn't been an arrest. Had Keating played a role in the man's death? If so—Tobias turned his attention to the watch before mounting horror suffused his face.

The watch was a large hunter with a case, but the back opened up to reveal a tiny boiler. It was almost burning hot to the touch, uncomfortable unless one held it by the chain. "A clever notion. I'd love to take it apart. But it hardly seems practical. You'd roast a hole in your pocket, wouldn't you?"

"We think alike, my boy." Keating gave him a sly smile. "I've had my doubts about Bancroft, but the jury is ready to see if you're cut from better cloth."

Tobias tensed, as if the floor were suddenly made of crackling ice.

He saw the steam baron had got the desired result. Keating's smile was reminiscent of a jolly crocodile. "Keep the watch. It's yours. The previous owner doesn't need it anymore."

"Previous owner?" Had he had seen the watch somewhere before?

The smile disappeared. "Aragon Jackson. My former aide."

His father had said there might be an opening on the Gold King's staff. Jackson had been a pet inventor of sorts, hadn't he? The watch felt slippery in Tobias's hand. "Former? Is Mr. Jackson no longer with you?"

"He was obliged to leave. Permanently."

Good God. Did irrevocable fate remove the right monster?

"I like to collect good people," Keating said affably. "Think about it, Mr. Roth. You could have a free hand and all the tools and supplies you need. You could spend day after day doing nothing but tinkering to your heart's delight. And I pay well."

It sounded like salvation and damnation in one tidy package. Tobias struggled between the urge to run and a desire to leap at the offer. "I'll think about it."

"Good." Keating patted him on the shoulder. "Come have dinner with my daughter and me some night. You know Alice, don't you?"

"Yes," said Tobias with a greasy feeling in his stomach. "I have the pleasure of Miss Keating's acquaintance."

"Excellent. We'll have a talk about things."

CHAPTER FORTY-ONE

NICK STARED AFTER EVELINA, NEARLY BLIND WITH MISERY. He shouldn't have kissed her, especially not like that. He should have just left town. Now even when he came back to London, he would have no right to see her.

Anger charred his veins, fueled by a horrible helplessness. What could he do? He already made the best living possible for someone with no last name, and that was chancy. All it would take was one fall during the show, and he would be done. But what choices did he have?

He looked around the room, suddenly unsure why he was there. None of this business with artifacts and thieves was his problem. Holmes had been a good sport to ask him along, but he didn't have a place in their story. Nameless Nick was just the bit of rough that gave the narrative spice and then vanished when it was time to light the fire and draw the drapes against the dangerous night.

Fly.

He looked toward the spot where he thought the voice had come from. Evelina had left her basket. It had been knocked over during their grappling kiss, the contents spilling out across the papers littering the desk.

Fly.

Nick took a step toward the mess, both repulsed by and reverent of anything Evelina had touched. As he reached out to right the basket, his hand tingled as if he'd been scalded.

There was an ugly lump of clockwork that looked as if it had been rescued from a fire. Or a shipwreck. Whatever it was had been damaged. Curious, he picked it up.

You came.

Nick stared at the thing. There had to be a deva inside, just as with Evelina's bird. "Who were you waiting for?"

Your fathers were my people.

"I have no father." But of course that was not true. Technically, everyone had a father. He just had no idea who his had been.

You understand my words. Others do not. You are of my people, the riders of air.

"What about Evelina?"

She was not the one. You are.

"Lucky me." He knew Evelina could hear air devas, just like he could hear those of the earth and forest, but he could hear animals sometimes, too. And, apparently, talking scrap metal.

That is your legacy. I waited and you came.

And then he noticed the silk bag in the bottom of the basket, a corner of something gold poking out the top. He put down the lump of metal and picked up the bag. When he dumped it out, a king's ransom in gold and stones poured into his hand.

Ship. You build. I fly.

Nick was good with his hands, but he didn't know how to build—not like Tobias or Evelina. He was about to say that, but then stopped himself. He couldn't be defeated before he'd even begun. Perhaps he wasn't an engineer, but it seemed he finally had the right Blood for something. Maybe for once in his life he was in luck—he had the airship plans, and he had Striker, who was aching to break free of the Gold King's leash. And then Nick looked at the cube, suddenly understanding what it was. Athena's Casket—the deva that the steam barons wanted to use for their fleet of lethal airships.

Dark hells, what have I stumbled on? Terror crept up his limbs as his fingers, with a will of their own, curled around the fortune in his hand. He had no right to any of it. Not even to escape the Indomitable Niccolo and become somebody else, someone with the kind of power *she* would be forced to notice.

Nick shook his head as if to clear it. Jilted love was a bad reason to decide anything—he was stronger than that. Whatever he did, he had to do because it was the right thing for Nick and no one else.

You came.

The casket hummed happily in the basket. It was ugly, stripped of everything that had once made it fearsomely beautiful, but it knew what it was for. Nick wished he had one iota of that clarity. "I'm not a thief."

But you came. I fly. You fly.

He dumped the gold back into the basket, his hands tingling with the feel of Evelina's body struggling against his. "I love her."

The deva reached out, touching his mind, like a mother soothing her heartbroken child. *Then win her. Make her see who you are.*

Like a frail twig, whatever had kept Nick on the side of the law snapped.

EVELINA SLOWED HER pace as she reached the gallery. She stopped just outside the large open room, forcing herself to take a moment to gather her wits. There was a marble stand with printed programs. She picked one up, pretending to read it.

It was all she could do not to turn around and walk straight back to Nick. She could feel him like a fire behind her, a warm, dangerous light in the darkness. But what purpose would running back serve? What exactly could she hope to erase? She hadn't meant to be cruel. Or had she been? She'd told him the truth.

A fresh wave of tears took over. She turned to the wall, burying her nose in the program for cover. She stiffened, forcing her shoulders not to shake. Fighting her body left her weak, her stomach aching as if someone had kicked her. She sniffed, pulling up the sleeve of her dress. Her wrist had blossomed with a bracelet of bruises where Nick had grabbed her. It still throbbed from the force of his grip. He'd been angry. She'd torn his heart out. But that didn't make hurting her right.

She tugged down her cuff before one of the other guests milling around got curious. Pulling out her handkerchief, she wiped her eyes and nose and wished she could wash her face. If only her face wouldn't show her emotions, but it was pointless. She couldn't seem to stop the slow, steady leak of tears.

Some women cried gracefully, but not her. She was doomed to go through the evening with a red nose and bleary eyes. There would be curious stares or, worse, sympathy. Some would put it down to a broken heart. Well, that was true. Just not in the simple way Lady Bancroft's novels would have it.

Evelina took a handful of deep breaths until the colors in the room stopped swirling around her. She folded the program in her hand, nodding and smiling as a couple walked by arm in arm. Their obvious contentment made her want to scream.

Instead, she strode briskly into the gallery and stopped next to her uncle, who had finally condescended to use the wheeled chair. She kept staring straight ahead. "You did not return to the office."

"I have been having some difficulty finding my way to Mr. Keating's side," he replied blandly.

She didn't believe that for an instant. The room was crowded, but that would barely slow him down, chair or no chair. "Nick found me."

"I thought he might."

"We argued."

"Ah." He made a face. "I'm sorry."

"You don't sound surprised."

"It was somewhat inevitable and, unfortunately, necessary."

"What do you mean?"

"I know foolhardy young men, having had personal experience of the state. They don't exit the stage quietly, even for their own good. Even if they have no immediate role in what is to come."

Her insides clenched. "How do you know all this?"

He gave her a grimace that said he detested the topic. "He has no role because you won't permit it. Therefore, his proud nature demands that he leave. The math is simple. I took advantage of it to play something of a long game."

She hiccuped, her roiling emotions at war with his so-called simple math. "I don't understand."

Her uncle waved an impatient hand. "Tears and explanations must wait. But remember I told you that your friends would be out of harm's way."

He had saved Nick. That was good, but what about the Roths? Panic seized her. Imogen and Tobias were in trouble, because there was no way Lord Bancroft was innocent.

Holmes gave her an impatient look as he read the panic on her face. "Focus. Right now the show is about to begin. Look carefully about the room and take note of who is here."

She did as she was told, beginning on her left and sweeping her gaze slowly to the right. Many of the guests were very familiar. The Roths, of course. Jasper Keating held court among a clump of hangers-on, his silver hair perfectly waving around his patrician head. She recognized Captain Roberts, a friend of Lord Bancroft, mopping his forehead from the heat. There was Professor Teasdale from Oxford, sipping tea and chatting with the Duke of Westlake. There was another man slumped against the wall, looking sourly at the others.

"Who is he?"

"Harriman, Keating's cousin and the owner of the warehouse you visited."

She took a second look. Harriman was younger than his cousin but had blurred versions of the same features, rather like a bad copy of a famous painting. "Very well, now what?"

"Take note of the exhibits. They are as advertised—bowls, wine jars, helmets, jewelry—Schliemann found a burial ground with considerable wealth. They are still translating the inscriptions, but it seems to be the property of a warrior king from Homeric times, but those details are irrelevant."

A glance around confirmed what he was saying. She thought of the bar of gold Grace Child had been carrying. The stones that had been with it were roughly cut, just like the gems set into the items on display. She suddenly jumped, an idea filling her with dread. "I left my basket in the curator's office."

Sherlock blinked lazily, then looked around for Watson. He waved him over. "Would you please retrieve Evelina's basket from the curator's desk? It contains vital evidence."

Watson nodded and left at once, apparently used to playing errand boy. Evelina pressed a hand to her mouth, a bad feeling filling her.

"Never mind," Sherlock ordered. "We need to press on."

She swallowed hard. "What next?"

"A bit of theater. I would like to topple that vase over by the window. The delicate one."

Evelina stared. "Why? It's incredibly old and valuable!"

"It is neither. As I said, these are copies. Do you have a means of discreetly knocking it off its display?"

"I do."

He opened his hands in a showman's gesture. "Then let the demonstration begin."

She slipped Mouse out of her pocket and dropped her program at the same instant. As she bent to retrieve the booklet, she set Mouse loose.

"Be careful," she whispered. "Don't get stepped on!"

It rose up on its hind legs, nose twitching. *I shall also avoid explosions. I'm not an exhibitionist like that wretched bird.* With that, it disappeared under the skirting of a display table.

She straightened. "Wait a moment."

Holmes cocked an eyebrow, but Watson returned before he could speak.

"I looked in all the offices," said the doctor. "The basket is gone."

"Did you see Nick?" Evelina demanded.

Watson shook his head. "No."

The meaning of that *no* had barely hit her when there was a metallic crash. For an instant, she imagined it was her heart. Then Evelina whirled around to see a pair of ladies leaping back from the vase, which had fallen, bounced, and was now rolling unevenly through the crowd. A gray shape streaked toward her on the floor. She knelt, catching Mouse safely in her hands. "Well done!" she whispered.

Piece of junk, that was!

And best of all, no one could blame her or Uncle Sherlock for knocking it over. She kissed Mouse's nose and put it back into her pocket.

"Clever," her uncle said softly. "Now watch everyone's reactions."

Jasper Keating had picked up the vase and was staring at it with a thunderous expression. Never a man to hide his displeasure, he vented his wrath in a spray of spittle. "It's chipped! The gold is flaking right off! But this piece is supposed to be solid gold!"

"They're running!" Evelina cried. "Look at Captain Roberts and the professor!"

"Never mind. Lestrade has his men waiting outside the doors."

"Then they'll catch Nick!"

"Do you really think so? From what I understand that young man has a penchant for crawling along rooftops. Now pay attention."

Jasper Keating exploded. "What is the meaning of this?" He rounded on his cousin, grabbing him by the arm and bodily dragging him over to the wreckage of the vase. "Explain!"

"Why are you looking at me?" Harriman raised his hands like a bank robber surrendering to Scotland Yard.

Holmes swung into action, ordering Watson to roll him forward. "Because you run an interesting business, Mr. Harriman."

"Who the devil are you, sir?" Harriman demanded, pulling out of his cousin's grasp to round on Holmes.

"Sherlock Holmes," Keating said with a satisfaction dreadful to behold. "Your ship is sinking, Harriman. Start bailing."

The man's jaw dropped, but nothing intelligent came out of his mouth.

"You used to employ a number of Chinese workers, I believe," Holmes said to Harriman. "They worked at the warehouse where the collection was unpacked, up until the time their dismembered bodies were found floating in the Thames. Some were goldsmiths."

Harriman remained silent.

Keating looked at his cousin, and the chipped and dented vase in his hand, then at Sherlock. "Tell me."

Her uncle pointed at the vase. "Evelina, hand me that travesty."

She took the offending item from Keating and handed it to her uncle. The once-beautiful object seemed naked and fractured. She couldn't help handling it almost tenderly, as if it were a patient.

He took it one-handed. "They made casts of your treasures, then replicated them in base metals, then electroplated them with a thin layer of the original gold so that it matched precisely. Gems were easily replaced with glass."

Keating had turned gray, looking from one display case to the next in visible panic. "Why did I not see the difference?"

"The replicas were cleverly done, though not perfect." Holmes picked up a graceful urn in his good hand, turning it over. "If you look carefully at the bottom of this one, there is the faintest trace of a seam from the mold."

"But surely this would be found out! This exhibit was to go to the British Museum!"

"Not before it was stolen," Holmes said with a tight smile. "Lestrade uncovered that piece of the plot after interviewing the finest among the brotherhood of London's thieves. Before the weekend was over, this entire collection would disappear in a robbery, and all evidence of forgery along with it."

They all looked at Harriman, who looked dumbfounded. Evelina guessed this was news to him, too.

"I don't understand," said the duke, shouldering his way forward. "Why go to such a fabulous amount of work?"

"I would have never known the difference," Keating rasped. "A staged robbery? I must have been robbed months ago, to allow enough time for the forgeries to be made. Even with slave labor, it would have been a long and expensive process." He turned on Harriman. "Where is my treasure?"

"Melted down," Holmes said to the man.

Lestrade had come forward and pinned Harriman's arms. The man glared at Keating with a hatred that made Evelina's stomach churn.

"I'm your kin, damn you!" the Gold King snarled.

"It doesn't matter," Harriman returned. "You lord it over all of us. What do you expect?"

"Those were priceless artifacts!"

"So was our pride."

"Who were your confederates?" Lestrade snapped. "We shall want a list."

"I doubt you shall ever find out," Holmes interrupted again.

Holmes cast a quick glance at Evelina, as if to say that no matter how he felt about the matter, Bancroft's fall would not come at his hand. But it was plain that her uncle's reticence would not be enough to save the conspirators.

Keating's jaw worked. "Leave Harriman with me and you shall have your list."

Harriman sucked in a whistling breath.

"He'll be off to Newgate," Lestrade said. "The rest of this conversation can take place there."

With that, he dragged Harriman toward the door. The crowd parted, and many hurried toward the cloakroom. The evening was over, and the entertainment had not been at all what they'd expected.

Keating fixed Holmes with a keen look. "Athena's Casket?"

Her uncle gave him a sorrowful face. "I suspect it's been melted. A tragedy."

The Gold King turned away for a long moment, his shoulders hunched. When he turned back, his face was stern but composed. "Still, I thank you for uncovering this treachery. If it had been allowed to fester, who knows what havoc Harriman might have caused. I underestimated him."

Holmes blinked lazily. "So it appears."

"You shall be recompensed." Keating frowned.

Sherlock glanced at his arm. "I shall remember to forward my bill."

With a stiff nod, Keating stalked away to salvage what he

could of the night. Evelina was free to scan the remaining crowd. "Where is Lord Bancroft?"

"He left as soon as the vase hit the floor."

She looked at Holmes sharply as suspicion changed to certainty. "So he was one of them."

"Undoubtedly. I suspect he was the key player. It remains to be seen whether Keating figures that out. I'm sorry for your friends, but it will be rough sailing for Bancroft if he does. That can't be helped."

She swallowed hard. He was telling her no more than the truth. "But what about Grace? And who shot you?"

Holmes made a face. His color had gone beyond white to a sickly gray. "The game is still afoot. It might be limping, but it's not finished yet. Unfortunately, for tonight, I am."

CHAPTER FORTY-TWO

IT HAD BEEN UP TO TOBIAS TO CALL A HANSOM AND BUNDLE his sister into it. Lord Bancroft had taken the carriage, and Tobias's first priority was to exit the scene before anyone noticed that he and his sister had been left behind. After that shocking scene with Harriman, who knew what scandalous whispers the slightest misstep would cause?

The pater's sudden departure said he was guilty, but how bad was it? Imogen had opened her mouth once or twice, but had not been able to force out a single word. Instead, she held her brother's hand as if to comfort him. She was probably comforting herself.

Poor Im. She's always the leaf caught in other people's storms. And she'd been looking ill again the past few days. She wasn't made to withstand so many shocks.

Jolting along in the cab, Tobias wrapped himself in the tense silence with a species of bloody satisfaction. Whatever his father had feared, whatever guilt he had tried to hide, little Evelina Cooper and her peculiar uncle had found it. It served his father right for keeping it—whatever *it* was—from his own son. He'd assumed Tobias was too incompetent to be of help, but who was the family disaster now?

Tobias let the petty monologue run riot around his brain until the hansom reached their house. Bigelow, with the instinct of a well-trained servant, had already opened the door before Tobias reached the front walk.

"What's going on?" Imogen asked once they were safely inside.

Tobias mused a moment, studying his sister's worried

face. The worst, he knew, was yet to come. "Go look after Mother. I'll try to talk to Father."

"Tobias," she grabbed his sleeve. "Grace Child . . ."

"You don't really think Father killed her do you?" He did. He had since the disastrous dinner with the detective.

"I don't know. There are moments I think I do. Other moments I'm so angry that I wish I could." Imogen's eyes were dark with fear. "But what do we do now?"

"We do what we need to." He kissed her forehead. "You're the sane one. The rock. You have to be strong for us."

"But I'm not strong. I'm the one who is always ill." Her voice shook just enough that he caught the tremor.

He wanted to take his little sister in his arms and hold her, but was afraid he might lose his courage. Instead, he gave her a little shove toward the stairs. "Go be the saintly daughter. See to Mother. I'll come find you later."

Tobias went to his father's study, but paused outside with his hand on the cold brass knob. It had been little more than a week since he'd been summoned there after the squid affair. His father had told him to seduce Evelina in order to prevent exactly what had just happened. *So I would have ruined a girl's life over what? Some gold pots?*

He turned the doorknob slowly, part of him hating Evelina. She and her uncle had turned everything on its head. But he'd felt her lean into him on the dance floor and in that moment of tenderness, he'd known nothing was simple for her, either. She'd been wise to say she couldn't afford him. And yet, despite her cool reasoning, her blood ran every bit as hot as his.

Only one thing was certain. Tobias was done being his father's puppet.

The door swung open. His father sat behind the desk, the tiger's head snarling above him. One of Lord Bancroft's hands rested lightly on his silver-handled revolver. Tobias's heart jerked in his chest, like a carriage hitting a rut. This was unexpected. For a moment, he nearly turned and ran.

He forced his voice to be light. "Are we so ruined that you need to blow out your brains?" He was being deliberately callous, but it got Bancroft's attention.

His father glared up at him through lowered brows. "Get out."

Tobias took a deep breath, forcing the air into lungs so tight they screamed a protest. Suicide? Truly? He'd always assumed his father too egotistical, but now he wasn't sure. Like everything else, this assumption was crumbling away, leaving him standing on air.

He stuffed his hands into his pockets and sauntered in. "You're guilty."

"Yes."

God help us. "How badly?"

Bancroft stared at the middle of the desk. His voice sounded already dead. "I organized the affair. I knew jewelers who could recut the stones and sell them for a sizable profit."

"Why do it?"

Bancroft made a minute movement, not quite a shrug. "Money. Ambition. Everything takes gold. I gambled and lost."

That made Tobias swallow. Would this be him in twenty years, disappointed and holding a gun? In ten? "The Gold King doesn't know you're involved. Not yet. Suicide is as good as admitting your guilt."

"He will. And a bullet might encourage Keating to spare my family." Bancroft's hands were starting to shake. He was a brave man, but no one could stay wound to the necessary pitch forever.

Tobias was counting on the fact. If he stalled long enough, his father would lose his nerve. "Don't be an idiot. Killing yourself won't spare us. It will shatter us to pieces."

Bancroft's hands clenched. He smelled of whisky. "Stop sniveling. If you'd been a man, if you'd stopped that girl, then none of this would have happened."

Tobias gave a dry smile. "But it seems that, at the moment, I have Keating's respect. He likes my spirit."

Bancroft's mouth worked. He'd never been able to bend. Now he was breaking. "Leave me."

Tobias was losing patience. "No. I'm tired of dancing in your wake. If it's not a scheme at Harter's, we're being Disconnected. One day you're asking me to seduce an innocent girl, the next someone is murdering our servants to get their hands on a collection of cursed automatons. The family cannot afford this insanity a moment longer." Tobias still wasn't satisfied by his father's explanation about the automatons, but this wasn't the moment to revive that argument.

His father finally met his eyes. His gaze was dull as rock. "How dare you presume?"

Tobias gritted his teeth, biting back his first retort. The second was only a sliver more civil. "I dare because if you don't act like the head of this family, I will. Splattering your brains on the wall won't fix anything."

A look of pure rage crossed his father's face. He gripped the revolver, raising the barrel to point right between Tobias's eyes. "Get out."

"What about Mother? What about Imogen's Season? How can she find a husband if she's in mourning? And Poppy is still a girl. She won't understand."

Defeat flooded Bancroft's face, turning his eyes raw with despair. "Don't you comprehend ruin? Those will be the least of their problems."

His father's face—that look of a drowning man—transfixed Tobias. He went utterly still inside, much the same way as when he was deep in the bowels of an engine. It was the same calm he felt memorizing how parts connected, cog and wheel, piston and pulley. He was a maker. Cause and effect worked the same way, inside a machine or out of it.

He had a flash of insight how his father, once a maker himself, got into the business of politics. It was all about pulling the right levers.

Tobias gentled his voice. "I understand there are broken things that need mending. I'll kiss Keating's arse if that's what it takes to bring him around. I'm exactly the type of bright young aristo he likes in his retinue. And I can build a better machine than that prat Jackson. I can save this."

For a moment they stood staring at each other. An understanding passed between them Tobias had never thought possible. It wasn't enough.

Bancroft shook his head. "I've always told you to be like

me, but I've secretly taken comfort in the fact that you weren't. You still have dreams. Don't give them up. Not for Keating."

"I'm doing it for us." Tobias reached for the gun, feeling exhausted and exhilarated at once. It must have been the way those Japanese warriors felt when they drove a sword into their own entrails. Sacrifice and honor.

Tobias's fingers brushed the silver grip of the revolver. Bancroft jerked the gun away. Tobias grabbed for it at the same instant, trying to wrestle it out of his father's hand. It went off with a thunderous pop, blowing a plume of sawdust out of the tiger's head. A fang clattered to the floor.

And then Tobias had the revolver. He was panting, more from nerves than from exertion. Bancroft looked amazed, then furious. The fleeting moment of understanding was over, and suddenly they were rivals.

"No!" Bancroft lunged across the desk.

Tobias had had enough. He'd had enough for years. "We're done."

"Stop being a child!"

Without exactly thinking, Tobias plowed his fist into his father's jaw. Bancroft sprawled backward into his chair.

"We're done," he said quietly. Nausea seeped upward. He'd crossed a line, gone to a place he couldn't retreat from. "I'm sorry."

The study door banged open, Bigelow an uncharacteristic tableau of panic. He'd heard the shot. Tobias held up a hand, signaling calm.

Bancroft touched his face. Blood welled on his lip. "You'll hate yourself for this."

"I already do."

It wasn't just for the blow. He'd taken authority from his father he didn't want. Now he had to keep his word if that gesture was to have an ounce of meaning.

Tobias turned and walked past the butler, still holding the gun.

CHAPTER FORTY-THREE

Any truth is better than indefinite doubt.
      —Sherlock Holmes, as recorded by John H.
Watson, M.D., "The Adventure of the Yellow Face"

HOLMES WENT DIRECTLY BACK TO BAKER STREET UNDER Watson's care. His wound had reopened, and the good doctor was ready to enforce bed rest at gunpoint if necessary.

Worry squirmed inside Evelina, pushing her into action. The Roths had left, Nick had fled into the night, and she needed to find a ride back to Hilliard House. She had to collect the last of her things and make her way to Baker Street. She'd been advised that morning that the moment her uncle was no longer an invalid, Lord Bancroft no longer wished to suffer her presence. She had delayed until after the gallery opening only because her uncle had required her presence and she had run out of time to pack. Now that Holmes had started a chain of events that would likely lead to Lord Bancroft's arrest, she would be lucky not to find her underthings in the street.

How much has changed in such a short span of time. She stood at the curb in front of the gallery, looking for a hansom to hire.

"Miss Cooper." She turned to see the Gold King standing beside her. He gave a slight bow.

"Mr. Keating." She gave a small curtsy.

"Allow me to loan you one of my carriages for the night."

"Thank you," she replied. "But I am quite comfortable hiring a cab."

"Perhaps, but I owe your uncle for his services. It was my

men that saw him home, and he specifically requested that his young relation be treated with all possible respect."

There was no objection she could make to that. Keating studied her a moment, as if seeing her for the first time. She noticed his eyes were a peculiar shade of amber, like a cat's. "I understand that you also played a role in uncovering the forgery scheme," he said.

"It was very modest, I assure you."

"I don't think so." A smile creased his distinguished features, but it had an edge. "I found your paper knife in the leg of my streetkeeper, and my agents found Miss Roth's calling card in the warehouse."

Evelina felt herself going light-headed. "A coincidence, surely."

He smiled with a quick shake of his head. "You have interesting talents. I am always keen to know more of clever young people."

"And I am gratified if I was able to assist in any way."

A small black victoria pulled to a halt in the street. One gray horse pulled it, and the top was up to shelter against the evening breeze. Keating gave another bow. "Here is my carriage. Again, I thank you. I'm sure we shall meet again sometime."

He helped Evelina up and closed the door, but his hand remained on the sill of the open window. "One piece of advice, Miss Cooper. It is clear that my foolish cousin is but one of a cabal of thieves, quite probably the least and last of their number. That is my mistake; I thought safely unpacking crates was well within his capabilities. Apparently, I was in error."

Evelina waited while he cast a glance around the street and then leaned closer to the window. "Captain Roberts is certainly among the guilty, and Lord Farley. I do not doubt those involved in the Harter Engine scheme attempted to recoup their losses at my expense. This bears the hallmark of someone with imagination and an understanding of craftsmanship and metalwork."

Understanding seeped in like chill, foul water. She turned

icy, her fingers trembling in her lap. *He suspects Lord Bancroft. Dear God, they're ruined.*

He narrowed his eyes. "When word gets out, there will be a metaphorical bloodbath in Mayfair, Miss Cooper, and I would be very surprised if your name was not dragged into the affair. I would advise you to forget having a Season and retire to the country. I'm sure what social events go forward would not welcome you."

She caught his gloved hand where it sat on the window. "Please, remember these men have families, and they are innocent."

The look on his face said she'd revealed something interesting to him. Her anxiety went up a notch as if a gear inside her had tightened.

"Calm yourself, Miss Cooper. I know very well about family affections, and I'm not a wasteful man." He rapped on the side of the victoria with his cane, and the Gold King's equipage lurched forward, rattling on the cobbles.

If his words had been meant to reassure her, they didn't. Evelina sank into the soft velvet of the cushions, horrified. *What is going to happen now?*

Once the carriage reached Hilliard House, she stood for a moment admiring the serene beauty of it, ignoring what it hid. She'd never completely fit into the world of the gentry. She remembered cowering in the cupboard under Grandmamma Holmes's stairs, afraid of a beating because she'd thoughtlessly picked the flowers in the formal garden. And she'd cried when she saw her brand-new bedroom, the one her mother had as a girl. It was so big, and so beautiful, but she had no one to share it with, and she would have to sleep in the huge white bed alone. And yet she'd persevered. She'd gone to school and learned to be a lady. She'd been presented to the queen and danced at a ball. She didn't *not* fit, either.

Quietly, she slid into the house and mounted the stairs to her room. Her trunks had already been removed. All that was left was a bag to pack with her last few things, and she wanted to avoid everyone until that task was done. Far bet-

ter to be ready to go before she went through the awkward-
ness of good-byes.

"It's my fault, you know. I should have left Grace Child
standing outside in the cold."

She turned. Tobias was in the doorway, his face haggard.
"That's nonsense," she said. "If anyone is to blame—" She
stopped. She was going to say it was her fault, or her uncle's.
But her intention had been to save Bancroft, and Holmes
had been hired to find the casket. Both of them had, in their
own way, tried to shield the family. In truth, the only person
guilty of Bancroft's ruin was Lord B himself—but that
wasn't what Tobias needed to hear.

"It doesn't matter," he said with a shrug. "What matters is
that everything has fallen to pieces since. It will seem odd
with you away. You've been Imogen's friend so long, I feel
like you're one of us. I can't imagine our house at Christmas, or five or ten years into the future and not seeing you
in your spot at the table. You've been one of the family for
ages. You're a habit I like."

She bit her lips together to keep them from trembling. "I
know. I feel it, too. But things will settle down when your
father realizes that everything is fine."

That statement fell between them like a concrete dirigible. Once Keating finished with Harriman, and got his list
of names, Lord Bancroft would be in very, very deep water.
"The Gold King warned me what was coming. He said I
should go to the country. Grandmamma isn't well. I think
I might go stay with her for a time."

"What about your Season?" he asked.

"There won't be one. Not for me, anyhow. I'll be fine. I
always am."

She saw her words strike to the quick. He blamed himself,
or at least his family, for what was likely to be her fall from
favor, too.

"It's all right." She whispered it, because she didn't trust
her voice. "You didn't cause any of this."

He smiled, but it was jerky. "I don't like it."

"But what you like doesn't count right now, does it?"

He took her hands in his, and she felt the rough spots

where he'd been handling tools. He kissed her fingers, looking up under his brows. She saw the fear and desire in his gray eyes. It was the look of someone seeing a door crack open—and praying it doesn't close. The naked, honest vulnerability of it squeezed her heart.

They embraced, hot and desperate. His mouth found hers, telling her without words how much he hurt. Evelina felt tears slip from under her lashes and she dragged in a shaking breath. "I don't want to lose you."

His hands slid over her ribs, over the flare of her hips. "I know."

And their lips met again, but this time it was slower, more deliberate, as if the alchemy of touching was turning their sorrow into something else. They kissed once, twice, then his fingers found the buttons of her fine lace collar and slid first one pearly sphere, then the next through the fine mesh loops that held it closed. Warm against her throat, his fingers were indescribably intimate, as if a great deal more of him were touching her.

An ache began low in her belly, a fire instantly stoked to life. She leaned into him, suddenly needing the pressure of his body like she needed air, and rested her head against his strong shoulder.

The lamp on her desk spilled light into the room, pulling the yellows and gold from the Turkish carpet, but it could not dispel the emptiness of the space. The dresser was bare, the wardrobe door standing open, the bookcase cleared of all her volumes. She had already left. This was just the denouement.

Tears coursed down her face freely now. "Tobias."

His hand pressed against her back, holding her to him. "I love you."

Evelina felt her body go limp. She didn't move a muscle, but felt like an automaton whose engine had just died. Then a wave of heat surged up from her feet, as if life suddenly returned in a glorious, delirious rush. *He loves me!* It was real. She'd heard it in his voice.

She raised her head to look at him. His eyes, too, were bright with tears, but he blinked them away. He no longer looked like an angel, just a weary, fallen man. She liked this version of him better. She could love him this way, not just adore him as a golden idol.

His mouth worked a moment before he spoke. "Look, things are at sixes and sevens. You might have to leave for a while, and I have to put things to rights. Keating has to be appeased somehow if we're going to keep going. I have to try, especially for Imogen and Poppy."

As always, she dove for the difficult question. "How?"

"I'll put my talents at the beck and call of Jasper Keating. I know it's dealing with the devil, but it's up to me to help make this thing blow over. If I do a good job, we need never worry about money."

About my pitiful dowry, you mean. "What about your own work? Whatever Magnus wanted to show you? Is there something there you could make your own?"

"He had some sort of a master plan he wanted me and some friends of mine to work on. He said he needed makers and that there was a part he was trying to get."

The airship. Magnus would need talented makers to put it together, but he had also needed Athena's Casket. She couldn't imagine the mayhem the doctor would have caused if he had possessed such a powerful weapon.

Tobias closed his eyes. "But in the meantime, he had built an automaton. He meant to test us with it. Incredibly beautiful, but it was—enchanted somehow. Maybe that was the test, to see if we would balk at the magic. I did." He visibly shuddered, wiping his face with one hand. "I never understood all the prattle about herbwives and sorcerers, but I understand it now. Evil stuff. Vile. No wonder the steam barons do everything they can to repress it. The Gold King is right about that much."

Evelina caught her breath, unable to speak, and her joy fluttered to earth, a moth with one wing. *He is afraid of magic.* Not only that, but she heard the subtle shift behind the words. Magnus had been his savior before. Now it was the Gold King. *He doesn't know how to save himself. For all his talk about independence, he needs a stronger man to follow and they're all monsters.*

She took a step back, but Tobias caught her hands, keeping her close. "Magnus is done. He's not a problem anymore." He gazed down at their clasped hands. "All the mysteries are solved."

But they weren't, not by a long shot. Evelina's brain suddenly skittered sideways, her fingers twitching in his. He released her hands. "What is it?" he asked.

"I understand now." She took a step back, folding her arms. She had figured out the murders. She thought of Grace standing in the cloakroom with her candle and her petticoat, unaware that she was minutes from her doom. "Grace was waiting for your father to meet her and collect the gold she was carrying. The killer probably came on her by accident that night."

Tobias looked sick and confused. "The killer? You mean my father?"

"No, it wasn't your father." Pieces of evidence clicked into place. "Bigelow found Lord Bancroft in the library when he went to raise the alarm. Your father had fallen asleep after drinking too much. He didn't murder the grooms, either. It was Magnus looking for the automatons, first in the house, then on the road. He'd somehow slipped into the house. That had to be him who passed me in the hall." And as a sorcerer, it would be no trouble to cloak his presence from sight. Excited, she went on. "The only reason his plan failed is that your father realized he was in London and moved the trunks before he got there. Magnus probably came in the side door, but when he tried to leave, Grace was there."

Tobias's mouth drifted open, horror mounting on his face. He snapped it shut.

Realization shocked her. "You thought your father killed Grace, didn't you?" Memory surged. She could see him putting the pieces together during the dinner when her uncle was shot, just before he left the room.

Her face went cold, a painful ache growing in her chest. Her feet backed away from him, almost by themselves. Tobias was known as a crack shot. He had been the first to leave the dinner table. Their eyes met, each reading the other perfectly. In that moment, she saw something in him change. The man who had just confessed his love vanished in a storm of fear. He was terrified of what she might know.

Evelina's mouth went dry. *You tried to kill my uncle. You thought he had figured out your father was guilty, so you tried to kill him before he could say anything—and now you know that I've guessed as much.*

But if she said it out loud, was he going to let her go? The unspoken dialogue between them stretched on, the fear on his face hardening to something else. There were moments when she was certain Tobias loved her, but there were also many when she was glad she hadn't poured out every ounce of her soul. *He fears magic. He feared my uncle. He would rather lash out than face the consequences of the truth.* Not a comforting train of thought.

That was the difference between them, and there was no chance for either of them to grow and change now. *This affair cuts love's throat as surely as it did poor Grace's.*

And this man—Tobias—had tried to kill Uncle Sherlock. She looked away, trying to hide the mounting horror she felt. *I wouldn't have believed it of him.*

Tobias watched her reaction, seeming to catalogue every nuance. His mouth twisted with bitterness. "My father isn't a murderer? I'm so relieved."

Yes, he knew he had made a mistake.

She felt a flash of pity, but it was mixed with fear. "Your father made a terrible mistake and things are going to change for your family. You can't preserve things the way they are. If you do that, you let Keating pin you like a specimen in a shadow box."

Tobias curled his fingers into fists. "I will protect the people I love."

You'll pick up a gun and start shooting. "At what cost to you? To them?"

He gave her a weary look. "I don't know, Evelina. My mother has already collapsed. I'll do whatever is required of me."

"How far will you go?" They both knew she meant with her.

He gave her a dark look. "If I think there is a threat, I will take care of it." Then he wavered, a little of the hardness falling from his expression. "I can't be the man either of us wants anymore. And there's too much between us now."

"You said you loved me a moment ago." But the words were pointless. He was right. *You shot my uncle.* That was bad enough. What was worse was that until she'd figured out the truth, he'd been willing to live with that secret every time he kissed her.

Tobias Roth was a coward and a liar. *I was right. I can't afford him.*

She wet her lips, at a loss for anything else to say. There was one more mystery solved, for whatever good it did her. "I need to leave. My uncle is waiting for me."

There was a tense moment. She had his secret. What was he going to do now?

"Then you had better go," he said at last. There was no warmth in his voice now, as if he had made some final decision to put his fate in her hands.

Evelina didn't want anything from him, least of all that.

She had finished packing. She picked up her bag. One foot shakily before the other, she made for the door.

"Evelina."

"Your secrets are safe," she said in a small voice.

"One thing you should know."

She turned, already sure it would be a mistake. "What?"

His eyes were hollow with dread and sadness, but there was ice there, too. "My father asked me to seduce you."

She flinched, as if his words were slender, deadly blades. "Why are you telling me this?"

"Everything I said." He sucked in a breath, his lips pressed together so hard they turned white. "Utterly false. Always."

Pain sliced her, bringing a flush of shame to her cheeks. She knew he was lying, lashing out through his hurt. Or maybe he was doing what he believed he had to, freeing both of them so he could save the family fortune.

He still wounded the most tender part of her soul.

"If that's how you want it," she whispered.

"It's better to make a clean end, don't you think?" His voice was as expressionless as lead.

Without a word, Evelina turned on her heel and walked away. She meant to stop and say good-bye to Imogen, but her feet wouldn't slow as she marched down the stairs. She couldn't face anyone right then.

Tears ached behind her eyes, waiting for the least excuse to fall, but she held them in. She was a lady. She had been presented to the queen. She was made of finer steel than Tobias Roth could shatter.

But defiance soured to uneasiness in the time it took to reach the door of Hilliard House. Tobias was willing to kill. She knew his secrets.

It didn't take a Holmes to add up that equation. There was no question of belonging here now.

CHAPTER FORTY-FOUR

EVELINA WAS EAGER TO BE GONE, AND LORD BANCROFT WAS eager for her to go. His own carriage took her to Baker Street, where she would stop for the night before returning to her grandmother in the morning.

She found her uncle was waiting up for her, browsing his books of chemistry. Dr. Watson wasn't there, apparently returned at last to the long-suffering Mrs. W.

"Uncle? I thought you would have retired for the night."

He raised a hand. "Please, I have had enough coddling from Mrs. Hudson and the good doctor. No more."

She didn't care. He looked awful. "Why are you still up?"

He settled against the cushions of the chair, his expression defensive. "I was merely reviewing the case in my mind. There is only one outstanding question."

She sat down wearily. "What is that?"

"The voices you heard at eleven o'clock the night of the murder."

"It could have been anyone," Evelina replied. "Does it matter?"

"Not necessarily." He snapped the book shut. "It's merely a species of maggot that will not leave my mind. I have expected all along to discover a witness who saw Dr. Magnus the night of the murder. The police sought reports of a lone man and found nothing. But there were many reports of a tall, dark man in company with a woman. Perhaps he had an accomplice? Did you not find a female footprint by Grace Child's body?"

"I did," she said, sitting up straight. She remembered the night Magnus returned Bird, when she was talking to Inspector Lestrade. What was it Bird had told her? *The hedge deva said the man and his shadow came here more than once.*

Tobias and Grace weren't the first couple outside the side door that night. She had utterly forgotten. "I'm an idiot. There was a witness—no one of importance," she said quickly in response to her uncle's questioning look. "There was another couple outside the door. I suppose it was their voices I heard."

"Then who were they?" Holmes asked. "Was Magnus working with someone?"

"Every time I saw the doctor, he was alone."

"No wife or lover? No one to play the accomplice in skirts?"

"No. None. Nick said he lived alone, without even servants. And the witness who saw the couple described them as a man and his shadow. Apparently they'd been there more than once."

"If they were the culprits who murdered Grace and stole the automatons, they were no doubt getting the lay of the land. But a shadow? Are we dealing with doppelgangers now? Crazed shadow-men with blades?" Her uncle grimaced.

"I feel like I've been chasing shadows." Evelina wrinkled her brow, speaking mostly in jest. "Is that our second murderer? A ghost with a blade?"

"How utterly distasteful. Not to mention preposterous. If maniacal spirits are the order of the day, I am retiring. I would rather believe Magnus wielded the knife himself."

Evelina wanted to say something clever to that, but weariness left nothing but a blank in her brain. "He did, didn't he?"

"It seems the likeliest answer, but the evidence is all circumstantial. There is nothing that would hold up before a judge."

That left a queasy feeling in her stomach. She wanted certainty, but Holmes wouldn't give it to her just for the sake of comfort. "Before you were shot, you said there were two unknowns. One was Harriman. Was the other this mysterious woman?"

"Perhaps. Recall also our two grooms. There was plenty of time for our killer to leave Hilliard House and catch up with them, but would one person have the strength to subdue two burly men?"

"There has to have been an accomplice," she said softly. "Magnus said that he didn't wield the blade himself, and I'm inclined to believe him."

"Hm. And we may never know who that was, beyond the suggestion that it *might* have been a woman. I have, of course, apprised Lestrade of the facts. If there is a hint of new information, I will follow it up, just as I am alert to any new information about the death of the Chinese workers. Lestrade will question Harriman about their deaths, but I want to make sure the case is closed properly. It is too little and too late, but we owe them justice for what was done to them on our shores."

"Indeed we do." She shuddered, remembering the gruesome news reports of bodies in the Thames. Grace's slashed throat. The grooms she'd spied on and then were later found still and cold. There had been too much tragedy.

At least Magnus was gone. It was some comfort. Evelina sighed. "I assumed somehow this would be resolved."

"You mean, when I arrived I would wave the stem of my pipe and all would become clear?" Holmes looked uncharacteristically sympathetic and rather amused. "You flatter me."

"But how will Grace get justice?"

"That is the sad truth of crime. She may not—but I will do my best to see to it that she does. Not all cases are solved overnight."

Evelina bowed her head. "I had no idea detecting took such stamina."

Her uncle snorted. "When Watson writes his stories he skips over the dull bits. Crime solving takes mind-numbing patience and rather a lot of hard work."

"So I discovered." She shifted wearily in her chair. "I finally have a true appreciation for what you do." And right now, she hoped to never need investigate another case. Detection sounded romantic and interesting on paper, but the real thing involved death and broken hearts.

Another thought inserted itself, seemingly at random. She spoke before thinking. "None of this would have any connection to this Baskerville business, would it?"

"No," Holmes said flatly, making her wish she'd held her tongue. "Various players in this piece have connections to the rebels and others I think wish they had, but the murder of the serving girl was an entirely different tragedy."

Evelina digested that and wondered why the topic made him so prickly. "Then you know who has rebel sympathies?"

"I'm speculating. Politics is Mycroft's area of expertise, not mine. I prefer pursuits based on some form of logic. Do you perceive any other loose ends in the case?" Holmes asked, clearly changing the subject.

Annoyed by his abruptness, Evelina couldn't help being blunt. "Tobias shot you."

"I know."

Of course he did, the wretch. "You might have mentioned it."

"I thought it best if you figured that out for yourself. You bore the young man some affection."

Evelina lifted her hands, then dropped them to her sides in a gesture of sheer exasperation. "I did. Both him and Nick. I wanted them to be innocent."

"Neither of them killed the maid."

"Tobias turned killer and Nick turned thief." Her voice rose with fury. "Are all young men so hopelessly thick?"

Sherlock raised his eyebrows. "They are both in love with you and both are pushed into impossible corners. Tobias is desperately struggling to keep his family from ruin. An admirable goal, although I question his methods."

"By killing you?"

"He isn't the first who tried." Her uncle gave a wry smile. "And your Niccolo is a bright young man with absolutely no legal method for betterment open to him. How is he ever to win your hand?"

All the dammed-up tears inside her started to fall. "I love them both. I ruined their lives."

"That is rather a dramatic assertion, and a rather egotistical one. I will grant you love is rarely convenient. I'm told that's part of its charm." With a vaguely disgusted look, Holmes produced a pocket handkerchief and passed it over.

Evelina sniffed, and there was nothing dainty about it. "I thought for a moment, right when I was being presented, that somehow my future would be guaranteed. That wasn't true."

"That's why I never approved of the presentation scheme. It wasn't my idea, you know."

She blinked at him. "It wasn't?"

"It was Keating's, and a waste of time. Empty ceremony was never going to contribute one iota to your ultimate happiness. You and I are sadly alike."

She had nothing to say to that.

Holmes waved a dismissive hand. "Perhaps by the time you graduate from your women's college, Tobias will be a steam baron in his own right and Niccolo will rule the criminal underworld. Then we can reassess your future plans."

"You aren't going to turn them over to Inspector Lestrade?"

"Heavens, no. This is far too interesting. Now go to bed."

Evelina obeyed, moving slowly. Mrs. Hudson stopped her on the stairs, handing her an envelope.

"This just came for you, Miss Cooper. A grim-looking gentleman he was, but he was nicely dressed. He just left it, and said he would call some other time."

"Thank you, Mrs. Hudson." Evelina took the letter, and continued on.

Exhaustion dragged at her feet, and she was infinitely glad to see the small, tidy room the landlady had prepared for her. Mouse and Bird were chasing each other over the dressing table in a complicated game of tag, bickering as they scampered over the soap and towels her hostess had left out. They had both volunteered to go with her to her grandmother's. Earth devas rarely traveled, and they were eager to see a new part of the world.

She took a closer look at the envelope. It was fine cream

paper addressed in a bold, sweeping hand. *Miss Evelina Cooper.* The red wax seal was marked with a plain circle. Curious to see who had sent it—she'd only been at Baker Street for a half hour, so who knew she was there?—she broke the wax and unfolded the note. It was dated that day.

> *Miss Cooper,*
>   *The Divine gave birth to Wisdom and gave Her the name Helen. He sent Her to comfort His creatures, and give them succor in their ignorance and pain. She dwells in the body of woman, the perfect soul incarnate in beauty. I have sought Her for millenia, even attempted to make Her with my own hands. Have I finally found Her in you?*
>   *As I suspected, your natural talents are unsurpassed. There will come a time when you want answers, when the mysteries shall be mysteries no more. Then I shall find you and teach you the vast universe of what there is to do and know and imagine, my luminous Evelina.*
>   *Dr. Symeon Magnus*

She dropped the note back to the dressing table as if it were red-hot. "Impossible," she said aloud. He was dead. Nick had seen him die.

"What is it?"

Evelina whirled around. Imogen was in the doorway, a plaintive look on her face.

Evelina was suddenly disoriented. "How did you get here?"

"For you, I climbed out a window and caught a cab. I'm not helpless, you know. You left without saying good-bye." Imogen's gaze went to the paper in her hand. "What's impossible?"

Wordlessly, she handed over the note. Imogen read, her hand coming up to cover her mouth as her eyes got wider and wider. "Dear Lord in Heaven. How is it possible he lived?"

"There are all kinds of death magic, and he's a sorcerer. Or this is just a vicious joke."

Without warning, Imogen flung her arms around Evelina in a fierce embrace. "Oh, don't go."

Evelina squeezed her eyes shut, forcing back another wave of tears. "I have to."

Imogen held her tight, her shoulders starting to shake with grief. "You'll leave me behind."

Evelina swallowed hard. "No I won't. I stick like tar, you'll see."

Then Imogen started to cry in earnest, her words crumbling at the edges. "If you go, that means we're at the end. My parents will marry me off to someone horrible and you'll go to school and I'll never see you. I've already lost one sister. My family is going mad. I don't want to lose you, too."

Evelina buried her face in Imogen's golden hair, hurting for her friend. Hurting for herself.

A young woman had been seduced and killed, and the killers still roamed free. The two young men she loved had been proven innocent of that crime, but were guilty nonetheless—and she had played a part in their fall. And now the dead were sending her letters, tempting her more than she cared to say. Evelina might have been dismissed from Hilliard House, but she wasn't walking away from anything.

"This isn't the end," she whispered to Imogen. "Not by a long shot."

The adventures of Evelina Cooper continue with a bang in

A STUDY IN DARKNESS

Book 2 of The Baskerville Affair
by

EMMA JANE HOLLOWAY

Be sure not to miss this thrilling sequel,
coming soon.

And the epic conclusion, *A Study in Ashes*,
follows shortly thereafter.

Turn the page for a special preview.

And, for any desiring bonus content, check out the
exclusive, FREE e-short "The Steamspinner Mutiny,"
currently available on
www.facebook.com/emmajane.holloway.

Not to mention, for those who missed it, the FREE e-short
"The Strange and Alarming Courtship of Miss Imogen
Roth," the tale of Imogen's secret engagement to one
Buckingham Penner.

THE DOOR TO 221B BAKER STREET OPENED AND A BODY hurtled over the threshold, causing Evelina Cooper to skitter backward. The body landed with a wheeze on the hot sidewalk, arms and legs sprawling.

In her haste to back up, Evelina stepped into the street itself and narrowly avoided collision with a speeding steam cycle. With a silent curse, she caught her balance against the wrought-iron post of a gaslight, wondering what sort of a mood her uncle was in. Projectile clients were never a good sign.

The man on the sidewalk moaned. One hand groped awkwardly, as if seeking any solid object to cling to, and fastened on her right foot in its gray kid boot. As the only weapon Evelina had was her parasol, she swiped at the importunate fingers, delivering a smart tap with the furl of pale pink silk.

"Sir, unhand my toes." She frowned. That hadn't sounded quite right.

The man didn't move, instead emitting another groan. She studied him for a moment, the August sun warm against her shoulders. His limbs appeared to bend in the usual places and no blood was pooling around the prone body, but he lay perfectly still. Delicately, she pushed his fingers away with the ivory tip of her parasol and wondered whether she should send for Dr. Watson. The good doctor had married and moved out of Baker Street, but he always came at once when her uncle required his services—which seemed to be with disturbing regularity.

Evelina's shoulders hunched. Passersby were giving her

strange looks. As she looked up, a lady with a perambulator crossed the street, obviously avoiding the strange tableau.

"Spare him no sympathy, niece of mine, he is but refuse tossed into the gutter." The voice came from the doorway. Evelina turned to see Sherlock Holmes glowering out at them. Tall and spare, his black-suited form was an exclamation point in the doorway. The long, lean lines of his face pulled into a frown. He jerked his chin toward the sprawling form. "That individual is engaged in a perfidious plot. I suggest you step away from him at once. Quickly."

They hadn't seen each other for months, and one might have expected a hello or a polite enquiry about one's health—but Evelina knew better than to expect social niceties from Holmes when there was a villain adorning the front walk. "A plot to what end?"

"Come inside and I'll give you the details."

"What about him?"

"I'll call a street sweeper," Holmes said mordantly.

Evelina caught a glimpse of movement from the fallen man, but her attention didn't stay on him. Suddenly the house rumbled, and then a cloud of thick black smoke belched from the upstairs study window. There was a female shriek behind Holmes.

"Mrs. Hudson!" Evelina cried, and Holmes turned to check on his landlady.

The man on the ground chose that moment to spring to life. He rolled away from Evelina, coming to his feet in a practiced move. She saw the shape of a gun as his coat swung wide with the motion. Acting on instinct, she thrust the point of her parasol into his spine, the force of the blow splintering the wooden handle of her makeshift weapon. He staggered forward with a grunt, but then he used the momentum to sprint toward the door, drawing the gun as he ran.

Panic bit hard and fast, freezing a cry of outrage deep in her throat. Evelina grabbed for the man, but her fingers just brushed the back of his wool coat. She followed as quickly as a bustle and corset would allow, skirts swinging like a bell, but he was already through the door. She grabbed the frame and hauled herself forward, narrowly avoiding a fall as her heel caught on the sill. She skidded to a stop in the dim light of the front hall. She was alone.

Her uncle had vanished, as had his attacker. Evelina turned slowly, taking in her surroundings. Smoke hung in the air like stinking black breath, but there was no damage she could see. The explosion—for that was surely what had caused the disturbance—had been confined upstairs. And where was Mrs. Hudson?

For a moment the only sound was the clamor of voices outside. A man with a booming voice was explaining that the detective who lived upstairs was a chemist, fond of smelly experiments. An old gent with a wheezy tenor was sure the radicals had struck. No one barged in with offers of help.

"Mrs. Hudson?" she asked in a stage whisper.

"I'm here." The housekeeper materialized at the door leading to the lower apartments. She was still a handsome woman, straight-backed and neat as a pin, but now her face was ashen. "That man chased your uncle up to his study."

Evelina edged toward the foot of the stairs. Pausing for a moment, she listened to the sudden, ominous silence. Her brain wanted to lunge forward, but her feet were obstinately glued to the carpet. Evelina didn't like the fact the armed man had the higher ground and the staircase offered no cover, but there was no alternative—except to do nothing.

A gunshot cracked overhead, echoing ferociously in the tiny front hall. Somewhere on the second floor, a window smashed. Evelina looked up at the sweep of the staircase that led to her uncle's suite. Feet thundered overhead. Evelina grabbed her parasol more tightly, and then noticed its splintered handle. It drooped like a wilted tulip. She tossed it aside and picked up the no-nonsense broom that Mrs. Hudson had left beside the door.

"You're *not* going up there, young lady!" Mrs. Hudson announced, grabbing Evelina's arm. "I'm fetching the constables."

The landlady was being perfectly reasonable, but the voices inside Evelina were not. She had lost her parents, and

Holmes was the one remaining relative who had shown her any understanding. She wasn't about to squeal and run away in a flutter of ribbons—and after growing up in a circus, she had more skills than the average debutante. "You go. I'll do more good here."

"Miss Cooper!" the landlady protested.

"I'll be fine." Evelina heard her voice crack with doubt, but somehow speaking the words broke her stasis. Lifting her skirts in one hand, she took all seventeen stairs in a single silent rush, the broom poised for action. She crept toward Holmes's study door, staying close to the wall. The smell of gunpowder was thick enough to make her nose run.

Crack! She heard a bullet hit the plaster on the opposite side of the wall, from within her uncle's study. It punched through the wall just above her head and dust rained down, tickling her face. Evelina hurried the last few steps to the study entrance, peering around the carved oak of the door frame. A quick glance told her the path to Dr. Watson's old desk was clear. Watson had always kept his service revolver there. She wondered whether her uncle, who adapted to change with as much ease as rocks learned to fly, had replenished the firearm drawer when the doctor had left.

But the thought went by in an instant, pushed aside by the tableau directly ahead. Holmes knelt on the bearskin rug before the fireplace, facing Evelina. The stranger stood with his back to her, his gun aimed at Holmes's head. Swirls of black particles sifted through the air, eddying on the warm August breeze and settling on the litter of papers and other debris scattered across the floor. The room—never exactly tidy—was in a terrible state, but she didn't take the time to thoroughly catalogue the damage. That could wait.

"We were having a conversation before you threw me out," the man growled at Holmes.

Evelina noticed the accent sounded neither working class nor quite gentry. That made him one of the many in between. These were hard times for men like that, so many trying to scrabble upward while most slid farther behind. And that fit with his clothes—tidy, but inexpensive, his shoes in need of patching. In any other circumstances she might have taken him for a clerk or a lesser type of tutor—almost middle-aged, nondescript, and the type one would pass without a second look. Of course, that might have been the whole idea.

Holmes said nothing, his entire body as communicative as the fire screen behind him.

"There's no point in keeping quiet." The man shifted his grip on the gun, as if his hand was growing tired. At the same time, he was using one foot to move the papers around on the floor, taking quick glances to see what they were. More correspondence had landed on the nearby basket chair, and he picked up a handful, quickly scanning the letters and tossing them aside. Clearly, he was looking for something.

At least that meant he was fully occupied. Silently balanced on the balls of her feet, Evelina eased into the room. She saw a minute tightening of her uncle's mouth, but he gave no other indication that he saw her.

Now what? She took another glance around the room. Some of the furniture had tipped over in the blast, but other pieces, like the table and desks, were still miraculously upright. Watson's desk was directly to her right, just past the dining table. If she moved in utter silence, she could open the drawer, grab the gun she hoped was there—and loaded—and shoot the intruder before he shot her or her uncle. If she remained utterly silent and if she were fast enough, her plan might work.

Or she could creep up and knock him unconscious with the broom handle. She might get shot that way, too, but the whole scheme sounded simpler.

"Even if you think your way out of this with that big head of yours," the man went on while throwing more papers to the floor, "someone else will come. I won't be your only visitor, I can promise you that. The Steam Council is on to you."

The Steam Council? That was what the men and women who ruled the great utility companies called themselves. She had met one of these steam barons—Mr. Jasper Keating, the one they called the Gold King after the yellow-tinted globes he used to mark all the gaslights his company supplied. They all indicated their territories like that—the Blue King, the Violet Queen, and the rest. At sunset, the multicolored globes turned London into a patchwork glory of light. It was a beautiful sight, even though it was evidence of the stranglehold the council had on London and all the Empire.

So what did the steam barons want with her uncle? As far as she knew, Holmes was in favor with Keating after he had exposed a forgery scheme that had robbed the Gold King of a fortune in antique artifacts. If they survived the next hour, she would have to ask.

Lifting the broom high, Evelina ghosted forward, walking slowly so that her skirts didn't rustle.

"Your brother knows who the members of the shadow government are. But he is a hard man to catch outside the walls of his home or club."

Holmes finally spoke, only the quickness of his words betraying his nerves. "If you believe that I have my brother's complete confidence, you are sorely mistaken."

"Putting a hole in your head might draw him out."

A derisive smirk flickered over Holmes's face. "I think not."

Evelina raised the broom high above her head.

"I'll give it a try anyhow. Unless you want to talk." The man snatched up a calling card, read the name, and flicked it aside. Then he adjusted his aim a fraction, focussing completely on Holmes. "The council has heard the name Baskerville. They'd like to know something about that."

Holmes lifted his brows slightly. "The steam barons have played you for a fool. Your only function here is to startle me into betraying my hand. It won't work, and you won't survive this."

Evelina struck. There must have been a noise—a whistle of air through the bristles, perhaps—because the man turned at just the wrong moment. Rather than knocking him out, the broom handle glanced off his temple with a hollow crack, sending him stumbling into the basket chair next to the rug.

Then Holmes was on his feet, hammering the man in the jaw with a hard right hook. The gun went spinning away, clattering under the table. The man dove for it, but so did Evelina, using her speed and smaller size to wriggle between the chairs first. For the second time that day, he grabbed her foot, this time trying to use it to drag her out of his way. Then Holmes was on him. That gave her enough time to grab the slick handle of the revolver. It was still warm from his hand.

Evelina kicked the man off and twisted around so that she was on her knees. Holmes hauled the man back and punched him again. This time the man stayed where he fell. Evelina felt a bit ridiculous, crawling out from under the table and trying not to get tangled in her petticoats, but she eventually got to her feet.

She pointed the gun at the writhing man's belly. "Don't move," she said, squeezing the weapon so that it would not shake.

"You bloody hoyden." The man's face twisted as red streamed down his lip and chin, bubbling with his wheezing breaths. "I didn't plan on killing you when I started, but I can see you're an apple off the same tree."

"Confine yourself to answering questions," she said crisply.

He wiped his nose on his sleeve, staining the fabric crimson. Evelina winced in sympathy—there was little doubt Holmes had broken the man's nose—but she kept the muzzle of the revolver squarely aimed. His eyes, red-rimmed and blurred with pain, were still bright with anger.

Holmes, with the air of one who is about to put out the trash, strode briskly toward them. He bent and, quickly and efficiently, searched the man for other weapons. He found a knife, a pocketbook—which he examined, taking out several papers and looking them over—a small flask—which he opened and sniffed—and a ticket stub from a music hall. Holmes set the items aside and took the gun from her. And however little she liked the idea of holding a man at gunpoint, Evelina felt oddly bereft as she surrendered it. A primitive instinct had already marked the intruder as her prey.

"My dear," Holmes said, "would you please reassure the crowd outside that nothing is amiss?"

She suddenly became aware of the hubbub in the street. "What shall I tell them?"

"Whatever you like, but if you see a scruffy young lad named Wiggins, would you ask him to call for, um, just to call for our mutual friend?"

Evelina stared for a moment but knew better than to ask for details. Gingerly, she picked her way across the blasted room. Shards of glass framed the view of the brown brick building across Baker Street, with its neat white sashes and bay windows. Mrs. Hudson's lace curtains lay in shreds.

Carefully, she put her head out the hole in the shattered pane. There was a crowd gathered below, their upturned faces all wearing identical looks of bald curiosity. Someone in the street shouted a halloo, and Evelina waved. "Nothing to worry about. Just an accident with the kettle. No need to concern yourself."

A boy of about twelve, wearing ill-fitting clothes and ragged shoes, cupped his hands around his mouth to yell up at her. "That musta been some cuppa!"

"Yes, it was a very large kettle," Evelina replied. "Are you Wiggins?"

"Indeed I am, miss."

Evelina cast a glance over her shoulder, but her uncle hadn't moved. She knew he employed street urchins from time to time as a kind of messenger service that not even the steam barons could infiltrate. Wiggins had to be one of them. She turned back to the boy. "Mr. Holmes wishes to speak to your mutual friend."

"Right you are." The boy did an about-face and bolted down the street at a dead sprint. Apparently that mutual friend was well known.

She pulled her head back inside, her curiosity getting the better of her. "Who is your friend?"

"Someone equipped to take this charming specimen into custody," her uncle said flatly.

The man swore.

Holmes gave him a freezing look. "Silence. There is a young lady present."

The man shifted, his face sullen.

"Mrs. Hudson already went for the constables," Evelina said.

"Won't find any," their prisoner put in. Perhaps he had friends who were keeping the local plods occupied. Evelina hoped it wasn't anything worse than that.

Holmes looked unimpressed. "Even so, we dare not waste time." Impatiently, he waved her over and handed her the gun again. "Keep him still."

With that Holmes crossed to his collection of chemical supplies and surveyed the racks of bottles intently, clasping his hands behind his back as if to deliver a lecture on the laws of aether. He stood for so long that Evelina grew bored and longed to let her gaze roam around the room rather than keep her attention on the man on the floor. She'd caught glimpses of the soot-stained walls, the paintings hanging crooked. The explosion appeared to have emanated from a spot near the window.

"What blew up?" she asked.

"A brown paper package." Holmes finally selected an amber glass bottle from the chemical supplies and then began rummaging in his desk. "It was badly placed and badly made, if the intent was to obliterate my rooms and everyone in them. Although this looks like a great deal of damage, an efficient bomb would have reduced 221B Baker Street to a smudge." Eventually he took out a leather case and opened it, revealing a hypodermic needle. He took it out and began filling it from the vial of liquid.

Evelina's stomach squirmed at the sight of the long, sharp instrument. "I hope that's a sedative."

Holmes gave a flicker of a smile, but otherwise ignored the question as he squirted a few drops out the needle. "This individual—Elias Jones by name, and his pocketbook concurs with that identification—entered the premises on the pretence of hiring my services. He brought with him a package wrapped in butcher's paper and string, and proceeded to spin a tale about a mysterious Dresden figurine I would find inside the box, and how it held the clue to the grisly murder of an elderly aunt and her fourteen cats, and how he had been cheated of his inheritance."

"Fourteen cats?" Evelina echoed in surprise.

"It was not clear whether they were among the victims."

Her throat tightened as he turned, hypodermic in hand. She tried to keep her voice light. "Perhaps the felines conspired to steal the old lady's fortune?"

He gave her a dry look. "My would-be client's laundry needed attention, and the box had a distinct chemical odor inconsistent with fine china. It was evident to me that he was attempting some sort of ruse. Accordingly, I refused his case and told him why. Then he became obstreperous and began demanding information. I summarily threw him out the door for his trouble, before he even had a chance to resist."

"Or draw his gun," Evelina observed, feeling more than a little queasy about what might have happened.

"Quite." Holmes looked uncomfortable. "I apologize for tossing an armed man so close to where you were walking. That was unforgivably careless of me."

"I'm sure you were quite occupied at the time."

"I was annoyed," Holmes replied. "Mr. Jones seems to be under the misapprehension that I know more than I do about Mycroft's work, and that either of us has a connection to the rebels."

That made Evelina's breath catch. The rebellion against the Steam Council was growing and had been more and more in the papers over the summer. Anyone identified as a rebel automatically faced the gallows.

"What about it, Mr. Jones?" Holmes asked in a terrifying voice, holding the needle just where the man could see it. "Did your masters give you the order to insinuate yourself into my confidence in the guise of a client, and then search my quarters for evidence of treachery?"

Evelina swallowed hard. Uncle Mycroft worked for the government, but the Steam Council had so many politicians in their power, it was hard to know where the elected officials ended and the steam barons began. Loyalties were nothing if not complicated—and it was far easier for her to concentrate on more immediate problems. "If he knew his cover story was blown, why run back inside?"

"Indeed, why?" Holmes asked, leaning yet closer.

Jones grunted, flinching away from the needle.

The detective gave a thin smile. "Very well, keep your confessions for now. I spoiled your plan when I saw through your nonsense and tossed you to the street. There was no means of gaining information from the curb, so you had to get back inside if you wanted to earn your pay. At that point, direct questioning at gunpoint had to do. Not very subtle, but what does one expect from someone who is little more than hired muscle?"

"I still don't understand the bomb," said Evelina. "Why blow up the very person or place that can provide information?"

Holmes waited, giving Jones a chance to answer for himself, but the man remained mute, holding his hand to his bloody nose.

"That is rather less clear to me," the detective mused. "He was carrying a small amount of a strong sedative, which suggests that he might have attempted to drug me. That would allow him to search my rooms at leisure, find a list of rebel names or whatever else he dreamed would be among my possessions, leave, and set off the incendiary device. Effective, since it delivers a supposed blow to the rebels and covers his deception in the same stroke."

Something didn't seem quite right about that. "But what if you asked to see the figurine in the box?"

"The box might have been constructed to accommodate both a bomb and a prop for his masquerade."

Jones made a noise that might have been agreement, but Evelina couldn't tell. "Perhaps, though why risk setting a timer when there was no way to tell when his search would be over? It would have made more sense to set it once his search was done."

She knew her uncle well enough to read the confusion under his insouciant mask. He didn't know the answer to that question any more than she did. "Accident? Stupidity?

You overreached yourself when you went up against me, Jones."

Jones squeezed his eyes shut.

Perhaps he bit off more than he could swallow, but even fools kill people. Evelina's skin pebbled with horror at what might have happened, and she looked down, thinking how easy it would be to pull the trigger on Jones right then and there.

And then, with a look of vague distaste, Holmes pulled a handkerchief from his pocket and tossed it to Jones to stanch the blood dribbling from his nose. As the man grabbed it from the air, Evelina noticed the smudges on his cuffs and understood the laundry comment her uncle had made earlier. "Gunpowder."

"Precisely. Careless inattention to detail."

Jones visibly cringed as he pressed the handkerchief to his face, but then he caught sight of Holmes advancing with the needle, obviously meaning to use it now. He made a low noise and tried to squirm backward. "Please, guv'nor, don't kill me."

Holmes was impassive. "You should have considered the consequences before you walked through my door with violence in mind."

Evelina's shoulders were in knots, the gun shaking in her hands. Elias Jones had tried to kill her uncle and had nearly blown her up in the bargain, but her insides still turned to ice. "Uncle?"

Wordlessly, Holmes caught Jones's arm and began unbuttoning the filthy cuff and pushing up his sleeve. The man struggled furiously, making a choking sound of disgust and fear as Holmes jabbed the needle into his arm. Her uncle's jaw twitched as he depressed the plunger, and Jones quieted at once, his eyes rolling back in their sockets. His silence disturbed Evelina almost more than his fear.

"Did you, uh . . ." she whispered, letting the gun droop.

"No." Holmes narrowed his eyes. "Although that might be his preference by the end."

Her mouth went dry. *What the devil is going on?*

There was a scamper of young feet on the stairs, followed

by a heavier tread. A moment later, Wiggins burst into the room, followed by a man. He was about thirty, tall and lean, with curling, sandy hair and small wire-rimmed glasses tinted a pale green. As he surveyed the room, he wore the look of someone who was perpetually amused and slightly dangerous.

"Allow me to introduce the Schoolmaster," Holmes said cordially, stepping away from Jones's still form as if drugging a man senseless were an everyday event.

The Schoolmaster? Evelina had never met a man with a code name before, but in her uncle's line of work she supposed such things occurred—and she would fall on her own parasol before letting on she was anything but au courant in the detecting game.

Holmes gave a brisk nod to the boy and tossed him a shilling. "Well done, Wiggins." The lad caught it and was out the door again in a flash.

Then Holmes turned to the Schoolmaster. "Look what my niece has caught for you."

"Indeed," The Schoolmaster grinned appreciatively at Evelina.

His easy smile brought heat to her cheeks and irritated her all at once. She wasn't in the mood for flirtation. "May I put this gun down now?"

Her uncle laughed. "And deprive my friend here of the spectacle of my lovely niece holding one of the prime villains of London at bay?"

"I will point out that I subdued him with a broom," Evelina replied coolly. "If he is a prime villain, then crime in London is in decline."

The Schoolmaster took the opportunity to flip Jones over and pinned his hands. Evelina stepped aside to give him room.

"Well, perhaps, he is a step or two down from prime," Holmes replied, turning to the Schoolmaster. "You'll be interested in this one. I had to confirm the identification, for I have not seen the man in the flesh for over a decade, but I recognized him. Moreover, I have current intelligence about his activities. Elias Jones works for the Blue King."

Evelina recoiled from the man. The Blue King—better known as King Coal—was the eccentric steam baron who ran the worst parts of East London. He squeezed whatever he could from the impoverished residents of Whitechapel and Limehouse. Anyone who worked for him either had to be pitied or reviled. Looking at Elias Jones, lying bloody and unconscious on the floor, she decided it was probably both.

The Schoolmaster withdrew a set of handcuffs the like of which she'd never seen before. He snapped a heavy cuff on Jones's right wrist, and then a tendril of steel automatically snaked out to catch the left. The steel was so many-jointed that it was almost ropelike, but it snapped shut with a sharp click. No sooner had the sound faded than another rope sprang out to catch the man's waist, then more slithered down his legs to hobble his ankles. Evelina was transfixed.

"How do those work?" she asked. The need to know was almost a hunger. She loved all things mechanical, and the design of the manacles was elegant, even fascinating, for all that they made her shiver.

The man gave her a sly look, as if it were a secret he would die sooner than tell, and then turned back to Holmes. "Jones? I know this one's reputation—a sly rat, if there ever was one. How long will he be unconscious?"

Holmes gave a slight shrug. "At least an hour."

"Good."

"He is really that fearsome then?" Evelina asked, still eying the manacles.

The Schoolmaster frowned, which she took as a worrying affirmative. "Why did the Blue King send him here?"

Holmes answered. "No doubt he wants what all men want from me—answers or silence."

No, thought Evelina, *it's not that simple*. Now that the crisis was past, her mind was churning out questions. She knew that her Uncle Mycroft had his carefully manicured fingers in a great many pies, both literal and figurative—and apparently at least one pie was volatile enough to interest a steam baron and to make Holmes hide that fact from Evelina. *A shadow government? Baskerville?*

The Schoolmaster glanced down at his prisoner. "Shall we take him in, then?"

She wondered where "in" was since she very much doubted that they were referring to the police. If her uncle had wanted Scotland Yard, he would have sent Wiggins for Inspector Lestrade. And who was this Schoolmaster? The steam barons would want to ask him a great many questions about those restraints. Makers weren't allowed to ply their trade without the Steam Council's approval.

Holmes looked critically at Jones. "We'll need a cab. The closer to the back entrance the better."

"I have a Steamer around the corner," the Schoolmaster replied. He turned to Evelina, touching the brim of his hat. "If you'll excuse us, miss."

She nodded mutely and turned to her uncle. "I was planning to have my trunk delivered from the station . . ."

"Oh, by all means," he said with a flap of his hand. "Mrs. Hudson has your room ready. When she's back from her quest for constables, perhaps you could ask her to sweep up and call the glazier. In the meantime, some letters have arrived for you. Invitations and whatnot. I'm sure they will keep you occupied until I return."